THE POWER OF MAGIC ...

"Imagine that this power lies in the earth the way oil sits in the bowl of a lamp. Certain things are needed to make that oil give light. A wick must draw the oil up to the air, and, once there, a spark is needed to start the flame. Do you see? Those with talent are wicks, Averil. Like young Flattery; the power comes up through him, but what is lacking is the spark. The spark, I think, comes from ritual, and the ritual is dependent on language. . . and elements we are only beginning to understand. But even now he draws the power up. At least that is their hope. And if it is true, well, strange things will begin to happen around him. Virtually every mage had some affinity with the animal world. This falcon. It was the first sign."

"I was a fool," Kent said bitterly.

"No, no. Do not whip yourself, Averil. You could not have known."

Kent shook his head, taking no comfort from Valary's words. "Do you know I am worried about the boy, as well. I know he is the focus of this blind madness, but he is not part of it—at least not yet. What will become of him? Precisely what do the others aboard the ship intend?"

"It is a worry," Valary said quietly. "You can see it throughout our history. Those who showed any signs of talent too often were victims of ignorance and superstition. Stoned to death or cleansed with fire before a mage could discover them or before the talent had truly taken form. But once the power is manifest, it will begin to protect its possessor—though to preserve itself, not Tristam Flattery."

SEAN RUSSELL
has also written

THE INITIATE BROTHER

GATHERER OF CLOUDS

Moontide and Magic Rise:

WORLD WITHOUT END

SEA WITHOUT A SHORE*

*forthcoming from DAW Books in Fall 1995

SEAN RUSSELL
WORLD WITHOUT END

Book One of
Moontide and Magic Rise

Owl's song on whispered shores
Where the silvered sea dies
Along the wake of a running moon,
Moontide and magic rise.

DAW BOOKS, INC.
DONALD A. WOLLHEIM, FOUNDER
375 Hudson Street, New York, NY 10014

ELIZABETH R. WOLLHEIM
SHEILA E. GILBERT
PUBLISHERS

First Printing, March 1995

1 2 3 4 5 6 7 8 9

DAW TRADEMARK REGISTERED
U.S. PAT. OFF. AND FOREIGN COUNTRIES
—MARCA REGISTRADA,
HECHO EN U.S.A.

PRINTED IN THE U.S.A.

ACKNOWLEDGMENTS

As always this book wouldn't have come into being without the input and support of many. Thanks go to Karen, of course; Jill, Walter and Chris at White Dwarf Books; Ian Dennis; my agent, Bella Pomer; my editor, Betsy Wollheim, and all the folks at DAW; Sean Stewart; Stephen and Petra; Margo; Rory MacIntosh for geological information; Elizabeth Towers and Mark Hobson for their help with the natural history; Don and Michael; and John Harland and Mark Myers for writing their impressive *Seamanship in the Age of Sail*.

For Karen

Would it be too bold to imagine, that in the great length of time, since the earth began to exist, perhaps millions of ages before the commencement of the history of mankind, would it be too bold to imagine, that all warm-blooded animals have arisen from one living filament which the Great First Cause endued with animality. . . and thus possessing the faculty of continuing to improve by its own inherent activity, and of delivering down those improvements by generation to its posterity. . . world without end!

—Erasmus Darwin,
"Zoonomia" (1794)

One of the two horns of my dilemma.
—Laurence Sterne,
"The Life and Opinions of Tristram Shandy."
(1760)

NOTE TO READERS

Scientific names, originally in Old Farr, have been rendered in equivalent or near-equivalent Latin.

ONE

The drama unfolding in the field below seemed so improbable that it could have been nothing more than two groups of players preparing a performance—the duel that would bring down the curtain on the first act.

"I've forgotten my field glass. Hawkins? Can you see what they're doing?"

The driver had been pacing, almost silently, back and forth between his team and the door to the carriage, but he stopped now and shielded his eyes with a callused hand. "It is not yet clear, sir. They remain standing in their separate groups, and no one is stepping forward." The driver stayed in his place for a few seconds and when it appeared that his employer would have no further questions, at least for a moment, he returned to whispering to the gray mare and gelding.

The man who watched shifted on the seat of his carriage and realized he was gripping his cane so tightly that the joints in his fingers had begun to ache. The gestural language of the theater was well known to him, and what he saw transpiring on the field bore the unmistakable signs of unfolding tragedy. Signs he had seen often these past months. The emotions that a pending tragedy engendered were also very familiar: the overwhelming sense of helplessness; the firm knowledge that the small justice of men was of little consequence on the larger stage; and then the growing horror.

He gazed out over the field where the curious whispered among themselves, as people did before the curtain rose. Somewhere a physician stood by with his bag of dressings and instruments.

The man who had come to witness this renewal of the art of the duel was not one of the idly curious. Unlike most of those who stood about the field, he had fought a duel, though it had been long ago. That was one memory that did not fade. He knew what it felt like to turn away from one's second and come suddenly to a full understanding that this was no longer the practice floor. These could be the final moments of one's life. He had hefted a blade to test its balance and felt that second sharp stab of knowledge: what he held in his hand was an implement to end life.

He had been fortunate and never killed a man. True gentlemen did not demand another's life to assuage their pride, for pride was invariably at the center of these affairs—not honor. The man in the carriage had long ago seen past that particular myth.

On the field, too far off for him to discern detail, a tall, angular man had removed his frock coat—snow white linen against the green. The Baron Ipsword. Never graceful of movement, the baron appeared puppetlike now, moving jerkily on the stage. And he stayed near to his supporters; too close, in fact. They were all afraid.

The forces that had animated this puppet for so many years had fled. The aggressive pride, the jealousy, and outright malice had been replaced by overpowering terror. The baron was not, it appeared, a courageous man—which might have explained why he was so vicious in attacking others. But a quick tongue would not shield him today.

Beyond the site of the duel a thin covering of ground-mist still resisted the sun. It hung over the river, obscuring the boles of poplars, like the vapor one would imagine rising from molten gold. A summer morning so still the sky seemed to hold its breath. Then came the quick flick of a horse's tail and the impatient shaking of harness.

The second swordsman could be seen now, stepping

away from his fellows. This would be the Viscount Elsworth, as tall as his opponent but athletic and graceful. Even with poor vision, the man who watched could see these qualities. If Ipsword was a puppet, this man was an acrobat, a tumbler—nimble, flexible, and strong. He cut the air three times quickly with his blade, testing the balance of the weapon, and then pivoted, flexing one knee. Satisfied, he strode forward a few paces and stopped, staring expectantly at the party huddled under the elms.

A good actor could express a great deal at a distance, even to those sitting at the furthest extremes of a theater, but no actor could ever convey the complexity of emotion that Ipsword displayed as he walked forward to duel; terrified, enraged, sullen, meek, almost ready to beg, prepared to do murder. Only enough pride and arrogance remained to carry him to this place.

It was common, the man in the carriage thought, that the actors could not see the signs of impending tragedy. *"Poor fool,"* the man whispered. *"It has almost nothing to do with him."* He shifted again on the seat, the leather squeaking. If he was right in what he guessed, then first-blood would not end this affair. Ipsword might have been carried here by the remains of his pride, but Elsworth was likely concerned with neither pride nor honor.

"Pray that I am wrong," the man who watched said aloud.

The two swordsmen saluted with their rapiers and then stepped to the guard position, one so tentatively that it seemed he might break and run. A third man raised aloft a white handkerchief, like a flag of peace . . . and then released it.

The man in the carriage thought afterward that he must have blinked, for he did not see the thrust. Only Elsworth bent forward over a flexed knee, poised like a dancer, sliding his blade from the chest of the collapsing baron.

"Flames!" the man in the carriage whispered.

The viscount stood for a moment, looking at the fallen man, and then he turned and handed his blade to another. His second spoke to him and then went slowly over to the men gathered around the injured baron. He hovered on the edge of this scene for a moment—the faithful gathered around the fallen hero—perhaps he spoke, and then crossed back to the viscount, who stood now with a coat draped about his shoulders. They nodded to each other, like men of business at the end of the day, and then went directly to a large carriage drawn up under the elms.

The man watching realized he had raised his hands in horror and half covered his face. He took hold of himself as best he could. "Hawkins?" he said, leaning out to speak to his driver, his voice trembling. "Will you go down?"

The driver nodded stiffly and set off, picking his way hurriedly among the brambles down the slope to the open field. The man sat back in his carriage, breathing in short gasps, and then banged his cane hard on the floorboards. He had *so* hoped that he was wrong.

It was only a few moments until a gentle tap sounded on the carriage door.

"Hawkins?"

"It would appear to be a thrust to the heart, sir." A pause. A breath roughly drawn. "I think he still lives but can't continue much longer."

"No, I'm sure he can't." The man looked out at the field once again. The retreating carriage. The small group bearing up their dying companion. He could almost see the horror on their faces. None of them had expected this—an accidental injury, perhaps, but not this.

"Shall I take you back, sir?" the driver asked quietly.

The old man shook his head. "No. We go on. You must have me in Merton by nightfall."

TWO

*What are the beliefs of this "Man of Reason?" That the
application of reason to all areas of life will lead mankind into a golden age of peace, knowledge, and prosper-
ity. That religion and nationalism, are merely guises of
tribalism—manifestations of base passions unbridled by
reason—and all lead us away from the "reasonable
world" into ignorance and endless cycles of violence.*
                                Beaumont: The Man of Reason

The sloop of war that carried Tristam Flattery to
Avonel was named *Mysterious,* and he saw irony in
that. He stood at the ship's rail watching the eastern
shore of the sound creep past, listening to the slap of
small waves against the hull.

"We will certainly make harbor this evening, Mr.
Flattery." It was Hawksmoor, a minion of the King's
Man—the one who pried.

"So perhaps now you can tell me the reason I have
been summoned?" Tristam did not turn to look at the
man. The ship moved slowly through the long shadow
of the western shore, and Tristam found he did not
want to take his eyes from the area still bathed in sunlight.

"I cannot, Mr. Flattery. In fact, I don't know myself.
I was told to be sure you were the Flattery who assisted Professor Dandish with Baron Trevelyan's collection. No more. You may draw whatever conclusions
you might from that."

"I have misclassified some rare flower and shall be
sent to the tower for my sins?"

Even the man's laugh was artificial. "For such a crime a beheading is usual. A Royal Summons, Mr. Flattery. A chance to serve the King. People dream their entire lives of such an opportunity. You should be glad of it."

Tristam felt his shoulders shrug. In truth he was very pleased by the prospect of serving the King—but this *"man of the King's Man,"* as Hawksmoor liked to name himself, was irritating beyond reason. Tristam was sure Hawksmoor knew full well why Tristam had been summoned—but kept it secret because it allowed him to feel some small sense of being in control of the situation. Tristam had seen this characteristic in men before. He would be willing to wager that Hawksmoor was used to being dealt with in this same manner. Pettiness begetting pettiness.

"The anchor will be down an hour after dark, Mr. Flattery. We should be ready to disembark immediately." Without awaiting a response Hawksmoor was gone, leaving Tristam standing at the rail, shaking his head gently. There must be something about the King's Service that shriveled a man's spirit, Tristam thought, for the pettiness of bureaucrats was unparalleled.

Tristam had not been to Avonel in two years and he realized some of his sour mood was due to this return. The place called forth his particular ghosts and no amount of time appeared to alter that.

"The studding sails are set and drawing, Mr. Flattery," came a voice at his side. Tristam glanced over at young Jack Beacham, midshipman in the King's Navy and Tristam's self-appointed mentor in things nautical.

"I can't tell you what pleasure they give me," Tristam said, hiding a smile as he looked up. The maintop, as the upper mast was named, was still in sunlight, the weathered canvas appearing stark in contrast to shadow and the evening-blue sky. Tristam often found himself teasing this good-natured young sailor, for it was obvious that the midshipman believed the sailing ship was, without question, man's greatest accomplishment.

"They are a beautiful sight, sir," Beacham said, almost wistfully. He continued to stare up at the filling sails for a moment and then seemed to remember his obligations as tutor. "Unfortunately, Mr. Flattery, these are light air sails, and it means the wind's dropping and the master expects it to fall lighter yet."

Tristam raised his eyebrows as though impressed with the master's great insight.

Beacham was a stocky youth, in his middle teens, perhaps. An officer in training, and well suited to the calling, Tristam thought, for the boy viewed life on land the way some feared prolonged illness. Tristam had not known the word *"landsman"* could be spoken with such heartfelt disdain.

The young sailor pointed a callused hand toward the shore. "But there's a wind line there or my name isn't Jack. Every evening about this time, if there isn't a gale to interfere, a breeze comes down off the hills. Cooling air, some have it . . . though you'd know more about that than myself, I'm sure."

Beacham, whose name certainly wasn't Jack (it was the name given to every new sailor, though Beacham seemed overly pleased with it), was mightily impressed with Tristam's education and became even more so when he discovered that Tristam knew as much, or more, about the geometrics of the sphere and the theory of weather as the officers aboard.

The two young men stood, staring off toward the eastern shore as the ship moved slowly through calm water. Across this narrow arm of the Entide Sea the crags rose up, supporting rolling fields which spread out toward hills, faded and distant under the summer sky. The land seemed fair to Tristam, and appeared very firm and secure, no matter what the young midshipman might think.

Hedgerows crisscrossed the downs, laid out according to no apparent design or discernable logic, they traced the contours of the land, standing out from their long shadows in the evening light. To Tristam they looked like the supporting framework of the countryside, forming an infinitely complex web of branchings and intersections, dividing one field neatly from the next, the holdings of one family from those of their neighbor. Though no two fields were alike in shape or size, Tristam saw a comforting order displayed on the downs which was almost restful to his spirit. It also said much about life in the Kingdom of Farrland.

"Excuse my manners, Mr. Flattery," Beacham said, still staring up, "it is not my meaning to pry, but are you any relation to Admiral Flattery who had command of the Blue Squadron at Cape Locke?"

"Oh, very distantly, I'm told. All landsmen in my more immediate family, I'm afraid."

"Well, sir, there have been many fine landsmen," Beacham said quietly, an obvious concession on the young sailor's part.

"Kind of you to say." This time Tristam hid his smile by shading his eyes to look aloft. Silence returned and Tristam waited for Beacham to screw up his nerve enough to ask the question that was no doubt gnawing away at him. It took some little while.

"We were wondering, my messmates and me," the lad began, "if you might be kin to Erasmus Flattery, then ... ?"

Tristam lowered his shading hand but kept his attention fixed on the uppermost sails. "My late great-uncle," he said with some resignation.

"Ah." Beacham nodded as though he had been proven right. Apparently unaware of the sour note in Tristam's voice, the midshipman plunged ahead. "Was it true, then, that your uncle was apprentice to Lord Eldrich? It's often said that he was."

Tristam nodded, keeping his eyes on the men working the ship, coiling the myriad lines, going about their business without a word. "He never spoke of it to me, but apparently he served in Lord Eldrich's house for some short time. Eldrich must have been very old, and my uncle very young."

"Do you think it was true, then, that Lord Eldrich was a mage, as everyone said?" Youthful curiosity and enthusiasm overcame all other considerations.

Tristam heard himself release a hollow laugh. "To be honest, Mr. Beacham, I probably know less about Eldrich than you do yourself. Certainly my uncle was the most ordinary of men—except for his intellect and an impressive variety of eccentricities. There was nothing in his life that would make one believe he had abilities we poor mortals lack."

"I have never had the pleasure myself, Mr. Flattery, but those that have tasted them say the wines made from the Erasmus Grape have a bit of magic in them."

Tristam smiled. "A magic you could learn yourself. Breeding a new varietal and a structured inquiry into the process of fermentation. The magic of knowledge, Mr. Beacham, no more. Though that is magic enough for me."

Tristam never learned what the lad intended to say next, for the voice of the ship's master cut him off just as he opened his mouth to speak.

"Mr. Beacham. Would you be so good as to find me the ship's carpenter."

"By your leave," Beacham almost whispered, giving Tristam a nod and setting off at a trot looking for the drunk who, apparently, was also referred to as the ship's carpenter—the kindest appellation Tristam had heard thus far.

A small alcid surfaced alongside and then dove at the sight of the great, looming ship. Tristam stared down into the dark waters for a moment, trying to see if the bird swam using its wings as some said it did. Too dark.

Something faint and milky-white, almost apparitional, appeared in the water and it took Tristam a second to realize that this was not in the depths but a reflection. The city of Avonel, still aglow in the last light of the day, had chosen that moment to appear over the shoulder of a hill.

Tristam looked up to the rising towers and sloping slate roofs, not sure if he felt ambivalence or real animosity. *Why,* he asked himself, *can't I bury all my past associations with this place and see it anew?* He squinted a little as though it might help him with this exercise. Perhaps the city was too familiar, for the shift he looked for did not occur. It remained as it had for two centuries, a lovely city spread out beneath a graceful skyline—and greatly unaffected by Tristam's feelings toward it.

There were, even Tristam had to admit, a few things about Avonel which were undeniably admirable. The whitestone from which it had been built was a naturalist's dream—riddled with the fossilized life of ages long past. Almost every stone appeared to have carved upon it the shapes of sea shells, of crustaceans and all manner of marine life, some of it quite unknown today and steeped in mystery. Tristam, like many of his fellow scholars at Merton, often wondered what had befallen these creatures.

Avonel was also unique in all the cities surrounding the Entide Sea, for it had not grown haphazardly over the centuries, one period of architecture thrown half atop that of another. The city of Avonel was the result of the vision of one man, Prince Kirstom, who had been given the responsibility of rebuilding the city after it was razed by the armies of Entonne in the Winter War. The intervening two hundred years had added much to the great designer's work. The color of the stone grew warmer with age, trees and gardens matured, and ivy, wisteria, and columbine draped the walls and eaves.

In the fading light Avonel began, finally, to change character, elements disappearing into shadow until the scene became unfamiliar, foreign. Tristam could now easily imagine that he was approaching an unknown city, seeing a new land from the deck of a ship fresh from the open sea.

As the very last hint of light disappeared, Avonel looked like the ruin of an empty city, mysteriously abandoned. And then a streetlight flickered into being, and then another.

This nineteenth day of June, 1559.

Arrived in Avonel late this day and am installed in a suite of rooms at the Queen Anne—I feel rather like a gentleman of means. No one has yet bothered to tell me why I have been summoned to the palace and my curiosity is swollen to near bursting. I shall hardly sleep this night.

I'm grateful that the Queen Anne does not afford me a view of the old theater site. Martyr's flames, how I wish they would erect a building there! Dandish always told me that if all men felt shame for the follies of their fathers every man in the country would live in constant disgrace. Good advice, I'm sure, but from someone whose father did not, to my knowledge, have any great failure attached to his good name—let alone a failure of vast proportion and infamy. And to suffer this ruin over something so frivolous as a theater! Why couldn't my father have failed in a nobler cause at least? And why must I always come back to this same matter? I am like a compass—turn me as you will, but I seek my one true direction. It is the anxiety of this strange summons that has led me into these too familiar paths of thought. Once I am actually employed in my task, whatever it might be, I'm sure these feelings will come under control again . . . for a while, at least.

THREE

Sir:

It would appear that Mr. Tristam Flattery is a man of great interest to us, though his connection with Erasmus is still troubling.

Briefly: Mr. Flattery is, at the time of this writing, twenty and three years of age and has recently left an appointment at Merton College: the same institution from which he graduated some three years past.

The sad tale of Mr. Flattery's father, the Honorable Morton Flattery, is well known; his marriage, against the wishes of his family, to an actress of vastly inferior social status; and then the final folly of the Grand Avonel Theater. The collapse of this endeavor led Morton Flattery to self-murder at the age of twenty-nine, and then, the following year, his wife was carried away in the terrible influenza epidemic. The child was then aged eight years. Subsequently, Tristam Flattery was raised by the senior member of the Flattery family, the well known Erasmus, though the uncle seemed to take small interest in his charge—his attentions being focused elsewhere, as might be imagined.

The child was an excellent student at Edington School, where he lived until graduation. There is little more to say of those years except that, unlike many of studious nature, Tristam Flattery proved himself a gifted athlete, showing skill with the bow, riding, fencing, rowing, and, due to instruction by his great uncle Erasmus, he also swam.

As one would expect, Mr. Flattery went on to

Merton College. Here he came under the influence of Professor Sanfield Dandish, the celebrated botanist, and discovered the empiricists, joining the ranks of the, so-called, "men of reason": those who believe, among much else, that one should be of good character because it is sensible! For two years after graduation he assisted Professor Dandish in the taxonomic classification of Baron Trevelyan's great collection.

On the surface it would appear that he is a normal enough young man—perhaps a cut above the average in intellect and other gifts—but I discovered two incidents from his years at Merton that set him apart most distinctly. The first took place in a class exploring the arithmetical relationships of chance. I do not know the precise details, but no doubt it was a lesson much like we have all attended; discussion of ratios and odds etcetera. The salient detail is that Mr. Flattery was able to predict the outcome of a coin toss more than twenty times without mistake! (I have this on good authority, as there were a dozen students in attendance as well as the instructor.)

Being the most conventional of young men, and refusing to take risks (the lesson of his father) he will neither dice nor play at cards so it cannot be known how frequently Mr. Flattery might be able to perform feats of this nature. I do not need to say how great are the odds against such a thing!

The second incident concerned the so-called "ghost boy of Merton," the apparition that is said to have been wandering the town since the days of the first true plague—some two hundred years. I will not go into the details and history of the story for I am sure you are aware of them. Today's "men of reason" do not believe in this apparition, of course, and several pranksters have been caught with younger brothers dressed up in the appropriate costume which has discredited the story even further. In his second year at Merton Mr. Flattery encountered a small boy, dressed for the part, who actually approached him as though to speak, but, as this took place on the edge of a central common, several *other scholars witnessed the meeting and gave chase to the "ghost." The boy ran into the common and around a tree but, true to all tales, was not to be found when the scholars arrived in hot pursuit. Nor had this child climbed up into the branches. A concerted search revealed no clue as to the child's disappearance. The scholars believed (and still believe, apparently) that Tristam Flattery had practiced upon them in a most clever way, though, for his part, young Flattery claims he was the victim of the prank. From the little I have seen I would venture that such a stunt would not be in keeping with the character of Tristam Flattery.*

Perhaps here is our lodestone at last! Certainly he is as promising as any I have known.

If the opinion is that Tristam Flattery is a man of interest to us (and I would argue strongly that this is so) then it would seem prudent to find some way to shift his residence to Avonel.

I remain your servant,
E. D. H.

Sir Roderick Palle folded the letter and sat watching the ballet of flames in the hearth. Quiet moments were few in his life and found usually late at night—the price one paid for being the King's Man. A book he had been trying to finish for several months lay on the small table beside the chair, but—like most nights—the real world would not allow him escape.

He raised a glass of wine, taking great pleasure from the play of firelight in its dark ruby center, as beautiful as any gem to his eye. Knowing the history of the grape could not spoil that—at least not entirely.

He looked back at the letter he had laid on the table. There had been too many blind ends over the years for Palle to allow his hopes to rise. Keep the mind on the task at hand, that was his creed.

In the midst of savoring his wine a soft knock sounded—as though delivered by a hand lacking bones.

"Drayton?"

His man servant appeared, solemn as always. "Sir Benjamin, sir," he said, using the tones usually heard at funerals.

"Please bring him up. And Drayton? A second glass."

Benjamin Rawdon appeared, his handsome face seeming a little careworn.

"You are up late, Benjamin. Seeing to your patient, I presume?"

"The dreams again. I think they are almost unbearable sometimes." The physician, too, kept his voice low, as though afraid of waking the rest of the palace. He sat opposite Sir Roderick, accepting wine with some relief, his host thought. "I left Teiho Ruau singing—songs from his own land. Very haunting and beautiful."

"Music to soothe the troubled soul." Roderick raised his glass. "The King's health."

They each drank and then sat without speaking. There was something on the Royal Physician's mind, Palle was sure. Rawdon was not one to seek out the comfort of another man's company—the physician was of the type who could only be truly at ease in the company of women.

Palle decided not to ask what the problem was. He knew this was a little perverse, forcing the doctor to bring it up himself, but the man's reticence could be a bit annoying sometimes. The silence soon began to unsettle Rawdon.

"You have not had a reoccurrence of the pain in your legs?"

"No, I've been perfectly hale. Kind of you to ask."

Rawdon sipped his wine, nodding in response just as the glass touched his lips.

Sir Roderick continued to stare at the doctor. He had often been told that his gaze unsettled people, and at times he found this ability useful. Rawdon had interrupted this little bit of time alone and the King's Man realized he was making the doctor pay for that small offense. *Petty,* he told himself but kept his gaze fixed on the doctor.

After another moment of awkward silence he relented. "I take it there is something on your mind, Doctor." He made his tone kindly. Foolish to act this way toward Rawdon, as though the man had not had enough troubles of late.

The Royal Physician nodded. "Yes." He looked out the window. "Some of the others are concerned about this young Flattery."

"Are you speaking for them? Expressing your own concerns? Or are you merely keeping me informed of the mood of our colleagues?"

"I—I speak for no one else."

"Then you are concerned yourself?"

"Yes. . . ." He looked down into his wineglass. "Yes, I am. It is this family connection. . . . Doesn't it worry you?"

The King's Man held his wine out toward the physician as though it were, in itself, an answer to the question. "The great nephew and heir of Erasmus?" He paused, looking into the fire. "I understand why you are reticent, but I think it is not really such a risk. And the prince would like to see greater efforts made. . . . I want to have a careful look at this young man in any case. I showed you this?" He indicated the letter he had been rereading earlier.

The physician leaned over to look and then nodded.

"Even with his connection to Erasmus, we cannot ignore this." Sir Roderick laid his head back, suddenly tired. He closed his eyes and felt that slight acidic burning of exhaustion—a sign he habitually ignored. "We know so little of Erasmus . . . and his intentions." Roderick opened his eyes and looked over at his visitor. "The man laid down so many false trails. As I have come to the end of each, invariably I have had this feeling that it amused him to lead me on." He held up his glass again. "The finest grape in the known world. It is a measure of his genius for revenge. I taste it daily."

The physician's nod was so distracted that Roderick wondered if he listened at all.

"Well, I am glad it's you, Roderick, who will have young Flattery in hand."

This brought a silence in which both sipped at their wine. The flavor was complex, Roderick felt, the bitterness undetectable to most.

"Do you not worry, Roderick, that we might have miscalculated?" Rawdon asked, the tone of his voice admitting that this was his real concern. "We have made such crucial decisions based on so little knowledge."

Roderick did not hesitate before answering. "And what other choice can you see? We have the Entonne to consider, as always. And I am confident that much good will come of our efforts—as you should be, Benjamin. You of all people." The King's Man looked over at his companion. "Your life has been most difficult these past months, fraught with ill luck: at such times it becomes easy to believe a pattern has been cast. But be of good heart, Benjamin. Your wife is recovered. The King is hale. And our own endeavors proceed apace. Do not let pessimism and melancholia take hold of you, Benjamin. Once they have sent their tendrils into your heart, it is most difficult to free yourself again. And they have only found purchase because of your recent troubles—none of them of your own making."

The man forced a tight-lipped smile, though his eyes did not quite agree. "I'm sure you're right. I am easily unbalanced by things these days." He sipped his wine, without proper appreciation, Roderick thought. "You heard of this bloody duel?"

Roderick nodded. "Yes. No accident, I am told."

"Completely intentional! I spoke with the physician who attended. Has the word *gentleman* lost all meaning?

"Yes, in fact, I fear it has—for many, at least. Though it is good to remember that Elsworth takes his instructions from a lady. Unfortunate the fools did not run each other through so we could be rid of them both."

"That is harsh judgment," the physician said quietly. "I thought Ipsword a fool—but nothing more."

Roderick laughed softly. "Is it harsh? Yes, I suppose. And I know folly is not the exclusive domain of the foolish. Look at this young Flattery's father. No fool, no matter what people say. Wed to ill luck, that was all—betrothed at birth. We who have fortune smiling upon us must not lose sight of that. One can too easily focus on only the bad. It is a tendency one should be wary of."

"I tell my patients as much," the physician said, displaying the mildest surprise, as though he had never considered this advice to be anything but words.

"And you are telling them true, Benjamin." Sir Roderick lifted his glass again. "Long life, sir."

"Yes. Long life."

FOUR

The dream never varied. Tristam would become conscious in the dark, but he could not move, even to open his eyes. And then he would realize that he was aware within a dream—unable to wake. No amount of effort would allow him to move even a finger, to open his mouth to scream. It was like being buried alive. And then, finally, he would awake, gasping for air, his heart pounding. After that, sleep came with difficulty, or not at all, for, if he did sleep, sometimes the dream returned.

❧   ❧   ❧

Tristam woke to the sound of carriages passing beneath his window. A sudden fear that one of these might bring the King's Man propelled him half out of bed where he stopped, staring dumbly at the clock face. After a few "ticks" the position of the hands registered. Half-six. There was time yet.

Tristam fell back into the bed and let his eyes close. Even before anxiety about the day could begin, he felt the emotion left by the dream still clinging to him. It had been a few months since the dream had haunted him, for that was how he thought of it—*haunting*.

It is brought on by anxiety, Tristam told himself. *My coming appointment at the palace.*

Sleep, always elusive in Tristam's world, was not going to return, so he forced himself up.

As he stropped his razor, Tristam tried to shake off

the emotion the nightmare left behind like a residue. He tried to force his mind into the day and out of this state of enervation—neither awake nor asleep.

Dreams plagued him, and often, try as he might, he could not remember what they had been about. They would hover on the edge of consciousness, like a face just at the periphery of one's vision. Tristam often wondered if his nightmares were part of the cause of his insomnolence, for he was plagued by that as well—an inability to find sleep. Certainly he did not really like the dream state; to his mind the reoccurring dream was proof of that.

He stared at himself in the mirror. *Try to appear more in control,* he told himself. With his green eyes set too wide apart, Tristam thought he always looked as though he had just been startled—a man constantly surprised by the world in which he found himself. He was sure this was one of the several reasons that women did not throw themselves at him as they did at his blue-eyed cousin, Jaimy. The reflection in the mirror was less than he'd hoped, in fact. Nose not large but not finely formed either; mouth acceptably shaped, lower lip protruding marginally too far. Only his high broad forehead was admirable, and perhaps his hair— thick, dark blond, and given to curls. Still, his would never be a portrait that inspired women to sighs, he was sure of that.

His mind returned to the coming appointment. Despite the look that he believed was written large on his face, Tristam was not a person who liked surprises. This secrecy surrounding his summons was driving him a little mad.

Not much longer, he told himself, though it didn't seem to help.

Unwilling to wait for hot water, Tristam suffered a cold water shave, and nicked himself twice for his lack of prudence. He proceeded to dress with extreme care—a knight donning armor could not have been more thorough—as though the slightest flaw in his attire might leave an opening through which a blade might slip. His conduct and appearance seemed the only things, in his present circumstances, over which he could exercise any control, so he put his energies there.

Tristam emerged from his rooms looking like the scion of an important family. Nervousness, he hoped, remained hidden behind the costume. He locked his door with a decoratively cast key and set out in search of the dining room, wondering if his stomach would tolerate food.

Although Tristam would normally have chosen to break his fast in one of the establishments that represented the latest fashion in Avonel, a coffee house, he was afraid to stray far from the Queen Anne for fear of missing the arrival of Roderick Palle. This despite the fact that the appointed hour was still some time off.

A servant led him into a sunny courtyard to a table set beneath the boughs of an ancient butternut tree. Finches sang among the leaves, and kinglets flitted through the curtain of ivy that covered the courtyard walls. It should have been a perfect morning.

Anxiety be damned, Tristam thought, *I cannot begin such a day without coffee.*

When food came, Tristam registered on some level that it was very good, but even so he was not able to enjoy it to any degree. Instead he sat sipping coffee, musing on his coming appointment and occasionally trying to turn his mind elsewhere. The gardens provided some relief, for Tristam was not only a botanist by training but a gardener on no small scale at his own home. This was the influence of Dandish, though Tristam's great-uncle Erasmus had made a contribution as well, leaving behind a beautiful mature garden, which Tristam had done much to improve.

"Mr. Flattery?"

Tristam looked up to find a gentleman of round features looking down at him.

"Roderick Palle," the man offered.

Tristam almost jumped to his feet, only barely remembering to make a leg. "Sir Roderick. Have I mistaken the time of our meeting?"

"No, I believe, by some near-miracle, my driver has brought me early." He gestured to a second chair. "May I?"

The King's Man took the seat, looked around the courtyard briefly, and then produced a beautifully made pocket watch. "We have some few moments yet. Just time for a draught of their fine west island *coffea*." He offered Tristam a stiff smile as though this was something he did infrequently. "It is healthful, I'm convinced. My own physician recommends coffee highly. 'Drink in the morning until there is a slight tremor in the hands, and then the same at supper.' It sets one up marvelously, don't you find?"

"I'm sure there's nothing quite like it." Sir Roderick Palle did not fit Tristam's image as one of Farrland's most influential men. Portly, soft featured, eyes perpetually half-closed. The man dressed in the most conventional manner and colors. Tristam had seldom met anyone who more suited the part of gentleman's gentleman.

What does this man want from me? Tristam wondered, all traces of appetite gone.

Sir Roderick's coffee arrived and as he tasted it an almost imperceptible easing of tightness around the eyes might have been an indication of satisfaction, though Tristam could not be sure.

"I have the pleasure of being acquainted with several members of your family, Mr. Flattery: your uncle, the duke, and the good duchess also; the Earl of Tyne, though not so well." He hesitated and Tristam felt his own face grow warm. "I did not know Erasmus Flattery, though he is something of a hero to me." He held up his cup. "I would find a morning without coffee difficult, but I am in thrall to the Erasmus Grape. Your great-uncle shall have my undying gratitude for his efforts in viniculture."

Tristam managed a smile, relieved the man had not brought up his father.

"I understand you are the heir of Erasmus? Do you pursue his interests?"

Tristam shook his head. "No. Viniculture was my uncle's special province, Sir Roderick. I shall not attempt to compete with him there."

"I wish I had known him, but it was always said that Erasmus was not a social man."

Tristam was used to this by now. Those who knew of his uncle at all were usually a little fascinated by his life. "The truth is, I hardly knew him myself. Deeply and incurably reclusive is how I would describe my uncle. I always lived at school."

"As I did myself. Which was a great blessing—my parents were famous bores." He tried the smile again to only marginally better effect. "And what lies ahead for you, Mr. Flattery? Finished at the university, I collect. Have you considered the service of the King?"

Although Tristam had dedicated some time to imagining the possible conversations he might have with the King's Man, this was not one that he had considered. He was a little taken aback. "To be honest, Sir Roderick, the thought had never occurred to me."

Roderick nodded. "But you should allow it to occur to you, Mr. Flattery. There is much work to be done and too few to do it. Too few of ability, that is." Roderick's tone and manner would suggest he spoke half in jest, yet Tristam had the strongest feeling that he was completely serious. The younger man found himself looking quickly around as though he might need to bolt. His journey with the detestable Hawksmoor came back to him. Not for him the life of a bureaucrat.

"I often encourage young gentlemen of conspicuous ability to consider the King's service. We cannot all live at our ease, Mr. Flattery; someone must shoulder the burden. At times I feel as though I am a dike holding back a vast sea of foolhardiness." All the while he spoke, Tristam noted that the man's tone did not alter, always remaining carefully neutral. Tristam suspected it would remain so even in a fit of rage. "There are any number of well-meaning fools who would bring Farrland to ruin in a trice. Without stopping to think, they would undermine our strength and have us, in the end, little more than a province of Entonne. And do not think our neighbor would not pounce on any opportunity. . . ." The color had begun to rise in the knight's face, but as quickly as it appeared the man seemed to gain control. He took a sip of his coffee. "It would raise my spirits to know that another had joined my colleagues and myself in our efforts. Young shoulders, Mr. Flattery; there is no substitute. Wisdom may come with age but, alas, the energies flag."

Tristam did not know how to respond. There was little doubt in his mind that to tell Sir Roderick the truth in this—that he would consider *prison* preferable—would damage the man's opinion of him irreparably. "It is such a new thought, Sir Roderick, I shall have to take time to consider."

Roderick looked down at his coffee, perhaps disappointed by Tristam's answer. "No doubt you have set a course of your own—graduating first of your year, and your family is not without influence."

Tristam felt his face grow warm again. Palle knew more than a little about Tristam, apparently. "Medicine," and then he added, more truthfully, "perhaps."

Roderick smiled, a little brittlely. "And would that be your choice if you were not trying to win the favor of a young woman? One whose father might look kindly upon the suit of a physician?"

Tristam's cup stopped halfway to his mouth. Roderick was showing terrible manners bringing up such a thing—but then he was the King's Man, after all. He would be sure to know a great deal about any person he brought into the King's palace.

"Am I being too familiar, Mr. Flattery?"

"Not at all. I was just framing a reply. As you say, the physician's calling might not be my principal interest, but it is a noble pursuit and one helpful to all. . . ."

"But not where your true interests would carry you?"

Tristam realized he hesitated. "Perhaps not."

"And your true inclination is . . . ?"

Tristam expected Sir Roderick knew the answer to the question already. "I would continue my study of the natural world," Tristam said as though admitting a great flaw of character.

"A worthy endeavor, but I will tell you; not a few men have served their King in great capacity and contributed much in other fields as well. Such men do not lie awake at night worried that they have wasted the day." Roderick consulted his pocket watch suddenly. "Shall we . . . ?"

As they set out in Roderick's carriage Tristam had a sudden fear that they would pass by the ruin of the Grand Theater of Avonel, and found himself staring at the passing scene registering little. Roderick would certainly know the story of Tristam's father; all of Avonel did. Tristam had developed his own defense in this. Mention the Avonel theater and he would make the most disparaging remarks about his father. And then, afterward, he would feel cruel and disloyal. He forced himself to look at the street, consciously reading the shop signs, almost reciting them mentally.

He glanced over at Roderick, who remained absorbed in his own thoughts. For a second Tristam feared that he had already so disappointed the King's Man that Roderick could no longer bother to make conversation. The younger man tried to think of something to say, if only to gauge his companion's response.

You are just nervous, Tristam told himself. *No doubt this is what it's like to begin in a new position.* Never having known employment for wages, he could only guess.

All the while, Tristam paid close attention to their progress and was relieved when they turned away from the city's center.

Although the coaches of the wealthy were a common sight in the streets of Avonel, Tristam could not shake the feeling that he was an object of attention traveling in Sir Roderick's beautiful phaeton. Opposite him the King's Man lounged, a look of complete distraction on his face.

I am the country cousin, Tristam thought. Even though his uncles—his father's elder brothers—were the Duke of Blackwater and Earl of Tyne, respectively, Tristam had always lived on the edge of the charmed circle of his near-relatives. He had shared rooms with cousin Jaimy at the university (cousin Jaimy was the heir to the Blackwater title, and therefore addressed as "Lord Jaimas," though to Tristam he was "Jaimy" or even "J") and had often been a guest in his uncles' homes, though he had never felt completely at ease there.

It was the tradition in Farrland that orphans were raised by the eldest member of the family—an odd tradition, Tristam often thought. In his case it had meant being raised by a series of reserved, often uninterested, instructors. Tristam felt himself warm a bit toward the King's Man when he realized that Sir Roderick had endured the same fate.

Although Tristam had felt some jealousy of classmates who went home to families, he had been allowed a freedom that was the cause of great envy among his fellows. Tristam knew quite well that the adult world had felt some measure of pity for him—fatherless and motherless as he was—but Tristam had wasted little time on self-pity in this regard. The truth was his parents, when alive, had not had much time for him anyway. After his mother's death, Tristam had missed certain of the servants more than either of his parents.

The great "tragedy" of being orphaned, in Tristam's view, had merely served to make him extremely independent while still very young. "Loneliness," as other people described it, was something that Tristam had not experienced since he was very young.

If Tristam had any true "family," it was his cousin Jaimy, who was like a brother to him. Later there had been Dandish, of course, but he had been a mentor and a friend. Tristam did not subscribe to the commonly held belief that orphans sought out surrogate parents for the rest of their lives. Certainly he hadn't wasted his time in that endeavor.

The street they passed along was thronged now with carriages and wagons and men on horseback, and the walkways streamed with pedestrians. It was a street that wound its way up the side of the low hill over which the city of Avonel spread. The gray granite paving stones were so smooth and finely fitted that the well-sprung coach rode as comfortably as a boat on calm water.

Off to the south Tristam caught a glimpse of billowing white clouds on the horizon. An afternoon rain shower was likely, a common occurrence in this season.

The carriage passed a queue of people outside a small temple and Tristam saw Sir Roderick fix his gaze there for a few seconds, his countenance unreadable. Over the wide doors spread a relief of the Martyr upon the pyre.

We have a barbarous history, Tristam thought.

"Are you too much a man of reason to be a follower of Farrelle, Mr. Flattery?" Sir Roderick asked, much to Tristam's relief.

"I am a trained empiricist, sir. Superstition is not compatible with my pursuits."

"Ah, I wondered." Genuine amusement shone in Roderick's smile. "And I have been trained a pragmatist. Too much so to follow the path of the Entonne Martyr. You might say that religion is not compatible with my pursuits, as well." He tilted his head toward the line of believers. "Waiting to pay their tithes, no doubt. Money that could provide their children with educations is sent off to Entonne. Their own children! Ah, well, Lord Skye said, 'There is no other occupation in which idleness can be turned to such profit.' He knew something of priests, apparently—and perhaps *prophets* as well." Roderick rubbed absently at the palm of his hand. "They have become a nuisance, these priests of Farrelle; petitioning the government, stirring up their parishioners. Five hundred years since their power was broken and still they cannot accept that the church shall have no part in governing. Even the mages realized that government should be left to kings and their ministers."

The conversation ended there and Tristam decided to keep his thoughts on these matters to himself. There was nothing to be gained in arguing. It had been sixty years since the last war with Entonne, but many—and Roderick was obviously one of these—believed the long history of hostilities with this nation was not yet done. For these people, the Farrellite church was just another Entonne institution aimed at subverting Farr independence.

Like most of the students at the university, Tristam was an admirer of Entonne culture. War, he believed, was unlikely unless brought about by Farrland. Not something he could say to the King's Man.

There were fewer carriages on the road, and almost no pedestrians. A wide gateway led into an area of open lawns and carefully designed gardens: the famous parklands that surrounded the palace proper. But Sir Roderick's driver passed the gate by, paralleling the high, surrounding wall until he found a lesser gate, this one closed and locked. Two men, who were clearly not palace guards, appeared from the gatehouse and allowed the carriage to pass.

Roderick was alert now, looking about as they went. The driver took them along a narrow drive between closely planted trees and hedges—a path for the use of gardeners, Tristam was sure.

A cuckoo disappeared into a hedge, catching Tristam's attention for a second, and then the driver brought the carriage to a halt, footmen jumping down to open doors and lower the steps.

"I hope you don't mind a short walk, Mr. Flattery?"

"Not at all." Tristam stepped down and immediately the King's Man set off along a narrow, gravel walkway lined with flower beds and small trees.

The King's senior minister is trying to enter the palace secretly, Tristam realized. It was the last thing in the world that he would have expected. *He is attempting to spirit me into the palace unnoticed. But unnoticed by whom?*

Through branches moving in the breeze, the palace appeared, like an island in the waves, a rose colored cliff rising from a sea of green. The Farr flag rustled in the breeze; bands of blue, white, and deep crimson, the King's gold and black crest in the center.

The Tellaman Palace was the principal residence of the Royal House of Farrland, a family that had known as much tragedy as glory in the centuries of their reign. Tristam had never before been inside the walls and found now that he did not want that to change. His home in Locfal suddenly seemed a place of great peace and security.

Unlike the rest of the city, the Tellaman Palace was constructed of granite. Tristam had often hunted beetles in one of the quarries, so he felt an odd connection between that great scar on the land and the King's palace. Stone of both rose and gray had been used for the exterior and the roofs were of copper, weathered to green-blue. It was generally a low building, seldom more than three stories, four at the most, not given to soaring towers or high walls or other structures common to castle architecture.

The basic floor plan was in the shape of an "H" and, onto the main building, wings had been added, carefully maintaining the style if not the symmetry. Onto these wings other additions had appeared every few decades.

The door Roderick led Tristam to was not large but, as at the gate, two men awaited them. Both bowed to Roderick who did not bother to acknowledge them.

The *"young shoulders"* Sir Roderick had spoken of. The King's service looked even less appealing than he had previously imagined.

They were soon in a long hall lined with busts of the sovereigns who had reigned over Farrland since the restoration. Both Kings and Queens watched with equanimity as the two men passed. And there among them the child-King, Birchard, seemed to meet Tristam's eye with a look of infinite sadness. For a second Tristam felt that sadness, as though he were marching off . . . to what? To war perhaps, or something even more tragic, for Birchard's story was not a happy one.

Then Alecka, the Fair, the childless Queen, looked down upon him, her face saintly, at peace, and though the sadness did not pass, Tristam felt as though Queen Alecka had just granted him silent forgiveness, for what crimes or sins Tristam did not know.

This hall was well known in Farrland, for it was often used in Royal ceremonies; to be raised to the peerage, for instance, one must pass down this hall. Perhaps a new baronet must gain the approval of all the royal ghosts. But this morning only Tristam and Sir Roderick represented the living here.

They turned into a narrower hallway where guards saluted them through high doors into a long, bright gallery, lined on one side by leaded windows. Pale marble floors reflected the sun and lit the opposite wall, which supported massive canvases depicting the sea battles that had played such an important part in the shaping of the world over the last two centuries. After a hundred ships had slipped beneath the waves, they came to the hall's end where purple-uniformed Royal Guards let them through more doors.

Farrland was a wealthy country and the Tellaman Palace reflected that. The ceilings in this hall were thirty feet overhead and ornate, painted with scenes of wood nymphs and fantastic animals. Floors were of marble, with pillars of different stones. Tall windows at the hall's end cast a long rectangle of soft light, as though it fell through the boughs of a summer forest.

Into this setting a woman's laughter floated, like the first notes of an aria—borne up by promise. Tristam saw two women rise from a bench half-ridden by a column. They stepped out so that the soft sunlight bathed them in gold and illuminated their hair like halos of soft flame. Tristam was almost transfixed, certain that this must be Princess Joelle, wife of the Prince Royal, for one woman appeared tall and regal.

To his great surprise Tristam heard Sir Roderick curse under his breath, and then suddenly the King's Man reached out, taking hold of Tristam's elbow and bringing him to a halt.

The two women continued to walk toward them, one a servant, Tristam realized, and the other dressed in a gown of pale green and gold. Even at a distance of twenty paces, Tristam could see that the gown highlighted the woman's long, copper-gold hair perfectly.

"The Duchess of Morland," Roderick said, bending his head somewhat.

Realizing that he was staring, Tristam immediately cast his gaze down. The dowager duchess was a favorite, perhaps *the* favorite, of the King.

When only three paces separated them, Sir Roderick bowed, and Tristam did the same.

"Roderick, what a pleasant surprise, and unaccompanied by your gaggle of secretaries and ministers." Her smile, Tristam saw, would melt the coldest of hearts. "I cannot say what led us to walk here, but I count myself fortunate." She nodded to Tristam and he thought her gaze, which rested on him for the briefest second, took in a great deal. Her manner was a little triumphant. This, clearly, was the person Roderick had hoped to avoid.

Before the King's Man could speak, she extended her hand to Tristam. "Elorin, Duchess of Morland."

Tristam self-consciously touched his lips to her hand, thinking as he did so that he had just kissed the woman said to be the most beautiful in Farrland. He hoped his discomfiture didn't show.

"Duchess," Roderick said quickly, his voice perhaps a little tight. "May I introduce Mr. Tristam Flattery."

"Certainly, Mr. Flattery, you are the colleague of the renowned Dandish?"

Ah, someone who did not immediately connect him to the Grand Theater! Tristam could hardly believe that the Duchess of Morland had heard of Dandish, let alone Tristam Flattery. His opinion of her went up immeasurably.

"I was his student and later assistant, Your Grace."

"You are being modest, I think." She smiled again and Tristam felt her reputation was well deserved.

The duchess then turned to Sir Roderick. "You are on your way to the arboretum, Roderick. I shall accompany you."

Roderick bobbed his head, saying nothing.

The duchess dismissed her servant and the three set out along the hall. Tristam noted that the green of the duchess' gown set off the green of her eyes perfectly and the subtle use of gold, in her gown and jewelry, was reflected in the gilt used in the hallway decoration.

The realization struck Tristam suddenly. Her entry had been staged; the exact place chosen, the light perfect, the timing of her beautiful laughter precise. Tristam, of all people should have seen that immediately. His mother, after all, had been an actress.

"You are in Avonel for some time, Mr. Flattery?"

"I am not yet certain, Your Grace."

"At your leisure, I see. I have many friends whose interests are not so different from your own, Mr. Flattery. Perhaps you would enjoy an evening at my home . . . ?"

Tristam did not know how to respond. Clearly there was animosity between the duchess and Sir Roderick— but how could one refuse the Duchess of Morland?

"I am honored that Your Grace would ask," Tristam said, hoping it was a neutral enough response to offend no one.

She laughed. "No need to be so formal, Mr. Flattery. I have known your aunt, the Duchess of Blackwater, for many years, and the duke as well." She turned to him, her look coy, though it was clearly not to be taken seriously. "You needn't worry that we have only just met."

"I would be honored to spend an evening at your home, Your Grace."

"And bring yourself along as well, Roderick. The company of people whose opinions vary would do you good." A beautiful smile appeared on her face as she said this, as though she teased a dear friend.

Roderick's face pulled into a tight smile. He bobbed his head again. Apparently even the King's Man must bare his breast to the barbs of the King's favorite, and try to smile into the bargain.

What is it that these courtiers want of me? Tristam asked himself again.

Sir Roderick used a key to let them through a large door. Inside was a small antechamber with a tiled floor. Unremarkable, perhaps, but Tristam's nostrils were assailed by the dank odor of rich soils and vegetation. The air itself was quite moist and the temperature seemed to rise immediately upon the doors' closing: the arboretum mentioned by the duchess.

Tristam knew that the palace had a collection of the flora of Oceana that rivaled that of the university. Professor Dandish had spoken of it and had made several journeys there to compare specimens.

Tristam felt his excitement growing. The obvious animosity that existed between the two courtiers was forgotten. After all, involvement in petty rivalries was considered one of a courtier's vital signs.

Sir Roderick turned to Tristam. "I realize, Mr. Flattery, that you have been inconvenienced. Brought here without even knowing a reason. Soon, I hope to make it clear why this was so." He glanced over at the duchess, and then back to Tristam who was surprised to hear anything approaching an apology from the King's Man. "Before I begin, I must tell you that I am about to speak of matters of great sensitivity. No part of this may be repeated. . . ." He seemed to be waiting for a reply from Tristam.

"Of course."

"Professor Dandish has always been our advisor in matters concerning the palace arboretum. It is a collection dear to our sovereign's heart, for, as you know, Gregory was much admired by the King."

They passed through an arch and into the arboretum proper. Tristam stopped involuntarily. Under a sky of curving glass the dense green of a tropical jungle thrust upward, life seeking the air and water and light without regard for the artificiality of its surroundings. Tristam recognized the nut palm and the crest palm immediately. And there the hotu and a *Plumeria,* a frangipani, no doubt; flora he had spent so much time classifying that he knew it as well as he knew the trees and flowers of his own garden.

Suddenly, Tristam realized that Roderick had stopped in the midst of his explanation.

"Pardon me, sir."

"As I was saying, Professor Dandish has always been our advisor. But, as you know, the good professor has not been well, nor is he any longer a young man. Fortunately, however, he is not the only empiricist in Farrland with knowledge of the flora of Oceana. Your monographs on the collection of Baron Trevelyan have been widely appreciated, Mr. Flattery."

They proceeded along a brick walkway that snaked through the jungle. Despite the distractions, the gravity of Sir Roderick's tone kept Tristam's attention. They turned off a side walkway past flowering frangipani, then made their way through several turnings to stop before a brass-bound, wooden door.

Taking a key from the pocket of his waistcoat, Sir Roderick turned the lock and pushed the door open. "Please." He held the door for the duchess and Tristam and then locked it once they had passed inside.

They were in a gardener's shed, or so it would have been were it not part of a palace. Wheelbarrows leaned against the wall and gardening tools hung in their proper places. A mound of dark soil covered a square of burlap on a potting table and terra cotta pots were stacked to one side.

"Tumney?" Sir Roderick raised his voice to call. "He does not hear so well as he did, our good gardener. He can't be far."

Another door at the end of the workroom let into a smaller arboretum, and this was planted with neat rows of a single species; one that Tristam did not immediately recognize.

"This," Sir Roderick said, his voice almost solemn, "is Kingfoil, or so Captain Gregory translated the islanders' name for it." He reached out and very gently touched the waxy leaves.

Tristam realized that this was a species new to him. His eyes ran over the branches almost of their own will, looking for the taxonomist's clues. The leaves would be classed as orbicular in shape, or perhaps reniform, but were divided into narrow pinnate segments at right angles to the central stalk, somewhat like feather palms, but these leaves were barely larger than a man's hand. The branches were covered in a brown-orange bark, plated and appearing thick.

"I'm not familiar with this shrub," Tristam said, "though perhaps its family is *Verbenaceae?*"

"I believe that is true," Roderick said, and Tristam saw the duchess nod.

"The genus," she interrupted, "is *Spuriverna,* and it is represented by only this single species, improperly rendered as *regis.*" She was clearly intruding on Roderick's office here, and Tristam was sure that the King's Man was not pleased, though Roderick's face remained unreadable. "As can be seen, it is an ordinary enough bush by the standards of Oceana. But this plant is of grave importance, Mr. Flattery. Kingfoil produces a seed from which a physic can be made, a physic with healthful properties unknown to us before the voyages of Captain Gregory." The duchess spoke even more solemnly than had the King's Man. *"Regis* produces few seeds, most of which are infertile—they produce no seedlings. These, and a few plants in the next chamber, are all the Kingfoil in our land. For this, and other reasons, this plant is kept a secret of the palace, explaining why you did not encounter it in your study. The physic made from the rare seeds is necessary to treat an affliction suffered by our King." She met Tristam's eye. "I will tell you in all frankness, Mr. Flattery, that without this physic King Wilam will certainly die." The duchess' green eyes began to glisten with forming tears, but she blinked them back and no droplet appeared on her cheek.

Tristam felt suddenly overly warm and longed to shed his coat and loosen his neck cloth. He also felt his own throat tighten at the duchess' obvious show of emotion.

What have I fallen into? he thought. He had come expecting to act as a tutor to a royal brat and found, suddenly, that it was the life of the King set on the balance. He dreaded what would be said next as much as an accused man feared the judge's pronouncement.

"*Regis* bears male and female flowers on different plants," Roderick said, grasping the opportunity, as the duchess recovered her equanimity. "There is a word for this. . . ."

"Dioecious," Tristam managed through a dry mouth.

"Exactly. Kingfoil is dioecious. But recently the few seeds that germinate produce exclusively male plants and the females that remain produce fewer and fewer seeds. We do not understand why this is occurring, Mr. Flattery, but it is obvious what the result will be. Soon there will be no seeds to make the physic required by our King. Mr. Tumney, our worthy gardener, is not a man of education, Mr. Flattery. It is our hope that the methodology of a trained empiricist might provide some insight into this dilemma—perhaps solve it."

Both the duchess and Roderick were staring at Tristam in silence, trying to read his reaction, he realized. They wanted to be told that their problem would

be solved. They wanted to hear confidence in his
voice.

"I must begin by speaking with your gardener,"
Tristam said mildly. "Is there no monograph dealing
with *regis?* Perhaps Lord Trevelyan . . . ?"

Roderick shook his head. Tristam had not spoken to
give them hope or to deny it entirely, and this had been
duly noted. "Only Captain Gregory had knowledge of
regis. There is a brief monograph by Professor
Dandish, but it is not based on information collected *in
situ.* All of his observations took place within these
walls and were combined with information from
Gregory's unpublished writings." Roderick paused and
met Tristam's eye; the bright awareness Tristam had
now seen appear and disappear shone strongly. "Do
you think there's hope, then, Mr. Flattery?"

"I think it would be premature to say such a thing,
as much as I would like to. My inquiries may take several weeks, perhaps a few months."

"Indeed," he said quietly. Roderick caught Tristam's
eye and held it. "Mr. Flattery, I feel it is necessary to
say again that all information pertaining to Kingfoil is
to be kept in the strictest confidence. The health of the
King, as you must know, is a source of constant speculation. Even rumors can have disastrous effects on affairs of state—our present treaty negotiations with
Entonne are but one example. I charge you to speak of
this matter to no one not already involved: the duchess," he said; clearly a concession, "myself, Tumney,
and Professor Dandish. Any lapse shall be dealt with
without regard to your intentions, loyalties, or family.
I hope that is clear?"

"Completely, sir."

He glanced at the duchess, hesitating. "I will locate
our gardener." Nodding to her, he was gone without
further formality.

Alone with the Duchess of Morland, Tristam suddenly felt awkward. He turned his attention to the
Kingfoil, reaching out and touching a leaf, though his

mind raced so that it registered almost nothing of the foliage.

"Mr. Flattery?" The duchess' tone was quiet, almost intimate.

"Your Grace." It was impolite to look away while being addressed and Tristam turned and looked into the duchess' striking eyes.

"Roderick has been known to have titles and estates granted to those in his circle for accomplishing nothing more than constant agreement with his opinions, but those he has not befriended could save the kingdom and hardly receive a note of thanks. It is the way of the court and courtiers. But not everyone is so blind. Please indulge my forthrightness for a moment. If you find a way to make the Kingfoil bear seeds again or grow female plants that bear fruit . . . the gratitude of the King will be great, as will be the gratitude of those who know of Kingfoil and its value to our sovereign. A title and the favor of the King, Mr. Flattery, would aid you in any endeavor you could wish to pursue."

Tristam really did not know what to say. "I . . . I am overwhelmed, Your Grace."

She favored him with a radiant smile and touched his sleeve. "You may call me Duchess, if you will."

Not knowing what to say, Tristam bowed his head.

"I will leave you to your important task, Mr. Flattery. Sir Roderick has instructions to assist you in all things, but if this arrangement should not prove completely satisfactory. . . ." She pressed a calling card into his hand. "And I have not forgotten your promise to attend an evening at my home. A world of luck to you, Tristam Flattery." With a swish of her skirts, the Duchess of Morland turned and disappeared back the way she had come.

Tristam was alone in the arboretum, but the tension between the two courtiers remained behind, still vibrating along his nerves. A sudden need to sit came over him, but he could see nothing that would serve his purpose. Unable to continue standing, he crouched down as though he would examine the *regis,* but his brain registered nothing. The life of the King was suddenly in his hands, yet he was no physician experienced in maintaining his equilibrium in such situations. *The life of the King!*

He pressed his hands to his eyes for a second. Certainly, if he succeeded, the rewards would be great. . . .

"Mr. Flattery, sir?"

Tristam removed his hands from his eyes and looked up to find an old man gazing down at him with some concern, turning a hat nervously in his hands as he did so.

"Are you well, sir?"

Tristam rose to his feet quickly. He tried to remember the name Sir Roderick had called out, but it was gone. "Perfectly well. And you are . . . ?"

"Tumney, sir. King's Gardener, and your servant, Mr. Flattery."

Tristam smiled to cover his search for some appropriate phrases. "Well, Tumney, it appears we have a task laid out for us. Sir Roderick mentioned a monograph written by Professor Dandish?"

"Sir Roderick asked me to say that he would have it sent around directly. The knight also sends apologies—called away on the King's business." Tumney shrugged. "The King's Man, you see."

As they spoke, Tristam realized that he towered over the King's Gardener. Tumney was a very small man, though well formed. His brown hair had thinned on top and he grew it long on one side and combed it across, trying to hide the expanse of bare skin. A wig was not an appropriate accoutrement for a gardener—even a King's gardener. The man's dress was what you might expect of his trade, though he wore a surprisingly elegant waistcoat beneath his jacket, jade green just visible where the last button closed. Clean shaven though not terribly wrinkled and, Tristam would guess Tumney was seventy if he was a day.

Tristam reached out and brushed the leaf of a nearby

bush. "You tend the Kingfoil. Tell me, Tumney, when was it first noticed? The lack of female seedlings?"

Tumney stopped turning his hat and reached up and patted the hair combed over his pate: it was an unconscious gesture. "Well, Mr. Flattery, it was very gradual so as to make a beginning hard to tell for sure. You see, she has played such tricks on me before. Seven years past, I would think, this same trick to the letter. Fewer and fewer seeds from each plant. Each planting had more boys and fewer girls until there were no girl children at all. She only lives about ten years in all, the Kingfoil, and bears scarce few seeds the first year or two, so I keep a nursery always full of children, you see. These ones here," he waved a hand at the planting, "they are all three to seven. The prime years for making seeds. Or so it always has been." He looked more than a little troubled as he said this.

"But this time is different, Mr. Flattery. When she played this trick before, it lasted long enough—near to seven months. But this has been going on longer than that. Almost a year to the day, sir."

"When this happened before, was it the same season?"

"No, sir, of that I'm sure. It was winter, but she will still flower here in our own little piece of Oceana, no matter what the season. Midm'nth was when I first took notice, Mr. Flattery, Midm'nth in the last year. I scratched it in my almanac, where I keep my record of planting and flowering and such."

"You have a record, then, of how this whole business began?"

Tumney gave a crooked grin, baring very even teeth. "Yes, sir. Everything is writ down just as Professor Dandish wanted it. Dates and numbers of seeds taken from each plant. I give every plant a name and that's marked on a plan of the beds, sir."

"You give me hope." Tristam felt his anxiety subside a little. If Dandish had prescribed the method of keeping records, it would be flawless and detailed. "Your almanac will save us a great deal of work. There are other plantings beside these?"

"There's a nursery, Mr. Flattery. I can show you if you like."

"That is exactly what I would like."

Tumney led Tristam down an aisle that ran along the side of the planting. The old gardener walked with a stoop and an obvious stiffness in one leg, but his pace was not slow and he did not seem to labor to walk so. He was probably hardier than he looked, this man. Tristam had seen the type before.

They passed through a heavy wooden door and came into another small arboretum, this one less elaborate, as though it had been built in a rush. Here there were carefully spaced rows of Kingfoil, each row a different age, no doubt, from seedlings to plants two-thirds the size of the adults they had just left.

Many of the plants displayed small but elegant white blossoms. Tristam bent down to look at one of these closely. A pretty five-petaled bell with broadly curving petals, tinged in purple, and with a lengthened pistil. They were not large, the size of a new gold crown.

"There are no female plants in flower, Mr. Flattery," Tumney said quietly. "Nor have there been for some months. They grow well. They look perfectly healthy both in leaf and root, yet they produce no flowers." He removed his hat and patted his head again, then began turning his hat as he had before.

"I have no doubt that what you say is true," Tristam said, "but I'm obliged to examine them, leaf and root, as you say."

"Nothing would please me more, sir. Not one bit more. I'm a gardener by trade, Mr. Flattery. Prenticed under Hawthorne who was King's Gardener for thirty odd years. But I've never stepped inside the gates of a university and I never had no one like Professor Dandish to steer me straight. I hope that you find old Tumney has missed the obvious—a mite or a blight I've never heard tell of. Nothing would please me more. No, sir; not one bit."

A ringing bell interrupted them and Tumney gave a quick bob. "That will be the good professor's monograph, I should think. Excuse me, sir. I'll return directly."

Tristam was alone again. Genus *Spuriverna.* Family *Verbenaceae.* There were several plants in the family with known medicinal properties—or at least thought so by the islanders of Oceana. Healing burns came to mind. The Old Farr name meant "sacred herb." The genus name was a bit odd—more common in a plant found in northern latitudes—for it would be rendered as "false spring."

Against one wall stood a table set with a wooden frame divided into small, closely spaced boxes. Tristam walked over to examine them for they were probably planted with the seeds of the Kingfoil. He made a quick count and found one hundred and twenty boxes. Of these only six showed signs of a tiny closed fan of green pushing up through the dark earth.

"There will be a few more yet, Mr. Flattery. Perhaps ten in all, if things continue as they have. And there is no guarantee of that."

Tristam turned to find Tumney approaching, a quarto portfolio in vivid blue tucked under his arm.

"It isn't just that there are drastically fewer females: general fertility is decreasing, as well?"

Tumney stopped and scratched behind his ear, thinking. "That would appear to be the case, though the Kingfoil has never been a good bearer. From a hundred seeds planted I would expect to see twelve children, perhaps fifteen." He proffered the portfolio. "I'm sure Professor Dandish has recorded these things all in good order, sir. Much better than I could tell it."

Tristam took the slim portfolio from the gardener. "You haven't read this?"

"No, sir," he spoke a bit defiantly and Tristam suspected that it injured his pride to say it.

Tristam considered the warning of Sir Roderick and remembered that Tumney's name had been mentioned among those he could trust. "Would you care to see it when I have finished?"

The old man shrugged. "Well, I wouldn't mind, sir, if you think it would be all right." Tristam could see this small gesture of confidence pleased the man.

"I can't imagine why it wouldn't be. Is there a place where I might sit to read?"

"Follow me, Mr. Flattery. We're not entirely without comforts here."

They passed back into the larger arboretum and Tumney led the way to a corner, hidden away behind the tallest Kingfoil, and here there were a chair, a small table, and a lamp. There were one or two other comforts as well; a pipe stand and a tobacco humidor of the very finest craftsmanship, as well as a silver tea service, also very well made.

"There you are, sir, as homely as you could like, I should think." Tumney gestured to the chair and then stood with his hat in his hand again. He looked slightly embarrassed. "That humidor, Mr. Flattery, was a present from the King. Sent it to me on my fiftieth birthday with as nice a note as you can imagine—in the King's own hand, mind you." He flushed a bit with pride.

"And well deserved, I'm sure."

"I like to think so. The tea service is from the Duchess of Morland. And though some would speak ill of the duchess, to my mind there is not a more gracious woman in the Kingdom. Often the duchess looks in on my work and always has a good word. Even now, when the Kingfoil is not acting according to hopes, not a word of blame. As gracious as, as. . . . Well, I don't know, sir, but as gracious as a queen, I should think."

"You can't say fairer than that, Tumney." Tristam made a show of untying the ribbon that bound the portfolio.

"I have my morning tea at this time, Mr. Flattery. Could I bring you a cup?"

"That would be very kind of you, Tumney, very kind indeed."

The old gardener retrieved the tea set from the table,

with some reverence, Tristam thought, and disappeared down the aisle between the rows of Kingfoil.

Inside the portfolio Tristam found his teacher's familiar hand on a title page.

The Life History of Verbenaceae Spuriverna regis, with
Instructions for
Cultivation in Northern Regions.
Illustrations by the Author
1542

Tristam turned to the next page and read

The species regis, is the only known example of the genus Spuriverna, though its family is known to comprise approximately forty different species, virtually all of these within the genus Medicus. Regis, also called Kingfoil, is indigenous to the southwestern region of Oceana and is found almost exclusively on the island called Varua by its inhabitants (named New Blanshford by Captain Gregory and so noted on naval charts). Its existence on other islands of the New Blanshford group is largely conjectural and based on stories told to Captain Gregory on his first visit. These may have been apocryphal and Captain Gregory himself states that his understanding of the language was imperfect.

In its native environment regis will grow anywhere there is loamy soil and some shade (for it does not grow out in the open) up to about three thousand feet in elevation. Despite regis' simple requirements, it is surprisingly rare. The people of Oceana value it extremely and, in their culture of taboos and prerogatives, all plants found are considered to be the property of the King.

Regis seldom exceeds four feet in height and occasionally mature plants do not reach more than two feet eight or nine. Branches begin at about one quarter of its height and the main trunk often splits into two or three main branches not much above this and

*each of these secondary trunks will support several
branchings, often as close as every four inches.*

A detailed description of Kingfoil's appearance followed, and Tristam was able to compare this directly
with a mature plant not four feet away. As he expected,
it was precisely correct in every detail. Dandish did not
have his reputation without reason. At this point
Tumney arrived with tea. Tristam buried his head in
his reading and the gardener took the hint and went
back to his own duties.

*The King of Varua, who gave Captain Gregory the
seeds of* regis *as a gift to our own King, told the captain that it was possessed by a spirit that delighted in
the playing of tricks. Often the spirit would cause the
plant to stop producing seeds and it would then become barren; sometimes for several years or even
forever after. Naturally occurring plots of* regis, *where
the plant had grown for years, would suddenly die
out and this would precipitate a search for other
plots, with great rewards to the man or woman who
found one. Several annual ceremonies on the island
were apparently performed for the express purpose
of supplicating this spirit.*

The islanders do not attempt to cultivate regis, *or
did not at the time of Gregory's visit, but rely on finding places where it occurs naturally. Gregory was
told that* regis *invariably grew in stands and single
plants were never found.*

*Without doubt, much more could have been
learned of* regis *during Gregory's stay if his able
ship's naturalist, Mr. Trevelyan, had known of the
plant's existence and had been allowed to apply his
considerable powers of observation to* regis *growing
in its native environment.*

*We are left with Captain Gregory's account of the
Varuan King's words, for the captain states clearly
that, at no time, did he see* regis *growing.*

*The cultivation of Kingfoil in more northerly regions
must be practiced in sheltered gardens, preferably*

within an arboretum especially constructed for the purpose. Such a building must have provisions to block some portion of the summer sun, for regis *prefers to grow in shade. Temperatures must be maintained strictly and never allowed to fall below sixty-five (and even that for short periods only). An average of eighty degrees would create an environment much like its own. Whether one can create temperatures too hot for* regis *is perhaps moot, for it is difficult to maintain temperatures over ninety-five in our latitude and* regis *will be unaffected by such heat.*

A prospective grower of Kingfoil must pay strict attention to the soils used. Regis grows only in soils of decaying vegetable matter (commonly found in the jungles of Oceana) that are not overly acidic. Therefore, soils made of decaying needles of pine (pinaceae), *cedar* (cupresaceae) *or related gymnosperms should be avoided assiduously.*

There followed a treatise on soils and their makeup. Though not new to Tristam, he read it carefully in case there was information that would bear directly on the growing of *regis*. Meticulous in detail—that was the creed he had learned from Dandish and he had come to believe it as fervently as his former teacher.

Tristam looked up from Dandish's monograph and wondered how his life could have changed so much in so short a time. Only a few days ago he had been a gentleman of leisure with nothing that could even be seriously thought of as responsibility, and now the life of the King was dependent on his work. It did not seem possible. Not he, Tristam Flattery. Even for someone used to facing life alone, this was far too much all at once.

He glanced down at the monograph again and thought immediately, *I must write to Dandish.* The monograph had raised innumerable questions. The realization that his old professor was only a day's journey away took some of the weight off Tristam's chest and allowed him to breathe. Dandish might be old and of nervous disposition, but Tristam had never known his brilliance to fail. If nothing else, there was that to reassure him.

FIVE

The fluttering of wings called Tristam out of the warmth of a deep sleep. He rolled over and raised his head, confused, unsure of where he was. The room was dark, but a sound on the balcony drew his attention. Wings beating and a movement of white in the pale light of the moon. *"Pigeon,"* Tristam told himself. He let his head drop back to the pillow and continued to fall, into darkness and warmth . . . and then light.

A warm wind blew, and the fluttering of wings had not abated. There, out on the water. A bird Tristam had never seen, white as the distant line of surf. Two long tail feathers, elegant and exotic. The bird beat its wings, hovering over the turquoise lagoon, for that is where he was, standing on the white sand edge of a broad lagoon. The wind rustled the palms behind him; a sound he'd never heard though it was familiar in his dream.

Below the hovering bird a flower lay on the water, water so clear that the blossom, too, seemed to float in the air.

Hands appeared from below the surface, rising up, cupping the flower as though it were a treasure, an offering, lifting the blossom into the air. Perfectly formed hands—a young woman's hands. Tristam felt himself take a step forward into the warm lagoon.

A woman emerged from the water then, face and shoulders glistening wet in the sun, though, impossibly, her hair remained dry. Long black hair floating on the surface around her, blowing in the fair wind. With great care she placed the flower behind her ear and then she looked up and saw Tristam for the first time. A smile of delight lit her beautiful face.

She knows me, Tristam realized, though he had never seen her before.

Her dark eyes met his without shyness and she began to walk toward the shore. As she moved her beauty was revealed slowly, glistening skin that held no secrets from the sun. In water barely above her knees, the woman stopped.

She embraced him then, her wet skin warm against his own. He felt her lips touch his, touch his neck, and he kissed her shoulder—unimaginably soft. She pressed herself to him and Tristam felt a sharp, involuntary intake of salt air. He kissed a small breast and felt himself falling, back into water that caught them, surrounded them with soft warmth, supported them.

Without intending to he felt himself enter her, and they were moved by a slow, pulsing rhythm from the surf breaking on the distant reef. The flower fell from her hair and tumbled into the water. A swirl and a flash of white and the flower was gone, whisked down into the depths.

Tristam heard a moan and awoke to the sound of his own voice. He was tangled in the coverlets of his bed, blood pounding in his ears like drumming. It was dark and still. He lay trying to calm his heart, to catch his breath. Part of him reached out to hold fast to the emotion of the dream, but already the feeling was dissipating, like a spent wave. Ebbing back down the sloping sands—lost to him.

🎐   🎐   🎐

Tristam became conscious of light, of sounds. His attempt to seek his island woman back through the realms of sleep had been futile. If he had dreamed again, he recalled nothing.

It was his fifth day in Avonel and things were not proceeding as he hoped. The truth was Tumney had already performed virtually all of the procedures Tristam would have attempted. Despite Sir Roderick's reservations about the man, the gardener knew his trade. The inquiries that Tristam had begun were not yielding results of any significance, leaving him struggling against a feeling of failure which he knew was affecting his analytic abilities. It was, he decided, time to swallow his pride and seek assistance. He would write to Dandish again over breakfast.

He had sent a note off to the professor immediately after his visit to the palace, but that hadn't been a call for help—merely a few questions. Tristam hadn't understood the difficulty of the problem then.

Why entire stands of regis have periods of infertility or suddenly become barren altogether is unknown and requires much further study. It is most likely to be part of an extended natural cycle and therefore can be best avoided by keeping seeds from the earliest plantings and using these to regenerate the plots.

So Dandish had written. A simple paragraph suggesting a simple solution. But the professor had been wrong. Tumney had long since tried the obvious, to no avail.

The servants knew Tristam's routine now, and hot water arrived seconds after he rose. Even so he bathed and shaved without pleasure.

He had also written to Jenny, the young woman he courted back in Locfal; a letter which, he was embarrassed to admit, made his situation sound more glamorous than it truly was. Jenny, after all, did not share Tristam's interests. She would want to hear about balls and the theater and the doings of the Royal Family.

There had been at least two social functions at the palace since his arrival and Tristam had attended neither. There was only the hinted at invitation to the home of the Duchess of Morland—an invitation that had not yet materialized and looked less likely every day. Tristam had found himself occasionally taking out the duchess' calling card to assure himself that the meeting had not been imagined. Upon his return to Locfal, Tristam would have little to tell.

The truth was he had dug in the soil quite a bit. Examined roots and seeds, dissected flowers, devised complicated planting schedules, searched for mites, blights, rusts, and numerous other parasites and diseases—all to no avail. He had taken regular temperature readings of both soil and air; proving nothing. It was quite clear that unless one of his plantings revealed a clue to the mystery, no less than a miracle would be required to have the Kingfoil bearing seeds again. He closed his eyes.

It was a bit embarrassing to be brought all the way from Locfal with great expectations, and then prove to know nothing more than one very elderly gardener. So much for his years at the university.

Dandish. He hoped the professor was well enough to offer some advice.

A zephyr of the feeling from his dream encounter touched him. Jenny suddenly seemed an annoyance, his letter to her embarrassing. The truth was he had barely thought of her in five days. Hardly a mad passion, but then he was looking for a wife—someone who would be his companion and supporter over the years. A sensible mother to their children. At least that was what he told himself.

His mind returned to the problem of the arboretum. "Another Flattery fails spectacularly in Avonel," Tristam said ruefully. But at least his failing was not public. Something to be thankful for.

What exactly would he say to Dandish? The worthy professor would not think less of him for asking assistance. Not one bit. Dandish was the ideal empiricist. Pushing back the borders of ignorance, that was his only reason for living. Other empiricists might suffer jealousies and defend themselves and their work with an aggressiveness that would not be out of place among bulls, but not Dandish. The professor could not bear criticism himself and so would not inflict it on others in anything but the mildest terms. He hardly even noticed that Lord Trevelyan gave him little credit for his years of work on the classification of his great collection. No, he would not criticize or judge his former student. Only Tristam felt that he had failed—Tristam and the King's Man, and perhaps the beautiful Duchess.

He crawled out of the bath and began to dry himself, the warm breeze coming in through the open window reminding him again of his dream—lack of sleep making it harder to manage the transition into complete wakefulness.

A knock on the door.

"Yes?"

"Mr. Flattery," came a muffled voice. "Your breakfast and a letter, sir." It was an old servant named Benjamin.

"Leave it on my desk, will you?"

"As you wish, sir."

A letter from Dandish. Tristam's spirits rose perceptibly.

He dressed slowly, in no hurry to rush to the palace as he had been only a few days earlier—his opportunity for glory was quickly beginning to look like the field of his defeat.

As he entered the sitting room, the smell of coffee assailed his nostrils and provided him with something approaching pleasure. He tilted the silver pot, splashed the steaming liquid into a cup, and raised it to his lips. He was holding back intentionally, preparing himself to not be disappointed if Dandish's letter contained no revelations. He lifted the envelope and found the seal of the university pressed into wax.

The letter turned out to be from Cecil Emin, Dean of Merton College, a man who had been a friend of his father, and a friend to Tristam as well.

Dear Tristam:

It is my sad duty to inform you of the death of our colleague, Professor Sanfield Dandish. I know you will mourn his passing as much as I. The good professor passed away in his sleep last night. A great loss to us all.

I was fortunate to have visited Professor Dandish but two days ago, and he mentioned that you were engaged in some matter in the Royal Arboretum. I hope this letter finds you still in Avonel. As you may know, I am the Executor of Professor Dandish's estate, but I don't think you can be aware that you are mentioned in his will: no fortune, I'm afraid, but some of the professor's personal effects that may bring you comfort.

It would be a great favor to me if you could spare a few days to help in the formidable task of putting the professor's effects in order. I don't think there is anyone better qualified for this task than yourself as you were so often at Dandish's home and knew his study in the college better than he did himself. Of course, the King's business may not allow this and, if so, I certainly will manage. Please do let me know your decision.

> *Your servant,*
> *Cecil Emin, Dean*

Tristam sat down hard in a chair. He felt suddenly dizzy, disoriented. Something was very odd. He heard the muffled sound of someone sobbing, far off.

Farrelle's blood, he thought, *is that me? Am I weeping?*

❧   ❧   ❧

Sir Roderick was extremely kind and solicitous upon hearing Tristam's news. Of course, he had known Dandish himself and such things always made a difference. Once assured that Tumney could look after the plantings and gather all necessary information, the King's Man had been only too willing to release Tristam for a few days. At the same time Tristam had confessed that there was, as yet, no indication of what was causing the problem with *regis*. Roderick had only nodded and looked down at his desk.

To Tristam's surprise the knight had insisted on providing Tristam with a carriage and driver, refusing to let him post up to Merton on the public coach—an act of kindness that Tristam found quite touching. Perhaps there was a heart beating in Roderick's chest, after all.

It appeared that the King's Man had a weakness for fine carriages—the *Bronam* that he lent to Tristam was not only the latest fashion but it was a paradigm of the carriage maker's art.

So Tristam's journey to Merton, the location of the university, passed in relative physical comfort. Ironically, or so it seemed to Tristam, the day was perfect and the green countryside rolled past in ordered tranquillity, the death of a single man having shockingly little impact on the larger world.

The journey was familiar to Tristam, as he had made it often enough as a student. He watched the miles roll by, memories of his years at Merton surfacing, Dandish playing a part in many of these.

At a slough by the roadside he asked the driver to stop so that he could take his glass and search the shores and pools—a practice he had followed for years. He went and stood on the edge where the irises grew, their ornate purples and highlights of yellow seemed so exotic they might have been the creation of an artist. The flowers reminded Tristam of Dandish, whom he could hardly keep out of his thoughts anyway. Among all his interests the professor had a soft spot for flowers, and cultivated them with all the love another man might have lavished on wife and children. The pond seemed a sad and lonely place today.

An evening egret was Tristam's chief find and he was gratified to see them nesting so far from their common range. The slough had its usual complement of ducks and waders, and passeriformes—perching birds—of the sort that preferred the wet lands to the dry. As Tristam moved his glass slowly across the scene, all singing ceased and the smaller birds disappeared into thickets. Tristam lowered his glass in time to see a winter falcon float over the water above the level of the surrounding willows. It disappeared behind the branches of a tree, and though Tristam searched the area with his glass, it was to no avail. The bird did not reappear.

Better than an egret, he thought, for winter falcons were not commonly seen in this season, at least not so far south. But Tristam was sure of what he had seen. His uncle had been a falconer. When Erasmus had died, Tristam had released all of his birds; but one, a winter falcon, was still seen occasionally, sitting in a tree in the garden. Tristam had begun to think that his late uncle, the alleged mage, had put his falcon to watch his errant nephew. But it was a beautiful bird and Tristam never tired of watching it in return.

❦   ❦   ❦

Dusk was on the horizon as Tristam arrived in the town of Merton on Wedgewater. He took a room at the Ivy, an old establishment, covered, as the name suggested, in *Hedera helix,* the inside paneled in dark polished wood. A place suited to aging servants and hushed voices. Tristam requested supper in his rooms and ate by a window overlooking the inn's small park. A large elm grew nearby and the branches came close to Tristam's second floor window so that he felt he had moved into a tree house—and this idea pleased him as much as anything could that day.

As usual, sleep eluded Tristam, perhaps even more so that night. When it did find him, it was not sound. Again he was wakened by strange dreams several times, though in the morning he could recall nothing of them.

SIX

Before breaking fast his first morning in Merton, Tristam sent his card around to Dean Emin asking if he could call at eleven, and before long, a reply came saying that he would be expected.

Merton on Wedgewater was so small that Tristam elected to walk the short distance to the dean's. The town changed little over the years and Tristam half expected to meet his classmates on the street. It was the nature and part of the charm of Merton that scholars who had lived there even fifty years earlier felt the place virtually unaltered when they visited. A town that defied time, in its own small way.

Merton was "of a piece," the town's people liked to say. The architecture of the houses was generally a reflection of the university and, in any given street, one house was much like another, the principle differentiation applied was "old home" as opposed to "new." Old homes were built of uncut fieldstone and new of rough hewn. Of course, new homes were often two centuries old or more.

Eighteen Northmoor Road was a "new" house in a row of almost identical dwellings built hard up against each other. Their front steps emptied directly onto the walkway and if not for the evenly spaced chestnut trees growing before them the houses would have shown a particularly bland facade to the world. Fortunately, as Tristam well knew, they were more than comfortable inside. In fact, the dean's home could be described as rather genteel. His late wife had seen to that, and Dean Emin did not attempt to improve upon her work.

The row of houses on Northmoor overlooked a common, and as he crossed the lawn, Tristam could see the dean standing in his study window looking out toward the spires of the university. Having been acquainted with Dean Emin for many years, Tristam knew that the man's eyes would be focused on some point in the impossible distance and he would be slowly turning his pocket watch over and over, his thoughts as far off as the point he gazed toward.

Barnes, the dean's gentleman's gentleman, answered Tristam's knock and escorted him up the stairs where he tapped lightly on the study door.

"Yes?" The dean's voice sounded surprisingly frail to Tristam.

"Mr. Flattery, sir."

"Show him in, Barnes. Thank you."

The servant opened the door and, as Tristam passed, said softly, "Good to see you, sir."

Dean Emin turned from the window and attempted a smile of welcome, though he was clearly too saddened to manage it. "So kind of you to come, Tristam."

"I only wish we met under more pleasant circumstances, Dean Emin."

"That's the way of humans, I sometimes believe. We wait until there is a tragedy to bring us together. Unfortunate." He waved at one of two ancient leather chairs and both men sat down. Tristam had not seen the dean for more than two years and he thought the don had aged more in that time than in the previous decade. His white hair and mustache did not seem so thick and lustrous and, like many scholars, Emin showed signs of his sedentary profession, for he was somewhat given to portliness. Thick lips and a small chin both seemed out of place on the man's round face, and his skin was so smooth and delicate it appeared never to have been out in the sun. But it also seemed to be stretched too thin, the veins showing purple at the temples. His eyes, once a vivid blue, were drained of their color and had lately become very pale. The old man kept glancing at Tristam with a look that verged on pity.

They sat in awkward silence for a few seconds and Tristam, unable to meet the dean's gaze, examined the room.

The study had walls built of bookcases, apparently a small fireplace, the dean's desk, the two easy chairs now in use, and a small table bearing a chess board. There was no art on the walls, for the bookshelves left no room. The floor was bird's-eye maple, the planks all of ten inches in width, and in the center of this was a faded rug that had once been a work of some beauty. The only window to the study was taller than a man, for the ceiling followed the contours of the roof and Tristam estimated it to be at least eleven feet. It was the room of a don, there was no question; a scholar's retreat, insulated from the world of the everyday by walls lined with the works of great minds.

Unlike most studies Tristam was familiar with, this one lacked the bittersweet smell of pipe tobacco, for the dean's wife had forbidden him to smoke indoors and though she had now been dead almost as long as Tristam had been alive, the dean still would not go against her wishes.

"Well, it is a sad day for us both, I'm afraid," the old man began at last. "Sanfield Dandish was certainly of the very first rank. A scholar and an empiricist to be admired and, I dare say, emulated. He was a great example to our young scholars, and quite a number of graduates from his classes have become names to be reckoned with. And that is living praise for the man, to be sure." He leaned over and touched Tristam's arm, an unusual gesture for the old man. "Could you use a brandy as much as I?"

Though it was far too early for Tristam to feel such a need, he could not refuse a gesture of affection from Emin, knowing how hard such things came to the old man. "Yes, I think I could."

The dean patted his arm awkwardly and then rose and went to call Barnes. He returned to his chair immediately, as though age or exhaustion had left hm too weak to stand for long.

"I am loath to speak of practical matters at such a time, Tristam, but I must be at the college shortly and I will be unable to get free until this evening. Do you mind?"

"No, by all means. It's why I've come. Or at least part of the reason."

Barnes arrived with two brandy snifters on a tray. He retreated as silently as he had come.

"Well, the memorial service will take place the evening after next, the twenty-seventh, in Merton Hall. Will you want to speak?"

Tristam hesitated for a second. "I—I think not."

"It's a difficult thing to do and no one will think less of you if you don't. I'm expected to, of course, so I must do my best." The dean sipped his brandy and the awkward silence settled around them like a winter evening. Both men's thoughts returned to their friend, so recently gone. "He rallied a little at the end," the dean said. "I thought he might pull through. But then, the last two weeks. . . ." The old scholar pursed his lips tight together and closed his eyes. Tristam expected to see his shoulders begin to shake, but they did not. The dean glanced over at Tristam and attempted a weak smile, but it was so fleeting it appeared more a look of resignation and grief. "It is one of the most terrible aspects of growing old, Tristam; you begin to lose your friends. Men and women you've known for thirty and forty years—and more." He put a hand up to his face, and Tristam heard him sniff quietly.

To see this kind old man so grief stricken and dispirited affected Tristam. He wanted to reach out and touch him, just lay a hand on his arm, but he didn't want to add to the old man's embarrassment.

"The will reading can't take place before the memorial," Dean Emin went on, forcing himself to speak of the practical things, almost clinging to them—avoiding any words that reflected what he thought or felt. Only the tone of his voice and the barely contained grief spoke any truth. He paused to take a long breath. "Dandish and I shared a barrister. We'll meet in his office." His voice gained some strength now, as the dean mastered his emotions. "I'll let you know. He ... Dandish, left virtually all of his estate to his sister. A sad story really." The Dean cleared his throat. "She's mad, you see ... but this will provide her with some comforts she doesn't have where she is. I only hope she will be aware of them. His library, papers, and collections he left to the university, of course, with a few exceptions—and these exceptions he stipulated should go to you, Tristam. Things I believe you expressed admiration for at one time or another. His instruments also will be yours."

Tristam shook his head. He tried to find some appropriate words, but this faculty deserted him at that moment.

The dean went on, apparently wishing to have everything said. "Sanfield had no children, and though his students took the place of family for him, you, Tristam, were the favored son. He said as much to me on more than one occasion. Dandish had the highest opinion of your abilities ... as do many others."

Tristam took a drink of his brandy and discovered that his hand trembled.

Perhaps to save them both embarrassment, the dean rose and went over to his desk. From a drawer he removed a ring of keys. For a second he stood looking down at Tristam, care written on his face. He smiled, not the smile of happiness, but the soft gesture of concern and affection. "Could you use more brandy?" he asked awkwardly.

It almost made Tristam smile. "No, no thank you, Dean Emin. I am not overwhelmed. Please go on."

The old professor looked at him for a moment, as though trusting his own assessment more than Tristam's words. "These are to the professor's house and rooms at college," he said, lowering himself slowly into the chair and proffering the keys to Tristam. "I'm not sure which is which, but I'm sure you will work it out. My barrister, who is a sensible man, does not expect a full inventory of the professor's effects. The will is not so complicated and there aren't several parties vying for advantage, you see." He raised his glass thoughtfully, but then pulled his focus back. "Don't concern yourself with the extraneous. The books, monographs, correspondence; these are really our concern, Tristam. No one else will be able to discern their importance."

Tristam looked down at the keys in his hand, a ring he had often seen the professor produce from his coat pocket. "I'll do everything I can."

"I have no doubt. It won't be a small task, though. It might take several days. Then there are Dandish's rooms in college. Perhaps the two of us should tackle that tomorrow? Or better the day after? You'll let me know how you get on."

Tristam nodded. "When it comes to the professor's rooms at Merton, the more of us the better. Despite his great interest in the order of things, the professor managed to bring little of it to his own life. His rooms will be in a state of chaos, I fear."

The dean smiled. "It was a small flaw in a great spirit. . . . I'm sure you feel the same." He held up his brandy snifter. "To Sanfield Dandish. May his labors bear fruit for a thousand years."

Tristam raised his glass in silent salute.

❦   ❦   ❦

Sanfield Dandish had remained a bachelor all his life but, even so, he had lived in a largish house, well-suited to a family, set in a country-style garden. The house would not have stood out in Merton except that Dandish had designed a stone tower that was attached rather arbitrarily to one end of the structure. To a passerby this tower might have contained nothing more than a stairwell, but its upper story was actually a water tower. The water was pumped from a well up into the cistern by a wind-driven mechanism—another innovation of the professor's. Dandish's home boasted water piped into the water closets and the scullery as well. Tristam knew full well that the convenience of this had been of no consequence to Dandish—it was merely the delight in the design and execution that had led the professor to spend considerable energies in this project.

Tristam lifted the latch on the gate and stepped into the professor's world. The old man had done much of his own gardening, when he was able, and had closely overseen the rest. Several new varieties of rose had come from this very garden as well as variations on both ornamental and food plants.

"Look at what has been done to the breeds through animal husbandry! And in the world of horticulture," Tristam remembered Dandish saying, *"entire new varieties! If man can do such things in living memory, what could nature accomplish in a few million years?"* Which brought the professor down squarely on the side of *Constant Change* in the species debate, a debate that still raged. This belief in the transmutation of species had made the old pedagogue somewhat of a radical in his youth, and, though the tide was beginning to turn on that issue, it marked the professor as a man who stood by his convictions. As long as Tristam had known him, Dandish had never been afraid to entertain ideas that others scorned. Unlike many, age had not cast his mind into rigid patterns. Tristam had often thought the professor more flexible than his students. Certainly less sure that he knew the truth. Perhaps this had been what had made him so susceptible to criticism.

Tristam walked down a narrow gravel path between rows of exotic irises of different hues. Dandish had been a complex man. He had been quite surprised at his students' commitment to finding "the truth." *"In empirical studies,"* he once said, *"we formulate succeeding hypotheses to explain phenomena, each hypothesis fitted to our facts a little more closely. But ultimately, Tristam, I do not think we will arrive at truth. I think we shall arrive at a great mystery."*

For some time afterward Tristam had suspected the

professor of being a secret mystic, a transcendentalist perhaps, but Dandish had been as fixated on developing hypotheses as any empiricist Tristam knew. He had also said, *"A great hypothesis is like a great poem, as long as it explains something central to the human mind it will stand. When it no longer fulfills this promise something else takes its place. But we all remember the name of Maritain even if we no longer read his poems. And if not for Maritain, there would never have followed Bartram and Northrop. A poet's greatness is not just measured by how long his poetry is read."*

Despite all, Dandish had been as concerned with "immortality" as any of his colleagues. Tristam hoped the professor's work was substantive enough to assure it.

When Tristam had first come to know Dandish, he had been confused by the professor's penchant for talking about empiricism in terms of art and poetry, but over the years the student had slowly come to understanding. Dandish held the "fact collectors," as he called them, in disdain. The collection of information, to Dandish's manner of thinking, had one purpose—to support a hypothesis. Reason must be applied to guide the search for information and to interpret the findings.

To Tristam it seemed a statement of the obvious, but in the great debate between the "rationalists"—those who believed that everything could be understood by mere application of the mind, and the pure empiricists, those who believed understanding grew from one's experience of the world—Dandish had been attacked by both sides. Too much "rationalism" for the fact collectors and too interested in collecting facts for the rationalists. But this debate, too, was slipping into silence—the very word "empiricism" was changing in meaning, and the school of thought championed by Dandish and some of his colleagues was winning the field. Unfortunately, the personal cost to the hypersensitive Dandish had been immense.

Tristam strolled through the garden, partly to avoid entering the house, though he was not sure why. He was surprised to discover wet soil in the beds: someone had thought to come and water.

Although the professor had not been a large part of Tristam's life for the past two years, they had spent many many hours together during the classification of Trevelyan's collection. Dandish had been a reserved, distant man, not given to displays of affection or to discussing personal matters—Tristam had not known of the sister, for instance. Theirs had been an odd, unspoken friendship, more important to the professor than Tristam had realized.

To think that he remembered me in his will, Tristam mused. *I wish now that I had realized. I should have made the effort to visit. Had I only known he was so ill. . . .*

He knew that he would harbor some regret over this. Of course, Dandish may have preferred things that way. Friendship unacknowledged, unspoken. It might have been easier for him, for it did not seem uncommon in the reserved, rather cool, world of the Merton dons.

Tristam stopped and surveyed the garden. Thick hedges and stone walls, shaded from too much sun by ancient trees. It was the town of Merton writ small. Set off alone, a backwater into which drifted a certain type of man. Tristam had decided, years ago, that there must be more to life. There was a whole world beyond Merton, after all. Did not empiricism mean to experience?

So Tristam had left Merton and returned to Locfal, disappointing Dandish, perhaps, but the life of a Merton don was not for Tristam. It wasn't that he did not share their interests. Certainly he did, and he was not about to give them up. But he had realized that it was not a full life. It was *the life of the mind,* and there were other parts to Tristam—uncharted territory, nearly. Of course, he had not yet been able to decide what form his life beyond Merton would take. That was the real struggle.

Occasionally, he feared that he had taken up with

Jenny in hopes that the relationship would provide an answer. Now he feared it would not—and was not quite sure what to do about it. This line of thought always unsettled him, so he turned away from it and approached the house.

He tried the most likely looking key and the front door creaked open. The odor of stale tobacco smoke wafted out from the entry hall. Leaving the door ajar, Tristam walked quietly into the house as though afraid to awaken the occupants.

I believe in ghosts even less than I believe in magic, Tristam told himself, *despite pranks played to convince me otherwise.* Still, he felt uncomfortable alone in the house where a man had died so recently. He went into the dining room and opened the windows. On the table, at the professor's accustomed place, there was a book lying open. Closing it gently, Tristam saw it was Lord Trevelyan's *Propagation in Tropical Angiosperms.*

He passed through the spotless kitchen, seldom used except for the production of tea and coffee. It was the professor's custom to take his meals in the college dining hall or at an inn.

Tristam looked into all the ground floor rooms, opening doors and windows as he went, and a profound melancholy began to grow in him. The realization that all of the professor's mundane belongings easily outlived him, Tristam found very sad.

There was a narrow, back stairway to what would have been the servant's room, and Tristam followed it up to the next floor.

He avoided the door to Dandish's sleeping chamber—the room where the professor had died—and went directly to the library. Though he had never spoken of it, Dandish must have had some family money, for his library contained over three thousand volumes, and books were expensive things. A man on a professor's salary could hardly afford so many and such a capacious house as well. Most of the books were on the subjects dearest to the professor's heart: natural history, taxonomy in particular; all branches of natural philosophy; mechanics; and engineering. The breadth of the professor's interests was striking, for there were also many volumes of philosophy, poetry, linguistics, and history. He had even possessed a few novels.

The walls supported floor-to-ceiling bookshelves except for a bow window on one wall and a fireplace on another. Over the hearth hung an artist's study for a painting of sea lions in the surf. It was by a painter of some fame and Tristam knew it was one of Dandish's most prized possessions.

A complete collection of the *Annals of the Empiricist's Society* caught Tristam's eye and he found himself wondering if this set might be one of the things left to him. There were quite a number of gaps in the bookshelves and Tristam knew he would find the missing volumes lying around the house. Dandish typically read several books at once and he would leave them in different places around the house—some by his bed, the book in the dining room, one or two in the morning room, more by each chair in the parlor. The library, of course, had books on the tables and desk. Even the drawing room would have its opened volumes.

On the desk lay another of the professor's innovations—a copying machine, the frame bearing a mechanical pencil that reproduced every stroke made by a pen, allowing Dandish to make two of any letter or document he wished.

Tristam looked about, not quite sure where to begin, but then he removed his jacket and laid it over a chair, opened his neck cloth, and chose a corner of the room. Work would be the cure for this sudden outbreak of emotion.

It was a slow process, for the professor's books were poorly organized—astonishing he had ever found what he wanted. But, oh, there were some treasures!

Tristam stopped occasionally to admire a volume; many were first editions, some very rare, and often inscribed by the author. In a long life Dandish had met most of the eminent men in his field. He had also been a member of the Empiricists' Society for more than twenty years and that had provided innumerable contacts.

It was always Tristam's dream that the professor would one day put his name forward for fellowship. That would never be, now, and Tristam had yet to do the work that would qualify him for a place in that august company.

Midday arrived and Tristam, nowhere near halfway through his task, was suddenly stricken by hunger. Locking the door behind him he made a brief foray to a nearby shop and returned with bread and cheese and a flagon of perfectly serviceable ale. There was a bower in the garden where Dandish often sat and here were two wicker chairs and a small table. He set his luncheon there and slipped back in the kitchen door to find a book and a mug.

Stepping into the hall he almost ran down an old woman and he gave her such a start that she shrieked, scaring Tristam almost as much as herself. The two stepped back, eyeing each other warily.

"Mrs. Ebish?"

"And who might you be?"

"Tristam Flattery. I'm sure you don't remember. I was a student of the professor's." He smiled, he hoped reassuringly. This was the cleaning woman Dandish had employed. Tristam had met her once or twice and was astonished to have remembered her name.

"And what cause have you to be sneaking around here?" she asked, her voice sullen.

"Dean Emin, who is the executor of the professor's estate, asked me to come and itemize the books and papers. He gave me a key." Tristam removed the ring from his pocket and held it out as proof.

"Quite a fright you gave me," she said, obviously still not recovered and somewhat annoyed.

"Unintentional, I assure you. May I ask what you're doing here yourself?"

She looked a bit defensive. "I've been watering the plants," she said defiantly. "Someone's got to. Your

Dean Emin never thought of that, I see. This morning I did the garden, but I had no time to tend to the house." She gestured to the battered watering can she held, much as Tristam had done with his keys.

"That is most thoughtful of you, Mrs. Ebish." He wondered how much of the professor's silverware she might have in her apron and immediately felt mean-spirited.

"I haven't watered the plants in the upstairs drawing room. The professor always kept that locked and tended to it himself. I suspect the plants in there are as limp as old rags by now." She nodded to the keys Tristam held in his hand. "Have you one for that room as well?"

He looked down at the keys. He hadn't yet looked into the upstairs drawing room. "I confess I don't know."

"It would be a shame to let the plants die. They were a special study, he told me, and seemed very dear to him."

"Well, perhaps we should have a look," Tristam said and motioned for the old woman to lead the way.

She was not spry, but she kept a steady pace as she mounted the stairs, clutching the rail strongly. Tristam seemed to remember Dandish saying she had cleaned his house for thirty-some years.

"It will be quite a change for you, Mrs. Ebish, without the professor to look after."

"I dare say it will. Though I must admit, my old bones could do with a bit of rest. It was me that found him, you know." She was suddenly embarrassed. "I'll say no more than that."

They walked along the landing to a large oak door and here the woman stopped and stepped back to let Tristam try the lock. He thought she was doing a poor job of hiding her anticipation: she actually licked her lips. The third key drew the bolt. As the door swung inward, Tristam caught a whiff of something famil-iar—dank, organic.

He pushed the door wide, revealing a large, formal

room. All the furniture was stacked to one side and covered with sheets to leave space for the professor's "special study." There, before the broad windows, stood neat rows of copper-lined planting boxes, each filled with soil but empty of any flower or shrub. They lay like coffins in the squares of sunlight falling through the glass.

Tristam looked back at the cleaning woman and saw a clear look of disappointment.

"Well," she muttered. "Well."

"Not what you expected, I collect?"

She smiled, wanly. "I've often wondered. I thought there would be some beautiful flower that he was keeping so secret." She gave a short laugh. "Well. He must have finished with his study. Just like the professor to say nothing."

"Yes . . . exactly like him." Tristam turned back to empty boxes. There had clearly been something in them, for at regular intervals there was a depression in the dirt where it appeared some plant had been removed.

"Well, I won't have to worry about water here." She laughed, but it did not seem quite natural. "Good day to you, Mr. Flattery, and I wish you luck with your work. I can't say as I envy you; the professor's effects will be in a fine muddle, I'll warrant. Never a thought to the practical things, the good professor— rest his soul." Tristam listened to the woman's slow progress down the stair—the measured sounds of her step, the occasional squeak of her hand sliding along the railing.

Obviously, Dandish's secrecy had piqued her curiosity.

Tristam crossed the room and walked among the long copper-lined boxes. He sniffed the air, turning his head like a hound. A hint of a familiar scent lingered.

He dug in the soil and turned up roots that had been broken off, and though he could not say from such little evidence to what plant the roots had belonged, he was certain he had seen others quite like them. It was clear the plants that had grown here had been removed by main force—torn out of the soil—not carefully dug out to be moved elsewhere.

Tristam went to the window and looked down into the garden. Yes, it was still there—a small enclosure of brick for burning refuse. He glanced down at the empty planting boxes. "It is only a coincidence," he whispered. Locking the door after him, he went back into the garden.

The trash burner contained only fine ashes, but a subsequent search of the property gave Tristam the answer to his question. Caught in the branches of a laurel hedge he found a single leaf, curled and desiccated, singed on one edge, but it was unquestionably Kingfoil.

He stood, turning the paper-dry leaf over and over in his hand, trying to devise another explanation for its presence. He looked up at the empty windows of the drawing room and shook his head. There could be no doubt. The professor had been growing Kingfoil, and had destroyed it. Or someone else had.

A breeze brushed through the garden, an almost articulate whispering. He gazed up at the windows of the drawing room again and thought that the reflections of the surrounding trees could almost have been the leaves of *regis* pressed against the glass.

Clearly, Sir Roderick knew nothing of this or the King's Man would have said something to Tristam before he set out. This entire matter was taken so seriously by Palle that Tristam was sure it could not have merely slipped his mind. Roderick hadn't risen to such heights by letting things slip.

"There must be a perfectly reasonable explanation for this," he said aloud.

Tristam returned indoors and went resolutely up to the door of Dandish's sleeping chamber. Here he paused with his fingers on the handle, gathered his resolve, and pushed open the door.

The odor still lingered. Not unfamiliar to Tristam who had studied mammal taxonomy, but this he found unbearable. He held his breath and pulled aside the curtains, then threw open the windows. He leaned out for a second, taking a number of deep breaths. Here Dandish had died alone, Tristam thought, and this chilled him completely. Taking a last deep breath he went directly to the night table beside the bed. The drawer was locked but the smallest key on the ring fit perfectly and within Tristam found what he expected—three identical, leather-bound books. The professor's most recent journals. Locking the drawer, he retreated quickly from the room.

Back in the garden he took up one of the journals. The first entry was April, two years earlier, and contained plans for work in the garden as well as a detailed description of a spider uncovered in the woodpile.

Tristam found himself reading whole passages, comforted to know about the small events of Dandish's days. He could imagine the words spoken in the professor's slow manner, each word chosen with particular precision. Tristam could feel Dandish's delight at the first blossoms of spring, at a small discovery at the university.

Almost gently he turned the pages, looking for the last entry, and found instead a page over which ink had been spilled so that the entire leaf had been blackened. The ink had soaked through to the next page, though the blot was not so large; then to the next, the mark smaller again, until on the fifth page it was a stain no larger than a coin . . . And then Tristam turned the page and the mark was gone.

It was the point at which Tristam's mind finally grappled with the reality of his mentor's death. For the next hour he walked among the shrubs and flowers, gaining no comfort from their transitory beauty. It took some time for him to master this dark mood, but finally the discipline that Tristam had developed in all the years he had spent alone allowed him to turn his attention away from Dandish and his loss.

He returned to his chair wondering if poor Dandish

had become so ill that he had spilled ink into his journal. Or had the professor intentionally blotted out some pages? Tristam shook his head. If Dandish had wanted to erase something, far more effective to cut out the pages and burn them, as he apparently had done with the Kingfoil. If he had been able to.

He flipped back through the pages, reading randomly. Notes on meetings at the college. Inquiries the professor was conducting. Criticism of writings from several journals. References to correspondence posted and received.

A brief entry that described perfectly one of the scourges of Dandish's existence.

Ipsword has attacked me for the second time in a week. Not my work, but me personally! I cannot shake his maliciousness out of my mind and have barely slept or worked for seven days. I should not let myself be affected so, for the man is no empiricist at all. He is nothing but a blackguard!

Poor fragile Dandish. The entries for the days before this were all concerned with the same matter. What might the professor have accomplished if he had heard only praise? In truth, Dandish had not needed criticism from others—he had managed that well enough on his own.

Into the previous year Tristam finally found what he sought—a reference to *regis*.

I cannot understand why my regis *is suffering the same deficiency as the planting at the palace! My seeds came from the second crop, yet they are acting identically to plants grown from the later generations. Why??*

Dandish knew of the fertility problem before Tumney . . . and had kept it to himself!

An envelope slipped out of the back of the journal and Tristam pulled it free to find Dandish's writing across the face. It was clearly addressed to the Duchess of Morland.

Tristam felt his hands fall to his lap. He need not even open the letter. In a way he had known since discovering the empty planting boxes: the staged meeting at the palace; the duchess' interest in Tristam, completely out of proportion to his supposed accomplishments. Dandish had been growing Kingfoil for the Duchess.

Why?

A physic that kept the King alive.

Fierce competition among the courtiers for the favor of the King. Or at least between the duchess and Sir Roderick Palle. And somehow she had enlisted Dandish to her cause. Almost gingerly he pushed the letter back into the pages of the journal as though he could make it disappear.

Tristam looked around the garden as though it were not the home of his old professor, but some place he had never been. Try as he might, Tristam could not imagine a person less likely to be involved in the intrigues of the court. *And I thought I knew him.*

He stared off at the far border of the lawn where a stone wall stood guard between Dandish's world and the greater world beyond. Tristam had always believed that there was little commerce between the two worlds.

With a noise like a wing fluttering, the letter slipped from the leaves of the book again, and Tristam stared at it for a few seconds, as though fascinated by the texture of the fine paper. It seemed the most innocent of objects.

It is a letter addressed to the favorite of the King, Tristam reminded himself, and pushed it yet again into the book.

A few seconds of hesitation while Tristam struggled inwardly, but a sudden compulsion to know about this secret life Dandish had been living overcame all other considerations. No one could know of the letter's exis-

tence but Dandish and Tristam, that seemed certain.
And Tristam wanted to know why Dandish had become engaged in this matter behind the back of Sir
Roderick Palle. It made Tristam wonder about the motives of the King's Man.

That was all the justification Tristam required. He
took a small clasp knife from his pocket and cut the
letter open with some precision.

Your Grace:

*It is with deep regret that I write to inform you that I
am unable to continue the inquiry I had undertaken.
My health has grown worse and I will be forced to
give up most of my activities, including my position at
the university. Even so, I believe I can say at this
point that there is no answer to the problem.*

*I say this with complete awareness that I have
failed Your Grace in a matter of great importance: an
unworthy return for your confidence in me as well as
all of your kind attentions.*

*It has been the greatest pleasure and honor to
serve Your Grace in this matter and I only regret that
I cannot, in return, do more.*

*I have taken the liberty of destroying the plants in
my possession as I am sure they are of no value to
further study.*

> *Your servant,*
> *Sanfield Dandish*

It was clear which side Dandish had chosen in court
politics.

Once more Tristam turned the pages, looking for
what he did not know. He came upon the last entry
dated the twenty-first—Dandish had died sometime the
next night. He began to read down the page.

*Visit from Dean Emin. There is no denying the grav-
ity of my situation. The look on that poor man's face;*

*as though he had found a ghost propped up in my
bed.*

*My heart is not at peace this day, arrhythmic and
fluttering, and my breath does not come easily. I
must somehow find the strength to write Tristam, but
not today. How deeply I regret his involvement!*

A sudden roll of thunder pulled Tristam back into
the world. A blast of wind rustled the leaves in the garden like a hiss, and then there was a profound stillness.
A summer storm had swept down upon Merton, and
rain suddenly lashed the earth with the violence of a
great battle of men.

After rushing about closing doors and windows,
Tristam flung himself down in a chair in the parlor
to catch his breath. Outside, the trees swayed and
leaves tore free of their branches to disappear on the
wind.

Unable to return to his task in the library Tristam
found himself drawn back into Dandish's diary and
near the end of the final volume he found a brief entry
he had not seen. It had been written some four weeks
past.

*I am not quite the old fool the Duchess takes me for.
I shall get a letter off to Valary tomorrow.*

Tristam looked up from his reading. *Valary?*

"Well, here is one mystery easily solved," Tristam
thought aloud. Returning to the library he went to a
stack of wooden boxes in one corner. These contained,
in some semblance of order, the professor's volumi-
nous correspondence—some four hundred letters a
year. As a widely recognized authority in several disciplines, Dandish kept up a correspondence with innumerable empiricists in both Farrland and beyond and,
to keep his memory fresh, followed the common practice of making a fair copy of each of his own letters
before committing them to the post.

Two hours of searching produced no letters either

from Dandish to Valary or the other way about. Nor was there a sign of a correspondence with the duchess.

A sudden blast of wind shook the house and a loud banging caused Tristam to start. When he went to investigate, he found someone was pounding on the front door. It seemed impossible to believe that Dean Emin was capable of such violence, and, a bit warily, Tristam opened the door.

Before him stood the drenched and dripping figure of his cousin, who measured Tristam with a concerned gaze.

"Jaimy?" Tristam said dumbly.

"Ah, you do recognize me. Thank goodness." Jaimy tried a smile, though it was still touched with concern. "Will you invite me in or shall we converse while I shower?"

Tristam heard himself laugh; a great relief. He reached out and drew his cousin bodily into the hall. "What on earth are you doing in Merton in the summer?" Tristam was overjoyed to find his cousin—his ally in so many things.

"Visiting Flinders, of course. He's a junior lecturer now, or some such thing. With typical bad manners he has abandoned me to my own devises for the evening as he is out courting. Our friend Flinders has gone all to pieces over a winsome lass—or so he says—I can't vouch for the girl's alleged winsomeness." Jaimy's attempt at joviality faded suddenly. "Dean Emin told me I would find you here. I am sorry to hear about poor Dandish, Tristam, I know he was a particular friend to you." He paused. "Is there anything at all that I might do?"

Tristam's throat was suddenly tight again. "I'm touched by your concern, J, but you needn't worry. I say quite honestly that I am well with it. He was an old man and lived a full life in his own terms." He looked at his cousin and shrugged. What could be said in such circumstances? "Dean Emin asked me to come down to go through the professor's papers. The will hasn't been read yet, but it seems that the kind professor mentioned me—some books I expect."

"He held you in high regard, Tristam." Jaimy glanced about. "I thought you might need to break from this. Shall we go find a meal? It might cheer you. And then I will offer you all the help I can in your task."

"It might fortify me, which I feel I need more than cheering. One moment." Tristam went in search of his frock coat and then bundled up Dandish's journals, careful to put the letter to the duchess into the pocket of his coat so that it didn't slip out, as it appeared to have a tendency to do. It was then that he realized the burnt Kingfoil leaf was still in the garden. He rushed to the door and could see through the glass that the leaf was gone, probably swept away on the wind. For a second he felt a rush of fear, but then he realized that no one would ever notice—just another leaf on the ground. It seemed appropriate somehow.

Returning to the entry hall, Tristam found Jaimy standing before the shelves upon which Dandish displayed many curios of his trade.

"What on the round earth is this?" Jaimy was looking down at a roughhewn bust of wood. It appeared to be hollow and had a hinged jaw and rather too-human lips shaped of leather. The sculptor had carved only the suggestion of a nose and the eye sockets had been left eerily blank.

"You've never seen this? It was the talk of Merton and the Empiricist's Society twenty years ago. Even the King asked for a demonstration. Here, pump this." Tristam directed Jaimy to a bellows attached to the back. "There is a mechanism inside made of ribbons of the thinnest copper." Tristam took hold of the controls, trying to remember what Dandish had shown him.

When he judged that there was sufficient "breath" being created, he moved the controls.

"Ma'am," the head hissed in a breathy, childish tone.

Jaimy stopped pumping in surprise. "What in . . . ?"

"It was an attempt to reproduce the mechanism of human speech—or perhaps I should say approximate it. Of course, it is very primitive, but ingenious all the same. There was some debate about the origin of human utterances and Dandish concocted this to prove a point. It makes three or four other sounds, but I can't recall how they're managed."

Jaimy gave a shiver, as though suddenly chilled from his drenching. "It is a little macabre. I don't think that I would choose it as an ornament for my entry. And this?"

He pointed to a device of wood and metal set on its own narrow shelf.

"Rover," Tristam said, almost laughing at the memory. "A gift from someone or other. A barometric dog, so called. Changes in atmospheric pressure cause it to flex, and creep along the shelf. Even with great plunges of the barometer, its movement is painfully slow—a slug would appear a regular racehorse in comparison—but it works."

There were a dozen other devices, but the rain had fallen to a drizzle, so they took the opportunity to set out, first for the Ivy. Tristam felt a great relief at finding himself so suddenly in the company of his cousin, for truly Jaimy was his closest friend. They had survived the rivalries and petty squabbles of their youth and had forged a friendship of great importance to them both. No doubt part of the reason for the success of this friendship was their "fit," for more often than not where Tristam was strong Jaimy was less so, and vice versa. It was also true that the two could never be rivals, for Jaimy was the heir to both title and fortune and was socially successful in the extreme, while Tristam's accomplishments as a scholar and empiricist, both knew, Jaimy could never hope to equal.

They were alike enough in coloring and size to be brothers, and were often mistaken for such. Jaimy's eyes were blue, rather than green, and the bone structure of his face was perhaps a bit stronger, but there could be little doubt that much the same blood flowed in their veins.

Upon first meeting, many thought Jaimy to be the older brother, for he was confident and well versed in the social graces of his class, but those who knew the cousins better believed Tristam to be the older of the two.

They stopped only briefly at the Ivy where Tristam lent Jaimy some dry clothes, and at the same time, though he could not say why, he buried the professor's journals under his luggage inside a wardrobe.

At Jaimy's suggestion they set out for one of their old haunts. The proprietor recognized Lord Jaimas immediately and led them to a good table by a window.

Over dinner Jaimy steered the conversation with great consideration for his cousin's mood—neither allowing it to become frivolous nor too serious. No further mention was made of Professor Dandish, and though Tristam dearly wanted to speak with his cousin about the discoveries he had made, Sir Roderick's warning could not be forgotten. Better not to involve Jaimy, no matter how strongly Tristam desired his council. Dandish had almost certainly broken laws and his ally appeared to be a very well placed lady. So Tristam held his peace, and though Jaimy could normally guess when something was troubling his cousin, the death of Tristam's friend would seem a likely explanation for his mood.

The summons to the palace was another matter, for Tristam could not very well give no reason for his presence this far from Locfal, so he explained it as a mission to heal an ailing shrub and made it sound absurd—another example of the foolishness of courtiers.

Midway through the meal, Tristam thought he might ask a few innocent-sounding questions of his cousin, for Jaimy's knowledge of the workings of Farr society greatly exceeded his own. "J? Have you ever met the Duchess of Morland?"

"Once or twice. Why do you ask?"

"I met her at the palace. briefly. I was in the company of Sir Roderick Palle and got the distinct impression that they were cool to each other."

"I should say! Palle is the confidant of the Prince Kori, and the duchess is not popular with the princess. She is too close to His Majesty for the liking of Palle, you can be sure, and promotes the interests of her friends with great success." He flashed a smile. "The duchess is a great beauty. . . . Did you happen to notice? Watch yourself there," his cousin teased. "It is said the duchess enjoys the company of younger men."

Further questions were impossible, for Jaimy began to talk about his recent travels and was as entertaining as always, actually managing to distract Tristam from his troubles. The world began to look normal. The entire issue of Kingfoil and Dandish and the duchess began to seem rather impossible. Certainly impossible that Tristam could be involved in any such thing. Tristam Flattery of sleepy Locfal. The more ale he drank, the more it seemed that he must simply have blown matters all out of proportion—suffered temporary delusion.

Jaimy, it came out, had lost his heart to a young woman—the real reason he was in Merton—and was feeling very dejected because his suit was apparently not succeeding. Tristam was sympathetic, but a little surprised as well. Merton was not known to be the home of Farrland's aristocrats. "How in the world have you found a woman here?" he asked at last.

"Do you remember Professor Somers?" Jaimy said, still a little defensive, as though he expected to be laughed at.

"Of course. I even recall that he had daughters. Two, I believe."

"Four, in fact." Jaimy stopped to gather his

thoughts. "Somers has carried out the most noble experiment, Tristam. He has educated his daughters. I mean truly educated them. Not just taught them to perform pleasingly on the pianum, or to fill in a silence in the conversation with a few words carefully chosen to ruffle no one." His eyes sparkled now and he leaned forward as he spoke. "They have read, Lord Skye and Trevelyan; yes, and Halden, too. They know more about the significance of our treaties with Entonne than they do of the latest Entonne fashions. Why, just the other day in their garden, Alissa identified a beetle I could not name. The word education has a meaning in the Somers' home that it does not elsewhere."

Tristam was forced to remember that his Jenny played Brimm badly. "Alissa, is she not still a child?"

"Seventeen."

"Ah."

"Don't be tiresome, Tristam, her age is not the issue. Alissa is mature beyond her years. Beyond my years, I sometimes think. And she seems to care for me more than a little."

"And what of the good professor? How does he look upon this?"

Jaimy stared down into his brandy glass and then said quietly, "He thinks I'm a rogue, I suspect."

"Ah, cousin. This is most difficult."

"My father knows nothing of this, so you needn't ask."

"You don't think the duke would look upon this favorably?"

The young lord shrugged. "You know him as well as I."

"Not nearly as well, but I take your point." Tristam was having trouble maintaining his composure. "Well, cousin, you are about to be indebted to me eternally—that is, if you are truly serious about this young woman. Professor Somers is one of my great supporters. In second year I made a small contribution in his area of study and since that day, in the good professor's eyes, I can do no wrong. Leave this to me. I shall resurrect your reputation in the house of Somers, and all I ask in return is that you slave in Dandish's library like the most devoted of clerks."

SEVEN

After parting from Jaimy, Tristam found that he was not drawn back to his bed at the Ivy. Not that he didn't feel the weight of fatigue in his body, but even so he knew that sleep did not wait for him in his rooms. He wandered down the streets of Merton, stopping to lean over the rail of the bridge and listen to the flowing river.

The air was soft with dew and the earlier rain, and into this renewed atmosphere summer seemed to have released all of her perfume. Small breezes pursuing the mother storm sighed in the darkness, bending the cattails by the river edge and swaying the robes of the willows. High over the towers of the university Tristam could see the moon in its first quarter, floating among stars that appeared suspended in liquid, for around the largest faint haloes glowed.

A bell in the university tower sounded the night's middle hour, and the echoes answered, then faded until the whisper of flowing Wedgewater was the only voice.

Despite his clear awareness that he was not well versed in the ways of the human heart, Tristam had a sense of what he felt, for he had known it before. It wasn't just the loss of his friend, it was the sudden awareness of one's own mortality that such losses invariably produced. The sudden shift in one's view, as though a death opened a window that normally was kept shut and shuttered. Most of everyday life's great issues looked trivial when seen through that window.

What were these foolish courtiers up to and why had

they entangled Dandish in their schemes? All this so one very old man would look upon them with favor and forget to smile on their rivals. Oh, Wilam was not a bad king. Tristam did not wish him ill. But Wilam had had his own follies—most prominently, the last war with Entonne. If he passed on, the greater world would not likely be torn apart—but the lives of some courtiers would change irrevocably. So anything to keep him alive.

Tristam pushed himself away from the rail and walked on. Jenny had often hinted that Tristam was without emotion, always cool and detached. He was never quite sure what it was she expected of him. Her own beliefs in such matters were somehow different from his, but different in what way, he could not explain—nor could Jenny, it seemed. It was rather ironic considering that he had left Merton because he thought the life of the mind inadequate.

Tristam had come to believe that a life should be conducted in the light of reason. Love and passion had their place, certainly, but they should not rule. The idea seemed so eminently sensible that he could not see how anyone could argue against it. He wondered again about the course he had chosen. Tried to imagine life with this young woman who neither understood nor shared his interests.

He looked up at the stars, feeling again the stab of loss. If Jenny believed he was without feelings, then she should see him now. It struck him as rather sad that he could even consider that Dandish's death should serve to prove the existence of Tristam's emotions.

He turned into another street, lined with high elms. *I cannot sleep,* he realized, *and there is no profit in this line of thought.* Picking up his pace, he set out for Dandish's home. Damn the intrigues of courtiers. Damn sentimentality. Let the flames take even love, for the moment. He would go and apply himself to the task he had been given. Three hours of real work would drive out these demons.

He had some trouble finding the right key by moonlight, but then the lock turned and the door swung open, the familiar smell of stale tobacco smoke wafting out into the pure night, followed by a thump quickly muffled. Tristam stopped on the threshold, suddenly alert. He stood listening, holding his breath so that he might hear even the slightest sound. Nothing.

He almost laughed. Perhaps he had not closed a window properly and it had been found by a breeze. Somehow Tristam did not think Dandish was a likely candidate to return and haunt his old home. Not that the professor didn't have secrets, as Tristam was learning, but still, Dandish had been a largely benign presence in the world. Tristam cleared his throat audibly if only to prove that he could control his fears.

He would have to find the implements to strike a lamp, but he was sure such things must lie by the fireplace. Slowly he began to feel his way toward the sitting room, his eyes adjusting quickly. There was a little light from moon and stars filtering through the windows and Tristam began to distinguish objects; a chair here, a small table.

For no reason that he could name, Tristam regretted clearing his throat. *Be reasonable,* he told himself, *you are not afraid of the dark.*

As he was about to step through the door into the sitting room, he heard a sudden curse and someone large shot through the doorway, the collision propelling Tristam back into the stair rail. His head struck the oak with such force that he collapsed into a heap, his ears ringing, the wind knocked from his lungs. The front door banged open and Tristam heard boots on the gravel path, running.

"Farrelle's flames," he heard himself whisper, despite lack of air. He tried to rise, afraid he was in danger, but he could only manage to sit, gasping. "Blood and flames," he said. His head spun from the effort of moving and his eyes closed of their own will. The room seemed to tilt, first one way and then another. Tristam fought to remain conscious, as though the

darkness that tried to overwhelm him was death itself. He focused all of his will on that one act, opening his eyes just enough to see moonlight, to know that the world was not fading.

It took a second for the image to coalesce and register in his brain, but not three feet away, in the shadows and pale light, a small, frightened child crouched, his gaze fixed on Tristam. And then the room began to whirl again and he felt himself falling.

❦ ❦ ❦

Tristam was sure he regained his awareness in only a few seconds. For some time he lay still, like an animal trusting to darkness and lack of movement for protection. From his position by the stairs Tristam could see no one—neither men nor small boys. An urge to rise and run out the front door came over him, but then he remembered that the nocturnal visitor had gone that way. The house, Tristam reasoned, was almost certainly empty now.

He raised a hand to his head and assured himself that there was no great flow of blood. The skin had been broken, but barely, and a welt was rapidly rising. "I am whole," he said aloud. Very slowly Tristam pushed himself up onto moderately steady legs and held onto the stair rail, taking stock. He would do.

Not without some trepidation, Tristam passed into the sitting room, his eyes darting about as he went, searching the shadows. In one corner of the room Tristam saw a thin line glowing orange and he stopped in horror. And then he laughed aloud, crossing toward the dull light. As he thought, it was a storm lantern, light leaking from the crack on one side of the door.

He managed to open the lantern without burning himself and the soft, familiar glow of lamplight flowed out like a sigh, pushing back the pale light of stars and moon, pushing back the shadows. Tristam eased himself down into a chair for a moment.

Housebreakers. He had interrupted housebreakers.

Here, in Merton. Think as he might, Tristam could not recall ever hearing of such a thing before. It unsettled him completely.

I should wake Jaimy, Tristam thought. It would be good to have a companion in this situation. But then he remembered again that the housebreakers were outside, somewhere, and decided that staying in the house might be the most intelligent course. After all, if he left the house and anyone was watching, they might come back to finish the job. Whatever it was they intended.

Realizing the door was still open, Tristam scooped up the lamp and forced himself up. Beside the entrance to the sitting room he found a fireplace poker lying on the floor and picked it up, hefting it. He was completely sure it had lain by the fire earlier that day. The small lump he had on his head would be nothing compared to what this would have done.

Tristam bolted the door and decided that he would hunker down here for the night, with his lamp and fire poker. Kindle a blaze in the fireplace. Light more lamps. It was unlikely he would sleep, but he would keep the house—and himself—from harm.

🍂 🍂 🍂

When the dull pewter of impending morning spread into the eastern sky, Tristam could keep awake no longer. He slept lightly for perhaps two hours and awoke to early morning, the garden alive with the songs of birds, sun bright, and lamps guttering in the sitting room. After lying for a moment, almost unwilling to face the day, Tristam roused himself and blew out the lamps.

Immediately he noticed that one of the double doors opening onto the garden had a shattered pane, and shards of glass were scattered across the floor. Why, if this was the door used to gain entrance, had the vandal run Tristam down to get out the front? It made no sense.

Taking up his poker again, Tristam went from room

to room and everywhere met the same sight. The house had been ransacked. Cabinet doors hung open and the contents of drawers and closets were strewn across the floors. In the scullery a bowl lay shattered on the bureau, the pattern of yellow roses fragmented over the sheet-copper. He may have interrupted the housebreakers in their work, but they appeared to have been nearly finished anyway. The house was in ruins.

On the landing he found that the door to the drawing room had been forced, causing some damage to both door and frame. There was no harm to the room, however. The covering sheets had been pulled off the furniture, but all else remained untouched. Tristam continued his search and found the guest rooms had been given a thorough going over.

It was not until he entered the library that Tristam felt real dismay. Books lay everywhere, many torn and damaged, their covers hanging by a few threads or gone altogether. The drawers of the desk had been dumped out onto the floor and mixed with Dandish's correspondence. All of Tristam's careful work had been undone. The artist's study still hung in its place—not entirely a surprise—even though it was valuable and housebreakers usually knew their business.

The professor's sleeping chamber had been treated like all the others, though here the mattress and pillows had been slit. As he stood looking at the room, covered in a fine snowfall of down, a sharp rap caused Tristam to raise his poker in defense before he realized it was the brass knocker in the main entry.

Jaimy stood waiting on the steps, his most charming smile in place.

"Your clerk has arrived." The young lord looked down at the poker in Tristam's hand and then more closely at his cousin's face. "What is it?"

With some relief Tristam pushed the door wide. "I've just been searching the house. I came back last night and interrupted housebreakers, if you can believe it." Tristam bent to show his scalp to his cousin. "I received this when I collided with a vandal in the dark."

Jaimy carefully parted Tristam's hair. "Not too serious, I think. You will have quite a lump though. You are all right? Not light-headed? Not feeling ill? Your vision is unchanged?"

"I am perfectly whole. More than we can say for the house."

Jaimy looked around as though he suspected criminals to still be lurking. Tristam took his cousin to tour some of the wreckage.

"Is much missing?" Jaimy ventured.

Tristam shook his head. "I wish I knew. I had begun to inventory the library, but I was nowhere near finished. The house keeper might know, I suppose."

"If it wasn't her sons that did the deed."

"Mrs. Ebish? No, she will be quite innocent. 'Salt of the earth' is how you would describe Mrs. Ebish." Tristam picked up a piece of the shattered bowl, for they had wandered as far as the scullery. "I need to let Dean Emin know what's happened here. Would you watch the house for a while?"

"Of course, but it makes more sense for me to find the dean and you to stay here. You might begin to make some sense of this and I wouldn't know where to start."

Tristam looked around at the wreckage. "Yes, that would be best. The dean should be at the college, but if not he'll likely be at his home. Eighteen Northmoor Road. Do you know it?"

Tristam watched his cousin go, sensing how troubled Jaimy was by the set of his shoulders alone. *And he cannot imagine what this truly means,* Tristam thought.

Not knowing where to begin, Tristam returned to the library and started in on the chaos. He had not toiled long when he heard a frail voice wafting up from the garden. It sang a children's song.

> *Posies, posies, a-singing to the rosies*
> *A-courting gladiolies*
> *A-dancing with the snow lilies.*

There were more verses but she, for it was Mrs. Ebish, repeated this one again and again as though it were an incantation, a spell used to conjure lost youth.

Tristam went to the window and saw the old woman at work in the garden. She was stooped over and apparently evicting weeds from a flower bed. For a moment Tristam watched and felt a sadness come over him that he could not explain. There was something pathetic in the scene—the bent old woman weeding in a dead man's garden—as though her life had been pared away until only routine remained.

Tristam cleared his throat loudly; when that did not catch her attention, he called out, "Mrs. Ebish! *Hel-lo*."

The old woman stood up sharply, looking around, a hand pressed to her heart.

"It's me, Mrs. Ebish. Tristam Flattery."

She saw him now and gave a small laugh. "Must you always sneak up on a body, Mr. Flattery? My old heart is a-pounding like a great drum." She laughed again, obviously relieved in some way. "I thought it was the professor's ghost calling out and that I was about to cross over myself."

The mention of ghosts did not cheer Tristam.

"I am sorry. I hope you'll forgive me. You see, a terrible thing has happened. Someone has robbed the professor's home. I was hoping you might help me determine what has been taken."

"Well!" she said. "My word! The poor professor."

      🐛   🐛   🐛

The dean and Jaimy arrived as Tristam and Mrs. Ebish were trying to make some sense of the mess in the lower rooms.

"What a terrible thing," the dean said, as he surveyed the ruins. "You are unhurt Tristam? Did they attack you?"

"No, I was merely run down in the dark by some blackguard who was making good his escape. It seemed that I surprised him—or them—and they got away with little, perhaps even nothing at all." Tristam was not sure if he should alert the dean to his suspicions.

The dean nodded stiffly. The skin of his face appeared to have a layer of deep purple beneath it. "May I have a word with you, Tristam?"

The two stepped out onto the terrace, the dean pacing for a moment before turning to Tristam. "I was at the college this morning and there was an awful row going on. Dandish's rooms have been . . . *sacked* is the only word I can conceive to describe their state. And now his home, too. I can't remember such a thing ever happening before. Dandish was not a wealthy man, nor was there reason for others to think that he could have been. And, as you have said, things of value have not been taken. There is something very odd in all of this, Tristam, you mark my words. Can you think of anything that would explain it?"

Tristam looked down at the bricks of the terrace, shaking his head. "I can't say that I can, Dean Emin." There was a second's silence and Tristam could feel the don staring at him.

"Tristam," the old man said softly. "If I may be completely candid, you are the poorest liar. Lack of experience, no doubt—which is to your credit. But all the same, you are not telling me everything you know. Is that not so?"

Tristam looked up and met the old man's pale eyes. He felt shame burning on his cheeks. He nodded his head.

"But you are not inclined to speak further?"

"I'm not."

The dean looked out over the garden and took his watch from his pocket and turned it slowly, over and over. "I can't imagine either Danish or yourself involved in something of questionable legality."

"Nothing of the sort, sir."

The dean nodded. "Well, I am relieved to know that,

at least. This has something to do with the palace arboretum, I collect?"

Tristam hesitated. "I have been sworn to secrecy by the King's Man, Dean Emin."

The dean slipped his watch back into his pocket. If he was surprised by what he had just heard, he did not show it. "Say nothing more, then. I'm sorry to have pressed you."

"And I'm sorry to have lied to you, sir."

The dean reached out and put his hand on Tristam's shoulder. "I as much as made you do it, Tristam. Do not apologize. Let us go back inside."

Dean Emin soon left—called by his duties at Merton College—and Tristam, Jaimy, and Mrs. Ebish continued with the restoration of order to the professor's house. It was well past midday when hunger finally drove the young men out in search of food. Mrs. Ebish went off to perform some errand or other and they locked the house, wedging the back door as best they could. Tristam thought it was unlikely the house would be bothered in broad daylight, and besides, whoever was interested in Dandish had likely already finished searching for whatever it was they wanted. Whether or not they had found it was the question in Tristam's mind. Although he tried to keep up a front before the others, Tristam was deeply disturbed, and not just by this assault on Dandish's home.

The Ivy was not far off, so Tristam suggested they stop there for a meal. In truth, he wanted to check on the diaries in his room, for he was almost certain that the night visitors had been seeking Dandish's writings—anything he might have recorded about Kingfoil.

Excusing himself momentarily, Tristam went up to his room and was relieved to find the professor's papers still tucked away where he had left them. He was about to return to the dining room when there came a knock on the door and Tristam found a servant he had come to know standing in the hall.

"Pardon the interruption, Mr. Flattery. I saw you go-

ing up the stairs. There were two gentlemen here asking after you this morning, sir, and neither felt inclined
to leave so much as a calling card. I thought you
should like to know, sir."

Recent events had taken their toll and Tristam felt
immediately suspicious. "You can describe them?"

"I believe so. The first was a young man, sir, about
your age, I should think, and not unlike you to look at.
I thought he might be kin to you, Mr. Flattery."

"He likely was. And the other?"

"A bit older, sir. A gentleman. Dark hair, the finest
dress. Came in a good-sized carriage with footmen;
very close on the heels of the first gentleman, as well.
Handsome man, too, I should think."

Tristam racked his brain. There was no one he could
think of in Merton who would fit such a description
and certainly no one who would be traveling in such
style. "Well, I can't imagine who it was."

"He asked after you in such a way as to give the impression of friendship, sir, and when told you were out
said not to worry. I thought he knew where you must
be. I gathered he was off to find you directly."

"Well," Tristam said, trying to pass it off as unimportant. "No doubt he will catch up with me yet.
Thoughtful of you to remember."

"Not at all, Mr. Flattery."

Tristam had a sudden thought. "There is something
you could do for me, if you will. I need to wrap a
small parcel, about like so. . . ." He measured with his
hands. "Could you find me some heavy paper, or oil-
cloth, and string?"

Tristam took Dandish's diaries from the wardrobe,
and when the servant returned he wrapped them carefully and passed them into the man's care.

"Will you post this for me?" Tristam thought
quickly. He did not like the sound of unknown gentlemen asking after him at his lodgings. "To Tumney,
Tumney . . . what was his given name? Never mind: to
myself, Tristam Flattery, care of Mr. Tumney, King's
Gardener, the Tellaman Palace. Can it go off today?"

"By the evening coach, sir." The man showed not the slightest sign that he thought this an odd request.

Tristam locked his door, checking it with more care than usual, and hurried down to join his cousin.

"J?" Tristam said as soon as he was seated. "Did you call here this morning?"

"I did. I thought I should catch up with you before you left. Why?" Jaimy was already working on a mug of ale and wiped a mustache of foam off his lip.

"A servant just told me two men came by after I left for the professor's. I don't know who the second would have been."

Jaimy nodded. "Did your man say anything about your caller's appearance?"

"Tall, I think. Well dressed gentleman. Came in a good-sized coach with footmen."

Jaimy nodded, his brow furrowing as it did when he was truly worried. "As I was coming out of the inn, I saw such a coach stop outside. I didn't see the man who emerged, close to, but I was quite sure he was the Viscount Elsworth."

Tristam shrugged.

"The brother of the Duchess of Morland, Tristam," Jaimy said, a little exasperated.

"Ah," Tristam drank from his own mug, hoping his hand would remain steady.

"You must remember that business a few weeks ago. . . ? The viscount killed Baron Ipsword in a duel. Surely you heard?"

"Yes. Yes, I did hear something about it. Rather barbaric business, I thought. Though it could hardly have happened to a more deserving individual." Baron Ipsword had been one of Dandish's greatest detractors and a man who spent much time promoting himself and his "theories."

Jaimy looked hard at his cousin. "The duel was over an insult, I was told—a fine world it would be if we fall back on murder every time a man feels he has been paid an insult. I thought that foolishness had been left behind.

"Despite this blot on his character, the viscount remains, if not a central player, at least a member of the Royal Troupe. His sister, the Duchess of Morland, the lady you met, is the leading actress; center stage in the charmed circle. They have the King's favor and travel with the artistic crowd. Entonnophiles: far worse than any of our fellows here at Merton."

Tristam's mind went back to Dandish's diaries. Ipsword was a great opponent of transmutation. Over the years he had attacked Dandish savagely several times—never intelligently—but he had injured the highly-strung Dandish all the same, grievously on more than one occasion.

Impossible, Tristam almost said it aloud. Dandish was growing *regis* for the viscount's sister.... No, there could be no connection. It was too evil to even be considered.

"Tristam? Are you well? Let me look again at your wound. You are as white as a ghost."

"No, I am perfectly well." Tristam's mind was in a whirl. "Lack of sleep, I think. And I am famished as well."

A servant appeared at that moment, diverting attention away from Tristam. The subject was changed, but Jaimy did not lose his look of great concern and many awkward silences punctuated the meal—unusual for two who were so easy in each other's company.

As they walked back toward Dandish's home, Jaimy suddenly turned on his cousin, something verging on anger coming to the surface. "Shall I continue to act as though I'm too obtuse to notice, or will you condescend to tell me what it is you've involved yourself in?"

Tristam looked off, unable to meet his cousin's gaze, but even so he felt Jaimy staring at him.

"It isn't that I don't want to tell you, Jaimy. It isn't that. I.... To be honest I have been sworn to secrecy by someone of importance."

"This 'someone' would be Roderick Palle, I assume?"

Tristam looked over at his cousin. He should not have been surprised. Despite his easy-going manner, Jaimy was no fool of an aristocrat.

"Well, perhaps you should not speak, then," Jaimy said. "I cannot guarantee that I would bear up under torture." It was a jest but said without trace of humor.

Tristam remained silent, though with great difficulty. There was only one person he wanted to speak with more than Jaimy and that was Dandish.

"Precisely how important a secret can a shrub be, Tristam?" Jaimy said after a moment, obviously not willing to let it go.

"More than you would think. Certainly more than I ever imagined."

"Well, if you have the Viscount Elsworth asking after you, perhaps you do not exaggerate." Jaimy reached out and took hold of Tristam's shoulder. "I should remind you, cousin, that I have kept every secret you have ever entrusted to me, going back to our childhood. If you are involved in something as peculiar as I think you are, you know I shall never talk. And even Sir Roderick Palle does not bully the son of the Duke of Blackwater. Besides," he said, "you will need me. You probably didn't know who Sir Roderick Palle was before he summoned you to court."

They had arrived at the back gate to the professor's home and Tristam stopped, struck by the look of concern and determination on his cousin's face. "I do not jest, Jaimy, when I say you cannot repeat a word," Tristam said quietly.

"Not a syllable," Jaimy answered, the tiniest sign of relief in his tone.

They went into the garden and sat in the arbor. Tristam began with the arrival of a member of Roderick Palle's staff to his home in Locfal. Years of difficult study had sharpened Tristam's memory and he related the entire tale in great detail. For the most part Jaimy merely nodded, listening intently. Very occasionally he stopped Tristam to clarify some point, but the two knew each other so well that this was seldom necessary.

When Tristam finished, Jaimy rose and excused himself, leaving his cousin sitting in the sun-drenched garden. In a moment the young lord returned bearing two mugs of Tristam's ale, warm but welcome.

"Would you like to hear what I think?"

Tristam threw up his hands. "No. I have broken my oath to the King's Man merely that I might have company in prison."

Jaimy stirred at the head on his ale for second, as though he wrote something there. "To begin: this man Hawksmoor is Sir Roderick's most trusted minion—a man who would place himself in the way of a cannon ball if it would serve his master. Palle sends Hawksmoor on only the most sensitive errands. So why was it so important that he fetch you?" Tristam hoped that this question was not merely rhetorical, but after a moment of thought Jaimy went on without proposing an answer.

"Palle tries to convince you that your future success lies in service to the King," Jaimy said, his mouth turning up in a hint of a smile, "proving that Hawksmoor learned almost nothing about you on your voyage. Then, the Duchess of Morland offers you a title and whatever else you might desire if you can but make this recalcitrant plant bear seed. She even allows you, a comparative nobody, if you will excuse me for saying so, to address her as 'Duchess.' Quite suddenly, Tristam, you are the object of attention of two of the most powerful people in all Farrland. And despite their perfect manners and impeccable conduct, these are two people whom one never wants to cross." Jaimy leaned over and touched his cousin's arm. "I cannot stress this point enough. This incident with the viscount and Baron Ipsword is a perfect example. Trust that the late baron had run afoul of the duchess in some way. All this noise about him insulting the viscount was utter fabrication. Ipsword was a fool by any man's measure, and capable of offense, surely, when criticizing other empiricists, but he was not stupid enough to insult someone of Elsworth's reputation. Ipsword's only weapon was a razor-sharp tongue and an uncanny precision in its application, but he was no swordsman. I can't even imagine how he would have met the viscount."

Tristam looked away, Jaimy's words striking him like blows. "I think even you have missed the point," Tristam whispered, almost afraid to mouth the words, as though they were a spell with the power to create truth. "The late baron was an enemy of Dandish . . . Drove the professor into fits of despair and melancholia with his vicious attacks. After such assaults Dandish would be unable to work . . . for weeks sometimes. Unable to work on this study he undertook for the duchess. . . ."

The croak of a rook somewhere nearby. Then quiet.

"Blood and flames," Jaimy said almost under his breath. "You can't seriously believe he killed Ipsword because the man . . . criticized Dandish?"

"Because Ipsword affected Dandish's ability to pursue the duchess' inquiry."

Jaimy put a hand to his face. "Tristam, that cannot be. . . . It is more than monstrous. There would have been a dozen ways to deal with Ipsword short of murder."

"Yes, I'm sure there were."

Jaimy rose and paced across the arbor, overcome with agitation. For a few moments he said nothing, only staring down at the ground and combing his fingers into his hair. Finally he turned to his cousin, his distress clear. *"Tristam. What on this round earth have you gotten yourself into?"*

The two sat for a long time pursuing their private thoughts, trying to make some sense of what little they knew. It was Jaimy who finally broke the silence.

"Let us consider this logically, as you are prone to saying. The duchess and Sir Roderick are clearly at odds over this seed that produces the physic. Palle involves you in hopes of solving the problem. The duchess, however, has had Dandish attempting to solve the problem for some time—over a year, you say?"

"As much as three, I suspect."

"Yet you claim that the King's own gardener did not recognize the problem until recently." Jaimy put the tips of his fingers together and touched them to his chin—a posture almost of prayer. "How intelligent do you think the duchess is?"

Tristam shifted in his chair and cast a look over his shoulder as though suddenly afraid they were not alone. "It isn't a question of intelligence, really. It's training. The duchess could be a natural genius and still not see what needed to be seen. I have looked carefully at Tumney's records and, assuming they are accurate, I would say that it would have been impossible to recognize the existence of the problem before Tumney did so himself. Plants do not always bear consistently year to year. You know this—one year there are more apples than can be eaten, the next there is hardly one to be found. Even in a controlled garden such as the arboretum there are cycles. Two years in which seed production declines does not necessarily have meaning, if you see what I'm saying. I suspect this problem has been increasing slowly for three years now and still that is not necessarily significant. The Kingfoil could produce a bumper crop next year. Although I, personally, do not expect it to happen. But you see my point."

"I have not read Dandish's journals. Is it possible that he had begun by merely growing Kingfoil for the duchess and then recognized the problem later?"

Tristam looked up at his cousin. "I can hardly imagine that Dandish would be involved in such a venture. Even someone as unaware of politics as the professor must have realized that this would not be strictly aboveboard?"

"The duchess is a persuasive woman, Tristam. Who knows how she would couch such a request. Here we have an herb that will cure a disease, apparently. Dandish was a good man, concerned with human suffering. . . . Or it is possible that the duchess made it appear a request of the King—to be kept secret, even from Roderick Palle." Jaimy shrugged as though to say such a thing could be easily managed, and Tristam had to admit he was right.

"The Duchess of Morland is an animal of the court, Tristam. One would be foolish to presume to understand her motives. There is more than self-interest at work here, I think, but she is involved in so many machinations with such varied alliances that one could hardly imagine her intentions. The favor the King shows toward her makes the duchess much caressed wherever she goes. She need only speak a few words on someone's behalf and this person will find himself borne up—invited everywhere, feted—whatever you can imagine. The duchess' offers to you were not vain—granting such favors would be easy for her." Jaimy paused, looking off at the sky for a moment. "Despite all, the duchess must be getting rather nervous, for ultimately her strength is dependent upon a king who has lived well beyond his time. One would have to say that her ascendancy is near to its end. But, for the moment, if you are in some way a guarantor of His Majesty's health, well, the duchess will see that you are kept very happy, let me assure you." Jaimy paused, as though considering what he had just said.

"But there is something more here. It is almost as if the two factions in the court were vying for control of this seed. Is the King so weakened that he has allowed this to occur? The Prince Royal, of course, is close to Palle." He shook his head. "I can't quite force it to make sense."

"A hypothesis to fit the information," Tristam said.

"What?"

"We are looking for a hypothesis to fit the information. Some elegant explanation for everything we believe we know. Not so easy when it is human beings that we are dealing with. The courtiers are involved in a struggle over a seed that keeps the King alive. . . . Obviously the Prince Royal would gain the throne if the King were to die, and the duchess, as you have said, would lose her place at court. That fits most of what we know. Add to it the fact that Dandish clearly chose to support the duchess rather than Palle."

"You are suggesting that the King's Man, the sovereign's chief minister, is in league with the heir to 'dethrone' the King?" There was a little scorn in Jaimy's voice.

"It fits what we know," Tristam said, defensively.

"Flaming martyrs," Jaimy said, quietly. He finished his ale and looked reproachfully at the empty mug. "But why would Palle bring you to court? If he is trying to do away with King Wilam, it would be in his interest to have the Kingfoil never bear again."

"Hypotheses are built like this. A fact that does not fit must either be wrong or the hypothesis altered. And the truth is I do not know why Palle brought me. Perhaps he thinks me so incompetent as to be no threat." Tristam rose to fetch more ale from the house. A thought struck him as he walked.

"Jaimy," he said when he returned, "there is this entry in the journal about Valary. Do you know that name?"

"Another empiricist, I would guess. I'll make some discreet enquiries around the university tomorrow. Flinders might even know, or perhaps Dean Emin."

Yes—or no one might know. There was much that Tristam suspected was beyond conventional knowledge. The man he had collided with had been truly terrified, and it had not been Tristam who had inspired that.

I struck my head, Tristam told himself. *The child was merely a fabrication of light and shadow and blurred vision. Nothing more.*

❦   ❦   ❦

It was late by the time Tristam finally stumbled into his rooms at the Ivy. When the servant who lit the lamps had gone, Tristam pulled off his shoes and collapsed in a chair. Outside his window a breeze rustled the leaves of the old elm—a sound Tristam found almost hypnotic. He awoke with a start as his chin hit his chest and he forced himself up, looking around the room quickly to be sure no small boys lurked in the shadows.

Out of habit he went to the desk to keep his journal, but it was not where he'd left it. Nor was it in the drawer. Tristam came fully awake then and mounted a concerted search but the journal was not to be found. He sat thinking for a moment, but there was no doubt in his mind—he hadn't taken it from the room since his arrival in Merton.

The briefest sense of vertigo unbalanced him. He checked the pocket of his frock coat and found it empty. It was then he realized that he had changed coats that day. He went to his wardrobe where his fears were confirmed: Dandish's letter to the duchess was gone.

EIGHT

"I'm not quite sure how you did it, Tristam, but I really will be in your debt forever." A jubilant Jaimy sat across from Tristam in the dining room of the Ivy. They had spent the previous night at the Somers' home, and it had been agreed that Tristam and Jaimy would come up to the lake country late in the season to assist Professor Somers with his fossil quarry. A fortnight near the object of Jaimy's affections!

Tristam, however, was not feeling jubilant. Sir Roderick's coach was being readied for the return to Avonel, and Tristam was filled with apprehension. Someone possessed the letter Dandish had written to the Duchess of Morland and if that someone was Roderick Palle, then Tristam's situation was ... confusing, to say the least.

"You still think it was the duchess' brother who took the letter?"

Jaimy tilted his head and tried a half-smile. "You can't let this go, can you?"

"Nor could you if you were soon to be speaking with Sir Roderick Palle. And what am I to say? If he has possession of the letter, then he is now fully aware of Dandish's inquiry—and realizes that I know as well. If I choose to say nothing, then I am hiding things from the King's Man. If I speak, I will be incrimination the King's favorite as well as Dandish. And, as we have said, it might be the duchess who has the King's interests in mind."

Jaimy's manner turned serious. "It was also likely the duchess who had a man murdered for the crime of being an annoyance. Take no sides in this matter, Tristam. For my money, it was the viscount who took the letter and your journal. So say nothing to Roderick. Say nothing to anyone. Go about your task at the palace and then get free of this situation as quickly as you can. Let these courtiers have their battle without you. And, Tristam, don't let the duchess persuade you to take up where Dandish left off. Whatever you do, avoid that trap."

They finished their meal and walked out to find Tristam's carriage, but before they came within earshot of the driver, Jaimy pulled Tristam up short. "If you need me to, I will come to Avonel, but I caution you, Tristam—and I am not being melodramatic—trust nothing sensitive to the mails. Merely invite me to come visit you, or some such thing, but don't commit a word of this matter to paper."

"I can't thank you enough, J. I don't know what I would have done without your help."

Jaimy broke into a huge grin. "I have been paid back and double, Tristam, for I will have a fortnight in the lake country near my sweet Alissa. I am in your debt. Safe journey. Speak not to strangers."

As Sir Roderick's coach carried Tristam off toward the city of Avonel, the young naturalist began to suffer extreme trepidation. Any thought of his inevitable meeting with the King's Man caused his palms to sweat and his stomach to churn.

With some effort he turned his mind back to the occurrences of the last days and found himself wondering again why Dandish had been growing *regis* before the fertility problem had been recognized. Perhaps Jaimy was right and the professor's original intention had not been to solve the problem at all, even though it became his focus.

So the journey went by with Tristam's fertile mind creating one hypothesis and knocking it down, then creating another. There seemed to be no grand scheme that explained everything and this did not make him happy. When he faced Roderick Palle, as he was sure he must do, he wanted to be quite certain that he understood what was going on. Unfortunately, this did not seem very likely.

Some hours into the journey the driver stopped, jarring Tristam out of his whirling thoughts. He looked out the window and found they had come to the slough where they had paused on the way to Merton. The carriage bobbed as the driver stepped down to the ground.

"Thought you might like to have a look, sir," he said. "Or should I drive on?"

"No. Thank you. I shall look." One of the instruments Dandish had left to Tristam was his Fromme field glass. Tristam dug it out of a trunk and set out along the short path to the pond.

The Fromme glass was a relatively new invention—a field glass made up of three bronze tubes that collapsed one into the other so that it compressed to only a third its extended length. Far more convenient than the rigid glasses that had been made previously. But it was not just that innovation that made the Fromme instruments so coveted; it was the incomparable lenses as well. There was no glass so perfect, none with such ideal resolution. Tristam hefted it in his hand and then extended it for use. Inscribed on the inner tube he found the words:

For the use of Professor Sanfield Dandish, with thanks, R.M. Fromme.

Well, yes; the professor had many admirers. More than Tristam knew, it seemed.

He lifted the glass to survey the pool, and to his surprise found he could see nothing. Tristam shook the glass gently and thought he heard something move inside. A part of the instrument had come loose, apparently.

With great care he unscrewed the lens and tilted the glass to see if anything would slide out into his hand. The edge of a wad of paper protruded.

"What in . . . ?" Tristam breathed.

He tugged at the paper and pulled it free, fumbling to unroll it—a single sheet torn raggedly in half and awkwardly stuffed into the tube. Slough and Fromme glass were forgotten. Here was Dandish's writing, though firmer than usual, beginning in mid-sentence.

stronger those few days, and my arrhythmia was all but gone. I have used the last of the physic, and learn that to desist ravages both body and mind terribly. Do these people truly understand what they have discovered? I must assume they do. At least now their desperation to produce more seed can be understood—I'm sorely tempted to do so myself. But I will resist. The planting must be destroyed. Pray no one else discovers the solution.

Tristam looked up from the page. *Dandish had solved the* regis *problem.* Solved it and told no one. Then he destroyed the plants, all his notes but this fragment, and wrote the duchess saying a solution was not possible.

"He was too ill to write me," Tristam said aloud, realizing suddenly what this hidden message meant. Here were the last words of Dandish—to Tristam at least. And perfectly clear, except for what was left unsaid. Dandish had tried the seed; made the physic and experimented on himself. Infinitely curious Dandish—and not nearly so naive in the ways of the world as Tristam had believed.

He could almost hear the old man's voice. *"Do not attempt to solve this problem, Tristam."* That message at least could not be mistaken.

Tristam looked up and addressed his words to the infinite depths of blue. *But why?* was his first thought. Dandish had clearly not wanted to tell more. Good, unselfish, noble Dandish.

"I must trust someone," he said quietly, still addressing the sky. "And I'm sure you had your reasons, Professor, though I wish you had seen fit to tell me more."

He sat for a while, staring out at the dragonflies

weaving their intricate patterns over the slough, like courtiers in a dance. Then he took the lens from Dandish's field glass and used it to focus the rays of the sun, setting fire to the professor's final message. The ashes he committed to the breeze, watching them scatter across the still surface of the pond like wind-borne seed.

NINE

A letter had been awaiting Tristam for several days at the Queen Anne, but his immediate hope that it came from Dandish was quickly dashed. It was addressed in an unfamiliar hand. Tristam perched on the arm of a chair and read.

My dear Tristam:

I have only just learned the reason for your journey to Merton. This is the saddest news. Although I did not know Professor Dandish as well as you did yourself, I counted him a friend and admired his accomplishments, as any educated person must. Do accept my heartfelt condolences.

The King himself expressed grief at the loss, though His Majesty was reassured by my confidence in your skills.

If you return to Avonel by the last day of the month, and feel up to it, I will have an evening at my home that you might enjoy. Please do attend.

> *Yours,*
> *Elorin, Duchess of Morland*

Well, here would be the attempt to enlist Tristam in Dandish's place. Or had the duchess some other motive that Tristam and Jaimy had not even begun to guess?

A knock interrupted the pursuit of these thoughts and at the door Tristam found a liveried footman.

"From Sir Roderick Palle, Mr. Flattery." The man

proffered a sealed envelope—the second in a span measured in minutes. "Sir Roderick awaits your reply."

"Sir Roderick is . . . here?"

The man nodded. "In the lobby, sir."

Tristam's heart sank as he read standing in the open door.

My dear Mr. Flattery:

I realize you have just returned from your duties in Merton, but, even so, I thought you might care to join me for a Society gathering this evening. There will be an interesting paper, I think, and, as always, the best conversation in Avonel. I await your reply.

Yours,
Roderick Palle

"Flames," Tristam said under his breath. Indecision kept him standing half out in the hall.

Neither faction was wasting even a moment, though he was still not sure what anyone wanted of him. The bait being offered—an evening at the Society—was certainly perfectly chosen to lure Tristam, but even that could not overcome his trepidation about speaking with Palle. Of course, he could not avoid the King's Man forever, nor would it be wise to snub him: best to have it over with than live with the constant anxiety about what might come.

"Would you thank Sir Roderick for his kind invitation and say that I shall be down directly?"

"Certainly, sir."

Closing the door, Tristam began a desperate search for suitable clothing.

It seemed a shame that he would finally achieve one of his dreams—attending a meeting of the Empiricists' Society—and have the experience virtually ruined by his fears of the coming interview. He had always hoped Dandish would take him to a gathering of the Society, but Dandish almost never attended himself—

too much opportunity for conflict for the poor professor. The meeting notes in the quarterly *Society Annals* were a fascination of Tristam's, and he pored over them with a mixture of envy and vicarious pleasure.

Tristam was surprised to learn that Sir Roderick attended meetings of the Society. Was he a fellow, Tristam wondered? Certainly, to invite a guest, he must be.

Not fifteen minutes later he was flying down the stairs, three to a stride, making a most undignified entrance into the Queen Anne's lobby.

Sir Roderick rose from a chair, a half-suppressed smile enlivening his usually expressionless face. "Not to rush, Mr. Flattery. It is better to arrive with both legs intact. My driver informed me of your return. I realize you have had barely a moment to get settled, but I thought you might not want to miss the Society meeting."

Tristam nodded his agreement.

"We have time yet," Sir Roderick said. "I thought we might find something to eat—if you have not already supped?"

"I'm famished, actually."

"I am as well. Allow me to take you to an establishment I know. You will not have reason to disapprove, I think."

They found yet another of Sir Roderick's beautiful carriages outside and set off to the knight's promised meal. It was not quite dark—the lamplighters had just appeared—and Tristam caught glimpses of a vivid sunset here and there between buildings. The unhurried *clip-clop* of hoofs echoed in the quiet streets, preceding the carriage like a tired crier.

They passed into a neighborhood of fine homes where the driver turned out of the street and the carriage rolled slowly up a short drive, lamp-lit and garden lined. Tristam had not noticed any sign or device at the gate to mark the entrance as belonging to anything but a private residence.

"Is this a club?" Tristam asked.

"Of sorts. Though it has no official name or even a list of members. But I suppose it is a club as much as anything."

Servants appeared under the large carriage entrance and Sir Roderick greeted the steward by name. They were ushered inside a beautiful mansion dating, Tristam believed, from a century after the rebuilding of Avonel. It had that certain lightness, both in color and form, created by high ceilings in combination with carefully proportioned columns and openings.

There was little about the residence to indicate it was not a private home—though a wealthy family's home, to be sure. A servant led the way past the partially opened doors of a ballroom and from within issued the purest tenor voice Tristam had ever heard. Involuntarily, he stopped. The song was familiar, an aria composed by Ramsay for his great unfinished opera, and more moving for the knowledge that it had been the composer's last work. But it could have been anything; the voice was so sure, so devoid of artifice, so effortlessly powerful that it pierced the listener's heart.

The music ended to a riotous ovation, and both Tristam and Sir Roderick stopped in the hall and applauded as well. People began to stream from the room then, many greeting Sir Roderick with obvious pleasure.

The knight touched Tristam's elbow and they moved on.

"Teiho Ruau," Roderick said, quietly.

"So I expected. The descriptions I have heard were not exaggerated in the least. What an instrument that voice is!"

Ruau was an islander brought back from Oceana by Gregory. He was famous in all the lands surrounding the Entide Sea, and much caressed by the nobility. Even the King was known to be an admirer, often enjoying private performances.

"It almost makes one believe in gods and their

gifts," Roderick said. "That was not a voice you heard; it was a miracle."

Just then the crowd parted and a young man, dark of complexion and round of features, came through the doors. He was smiling broadly, and nodding to admirers on both sides. Tristam could not help but notice that he dressed as a dandy, his clothing of the most exotic fabrics and colors, and under his arm he carried an elaborate, white-plumed hat. It must have been the naturalist in him, for Tristam's eye was drawn to the man's belt which appeared to be made from the skin of a snake, but before he could be sure the man was lost in the crowd.

The people leaving the ballroom were flushed with apparent excitement and, to Tristam's dismay, he noticed they wore formal clothing.

"I feel I am not properly attired for the occasion," Tristam ventured.

"Not at all. We will take our meal in a private room. Had we come to the ball, that would be another matter. But for our supper and the Society later, we are both more than adequately attired. We do not all have to dress like our friend Ruau." He gave a gentle laugh and shook his head.

"You know him?"

"Oh, yes. Certainly. He is in the palace often. We share a tailor, though you would hardly know it." He indicated his own clothing which, though finely made, was quite conservative in style.

"Did I see a snakeskin belt?" Tristam asked.

Roderick laughed. "You did indeed. He can't be parted from it. You see, a bit of the savage remains, despite all of our efforts. Here we are."

They were led into a private room and there attended by servants of great skill and discretion.

"I see you are still wondering where I have brought you," Roderick said, alarming Tristam a little with his perception. "You have attended evenings dedicated to the appreciation of things Entonne?"

"At the university such things were common."

"I have no doubt. Well, in this place one can always find a celebration of things Farr—though celebration is perhaps not the correct word. Those of us who come here believe in the value of Farrland: her traditions, her culture, and art. You will never hear a word of Entonne spoken in these rooms, nor will you hear Entonne culture lauded at the expense of our own. We are not mad nationalists, by any definition, but we are a balance to this mania which promotes the worship of anything and everything Entonne. Does that set your mind at ease?"

"I was curious." So here was the center of the anti-Entonne movement in Farrland, Tristam thought. How was he to decline when he was invited to join, as he was certain he would be?

"You needn't look so concerned, Mr. Flattery. I brought you here only to find a private place to talk." Roderick smiled and lifted his glass in a toast. "I am aware of the feelings of our recent graduates toward overt patriotism of the sentimental variety. So let us drink to those things which are of value in all cultures." They toasted—Tristam sure his relief showed— and Roderick took a moment to examine his wine by the lamplight. It was, Tristam realized, excellent wine.

"You have traveled abroad, Mr. Flattery? You have journeyed to Entonne?"

"Yes, there and to Doorn as well one summer. Most pleasant." He could hardly be more non-committal than that.

"Do you share the Entonne fascination with the mages, then?"

Tristam realized he would never be able to predict where a conversation with Roderick Palle might be going, and though this sounded like nothing more than small talk, Tristam thought it would be wise never to assume innocence in anything this man did or said.

"No, though I find it a most curious thing. I have come to believe that the Entonne are more capable of embracing contradictions than we are ourselves. Something in the character. But they are in awe of the charismatic and I sometimes think their interest in the mages is related to this. Or so it would seem to me." There: some criticism of Entonne that he could make in good conscience. Perhaps that would prove he was a true citizen of Farrland.

"Yes, I would agree. How else do you explain this near-worship of Count Previsse? There was never a more despicable human being born of woman. And they think him a great poet and a painter as well as a statesman! It is beyond belief."

Tristam nodded. His classmates at Merton had all admired Previsse, for the high adventure of his life if for nothing else. A servant entered to pour more wine and his exit seemed like a signal for the conversation to change.

"I hope your journey to Merton did not leave you too out of sorts. It was a sad business."

Tristam nodded. "Yes. I will miss the good professor. He was a very kind and patient teacher to me, and I fear I was not the perfect receptacle for his vast knowledge."

"Let time judge that, Mr. Flattery. No man of the first rank is ever satisfied with his accomplishments, no matter what others make of them."

Tristam immediately thought of poor Dandish. "Well, that was true of Sanfield Dandish. If doubting the value of one's work is a measure of its importance, he approached greatness." *How in the world had such a man become involved in growing Kingfoil for the duchess?* Had he merely fallen victim to her charms? There was the note in Dandish's journal suggesting the duchess believed she was playing him for a fool. But he had played along, apparently, for reasons Tristam could not guess. And why had Dandish not allied himself with Sir Roderick Palle?

Jaimy was right, Tristam thought. It was best to stay out of this struggle between the courtiers at all costs. *I can't begin to see which side has intentions of which I would approve.* Tristam found himself looking at Roderick with even greater suspicion.

"Yes," Roderick said, "the professor was truly as modest as most gentlemen claim to be—though seldom are."

There was a moment of silence. Tristam felt a slow growing panic seize him. He could not think of what to say or how to begin describing what he had found in Dandish's drawing room. He was beginning to think that fear would not allow him to broach the subject at all.

"I have heard a rumor, Mr. Flattery," Roderick said very softly, "that Dandish's journals were not to be found. Perhaps stolen, in fact." This was said in the most matter-of-fact tone, but the King's Man fixed Tristam with his unfathomable gaze and did not look away.

Tristam nodded. He began to take a sip of his wine to steel his nerve, but his hand betrayed him and trembled so that he returned the glass quickly to the table. "Stolen is what I expect myself. I know that there were many volumes—perhaps fifty—yet they were nowhere to be found. Both Dandish's rooms at Merton and his home were broken into and ransacked, yet nothing of worth appeared to be missing."

Roderick nodded as though Tristam were merely verifying information from other sources, which disconcerted Tristam even more.

"An empiricist's journals are valuable, without question, but they are not valuable in gold and silver. What do you make of it?"

Tristam feared that he was betraying much. His mouth was dry and he clasped his hands together lest their trembling be noticed. Roderick stared at him and Tristam wondered what the knight knew already. The King's Man had resources that Tristam could only imagine and was proving himself perceptive in the extreme.

The best lies, Tristam thought, are made of half-truths.

"I fear, Sir Roderick, that Dandish's involvement in the palace arboretum has drawn the interest of others.

I can hardly imagine anything else that would lead to such a thing."

Roderick considered his words and then nodded. "I shall send Mr. Hawksmoor to Merton directly. He will get to the bottom of things."

Tristam felt his heart sink. It would not take a genius to guess what had been planted in the professor's drawing room. Half the truth, he reminded himself.

"One thing he will find is a number of planting boxes—their plants gone—kept in a locked room in Dandish's home.

This produced a reaction in the placid facade of the King's Man. The knight looked as though he had just received the worst possible news, but his response was not grief—it was anger. He pushed back from the table, opened his mouth as if to curse, and then it passed, like a strange fit. Only a darkness remained, as though Sir Roderick exerted himself to mask pain.

"You think the professor was growing Kingfoil." It was not a question.

Tristam nodded, almost afraid to speak now.

Although his eyes were fixed on Tristam, it was clear that Sir Roderick's focus was on something else. *"I should have known,"* he said, so quietly that he was obviously speaking to himself. To Tristam it sounded like self-accusation. *"Dandish,"* Palle said as though naming a betrayer.

And in Tristam's mind echoed this same word. *Dandish,* the most guileless of gentlemen.

Roderick's reaction was so genuine that Tristam was now all but sure that the duchess' letter could not be in his hands.

"Do you have any evidence beyond the empty planting boxes and the coincidence of the journals being stolen?"

There was no moisture in Tristam's throat, but he tried not to swallow hard. "The corner of a burnt Kingfoil leaf," he managed.

"Which could have come from the palace arboretum?" Roderick said.

Tristam shrugged. "Perhaps."

"Who do you think removed the plants?" Roderick asked suddenly, obviously not believing his own objection.

"Professor Dandish, I suspect. The room was locked when I first arrived there—the door had not been forced. I suppose it could have been done by someone else—between the professor's death and my arrival. . . ." Tristam had trouble forcing out the lies. It was not his nature to prevaricate and this man who sat looking at him spent all his days sifting words for truth. "I can't tell you how difficult it is for me to inform you of this, Sir Roderick. Professor Dandish was my mentor and friend. . . ."

"You knew him well?"

"So I would have said." Tristam heard some small distress in his voice.

Roderick stared down into his glass, swirling the wine gently in the bowl, as though his anger had been replaced by sadness. "Do you think he could have found the solution to our problem?" he asked, then glanced up at Tristam.

Tristam found that speech had deserted him altogether, as though he had reached the end of his capacity to lie.

Roderick continued to stare, mild surprise registering in the instant before Tristam looked away.

"I don't know, Sir Roderick."

"You seem unsure, Mr. Flattery. Do you think there's some chance that he did?"

Tristam felt his shoulders shrug. "I can't answer either way. His notes were not to be found—destroyed with the plants, I suspect." Tristam had a sudden wild fear that the diaries he had sent to Tumney had been brought to Roderick's attention.

"I don't think he solved the problem," Sir Roderick said firmly, surprising Tristam. "And do you know why, Mr. Flattery? Because it cannot be solved. That is my belief. Teiho Ruau is convinced the plants will never bear again. 'Spirits,' he claims. Once the Kingfoil stops bearing, the islanders say, it will never produce seeds again," he smiled suddenly, "unless the spirit can be appeased by ritual. Tumney has not solved the problem. Dandish could not solve it. Nor will you, I fear, Mr. Flattery. And that is no reflection on your abilities."

Servants arrived with food, interrupting the conversation. Neither man touched his supper. Roderick lifted his cutlery but stopped. "The circumstances of the professor's death were not unusual in any way?"

"Why, not that. . . ." Tristam felt real distress at this suggestion. "You have taken me aback, sir. Could there have been someone so desperate to have *regis* that they would commit murder?" He thought immediately of the death of Baron Ipsword.

"The life of the King. . . ." Roderick left the sentence unfinished and began to eat, almost mechanically, for he had obviously lost his interest in food. "One wonders what the man was thinking." Roderick shrugged and appeared to pull himself away from whatever thoughts he pursued. His equanimity returned as well, as though he had not just said, in effect, that the King would now die. "Unless you can say more, Mr. Flattery, I believe we should leave this subject for now."

Tristam nodded. "There is one other thing, sir."

Roderick looked up.

"My journal disappeared from my room in Merton."

"Had you written about Kingfoil in it?"

"Not a word, sir. I have kept all my notes in the arboretum."

"Very wise of you, Mr. Flattery. It is still a loss, of course. I hold little hope of these missing journals coming to light, I'm sorry to say." And that was all he offered on the subject.

Conversation turned elsewhere, to Tristam's great surprise. That was all? Somehow he could not believe his lies had been accepted that easily. Even Dean Emin had seen through Tristam immediately. But Sir Roderick gave no indication that he did not believe everything he had heard. And, undoubtedly, he did not need

Tristam to tell him for whom Dandish grew the Kingfoil.

It is how the game is played, Tristam told himself. *If Roderick believed there would be some advantage in exposing me in my own lies, he would no doubt do so—and easily, too.*

But Roderick appeared to have no intention of doing so. It was as though the conversation had never occurred, and Roderick's manner changed so completely—he became positively amiable—that Tristam almost began to wonder himself.

Another aspect of the King's Man was now revealed, for Roderick proved himself to be knowledgeable in many areas of natural history and natural philosophy, as well as a falconer and breeder of some real skill. The knight engaged Tristam in conversation, pulling him away from his own thoughts and fears so that in the end he gave in and allowed himself to pretend the situation was real.

❦   ❦   ❦

Supper over, the two men took to Roderick's carriage again. Their conversation, which had flowed so freely over wine and food, dried up altogether. Tristam found himself considering the King's Man, trying to remember what he knew of Sir Roderick Palle. Jaimy would have been able to go on at length on the subject, but Tristam did not have a memory for such things. In fact, he was usually not interested in the "who's who" of the Farr court. Something that was changing rapidly.

If Tristam's memory was not totally faulty, Sir Roderick was of a good family—cousin to the Earl of Mindon. He had risen through the army quickly, for his organizational abilities were superb, and was taken into the service of the King by a high ranking officer who was briefly a minster. Even when his patron was gone, Roderick Palle had continued his climb, having exchanged his rank as officer for a series of new offices.

It had been a quick ascent. Certainly, Sir Roderick

Palle was now, and for many years past, the most powerful man in the kingdom, after the sovereign and his heir, for the King's Man was the link between the ministers of the government and the crown.

Despite this, Roderick had refused all rank but the knighthood he had won for his service in the military—an uncharacteristic flouting of convention. Sir Roderick Palle was the first untitled gentleman to hold the position of King's Man ... ever.

Tristam was absolutely sure that Roderick did nothing without purpose, but he had no idea what was achieved by this refusal of rank. It was possible that Palle garnered a certain popularity with the common people by refusing a title, but somehow Tristam did not think Roderick the type to care about what the people thought.

Roderick Palle was quiet, almost unassuming considering his position, but he was more powerful than any of the nobles in Farrland, no matter their title or connections or wealth. Tristam wondered if his continued refusal of titles unsettled the aristocratic families. Despite his birth, Palle had made himself almost an outsider by his refusal to acknowledge that most significant indicator of a man's importance—a peerage—and he did not seem to care about that either.

The King's Man was, as far as Tristam could tell, an enigma—not just to Tristam but to everyone. And here he sat, across from Tristam, appearing for all the world like a distracted scholar chewing on a problem. A man without an apparent sense of self-importance, and without noticeable manifestations of imagination as well. *What a facade he has created*, Tristam thought, *as impenetrable as the ocean depths*.

They arrived at the mansion that was home to the Empiricists' Society—part museum, part clubhouse—it was the object of many of Tristam's dearest fantasies. He felt his excitement grow as the carriage pulled up before the doors.

The young naturalist was almost sure he had entered a dream, he even seemed to be floating, his mind registering things in a haze. The entrance hall was a marvel of pale veined marble—columns, floor, a sweeping stairway, and a high, domed ceiling—lit by a great chandelier so that the stone took on an aspect of almost liquid translucence.

A life-sized sculpture of Boran stood upon a low plinth in the hall's center, the father of empiricism holding out his arm in a sweeping gesture as though indicating the wonders of the world.

In a large niche in one wall the reconstructed skeleton of a dinosaur, *dracosaurus,* dwarfed everything and everyone in the room. Nearby, the imposing shell of *Tridacna gigas,* the giant clam of Oceana, sat upon a small pedestal.

Tristam realized suddenly that Roderick was watching him, gauging his reaction, perhaps.

"I must ask your indulgence for a moment, Mr. Flattery. I need to say a few words to Beall." He nodded toward a group of men gathered across the hall, absorbed in conversation.

"By all means. There is no lack of things for me to see."

Tristam was left alone and found himself wandering toward the side of the hall, as though he felt too conspicuous standing out in the center. A large canvas hung there and so disoriented was Tristam that he took a moment to realize it was the painting based on the artist's study he had inherited from Dandish. For some time he stood, lost in a close examination.

"A Hobbson," a voice said beside him.

Tristam turned to find an avuncular looking gentleman dressed in a style popular before Tristam's birth, including knee-high boots and a powdered wig.

"Averil Kent," the man said, offering Tristam his hand to clasp.

"Your servant, sir. Tristam Flattery." The man's name was familiar, but Tristam could not think why.

"It is a beautiful work, is it not?" Hobbson was a master, I think."

"I could not agree more. I have the artist's study for

this very canvas." Tristam said this with more surprise at his good fortune than from an intention to impress. But even so, the man turned to him with wide eyes.

"Do you indeed! Signed? What a treasure! How fortunate. Does it differ greatly from the final work?"

Martyr's blood, thought Tristam, *of course!* This was *Averil Kent*—a painter of great fame in his own right. He tried to gather his wits to answer the man's question. "Well. The study is very small, of course, so in detail it is far less complex. The composition is identical, to my eye," he added. "The palette here is generally more subtle, though this sunset is extremely vivid, perhaps creating greater contrast." Tristam looked over at the old man's kind face as he stared at the painting.

"I am intrigued, Mr. Flattery. To gain some insight into the inner process of Hobbson—that is the opportunity that such studies provide."

"I should be most happy to show it to you, if you would like," Tristam said, aware that it was most likely the man was merely being polite and did not really care to see the study at all.

"I should like nothing better!" Kent said warmly. "Do you live in Avonel? I collect you are a son of the Duke of Blackwater?"

"Nephew, in fact. I make my home in Locfal, but I'm in the city for a few days—at the Queen Anne. Perhaps we could sup together?" Tristam was gratified that the man's interest seemed genuine and he had not put him in a difficult position.

"How I wish I could, but my evenings are filled. If an afternoon could be made to suit, that I could arrange."

They agreed to meet for tea the next day and the artist continued his rounds, leaving Tristam feeling somewhat more welcomed and less like he had walked into a dream.

"I see you have met Kent." It was Roderick, returned.

"Yes. What a kind gentleman."

"There is no better sort. If he takes a liking to you,

he will introduce you to every empiricist in the charted world. He has been a fellow forty years or more. Knows everyone." A servant came to the door of the hall at that moment and, as softly as one could, blew a clear note on a conch shell—the tradition in this place.

"Shall we go in? I am told this should be an interesting gathering, though I must warn you—there will be a moment for poor Dandish. I hope you won't mind?"

"Not at all," Tristram said, hoping he told the truth.

They entered a sizable hall and found a place among the rows of chairs. The room filled quickly and the Speaker took the podium—none other than Kent, whom Tristram had just met.

"The pleasures of the evening to you, gentlemen." Kent surveyed the hall with a look of such apparent affection that Tristram had the impression the artist was looking out over his own, much beloved, family. "Before we begin with this evening's lectures and discussion it is my duty to report the sad passing of our colleague, Sanfield Dandish, Layel Professor at Merton College."

Kent had obviously prepared carefully, for he spoke with great knowledge of the professor's accomplishments and with some feeling about Dandish, the man, neither overlooking his shortcomings nor exaggerating his many fine qualities. It was a balanced and fair summary of the professor's life and work. The famous *Book of Fellows* was brought forward and a final date was entered after the signature of Sanfield Dandish—something many present found very affecting, for there was more than one throat cleared with difficulty.

In the moment's silence that followed, Tristram found himself thinking that in this very book Lord Skye had written his name, and Boran and Thayer . . . and his friend and mentor, Professor Sanfield Dandish. What honored company the professor kept! There could not be a better indication of a life well spent.

It made the professor's recent activities seem even more incongruous.

"If there are no pressing matters requiring our attention," Kent said quietly, breaking the spell, "I shall begin. . . ."

"Mr. Speaker." A voice familiar to Tristam punctuated the somber mood.

As Tristam turned to find the source of the voice, Roderick muttered, "Somers."

And indeed it was. The father of Jaimy's current passion.

"I have spoken before on the subject of female fellows and though I disagree utterly with the decision of my colleagues in this matter, I bow to the will of the majority." He bobbed his head. "Though we honor a female empiricist here in our own home with the dedication of the Marsfield Library for her contribution to medicine and human anatomy, still we do not allow ladies beyond our sacred doors. I would put it to my honored fellows that female guests—properly escorted, of course—should be allowed to attend our lectures. I know, myself, several women who read our annals with great interest and understanding and their presence here could only add to the discussion."

Somers was about to go on when Averil Kent took the opportunity to slip in between sentences. "Professor Somers, no doubt what you suggest should be given our most serious consideration, but this is not a properly constituted, voting assemblage. All matters pertaining to rules of fellowship etcetera must be put to the annual constitutional review board. I do thank you for bringing this matter to our attention and urge you to raise the issue again at the proper time."

Somers swayed on his feet for a second, then, with a nod, returned to his seat. Tristam heard the man directly behind him mutter, "Oddest notions, our Somers."

Kent turned back to his audience. "Before we begin, I would like to welcome our guests this evening. Count Massenet, Entonne Ambassador to the Farr court, and Doctor Paul Varese, distinguished empiricist and author." These gentlemen rose with an easy grace, bowing to the restrained applause.

Tristam had never heard of the ambassador, but Varese was certainly the Entonne champion of the Farrellite version of geological history—they denied Layel's hypothesis that the earth was immeasurably old, perhaps hundreds of millions of years. *How Dandish will love to hear of this,* Tristam thought immediately, as people often do of those recently gone—and then felt the loss heavily.

"We also have in our company this evening," Kent went on, "Mr. Tristam Flattery, colleague of Professor Sanfield Dandish and co-author of several widely admired papers on the collection of Baron Trevelyan."

Roderick touched Tristam's arm; he rose and bowed, feeling slight embarrassment. So that is why Roderick had excused himself earlier, he realized. The thought disappeared in the rush of emotion though. He was being applauded by the most accomplished empiricists in the land. Even without introductions he recognized some of them from portraits he had seen. He sat again, feeling a small rush of pride.

The first lecturer was introduced. His paper was entitled; *Predator Identification in Bivalvia.* A rather graphic demonstration preceded the actual reading, delighting the audience and making them very receptive to any subsequent claims. In a shallow, copper pan, partially filled with salt water, the lecturer placed a dozen *Pectinidae,* commonly called "swimming scallops." He then held up a starfish, the deep purple rays curling slowly. The instant the man placed the starfish into the water with the scallops the entire pan began to shake, water splashed out on the table and then the scallops began to shoot out of the pan until they all lay on the now sopping cloth, and the starfish was left alone. An explanation and discussion followed—all rather polite and low key.

But all the while Tristam could feel a tension growing in the room. It was as though a storm was about to throw itself upon the building and everyone hushed to hear its approach. Mr. Varese was apparently to speak next.

A brave man, Tristam thought.

Varese was of average height, a bit emaciated looking as though he had been ill or was simply too preoccupied to remember to eat, for he had that look about him as well. He went reluctantly to the lectern, it seemed, though he did not appear nervous about his coming encounter.

The Entonne took a moment to settle an oddly shaped pair of spectacles on his nose, looked down at the papers he had spread out on the lectern and then began.

"I speak, gentlemen, of a subject dear to all of our hearts," he said, his voice strong. "Dear to our hearts but hitherto unaddressed."

Varese's manner was not conducive to gaining the sympathy of an audience, Tristam thought. The man's Farr was very good, but his manner would have been appropriate to a schoolmaster who addressed a group of boys too stupid to appreciate what he had to offer. Tristam was not sure this was actually the man's attitude—he suspected by the choice of words that it was not—but it was obviously his common manner of speech and it seemed that Varese was too socially obtuse to realize the effect it had on others.

"It is the accepted conception of history that empiricism came into being the day Wilam Tomas Boran first published his great book, *The Role of Experience in the Study of Natural Philosophy, or An Inquiry into Methodology.* Of course the interpretation of this great text led to the schism between the 'empirics' and the 'empiricists' as defined by Noam and Jaspers. In recent years this split in approaches to natural philosophy has largely been healed by the all but universal acceptance of the Jaspers' interpretation of empiricism—observations interpreted by reason. Few, if any, ideas have had such impact on the lives of men.

"Like many another young scholar, I became enamored of Boran's book and to this day I continue to follow the basic tenets that Boran set down some seventy-five years ago." He looked up then, regarding the audience over his spectacles. "But I have discovered that this accepted version of history is no more true than any nation's official account of its wars. Boran did not formulate the ideas of empiricism first and it is possible that he was aware of the ideas from his reading of another."

The dramatic pause could not have been better timed. Boran was worshiped in these halls. To say that he did not have primacy in the creation of the empiricist creed was sacrilege. To suggest that he *stole* these ideas from another was blasphemy. And to judge by the reaction of the men around him, some were ready to kindle the cleansing pyres.

At least two men stormed noisily out of the hall. Others muttered among themselves or merely to themselves. No one looked pleased. Finally, the voice of Averil Kent was heard.

"Gentlemen, please. Doctor Varese has not yet finished. Can we not accord him the courtesy which all are due here, in this hall where new ideas have always been welcomed?"

Varese nodded to Kent and then looked back at his audience. "I do not make such a claim brashly. Boran, as I have said, is one of my true heroes. Nonetheless, I do say it. Over the course of my researches I found, in the correspondence of the Marquis of Reme, three letters written sometime between the years 1430 and 1450. All of them were signed with nothing but a very elaborate letter 'L.' The signature, as I'm sure you are all aware, of Lucklow." He stopped to drink, and refer again to his notes. At the mention of the mage, Roderick had suddenly moved forward in his chair as though straining to not miss a word.

"I have made every effort to compare the handwriting of these letters with other samples known to be the mage's, and I am convinced of the authenticity. It is, unfortunately, unclear to whom these letters were addressed, for the name of the recipient was certainly a diminutive. Due to the nature of this diminutive and the tone of the writing I suspect these letters were written to a woman in the house of the Marquis of Reme: likely the marchioness, the marquis' second wife. One immediately wonders about the nature of this, hitherto unknown, friendship. I will only say that these letters did not lie unread for over a century for no reason. This was an intimate alliance kept carefully secret. The fact that these letters were not destroyed is fortunate in the extreme, for there are indications that there existed a larger correspondence—no more of which has been found among the family papers. I shall also add at this point that the Marquis of Reme was briefly the patron of Wilam Boran during the years 1457 and 58.

"Much of what is said in these letters, written in Old Farr, is in the common nature of such letters, even if somewhat veiled: the inhabitants of one time expressing much the same sentiments as those of another. There are, however, a few paragraphs dealing with other matters: politics of the time; gossip; and a single paragraph that I shall now read to you." The man paused to drink again, for effect, Tristam was sure.

Tristam took that opportunity to glance around. The hall was as silent now as it had been noisy moments ago. Sir Roderick was not the only man straining forward in his seat. The Entonne Ambassador had actually half-risen and then returned to his chair, his face contorted in what appeared to be great distress.

"Here, gentlemen, are the words of Lucklow." He cleared his throat. "*'To suggest that one can deduce the workings of the world through sheer mental effort is a continuing fallacy that I cannot fathom. Haldbraith claimed the number of teeth possessed by a horse to be twenty, though he had never made the extreme effort of actually looking into the mouth of the beast. If one would know the number of teeth possessed by any animal, one must take the trouble to enumerate them, as one must do for the petals on a flower or the number of bones in the finger. Who could possibly believe that the exploration of the natural world was somehow akin to the study of abstract formulae, to be comprehended by mere logic?! In fact, to know the number of teeth possessed by a horse, one must count the teeth of one hundred horses to eliminate the possibility that some have been lost to accident and so on. Until such a numerative and empirical approach is taken up by our natural philosophers, they shall continue to fill book after book with facts created out of nothing but their own ignorance. Even the most illiterate shepherd will count his flock upon his fingers to see how many sheep he possesses. Only a philosopher would think to deduce the number according to some principle of logic.' "*

There was a moment's stunned silence as the impact of Varese's claims wore off a little and then the room erupted. Questions came from all corners and not a few of them were outright accusations. Voices began to rise as everyone struggled to be heard. Averil Kent reached the lectern at the same time as the Entonne ambassador and as Kent held up his hands, attempting to gain a respite, the ambassador leaned over and spoke in the ear of his countryman. Without further adieu, Count Massenet ushered his compatriot out the nearby door, bringing the gathered voices to a crescendo in both volume and indignation.

The meeting broke up then, the discussion fragmenting as the fellows retreated in groups. Some made their way to the smoking room, others to the library and still others to various rooms around the old mansion.

Roderick led Tristam to a large drawing room where groups were forming and the discussion was already animated if not heated. Surprisingly, not all the talk was of Varese and his sudden departure—proving the old saw that the Entonne would make their exits without taking proper leave—for many named him a fraud and a crank and put his claims aside.

Nearby, three men were arguing about the age of the earth, while not far off another group debated the feasibility and merits of connecting Wrightfield and Kuldern with a canal. It was a lively company.

Tristam was introduced around by Sir Roderick, and the young empiricist was thrilled to find himself in the company of several of Farrland's most eminent thinkers: Beall, whom Roderick had mentioned before; the great engineer, Wells; and Noyes who had designed Bolingbroke Palace as well as written a landmark book on the new agricultural methods. Tristam received a warm welcome, for it seemed everyone was familiar with the work done by Dandish and Flattery.

The group fell immediately into discussion, as though there were not enough time in the evening to waste more than a moment on pleasantries.

"How did you like that, Mr. Flattery?" Beall asked. "A fine introduction to the Society! It is not every night we have someone attack the reputation of one of our most eminent thinkers and run off without so much as a 'by your leave.' "

"Did you see the way Massenet whisked him off?" Noyes said, laughing. "I'm sure the count feared he was creating an international incident!" He laughed again. "The ambassador should have thought of that sooner."

"But he did not know!" It was Beall again. "I spoke with the count earlier and asked what Varese intended. 'Something to do with methodology,' he told me. Well, I should say so!"

The entire group laughed, though Tristam caught Roderick sharing a glance with Wells that did not seem humorous in nature.

"Enough of that," Beall said, as though making a pronouncement. "Now, Sir Roderick," he began, acting as spokesman for the others, Tristam suspected. "You are far too close on these matters you have been pursuing and we are all wondering when you will see fit to tell us, your friends and associates, what you have discovered or invented, if that is the case."

Roderick laughed a little as though slightly embarrassed, but it was, Tristam suspected, only more of his act. "But, gentlemen, my endeavors, compared to your own great works, are so modest that I hardly wish to waste your time."

"We will be the judges of that," Beall responded and the other added their voices in support.

"I see that I may keep my small efforts to myself no longer. If you must know, I have been writing a paper on the nature of artesian wells and I think I have explained this phenomenon at last. There, now, is that not an exciting subject?" Taking a mechanical pencil from a pocket and calling for paper, the King's Man began a drawing depicting stratification in the earth. It was a short but very clear thesis that Roderick proposed and Tristam could see the others thought it ingenious. When this was complete and the others had given this hypothesis some small criticism, Roderick then began a second drawing of the workings of a carriage. "I have seen over the years that the greatest cause of carriages tipping, and all of the subsequent injuries to man, machine, and beast—loss of both teeth and spokes, much to the confusion of those who study such things—is the loss of stability caused when the front axle is turned." He had drawn a rough T shape. "The entire axle pivots on this central point, of course, and in an extreme turn . . ." he drew the axle to illustrate this, "the support of the carriage in the front is made so narrow and the direction of the pull caused by the team is such that the carriage is often overset." The knight began a second drawing. "Here you see what I am proposing—in fact, I have made a successful model and am about to have a full-sized carriage so modified. The wheels pivot on their own individual points on either side so that the stability is not compromised. At first I thought they must each turn to the same degree, but this did not prove practical, for the wheels, as I should have realized, describe circles of different radii. Do you see? The circle scribed on the ground by the inner wheel is smaller than the outer? This, then, had been the difficulty. The geometrics I worked out easily like this. . . ." He drew a line through the rear axle and marked a point on this that became the center of the circles that the front wheels would scribe. "But to have the wheels somehow turn differently when the horses went off at an angle to the carriage, that was the problem. Can you think how I managed it?" he asked, a bit like a school boy impressed with his own cleverness.

The gentlemen present clearly loved a puzzle and in a moment suggestions began to come as they all bent over the drawing. After a few moments Sir Roderick, pleased that no one had seen the solution immediately, set his hand to the drawing again, showing how he had connected the two wheels and the draw bar by an ingenious series of rods and levers. "There, you see? Mr. Wells was coming close to the mark. If I have engineered the thing so that it will take the punishment from our roads, I think, gentlemen, that we shall have a much improved carriage." He was obviously quite pleased by the ingenuity of the design and Tristam was a bit in awe. No wonder Palle had said that he knew of men who served the King and made contributions to other fields as well!

At first Tristam was too intimidated to speak, but after a while he was asked his opinion on a particular point and he could see that those around him felt he acquitted himself well in his answer. After that he joined in, circumspectly, and was gratified to find that his opinions were not thought foolish by any means.

During the discussion Tristam looked up at one time to find Kent staring at him from across the room, a look of some concern on his face, but when Tristam met his eye the artist looked away.

After hearing Tristam's explanation of the movement of flower parts in carnivorous plants, Noyes turned to the King's Man.

"Well, Sir Roderick, when will this young man's name be put forward? He has a head on his shoulders, to be sure."

"We shall see." Sir Roderick nodded, as though considering. "Soon enough, I think."

Roderick was called away to give his opinion on the practicality of building the canal and Tristam excused himself briefly to find the water closet. On his return to the drawing room, he came upon Professor Somers and a young man in the hall. It was difficult to tell who was more startled, the professor or his companion. Both quickly hid their reactions but the professor only nodded as Tristam stopped to speak, leaving the young naturalist standing in the hall feeling a little foolish. *Well,* he thought, as he continued on his way, *Lord Jaimas has rather quickly worn thin his welcome at the Somers' home.* And Tristam had only left his cousin that morning!

He gazed around at the knots of fellows scattered about the drawing room, and realized for the first time that here was a gathering of the very species he was trying not to become. Despite all of his fantasies about the Society, what Tristam saw before him was a gathering of dry intellectual men—almost any one of them could easily pass for a Merton professor. Not that they were all like that, surely, but even so, Tristam had spent his life among instructors and had a pretty good eye for the type. *There is more to life,* he told himself and wondered, if he looked in a mirror if he would see a young don in the making.

His own group had dispersed and could be seen engaged in other conversations about the room. The students he had known at Merton would die to be in his place, Tristam realized, for it was a particularly august company in attendance that evening. No one from his year had yet been made a fellow of the Society and it occurred to Tristam that he could still be the first. He did not know if this thought pleased or frightened him.

Certainly one can be an empiricist and escape the mold, he thought.

An enormously large man sitting alone and leaning heavily on a cane nodded his mane of silver hair to Tristam and then motioned for the young man to join him.

"Baron Trevelyan," the man said quietly as Tristam approached. He nodded to a chair.

"Your servant, sir. Tristam Flattery." Tristam took the chair, feeling suddenly awkward. This was the naturalist who had accompanied Gregory on his first two voyages! "This is a great honor, sir. I was Professor Dandish's assistant when he toiled classifying Lord Trevelyan's magnificent collection."

The baron nodded shyly and spoke, his voice so soft and reticent that one had the impression of being addressed by a small child. "Yes. Poor Dandish. All that effort must have killed him. Glad I didn't do it myself." He looked away almost coyly.

Tristam was taken completely aback.

"Mr. Flattery. . . . You are the son of Erasmus, I should think. How unfortunate for you." He leaned toward Tristam and then whispered. "They will be after your blood, sir. I advise you to flee before you are entangled." The baron tilted his head to the room, and moved his eyes as though indicating the men standing nearby. "It happens without you knowing, sir. It happens as you sleep. Eat nothing they offer, drink only spring water." He nodded, as though acknowledging the wisdom of his own prescription. He motioned with his hand to have Tristam lean closer. Not sure what to do, Tristam bent forward as little as possible. "I knew Lord Eldrich," the old man said, his voice so low Tristam strained to hear. "Erasmus, too, but it was Eldrich brought the great evil. Skye. Oh, I knew them both. Trust no one, drink only water from the purest spring. Collect it at sunrise." He looked at Tristam imploringly, as though terrified his advice might not be heeded.

Tristam realized that several fellows kept glancing his way, some amused and others showing what appeared to be pity. Clearly, the baron was not entirely well.

Suddenly, Trevelyan banged his cane on the floor with such force that Tristam jumped. "Look at them," he hissed, his voice rising in both volume and pitch. "They will open the doors to darkness. To naked women and children. Bastard son of a bastard son. Cross-pollination—shouldn't be done, I tell you, Flattery. I told your father as well but Erasmus heard only his own voice. His visions and his voice. Poor fool.

Our world wasn't ready. Still isn't." He looked about him then, his face red with rage and then, suddenly, the anger was gone and he spoke in his pitifully childish voice. "I would like some tea, I think. Wouldn't you?" He said this with such lack of confidence—as though Tristam would refuse him this small request—that Tristam felt a wave of pity. This man was . . . had been one of the great empiricists of their time. A great man in every sense.

"The pleasures of the evening, Lord Trevelyan." It was Roderick, performing a graceful leg.

"Pleasures? Yes," he said squinting up at Sir Roderick as if not sure that he knew this man. "That's the dark secret in our hearts."

"Would you mind if I took Mr. Flattery away for a moment?"

"Mr. Flattery? Ahh, yes. He knew Eldrich, you know. We have just been talking with him."

"I'm sure. Excuse us, Lord Trevelyan, if you will."

"How's the old fossil in the palace?"

Roderick took Tristam's arm, drawing him to his feet. "Ah. The palace fossils are well, Lord Trevelyan. Kind of you to ask."

Trevelyan looked up at Sir Roderick, his face set into the look of an earnest child. "Tell him . . . tell him no one lives forever. Even a young wife can't gift you that. Even . . . even a princess." He waved a finger at Tristam. "Only spring water. Never forget."

Roderick led Tristam away as two other fellows approached the baron, speaking in soothing voices as though they addressed a child.

"My word!" Tristam said as they left the room.

"It is very sad. The baron will get quite out of sorts if he's allowed to go on. That was a mild outburst compared to others I've seen. Very sad. Yet he still comes out. Strangely, he can be quite lucid at times. I've witnessed it. As though he were perfectly well. You haven't met him at his best, I'm afraid.

The evening came to an end, far too quickly in Tristam's view. As they left the brightly lit mansion, he felt he was being cast into the outer darkness. He stood waiting for Sir Roderick's coach, and turned to look back at the columned entrance, the light pouring out of the open doors into the dark night, which Tristam thought an appropriate metaphor. It was the efforts of the men who walked, and who once walked, these halls that had pushed back the darkness of ignorance.

Just then Baron Trevelyan appeared in the doorway flanked by two men who supported and guided him, for he seemed to have lost his way and kept turning as though he would return indoors.

They ushered him down the few stairs toward a waiting carriage, and as they came closer Tristam could hear them speaking.

"But I must warn him. . . ."

"There, there, Lord Trevelyan. I'm sure he understood you perfectly well. Here is your carriage, sir."

"But, no," his eyes suddenly fixed on Tristam and he struggled to stop. "Mr. Flattery!" He waved his cane. "Flee! Flee while you may!" The two men tightened their grip and began to move the old man forward again. With surprising strength the baron brought his cane down sharply across one man's shin. "It is your blood! They will have your blood, sir!" Two other men stepped up and helped push the baron into his carriage. The last sight Tristam had was of the old man's face in the window, struggling to lean out, his eyes still riveted upon Tristam. And then the carriage was gone, its lamps disappearing down the drive, flickering through the trees like fireflies.

Sir Roderick stood shaking his head, looking off toward the gardens. "I can hardly bear to see it," he said with some feeling. "That such a great mind should give way so completely. . . . It is the cruelest thing I can imagine."

Sir Roderick's carriage stopped before them and they quickly climbed in, as though to escape the air of embarrassment that was left in the baron's wake.

The drive through the night city passed in silence. Roderick stared fixedly ahead and Tristam thought the man so distressed by their encounter with Baron Trevelyan that he did not know what to say.

Tristam also was disturbed by his meeting with the baron, but he could not help but dwell upon his good fortune. *He had attended a meeting of the Society!* Lest in time he forget, Tristam tried to recall every word he had heard, attempting to etch them into his memory.

The silence lasted until the carriage rolled to a halt before the Queen Anne.

Tristam turned as his foot touched the paving stones. "I can't thank you enough, Sir Roderick," he said with genuine feeling.

"It was my pleasure, Mr. Flattery." Roderick paused. "I fear we shall require your services no longer." He tilted his head slightly to one side as though saying, "you understand." "I shall have Mr. Hawksmoor settle our affairs. It was kind of you to come so far. The pleasures of the evening, Mr. Flattery."

And Tristam stood watching the beautiful carriage disappear down the dimly lit street. What in Farrelle's name?! They had brought him this distance to dismiss him so quickly? What had Roderick guessed from their conversation that Tristam did not see? Had he realized that Dandish had found a solution? And, if so, how did he intend to pursue it without Tristam's help?

He does not intend to pursue it, Tristam realized. *It is the last thing he wants.* And, strangely, it had also been the last thing that Dandish had wanted.

TEN

Roderick Palle stood before a table in his study, rolling the model of a carriage back and forth, his mind running over the details of the design and then turning to the events of the evening and their ramifications, and then back to the model. A knock on the door sounded so softly it hardly deserved to be called a knock at all.

"Sir Benjamin has arrived, sir," came the low voice of his man servant.

"Good." He rolled the carriage forward once more, observing closely the wheels, then turned away at the sound of footsteps. "Benjamin. Kind of you to come so quickly."

The Royal Physician stood beside the door looking, as he invariably did, like a man who had not enjoyed a full night's sleep in a very long time. He nodded, but said nothing, as though he could not muster the energy at that moment.

"You have heard about the Society meeting?"

He nodded again. "Thirdhand," he managed to say.

"Well, let us sit and compare tales—first and thirdhand versions." The two men took chairs in the alcove overlooking the Royal Gardens. Night may have hidden their splendor, but the perfume was carried into the room on the smallest breeze.

Rawdon sat stiffly, his look slightly dazed—if such a regal looking man could appear dazed.

"No doubt you were told about Varese and his claims?"

Benjamin nodded. "I cannot believe Count Massenet could be caught so unaware."

"Nor could I, but I saw it myself. Beall had spoken to Massenet earlier and asked him what Varese intended. 'Oh, something about methodology,' was his answer. I'm sure the man has never felt such a fool in all his life!"

"You think this letter is real, then?"

Roderick considered a moment. "Wells would have to see it to be sure. But, whether it is or not, we'll hear from Count Massenet in a few days; 'the letters need to be authenticated by other scholars of this field,' he'll begin. In a week's time there will be 'grave doubts.' By next month they will be nothing but 'brilliant forgeries'—and such forgeries might even be produced as proof. All the while there will be a concerted search to be sure that there are no other letters to the marchioness left lying about in some relation's attic. Varese, of course, will suffer embarrassment, but he will be called a 'victim of some other man's fraud.' The Entonne King will grant him a knighthood and perhaps even a sizable pension for his other noteworthy accomplishments. And in years to come all that will remain is a story of the night this Entonne doctor appeared before the Society and cast aspersions on the memory and reputation of Wilam Tomas Boran." He paused for a second. "It will certainly not be remembered as the evening we mourned the passing of Sanfield Dandish." Sir Roderick told the physician of his dinner conversation with Tristam Flattery.

This jolted Rawdon back to his senses. "And we thought the murder of Ipsword a fool's argument." Rawdon looked out the window, seeming suddenly fragile, his movements those of a sick man. "I will tell you, Roderick, I would never have imagined betrayal by Dandish."

"No." Roderick said quietly. "Nor would I. It is a lesson we learn again and again: we must never underestimate the charms of our duchess."

Rawdon rolled his eyes. "No, if she so much as sneezes, His Majesty will have me attending to her at all hours—sitting outside her bedchamber in case she coughs. But then, I will confess, even I have enjoyed her company on occasion—her dinner conversation is full of wit, and the duchess is the most graceful dancer in Avonel. Her charm is genuine, even if it is designed to beguile."

"Benjamin, you should never confess such a weakness to me. Have you not heard that I suspect everyone?"

"Why else would I make such a confession? Anyone foolish enough to speak against himself must certainly have the most innocent intentions."

Roderick smiled. It was good to hear Benjamin even attempt a jest—he had been too long a victim of melancholia. It had been more than worrisome.

"Lady Rawdon is well, I trust?"

"Perfectly well," he said quickly.

"I am glad to hear it, Benjamin. The duchess may have her superficial charms, but there is not a more noble soul in all of Farrland than your fair wife, and this past year has proven that beyond a doubt."

The doctor nodded, looking down at his hands in his lap and then out into the darkened garden.

"You will be glad to hear, Benjamin, that I have decided to send young Flattery back to Locfal. No doubt he will have his use yet, but for now I think we should keep him out of harm's way."

Rawdon brightened a little at hearing this. "I'm sure you know best."

The King's Man nodded. "You will see to the baron?"

"First thing in the morning."

ELEVEN

Averil Kent appeared at the door of Tristam's suite precisely on time. The leather of his high boots squeaked as he crossed the threshold and the scent of his freshly powdered wig wafted in behind him. He cut such a figure in his old-fashioned dress that Tristam thought it unfortunate that the wearing of swords had gone out of fashion, for a rapier swinging at the painter's side would have made the picture complete. Despite his odd notions of style, Kent did not for a minute appear foolish. If anything, he seemed like an historical figure come to life. One immediately treated him with deference.

"I have not been in the old Queen Anne for many a year," Kent said, looking about. "I used to lodge here often, years ago. I believe I have let these very rooms." He smiled at Tristam and took the offered chair.

Tristam had placed the Hobbson study up on a bureau so that it would receive the most pleasing light and then arranged the chairs so that it could be best appreciated.

"Ah!" Kent removed a pair of spectacles from his jacket and, adjusting them carefully, leaned forward, his entire attention given to the painting. After several moments of silent examination, the man sat back, removed his spectacles, and briefly held a hand to his brow, half-covering his eyes, which were pressed tightly closed as though he were overcome with emotion. Tristam found that this display of feeling moved him as well.

"I will tell you," Kent said, slowly easing back in

his chair as though he had suddenly aged, "I have spent almost my entire life trying to capture something so elusive, so damnably inexplicable and with so little success as to make a man mad ... and here. ..." He waved a hand at the painting. "In little more than a sketch Hobbson has managed it better than I in all of my work." He shook his head half in sadness, half in awe. "It is a beautiful little piece, Mr. Flattery. I give you joy of it."

Tristam hardly knew what to say, and he found himself looking at the painting as though he had not seen it before. Suddenly he became self-conscious and turned away to pour the tea.

"How in the round world did you ever come by it?" Kent asked as he took up his cup.

"It was left to me by Professor Dandish."

"I see. Yes, of course. I knew Dandish—though not as well as I would have liked—and I esteemed him greatly. I dare say you shall think of him every time you look at this painting. What finer memento could there be?"

"None, I'm sure. The professor could not have been more generous. He kindly left me a dozen books—a first edition of Boran's great work—and all of his instruments, including a new Fromme field glass."

"I have a Boran as well, but there are not more than a thousand of the first printing in all of Farrland. Almost national treasures. Do not hide it away in some dark library, but preserve it from the dampness." Kent shifted in his chair, musing. "The Fromme glass will serve you well. I have been in line for one nearly three years now—Fromme makes so few." Kent sipped tea from the dainty cup. "Do you have it here?"

Tristam nodded. "I do. I'll fetch it." He excused himself and went to the other room. When he returned, he found Kent standing at the open double doors looking down into the street.

"Ah. And there it is! Now here is a different type of beauty. May I?" He took the glass from Tristam with some reverence. He extended the tubes and began to scan the street. "This is a noble instrument, Mr. Flattery. Why, I can almost read the words in that man's book. Have a look." He handed Tristam the glass and pointed out a man sitting on a bench opposite the hotel, as though Tristam had never looked through the glass before.

Tristam did as he was told and to his surprise found that he was looking at Sir Roderick's driver. The man who had taken him to Merton and back. Tristam realized that he had lowered the glass and stood staring somewhat slack-jawed.

Kent did not seem to notice but relieved Tristam of the glass and swept the horizon like a captain aboard his ship. Tristam thought the man's mood had changed, though; as though the glass had revealed something unpleasant.

They returned to their tea and then, after a difficult start, the conversation flowed again. The painter spoke like others Tristam had met who had lived full and satisfying lives—there seemed a sense of sadness that such a life could be drawing to its end, but this was mixed with a realization that, having experienced such good fortune, one could hardly ask for more.

As Sir Roderick had said, Kent knew everyone and he spoke of famous empiricists, both living and dead, in the most familiar terms. "Hobbson was very kind to me. I was so young when I met him and he was very encouraging. When I look back, I can't imagine why. My early work showed little that would indicate talent." He laughed. "I was not a protegé by any means." His attention was taken by the painting again.

"You speak Entonne, Mr. Flattery?" he said after a moment. "You know the word *isollae?* 'Loneliness in the face of beauty' is how it is sometimes explained, though it has many shadings. It is a word much loved by the Entonne. 'Melancholy' it is sometimes translated. Or sadness. Estrangement. Or 'isolated,' for it derives from the same root. But loneliness in the face of beauty strikes closest to the mark, I think.

"Evoking this emotion, *isollae,* is Hobbson's great

skill. The empiricists praise him for his dedication to presenting nature accurately, but that is something that can be learned through careful application. *Isollae* is far more elusive." The painter took out a square of cloth and began to clean his spectacles—an unconscious habit, Tristam was certain.

"I look at this simple sketch, Mr. Flattery, and I am suddenly *caught,* for here is a perfect moment of our world, as beautiful as any, and I know it passed almost before Hobbson could mix his paint. And I feel that loneliness—the sense that our existence is so brief and the world so large and filled with moments as beautiful and fleeting as this one captured here.

"The Entonne poets say that *isollae* is the beginning of wisdom." He looked at Tristam as though he suddenly wondered if he were talking sense. Seeing that Tristam listened raptly, he went on. "Isn't it odd that the painter most admired by the empiricists was actually trying to capture something that our pragmatism and 'reason' seem not to recognize? A sense of wonder and awe."

He sipped his tea and gazed at the painting again. Tristam did not dare speak for fear that he would shatter the mood.

"During the era of the mages, I believe wonder and enchantment were the order of the time. But now we see the world as a specimen to be examined under a magnification instrument, to be dissected, and ultimately understood according to laws which are rational and logical. How our view has changed: from seeing the world as a place of wonder and enchantment, where a tree was alive and sentient in the same way that we are alive and sentient; to our present view where the tree has become a member of a lower order that one day will be understood in all of its parts—how it takes sustenance from the soil and air and sunlight, how it passes on life through a seed. How it can be rendered 'useful.' " He held Tristam's gaze for a second.

"The rational mind does not admit *isollae,* Mr. Flattery, and we are in danger of losing much because of it." He fell silent, staring at the painting.

"I believe the transcendentalists say many similar things, sir," Tristam said quietly, touched in some way by the artist's words.

Kent laughed gently. "Oh, yes, they do. And much else that is less sensible to my way of thinking. But in this I am forced to say I agree with them. And for all that, I am an empiricist as well. As fascinated by the workings of the world as any fellow of the Society. Perhaps I am just growing old and beginning to ask other questions as well. Or perhaps *isollae* is only experienced by esoteric Entonne poets . . . and painters who've grown long in the tooth."

Tristam looked at the painting, at the sea lions playing in the surf as they had likely done in that very spot for thousands of years. "I suspect it is just that most of us are not aware of its value . . . but I know the emotion of which you speak. I feel it when I look at the world sometimes, but I quickly forget or turn my focus elsewhere." Tristam ran out of words.

"Well, perhaps you have begun your journey toward wisdom, Mr. Flattery," Kent said seriously. "We have such a short time and the journey is so terribly long. One cannot begin too soon."

❧   ❧   ❧

Once Kent had gone, Tristam went to the window again and focused his glass on the man reading on the bench. There was no doubt: this was Sir Roderick's driver. The feeling of relief that Tristam had experienced since his discussion with Sir Roderick suddenly disappeared. And there was more than that. He was not sure that Kent had pointed the man out to him merely by accident. Kent?

A knock on the door drew him away and as he crossed the room he realized he felt a certain sense of dread. "Blood and flames!" he exclaimed. "I will become mad if I start to worry about who is at my door."

Whoever it was Tristam feared, he found only an old servant standing in the hall bearing a simple envelope with nothing more than Tristam's name on it. No post mark—nothing to indicate from where it had come.

Tristam slit the letter open and inside found a short note in a precise hand.

My Dear Mr. Flattery:

I feel I must make an apology for last night. I was, as you saw, not well. Please do not judge me by this one meeting. I have long wanted to make your acquaintance and to thank you for the difficult labor you undertook with Professor Dandish in classifying my collection. Is it possible that we could meet today? Would four o'clock suit? I am not always able to have visitors, but today I seem to be myself. Please come if you are able. No need to send word, but only arrive.

Your servant,
Baron Trevelyan

The letter was obviously the effort of a sensible mind, Tristam thought. Had not Sir Roderick said that the baron could be quite lucid at times? Tristam pulled his watch from his pocket. There was time.

Well if nothing else, he thought, *I shall be able to say I made the acquaintance of Averil Kent and the great Trevelyan.* They were not names that would impress Jenny, perhaps, or many in Locfal, but they were men that Tristam was proud to know.

As he locked the door to his room, Tristam thought again of Sir Roderick's driver sitting across the street. *Yes,* he thought, *and the man was in Merton all that time. There when Dandish's home and rooms at college were broken into.*

Checking the door twice, Tristam set out along the hall.

When he left the Queen Anne, Tristam made very

certain that he did not look toward Roderick's driver, but set out leisurely along the street. After half a block he stopped to peer in the window of a shop and then risked a glance back. The man had not gone into the hotel as Tristam had half-expected but had risen and walked in the same direction as Tristam, though along the avenue's opposite side.

Tristam set out again and in a few minutes was quite sure that the man followed him.

How long has this been going on! he wondered. *Well, if I have been the fool until now, that is about to change.* How had Kent known? Or had it been mere coincidence?

Tristam turned into the courtyard of a hotel and quickly exited through a second gate onto the side street. Here he increased his pace for a moment and then started up a narrow flight of steps leading left. No one was on the stair, so Tristam ran to the top and stopped on the landing where a vine hid him from the street. A moment later Palle's driver passed, obviously looking about anxiously.

That will do, Tristam thought, somewhat satisfied, and he set out quickly for the home of the baron, though not without many a backward glance.

It was almost an hour's walk, but Tristam elected not to hire a hack as he wanted the ability to easily watch behind him and to slip up stairways and down alleys if necessary. He wondered what had led Sir Roderick to have his activities monitored and realized there were several answers. It might well have been agents of the King's Man who had broken into Dandish's home, as well as stealing Tristam's journal and the letter written to the duchess. This would mean that the knight knew Tristam had not told him everything and thought it prudent to monitor Tristam's actions. The other possibility was that Tristam had been entrusted with state secrets and Sir Roderick had been watching him all along—which made Tristam deeply regret his conversations with Jaimy.

The entire affair seemed to be running down tracks

that Tristam did not understand, and he felt more and more that he was floundering—like a man waking suddenly to find himself being swept out to sea in darkness, unable to know even which direction could lead to safety. He stopped and examined the leaf of a tree, checking behind him.

It was quite a relief to find the baron's street empty of all traffic. He had managed to arrive here without being followed; though he felt some satisfaction at this feat, he was not sure precisely what purpose it served. So what if Roderick knew he visited the baron? The knight himself spoke of the old man with some affection. All the same, Tristam felt better to think that his actions were known only to him.

The house of Baron Trevelyan was set well back off the street behind tall oaks and willows and weeping birch. Letting himself through the iron gate, Tristam was immediately struck by how ill-kept the grounds were; gardens grown over, the underwood flourishing. It seemed as lacking in order as the poor baron's mind. Birds were everywhere in the trees and under the bushes. Squirrels flowed among the branches, and then, across the gravel path, a fox appeared. It stopped for the briefest second to stare at the intruder, and then disappeared into the dense brush.

"This is no accident," Tristam whispered. The baron had given the grounds back to nature, the object of his lifelong passion.

The house had been constructed of the same whitestone that had been used in the building of the city, and though it was well covered in curtains of ivy the whirls and skeletal markings of the fossils stood out like the work of some unbalanced sculptor: a thought Tristam did not like.

A brass-handled bellpull was set into the frame of the door. Tristam sounded it and waited, not knowing what to expect, for the character of the place was so peculiar that one hardly anticipated the door to be opened by one of Avonel's typical somber domestics.

And it was not. A handsome gentleman answered

the ring and stood appraising the caller for some seconds before he spoke. "Sir?"

"Tristam Flattery. I have an appointment to see Lord Trevelyan." The man was so well turned out and so regal looking that Tristam found himself suddenly a bit intimidated. Dark, dark hair, thick and perfectly groomed, graying at the temples. Eyebrows so heavy and black they would have dominated the man's face had not his eyes been even darker.

"Ah, Mr. Flattery. I wish I had known, sir. I would have saved you the trouble. Benjamin Rawdon; Lord Trevelyan's physician," he said but did not offer Tristam his hand to shake. "The Baron is indisposed this day, I regret to say. You are aware that Lord Trevelyan is not well?"

"Yes. Yes, I am. I'm terribly sorry to hear he is beset by . . . troubles today. I received such a kind invitation that I had hoped. . . . Well, may I leave a note to say that I called?"

"You may, or I will gladly convey your regrets. Whichever you prefer." The man stood blocking the half-opened door as though he felt it necessary to doubly convey the message that Tristam's presence was unwelcome. He made no move to invite Tristam into the hall or even to find him writing utensils.

"Please say I called and thank Lord Trevelyan for inviting me. I should certainly come again if it were ever possible."

The man nodded, a slight bow, and backed away half a step as though ready to close the door. "I'm sure Lord Trevelyan will be very sorry to have missed you, sir. The pleasures of the day."

"And to you, sir."

Tristam turned and started back toward the street, certain the man would have shut the door in his face had he continued to stand there. It was not common to meet a gentleman of such poor manners in hyper-polite Avonel.

Very odd, he thought. The note had seemed perfectly lucid.

The physician was not the city's most gracious resident, that was certain. But it seemed even more odd than that.

He shook his head. *Look how this goes,* he thought. *I discover I'm being watched and suddenly everything appears suspicious, everyone's motives questionable. I will become as mad as the baron if I am not careful. I'll be drinking only spring water . . . collected at first light.*

TWELVE

The carriage, Tristam realized, was becoming the metaphor for this period of his life: he neither owned, drove, nor directed one in any way but was simply carried along. And here he was yet again—riding in a coach driven by a man whose name he did not even know.

Jaimy would call me a fool.

This particular carriage belonged to the Duchess of Morland. When he'd returned from the baron's, a note awaited, informing him that a carriage would call at half-seven to carry him to the home of the duchess. Tristam knew he should have answered immediately with polite excuses, but he hadn't done so. And he could not say why.

Curiosity, he told himself, dragging out that old excuse. He wanted to know why Dandish had been growing *regis* for the duchess while at the same time telling Sir Roderick that he was too ill to labor in the king's arboretum. Why the professor had later written to the duchess to lie about his success with Kingfoil. *Tristam wanted to know what in Farrelle's name was going on.*

No doubt this was true . . . but why couldn't he erase the vision of the Duchess of Morland rising from behind a column into soft light, melodious laughter preceding her like a delicate overture. This image unbalanced him. Every time he thought of the duchess, he felt as though he were losing his balance and had to exert himself to take control.

Vertigo, he thought, *a condition without known cure.*

Frightening to those who walked through life as carefully as Tristam Flattery.

Jaimy would think him doubly a fool for doing this. A rather vicious and petty baron had died beneath the famous elms beyond Avonel for running afoul of this duchess.

A more critical condition yet: desire heightened by a sense of danger.

Perhaps the real reason Tristam had accepted this invitation was even more tawdry. The Duchess of Morland was widely considered to be the most desirable woman in all of Farrland—and she wanted something from Tristam. He simply could not return to Locfal and wonder for the rest of his days what it was she wanted, and how sweet the rest of the overture might be.

🐛　🐛　🐛

Tristam could hear a bell sounding deep inside the mansion in response to his hand on the tasseled pull, but it hardly compared to the jangle of his own nerves.

A moment later a servant ushered Tristam through the doors that all aspirants to fashionable Farr society hoped one day to pass. According to the judgment of many, Tristam Flattery had arrived.

He followed the elderly manservant into the temple of the charmed circle. Everywhere Tristam's eyes came to rest, he found evidence of the sophistication of the Duchess of Morland, and the contrast between her elegant and carefully planned rooms and his own rather rough and well-worn home caused him a little embarrassment.

Nowhere in his uncle's home could one find anything to compare: the careful matching of pale colors, the creation of atmosphere—here an alcove arranged for intimate conversation, here a morning room to bring light into one's very soul. Every object had its purpose in the composition and yet nothing seemed contrived. Tristam knew that he was quite ignorant of current fashions in interior arrangements, but even so this home struck him as being an enormously detailed and successful work of art.

A door opened and the duchess appeared, her face lighting up in a smile of welcome. It was then that Tristam first realized that it was this smile—showing just a bit too much of the upper gum to be perfect—that he found irresistible. How could a man not be charmed by that open, innocent smile in contrast with those green eyes that challenged and mocked and claimed knowledge of what lay hidden in one's heart?

In her dress and bearing the duchess was a study in contrasts; at once a girl in the blush of youth and at the same time the duchess of a great house, dignified and gracious. The tiniest change in her face or the movement of a hand would transform her from one to the other more quickly than the eye could follow. With skin that would be the envy of a debutante, and tresses thick and lustrous, the duchess could play either part as she chose.

"My dear Tristam," she said in Entonne. "You cannot imagine what pleasure you give me." She smiled and flickered into youth before his eyes.

The duchess held out her hand to be kissed, and Tristam touched the soft skin with his lips. He was sure his nervousness must show.

"The pleasure, Duchess, is mine," he managed, and no more.

The woman took his arm and walked close beside him down the hallway. "I am so glad you felt able to accept my invitation. After your recent loss, I'm quite sure you need an evening of diversion." She squeezed his arm gently. "Banish all cares this night, Tristam Flattery. You have passed through a portal into the private realm of the Duchess of Morland. Wearing the current fashions is not enough to gain you entrance here. It is a world of the individual—we live by the strictures of no land. Convention is cast aside and we find our own way with only our true hearts as guides."

She turned her green eyes on Tristam, and he felt

himself nod, approving of what he did not know. The pressure of her hand on his arm and, indeed, her closeness had taken his voice away. In the presence of the Duchess of Morland, any sense that he had achieved worldliness evaporated and he felt awkward and young.

"I hope you will come to see me often," she said softly, and these words were enough to cause Tristam's balance to waver.

"I should like nothing more, Duchess, but my appointment at the palace is at an end."

The duchess stopped him, taking one of his hands between both of hers. "Do you say that Roderick has released you? We are to give up all hope?" Tristam could hear genuine distress in her voice.

He nodded but said no more.

The duchess looked down at his hand, apparently, and bit her lip delicately. "Why has he done this? Did you learn something on your journey?"

Tristam hesitated before he spoke. "Sir Roderick seems convinced there is no solution to the *regis* problem. He told me so himself."

"So suddenly? Why has he decided this?"

She looked up and Tristam could see no mockery in her eyes now, only sadness and concern. He was not sure how to answer. He searched among the possible lies and none seemed adequate. The truth—*I told him Dandish had been growing Kingfoil and likely found no solution*—would hardly endear him to the duchess.

Applause caused them both to look up toward a door at the hall's end.

"We must return to my guests, Tristam. May we speak of this later? I am greatly disturbed by what you say."

Tristam nodded his head, hoping an answer would suggest itself in the interim.

As they walked toward the room from which Tristam could now hear music emanating, he stopped before a portrait.

"Who is this?" he asked.

"The Countess of Chilton," the duchess said, nodding at the woman in the portrait as though their eyes had just met across a room. "In her day she was the most celebrated woman in all of Farrland and beyond."

If the portrait was an indication Tristam could believe this was true: an astonishing cascade of black hair framing a heart-shaped face and a full mouth. Dark eyes that appeared to be focused on Tristam. Something told him that the artist had been under the woman's spell, for the painting had a quality that could not be explained otherwise.

"My uncle kept a portrait of this same woman in his home. I remember it well. I always wondered who she was, and what became of it."

"This is Erasmus Flattery you speak of?"

Tristam nodded.

"I'm surprised," the duchess said. "But then the countess was admired by everyone—certainly every man, at least. I was presented to the countess once when I was a child. I thought she was a goddess, more beautiful than the painting by far. She is a recluse now, and must be very old. It is said that the countess wishes to be remembered as she was. None but her servants have seen her these past thirty years. But the Countess of Chilton reigned over Farr society for almost two decades." She made a half curtsy to the dark-haired woman. "Let me introduce you to my other guests."

The sound of a pianum came from beyond a door though Tristam had not registered it before. The duchess let them into the room with care, as though a child slept within. Two gentlemen and three women were revealed, their backs to Tristam, obviously entranced by the virtuosity of a young man seated before the pianum.

Pushing the door closed with the same exaggerated care, the duchess nodded to a divan out of everyone's line of view. Tristam took his place beside her, closer than he felt was proper, but the seat was small. The duchess did not indicate by even the smallest sign that she was aware of how near they sat.

The young musician was completely absorbed in his playing. His expressive face changed as fluidly as the melody, reflecting the music as though it flowed out of his heart more naturally than tears or laughter. Tristam was not overly knowledgeable when it came to music, but he could see that this man exercised astonishing control of his instrument. The subtle shadings of expression, the nuances of time—lingering on a note, hurrying over others. Here was a player of some genius, Tristam suspected.

The composition was long and, when done, the player seemed to collapse where he sat. The others leaped to their feet and rushed over, one man pumping the musician's limp hands, the women caressing his shoulders and neck and showering kisses on his brow and cheeks. All the while they cried praises in the language of Entonne.

"Duchess," one of the women said, "is he not a marvel? A genius? A master of the pianum?"

"He is, Lucin, all that and more. Let me introduce my particular friend, Mr. Tristam Flattery of Locfal," and then she smiled at him, "and Avonel, we hope."

The three women and one man, Tristam learned, were all members of the cast of an Entonne opera preparing a performance for the citizens of the capital. The musician, however, was Charl Bertillon, a man of such wide repute that even Tristam recognized his name.

It was not a surprise when the last man was introduced as Julian Burne-Johns, the Viscount Elsworth; the duchess' brother. Tristam took his hand with some misgivings, though he hoped it did not show, and felt a little nausea when he released it. The hand that had murdered Ipsword had been offered so casually.

The gathering repaired to a dining room where the table was set with fine crystal and silver and porcelain that picked up the colors of the room and would, no doubt, reflect some element of the view if it had been daylight. This was not one of the endless tables at which Tristam had often been seated but a small affair set for an intimate gathering of friends.

The company was high-spirited, but Tristam thought the duchess did not fully participate. Her gaze kept clouding over, and he would occasionally see her lose track of the conversation only to recover with enormous grace and ease.

The finest foods and wines seemed almost to wash over the table in apparently endless courses, like waves on a beach. At one point the gentleman from the opera troupe stood and literally sang the praises of the table. He was definitely in his cups, but amusingly so, and the wine had not spoiled his voice.

Although everyone was welcoming, Tristam still did not feel very comfortable. Most of the talk was of art and music and the latest plays and books, things he paid some attention to, though he certainly was not nearly as well informed as the present company. Jenny had often told him he was too much the dedicated empiricist, and a gathering such as this made him think she was right.

It was not that he couldn't enjoy himself entirely in this setting, but a discussion of Skye's laws of motion or recent theories about elliptical and circular planetary orbits would make him more comfortable. One of the young women, Lucin, sat to his right and she kept calling him *my pet* and *my peach,* common endearments in her own language, but a little absurd to Tristam's ear.

"Listen to Tristam's Entonne," she ordered at one point, stopping the conversation. "Our voice instructor would delight in such a student." She turned to Tristam. "Say . . ." and she asked him to pronounce one of the several words that those not raised to the language of Entonne found virtually impossible.

Tristam did as he was instructed, and she clapped her hands and bussed his cheek. "He has the heart of an Entonne, Duchess. What charming friends you have."

Bertillon loved to hear himself speak and held forth

at length, obviously used to being surrounded by devoted admirers. Fortunately, unlike many who insisted on dominating the conversation, he was not a bore, and often made people laugh, mimicking the accents and mannerisms of a host of public figures. The women present obviously delighted in his company.

But to Tristam's utter surprise, they were clearly quite taken with Julian Burne-Johns as well. Judging by the posture of the Viscount Elsworth, his hand was in the lap of Monay, the woman to his right, and she was having trouble maintaining her composure—her face quite red, and not entirely from drink.

The Viscount Elsworth was a large man—just taller than Tristam but broader of frame—in his early thirties, perhaps, and though dark-haired, handsome enough to have come from the same stock as the duchess. Despite his size the viscount had surprisingly delicate hands—hands one would have expected of Bertillon (though the musician's were actually unremarkable)—and the dark brooding eyes of a young poet.

Burne-Johns seemed as out of his depth in this conversation as Tristam, but the viscount did not seem to care in the least. He laughed at every joke—a great uninhibited laugh, full of his own pleasure—and partook of wine and food with great relish. It was difficult to imagine that a man possessed of such an easy nature could bring himself to kill another.

As a skilled hostess, the duchess occasionally steered the conversation this way and that, attempting to include everyone.

"This wine," the duchess said, holding up her glass, "is made from the famous Erasmus Grape, developed by one of Tristam's many illustrious relations. Are you not his heir, Tristam?"

He admitted that he was.

Upon hearing this news, the viscount showed surprise. "But is not Locfal rather far north for the grape to grow? Erasmus must have truly been a mage to accomplish that."

"My uncle had a small estate on the island of Farrow, Lord Elsworth. The Erasmus Grape, as it is now called, came from his years there."

"You possess an estate on Farrow, then? A winery?" the musician asked.

"Not a winery now. A vineyard. The harvest is sold to certain wineries and they are responsible for this." He held up his glass. "An art, perhaps not equal to yours, Mr. Bertillon, but an art in its own right."

Too used to compliments, Bertillon hardly acknowledged this one. "I have always wanted to travel to Farrow. You have seen the famous Ruin?"

"No. Unfortunately, no. Though I own a property on Farrow, I have never made the journey there myself. I plan to do so."

"Perhaps we could go together," Bertillon said. "I would find it fascinating, I think."

"Tristam," the duchess said, falling into the Entonne custom of using first names, "is also an empiricist of growing reputation."

Lucin made appreciative sounds.

Expected to continue, Tristam described the demonstration he had witnessed at the Society.

"All of them, out of the pan?" the viscount asked, a little incredulous. "Amazing! I should have liked to have seen that."

"I spoke with someone who was there, as well," Bertillon said quietly. "He told me that a man named Varese made a very bad impression by attacking the illustrious Boran."

Tristam nodded. "Yes. Yes, he did. Provoked quite a response."

Bertillon raised his eyebrows. "What did you think, Tristam? Is it possible that Boran could have borrowed his method from Lucklow?"

"I don't know. It all hinges on this letter he claims to have found." Tristam quickly told the others what had happened. "If it is authentic, it will shake Boran's great reputation, that is certain."

"But mages were not empiricists," Bertillon went

on. "They were practitioners of dark arts, it is said. Not even natural philosophers. *The dark arts*. The antithesis of empirical studies, it would seem."

"Dark arts," the duchess laughed. "Really, Charl. Lord Eldrich certainly expressed interest in geology, astronomy, and much else as well. Even music. What do we really know of mages? Perhaps they *were* natural philosophers. There are some who say that all the 'magic' of the mages was contrived by ingenious engines and chemistry."

The musician smiled and shrugged, conceding quickly to his hostess. "And perhaps they are right." He raised a glass. "To the arts—dark, light and all tones between."

The people present were prepared to toast almost anything, especially, Tristam suspected, if it would get them back to the topics that they found of interest.

Servants refilled glasses and Bertillon leaned forward, speaking low. "They say wine will kill you slowly." He nodded his head solemnly. "But that's all right, we're in no hurry."

Everyone laughed.

"Are you a fellow of the Society, my peach?" Lucin asked.

"I was the guest of a fellow," Tristam admitted. He realized he had hoped no one would ask and simply assume that he was.

"Soon enough, my dear Tristam," the duchess said, saving him an awkward moment. "I have it on good authority."

"To Tristam's pending fellowship, then," Viscount Elsworth offered, holding up his glass in his free hand. The toast was enthusiastic and Tristam realized how much he had drunk when he felt no embarrassment.

The musician leaned forward and stared carefully at Tristam in such an odd way that the others began to titter. "You see the high, strong forehead?" He nodded toward Tristam after a moment. "It is the mark of a superior mind, an intellectual's mind. One could know Tristam as a formidable thinker without exchanging a word." He tapped his own forehead. "The mark is un-mistakable." And then his face split in a smile; Tristam had been a little afraid the man was serious.

"Like Jons'," the woman beside the viscount inter-jected, making everyone laugh, including Jons, who was without question the quietest and most inebriated person at the table. His forehead was unremarkable as far as Tristam could tell.

This theory that related the shape of the head to characteristics of the mind was currently in vogue, though given little credence by true empiricists.

The musician continued. "Lucin has a strong fore-head, as well. There is no doubt."

The third woman, Tenil, leaned toward Lucin. Tenil was the youngest of the singers, and generally quiet, but Tristam had seen indications that she was pos-sessed of the sharpest wit. "Ah, poor Lucin," she said, "such a neckline . . . and gentlemen remark on your forehead."

There was much laughter at this, for Lucin wore the most revealing gown of all—which was an accom-plishment in this company.

"Now for all of those present who do not believe in the dark arts." Bertillon nodded to the duchess as he said this, but he was smiling. "I shall make a demon-stration. Are we finished with this glorious meal? Then we must have the table cleared."

Servants did as requested and at the musician's in-structions also brought him eight fresh candles set in holders. These he passed around the table so that each person had a lit candle. A single yellow rose in a nar-row glass vase was moved to the table's center, and this Bertillon proceeded to douse in fine brandy, until a layer of the liquor floated upon the water.

"If you intend to turn this rose into a beautiful prin-cess, Charl," Tenil said, "at least Her Highness shall be as soaked in spirits as the rest of us."

"I would like to speak with spirits," Lucin said a lit-tle breathlessly. "Someone famous and wicked."

The other lamps and candles were removed or put

out so that only the eight candles remained. This still left quite a bit of light though, too bright really to create the needed atmosphere, Tristam thought. He had been involved in such things before. Some of them merely larks where nothing happened and others where elaborate hoaxes had been prepared. This had all the earmarks of a lark, he thought.

"Now," Bertillon began, making his voice low and solemn, "we must all join hands to form a chain, of course."

Tristam took the hands of the duchess and Lucin, feeling the softest pressure from the duchess.

"I will perform the incantation, so you must all be silent. Stare into the heart of your candles until you have fixed the image in your mind. Now, for a moment only, we must close our eyes. Clear your brain of everything but the image of the flame."

The table shifted suddenly making someone squeal.

"Lord Elsworth!" Monay said, as though addressing a naughty child. "He does this with his knee."

"This will never work if we do not cooperate." Bertillon said, his voice more serious. "Close your eyes again."

Tristam did as he was told, conscious of the contact with the two women.

"Curre d' Efeu," Bertillon began, his voice strong. *"Vere viteur aupel e' loscure. Vau d' Efeu. Ivanté! Par d' embou vere fant!"*

The tittering stopped while Bertillon spoke these words, if words they were. Tristam had never heard this language before, but if it was mere nonsense, it was convincingly done. To his ear it sounded like very archaic Entonne. Given time, he might work it out.

"Now, in turn, we must each blow gently on the flame of our candle. Not so hard as to put it out, but enough to bend the flame away from you. We begin with the duchess and then myself."

Extending her neck so that she was level with the candle, the duchess blew gently, making the flame waver.

175

"A bit harder, Duchess," Bertillon whispered.

The duchess increased her effort and the flame licked out toward the rose, perhaps an inch, and then snuffed out, a ribbon of smoke spiraling upward in the light of the remaining candles.

"I am next," Bertillon said softly. Like the duchess he began gently, and the flame flickered in response. With great control he kept it up until the flame lay over, wavering so quickly it almost pulsed, and then it, too, was gone, the pungent aroma of the smoke filling the air.

"Ah," someone whispered, disappointed, perhaps.

Each went in turn, with varied success—for no one really understood what they were trying to accomplish. Jons blew his candle out immediately. Tristam had half expected the man's breath to burst into flame.

Lucin followed the others, the room almost dark now. The mood was changing as the room fell into shadow, as though everyone feared the blackness suddenly.

Tristam followed Lucin—the last to go and glad to see the end near. He blew with the same exaggerated care Bertillon had exhibited and watched his flame quiver, trembling like a crimson leaf in the wind. And then the flame began to elongate, not much but longer than the duchess had managed. And then it flared and was gone. At the same instant, the rose burst into blue flame, with a sound like an exhalation of breath long held.

Everyone started back, eyes wide, and then began to laugh, a release of tension. Everyone but Bertillon, who seemed to have been thrown back, asprawl in his chair, his eyes fixed on Tristam, the cold-burning rose between them.

Tristam focused on the ghostly flames as the alcohol-saturated blossom began to darken and curl. The duchess squeezed his hand gently and then released it, but Lucin clutched his hand like a frightened child. She giggled nervously.

"Now what is the trick, Charl?" the viscount asked, his matter-of-fact tones breaking the mood.

Bertillon sat up in his chair, pushing his charming smile back into place. "Trick? Tristam is the empiricist, Lord Elsworth, perhaps he will tell us."

"Dark arts, Lord Elsworth," Tristam said, but the laughter this brought was weak.

"Does it take a moment for the fumes to accumulate?" the duchess asked, anticipating Tristam's explanation.

"Perhaps," Bertillon said. "I don't actually know. Often it doesn't work at all. Not a very reliable parlor trick, but exciting when it succeeds."

"And the incantation?" Tristam asked.

"Part of a children's nonsense rhyme. You hadn't heard it before?"

No one had, apparently.

"There is quite a bit more, but I can't recall it now. Lost with my youth." Bertillon smiled again, moving his shoulders as though to loosen the muscles.

Servants returned to replenish everyone's glass and the duchess rose, composing herself like someone upon a stage. "And now, for your continuing pleasure, gentlemen and ladies all, certain of my gracious guests have kindly offered to display," she pronounced the words with conscious precision, "their arts."

The gathered guests rose unsteadily to their feet, and while Tristam, the viscount, Monay, Jons, and Bertillon followed the duchess back into the room where the pianum awaited, the others left by a different door, making rough sallies about their "arts."

"Do make yourselves comfortable," the duchess said as the gentlemen found chairs, in Tristam's case quite thankfully. "Charl has kindly offered to perform the accompaniment to our little entertainment." She reached out and touched the musician's arm, holding his gaze for just a second too long.

Tristam felt the sting of jealousy. Clearly it was not Tristam the duchess was trying to impress, and this realization caused some private embarrassment. He turned away from the two, taking a glass of brandy from a servant.

The room was lit only by candles now and the furniture had been rearranged so that the focus of attention was no longer the pianum but one wall. The servants were suddenly gone.

Tristam found that if he closed his eyes his head spun a little. He took hold of the arms of the massive chair, realizing that his wits were more addled with drink than he had thought.

A door opened a crack and Tristam saw Bertillon nod. He began a slow, almost folklike melody, deceptively simple but very evocative.

Tenil, of the well-sharpened wit, appeared, dressed as a girl of the country, with a long, full skirt and a peasant's open-necked blouse.

Reaching up, she began to unbind her hair so that it fell in strands that shone in the candlelight. Tristam had not previously appreciated how lovely Tenil was. And then she began to sing, a sad air, her voice rich and filled with the tones of a woman reaching out, singing from her heart. And this ability seemed so alien to Tristam's nature, that he could hardly bear to hear it, yet he could not have left if he had wanted to.

She sang in the language of Entonne—about a love, distant and uncertain—and after a moment a second voice joined her from the back of the room. Lucin appeared in the light of the few candles that lit the scene. Sisters, they sang to console one another for the lovers who were in a distant war.

The two women, their hair unbound, told the tales, in song, of each first meeting their lover when peace had ruled the land.

It was an opera Tristam knew by reputation, though he had never actually seen it performed. Two sisters in their room at night preparing for bed. The opera had all but scandalized the people of Farrland when it had first been introduced some years earlier. For the women would step behind a screen to disrobe, appearing again in their sleeping gowns having actually undressed on the stage, though all but out of sight.

Here there was no screen, and to Tristam's utter surprise that did not seem to matter to the singers. As she sang, Tenil continued to undress.

Tristam moved a little uncomfortably in his chair, embarrassed by his own response. He did look away for a second and discovered that the viscount and Monay were entangled on a divan in the corner, her skirt pushed up so that one long leg draped over the back of the viscount's thigh—a white petal against dark wood.

Jons was passed out in a chair and the duchess stood behind it, her hands resting on the back. She moved her head, swaying slightly, in time to the music, her eyes bright and following the movements of the singers.

Lucin was singing now as she crossed the room, blowing out candles as she passed. Tristam wished now that he had not drunk so much, for his mind was unable to grapple with the situation. What was expected here? How was he to act to not look the fool?

He found his breath coming with some difficulty and he could feel himself responding to the erotic charge in the room.

Lucin glided past his chair, draping her blouse over the arm as she passed, and caressing his neck. There was only a single candle left now, burning on the pianum for Bertillon. Tristam realized that Tenil was singing to him, coming toward him with her hands outstretched. She was clad now in only an undershift, very sheer, her long hair falling in a cascade about her lovely face, the fabric of her robe moving and clinging as she walked.

She took his hands and gently tugged him to his feet to lead him up near to the pianum. There was no music now but for the voices of the two women as they came to the end of their song. The last candle was blown out as they held their final notes. And then there was darkness and silence.

Tristam felt the young singer press herself to him, kissing his neck and then seeking his lips. A long sweet kiss. She stepped back from him, squeezing both his hands—then she was gone.

Tristam stood wavering in the dark, feeling abandoned and foolish. He reached out and found the cool edge of the pianum and then lowered himself onto the empty bench, accidentally setting his hand on the keys.

In the darkness he heard the rustling of fabric, a soft moan. Harsher breathing and bodies meeting in rhythm on the divan in the corner. Whispers. A laugh of delight.

Well, here you are, Tristam thought. *The evening you dreamed of through so many lectures and you are left sitting alone in a room where there are four women and only three conscious men.* He touched the keyboard a second time—an accidental trill.

"I thought I'd lost you," came a voice speaking Entonne.

Tenil! She had not abandoned him after all. Or perhaps the partner of her choice was already occupied. A vision of Bertillon entwined with the duchess and Lucin came to mind.

A sharply indrawn breath that became a moan of pleasure. Clothing slipping to the floor.

Hands found him. A woman, her breath sweet with wine, kissed his face, her hair brushing his cheeks and neck. Tristam found himself stumbling as he was led through the dark, out a door into the next room, as black as the one he had just left.

A thought of Jenny came to him, but was lost in a long kiss as the woman turned and embraced him. Tenil, Tristam thought, was very beautiful and at the moment only her presence mattered. He was awash in her perfume and the darkness of the room, blind to whatever lay beyond.

She stepped away, and Tristam heard the sounds of fabric rustling and then she pressed against him again. His head spun from drink and growing passion. He ran his hands up her naked back as she pulled his shirt open. They kissed and touched with more urgency.

Tristam was led again, a few steps this time, and he heard Tenil settle on a divan beneath a dark rectangle of window. He shed the rest of his clothing and joined her. Although Tristam's experiences with women were limited, he had drunk enough that he did not care. His passion was leading him and he had no time for doubts.

Tenil stroked his chest and his back, and he could feel her excitement grow as she touched him.

"What a beautiful boy you are," she whispered in his ear in Entonne. "You have skin like a baby, like silk, so smooth, so smooth," she cooed. Her fingers combed into his hair and he felt the ribbon tugged free so that his hair fell about his face.

In his other encounters Tristam had never felt such urgency in a woman, yet there was also a concern for his own pleasure, a desire to please him. Her kisses were both soft and demanding, and her hands were never still. "Oh, my pet—oh, my child," she whispered into his ear.

Reaching down, she guided him into her and Tristam was swept up on a wave of pleasure, his senses and those of Tenil entwined so that part of the fabric of his pleasure was her own. It seemed that the limit of his senses—of both their senses—was the boundary of their world. Nothing lay beyond.

"Oh, my gorgeous one." Her whisper became a cry. Suddenly she spoke in perfect Farr. *"Oh, my pet. Oh, Charl, Charl! Ohh!"*

Tristam's head spun. *The woman beneath him was the Duchess of Morland, and she believed he was Bertillon!*

He was frozen in place, unsure of what to do. She stroked his back tenderly. "It is not just the pianum you play so well, my sweet. You have many skills." She gave a small laugh of pleasure.

Tristam said nothing. He felt himself begin to

shrivel, which produced a sound of disappointment from the duchess. He rolled to one side gently and heard her sigh.

She sat up slowly. "Oh, my. Such good wine, and so much of it." She found his face and kissed him gently. "Do not disappear, my gorgeous child. Your devoted Elorin will return immediately."

Tristam heard the rustle of clothing and then a door opened. "Find a candle, my pet," she whispered and then disappeared. Tristam sat up quickly and was rewarded for this imprudence with a spell of dizziness that had him holding onto the divan. He found his clothes and began furiously to pull them on. He must be gone when she returned.

Blood and martyrs, Tristam thought, *what have I done?* He knocked over a chair searching for the door. In the next room the evening was not over, it seemed. The sounds of love and laughter emanated from the darkness and the air was musty and thick.

Tristam stumbled into a piece of furniture and regained his balance by pushing on some very soft flesh. A woman shrieked in surprise and then laughed. A doorknob came to hand and he let himself into an unlit hall, reeling as though he'd found himself aboard a darkened ship in a gale, the hallway rocking and plunging.

Tristam could not remember how he got out of the house, but he found himself leaning against a lamppost in the drive. Looking back, he saw the duchess standing at a dimly lit, upper window, a look of great concern on her lovely face. Ever so slowly, she ran her fingers over her cheek, as though exploring a bruise.

Tristam forced himself to move and staggered into the darkened avenue. A wave of nausea drove him to his knees. He vomited wretchedly and knelt for a long time breathing hard, the acid taste of bile burning his mouth and throat. Finally he rose to his feet unsteadily and attempted to clean himself with his handkerchief. It was only then that he realized he wore no shoes.

Unsure of where he was, Tristam became lost in the twisting streets, but overall he was sure he made his way down toward the Queen Anne. Occasionally he sat and struggled against a wave of nausea, breaking out in a cold sweat and gasping. The moon floated high, two days from the full, hidden now and then by great forests of cloud.

It seemed to be hours before Tristam arrived at the entrance to his lodgings. He was forced to ring the bell to gain entrance and felt the sting of humiliation at his state, which, upon looking into a mirror, he realized was far worse than he'd imagined. Even his hair was clotted with gorge.

He stripped himself and washed in cold water as best he could, thinking all the while. *What have I done?* It was almost a rape. *The duchess believed me to be someone else. . . . But I acted in all innocence,* he told himself again and again. *I did not know.*

He cursed the red-eyed reflection in the mirror. "What a terrible thing you've done." It occurred to him that either the viscount or Bertillon might demand satisfaction. This sent a shiver through him as he pulled on a clean shirt. Bertillon was probably far less adept with a blade than Tristam, but the viscount. . . . It was time for Tristam to leave Avonel.

Even as these thoughts went through his head, there was a part of him, a part he did not want to acknowledge, that whispered, *you have made love to the Duchess of Morland! The most desired woman in all of Farrland lay beneath you and shuddered and moaned with pleasure. What a night to remember!*

❧   ❧   ❧

The day was no longer new when Tristam fought his way back to consciousness. He called for bath water and coffee. *Wretched* was the word that best described how he felt. Wretched and at a slight remove from the world. Dull pain coursed through his head at each beat of his heart, and his neck and back felt as though they would snap unless he moved with considerable care. The state of his stomach could not be made worse by the drinking of a vial of acid, and his hands trembled whenever asked to perform—and that did not complete the catalog of his ailments.

The previous night was half a blur. Tristam was not sure that his memory was accurate. Perhaps nothing had occurred the way he remembered. He could hope.

After a bath and a shave, he donned fresh clothing and realized he felt only marginally better. His malaise was more than physical, he realized. The events of the previous night weighed on him. *There'll be no more drinking like that in the future,* he told himself.

Packing was also on his mind. Packing and leaving the city with haste. What would happen to the health of the king he did not know. There was a public coach going north late in the day and Tristam decided that he would be aboard it. He would leave Avonel behind and return to the familiar world of Locfal. *It is a good place for me,* he thought. *I am not meant for the court and its intrigues.*

The act of preparing for the journey hardly lifted his spirits though the thought of leaving a most awkward situation behind brought some relief. Before an hour had passed, Tristam had convinced himself that everyone had drunk so much the night before that what had occurred would never be known—even by the duchess. It began to seem a bit funny, in fact.

"I had love with the Duchess of Morland," he whispered. "And she will likely never know." His feelings were in such conflict that one moment he almost laughed and the next he felt the deepest shame.

A knock took him away from his task and he found Benjamin at the door. The old servant passed a note to Tristam.

My dearest Tristam:

Excuse my manners, but I believe I am in possession

*of some of your belongings? Do you have a moment
to spare me? I will come up, if so.*

Elorin, Duchess of Morland

"This is from the Duchess of Morland," Tristam said
stupidly.

"The lady did not identify herself, sir."

"The duchess is downstairs?"

"The lady who wrote the note is certainly there, sir."

"Blood and flames!" Tristam quickly dashed off a
reply and went looking for a neck cloth and frock coat.

The duchess arrived moments later, accompanied by
a footman she left outside the door.

To Tristam's great relief, she said pleasantly, "You
look a little white, my dear Tristam. I hope the evening's entertainment did not disagree with you?"

"I think I may be a victim of my own grape. The
wine was perhaps too good, Duchess, and I overin-
dulged. A terrible weakness, but the flaw is mine entirely."

She gave a tiny smile. "Yes. I dare say there are
others not at their best this morning."

As far as Tristam could tell, the duchess would not
be among these: she looked as ravishing as always.

"May I sit?" she asked pointedly.

"Excuse me. I am addled. May I offer coffee or
tea?"

"Kind of you. I can't stay long, however." She
reached into an embroidered bag and removed a pair of
shoes—Tristam's shoes. She raised her eyebrows.

"Ahem. Yes, I do seem to have misplaced a pair
quite like them."

She stared at him in reproach for a moment and then
broke into a delightful laugh. Tristam could not help
himself and laughed as well.

"Your stockings must be a sight," she said.

"I ordered them burned."

"No doubt." The duchess fixed him with a look that

he could not fathom, but he was sure it held no anger or resentment.

She does not know, Tristam thought, *though I wish that she did, and looked at me so kindly.*

"Tristam," she said, suddenly serious. "May I speak to you of your friend, Professor Dandish? Will it be painful for you?"

"No . . . it won't. Please, say on." He hoped he told the truth.

The duchess reached down and ran her thumb across a pulled loop in the bag's embroidery, then looked up and met Tristam's eye. "Do you have his missing diaries, Tristam?"

Tristam had wondered if this would eventually come up though it was Roderick he had expected would ask. He watched the duchess carefully as he answered, wondering all the while: *but are they not in your possession, Duchess?* "They were taken from his rooms at Merton, I believe."

The duchess stared at him for a moment. "I think you owe me better than that, Tristam." She reached into the bag again and removed a blue velvet ribbon—the one that had been used to tie his hair the previous evening. A memory of her pulling it free came to him. She held it out as though it were evidence of his offense—proof of his indebtedness. Tristam took a long breath. "It was dark, Duchess, I did not realize . . ." he whispered. "I can apologize, but it will change nothing."

"You could tell me what I want to know. Is it really such a difficult question?"

"I was sworn to silence . . . the King's Man. . . ."

"The King's Man!" Her voice was sharp. "Do you really believe that knight in his armor of self-righteousness cares more for the interests of the King than I?"

Tristam shook his head.

"I think you understand my concerns, Tristam. Do not play the fool. It is beneath you, and I won't believe it."

Tristam looked down at his hands for a moment. "Sir Roderick knows nothing of . . . the matter that concerns the duchess. If that is a comfort."

"I care less for what Roderick thinks than I care for the health of our King. Dandish's notes, his diaries? Where are they?"

"All but the last three volumes did truly disappear."

"Thank you, Tristam. You have these three volumes here?"

He shook his head. "I did not feel they would be safe here." He looked up and met her eyes. "They contain no references useful to our area of concern, Duchess."

"What do you honestly think, Tristam?" she said with great familiarity, as though they knew each other well. "Did Dandish solve the problem? Did he find a way to make the plants bear seed?"

Why did Dandish lie to this woman after he had taken on the task of growing Kingfoil? Tristam was not sure, but it was all the information he had to go on—that and his warnings from Jaimy.

The room swayed, just perceptibly, like an aftershock from his night's drinking. Or it might have been the presence of the duchess, who always unbalanced him. There was a part of Tristam that wanted to please this woman, to gain her favor. The memory of her beneath him in the dark came to him strongly. The air stuck in his lungs for a second.

"I . . . I am not certain what went on at Dandish's. I found empty planting boxes. And then someone broke into the house, looking for what I am not sure. I searched through the three volumes of his journal, but he had erased some entries. Only one escaped his notice, and that gave no indication of his success. In fact, it would indicate he was not succeeding, though it had been written over a year ago. Why was Dandish growing Kingfoil for you, Duchess, out of Sir Roderick's sight?"

She gazed at him for a second. "Roderick has his own designs. If preserving the life of the King was part of them, would he be sending you back to Locfal?" The duchess fell silent.

Though he never expected to be able to tell what this woman was thinking, there could be no mistaking her reaction to Tristam's words. She actually looked away, trying to hide her disappointment. "Tristam," she almost whispered, "you are telling me the truth now, aren't you, my dear?"

"I am, Duchess."

She shook her head and gave him a wry smile, her recovery almost complete. "I must have time to think." She looked at Tristam then, as though making an assessment of his well-being. "Tristam, I may need your help in this matter yet. It is the life of the King I speak of. Do you understand?"

Tristam nodded.

"May I count on you in this?"

"I am the duchess' servant," Tristam said very quietly, hoping that he would never have to live by these words but unable to stop himself from uttering them.

She reached over and took his hand, her eyes on his, and what remained unspoken in this gesture plunged Tristam into confusion. Perhaps he had meant every word of his claim of servitude.

"Thank you, Tristam," she said, and then withdrew her hand, sitting back in her chair. "Poor Sanfield. He was not young when he took this on. I'm sure he tried everything."

"I believe he did."

The duchess pulled the bag into her lap as though she would rise—but stopped. "Although it hardly matters. . . . There may be certain . . . references in those journals that would be better expurgated. Do you take my meaning?"

"It shall be done, Duchess. And please trust that I shall show them to no one."

"Roderick has not seen them?"

Tristam shook his head.

"Why, Tristam. . . . Did you think you were protecting me?" She reached out and squeezed his hand again.

Despite her obvious haste, she rose gracefully. "I am to meet the King, Tristam, so I cannot tarry ... as much as I would like to," she added, almost stopping Tristam as he began to rise.

Exercising great control to maintain his balance, Tristam accompanied the duchess to the door, her suggestion that she would prefer to stay echoing in his mind.

At the same time Tristam was relieved that there would be no enraged gentlemen sending their seconds to call. As his hand touched the handle, the duchess stopped and met his eye again.

"It was a lovely evening, was it not?"

"I am certain that I shall never know another like it," Tristam said, believing every word.

"You are sweet." She leaned forward and kissed his cheek.

The duchess was gone, leaving Tristam afloat in an eddy of perfume, the sensation of a soft kiss rapidly fading to imperfect memory.

Tristam stood by the door for some time, lost in thought, and then he shook his head and went back into the room. His eye was drawn to the blue ribbon. Did Bertillon not have straight hair?

❦   ❦   ❦

Tristam could not imagine that he would ever see the inside of the Tellaman Palace again so, on this last visit, he was attempting to fix the details in his mind as he passed through the corridors. There were only three errands remaining to be dispatched; say good-bye to Tumney, return the key for the arboretum, and retrieve Dandish's journals. These last were hidden in Tumney's workroom, a place Tristam thought unlikely to be searched, and, even so, the room was such a clutter of flotsam and jetsam that Tristam was sure his treasure would not be found.

The bronze key Tumney had provided turned the lock to the *regis* arboretum and Tristam entered the arena of his greatest failure—not without complete awareness of that very fact.

The air here was something Tristam was sure he would never forget, the dampness, the odor of rich soil and the distinctive scent of the Kingfoil blossoms, like a hint of an exotic spice.

After listening for a moment to be sure he was alone, Tristam uncovered his bundle and put the journals into a small carrying bag he had brought for the purpose.

Tumney could not be found, which was not surprising. His role as King's Gardener took him all over the palace grounds, though Tristam had the impression that the old gardener had able assistants and his supervision was more for the sake of form than of necessity. *Regis* had been Tumney's only real charge for many years.

Tristam paused for a moment to look at the Kingfoil planting and muse on the matter he had been unable to solve. The Varuan King's story of the spirit that inhabited *regis* came back to him and magnified his sense of failure. What had Dandish discovered? It was a question that he knew would plague him forever.

Tristam suffered a near desperate restlessness that morning and decided to go in search of Tumney rather than wait for the old gardener to appear. Locking the heavy door behind him, Tristam immediately encountered one of Tumney's gardeners who directed the naturalist through doors into another inclosed arboretum—one which Tristam had not been aware of previously.

Calling out Tumney's name was as useful as shouting the name of a tree and expecting it to uproot and walk—the man was deafer than most realized—so Tristam went in, searching.

There was more of the flora of Oceana here and Tristam found himself progressing slowly as he paused to examine various specimens. As he bent to look more closely at a complex flower, a butterfly appeared at the edge of his vision: wings of delicately veined white, a flash of deep red. The insect alighted on a leaf within

Tristam's reach but, as the naturalist turned his head for a better view, it took to flight.

"Flaming martyrs," Tristam whispered. "A crimson tip." It was a species from Oceana, he was quite certain. The pale wings appeared among the dark foliage again, and without hesitation Tristam stepped off the path and into the artificial jungle, careful as he went, but determined to have proof of what he'd seen.

The flora had been planted to represent some zone of Oceanic vegetation; a particularly rich and dense zone. Another glimpse of the gossamer wings fanning the air drove him on and in a few paces he came out onto a walkway. Much to his disappointment, the crimson tip had disappeared. Moving as slowly and carefully as possible, Tristam searched his surroundings. Just as he was about to give up, he saw the pale wings move. There! It was perched on the frame of an open transom window set above a wooden door.

He took a step; ever so slow, and then another. There was no doubt; the tip of the forewing was blood red. Halfway through a third step, the insect spread its wings and disappeared through the opening.

"Damn!" Tristam said aloud. He rushed forward and tried the handle, but the door was locked. "It is the worst luck," he whispered. "That would have been an addition to my collection, to be sure." But how had it come here? He had heard nothing of a butterfly enclosure in the palace.

Perhaps he could find Tumney and beg entrance to whatever hall this was. Immediately he was reminded of his errand and, on impulse, removed the key and tried it in the lock. The bolt turned soundlessly. Tristam looked around, a bit of guilt surfacing at making so free of the King's palace. *No one will care,* he told himself, *I've already been granted access to the greatest secret in the gardens.*

He pushed the door open, careful to turn the lock again as he passed. The butterfly was not to be seen and Tristam ascended a short flight of steps, regretting his lack of a proper net. At the top of the stairs a pathway of fine sand wound into the foliage of yet another entrapped Oceana. *It is like a puzzle,* he thought, *one inside another, inside another yet.* He stopped after each stride to search for the crimson tip. The sounds of a fountain bubbled through the dense trees and bushes. He almost expected to hear the wind in the palms as he had in the dream.

Overhead an intricately supported dome of glass showed a sky rapidly filling with clouds. Something moved. A glimpse of white in the dark green of the jungle. Tristam stepped off the path. The undergrowth was not so thick this time, and he moved more easily and more quietly. In the voice of the fountain Tristam could almost imagine a trill of laughter.

Again—white wings like a lady's scarf snatched away on the breeze. He began to make out the far side of the structure in glimpses through the flora—gray-stone, he thought. The sound of laughter came again, and Tristam was almost sure it was not the voice of the fountain. And then he saw water falling. Two more careful steps and he realized that there was no fountain at all; this was a waterfall cascading over rock into a clear pool. A natural composition from Oceana had been reproduced with enormous care.

The laughter came again and this time Tristam knew it was no auditory trick. It was a woman's laugh, though bitter and lacking joy.

"I despair, Your Majesty, of ever seeing our way through this," Tristam believed the woman said, though the falling water made hearing difficult. Even so the voice was known to him—a voice he had heard cry out in passion—the Duchess of Morland and, by the form of address, she could only be speaking to the King.

The young naturalist began to take a step back when a flash of white called his attention. The duchess' gown, and then the duchess herself, appeared through the leaves. Tristam sank to his knees. He could see the woman plainly now. She paced to the edge of the pool and stared into the falling water. This might be the duchess, but Tristam had not imagined her like this. She looked tired, defeated, overwhelmed by sadness. After a moment, she turned away and disappeared behind foliage.

How do I get myself into such situations? Tristam wondered. *Martyr's blood.* He started to retreat, but the duchess appeared again, preventing his withdrawal.

She stood at the edge of the pool, speaking over her shoulder as though she could not bear to face the man she addressed. "If you cannot bear up, how will I?" she asked quietly, but there was no answer. "The thought of what they might do. . . ." She shook her head as though this idea were too painful.

There was a long silence and the duchess moved back out of Tristam's view. He retreated a step, then another. A window opened in the foliage, and he could see the duchess again. She appeared to kneel in the sand. Tristam froze in place.

"I don't know where we shall find the strength," the duchess began and then her voice, pleading, fell so low he could not hear it. Then she spoke plainly again. "These last thirty years—they have been a golden age in Farr history. Without your wisdom, Wilam," she said, using the King's name as though she were a sovereign queen herself, "there would have been endless war. And now this." The melancholy in her voice touched Tristam.

She reached out and Tristam saw her take the dark spotted hands of a figure seated before her, a figure hidden by the jungle.

"Yes. Nothing but old men standing between sanity and chaos," a voice said and the sound rocked Tristam. He had never heard such a voice! It was not a man's voice at all but an echo of a voice—distant and distorted as though it came from infinite depths and distances, funneled up an endless well.

"Do not cry, child. I have passed my time, passed my golden age by far. I cannot continue. The dreams . . . nay, nightmares have begun to haunt my days as well as my nights. If I let my mind wander for an instant,

they are upon me like howling wolves. The wolves of madness—Farrelle protect me. If only I could leave my throne to you, Elorin, I would pass on in peace at last. But there is no peace for me. I know now that one can outlive one's time on earth. My entire generation is gone. You cannot know what terrible loneliness that brings. You are all the joy that is left to me." He paused and Tristam saw the duchess pulled gently forward, disappearing into the King's embrace.

"Elorin, I am sorry," the awful voice went on. *"I grow selfish and difficult. I do not mean to hurt you, child—you, of all people. I will not give up, just yet. Farrelle forgive me, but I will continue a little longer."*

Tristam slipped back several paces on hands and knees and then turned and fled as though he himself were hunted by wolves.

THIRTEEN

Tristam was walking on the hill above Highloft Manor, a canvas shoulder bag bouncing against his thigh, his ash-plant punching the soft ground at every other step. A wide-brimmed hat protected his face from the maturing sun, but even so his arms and neck were the nut-brown of a haymaker's.

A flicker of yellow in a holly had Tristam pulling Dandish's Fromme glass out of the shoulder bag—but even that instrument could not entice a bird to appear if it were disinclined to cooperate. A half-hour's wait produced nothing, and Tristam gave it up and passed on. Usually he would take such a thing as a challenge, but today he did not feel his usual self—nor had he for some time.

A long month had passed since his return from Avonel, and Tristam had become progressively more downcast and enervated with each day. It was not at all like him, he knew, but he could not shake himself out of this funk. High summer had come and gone and the season hovered now on the cusp of late summer. A stay in the lake country with Jaimy was looming. Tristam was not looking forward to it at all and had begun to consider possible excuses.

He sat down on a stone perched on the roll of the hill and opened his water flask. Below him the Tithy ran, its narrow course tucked under the hill's curving shoulder. Tristam surveyed his world: the old manor house with its various roof lines sloping off, each with its own idea of "level"; his uncle's eccentric gardens defying the laws of taste in both design and color; dilapidated outbuildings, each original only in its progress toward utter ruin. The pasture land, divided by a web of drystone walls and hedgerows, ranged outward to the surrounding hills crowned with nodding green woods. Today it did not seem the wonderful gift it once had.

Nothing had gone well since his return to Locfal. Jenny and her infernally pragmatic father had welcomed him home as the returning hero, but Tristam had not responded as he thought he would to this turn of events. In fact, he had become more and more distant, and this had caused a cooling in return. He could not help but think Jenny was a little relieved at this. They were not a match, he had realized.

His lack of success at the royal palace was weighing heavily on him—not that he had been given half a chance—but even so he had begun to feel that this had been a blessing in disguise. It saved him from having to fail in everyone else's eyes. Allowed to continue, he was now convinced, he would not have discovered the solution—Dandish's solution.

Something else to add to his growing melancholia.

Tristam had once thought that his estate would provide him with a lifetime of study in natural history, but recently it merely looked small and somewhat rundown. The journey to Avonel, he realized, had brought about a change in his perception . . . but it was a change he did not yet understand.

He told himself over and over that his encounter with the Duchess of Morland had no bearing on his present state. She was, after all, coldhearted and manipulative. Someone better kept at a distance. But the truth was, his thoughts never strayed from the duchess for long. Nor did they stray far from the last, overheard, conversation.

More than anything, Tristam felt as though he had been swept into a whirlpool, spun about several times, and then suddenly ejected into a sleepy backwater. His time away had left him in utter confusion, and the more time elapsed the less certain he was of the few things he thought were clear.

What in the round world was so important about *regis?*

"It is all a muddle," Tristam thought aloud. "A puzzle within a maze."

At least he had discovered the identity of Valary, or, thought he had. An eccentric historian—more highly regarded by Entonne scholars than he was in his own land. Tristam had written the man, hoping he was the Valary mentioned by Dandish, but so far he had received no letter in return. In his present state, Tristam had even begun to think this was somehow his fault.

Dandish's journals had been the subject of endless scrutiny this past month. Every word mulled over. Any sentence the slightest bit obscure analyzed for hidden meaning. This had led to such flights of fancy that Tristam had begun to doubt the soundness of his own mind and had put the books away.

And then there was the fragment hidden in the field glass. A warning Tristam still believed. Well, Dandish would be pleased by one thing. Tristam was as far from this matter as one could be and still remain in Farrland. If only he could shake it out of his mind.

Tristam had spent many a sleepless night wondering how Dandish had solved the *regis* problem. He had spent almost as much time in this as he had reliving his brief evening of love with the Duchess of Morland. Had she really thought he was Bertillon?

He pushed his hair back from his face, letting out an involuntary sigh. More than anything, he had begun to feel that he needed to get away. Escape for a few months. He had even considered a trip to his vineyard on the island of Farrow. At least he would be engaged in something.

Tristam's aging retriever came panting up the hill and threw itself down at his feet. He reached out automatically and scratched behind its ears.

"Well, should we go down and find you some supper? Eh?"

Sean Russell

The dog managed three beats with its tail, the normal response to being addressed on matters not completely clear. Man and beast followed a well-worn track down the hill, the ash-plant punctuating the sounds of their passing with perfect regularity.

Tristam hung his bag on a hook in the hall, tossed his walking stick into a corner and proceeded into his uncle's comfortable old home. His housekeeper, Mrs. Cowper, was dusting in the parlor and, without being noticed, Tristam scooped the day's post off a stand and made a quick retreat out onto the small terrace.

He collapsed into the best of several decrepit chairs and examined his mail. The first was a letter from Jaimy and he tore this open immediately.

My dear cousin:

I apologize for not writing sooner; I have been terribly busy helping the Somers' household prepare for a stay in the lake country.

It shan't be long now! I'm looking forward to our idyll with an enthusiasm that you may only begin to imagine; not least for the opportunity to see you again and to smash away at some promising rocks as well. I do intend to help and not spend every minute with my sweet Alissa, as much as I would like to (note: I said idyll not idle).

Now. . . . I have an answer to your inquiry. No, Professor Somers has not soured on either of us (quite the contrary, I think). I will tell you why he was so cool to you at the Society meeting but you cannot, you must not, breathe a word of it.

You may or may not remember that the good professor was accompanied by a young man? Perhaps you didn't notice. All the same, it was hardly a lad at all, for it was my own Alissa (with her beautiful curls tucked up under a wig) dressed as a young gentleman!

It says much for the powers of observation of our most skilled empiricists that not one of them noticed—including yourself, Tristam. Of course that

198

*is why Somers avoided you; he thought you might
recognize Alissa and give the game away—though I
am sure you wouldn't have done so intentionally.*

*Now you are a party to the secret and I trust you
will not say a word. Alissa gave me a full account of
the evening, which you must have enjoyed. Professor Somers assures me your name has been bandied about as a Fellow-to-be. You need only produce
a substantial piece of work and the ring is yours!*

I must run. Write if you get a chance.

> *Yours in haste,*
> *Jaimas*

*PS: I have thought a great deal about various matters and look forward to discussing these with you
again. All my preparations are complete. How go
your own?*

Tristam dropped the letter onto a bench and stared
off across the garden. Jaimy's overflowing happiness
made him feel even more desolate. He was jealous, he
realized. Not that he begrudged happiness to his
cousin, whom Tristam felt was a deserving individual
indeed. It was merely the contrast between their states
that struck him.

"Well, good for J," Tristam muttered. As he said
this, he noticed, in the shadowed branches of an ancient hornbeam, the pale shape of his uncle's falcon.
"My familiar," Tristam said. And then to the raptor;
"He is gone forever, you foolish bird. Be off."

"Who is there!?" Mrs. Cowper's voice came from
inside the open doors.

"Tristam, Mrs. C." Tristam called out.

The grandmotherly housekeeper appeared in the
doorway, wiping her hands on her apron. "Oh, there
you are, Mr. Flattery. I am deafer by the day, I didn't
hear you come in." She looked around. "Were you
speaking to someone just now?"

"Just a bird."

"Oh . . . I thought I'd heard something. Well, do excuse me." She turned back to her chores but stopped. "I've almost forgotten." She began fumbling in the pockets of her apron, and finally produced an envelope. "I had meant to give this to you straight off when you came in—had I heard."

Tristam took the envelope. It was postmarked from Avonel.

"I hope it's something to cheer you, sir, and not. . . ." She trailed off.

"Thank you, Mrs. Cowper." Tristam tore at the flap and then realized the housekeeper stood looking on. *"Thank you, Mrs. Cowper."*

She reluctantly disappeared back into the house and Tristam removed the single sheet of paper, a slight tremor in his hand. A letter from the duchess was what he hoped for, but a note from Tumney was what he expected; not what the envelope, in fact, contained—a brief note from Sir Roderick Palle.

Dear Mr. Flattery:

I write trusting that you will treat everything said in the strictest confidence. As we hold no hope of our Kingfoil ever bearing seeds, His Majesty's government has issued instructions to the Admiralty for the preparation of a voyage to Oceana. The purpose of this voyage will be to procure fertile seeds or plants of the regis *variety. As this purpose is to be known only to the senior officer and to a naturalist, your name immediately came to mind. It is the greatest good fortune that you are both qualified and already aware of our plight. I must say your reputation, and the high regard of several of your professors has also been a factor.*

Therefore, I am offering the position of naturalist on said voyage to you. Due to the gravity of the matter, a ship will be made ready with all haste to sail before summer's end. I require your decision in the return post. This gives you little time to consider, I realize, but it cannot be avoided.

I would say, if I may write candidly, that, though such endeavors are not without risk, similar voyages have made the reputations of our most eminent empiricists. There is also the possibility of finding some clue as to the fate of Gregory, not to mention performing an invaluable service to the King.

> *I await your reply,*
> *Sir Roderick Palle*

Tristam looked up, his gaze climbing over the nearby hills. In the sky beyond he could see clouds borne up on a distant wind. He realized that if he had prayed, this letter would be the answer to that prayer.

FOURTEEN

The vessel in question was built at Crouch by Fishborn and Daly, her present age three years seven months. She is full built, single bottom with galleried stern and comes nearest the tonnage mentioned in your warrant and is not so old by 15 months. She is 90 feet in length of upper deck; of extreme breadth 24 feet 4 inches; in draught 11 feet fully laden. Her burthen in tons 290 71/94. I cannot conceive of a more fitting vessel for service in remote parts. The survey indicates a refit necessary as her use has been hard, though she is sound in all her parts. Swallow *could certainly be made ready for sea by the date required.*

"So that is your ship, Mr. Flattery," Sir Roderick said, "though we may hope that not all the claims prove as false as that in the last line."

"She is ready for sea now, though?" Tristam sat in Sir Roderick's office looking at a letter from the Surveyor's Office of the Navy Board to the Admiralty.

"Yes . . . well, there are some special arrangements required to accommodate her officers and passengers. But they should be all but complete now." Roderick stood, leafing through a pile of papers on his desk.

Tristam turned and gazed out the window which overlooked the grounds of the Tellaman Palace. Trees were showing hints of the colors they would soon wear in full glory. The autumn migration was well advanced.

Roderick sat down and looked directly at Tristam. "It has come about that you will have another aboard whose concern is the *regis* plant." The King's Man paused. "The Duchess of Morland is determined to make this voyage and, remarkably, the King has allowed it."

Tristam could not quite believe that he had heard correctly. "The *duchess . . . ?*" he said stupidly.

Roderick nodded.

Tristam shifted in his chair. His thought processes seemed to have paused. The conversation he had overheard months ago in this very building came back to mind, but suggested no explanation.

"I was against it, as you might imagine. And the Admiralty refused—initially." The knight shook his head. "But we have orders from the King . . . so the duchess will be aboard when the *Swallow* weighs."

But I have signed aboard this ship to escape, Tristam thought. *Escape from this woman among a hundred other things.*

Tristam had hoped this would be a curative voyage, ridding him of his mild obsession with the duchess, restoring his spirits. And now she would be aboard the same vessel.

To his chagrin he felt his hopes rise at this news as well.

"The Duchess," Roderick began, interrupting the younger man's thoughts, "has not undertaken this voyage for her health. You understand, Mr. Flattery, that any Kingfoil or seed procured is the express property of the King of Farrland? To treat it in any other way would be treason."

What had Palle just said?

"I . . . understand completely, Sir Roderick."

Palle managed a thin smile, almost a facial tick. "You will find the captain a solid man; not *all sail and no ballast,* as the saying goes. Captain Stern, by name. He was not given command of this voyage without reason, Tristam. I can say with assurance that Captain Stern will not be swayed from his duty, no matter what occurs.

"He was senior lieutenant on Gregory's first voyage

and would have sailed with the great navigator again if
he had not been appointed to his own command. An
amateur natural philosopher of some knowledge:
Gregory's influence, no doubt. I'm sure you will find
much in common." Roderick appeared to consider for
a moment as though there were something to remember. "Stern is much like his mentor Gregory in other
ways as well, Mr. Flattery. He is very concerned that
officers aboard his ship conduct themselves in a gentlemanly fashion. Not that I think you would ever do
otherwise, mind you, but much of the irreverence that
is common among university men would be . . . misunderstood by Stern."

"I take your meaning, sir. I shall be on my guard."
Tristam paused, then offered. "Stern seems a doubly
likely name for a ship's captain." How could he find
humor in anything at this moment?

Roderick was leafing through his papers again and
did not smile. "I dare say."

Obviously much had been going on in the court in
the past months. He gathered his nerve for a few seconds. "Sir Roderick? If I may ask; what has inclined
the duchess to undertake this voyage? It shall not be a
comfortable outing, by all accounts."

Roderick leaned back in his chair and sighed. Exas-
peration was not something the King's Man displayed
often. "Mr. Flattery, what the Duchess of Morland in-
tends at any given time is one of the great mysteries of
our age. But the King is under her spell. . . ." He
looked at Tristam and raised his eyebrows. "This herb,
Tristam; it keeps the King alive. Never forget that. It
has caused no end of folly among those who know of
its existence. Consider what you yourself discovered
about Professor Dandish. . . . I wish you good fortune,
Mr. Flattery."

FIFTEEN

The fountains before the Tellaman Palace were known throughout all the lands of the Entide Sea for both their artistry and their technical ingenuity. The bronze sculptures were leafed in gold: ancient gods and goddesses; characters from mythology; historical figures; and fantastic creatures of land, sea, air, and combinations thereof. Water jets would suddenly erupt, rise to the height of the palace, and then subside or disappear altogether. At times, thirty-some different fountains would spout simultaneously.

Roderick stared out over the pool to the island on which the main fountains stood. An ancient god rode a giant seahorse that sprayed a fan of water from its mouth, while porpoises leaped around them, water spouting from their blowholes. Roderick had often wondered why the sculptor had chosen to portray this god of the sea as he had—a strong, handsome face contorted in anguish. There was no myth that Palle knew that would explain it. The knight had come to believe that this anguish was the emotion of the artist who had designed and built the fountain—completing it just before his own death.

Alone among the other figures this one seemed to be of the real world, Roderick thought: a god learning that he was mortal after all.

Hawksmoor interrupted the knight's contemplation of the fountains.

"There is little to tell, Sir Roderick. The Entonne are showing Varese's letters to no one, though I expect there will be some forgeries produced before long. I have, however, learned one thing of interest. When Varese first found them, he took the letters to a man named Valary to have them authenticated. This would have been some months ago."

Roderick nodded. He had not expected even Hawksmoor to be able to get access to these letters, for they were undoubtedly in the hands of Count Massenet. "Valary? Should I know this name?"

Hawksmoor looked down at the ground for a moment. "No, I don't think so, Sir Roderick." He paused again. Unlike the man to be reticent.

"Out with it, Mr. Hawksmoor."

The man cleared his throat. "Well, the man is an historian—something of a rival to our Mr. Wells, it would seem. Mr. Wells maintains the man is a fraud. . . ."

"And . . . ?"

"I am afraid that professional jealousy can occasionally cloud anyone's judgment, Sir Roderick."

Roderick used his foot to brush a small pebble into the water.

The two stood on the edge of the pool, backed by an area of open lawn. Not the best point from which to observe the fountain but a perfect place to speak privately. The day was warm, autumn—the flowers now outdone by the vivid colors of the trees.

"This man Valary wrote a book about the mages—translated and published only in Entonne—which would explain how Varese knew of him. It would seem that Valary is highly regarded by our friends across the water."

"And we have not seen this book?"

Hawksmoor hesitated. "No, sir," he answered quietly.

"Find me a copy, Mr. Hawksmoor, and we need to know more of Valary. He dwells in Entonne?"

"No, sir. Though I believe he travels there often."

"Well, I do not like the sound of a Farrlander being regarded as an authority on mages by the Entonne."

"No, sir."

Roderick moved a few paces down the stone walk and then stopped, Hawksmoor keeping pace, moving almost silently, the knight realized.

"I believe there has been no contact between Mr. Flattery and the duchess, Sir Roderick, if that is of any comfort."

Roderick shrugged. "That is about to end. He didn't seem to be suffering from melancholia when I met him...."

"No," Hawksmoor said. "I think the prospect of this voyage has lifted his spirits. Which is a good thing—I was afraid young Flattery might follow the example of his father."

"A concern of mine, as well," Roderick said. He glanced out at the sea god astride his mount. "I do hope he does nothing so rash. We may have need of Mr. Flattery."

"Not for two years, I hope. Our efforts go well, I trust?"

Roderick tilted his head from side to side. "Well enough." Roderick looked out again at the anguished god half lost in the mist. "What of Massenet?"

"If he were not the most social man in Avonel—and the most popular—I would be able to tell more of his purpose. As it is...." Hawksmoor stopped, thinking. He never offered more than he actually knew, no matter what, and that was one of the many reasons Palle valued him. "The count is so skilled, sir. I will tell you truthfully that I have some admiration for the man."

"His weakness is the ladies of Avonel. Realizing his country will not soon conquer us in the field, I think this count has decided to make his conquest of Farrland in the bedchamber. That is where Massenet will make his mistake."

"I'm sure you're right, Sir Roderick, but he has not done so yet."

"Never fear, Mr. Hawksmoor, men are betrayed by their appetites." Roderick turned back toward the palace, but stopped. "Valary—everything that can be learned about him. I will deal with Wells."

"Immediately, Sir Roderick."

The King's Man nodded, and set off briskly toward the palace, the anguish of the god forgotten for the time being.

SIXTEEN

"Flames, I wish you had spoken to me before agreeing to this voyage, Tristam," Jaimy said. "I think it is a terrible error."

They had been over this before. Tristam tried not to show annoyance. "My answer was required by return post, Jaimas. I am not the only trained naturalist in Farrland. Hesitation was not possible."

Tristam and his cousin sat in the window of an ale house overlooking the harbor of Avonel. Out among the many ships they could make out the bark, *Swallow,* lying at anchor, her decks and rigging teeming with sailors who appeared to be running in all directions simultaneously.

Tristam's mind was in a similar confusion, for preparations had been lengthy and complex. At the last moment, the Society had requested that he perform a number of tasks for various fellows and, though Tristam had been delighted to oblige, it had not made things easier.

But there was something he had meant to tell Jaimy. . . .

"I had a letter from this man Valary, at last."

Jaimy's expression changed immediately—interest kindled.

"It was lucky he replied when he did or his letter would have lain unread until my return." Tristam reached into an inner pocket of his coat and retrieved an envelope, his name and address across the face in an odd, irregular hand. "I'm afraid you will have a time deciphering it, the man's writing is abominable."

He handed the letter to his cousin, anxious to hear Jaimy's response.

My dear Mr. Flattery:

I am sorry to have taken so long to reply, but I have been abroad these last months and your letters lay in a mountain of others awaiting my return. I am greatly sorry to hear of the passing of Professor Dandish, for, though I never had the honor of making his acquaintance, I had great respect for his work. It was very considerate of you to write and inform me of his passing.

In answer to your question: yes, I did correspond with the professor, though one letter only. I am not certain what bearing, if any, it might have upon this inquiry of the professor's that you attempt to complete, but I will write you out a copy and send it along. The letter was not of a personal nature and I'm sure the professor would not mind. Interestingly, I had cause to mention Erasmus Flattery in this letter, whom I assume to be a relation of yours?

Good luck to you, sir. Do not hesitate to call upon me at any time. I am always willing to offer any assistance to a colleague of the professor's.

Your servant,
F. T. Valary

My dear Professor Dandish:

I cannot tell you my delight at receiving a letter from a gentleman I have so long admired! I will confess that I felt some pride that a man of such learning would approach me for information. But I fear I shall not provide answers that you will find satisfactory, for, in my pursuit, things are not easily measured or verified.

As the professor is no doubt aware, the mages were enormously secretive about their arts. I fear the result of this has been endless conjecture over some fifteen hundreds of years. Sifting this, looking for "truth" is a pursuit with few rewards, though occasionally one strikes a rich vein. Several of the matters you refer to are likely not verifiable and, in my opinion, not accurate. They had their root in an odd little book written by a man named Decker, who served in the house of Lucklow. The man was a servant and upon Lucklow's death thought he could earn some money from an account of his years with the mage. I suspect a true account would have held little of interest for the reading public at large, so much was fabricated (perhaps by the book's publisher, as is their wont).

As to the longevity: I think there can be no question. Certainly Lord Eldrich, whose birth and death were carefully recorded, lived to be one hundred, seventeen years. And I am quite sure that Dunsenay could not have been less than one hundred, thirty-three—and perhaps several years older. Most men in the time of Dunsenay could not have expected spans of more than fifty-some years. I will say, categorically, that Pylf did not see two hundred, twenty years, or even anything like it. This is a popular myth, I'm afraid, but typically the mages lived many years more than their contemporaries and there is no evidence that any succumbed to the common ailments or even to the terrible epidemics of their own ages. I often think that most people's fascination with the mages is inspired by curiosity about this great longevity and nothing else. Of course their longevity is, in most cases, quite beyond dispute whereas so many other things attributed to them are difficult, if not impossible to verify. Magic, people have come to doubt, but to live to twice, or even thrice, man's common span—that is too tempting to disbelieve!

Herb-lore, as you say, was the province of the mages, and it surprises me that gentlemen of your pursuit have not paid more attention to this. Certainly they knew much of healing, and some of this knowledge they did not hoard so carefully. I could, if it would be of use to you, trace a good number of common herbal remedies that had their origin with one or other of the mages. But if they were free with some *knowledge, they were extremely close with far more, and, like all of their arts, this one has passed from knowledge. I spoke at length to the late Erasmus Flattery about this and though that worthy gentleman said a great deal, when I reflected upon his words, I could find little to profit me. Rather like the writings of students I'm sure you have had occasion to see, where the author hopes to hide lack of inspiration behind a wall of well-wrought prose. Now Erasmus Flattery was a man of some substance, I am well aware, but whatever he learned from his three years in the house of Eldrich he took to his grave.*

I remember well that this worthy gentleman questioned me much about my own work, which flattered me more than a little at the time. Later, I had cause to reflect that Mr. Flattery's interest was as keen as my own, and I suspected he had not been so free with his knowledge as I had been with mine. But he did tell me, and I think he let this slip, that Eldrich had once intentionally infected himself with the yellow fever merely to observe the effects! And then, in a matter of days, grew well again! I do not think it possible that he observed this himself but more likely was told it by someone else in the house.

Specifically, was there a link between some course of herbal physic and longevity? I cannot answer with any certainty. Certainly there is evidence that this might be the case, but equally there is evidence that this great age was achieved through other, more arcane, methods. Holderlin, who developed a great friendship with Queen Vaill, wrote many letters to Her Majesty and I think he dearly enjoyed dropping hints about matters "magical." In one such letter he wrote: "It is true, Your Majesty, that to extend the life of a great ruler would benefit everyone in Farrland, and perhaps beyond, but long life is not a gift a mage can offer. To live to the age that some have, one must follow the art with an unwavering, iron discipline, else one would pay a terrible price."

He said nothing more that I am aware of on this subject, but this (rather dark) hint was quite uncharacteristic of the mages. One is left with the impres-

sion that, whatever the mechanism by which they extended their lives, it was part of the larger discipline, perhaps a result of practicing the art as a whole.

Now, to your final question: do I believe, myself? Well, sir, to answer in the affirmative would open me to the ridicule of my peers and would also cast my own objectivity into question. This particular area of scholarship has suffered such raillery over the years that I am loath to endanger any respectability my studies have finally achieved.

Have I danced enough? Let me simply say this. Men of obvious power, the nature of which is difficult to explain by currently accepted methods, lived among us until quite recently. I am convinced that at least some of the feats attributed to them actually did occur—how they were achieved, again, I cannot say. Are there still mages among us—hidden? No, I don't think so. I believe Eldrich was the last, and it would appear that he was not even a particularly powerful practitioner of the art. I believe their time had passed, for reasons that we do not understand. Perhaps even the mages did not understand themselves. And they were very careful to take their knowledge with them—a fact which is more suggestive of their intentions at the end than anything else we know. Except perhaps this: Eldrich is buried in the grounds of his family home and no one is allowed near the grave—but I have been told by someone who is in a position to know that the inscription on the headstone reads:

> The last to begin
> The journey out of darkness
> Takes but a lifetime

As cryptic as anything that can, with any certainty, be attributed to a mage (and not helped by the lack of punctuation), but, "the last to begin" would appear to mean the last of the mages. Or so I surmise.

I hope, sir, that this has been of some use to you. Please do not hesitate to write again if I may be of

*further service. I have information about herb-lore
that I believe you would find of interest.*

> *Your servant,
> F. T. Valary*

Jaimy looked up. "Flaming martyrs," he managed.
"Not what you were expecting?"

"I. . . . No! What in the round world does this
mean?"

Tristam had been pondering that very question day
and night for the past week. "It is quite clear what it
means, I think. That isn't the problem. The difficulty is
accepting the implications." Tristam glanced out the
window and then back at his cousin. "Dandish must
have believed this herb had something to do with
longevity—the King, after all, is very old, past his centenary now—and connected it somehow with the only
other group known to have achieved this much-sought-
after lengthening of years: the mages. It would seem
that, for reasons unstated, Dandish saw some danger in
this and destroyed his planting and the notes of his inquiry. I can't think of another explanation."

"But, Tristam, the Kingfoil was first brought from
Oceana by Gregory—only some thirty years past. It
cannot have any connection with mages, the last of
whom died near to half a century ago."

"The logic of that is impeccable, cousin."

"And this talk of our Uncle Erasmus. . . . Well, we
both know that it is completely absurd. Erasmus was
no more 'magical' than this mug of ale." He shoved
his glass toward Tristam. "Dandish didn't believe this,
did he?"

Tristam pressed fingers into the corners of his eyes.
He was tired and struggling to make his brain function.
"Perhaps. . . . Perhaps not. But what if he thought others believed? I think we are too young to really understand what it means to age. But it has driven people to
mad desperation often enough. Think of the number of
people who have been duped by charlatans who prom-

ised a return of youth? Some of our earliest voyages of exploration were motivated by rulers who sought rejuvenation. The *'apples of immortality'* is not just a phrase in a hundred bad poems—people once believed these apples existed. Fountains with enchanted waters. Elixirs. Potions. It was not so long ago that men sought the secret of turning lead into gold. Turning old age into youth—it is an irresistible myth, as Valary says.

"If some people believe, it would explain a great deal, I think. It might even explain why the professor destroyed his planting. He was an old man himself—he probably understood the lengths others might go to."

Stronger those few days and my arrhythmia was all but gone. The phrase surfaced unbidden.

"Blood and flames, Tristam. You think these people are seeking some elixir of youth?" He gave a short laugh, almost a snort. "Courtiers have always been notoriously foolish, but this is beyond all. Roderick Palle? He is not a foolish man, Tristam; I have met him." Jaimy took a drink of his ale, his focus inward. "Who is this man Valary, anyway?"

"That I can answer, at least somewhat. He is an historian of some note. Well respected in his own area. But apparently he has as a hobby the study of mages. He has even written a book, a history, though he could not find a publisher in Farrland, for the book is apparently not very sensational—an academic study, in fact. It has been translated and published in Entonne, however. You might find a copy of it while I'm away."

"But he is a crank, wouldn't you say?"

Tristam shrugged. "You read the letter. Was it the work of a crank?"

Jaimy picked up the letter and stared at it for a moment. "I know what you mean, but the most successful charlatans are those who seem the most reasonable."

"Whether he is sincere hardly matters, Jaimas. My guess now is that at least some believe this herb we seek has the property of extending one's years—the King's great age, you see. Pathetic really, for I'm sure this will turn out to be no more substantial than the

'apples of immortality': the King is old, but not yet unnaturally so." As he said this, he remembered the voice
he had heard in the arboretum—hardly natural. "If
even one person is desperate enough to believe, what
would he not do?"

"Ipsword," Jaimy said, as though it were a word
with intrinsic meaning.

"Exactly. The professor must have heard of the
man's death. Dandish was no fool. He would have realized immediately what this meant."

Jaimy looked out over the harbor and then quickly
turned back to his cousin. "It isn't too late to give up
this voyage, Tristam."

"No, it is too late." Tristam looked down at the table, unable to bear the concern in his cousin's eyes.
"No, I will go on. To bring us back some answers if
for no other reason." He shrugged, offering up his
hands as though they bore an explanation. "It is the opportunity of a lifetime, Jaimy, as you realize. A chance
to make my name in my field. I can't give it up because of the foolish beliefs of some courtiers. And it
seems likely that this seed does have some medicinal
purpose: it keeps the King in health. That much seems
true, and for that reason alone it is an endeavor worth
pursuing. I will go, J. I seem meant to go, really. I was
Dandish's protégé. I worked on Baron Trevelyan's collection. This task is for me to complete, I'm sure."

Jaimy nodded, the concern not leaving his face. "I
should be going with you," he said quietly.

"Your fiancée would not approve." Mention of
Alissa gained a small smile. "I told you that Viscount
Elsworth is coming as well?"

"You did. Seldom has one of His Majesty's survey
ships had such an esteemed company," Jaimy said
dryly. "A duchess and a murderer. One hand of velvet
and one of iron. I would imagine the duchess must
consider missing an opening night at the theater an intolerable hardship, and yet she takes on this. . . ."
Jaimy eyed his cousin. "She can't possibly believe she
can maintain her youth? The duchess is certainly not

that foolish," Jaimy said, and then almost smiled. "Her decision has the cream of Farr society in a whirl of constant speculation."

Tristam tried to smile in return. "Well, I will let you in on the real truth: a race of talented milliners and dressmakers has been discovered dwelling in the great southern ocean. You know what lengths some will go to for fashion."

One of Sir Roderick's footmen came rushing into the room at that moment and, seeing Tristam, made a bee-line to his table.

"Excuse me, Mr. Flattery, but some sailors have taken all your baggage. I couldn't stop them."

Tristam bolted out of his chair. "Blood and flames! Were they drunk?"

"Not so's I could tell, sir. I was told to say it was Jack Beechnut transported your things to the *Swallow*." The poor man was obviously wretched. "I am sorry, sir, I know you charged me to let no one touch them."

"About this tall?" Tristam held up his hand. "Curly, almost-blond hair?" The footman nodded, and Tristam burst out laughing.

"You know him, sir?"

"If his name was Beacham and not Beechnut, I do indeed." He sat down again.

"It might have been Beacham, sir. I didn't take proper notice, I'm afraid. Is there anything I should do, sir?"

"I think my baggage is in good hands. Please take Sir Roderick this note, with my regards and thanks. He has been most helpful, as you have yourself." Tristam quickly wrote a note for the footman and gave the man a coin.

When they were alone again, the two young men sat in silence for a few moments and then Jaimy turned to his cousin, his face serious. "You be careful, Tristam Flattery. Watch that bloody-handed viscount. You're the only cousin whose company I can bear for more than half of an hour. I should not want to lose you."

"And I don't want to be lost. I shall be on my guard

at all times." *And drink only spring water, gathered at sunrise.*

❦   ❦   ❦

The Admiralty was housed in an ancient building that stared down, many-eyed, upon the harbor of Avonel. It was here that decisions were made to send ships out to explore the globe, to blockade harbors, or to bring war to an enemy. Here was the brain of the great beast that was spreading over the oceans of the globe.

Inside the Admiralty, oak floors, which appeared to have been heaved by frost, creaked loudly as men set foot upon them, in stark contrast to the somber voices, the hushed conversations. Captain Josiah Stern had been in the building before, but this was his first visit to the fifth floor. It was here that the Sea Lord and the senior admirals had their offices. It was on this floor that the war room lay, waiting patiently, its massive charts changed every fortnight as new information was received from merchant ships, surveying vessels, and ships of war—the mysteries of the world being revealed inexorably.

A "midshipman" led Captain Stern along a corridor, the floor marking their passage with groans and creaks, as though they were the protests of a living thing. Despite his uniform and rank, the young man who escorted Stern was merely an office lackey, but this was the Navy and every man in it held a rank, whether or not he had set foot aboard a ship. This lad had not, Stern was quite certain. And in ten years he would be deciding the fates of seamen, like Stern himself. The captain felt a surge of resentment toward this boy—a mere teenager, and not overly impressed by the captain who accompanied him, that was obvious.

At least the men who held the high offices had once been sailors. The present First Lord of the Navy had spent a life at sea: Admiral Sir Jonathan Gage, a man Stern had once glimpsed as he passed in a carriage.

The distance between a mere post captain and the Sea Lord was far greater than the few floors that commonly separated them would suggest.

The midshipman turned Stern over to Admiral Gage's secretary, an efficient middle-aged man in a post captain's uniform, but a bureaucrat nonetheless.

Seated to await the Sea Lord's pleasure, Stern was given a cup of tea and time to ponder. It was highly unusual for the captain of a survey vessel to be called to the office of the highest ranking officer in the service. Unheard of, might be more accurate. Of course, not every survey ship had members of the king's court aboard—and one a woman, at that. He sipped his tea and looked over at the secretary who was busily arranging papers on a massive desk.

Stern wondered what in the name of Farrelle had brought the Duchess of Morland aboard his cramped little ship. When he had first been told, he had not asked: one did not question orders. Not if one wanted to advance. No matter what kind of fool's errand a man was sent on, he did not think to question its value or even its practicality. The naval officers took pride in their dedication to duty. Every one of them would sail their command into certain destruction if ordered to do so. And the men before the masts of five hundred other ships would sing a sad song of it—sad and proud.

But this did not stop a man from wondering, in the privacy of his own thoughts, of course. The Duchess of Morland?

Stern was not a well connected officer. He had come up through the ranks—the son of a mildly successful banker. His patron in the service, Sir Josiah Fitsch, had died years earlier leaving Stern "orphaned," as the saying went. But Stern had managed to rise on merit alone—although slowly. Sailing as first officer to Gregory had been a boost. Then he had made his post. But he was forty-four now, an age when many another led squadrons, flew the pennant of a Rear Admiral, or even more. Such was the nature of the service. Not that the incompetent necessarily rose simply because of their family or connections—but even the skilled officer needed support from someone within this building. And the sons of mildly successful bankers did not hobnob with the right crowd to find that support.

The death of Fitsch (a man married to an aunt of Stern's mother) had been more than the loss of a mentor, a friend, and a good officer. It had likely been the death of Stern's career as well.

For that reason, Stern was more than a little surprised to find himself here. He could not help but hope this might be an indication of some change—a sea change.

"Captain Stern?"

The secretary stood before him, his head bent a little, like a manservant. Stern had obviously been lost in his thoughts.

"Sir?"

"The admiral will see you now."

Stern set his cup back onto the silver tray and stood, taking up his tricorn and tucking it awkwardly under his arm. He wished he had a glass in which to check his uniform.

The large doors to the Sea Lord's office were opened and as Stern was about to enter, the secretary whispered, "Sir Jonathan:" the admiral's preferred form of address—something known by every man in the navy, Stern was sure. Decidedly nervous, Captain Josiah Stern put one foot before the other rather stiffly and went to see what the future might hold.

The admiral sat at a desk so large that it immediately brought to mind the deck of a ship of war. It even had a miniature cannon positioned on one corner. Admiral Gage was a man of about seventy years, his skin and hair giving the appearance of having had the pigment bleached out of them until they were as white and clear as sun-melted soap.

The man bent over a stack of papers on his desk, his face so close to the page that his long nose could almost have come away with ink on its tip. Although the admiral was a man of normal size, behind this desk he appeared to be as small as a child.

Hearing the door close, he sat up, a look of slight confusion on his face. Stern quickly made a leg.

"Ah, Burns. . . ." The Sea Lord said, and waved a hand at a chair. "Please, be comfortable."

"Captain Josiah Stern, Sir Jonathan."

"Stern, yes, of course."

It was a clear day, sunlight streaming in the huge window with such strength that Stern half-expected to see some of it filtering through the admiral—but there was a shadow on his desk. Gage looked back to his papers, signed something with a quick scrawl, and then turned his attention to his visitor.

"So, we have you going back to the Great Ocean?" he smiled, his almost colorless lips pursing.

Stern nodded.

"Well, I'm sure you will perform your duties with competence, as usual." The man rose a little stiffly, steadying himself with a hand on the back of his chair. He stretched his back, clearly with some pain, and then walked to the window where he stood peering down at the harbor, his hands clasped behind him. To the admiral's right a large telescope stood mounted on a bronze tripod, its glass eye pointed toward the ships anchored in the harbor.

"We are both busy men," the admiral said suddenly, turning away from the window, his face a little troubled, perhaps, "so let us not waste time in needless pleasantries. You have read your orders?"

"I have, sir." These had not been the type to be opened only when the ship was safely at sea.

"This young man, Flattery; he is well versed in the botany of Oceana, so there should be no trouble there. The situation, however, is more complicated. This herb the palace wants us to find—it is sacred to the Varuans. A level of diplomacy will be required to procure it."

Stern nodded.

"You have had good luck with these islanders before, Captain. I'm sure you will get on without troubles. Of course it is all a bit pointless, really," the admiral said suddenly, looking Stern directly in the eye.

Stern felt his eyebrows raise as though he asked why.

The admiral returned to his desk and picked up a mechanical pencil made of gold. "This herb, it alleviates the suffering of the King. . . . His Majesty is not entirely well, you understand. But the King is *very* old." He shook his head. "It is sad, really, for it is beyond imagining that His Majesty will. . . . Well, let us just say that two years has an entirely different meaning to those of advanced years." He raised his hands a little. "Even so, we must send out a ship—the palace has requested it. But Captain . . . do not waste the opportunity entirely. There is much that can be done: past discoveries that have not yet been properly charted, and you will have this naturalist along as well. Quite skilled by all accounts. Do what you can as you go. Any addition to our charts might save lives one day. Yes?"

The admiral set aside the paper he had signed and glanced at the one beneath. "Now, as to this matter of the Duchess of Morland, and Lord Elsworth." He kept his eyes on the papers before him. "It is a complicated business—the court, you know. . . . One faction vying with another. They would let the country go to ruin rather than give up the slightest advantage. I cannot fathom what drives such people. And within the palace there are some who do not trust us to do our duty, Captain." He said this with a little indignation. "And the duchess. . . . Well, what advantage will be gained if she returns to find that King Wilam has finally gone to his much deserved rest? Though I pray this will not be so, of course."

He looked up from the desk then. "Be certain, when you return from Oceana, that this herb is in your possession, Captain Burns. Otherwise you shall receive scant credit for your efforts. Do you take my meaning? Good." He looked back to the page, raising a corner to see what lay beneath. "It is a voyage for which you will get little enough recognition as it is. You understand that you must not speak of this herb? Yes?

"But rest assured that I will not forget you, Captain, even if the palace does not take great notice." He smiled at Stern, who was not terribly reassured—the admiral clearly did not know his name to begin with. "Now, the duchess. . . . I realize the situation shall be difficult for you. This is a woman well used to having her way. But command of the voyage is yours, Captain. I am relying on you to treat the duchess as someone of her station deserves, and yet discharge your obligations with alacrity. Not an enviable position you will be in, but I have complete faith in you. Perhaps all these damned delays will work in your favor. It is much more likely that you will get a good blow between here and Farrow at this late date. That might be all it takes to dissuade the duchess and her retinue." He smiled at this thought. "We can only hope. Good fortune to you, Captain."

SEVENTEEN

It was dusk before the *Swallow*'s deck was cleared of enough debris that Tristam was allowed aboard. The yawl boat bumped gently against the dark hull and Tristam was directed to the rungs of a crude ladder. This he climbed by touch alone and pulled himself over the bulwark onto the deck of the small bark.

"Mr. Flattery, is it?"

"Why, Jack Beacham! The pleasures of the evening to you."

"And to you, sir." The young midshipman appeared in the light of the stern lamps. "I must say that your prediction has not come true, Mr. Flattery."

"I should give up making predictions. They never work out. Remind me—what was the nature of this one?"

"When last we parted, I expressed the wish that we might sail together again and you said I would likely be an officer before such a thing would come to pass."

Tristam laughed. "Well, I am sorry to hear my prediction failed you, but I am glad that you will be aboard. It's good to have a true sailor around to keep the landsmen out of harm's way."

"Well, sir, I will do everything I can. Perhaps we can make an arrangement. I will teach you the ways of a ship if you might be so kind as to set me straight with weather and the geometrics. The geometrics of the sphere do seem to have me flustered, Mr. Flattery." In the poor light Tristam could see the lad shake his head, and his tone was one of concern.

"Well, I'm sure we can steer our way among the

shoals of spherical geometrics, Mr. Beacham, and the channels and capes of weather can be even more easily navigated—though, of course, nothing is so sure in that particular study."

Beacham looked somewhat relieved by this. "I would be in your debt, Mr. Flattery. I took the liberty of bringing your baggage aboard, sir, but I should present you to the ship's master before we see to it. The captain and first lieutenant have gone ashore but Mr. Hobbes, the master, will wish to make your acquaintance. Can't have strangers walking around on the decks of His Majesty's ship. You could be an Entonne agent."

Tristam responded with a few words of his best Entonne.

"You speak it, then?"

"After a fashion."

"I wish I had your education, Mr. Flattery," Beacham said with great sincerity. "Knowledge is a wonderful thing."

"Do not be too impressed by my own, Jack Beacham; it is as thin as an old copper . . . and of similar value."

Beacham found the ship's master and the boatswain crammed into a small cabin, pouring over records of stores. Mr. Hobbes, the master, was a tall-built man, very angular—all of his features large. One of those men whose frame was so big that there did not seem to be enough flesh to cover it properly, yet he appeared very strong. Tristam had never seen a man whose appearance was more uniformly gray: iron gray hair, stiff as wire; pale skin with a dull cast. Even the man's eyes suggested gray they were such a pale blue. His callused hand enveloped Tristam's in a firm clasp and the naturalist was surprised at the gentleness of the man's tone and manner.

In contrast, Mr. Pickersgill, the boatswain, was a small round man with a joyous smile and an ease of manner that must have won him many friends. He winked at Tristam as though they shared a private jest and Tristam could not help but smile in return.

"So that's the famous Mr. Hobbes," Beacham said as soon as they were out of earshot, and making their way through the poor light below decks. "He sailed with Gregory as did our captain." Beacham said this in a near whisper, as though the statement filled him entirely with awe. "Not a man will need be pressed to make up his crew. Every man Jack of them knows our master and captain will bring the ship back whole, and the crew as well."

"Pickersgill seemed a pleasant sort," Tristam said.

"I should say, though as great a blackguard as any boatswain in the King's Navy, I shouldn't doubt. 'Mr. Handy,' he is called."

"Really?" Tristam was taken aback by Beacham's response. He had thought the lad so open of nature as to be incapable of criticism.

"It's the way of them, sir. Sell the sails out of the lifeboats. Sell the provisions if they could. Farrland needs a special prison just for boatswains, if you ask me." The thought of provisions appeared to cheer Beacham. "Did you know, Mr. Flattery, we have tinned victuals aboard! Can you imagine? They say it will last years and the tins are proof against weevils and the like, though you have to paint them to keep away the rust."

"Paint the weevils?"

Beacham laughed at this weak jest. "Paint the tins, sir."

Tristam followed Beacham forward to see his cabin, although the term *closet* might have been more accurate.

The cabin appeared to be square and wedged tight up against the curve of the hull. Inside the door there was a tiny open area less than two feet square, to the right a tall locker, to the left a type of desk, and against the hull a cabinet with doors and drawers. Tristam saw no bed, or berth, if that is what such things were called aboard ship. Air and presumably light, if it had not been dark, would come from a tiny, bronze port set into the break in the deck, for Tristam's cabin was built against the forward end of the quarterdeck.

Beacham apparently read the look of confusion on Tristam's face. "There is a hammock here, Mr. Flattery." The midshipman dug into a corner the lamplight did not penetrate and unrolled a contrivance of fishnet and canvas. This was stretched corner to corner cross the cabin and tied into an iron ring-bolt. Beacham hopped up with an enviable grace and swung into the hammock to demonstrate the proper method of boarding and sleeping in such a contrivance.

"You'll soon get used to it, Mr. Flattery. Far more comfortable than a bunk and leeboard. A hammock swings with the ship—which is to say the ship swings and the hammock maintains its position relative to the earth—more or less. Have a try." Beacham rolled out, landing easily on his feet.

The young sailor did not hide his glee well and Tristam knew there must be more to it than there appeared. He contrived to copy Beacham's movements as closely as possible and in this his greater height was an advantage. He launched himself into the contraption and, to Beacham's disappointment, managed the thing without mishap.

"Why, that's it, sir! You've the way of a sailor, to be sure."

Tristam managed the exit almost as well, only banging his elbow a little. "About my baggage?"

"I commandeered a corner of the 'tween decks mess and piled your things there with threats to all should anything untoward befall them. It seemed that piling them in your cabin would leave no room to work at stowing them away."

Tristam followed the ever-resourceful (or so he was beginning to believe) midshipman into the 'tween decks mess. Two other young midshipmen were there and Tristam was quickly introduced. He got the impression that Beacham may have been talking him up a bit, for the young gentlemen were very respectful, even a bit nervous.

Tristam stared at the massive pile of his equipment and clothes and various stores. "Where in the world will I put all of this?"

"In your cabin, Mr. Flattery. Why, I could fit twice this in and still leave room for a hornpipe. You'll see."

The two worked away at the task of stowing Tristam's baggage and Beacham kept up a flow of conversation the entire time. He related the history of the ship and assured Tristam that she was a "lucky" vessel, and he talked of the ship's crew, some of whom he had sailed with and others whom he knew by "scuttlebutt." The midshipman showed great surprise when Tristam confessed he had never heard tell of "the famous" Mr. Hobbes before their recent introduction.

"I thought all of Farrland knew of Mr. Hobbes, sir." Beacham stopped emptying a crate of instruments. "Nothing else was spoken of for months on the docks and in the ale houses. You did not hear of the decision of the Navy Board?

Tristam had only recently heard of the Navy Board.

"Well, Mr. Flattery, I can tell you justice was never so poorly served in all of history." He said this with utter conviction. "You see, Mr. Hobbes was once a lieutenant, one step away from being made post captain, or so everyone says, and I believe it. He was given command of a rotting little scow called the *Briss,* which is Doorn for 'breeze,' though I'm sure you know that," he added quickly. "A surveyor by training, Mr. Hobbes and his command were sent to survey in the Archipelago above fifty—fifty degrees that is. Well, like every good officer Mr. Hobbes began by surveying his own vessel and discovered that she was not as fit for sea as the Navy Yard had made out—too much of the money for her refit had gone into the refitting of gentlemen's pockets, if you take my meaning, sir. Well, Mr. Hobbes wrote to the Navy Board with his complaints and the upshot was that he was ordered to sea, if you can believe it, in a vessel that was near to sinking at the wharf! You can see what would happen.

"Somehow the *Briss* made it through the summer months without disaster, but on their return voyage to Farrland they were set upon by a great blow of an autumn storm, sir, and the boat foundered." Beacham banged his fist on the door, clearly outraged. "The company, or most of it, got into the ship's boats, for survey vessels often carry three boats, Mr. Flattery: a yawl-boat, a cutter, and a long boat as well. The long boat, commanded by Mr. Hobbes, made the crossing with great hardship, losing only one man—almost one hundred twenty leagues! Near to two thousand miles! And at a terrible time of year as well. The other two boats. . . . Well, they were never seen again, Mr. Flattery, unless it is while haunting the nights of certain gentlemen." He took a long breath before continuing his story. "But was Mr. Hobbes thought a hero? Was he given his post, as well, and a pension from the King? No, sir! He was taken before the Navy Board and broken of his rank! That is how they rewarded him for preserving twenty-six lives! The letter Mr. Hobbes had written was 'lost' and he was charged with setting to sea in a vessel he knew unseaworthy. That is the truth of it, sir, I'm sorry to say. And the gentlemen who lined their pockets with the monies meant to refit the *Briss* . . . why, Mr. Flattery, they pay for their servants with that money. They pay for fine carriages, too!"

"I see what you mean," Tristam said quietly.

"Since Admiral Gage was made Sea Lord things have changed, but poor Mr. Hobbes will never pass beyond the rank of master even though he sailed with Gregory and Pankhurst and is one of the most respected seamen in the navy. He has the love of the Jacks, though, I'll tell you that. When they were crossing the Gray Ocean in the early winter, and in an open boat too, often as not he gave his ration to the weakest man. And without so much as a compass, he sailed to Farrland by the stars, making as fair a landfall as a ship of war. Sailed in the entrance to Wickham Harbor in the fog, sir! Sailed in as though it weren't impossible. There is not a Jack in the navy that wouldn't put himself in the way of a cannonball for Mr. Hobbes. You will see, Mr. Flattery. You will see."

After this outburst, they worked on in silence for some time.

True to his word, when everything was stowed away, there was room for a hornpipe, albeit danced by a dwarf. Through casual questioning as they worked, Beacham learned that Tristam was lacking certain articles that would make his life aboard easier; when Tristam went ashore, he had a list of things to purchase before the *Swallow* sailed, as well as instructions as to where such articles could be found and what price should be paid for them. Beacham was a thorough young man and Tristam had the impression that he did not think a landsman could be trusted to shave himself in anything but a flat calm.

As soon as his mind was free of his task aboard, it returned to his real concern. This voyage would not provide escape from the intrigues of the court, nor would it give him the time to heal as Tristam had hoped. But far worse: how was he to live, for two years, only a few yards from the Duchess of Morland? What if she were to find a lover among the officers? Once they passed through the archipelago, there would be no hope of leaving the ship. No escape at all.

EIGHTEEN

Having now circled the globe entire, and having looked upon strange and foreign lands perhaps more often than any man alive, I have come to realize that this great endeavor of "discovery" is vastly misnamed. Almost without exception we have found men living in these distant lands, and in those places thought uninhabited we have often found evidence that humankind once made homes there. The true age of exploration and "discovery" took place long ago; unheralded, unrecorded, and with great hardship I am sure, but in ages before our own civilization came into being. When one considers this lost history, the world seems endless indeed.

Gregory: Voyages

The fifteenth day of October dawned clear and autumn-warm, a fresh breeze sweeping down from the hills, spreading the scent of land out over the sea. Gulls searched frantically among the great ships at anchor, filling the air with their forlorn cries. And high above the bay an osprey hunted, as stationary as a kite on a string, as patient as a mage.

Tristam stood at the stern rail, out of harm's way, as the crew and officers prepared to make sail. He tried not to let his glance stray to the Duchess of Morland who was plying the officers with her considerable charms. Although Tristam knew that meeting the duchess again would not be easy for him, he had underestimated his reaction substantially. The cries of the gulls were like echoes of his own anguish.

Orders were given to weigh anchor when an officer noted a cutter, flying the flag of the Admiral of the Fleet, sailing quickly toward the *Swallow*. As it drew alongside, an officer stood up in the stern and called out, "The compliments of His Majesty, to the Duchess of Morland, Lord Elsworth, Captain, and crew, wishing a safe voyage for all." And then, to everyone's delight, Teiho Ruau, the Varuan, rose in the bow and began to sing.

It was the same unworldly tenor that Tristam had heard with Sir Roderick, but it was a song from Oceana, soft and haunting—words that Tristam did not understand but which affected him nonetheless. A song of farewell, Tristam realized, though he could not understand a single word. The entire crew stopped their work and stood silently along the rail, listening. Even the most hardened-looking Jacks appeared to be moved by the music, and unembarrassed to be so.

A voice to pacify the brutal soul, Tristam thought. Interesting that Ruau, from a race whose culture did not compare with that of Farrland, appeared more civilized than the poor Jacks of the *Swallow*. Yet even as he thought this, Tristam saw the islander was wearing his belt of snakeskin—a talisman of some sort.

His song done, the Varuan doffed his white plumed hat in a sweeping bow, and the cutter pushed off and was soon lost among the other ships.

Immediately, the boatswain blew his pipes, breaking the mood, and the capstan began to turn from the efforts of men at the bars. The chain cable rattled slowly through the hawsehole, and finally, after great effort, the laboring Jacks stumbled forward a step as the anchor broke free of the harbor bottom. Sails were loosed by the crewmen aloft and the survey vessel, *Swallow* turned her bow toward the open sea.

As the ship left the harbor Tristam found that his gaze was drawn back, not forward. He wanted to linger on the sight of land rather than gaze out toward the empty horizon.

❦ ❦ ❦

The great cabin of the bark *Swallow* spanned the ship's entire beam, making it the only civilized accommodation aboard. Light and air were provided by an arc of transom windows and a skylight set among the heavy beams that supported the quarterdeck. Even on this late evening the cabin remained bright, for the overhead was painted white as was much of the other woodwork.

Captain Josiah Stern stood near the table, the brass buttons of his jacket reflecting in the polished surface. He was apparently unaware of the motion of the ship, for his large workman's hands hung easily at his sides, clearly not poised to make a desperate grab for a handhold. In this he differed noticeably from the others present.

The captain, Tristam guessed, was in his middle forties and appeared to have the build of a bricklayer, a fact which was at odds with the man's careful dignity, for Stern appeared to do everything with great deliberation, as though he thought every action through at length. Tristam suspected the man of being somewhat like the great ships he commanded—slow to get underway but, once moving, very difficult to stop.

In his habits of dress, Stern was obviously fastidious, his uniform carefully tailored and impeccably clean. *"He likes to think himself a gentleman,"* Beacham had noted, *"but he will not brook dissent, Mr. Flattery."* Beacham had lowered his voice at this. *"The most pleasant officer afloat, sir. But he is not to be argued with. Not our Captain Stern, for he will change as quick as the sea beneath a squall."*

Tristam sat on the sill of an opened transom window, bracing himself by spreading his feet wide and pressing his back into the hard wood of the window casing—one hand grasped the sill and the other occasionally twitched in his lap as the ship lurched. He had chosen this position, for it afforded him a good view of everyone in the room, especially the Duchess of Morland.

The duchess perched in a chair that had been removed by several feet from the table end, so that she would not have to look up too abruptly at the captain. As always, she seemed utterly composed, waiting with, if not a smile, a look of pleasant expectation on her face. A few errant strands of golden hair had come free of her combs and Tristam thought the wind had given her face the most innocent blush. The naturalist forced himself to look away, thinking that her brother might feel that he stared.

When she had arrived aboard, the duchess had greeted Tristam like a long lost cousin, kissing him on both cheeks, making great show of her affection for him. Not a word for months, and then she responded as though she had missed him every second they had been apart—and said almost as much. He was sure that he had been the envy of every man on the deck—her intention, undoubtedly. And this had left Tristam in the grip of such confusion—resentful, delighted, hopeful, even a bit proud that such a woman would offer this public statement of her affection for him. He carried that confusion around with him now, like a chronic ache in his chest.

"I thought it important," Captain Stern began, interrupting Tristam's thoughts, "that we have a word before our wake has stretched too thin." He tilted his head slightly toward the duchess as he spoke. Some form of acknowledgment, Tristam thought.

The viscount sat in a second chair, which he had braced against the leeward of the cabin's two berths so that the slight heel of the ship held him firmly in place. He propped an ankle up on the opposite knee, and leaned back in his chair, smiling like an amiable drunk. Tristam was struck again by the size of the man—as large as any of the Jacks who worked the forecastle, and they were the most powerful of the sailors.

Tristam glanced over his shoulder at the ship's wake stretching out astern toward the hills of Farrland, floating dusky purple on the horizon like an exotic island. A gull, borne upon a current of air made by the passing ship, kept cocking its head reproachfully at Tristam, as though he were expected to throw something edible into the sea.

"Although I have had peers aboard ships of my command in the past," Stern went on, "they were always admirals or members of the Admiralty. Men who knew the sea, as well as the service and her ways."

The emphasis, Tristam noted, had been on the word "men." Stern, put one hand behind his back—a rather courtly gesture.

"Even when I have had an admiral, a gentleman of title, aboard my ship, there has never been any confusion about who was to command—who was to give the orders to officers and men. It is a long tradition of the navy. A ship can have only one commander, or she will soon be torn apart. A vessel cannot follow two courses; and the Jacks ... well, they must have a consistent routine and fair but strict discipline.

"The Admiralty has seen fit to give me command of both this ship *and* this expedition." He paused, meeting the eyes of each person in turn. "I hope that is perfectly clear?"

Tristam nodded quickly, but the duchess' only response was a slight tightening of the lips—not really a smile. The viscount's look of vacant foolishness did not change.

Chain of command, Tristam thought. *It is the litany of the navy men—their central belief.* He had been wondering how Stern intended to deal with the duchess aboard.

"Two years or more on a small ship ... this takes greater effort on the part of everyone aboard than most realize. The smallest annoyances, things we should hardly notice ashore, have led men to violence after months at sea. But if a strong captain, known to be just, sets the tone of the voyage—clearly marks the boundaries of acceptable action, and sticks to these with an iron will—then life aboard can be perfectly pleasant, if not as comfortable as some are used to. Discord is a disease and I shall not hesitate to wield my scalpel to cut it out." Again he met each person's eyes in turn. "In this I require your unwavering support. Aboard every ship there are those who are less than satisfied with their lot in life, and, instead of exerting their efforts to improve that lot, they channel their energies into disruption. It takes very little to encourage them in their natural ways. If they find one or two others of like mind among the Jacks, that can be cause enough for mischief. But if they believe there is support for their disaffection from officers or others aboard. . . ." The captain motioned up toward the deck, raising his heavy eyebrows. "I shall ask you to speak no ill of the navy, nor of the officers aboard, no matter what your opinion. Even in private be circumspect, for I will warn you also that privacy aboard ship is illusory—hardly more than a convention we have all agreed upon."

Stern looked down at the table, rubbing one hand across the smooth surface. As he did so, the captain turned just enough that Tristam could see the hand behind his back was knotted into a tight fist.

"At the various naval stations, you will often find that the officers have their families with them—wives and children. And these ladies have traveled out aboard His Majesty's ships. It is, therefore, not unheard of to have ladies aboard. It is, however, uncommon for women to travel on a voyage of such length." He glanced up, a bit embarrassed, Tristam thought, though he sailed on. "I anticipate no problems in this regard. The Jacks know full well that to offend the duchess or her maidservant in any way would elicit the harshest possible response from me. But if you would not mind speaking to your servant, Duchess, and suggest that she should, at all times, comport herself most circumspectly so that her actions could never be interpreted as encouragement. . . ." He raised his eyebrows, looking at the duchess, but she refused to reach out her hand to the drowning man. Tristam hid a smile. The captain had a great deal to learn about the Duchess of Morland.

Stern looked down at the table again, perhaps hiding his annoyance at the woman's response. "I'm sure you take my meaning. We are fortunate to have a good crew aboard. No man was pressed. The stories of Oceana brought volunteers enough to man five ships or more. Hobbes and I chose among them with some care. The First Lieutenant, Mr. Osler, is but a step away from his own command, and an officer I trust implicitly. And Mr. Hobbes . . ." He glanced up at those present and Tristam thought the man's look a bit defiant. "No matter what you may have heard, Mr. Hobbes is the finest noncommissioned officer in the navy. It is my opinion that he should be a post-captain today if not for. . . ." Stern caught himself, stopping awkwardly.

Tristam was not sure if the others present knew the story of Mr. Hobbes, which Tristam felt might not have come to him from the most disinterested source. But obviously Stern's view was similar to Beacham's.

"They are fine officers," Stern said quietly, "gentlemen all." He looked up again, this time fixing his sea-blue eyes on Tristam. "And I use the word to describe a man's way of going through the world—his manners and actions—not the circumstances of his birth. I am sure I can rely on you gentlemen to treat my officers as they deserve. It shall make all of our lives easier over the next two years."

Tristam nodded immediately. Lieutenant Osler had come from a situation not unlike Tristam's own—the young seaman's grandfather had been the Earl of Firthe—and as for the famous Mr. Hobbes. . . . Well, Tristam thought of himself as being above the prejudices of his class anyway, but he was prepared to treat Mr. Hobbes with deference, and especially so if the man's story proved to be true.

"You will not find me a difficult man to sail with," Stern went on. "I am not one of those martinets whose only purpose is to subjugate everyone aboard to his will. No, I think you will find me a reasonable man.

My creed is simple: duty to King and service; a gentleman always, to both friend and foe; tread upon no one else to raise one's self higher, but progress only according one's own merit. Old-fashioned, you will no doubt say, but those are my beliefs, and I have yet to meet a man who could find fault with them."

Tristam thought of the warning he had received from Beacham about not gainsaying the captain. It was no wonder Stern's beliefs had not been challenged. They could probably be far more objectionable than these banal homilies and Stern would never hear a word of criticism.

The officer brushed his hand across the table again as though attempting to erase the reflection of his gleaming buttons. "I will tell you honestly that there were those in the Admiralty that were against the duchess taking ship," Stern said, glancing up from the table.

Tristam could almost feel how tight the captain's fist was now. The man spoke as if he were straining to lift a heavy weight.

"And I will be perfectly candid, Duchess, Lord Elsworth——I feel that the task I have been given is well within my powers." He nodded toward Tristam. "With Mr. Flattery's skills and my own, I am sure that we shall succeed. And, despite what many seem to think, I am not the minion of any minister or courtier. I serve the King." His voice almost trembled as he said this. "It will be a long, arduous voyage, and not, I must tell you, without dangers. There will be an opportunity to reconsider when we reach Farrow and again at the Queen Anne Station.

"The Duchess, of course, is welcome aboard my ship," he added quickly. "And yourself, Lord Elsworth. Please do not misunderstand me. I only wish to offer assurances that my interests are those of Farrland and her sovereign. I have never yet failed to fulfill my orders."

"And what are those orders, Captain Stern?" the duchess asked evenly, her voice almost sweet. She fixed the officer with the same gaze she had turned on Tristam in the past, and the naturalist wondered if it unsettled Stern as much.

"I hope the Duchess will forgive me. Orders from the Admiralty are not to be discussed." He looked very grave as he said this, but Tristam thought he detected a certain amount of satisfaction in making this pronouncement.

"Have you other orders, other tasks, besides the one that concerns us all, Captain Stern?"

"Again, Duchess, forgive me, but I may not speak of this."

The duchess was not so easily put off. "I am not asking that you reveal the specifics of your orders, Captain, but only to tell me if there are other tasks assigned to this voyage. I am sure you cannot be accused of treason for revealing that?"

"I do apologize, Duchess, and to you gentlemen as well, but I am unable to discuss my orders. Even my officers have only the most general understanding of what we intend—and they know nothing of this ... other matter," he added, leaning forward and almost whispering. "They know that we are a survey vessel and that we have been sent out equipped to perform that function. We sail to Oceana, west-about, and shall carry a chain of measurements as we go. That is, Duchess, what my officers have been told and it is true enough." He smiled as he finished, as though he had just made an enormous concession to "getting along."

"Well, Captain Stern," the duchess responded, obviously not appreciative of these crumbs of information, "I only hope these tasks you allude to will not interfere with our true purpose. That is, you should know, one of my deepest concerns. For my part, and I think I may speak for Lord Elsworth in this, we intend to cooperate to the greatest extent of our abilities. You shall not find us interfering in the running of the ship or in the routines and discipline of shipboard life. We are out of our depth here and place ourselves entirely in your hands, deferring to your great experience and judgment. As to this other matter . . . I am aboard your ship for one reason and one reason alone, Captain, and that is to see that the intrigues of the court have not stowed away aboard, secretly. Like you, I, too, serve the King. That is why I have inquired about the exact nature of your orders. I would not think to challenge your knowledge of the sea, Captain Stern, but I have my area of knowledge. Your orders, despite their appearance, might not be in the best interests of the King, but instead might reflect the interests of others within the court. It would not be the first time."

Stern placed his other hand behind his back and stood very erect. "Allow me to assure the Duchess that this is not the case."

The duchess did not respond, but she and the captain had locked eyes and neither looked away. No doubt, Stern, who did not care to be gainsaid, was not used to being so confronted aboard his own command—and by a woman at that. There would be nothing in the seaman's vocabulary of responses that would suit the conditions. This woman was the favorite of the King of Farrland, after all.

"It is a more complex situation than most realize," the duchess said, giving not an inch.

Stern considered this a moment and then said, evenly, "I may be only an uneducated sea captain, Duchess, but I am not a fool."

"And I would never suggest that you were, Captain. Let us say that, for the moment, I am reassured." The duchess smiled suddenly, and Tristam saw that this affected even Stern. Threw him off balance, as though he had misunderstood the entire interchange—had taken it far too seriously—making the man wonder if he had just looked like a pompous fool. The captain reached up and took hold of the beam close overhead.

Yes, Tristam thought, *welcome to the world of the Duchess of Morland, Captain.*

"I hope you might all join me for supper this evening?" the duchess went on sweetly, looking around at each man in turn. "You do not all have other social en-

gagements? Your calendars are not too chock full?"
She smiled again, transforming herself in that way
Tristam had seen. Despite himself, he felt a smile ap-
pear in response.

"You are all very kind." She turned then to Stern,
her manner still animated. "Do not concern yourself,
Captain. We shall make every effort not to disrupt the
sacred routine of the King's Navy or to upset the delicate balance of this vessel."

Stern smiled in return, bowing his head slightly, as
though he had just received a compliment from a
queen.

❦   ❦   ❦

It must have hurt Stern immeasurably to give up his
accommodations to the Duchess of Morland, Tristam
thought, looking around the great cabin. There was no
other cabin aboard that compared—certainly not the
cubbyhole the captain was in now, hardly bigger than
Tristam's own. Stern, more than many others, must
know what it would mean on a two year voyage.

Tristam sat on the sill of the transom window,
watching the Duchess' Entonne maid putting the final
touches on the table, set for eight, though it would
have been crowded to seat six. The duchess stood
looking on and giving the maid and the captain's steward last minute instructions. For a woman used to a
staff that would number in the twenties, she seemed remarkably calm.

The steward tried twice to interrupt—something
about how tables were to be set in the navy—but the
duchess would have none of this. They may be aboard
a ship, but her table would be set according to the
standards of Avonel, or as near as could be managed
under the circumstances.

Tristam glanced out at the water bubbling out from
beneath the stern. Five knots he had been told they
were traveling, but if one looked directly down into the
water, it seemed much faster. The swirls and bubbles

of white, whirling off astern, were lost in the waves and the frothing wake. He felt a rush of joy at this sight, joy in the movement and the power of a ship under a sail. Rising on each swell, surging forward as she passed the crest, then settling into the trough, the sound of swift flowing water changing tone as the ship slowed, only to lift and surge forward again. Relentless rising and falling on the heaving breast of the great ocean.

Tristam was beginning to think that he might just survive this proximity to the duchess after all. He felt much relieved now that the ice had been broken. Her manner toward him was very kind. One would have thought Tristam was an old and dear friend. He still felt the incredible physical draw toward her, found it difficult to keep his eyes off her when they were together, but perhaps that would pass.

Below, the sea foamed and rushed.

"You are not ill, are you Tristam?"

Tristam turned away from the sight of the passing sea and forced a smile on his lips. "Not in the slightest."

The duchess looked at him, a bit concerned, it seemed. Tristam thought she was about to speak when a precise knock sounded on the cabin door.

"Your guests, Duchess," Jacel said.

Captain Stern made way for Doctor Llewellyn, a physician who accompanied the duchess, for the King had insisted she not sail without one, and then the captain entered followed by the navy men, scrubbed and fresh-shaven, their uniform buttons gleaming.

Tristam thought it possible that Osler, the first lieutenant, was not a total stranger to society, but certainly none of the navy men had ever been invited to dine with anyone of the duchess' station. The duchess, however, set about banishing their discomfort immediately. She greeted them all by name, her demeanor indicating she could not have been more delighted with her guests if they had been members of the Royal Family. Of course, they were all men, and the duchess was utterly confident in her affect on men, nor was she wrong in this.

In the babble of greetings and beginnings of conversation there was suddenly the most awkward pause, broken only by the voice of the physician who seemed unaware of the silence. Tristam had risen to greet the guests, but he stopped, surprised by the reaction. The navy men stood for a second, gazing at the table, and then they all looked immediately to the captain.

The duchess put a hand on the physician's shoulder to silence him and turned to the others.

"I fear I have committed some breach of etiquette, Captain Stern?" she said quietly.

Stern tried to smile. "It is just an old superstition, Duchess. The first night at sea the table should be made up of seven. It slipped my mind in the confusion of setting out: I apologize for not bringing it to the Duchess' attention."

"Well, we are all people of education," the physician interjected. "Not superstitious old shepherds. I will sit at a table of eight—or thirteen, for that matter."

The navy men all kept their eyes fixed on neutral points in the cabin, their features frozen—clearly horrified by the doctor's suggestion.

"Will you forgive me, Your Grace," young Osler said, trying not to appear awkward. "I should see to the running of the ship."

"Now, Mr. Osler . . ." Stern began, but did not finish, obviously as distressed as the others.

"I hope, Mr. Osler," the duchess said warmly, "that this doesn't mean you will not join me another evening?"

"I would be honored, Your Grace," he said, bowing slightly.

"Then I shall allow you to reduce our numbers at table appropriately. Thank you, Mr. Osler." The duchess curtsied to the lieutenant, having turned him into the sacrificing hero. Tristam felt a flash of jealousy and realized that perhaps life around the duchess would not prove so easy after all.

Before Osler could back from the room, the captain's steward pounced on the offending place setting, collecting it up as quickly as his hands would move.

From the forced manner of the sailors, Tristam guessed that, despite Osler's retreat, they believed the damage had already been done—the offense already noted by whichever sea god monitored such crimes.

The remaining dinner guests were seated, and a rather forced conversation began. Tristam, who was not feeling in the least social, found his mind wandering, and his gaze drawn again and again to the duchess, who was the focus of everyone's attention anyway. Tristam could not imagine that nature had ever created a more perfectly formed woman. If he closed his eyes for a second, even the sound of her voice enchanted him.

He wondered now if he would have escaped the duchess even if she had not come on the voyage.

Tristam tried to concentrate on the men seated around the table—an exercise he undertook halfheartedly. Stern, with his impeccable uniform and his close-cropped beard that could easily have been modeled on the beard worn by Jaimy's father, the Duke of Blackwater. A man displaced from his position as axis around which life aboard would turn. He was doing the best he could to appear unaffected, but even Tristam, who did not know the man, could see it was an effort.

Taine, the ship's surgeon, who in contrast to his captain was a little shabbily turned out, grime apparent on his cuffs and collar, a cheap scent masking his lack of a recent bath. The man must be feeling more than a little displaced himself, for it was commonly the surgeon who acted as the ship's naturalist, or at least made what collections he could. And here was poor Taine aboard a ship with a trained naturalist and a real physician, too—a physician who had apparently once served the Royal Household.

This physician, Norrish Llewellyn, was an odd man. Too talkative and completely insensitive of the fact—his manner condescending, which Tristam could not bear. The doctor had a small mocking laugh which was often released when he was asked a question, as though foolish queries brought him some amusement.

"Do the Varuans suffer from the scurvy?" the duchess had asked, and this had triggered Llewellyn's mocking laugh.

"No, Your Grace, the scurvy is a disease brought on by improper diet, as Gregory proved, and the Varuans have a healthful diet. Nor will scurvy touch a soul aboard this ship, for we have all the tried and true antiscorbutics aboard. Limes and sour-cabbage and beer brewed from the spruce." He looked up at the duchess, his lips twitching into a small smile of amusement. "You have Llewellyn aboard—a physician of the Royal College. It will not be disease that brings this voyage into danger, that I assure you."

Tristam was not sure who was more enraged: the duchess, who could not bear condescension; the surgeon, who was a graduate of the lowly Naval College; or the officers, who did not like to have it implied that the only danger that existed was mismanagement of the voyage. Somehow Llewellyn had missed offending Tristam. And the physician was unaware that anyone could find this insulting—he was, after all, only speaking the truth.

It was immediately apparent, though, that the doctor was a scholar of some real knowledge—as he made sure everyone knew—for he spoke several languages, and was a good amateur naturalist. But to Tristam's eye, Llewellyn had all the signs of a man who, though he knew much, had lived little. Fifteen minutes of conversation had not been needed for the physician to alienate almost everyone at the table, and the poor ship's surgeon most of all. Llewellyn corrected the man twice, before everyone, as though Taine were a lowly apprentice. He then made several mocking comments about the superstitious, as though he would, by such ill contrived "instruction," change the beliefs of the sailors present.

Tristam had seen teachers do the same in his school

days—always the instructors most hated by the students, and least effective in the practice of their profession.

Even the duchess did not find it easy to wrest control of the conversation from the irrepressible doctor, for he did not notice hints, even of the less subtle nature. In turn, she gave everyone at the table permission to address her as 'Duchess,' with the exception of Llewellyn, and even this took a moment to make an impression on the man. But finally he fell silent, perhaps realizing that even the lowly surgeon had been granted a favor that he had not. He was to remain in his place as her employee and address the duchess as "Your Grace."

"Captain Stern," the duchess said, rather solicitously, for she was obviously aware of the captain's loss of social standing that her presence had caused. "I wish to propose a toast but do not wish to compound my earlier error. Is there a tradition in this as well?"

Tristam thought that Stern noted her sensitivity to his position and seemed genuinely affected by this. "There are only a few areas one should beware of, Duchess. One never whistles aboard ship, for it is believed to bring storms. Likewise we never toast, 'fair winds' or words to that effect—which can leave one becalmed for weeks, or so it is believed. It is considered bad luck to give voice to specific kinds of fears, such as saying that one hopes we do not founder. All things supernatural are feared by the common sailors and not spoken of. It is bad luck to leave port on Friday." He laughed suddenly as he realized how quickly the catalog grew. "At its outset, we commonly toast the success of the voyage, Duchess, and at each meal we drink a glass to the health of the King."

"To the success of the voyage then, gentlemen," the duchess said, "and to the King's health."

Tristam saw the tightening around the eyes as she said this, as though the thought disturbed her. Perhaps the duchess had superstitions of her own.

"This is very fine wine," Llewellyn said, and

Tristam was not sure if he intended this compliment to make amends for his earlier offense or whether this was merely another opportunity to display his store of knowledge.

"It is from the grape developed by Erasmus Flattery," the duchess interrupted quickly, "whose heir graces our table."

"You are the son of Erasmus Flattery," Stern asked, his glass stopping in midair.

"He was my great-uncle, Captain."

"Well, you should keep that information to yourself, Mr. Flattery," Stern said, shifting in his chair. Then he looked around the table. "We should all keep it quiet. I'm sure there is no truth to it, Mr. Flattery, but the rumors that connect your great uncle to Lord Eldrich are well known. The men before the mast, the common Jacks, they would be genuinely frightened to know the heir of Erasmus Flattery sailed with us."

Stern attempted a reassuring smile, but it failed to do its duty. Tristam felt a flush of anger, coupled with a mild fear. Something else he did not seem able to escape.

The conversation went off in various directions after that, but Tristam hardly followed it. The duchess made great efforts to include everyone, but she obviously concentrated her charms on the ship's master, Mr. Hobbes. The master may well have suffered at the hands of the lords in the Admiralty, but it was clear he was ready to absolve the duchess of any connection to this group. It was a rather astute and totally cold-blooded strategy on the duchess' part. Hobbes was worshiped by the Jacks. Winning his approval would assure the duchess' acceptance by the crew.

Tristam took a deep drink of his wine—a private, unspoken toast to her genius. Stern might be so committed to duty that he could not be influenced by the duchess, but Tristam was willing to wager that no one else aboard would offer the same resistance. No, the *Swallow* would be the first ship in Farr history to surrender without the crew even being aware that they had done so.

      ❦   ❦   ❦

Tristam watched the stars, picking out the constellations he knew, focusing his glass now and then on a familiar point only to find the many more suns that lay behind—the infinite number of stars wavering in his lens. It was the night of the new moon and there was not a better time for viewing the heavens. Tristam felt as though he had slipped away into his own element. Dinner had not been easy.

Running away to sea was not proving very successful.

And his simple life as ship's naturalist was now complicated as well: court intrigue proving as difficult to elude as the duchess.

And yet there was a part of him that could not believe his good fortune. Two years aboard a ship with the most desired woman in all of Farrland! And it did not seem likely that he had a rival here. Had she not seemed genuinely delighted to see him when they met?

She is a dozen years your senior, he told himself, *of the very highest strata of Farr society, the favorite of the King, and a woman famous for her ability to manipulate—especially men.* Jaimy would think him a proper fool, Tristam realized. He knew what the word "obsession" implied.

But when I am with the duchess, Tristam thought, *I feel as though my entire being has been engaged—intellect, heart, desire. It is like suddenly waking. Unlike my days with Jenny,* he realized.

Do not be a fool, Tristam Flattery, he told himself. *The Duchess of Morland is not interested in a relatively poor naturalist from Locfal—beyond his, possibly useful, botanical skills.*

Of course it would be easier to conquer his feelings if he had not once felt the duchess beneath him crying out in pleasure—not that it was his name she had been crying!

"There you are, Tristam," the duchess' voice came out of the dark behind him. He felt his eyes close involuntarily.

"I had hoped you would stay a while and keep me company."

She came to the rail beside him, wrapped in a dark shawl, the starlight playing in her uncovered hair.

"Are you communing with nature? Is that what naturalists do?" she asked, her manner teasing but her voice quiet, perhaps remembering Stern's warning about privacy aboard ships.

"I was thinking of a conversation I had with Averil Kent," Tristam lied. "Do you know him?"

"Anyone who travels in society in Avonel knows Kent."

"He spoke to me at length one day about art, and about the Entonne word *isollae*. 'Loneliness in the face of beauty,' he translated it. I wonder if it describes what I am feeling."

The duchess did not answer, but he heard her stir beside him, the soft rustle of wool moving over her gown. They stood silently looking out into the depths of the sky and at the surface of the sea, faintly illuminated by starlight. A wave rolled by beneath them with a sound like a long exhalation.

"There is more to you than meets the eye, Tristam Flattery," the duchess said. "But does the word not also mean 'isolated'? I hope that is not what you feel."

Always, Tristam thought. "No, of course not."

The tips of three fingers touched his shoulder. He could feel them even through his coat. "Listen to me, Tristam. As much as I wanted to write you these past months, I could not. I could not draw attention to you and to us. But we are together in this matter. . . ." She paused; Tristam could sense her thinking. The pressure of her hand disappeared from his back. "Allow me to give you some small piece of information, Tristam. That is what empiricists seek, is it not?" She paused again, wrapping her shawl more tightly about her shoulders. "I knew your father, or perhaps it would be more accurate to say I observed him. I have always had an interest in the theater, the opera, even when I was young, so our circles were not so different despite our disparate ages. Your father was caught up in the cult of sensibility that swept through Farr society fifteen years ago, and has now, mercifully, all but disappeared. But I felt even then that the cult of sensibility gave your father an opportunity to express something that was true in himself. I am not telling you anything new to say that Morton Flattery experienced all his emotions in extreme. When he felt joy he was in ecstasy; when he felt passion it was near to madness; and when he knew despair. . . ." The duchess turned to Tristam, staring up into his face so that he could not look away. "But you are not like him, Tristam, not like him at all. You need not live in fear that your course in life follows his. It does not. You need not deny so much of yourself. To open some small corner of your heart will not bring you to ruin. Do you understand what I'm saying?"

Tristam felt his hand gripping the rail as though afraid he would lose his balance and pitch into the night sea. It was as though she had known his thoughts. He could not find words to answer, but nodded his head, feeling that the eyes searching his held as many mysteries as the night sky.

She turned back to the rail. "I hope you do."

"All those around me, as long as I can remember, have engaged only my intellect, Duchess." A long succession of instructors who smelled of pipe smoke and closed rooms. "There has never been anyone to speak to my heart."

She glanced up as though surprised. "Do not look to me for this, Tristam," she said, softly, almost imploring him. "Please. Hearts have never been safe with me. I say this only because I care for you." She reached out and laid her hand on his arm. "We must not start the crew gossiping. The pleasures of the evening to you, Tristam Flattery."

He listened to her footsteps as they crossed the deck. The night seemed to have grown a little cooler suddenly, as though the breeze had risen. The ship lifted on a crest and then settled slowly into the trough, making sounds of disappointment. A sheet stretched in its block, releasing a long, indescribable vowel that seemed almost an animal expression of sympathy.

"Isollae," Tristam whispered.

When he finally went down to his cabin, Tristam discovered an envelope tucked under his door. He opened it by lamplight and found a note scrawled across the top of more neatly written text. *This is the letter I wrote and should have sent,* it said, and was dated the thirtieth day of July.

My dearest Tristam:

I hope this letter reaches you before you hear from Roderick Palle. In this past month there has been a struggle in the court such as I have not seen in some years. But in the end His Majesty's government has ordered a voyage to Oceana to seek the elusive herb. I have made every effort to influence the selection of the members of this voyage. I can claim only partial success—but I have managed to have you, Tristam, named the prime candidate for the position of ship's naturalist.

I am sure you will feel some reservations about involving yourself in this venture, given what you have experienced of court intrigue, but the herb must be found, and quickly. There is no one in all of Farrland more qualified for this position than yourself, nor is there anyone more likely to succeed. So much is at stake in this matter—I hope some day to be able to tell you exactly how much.

Please, please, give this appointment your most serious consideration. I shall not know a moment's

*rest until you have said yes. And if you do consent,
I shall be more grateful than you can imagine.*

*I realize that such an undertaking has its dangers,
and not only shall I miss your company for the duration but I will worry constantly. I should never choose
to send you off if it were not so crucial. Please write
to me immediately, and, if you can, come to Avonel
so that we may discuss it at length.*

*Yours,
Elorin*

Tristam lay in his hammock, listening to the sea gurgle and splash as it passed over the hull outside his
cabin. So varied was the vocabulary that he almost
found himself trying to understand, listening for words,
attempting to sense the mood of this discourse.

NINETEEN

The carriage tilted abruptly to the right and then jolted back upright. Kent grasped tight to the leather hand-loop, but when the road ran on more or less smoothly for a hundred feet, he loosed his grip and returned the gloved hand to the head of his cane. Despite lack of moon and stars, the branches of trees could just be seen, swaying erratically as though they tried to shake free of the wind that pressed them down. The last leaves of the year fluttered, batlike, around the carriage. Occasionally, one flattened itself to the carriage window like sodden paper. Now and then the wind seemed to find a tunnel through the forest and the entire carriage would sway and rock like a boat on the sea.

It was not much farther, he was sure, though at the pace they traveled, it would still take a precious half of the hour.

"What a fool I have been," he said under his breath, and not for the first time. He had been mumbling the same litany for several days now, and thought it might be some time before he stopped—if ever.

"An old fool," the painter whispered bitterly.

A sudden lurch of the carriage had him reach out and take hold of the loop again. They were turning. It must be the gate.

"Fool," he said, as though getting in one last blow.

The driver gentled his team to a halt beneath a covered carriage entrance which allowed Kent to disembark—something he no longer managed so spryly—and still remain dry. On either side of the doors of the old mansion flickering stormlamps appeared to be standing in challenge to the elements, the circle of their light swaying and contracting as the wind swept beneath the eaves, moaning as though the voice of an ill earth.

Logs burned in the fireplace of an entry hall decorated in the "old style," and the painter was not sure which warmed him more. The same servant he had seen here for he could not remember how long took his hat, coat, and cane, and led him to the familiar sitting room. Here a fire burned, as well, and on the table beside a chair by the hearth stood a decanter of brandy, a cut-glass snifter, and a warmer, already lit. This would be his chair for the interview, or perhaps "audience" would have been a more appropriate term.

He poured the brandy and slowly turned the glass over the blue flame of the warmer, taking in the exquisite smell of the liquor.

There was not a single lamp in the room, so it was difficult to tell if the room had been altered; somehow he was quite sure that it had not. The weak light from the fire didn't penetrate many shadows. Here he could see part of one wall, there a well-used chair, and before him a painted screen.

A door opened, and that was followed by the unmistakable swish of a gown, sounds that always made his heart respond.

"I am so happy to see you, Averil." The voice had not changed either. Not cold but unexpressive, almost without inflection.

The countess took her seat in the chair beside the screen, arranged perfectly so that the light from the fire could not illuminate her face. She sat, as always, in shadow.

"And I am delighted to be in your company, Lady Chilton."

Her gown was deep blue, almost black, with white lace at the neck, he was sure. White lace at the sleeve cuffs covered her hands, though not completely, and these she clasped in her lap. He knew as the evening wore on, the hands would move more and occasionally even extend out into the dim light of the fire—and this was all he would see of the woman once thought to be the most beautiful in all the countries surrounding the Entide Sea.

"You are well?"

"I am. And I hope Lady Chilton can say the same?"

The head nodded. His eye was adjusting to the dark now—the trick was not to look at the fire, keep the pupil open. Her hair must be dyed. More likely, it was a wig, for he could see long dark tresses, even against the deep blue of her gown.

"Your letter has caused me great concern, Averil. Shall we speak of this?"

"Yes, certainly." Kent stared at the hands lying so still. "I fear I have made a grave error."

A nod, the dark coils of hair moving ever so slightly.

"They have sent young Flattery off on a ship bound for Oceana."

"We thought they might."

"Yes, but it never occurred to us that the Duchess of Morland and her brother would go as well," he said, as gently as he could, as though relating the death of a loved one.

The hands pulled back into the darkness. He followed the white of the lace. She pressed her hands to her face, he thought.

"*Elorin,*" she said softly, with almost a hint of affection. "Tell me what you have learned, Averil."

Kent took a long breath. "I have . . . made mistakes, I fear." He paused again, the rehearsed speech suddenly forgotten. "Professor Dandish, I'm quite sure, was growing the blossom in his home. I had not realized it. I . . . I thought he was merely engaged to oversee the planting at the palace. Stupid of me. Once I became certain that he was not involved with our friends, I spoke to him. Told him just enough to alert him to the dangers, or so I thought. He wrote to Valary. At least, I predicted something correctly. Valary responded with just the right letter and the professor burned his Kingfoil almost immediately. I think no harm was done."

The hands returned to the lap where one scribed a small circle on the dark satin. "Certainly Dandish did not grow the plant for himself?"

"No. I think . . . I'm quite sure he grew it for the Duchess of Morland."

The hands found each other, and then became suddenly still. "The duel with Ipsword," she whispered.

"Yes. . . . And to think, she cites the Lady Chilton as her model." He paused, suddenly realizing that this might wound the woman sitting in the shadows. He forged on. "Flattery . . . that is Tristam Flattery, has become a great interest for them."

"They seem surer, now. Do you feel that as well?"

Kent nodded. Yes. They were more sure. "I still have fears that Eldrich did not, or could not, destroy all of his writings. Or perhaps Erasmus did manage to spirit something away, though how I can't imagine. They are more sure. As though they have a rough translation of some significant text. I can't believe they have gone beyond that, and none of them have talent, that is certain."

The hands moved into the darkness again, perhaps pressed to the heart. "And this young man. What do you make of him?"

"Well, I have met him." Kent thought a moment of the serious young man he had found wandering at the Society evening. "I think he is not one of them, though I'm sure they have hopes. He believes himself to be, like most of today's educated gentlemen, a man of reason. I sounded him quite thoroughly. He would laugh if we told him our fears. No, that is not true. He is far too polite to laugh, but he would certainly think us unbalanced or at least, irrational—which means he would react the same if he were approached by others. Despite this, I would say he is intelligent. Well educated, certainly, and not just as an empiricist. I'm told he speaks Entonne like a native, and knows something about art as well."

The head shook slightly.

"He is naive, and terribly so. Certainly completely unaware of what he is involved in. I would also say he is by nature a good man. Too trusting, and a little . . . romantic, I think."

"I did not think empiricists were romantic."

"No? Listen to them rhapsodize about the perfect world that reason will build. . . ." Kent poured himself more brandy.

"Do you think he is the one they are looking for?" Dread . . . she hid it well, with her flat tones, but still, Kent could hear it.

He turned his snifter slowly over the flame, watched the steam condense on the glass. "I fear that it is so. I waited far too long. I wrote you about the coin toss and the encounter with the ghost boy?"

The head nodded.

"And we can see now how his involvement has grown. Merton College. Dandish's prize student. Botany. Trevelyan's collection. Like a salmon nosing up a stream. Then he is called to the palace. Kingfoil." Kent stopped, dismayed for a second by his own catalog of "coincidences." "The night Sir Roderick brought him to the Society Trevelyan was there, if you can believe it. Another strike. And the Baron tried to warn him! Tried to warn Flattery! Everyone thinks him quite mad, fortunately, for you would not have believed what was said. And then there was this Entonne doctor, Varese, with his letters from Lucklow. You see how it goes? Tristam Flattery has no more awareness of what he is doing than the poor brute of a salmon, but he is in the stream. He senses the current and he is tracing it toward the source." Kent took his glass from the burner and cupped it in his hands. He found it too hot but held it all the same—penance. "I was a fool, Lady Chilton. I did not realize they had progressed so far."

"But you say he is intelligent, Averil. How long can it be before he will realize what occurs around him? Certainly even a man of reason cannot rationalize these things as coincidence forever."

"No," Kent admitted. "Even a reasonable man will be forced to see, eventually. What he will do when he realizes . . . I do not know. He will be in the company of the duchess when he finally wakens . . . the Duchess and whomever Palle has placed aboard. My fear is that Flattery will have performed the task needed of him . . . and then, even if he rejects the aims of the others, well, they can find another with talent—eventually. Tristam Flattery will not be necessary then."

"You are sure that it was not this very Tristam Flattery who found the book you say his uncle stole?"

"*Might* have stolen, Lady Chilton. Might have. One would have to meet the young man," Kent said, sure of this one thing at least. "Flattery would have to be the greatest actor in Avonel to put forth such a facade of sincerity—such genuineness. No. Tristam is what he seems, I am sure. Too thoughtful. Views himself as a man of the intellect, but his nature is broader than he realizes." Kent drank the hot brandy, coughing lightly from the fumes. "I have not told you of the bird?"

The hands opened.

"I have seen it myself now, and others have noted it on several occasions. A winter falcon, Lady Chilton."

"I think you know I have not studied ornithology."

"Excuse me. It is a large falcon that makes its natural home in the north, but it is much prized by falconers. Erasmus had such a bird, and now there is one that follows the nephew. Blood and flames, it is almost a familiar!"

The countess' reaction made Kent wonder if this was less significant than he had believed, in which case he had just looked the fool. She raised one hand to her mouth and seemed to consider.

"That is not necessarily a bad omen." The head shook. "It is difficult to say." A pause, then the flat voice again. "What will you do now?"

"Where to begin?" He fell silent though he felt he must speak to hide his fears, his growing panic. "We are not yet strong, Lady Chilton. We must move so slowly, like a man standing before a viper—we are invisible when still. A word to the wrong person and we are lost. I must be so very careful. I did not dare speak to young Flattery, even though I was so sure. . . ." *Was that my mistake?* Kent wondered. "I have made arrangements, though hurried and makeshift. I have also sent a message ahead to Farrow with a ship of war. We will wait and see what we hear."

"Farrow." The hands clenched into small fists.

"Oh, yes. As I have said, he is the salmon in the stream," Kent affirmed. "The hound on the scent."

The countess shook her head. A pure white finger raised. "It is like life, Averil. Do you see? Seeking only to live. Seeking to be born anew." The finger disappeared and the white lace sleeves appeared to hang loose, like a doll's. "Is there anything else I should know?" she asked, her voice even more devoid of expression, if that were possible.

"Dandish was not as careful as he thought. Several parties know of his planting."

"But it was destroyed?"

"Yes. But still, they know." Kent hesitated before he spoke again. "I am also beginning to believe that all of the activity of Entonne agents in Avonel is not due to the treaty presently under negotiation." There, it was said.

"Palle is a fool!" she spat out, her voice suddenly coming to life with anger.

"No," Kent responded softly. "He is no fool. Ignorant of what he has begun, yes. Obsessed with the 'Entonne threat.' But no fool." He looked into the flames in the hearth, forgetting that he had intended not to. "Curiosity. It is our nature. The search for knowledge is presently enshrined almost as a first principle for the men of reason. Though others have learned that some knowledge should never be sought."

"The past," she said, her voice quavering just a little, "it always haunts us."

They did not speak for some time. Kent noted that the storm still assailed the world outside, and he did not look forward to leaving the warmth of the fire.

"You have been very busy, Averil," the countess said. "I am always impressed that the most innocent seeming gentlemen should be so cunning."

Kent gave a short laugh. "But I have survived as an artist all of my life, Lady Chilton, and done rather well. There is no courtier half so cunning as an artist, I will tell you."

The countess laughed, and it was like some part of her youth emerging, unbidden. Kent had never forgotten that laugh. Even an echo of it cut into his heart like a lash.

How have we grown so old? he thought, and realized he had pressed a hand to his eyes.

"Averil? Are you well?"

He pulled his hand away and nodded.

"There is nothing more, then?"

He almost dropped his glass as he set it on the table. "Just this," he managed and reached into the pocket of his coat to remove a small leather bag. He worked free the knot and pulled out a neatly folded handkerchief. This he unfolded with some care, laying it open to reveal three small seeds, one half-decomposed. He leaned forward and held these out to the woman in the shadows, looking down at the floor as he did so, despite his true desires.

The square of linen was lifted from his hands, and he sat up. There in the shadow he could see the countess peering into the folds of the fabric. Kent could hear her breath coming in short little gasps. Unexpectedly, she leaned forward into the light, but her hair fell in such a way as to hide her face.

"I dug them from the boxes Dandish had used for his planting," Kent said, hiding his disappointment, he hoped.

She leaned back, her head resting against the chair. He could almost make out a profile—white skin against raven black hair. "There is so much we don't know." He saw the head roll back and forth. But then she forced herself upright, sitting with the seeds cradled in her hands. "I have taken a precaution, Averil, in case something untoward occurs. I have written out the little I know regarding these matters. Don't worry, it is well hidden. You will receive this document if. . . . Well, you understand. There is much at risk."

He nodded, almost raising his hands to stop this line of conversation, but instead he reached out and lifted his glass again. He peered down at the burning logs. For some moments they did not speak, and he became lost in the maze of questions that he pondered through virtually all his waking hours. For the briefest second, the idea of being left the countess' document thrilled him, but then his saner self took hold. No, no. Better to remain ignorant. Far better. And the countess . . . he could not bear the idea that she would be gone.

"I think you must have spent some considerable sum of money in this endeavor, Averil." The voice was expressionless again except that it had become soft.

The painter looked up and then quickly down again. He nodded.

"I have meant to say that I feel very strongly that I paid far too little for the last painting I purchased. It is a work of some considerable merit and gives me constant pleasure. You are too kind to your friends, Averil. Too generous. We take advantage of you. I absolutely must make amends. No. Do not protest. I will not hear it."

TWENTY

After two days at sea Tristam had adjusted to the constant motion of the ship and it was unusual for him to need to put out a steadying hand—something he took a little pride in. If he was to spend two years on this voyage, it would be best to adapt to the conditions as completely as possible.

The lieutenant, Mr. Osler, had allowed him to climb aloft, though Tristam had only gone as high as the lower yard—the "main top," this small platform was called—but even there the motion was much greater than on deck. Even so, Tristam had wanted to stay, high in the branches of this strange tree, with its massive trunk and tracery of supporting vines. The swaying of this tree in the wind was almost hypnotic and the feeling that he stared out over a vast, empty plain Tristam found strange and compelling.

Glancing down, he noticed the duchess shading her eyes, looking up at him. She waved and that smile appeared. Tristam raised a hand in return. He felt a pull, as though gravity tugged at him, but he resisted. *But it is inevitable,* he admitted. *I will go down. My resistance will crumble.*

He had spent most of a sleepless night mulling over the conversation with the Duchess of Morland. *"But you are not like him, Tristam. Not like him at all."* It had seemed such a genuine expression of concern. . . . And somehow Tristam felt that the duchess had believed what she said. Even her warning against trusting his emotions to her had seemed to come from the heart. A warning he knew he should heed.

The contradictions were too great, and so Tristam remained at the crosstrees, hoping the wind would eventually clear his mind enough that all contradictions would find resolution like the image in a glass as it was brought into focus.

One moment he found himself questioning his earlier cynicism about the duchess, and the next, some remembered incident would prove the feeling reasonable. The murder of Ipsword kept coming to mind, like a whispered warning. The viscount followed the orders of the duchess, or so Jaimy claimed, and Tristam thought it unlikely that his cousin was wrong. *Ipsword.* The name had taken on its own meaning, like an incident of history—a tragic incident. *Ipsword.*

All so confusing. Even the fresh sea wind did not clear his mind sufficiently that he could see his way through the maze of other people's motivations.

For several hours he stayed, sweeping the ocean with his glass, hoping to see whales or the low skimming albatross, trying to force his mind away from his problems—and from the duchess.

There was something purifying about sitting up on the crosstrees among the swelling sails, anointed by the wind. If it did not help him solve the mysteries surrounding this voyage, Tristam felt that at least he gained some peace of mind from the experience.

When hunger finally drove him back down to the deck, he felt a sense of inner calm, as though the machinations of men were short lived and of small import when compared to the timeless grandeur of the sea.

As he descended the companionway, Tristam was met by the duchess' maid who addressed him in Entonne, perhaps happy to hear her own language. The duchess, she said, had invited him to tea. His return to the real world was going to be abrupt.

Jacel was petite, red-blonde, and pretty in a day-to-day fashion—she did not possess the regal beauty of the duchess, and her movements all seemed small, controlled, fearful of offering offense—but there was some part of Tristam that appreciated her more for that. Jacel dimpled when she smiled, and Tristam found immediately that he would make small jests with her in an attempt to cause these dimples to appear. She had told Tristam that she suffered from the sickness of the sea and he thought she looked a little desolate—as though she dearly wished her mistress had not chosen to make this terrible voyage.

Tristam slipped into his cabin and put his Fromme glass away, dug out a neck cloth, and proceeded to the door of the great cabin. He found the duchess, wrapped in a heavy woolen shawl, playing a solitary card game. She looked up as Tristam came in and greeted him in the language of Doorn—a common practice of the Farr aristocracy: to speak a language not accessible to their servants.

"Do you know, Tristam, I have already read an entire novel since we set out. I fear now that I have not brought nearly enough books. I hope we shall be able to exchange . . . ? Stern and Osler, it turns out, are both readers as well, so we might hope their interests are not too . . . seamanlike."

"I have brought, almost exclusively, the reference books of my trade, Duchess, space being so limited, and have only a handful of other things. But if you want to read botany, ornithology, marine biology, geology, I have sufficient numbers of these texts to last this voyage and more."

The duchess laughed, transforming herself into a charming innocent girl. "I should not even have asked. But I will not make fun. In a few months even geology might seem fascinating."

Tea was offered, for the afternoon wore on, and Tristam took a seat at the table.

"Do you think we may speak privately like this?" the duchess asked, glancing up at the deck.

"Sailors travel, Duchess. Doorn is visited often. We should take no chances."

"Then move closer, Tristam, for I want to hear your thoughts."

For the first time that day Tristam reached out to steady himself, moving his chair so that it was near to the duchess, gripping the table as he did so. Her knee pressed against the side of his thigh, and when she did not immediately move away, Tristam felt his body respond to this closeness.

"I wanted to talk to you about Professor Dandish," she whispered. "I have thought much about him." She paused to stare directly into Tristam's eyes, as though she were gauging whether or not he could be trusted. He was not sure what she decided. "It seems to me, now, that the professor gave up too soon. Does that not seem true to you?"

Tristam felt his anger ignite, surprising him completely. Whatever his thoughts had been of the duchess over these past hours, his sympathy was suddenly erased. Why had she drawn poor Dandish into this?

She must believe me a terrible fool, he thought. This suggestion of intimacy was obviously designed to have him open his heart to her, to tell her the things he might have hidden in the past. After the genuineness of their discussion the previous night, this caused Tristam some pain. He made an effort to keep his voice neutral. "I am not sure how long Dandish was engaged in this inquiry, Duchess, but it is my belief that the professor knew his health was precarious and destroyed his study so that it would not be discovered."

"You think that's it, then?" Those searching eyes held his, causing the anger to soften a little but not erasing the pain.

He shrugged. "It seems likely."

"There is no chance that the professor solved the problem?"

"Nothing is impossible, Duchess."

"Perhaps your explanation makes sense, but there is just something . . . I cannot explain it, but it seems like the professor acted so rashly. He was not rash by nature, Tristam, or so I thought."

"Perhaps it was something else, then?" Tristam said it with difficulty, led on by his resentment.

"What do you mean?"

What had Dandish written? *"I am not quite the old fool the duchess takes me for."* Nor am I the young fool, he thought, *and she might as well know it.* "The destruction of the planting, Duchess, it took place immediately after the death of Baron Ipsword." He heard himself inhale as though strongly in need of air.

Her mouth lost all of its soft beauty. She turned away and nodded, as though saying, *yes, it was only a matter of time.*

He expected her to explode in sudden anger, or to plead ignorance of what he implied, but instead she spoke very softly.

"Tristam, it was never my intention that the baron would be harmed." She stopped, closing her eyes for a second. When she looked up again, a tear had streaked her cheek, like the ocean's spray on clear glass. "Julian . . ." she looked away, touching delicate fingers to the bridge of her nose for a second. "He swears it was not intentional. Others . . . others say differently, I realize. I was not there. But I never intended anything more than to have Ipsword leave poor Dandish alone. He tortured him, you know that. Dandish had no defense against this irrational hatred. Ipsword's attacks—merely jealousy—caused the professor terrible anguish. I did what you probably wished to do yourself." She formed a fist and beat time on the table to the next words. "I wanted Ipsword to leave the professor in peace. That was all. But Julian. . . ." Her voice caught as she said this, her fist opened and spread flat on the dark wood. "I swear, Tristam, that no such thing will happen again. I could not bear it." Again the duchess looked away, turning in her chair to stare out the transom windows. "Some need protectors," she said so quietly that Tristam was not sure he had heard correctly.

❦   ❦   ❦

Standing at the rail, watching the sun set, Tristam felt the cold of the sea air. The master stood at the opposite rail, waiting with his sextant to shoot the first stars to appear—something that normally would have interested Tristam. But not this evening. Even the sunset, which was spectacular, barely drew his attention.

A litany of questions repeated themselves over and over, all to do with the true nature of the Duchess of Morland and her intentions—and with his own nature as well. Was it true that the viscount had not followed her instructions? Somehow Tristam could not imagine the duchess issuing an order to have a man murdered. She was not a criminal. Tristam thought of the viscount and felt a shiver course through him. He seemed like the most amiable of men. . . .

I am being buffeted about like a feather on the winds, Tristam thought. He wondered if his character really did differ fundamentally from his father's? He wondered if it was possible for someone to be coldly self-interested, manipulative in the extreme, and still have a heart? Human beings seemed capable of embracing such contradictions.

TWENTY-ONE

A gale found them on the fifth day beyond sight of land. It was not a bad gale as such things went, or so the sailors said, but it was enough to lay the green hands and passengers low with the sickness of the sea and keep them in a state of constant fear. Even Tristam suffered, though he managed to eat and retain the bit of food he forced down.

On the second day of foul weather he tumbled out of his hammock and struggled into the oilskins Jack Beacham had urged him to purchase. Although Tristam had found the sounds of the gale frightening from the comparative protection of his swinging hammock—the thunder of waves reverberating through the hull with such force that he was almost certain the ship would not stand it—he was truly alarmed when he made his way up through the hatch. The sounds of the seas pounding the hull were not as pronounced, but the wind in the rigging produced a chorus of screaming and wailing that he realized had been much muffled below. It was quite unnerving. And the seas appeared truly monstrous.

The deck was wet and slick from spray and the crests that broke over the forward quarter. They foamed down the lee deck and filled the scuppers so the bulwark looked to be a short wall standing in the midst of a chaotic sea. Tristam braced his feet against the hatch cover and grasped the lifeline that had been rigged at the onset of bad weather.

The rain had abated, but clouds flew low overhead, their gray presence threatening the deluge. Topsails whipped and cracked each time the ship labored to the top of a green crest and the wind howled in the rigging, changing pitch with the gusts: a most disconcerting chorus.

The *Swallow* was "lying to," which Beacham had explained meant riding to reefed topsails, and she made no headway, or movement forward, but only held her own against the head winds, making half a knot of leeway—the term used to describe the ship's sliding to one side. Tristam watched the spectacle for a long while, until the little ship's rise to every wave began to inspire a semblance of confidence. Once he felt his fear begin to subside, the naturalist in him began to observe, for he had only experienced such weather upon the land. Each time the ship rose and shook off the water that had crashed aboard, Tristam felt a little triumphant. On top of each wave he gazed down the long, reptilian spine of the crest, thinking how much it looked like a living thing. And then it passed beneath, shrugging the ship aside, the crests tumbling and blowing off in white spume.

"Your first gale at sea, Mr. Flattery?" a voice shouted above the tumult. Tristam turned to find Captain Stern calling out from down the quarterdeck. Tristam nodded and forced a smile. He made his way, hand over hand, along the lifeline and joined the captain at the binnacle. Behind him two sailors tended the helm, one steering and one standing by to assist.

The captain grinned at Tristam. "We've weathered the worst of it. I think we will be under way again before dark. The wind is abating. Can you feel it?"

Tristam could not, but he held up a hand as he'd seen sailors do and nodded to the captain, hoping he did not look completely foolish.

"Already it's veered a point or more. Not much of a gale, really, just enough to ruin our two days' run and test the green hands. You seem to be recovering quickly? Have your sea legs now, eh?"

Tristam nodded, hoping this was true.

"You might look in on Doctor Llewellyn, Mr. Flattery. The poor man has become the physician who can't cure himself. Mr. Taine has been trying to tend him, but he has two seamen who slid across the deck and have real injuries. Nearly lost them over the side." The captain shook his head, alarmed even at the idea.

"I'll see to him immediately."

Tristam climbed back down the companionway and into the dim bowels of the ship, where all the hatches had been closed against the weather. Below it was more difficult to keep one's balance, for there was no horizon to fix on, and Tristam was relieved to find that his nausea did not return immediately.

Passing forward through the ship, Tristam knocked at the door to the doctor's cabin. When there was no response, he became alarmed and tried the door, which was not locked.

"Doctor Llewellyn?" The cabin seemed even darker and more airless than the rest of the ship. Something shifted in the shadows.

"Mr. Taine?" came a hoarse whisper.

"It is Tristam Flattery, Doctor. The captain asked me to inquire after your health."

"Ah, Mr. Flattery," the doctor rasped. "I am as wretched as a man can be. The ship still swims?"

"Sir?" Tristam realized suddenly what the doctor meant. "Oh, yes. The gale is blowing itself out and the ship is riding like a duck. Captain Stern says we shall make sail before sunset."

"Thank Farrelle for that," the man said with real feeling. "How fares the duchess?"

"I don't know, Doctor; I have only just found my sea legs, as they say. Shall I look in for you?"

"Would you, Mr. Flattery? I have been poor help."

"I shall be glad to." Tristam closed the door and left the man to his misery. The young naturalist found himself smirking. There was, Tristam had to admit, some satisfaction in seeing a man convinced of his own superiority reduced to a condition of utter humility. And the good doctor was thanking *Farrelle!* Tristam laughed aloud. Some "man of reason."

In the poor light Tristam found the door to the great cabin and knocked.

"Yes?" came the voice of the duchess. It did not seem to be greatly affected by the gale.

"It is Tristam, Duchess."

"Do come in," the woman called over the sounds of the wind and sea.

Tristam pushed the door open and found the duchess sitting on a low stool wedged into a leeward corner of the cabin. She held a steaming cup in her hands and leaned over a berth rigged with a lee board. It appeared that the duchess wore her warmest possible clothing and was wrapped as well in several woolen blankets. The effect was incongruous, for she looked like a wealthy beggar, a vagabond duchess, if such a thing were possible. On the berth beside her lay a motionless form, apparently much reduced by the ravages of her condition. Poor Jacel.

"I am glad to see that at least one landsman has survived," she said her voice hale and spirit apparently as strong as ever.

"I seem to have found my sea legs," Tristam said. There was something irresistible about the sailors' language to Tristam and he used it whenever opportunity presented itself. "The Duchess is well?"

"Yes ... though I'm supposed to be a delicate flower, Tristam, in truth, I have the constitution of a mule. Poor Jacel has not done nearly so well." She turned to the inert form and said in Entonne, "Have you, my pet?" There was no response.

The duchess sipped from the cup. "I am grateful to cook who brought me this broth. I would be a block of ice without it—almost am, in fact. I never thought such wretched fare could be so welcome." She sniffed the cup and wrinkled up her perfect nose. "I didn't realize that they poisoned the crew thrice daily. It is a miracle they survive."

Tristam laughed, half from mere relief.

At that moment the maid rolled toward the edge of the bed and the duchess deftly scooped up a bucket.

Tristam backed from the room at a nod from the duchess but not before he had glimpsed the strangest of sights: the Duchess of Morland holding a bucket into which her maid was terribly ill. And odder yet, the duchess seemed amused by this as well.

Tristam went looking for his mentor in the ways of the sea, Jack Beacham, but when he could not find the boy in the 'tweendecks mess or the midshipmen's berth, Tristam climbed out onto the deck once more. He was not sure, but the winds seemed to be falling— and the seas, though still large, did not break so regularly.

Hobbes stood at the rail, a glass trained out to sea on the starboard quarter. Stern stood at his side, gazing in the same direction.

"The *Raven,* I would say, Captain."

Stern nodded. "Nash has had her this past year. Their destination will be the same as ours, though look how they come! See how they are pushing their ship!"

Tristam moved a little closer. He scanned the waves off in the direction which the officers stared. There did seem to be a small dot of white that did not appear and disappear the way the crests did.

"Ah, Mr. Flattery," Stern said, noticing Tristam. "Here is a sight to chill your heart. Fortunately, she is one of ours." He handed Tristam a well-used field glass. "There. A ship of war," he said, his voice filled with admiration. "Now there's beauty for you!"

Tristam took the heavy naval glass and, after a moment, found the ship—appreciating all the more his gift from Dandish. The black hull was throwing spray as she pounded into each sea. After Stern's words Tristam did find the sight ominous. "I am glad she is ours, Captain Stern."

"And for good reason, Mr. Flattery. The *Raven* would make short work of our little *Swallow.* But not to worry, even if we are wrong and she is not the *Raven,* there are no unfriendly ships in these waters." The captain took a watch from his pocket. "She will overhaul us before dark, Mr. Hobbes. Have the signal man stand by."

Tristam stayed at the rail for some time watching the great ship of war as she bowled along in a headlong rush over the dark ocean. Poor undermanned, under-canvased *Swallow* must lay to in such conditions, Tristam thought, and uncomfortable she was, too, but the great frigate, he could see, had reefs only in her top gallants, though her royal masts had been housed or sent down, Tristam could not tell which.

Under the oppressive gray of the passing gale, the black ship came abreast, though she stood off a quarter mile. *Raven* only luffed her sail a bit, slowing like a great horse, rolling its bit and dancing in place. A hoist of signals appeared, causing Stern and his officers some consternation, Tristam thought, though he could not hear what was being said. This was navy business and not for the landsman to know.

Stern had his signal man answer, and then the *Raven* dipped her ensign, trimmed sail, and gathered way again. In only a few moments she was throwing spray thirty yards off her bow. Tristam watched her go, her great galleried stern bobbing over the waves.

It was time, too, for *Swallow* to be off. Reefs were being shaken out of the topsails by the topmen and upper staysails were being set. Tristam watched the procedure, or "evolution" as it was called, as the men fought the wet canvas and the motion of the ship. It took a long hour, for the *Swallow*'s crew was small compared to a ship of war, and the master did not call all hands unless it was truly necessary, preferring to let the watch below have their rest.

It was dusk when the Jacks scrambled down the ratlines and most disappeared below for their supper, only a few remaining on deck to coil lines and to stand ready to do the deck officer's bidding. Tristam noticed the captain had gone below, to his own meal, no doubt, in the tiny wardroom that served the senior officers.

Overhead the cloud cover was finally breaking and there would be a quarter-moon that night, or so Tristam estimated. He moved to the rail and peered out into the growing darkness, certain he had seen the shape of an albatross sweep by close above the rolling sea. For some time Tristam stood staring out into the dark on an almost deserted deck. It was eerie, hearing the great sweep of the seas left by the passing gale, feeling their power even as it diminished. Again Tristam had that sense of loneliness in the face of the great ocean's strength, which made him think of Kent.

Suddenly there was a fluttering before him and he started back, thinking a piece of the rigging had torn free. But it was not so; a white bird hovered before Tristam, beating the air with its wings, and even in the darkness he was sure it was a falcon.

"Begone!" Tristam said, waving his hands. *We are hundreds and hundreds of miles from any shore!* But the falcon would not go. It hovered before him, reaching with its talons as though expecting him to hold out a falconer's glove. Tristam pulled a belaying pin from a pinrail and thrust it at the bird. "Begone!" he exclaimed. But the bird would do nothing of the sort. It grasped the pin and Tristam found himself supporting the bird as it tried to adjust to the ship's motion.

A noise behind caused Tristam to turn, and there in the main hatch stood a Jack, eyes wide. He made a warding sign and hurried below. Tristam pushed the belaying pin out into the darkness, letting it fall into the sea, and the bird took to wing and disappeared.

"Blood and flames!" Tristam whispered. "We are hundreds of miles out to sea. This isn't possible."

❦   ❦   ❦

Tristam had slept fitfully, not uncommon for him, his dreams disturbing but only half-remembered—gone entirely by morning. The motion of the ship had eased considerably during the night and was very near to normal now. There was also sun, Tristam could tell by the light in his tiny port, even though he had hung a cloth over it for privacy. Footsteps descended the companionway ladder, not far outside the door of Tristam's cabin. These footsteps came from leather shoes, so this was a midshipman or officer—not a barefoot Jack—and the owner of these shoes was in a considerable hurry. Jack Beacham or midshipman Chilsey.

A knock sounded on Tristam's door.

"Yes?"

"It is Jack Beacham, Mr. Flattery," an anxious voice said. "I think you should come on deck, sir."

Tristam was not sure what this was about, but he rolled out of his hammock immediately. "I'll be along directly."

Tristam threw his clothes on and thumped up the ladder to the deck. Beacham waited at the stairs descending into the ship's waist. There was a gathering at the mainmast where Tristam could see the tall gray form of the ship's master standing out among the others.

As he approached, Tristam realized there was something on the mast that had drawn everyone's attention. His first thought was that it was a bird or something else of interest to an empiricist, but then the unnatural silence struck him. When the Jacks saw him, they all stepped back, their eyes fixed on him in a manner that was not friendly.

"Do you recognize this, Mr. Flattery?" Hobbes asked, pointing to an opened book pinned to the mast by a knife driven through its spine—like a dead butterfly tacked to a board. It even fluttered a bit in the breeze.

Tristam found himself unable to answer but managed to nod, adding to the silence.

"Take it down, Mr. Hobbes," came the captain's voice. "May I speak with you, please, Mr. Flattery?"

❧   ❧   ❧

"I realize it is difficult to take such things seriously, Mr. Flattery, but it is one of the central superstitions of the Jacks." Stern looked a little ill, Tristam thought.

"To drive a knife into the mast will bring winds, usually a full storm—a hurricane, as you call it on land. But it is believed that men caught for weeks in the doldrums have done it out of desperation: usually with calamitous results. That is the root of it. But to take something that belongs to a man and spike it to the mast with a knife is to bring calamity upon the man himself."

Stern sat at the table in the small wardroom the officers used for their meals. Tristam was not sure if the captain was this subdued because he was embarrassed by the actions of his own crew or whether this ominous calm had some other cause. To the captain's right stood Mr. Osler. The officer's manner gave Tristam his only hint. Osler was almost rigidly still, spoke only when addressed, and then quietly and with deference. Tristam found that he was unconsciously imitating the lieutenant's manner—like two truant school boys.

"Now tell me, Mr. Flattery: we are seven hundred and fifty nautical miles from land. *Fifty leagues.*" Stern paused looking up into Tristam's face. "Is it possible that this hawk could fly so far?"

Tristam suppressed the response that came first to mind. ("How else do you think it came there, Captain? Magic?") The truth was that though land birds were sometimes seen far from land—blown out to sea by storms, some thought—Tristam knew of no sighting of a large powerful hawk so far out to sea.

"I don't know, Captain Stern," Tristam offered in a small voice. "It seems unlikely but . . ."

"How do you explain it, then?" Stern said, not so quietly, his voice clearly accusatory—an attitude that the naturalist did not like.

"I cannot, sir, though I think it was a trained falcon, for it seemed to want me to give it my wrist upon which to land."

"Captain Stern?" The physician's face appeared in the open doorway. "If I may, sir?" Llewellyn was still pale and weak but showed signs of returning to his normal manner.

Stern glanced up at Osler quickly, but the young officer did not meet his captain's eyes. Llewellyn should not have been interrupting. But then Stern shrugged.

"Yes, Doctor?"

"As a naturalist myself, I thought I could shed some light on this matter." Llewellyn pushed the door open and entered, taking a chair, though it was not offered. Obviously, the man had been listening from beyond the door. "It would seem likely that this was a falconer's bird, escaped, no doubt, from a passing ship. Coming upon the *Swallow,* it tried to land. In its exhaustion and confusion at finding itself at sea, the bird took to the first man it saw, as it would to its own master. I do not doubt that the bird would have responded thus to myself, or to yourself, sir, had we been the first it saw. There can be no other explanation."

The captain looked at his lieutenant, who nodded. "Well, that does make some sense," he conceded. "Though it will take more than a cogent argument to convince the Jacks, damn their superstitious ways!"

The captain fixed Tristam with the look he no doubt used to reduce sailors to the consistency of jellyfish. "Had I known you were the heir of Erasmus Flattery, I tell you honestly, I would have thought twice before having you aboard."

Tristam felt his timidity passing and his own anger beginning to stir. "I am his heir, Captain, but I hardly knew the man. I am not his direct descendant, nor am I his protegé in any way. I am almost as closely related to Admiral Flattery who had control of the Blue Squadron at Cape Locke." This was not strictly true, but Tristam was grasping at anything that might keep him afloat.

The captain considered this for a moment, tugging at his close-trimmed beard with long fingers. His voice softened just perceptibly. "Well, no doubt what you say is true, Mr. Flattery. And I believe none of this mage business myself, mind you. It is only the poor ignorant men before the mast who I am in consideration of. Foolish and ignorant though they be, they are necessary to the success of this voyage and if the Jacks think you are the heir of a necromancer . . . well, they are a superstitious lot and there's no telling what they might do."

"Do you mean that Mr. Flattery might be in danger, Captain Stern?" the doctor was clearly shocked.

"Oh, now, Doctor Llewellyn, I would not say that. No indeed. But their beliefs and fears will affect their service. I have seen it before. There will be no violence against an individual on a ship that I command, you can be sure of that. But the Jacks may not make Mr, Flattery welcome, and that is a hard thing when you are on a small vessel for two years."

The physician straightened in his chair. "Well, the lack of understanding; nay, the jealousy of the uneducated is not something we are all strangers to, Captain. Be of stout heart, Mr. Flattery, the approbation of the ignorant is a worthless coin, I can tell you."

Tristam did not know how to respond. He felt like he was on trial here, when he had done absolutely nothing wrong. He had known the navy men were superstitious, but he did not imagine it could be taken to such absurd lengths.

The captain turned to his senior officer. "We will have to try to control the damage that this incident has caused. Fother the hole, as it were. Mr. Osler, you will spread the word that this was a domesticated hawk—a falconer's bird escaped from a passing ship—that happened to find Mr. Flattery on deck when it looked for a place to light. Speak to Mr. Hobbes . . . you know how the Jacks hang upon his every word. If he were to say he once saw such a thing when he sailed with Gregory . . . well, the men would be touching Mr. Flattery for luck. Though I don't imagine Hobbes would agree to lie. Still, if he does not give credence to this mage business, it will help immeasurably." The captain turned back to Tristam and tried to smile reassuringly. "Don't be too concerned, Mr. Flattery. I'm sure this will pass. Just carry on as though nothing has happened. It is always the best course."

The naturalist nodded. "Yes, sir," he said and went out of the wardroom toward the companionway, feeling as though he had just been before the headmaster—something he thought was well past in his life.

Tristam emerged on deck into bright sunlight. There was no sign of the gale that had halted their progress, and *Swallow* was bowling along with a fair wind over a blue sea. Jack Beacham was loitering by the rail, and when he saw Tristam, he crossed over to the naturalist immediately.

The young man examined Tristam's face as though looking for damage. "A word, Mr. Flattery," Beacham said, and then cast a worried look along the deck. "A Jack named Kreel. A big man with a scar over his right eye. Dark hair and complexion. It would be wise to stay clear of him, sir." Beacham broke into a sudden smile as though they shared a jest. "Pleasures of the day to you, Mr. Flattery." And the lad was gone.

Tristam did not know the code of the sailors, but he was quite sure that Jack Beacham had just breached it—or perhaps officers in training stayed aloof from such things.

Tristam had this sudden impulse to go talk sense to the Jacks—even to this man Kreel. But he knew that Captain Stern had believed the explanation of the tame falcon because it fit into his beliefs. The Jacks would believe their own explanation—that Tristam was somehow the spawn of a mage—because it fit theirs. Though what they thought this meant, other than bad luck, Tristam was not sure.

Sweeping his gaze the length of the ship, Tristam found the duchess perched on a bench the carpenter had built so that the two women could sit in relative comfort on deck, with their backs to the rail. She clutched a book in her hands and stared up, shading her eyes with a gloved hand.

Needing the company of someone who did not think him supernatural, Tristam crossed the deck to the duchess.

"Tristam! The pleasures of the day to you." She

smiled and Tristam noticed that the sun had given her face a very appealing blush.

"And to the Duchess. It is a fine day."

"Indeed, it is." She pulled her skirt closer and motioned for Tristam to take a seat beside her.

"What is it you read?" Tristam asked, for he could not bring himself to broach the subject that concerned him. He realized then that he missed having a true friend—someone like Jaimy—in whom he could confide.

She held up a clothbound book so that he might read the title. It was Bedwell's *A Young Seaman's Manual.* "I'm quite tired of not understanding the half—nay, far more than half—of what is spoken aboard this ship. I have set out to learn my ropes, as they say. I thought it would pass the time as well."

Tristam found himself smiling at the idea of the Duchess of Morland learning to speak like a sailor.

"You needn't look so amused, Tristam, I am just as capable of learning such things as any half-educated farmer's son. Now," she waved the book at the ship, "perhaps you can clarify a few matters for me, since you have become such a seaman yourself. What area, precisely, is referred to by the word 'focs'le'? I hear it spoken of constantly, yet I cannot find reference to it in this little book."

"The seamen say, 'focs'le', Duchess, but it is properly written 'forecastle.' No doubt you have found it spelled so in your book."

"Ah, that is the way of it."

"There are a number of terms compressed in this same manner." Tristam pointed to the rigging. "These lines the Jacks use to climb aloft . . ."

"The ratlines."

"Precisely. They are referred to as 'ratl'nes.' Just as the word inscribed as 'gunwale' is pronounced 'gunnel.' 'Boatswain' is said 'bosun.' 'Studdingsails' are 'stuns'les.' "

"I begin to see." The duchess waved the book again.

"And this mast—the small one at the back—it is the mizzen?"

"It is, indeed, though one should properly say 'aft.' "

"Aft it is. The large one in the center is, quite logically, the main mast, and the smallish one on the forecastle," she pronounced the word correctly, "is the foremast?"

"Correct in every detail."

"Now perhaps you can help with this cloud of sails. There seem to be so many . . ."

All of Tristam's reservations about the duchess disappeared in the next hour, as they tended to do in her presence—when she was not obviously manipulating him to some end. Tristam realized that she had sensed how alienated the incident with the Jacks had left him feeling and she focused all of her charm and wit in an effort to combat this. It was, Tristam thought, like finding oneself suddenly in a shaft of warm sunlight after the cold and rain. His mind was taken completely away from recent troubles and Tristam found himself actually able to laugh.

He was also impressed with the pace of her learning and realized that in no time she would be able to talk ships and sail in a manner which would no doubt set all the officers' hearts aquiver.

The watch changed, and the seaman who came to the wheel nodded graciously to the duchess but conspicuously ignored Tristam.

The men detailed to stream the log acted in the same manner.

The duchess touched Tristam's arm. "This foolishness about your uncle has become tiresome, has it not? Do these Jacks think you will turn them into toads?"

Tristam shook his head. "I do not understand it myself. I wish that I could perform magic. I would live a different life, that is certain.

"Well," the duchess said very quietly, "I have often wondered if you once took on the appearance of an Entonne musician?"

The change in Tristam's face must have been extreme, for the duchess patted his hand. "I jest, dear Tristam. I try to cheer you. It was dark, everyone had consumed too much of the Erasmus Grape. . . ." She looked at him slyly. "Do such things often happen when you drink the Erasmus Grape?"

"Duchess, I am at your mercy in this, as you well know. I—I do not know how to make amends for what occurred. Tell me what you would have me do and I will gladly do it."

"Such an offer, Mr. Flattery! I must consider this seriously. Perhaps . . . well, no. Let me think a while."

She was, Tristam knew, taking the greatest pleasure from his discomfiture.

The duchess' attention was drawn away. "Tell me, when they heave the log; that is to tell the depth of the sea?"

The change of subject was abrupt, and Tristam almost shook his head to get his wits clear. "They 'stream' the log, I believe, and 'heave' or 'swing' the lead. The log is a device to measure the ship's speed through the water, something that must be known for accurate navigation. They stream the log aft—it is a device that will stay more or less still in the water— and they count the number of knots on the streaming line that pass in a measured period of time. Thus the nautical term 'knots.' We are making five knots.

"The lead, or lead line, is a weight on a graduated line that is lowered to measure the depth to the bottom. Beacham let me heave it once in the harbor of Avonel. I was surprised to find that one can really feel when it contacts the earth. There could be no mistake.

"The sailors sometimes put tallow into a depression in the bottom of the lead and material from the sea bottom will stick to this and indicate something about the nature of the ocean floor. Quite ingenious."

"I see. Stream the log, heave the lead."

Hobbes, the ship's master, came up then, speaking to them kindly and jesting with Tristam in a way that would indicate friendship between them. Tristam knew the old sailor was doing it at the order of his captain, but, still, he felt tremendously grateful, for even the man at the wheel nodded to him when the master had gone off to his duties.

The duchess decided she had been too long in the sun and excused herself, and Tristam went below to his closet, suddenly afraid that a falcon would appear, as impossible as that was so far out to sea.

🐦   🐦   🐦

They were seven days to their next landfall, the island of Farrow. The place where Tristam owned a vineyard. During that week Tristam tried not to constantly scan the skies for white birds, but lost himself in his duties. He dragged a net behind, four times a day, and spent hours examining what was caught under his magnification instrument—plankton, largely. Sometimes the physician would come to look into Tristam's instrument and discuss what had been found, and sometimes Beacham or the duchess would drop in to see what had been caught in his net. The microscopic world was fascinating to most, Tristam found, and even those with no previous interest in natural history, such as the cook and boatswain, took their turn peering into the lens. Jack Beacham was by to peer into the instrument so often that he was almost an annoyance, though he was too good-natured to be truly a bother.

All the while Tristam kept careful journals of what he saw, of weather and sea conditions, birds and sea life. The master and his mate used a *deep line,* a lead line used for measuring the ocean depth, and carried a set of measurements across an area of sea that had not formerly been investigated. Tristam examined every sample they brought up from the bottom and was rewarded with two species of *Onuphis* he was sure had not been previously recorded, and at unheard of depths—which made Tristam wonder if they were not some other genus that displayed similar characteristics. The complexities of taxonomy aside, the problem of finding an appropriate name for his first discovered species was rather pleasant. He would have liked to name a new species for the duchess, but a sea worm did not seem appropriate.

He spent some time each day with the duchess, often talking about natural history, for she had such a lively mind she seemed interested in everything. Tristam spent even more time than usual wondering about her own feeling for him, but as life aboard ship offered them little privacy, there were no awkward situations as a result.

The duchess was always kindness itself to him, but she also treated him like a favorite younger cousin, not a potential suitor. But just when Tristam convinced himself that her feelings to him were purely innocent in nature, she would do something to set him wondering—lay her hand on his arm in a most familiar manner and hold his eye just a little longer than was proper. One night, as he left her company, she leaned against him so that he felt the swell of her breast, and then she kissed him tenderly on the corner of his mouth. Of course, aboard ship people often lost their balance, but Tristam did not think that was the explanation. At lease he preferred not to think that.

During those days Tristam seemed to swing between feelings of joy and utter desolation depending on what occurred between him and the duchess—or it might have been more accurate to say, according to his current interpretation of what occurred between them.

On the morning of the sixteenth day at sea they raised the island of Farrow. It floated on the horizon under a pile of white cloud, as islands often do: two graceful purple hills rising out of the blue sea.

TWENTY-TWO

As the *Swallow* drew closer to Farrow, Tristam realized that not all the cloud hanging over the island was composed of water vapor. Some of it was certainly smoke.

"I have not seen that in twenty years," Stern said as he lowered his glass.

Tristam kept his own instrument trained on the lip of the volcano. There was smoke, to be sure, but very little.

"Mount Forwood has done this off and on since the discovery," the captain mused, "I can't think why it would stop now."

"Sail, Mr. Osler! Two points off the larboard bow," came a cry from aloft.

Tristam swept the area off to larboard.

"The mail ship, sir," the lookout called down.

There was a general moan among the crew and officers alike.

"That is bad luck," Stern said. "It will be two weeks before our letters go off now."

"Shall we try to signal them, Captain?" Hobbes stood shading his eyes and looking off at the distant ship. Tristam got the impression the old mariner did not need a glass to see so little distance; his eyes were not like those of mere humans.

The captain considered for a moment, perhaps measuring the distance. "They cannot have seen us, or they would heave to and take our mail. Try a gun to larboard with a flasher. Have the signal man stand by if that draws any attention."

Tristam watched as one of the bronze three-pounders

was uncovered, primed, and run out for firing. The speed and precision Tristam expected did not occur and he realized that this was not a ship of war which exercised her guns several times a week. It was the first time a gun had been unhoused since they had set sail.

"There shall be a prodigious cloud of smoke, Duchess," Stern said, "and an alarming crash. Would you prefer to go below?"

The duchess tore her eyes from the preparations, which she had been following as raptly as the cabin boys. "I have heard so much about the skills of the navy's gunners, Captain, and this terrible invention of Lord Skye. Why, I would not miss it for the world."

A moment later the air exploded in the most almighty crash, and the ship was enveloped in a thick, choking smoke. The breeze took this cloud off to leeward and amidst the coughing Tristam heard the lookout call down.

"She's holding her course, Captain."

Stern nodded. "Stand in to the harbor, Mr. Hobbes."

A fair wind and a slack tide welcomed the *Swallow* into the anchorage. Stern wanted to put on a display of seamanship for the other ships and those watching from shore. He intended to enter the harbor under full sail. *"We may be an undermanned survey vessel,"* he had said, *"but that doesn't mean we don't know our business. Call all hands."*

The boatswain's pipe shrilled and the sound of feet pounding the deck as men took their stations reverberated through the hull like a beaten drum. Almost every able-bodied man in the crew was given a place and Tristam volunteered to haul with those squaring the fore topgallant yard.

"Clap on to the bitter end, Mr. Flattery," Beacham instructed, his color higher than usual. "We'll show these fancy frigate men that we know what we're about."

A silence fell then and Tristam could tell that every man was anxious that he not let down his mates and embarrass captain and ship. Looking along the deck, Tristam could hardly believe his eyes, but there, on the foredeck, was Viscount Elsworth, stripped to shirt and breeches and hardly looking out of place among the huge forecastlemen.

Garvey, the master's mate, took the wheel, for he was acknowledged to be the most able helmsman aboard, and the captain stood by speaking quietly to his officers. As the ship passed between the two stone towers that guarded the harbor entrance, the ship's number was run up and the identifying codes were sent aloft as well. The flag dipped above the ramparts and four guns were fired to acknowledge a friendly ship.

The breeze was affected by the land formations, and suddenly the *Swallow* surged forward across the flat water of the bay. The staysails came down at a quiet order, but the ship slowed only marginally.

"We do seem to be moving rather fast," Tristam ventured, trying to sound calm.

Beacham put a finger to his lips and then must have realized that Tristam was exempt from normal ship's discipline—maintaining silence during evolutions was expected. "We'll round up into the wind and back the topsails." Beacham whispered. "You'll be surprised how quickly she will lose way."

The ship continued her headlong rush into the harbor, passing the stern of an anchored ship, which gave the impression of even greater speed. Tristam could not count the anchored ships, but there seemed a good number for such a small bay, though he kept his peace on this point, not wanting to get Beacham into trouble. The ripple of the *Swallow* passing through the water and the Jack standing in the chains heaving the lead and calling the depths were all that was heard.

The master's mate put the helm over at an order from the lieutenant, and Tristam missed the rest of the maneuver for Beacham whispered, "Haul away, brightly." And Tristam put his weight into the work, feeling the coarse hemp, pulled tight, resist their efforts, but then give way a little each time they heaved.

When the yard was squared, Tristam jumped to another line, but the Jacks did not make room for him there and Tristam was left standing, realizing that the foolishness of the Jacks was not going to pass as quickly as he hoped.

"Let go stock and fluke," someone called and then Tristam heard the slow rattle of chain running out as the ship settled back onto her anchor. Tristam stepped clear of the Jacks working. Those around him seemed to feel some euphoria at their success and their safe arrival, but Tristam didn't feel part of this.

"Make the ship secure, Lieutenant." The captain's voice was quiet and calm. "Mr. Hobbes . . . hoist out the cutter. A tot for the men should be in order, Mr. Osler."

"The island of Farrow," the duchess said at Tristam's elbow. "You have not visited here before either?"

Tristam shook his head, his eye drawn to the shore. Although the island of Farrow consisted of two volcanoes thrusting up from the sea, they were very ancient volcanoes. Layel had written a monograph on the geology of the island, and Tristam remembered that the last eruption had certainly not been in the present millennium. From the harbor only one of the two cones could be seen, Mount Forwood, sloping gently down to a flatter plain a hundred feet above the sea, and then plunging more steeply to the shore.

The island was green and fertile with a climate that many thought ideal. A warm ocean current kept the winters at bay and the almost constant breeze ensured that summers were never unbearably hot. For much of the year there was sun, though rain fell in quantities enough to sustain a productive agriculture. The southeastern slopes of both cones were given to vineyards, as these were protected from the westerly winds, and it was upon this crop that the people depended for most of their livelihood.

Terra-cotta roofs dotted the open green landscape and the roads and hedges and fields all seemed miniature versions of the real articles, made to the scale of the island.

"It is charming!" the duchess said suddenly. "I expect the people to be the size of children, and draft horses the size of ponies." She laughed.

Stern turned from saluting an officer on another ship. "We must go ashore and pay our respects to the governor. I'm sure the worthy gentleman will wish to make your acquaintance, Duchess, and Lord Elsworth's as well."

"I shall be ready in a trice," she said cheerfully.

"And, Mr. Flattery, you are a landowner here, I collect?"

"That is so, though I have never seen my vineyard." He thought of his small home in Locfal. "It might be a sad affair, I fear."

"Never mind, sir. You must come along as well. Here you will not be looked upon askance, for the name of Flattery is well loved on this island. The Erasmus Grape has greatly increased the fortunes of the islanders."

❦   ❦   ❦

In the end Doctor Llewellyn joined the shore party also, making the cutter a crowded vessel. The coxswain and six oarsmen dressed alike in white trousers and blue jackets and, with their varnished straw hats bearing the ship's name, Tristam thought they must make a very nautical sight crossing the harbor—the captain sitting in the stern, the ship's guests in the bow. The day was warm and the contrast with the temperatures they had experienced at sea—even five minutes out of the harbor—was great.

I will have to record some temperatures here and as we sail off, Tristam thought.

Rather than coming to the quay or to a dock, the boat fetched up on a section of pebble beach, where the men disembarked, and the cutter was shifted up onto the land so that the viscount and captain could assist the duchess ashore.

"My, what is this?" she said as she found her feet. "The island is swaying as much as the *Swallow*. It must have slipped its mooring, Captain."

Stern laughed. "The feeling will pass directly, Duchess. One must adjust to the movement of the ship and then, once that is accomplished, to the stillness of the land again. But it does not make a friendly port less welcome, I find."

They walked the few paces up the beach and were met by the governor and his party.

Sir Stedman Galton had been the governor of Farrow for twenty years or more and was almost as much a Farrower as those born to the island. Most in the King's service felt the small island to be a posting on the edge of nowhere—and leading to the same place in the King's service—but it seemed to suit Galton. And the islanders were happy to have him stay. He was a fair man and known to promote their interests well.

"The pleasures of the day to you, Lord Governor," Stern said warmly. "It has been too long. It is my great pleasure to present the Duchess of Morland."

Introductions were made, and the governor's delight at the coming of such company was obvious. He was perhaps sixty years in age, Tristam judged, with hair that was a mixture of white and faded blond, for wigs were not fashionable on Farrow. His girth was great and Tristam noticed that he seemed perpetually out of breath, perhaps a congenital condition, and his color was high.

"Mr. Flattery." The governor looked at the naturalist with great interest. "Welcome to Farrow. The word quickly spread that the heir of our own Erasmus Flattery was to pay a visit. You will be more welcome here than you can imagine. Your uncle is something of a hero to the people of Farrow." He waved them toward a waiting carriage. "Lady Galton sends her apologies, for she is not well today. I hope she will be recovered for the ball this evening. Would you come to tea?"

And so they went to tea at the home of the governor of Farrow. It was a spacious house built in the style of the island—plaster over light-brown stone, for the underlying structure could be seen where the plaster had cracked. The roof was tiled, like all the others Tristam had seen, and there were covered porches and tiled terraces. The house overlooked the harbor and was nestled among olive and tall, elegant cedar trees. The party sat on a shaded porch and looked out over the Gray Ocean, which belied its name for it was certainly very blue in this area.

"Captain Nash of the *Raven* gave us news of your coming. Of course, Sir Roderick had written weeks ago, but we were unsure of your time of arrival. Nash was in here like a hurricane chased him. Watered and provisioned his ship and was off, making all possible sail." The governor shook his head.

"Nash is an able commander," Stern mused. "A man who can fight a ship. I have no doubt that he will see the thing done."

The thing, which could not be discussed before mere citizens, even Tristam could guess the nature of: corsairs were making themselves known in the archipelago again. Nash had undoubtedly been dispatched to strengthen the station there.

"It will have nothing to do with your business, I am sure," the governor hurried to add. He smiled reassuringly at the duchess, then turned to Stern. "I hope you will stay longer than Captain Nash?"

"Several days, perhaps a week. I have a small crew so we must rig, if not merchant-fashion, at least in a manner that will allow us to work our ship and not diminish the crew. It is a long way to Oceana."

This was something that Beacham had explained to Tristam, and which seemed like the worst foolishness. Survey ships, like the *Swallow,* came out of the Navy Yard rigged to navy standards, yet typically carried crews too small to make the best use of such a rig. Even though it was well known that these survey vessels altered their rig at first opportunity, the navy persisted in following regulations and continued to turn out survey ships with "proper" navy rig. It was bureaucracy run mad, Tristam thought.

"A week," Galton said, perhaps a bit disappointed. "Well . . . that is good news. Lady Galton will be so glad to hear it. There is much to do and see on this island, far more than its size would indicate. And perhaps you saw that Mount Forwood has taken to smoke again? Why, Mr. Flattery—and yourself, Doctor Llewellyn—such eminent empiricists will not want to miss such a natural wonder. There is a carriageway more than halfway to the crater rim and from the end it is a short walk to the Ruin and then a brisk tramp to the top." The governor spoke with the excitement of one who wishes others to love his home as he does. Tristam wondered if his seeming respiratory ailment stemmed from this propensity to talk without taking a breath.

"And, Duchess, the Ruin can be easily reached and is not to be missed. Still a mystery, as you know. Who built it, no one can say. Even the famous Erasmus Flattery spent some time in an inquiry, though if he learned anything, he did not tell it. There are strange letters, or runes, carved into stone that no one has yet deciphered. It is the most wondrous thing you can imagine."

"Why, Sir Stedman," the duchess declared, "you make me want to set out straight away. We must arrange an outing."

Tristam agreed immediately, for he had hoped to have time to visit the Ruin. It was every bit as mysterious as the governor claimed.

"And the wineries . . . you shall not want to miss those. And our absurd cranes that live in the crater lake in Mount Sedgel. They make a sound like a child's trumpet and aren't the least bit distrustful of people. And there will be a ball. You will not be bored, I can tell you. . . ."

🐛   🐛   🐛

To Tristam's great relief, the governor insisted that Tristam, the duchess, Viscount Elsworth, and the physician stay with him and his wife while the ship was being rerigged. A week away from those superstitious Jack-fools, Tristam thought, and his spirits lifted immediately.

Captain Stern begged leave to remain on the *Swallow,* citing duty, which the governor could not argue with. After tea, Tristam was shown to a room, and servants were sent off to gather up a list of his belongings that would be wanted for a week ashore. He also wrote a note to the proprietor of his uncle's vineyard, for so he still thought of it, and the governor had it delivered.

Tristam felt both excitement and apprehension about this property. Oh, he wanted to see it, there was no doubt of that, but he was curiously afraid that he would be disappointed.

"Absurd," Tristam said to the room. "It is only a bit of land and some buildings. One would think it were a woman."

There was, Tristam realized, more to this than a bit of land and a few buildings. Despite the fact that Erasmus Flattery had dwelt at Highloft all his life, and the house was obviously well lived in, there was little there that revealed anything of significance about the man himself. Tristam's claim that he had hardly known his uncle was not an exaggeration. In the years after his parents died, Tristam had lived only parts of three summers at Highloft; the rest of his time was spent at boarding school or visiting relatives.

At Highloft, though his uncle had not been unkind, he had never been very attentive, leaving Tristam much to himself. The only exception occurred when Tristam had nearly drowned himself in a nearby pond and then his uncle had spent several days teaching his nephew to swim, an activity the old man did almost every morning that weather allowed. It was just another eccentricity of his uncle's, for almost no one in Farrland swam, including sailors and fishermen. It was said to be injurious to one's health, especially to the respiration.

Erasmus Flattery passed on, not apparently as a result of swimming, leaving no journals or letters. His monographs on various herbs and other plants went to the university; and that was all the writing that Tristam had ever discovered. So now he found himself hoping there was some key that would unlock the enigma of Erasmus Flattery at his estate here on the island of Farrow. Thus Tristam's contradictory feelings. If he found nothing, the secret of who Erasmus Flattery had been would never be revealed. That was his dread; this was the last and only chance he would ever have.

Tristam walked out onto his own low balcony. "Why does it matter?" he asked the trees. But no one knew the answer to that question, least of all Tristam. It was important. That was all he knew.

❦   ❦   ❦

The ball that night drew all of Farrow society, such as it was. To say it was a small affair by the standards of Avonel would have been speaking kindly: it was even small by the standards of Locfal. Despite this, Tristam enjoyed himself, for the islanders were friendly people and decency seemed to be their most common trait. The orchestra was passable, and one violinist was very good indeed.

The Duchess of Morland was treated like a queen and Tristam heard any number of residents note that, *"the duchess does seem to be enjoying our little affair."* There was a certain tone of relief when they said this—and perhaps a little pride. Lady Galton did make an appearance and spent much of her evening talking to Doctor Llewellyn, who spent much of his evening looking professionally solicitous and the rest holding forth on subjects that Tristam could only guess at. He avoided that corner of the room.

Though the island of Farrow seemed well endowed with comely young women, Tristam realized that their attentions meant little to him. He often found himself searching among the faces for a glimpse of the duchess.

A niece of Lady Galton was visiting from Farrland and she was clearly not interested in the many suitors from the island and so spent some part of the evening speaking to Tristam. Later he saw her dancing and laughing with a young lieutenant from one of the ships of war and discovered that, though he was not interested in her in the slightest, his pride was wounded a little all the same.

"Don't stare, Tristam, it is unbecoming." The duchess had come up behind him and spoke quietly near his ear. Tristam turned a little red.

"Any woman foolish enough to consider a naval officer is not worth a moment of concern. Imagine marrying a man who came home once every two years to make a child on you, pat his latest progeny on the head, and then go out to drink and gamble with sharpers. You can find a brighter woman than that. You do want a woman who has a mind, don't you, my dear?"

"And a heart as well, Duchess."

The sounds of music and laughter were not louder than the duchess' silence. "I see," she said rather coolly.

Tristam felt immediately ashamed of his remark, and not sure why he had made it. "Please . . . I meant nothing by it, Duchess."

"Nothing, Mr. Flattery? I am confused. You want a heartless woman, then? There are some, I think, but they usually marry for money and rank." She reached out and tugged Tristam's arm. "Now here is a tune that one can actually dance to. Come, Tristam, you have not been paying attention to me as you should."

They took the floor, Tristam certain his remark still hung in the air between them. They did not speak for several minutes, but danced on.

"Why, Tristam!" the duchess said suddenly, her voice filled with its normal warmth. "You play the country squire so convincingly that I am often fooled.

But you are the finest dancer here, by far, and would be among the best in Avonel. Wherever did you learn?"

Tristam hoped this was a sign that he had been forgiven. "At school. It is one of the arts taught to young gentlemen. We were forced to dance with our classmates, something very few enjoyed."

The duchess laughed her delightful laugh, youth appearing like a blossom. "Well, I have danced with many a graduate of your school and none stepped so fairly as you."

"The Duchess is very kind, and certainly the finest dancer I have had the pleasure to meet."

"Better than your classmates, even? I see why you were named flattery." The duchess met his eye. "Oh, my. I see you have heard this before. And I thought it so original." She looked at him slyly. "Though I'm sure it would pass as wit here." She laughed at Tristam's look. "Now I *have* said the wrong thing."

They spun at the end of the dance floor and, for the briefest second, she pressed herself closer to him than was strictly proper. Tristam almost missed a step.

"You have partaken of the Erasmus Grape, I assume?" The duchess did not wait for a reply. "I have been watching you but see no signs that you have begun to shape-shift. You are a bit redder than usual, but that might mean nothing. I will certainly look carefully at all my partners this evening, though."

The music came to an end, and the duchess took Tristam's arm. "I must have some air. I believe it is one of the arts of young gentlemen to escort ladies onto the terrace."

The moon was just past full, and that was all the light the terrace required. A group of men gathered at the leeward end, smoking pipes, and a few couples stood speaking quietly by the balustrade, ostensibly enjoying the moon. The duchess led Tristam there, keeping a distance from the others.

She looked out at the moonlight on the sea. "I like

Farrow more than I could have expected, even if it is rather sleepy."

Tristam nodded. It seemed appropriate, somehow, that the duchess would make her decision so quickly. "It does have a charm, as you observed when we arrived."

"We have Sir Stedman and Lady Galton to thank for that. Have you spoken to Lady Galton?"

"Just to meet her."

"Well, do better than that. It is she who looks after the interests of this island and its people, for which she is well loved. Lady Galton is a cousin to Princess Joelle, you know."

"I did not know." Tristam was surprised. The Princess Joelle was the wife of the Prince Kori, the heir to the throne. "And she stays here?"

"Yes, it is her health, and Galton's as well. You have noticed his breathing? They must have the climate. But they seem very happy prisoners, to my mind. Farrow has become their cause, in a way. You no doubt remember the passing of the Daye Laws a few years ago?"

"I'm afraid not."

"Tristam, really!" She gave him a searching look, as though discovering a case of mistaken identity. "It affected your fortunes, without doubt. Previously, the wineries of Farrow could not sell their wines to foreign countries but must sell them only to Farr companies who had been granted a charter, oh, two generations ago at least. It was rather a good thing for the Farr companies, for selling the wines took no effort and it was profitable in the extreme. But the Daye Laws allowed the wineries of Farrow to form their own company and trade their wines abroad. It was a difficult thing, for the men affected were not without influence; yet the Galtons managed it. She is a woman of parts, our Lady of Farrow. You would do well to know her better."

Tristam felt his face burning a little. He had known nothing of this. "You are well informed, Duchess."

"Aren't I? You would do well to be so yourself, Tristam. There is more to life than herbs and birds, or birds and bees, for that matter." She turned her head as the orchestra began another melody. "That will be the last dance, and I certainly must have it with the governor." The duchess looked around quickly and then gently pulled Tristam behind a column. To his surprise, she proceeded to give him a long kiss of such sweetness that he was left breathless. She stepped out from behind the column and curtsied primly. "Good night to you, Mr. Flattery. I enjoyed our dance." She swept up her skirts and disappeared back into the ball.

The evening drew rather quickly to a close, for Tristam learned that, unlike Avonel, on Farrow such affairs ended when the music stopped.

Upon returning to his room he found a soft breeze wafting through the balcony doors; welcome after the heat of the ball. He shed his coat, neck cloth, and shoes and walked in stocking feet out onto the balcony. There was a hammock here, not the narrow shipboard type but one with a wooden spreader at each end. He swung himself into this device and stared out over the garden. The duchess' kiss brought back memories of a night in Avonel. And this disturbed him in two distinctly different ways.

The duchess was a bewitching woman. She seemed to both encourage and discourage him, and he was so confused by this that he was not always sure it was true. Tristam found himself drawn to her in a manner he could not explain even though he knew that she manipulated him as easily as she released her lovely laughter. Part of him resented this quite profoundly and another part of him was thankful for even that attention. "Pathetic," he said to himself. "She is cold-hearted and manipulative, and you would do well not to forget it."

He lay in the hammock a moment longer and then went inside and prepared for bed. If sleep sought him, it was spectacularly unsuccessful. After an hour he stripped the coverlets from the bed, took a pillow, and arranged himself in the hammock.

The balcony was low, for his room was on the ground floor, and he had a view across a stretch of lawn to a row of lemon trees. A sound drew his attention and he saw one of the Farrow deer, a tiny species that had been found upon the island's discovery, though certainly not native. It had been introduced, no doubt, by the same race that had left the Ruin on Mount Forwood.

He closed his eyes and slipped into a dream.

Something brushed his shoulder. His hammock continued to rock gently to the motion of the sea. Something soft caressed his cheek, and he awoke with a start. His hammock was indeed swinging.

"Shh."

He twisted around to find a woman standing by his head, her hand resting upon the netting, rocking him gently. Even in the dim light he knew it was the duchess. Tristam was so used to waking in his dreams that he was not sure for a moment if he waked or slept. The duchess looked down at him with what appeared to be genuine affection.

"How pretty you look in your sleep," she whispered.

Her fingers combed into his hair. Unbound, her curls fell about bare shoulders. She was wearing only a sleeping gown of pure white and truly seemed an apparition—but Tristam realized now that she was not.

Taking his face between her hands, she bent so close that her breath caressed him. *"It is so far to Oceana."* Saying this she kissed him, though not so tenderly as earlier. There was desire in the kiss, and Tristam was swept up in his own response.

Taking him by the hand the duchess led him inside. "Draw the curtains," she instructed.

Tristam did as he was told, pulling the light curtains to, where they were easily wafted by the breeze. He turned to find the duchess' gown gliding to the floor, and he joined her in the bed.

Almost immediately he realized how dulled his

senses had been in their previous encounter, for every nerve in his body seemed doubly alive now. The duchess touched him and stroked him and kissed him, and he could feel this excited her as much as his own attentions.

"What a gorgeous child you are, Tristam," she whispered in Entonne. "You have not a hair on your perfect chest. As smooth as a child's." She ran her cheek from his shoulder to his stomach and then kissed his navel.

Despite her passion, the duchess was in no hurry to have it slaked, and Tristam discovered what a truly skilled lover was.

Morning was not far off when he lay, spent, and more confused than ever. The duchess sat staring down at him, twisting a lock of his hair around a delicate finger. He had realized something as they made love; more than anything it was his youth that excited her. It was obvious, when his wits were not addled by drink.

"My poor Tristam. You look entirely out of sorts." She smiled sadly. "Caught between reason and passion. . . . I wonder which you will choose? It seems that you love me a little, and hate me a little, and are angry at yourself for feeling like this." She caressed his cheek with the backs of her fingers. "Do you really think I am a . . . cold-hearted manipulator?" She laughed at the look on his face.

"It is a lesson that awaits us all. So many years of schooling provide so little education." She took her hand away and hugged her knees to her like a girl.

She took her eyes from him and gazed at the wall. "You have no notion of my life, Tristam Flattery, none at all. I lost my duke . . . many years ago now." She paused, but he could not read the look on her face. "I am thirty-seven years old . . . and this face that I have been gifted will last, perhaps, another five years." She took his hand and pressed it to her breast. "This skin will wrinkle and sag and . . ." She met his eyes. "Do you know that Lady Galton was once a great beauty?

"You think I am a manipulator, and I will not deny it. When Sir Roderick waves his hand and changes your life, you do not feel anger and resentment as you do toward me. But he has his power and I have mine. Men are not resented for being strong, for being cunning, for being leaders. Yet these powers allow them to manipulate others. The difference is less than you think.

"I have an excellent mind, you know, but I am a woman and can never be the King's Man. . . . My husband is gone. And my protector has grown so very old.

"You wonder what has led this pampered duchess to take ship to Oceana? It should be obvious that when the King dies I will move to an estate in the country and quickly fade from people's memories. I keep the portrait of the Countess Chilton in my hall to remind me. That is reason enough. So His Majesty's health is of great concern to me. Selfish, you think? Cold-hearted? Everyone at court is scurrying to protect themselves against the day the new King takes the throne: not least among them, Roderick Palle. He has ingratiated himself into the favor of the heir, something I will never do, for the Princess Joelle disapproves of me as much as you would like to." The duchess gave a short laugh.

"Am I cold-hearted?" She shrugged. "I care for the King, though many do not believe it. And there are others. . . . I told you of the Daye Laws. It was your clever duchess who convinced the King that they were unfair. His Majesty spoke to the Prince Kori, whose wife had been applying her own pressure on behalf of her cousin—our Lady Galton. So Princess Joelle—who would go to some lengths to thwart me—assisted in this matter, though I'm quite sure she was unaware of my part . . . at the time. Friends of Roderick's lost their lucrative monopoly." She laughed aloud. "*Gentlemen who value things Farr,* or so they style themselves. Lady Galton is in my debt over this. And Roderick would like to wring my neck." She shrugged and caressed his chest.

"So you see, that is the way of it. I do what I must. . . . And I must keep the King alive. His Majesty requires his physic. But I am certain Roderick has not given Stern instructions to find *regis* at all costs. The captain believes it is a minor task on a voyage of surveying and discovery. He does not understand the true importance. Only you, and I, and Lord Elsworth realize what hangs in the balance. Only we three can preserve the life of the King."

"But Duchess," Tristam whispered, "the King is so very old. What if . . .?" He could not finish. One did not suggest the King might die—especially to one who cared for him.

"The King will not die," she said firmly, "unless we are unable to return with the seed in two years' time." She nodded her perfect chin. *"He will not die,"* she said, though quietly as if reassuring herself.

The duchess fell silent again, stroking Tristam softly. Her gaze met his in the darkened room. "And so I come to you," she said, "my ally, I hope." Reaching out, she took his face between her hands and stared into his eyes. Then let him go, stroking back his hair. "I prey upon you, don't I, Tristam Flattery? But I do try to give something in return." Saying so, she bent and took him in her mouth, something no woman had done before.

Tristam's surprised intake of breath turned into a moan. The soft warmth of her mouth and the caress of her hands quickly brought him to a climax and he lay trying to catch his breath.

Without a word the duchess slipped off the bed, gathered up her gown, and disappeared through the wafting curtains. Tristam sat up, looking after her, his mind and heart in such turmoil that he felt tears sting his cheeks.

TWENTY-THREE

The governor's carriage rolled slowly up the slope of Mount Forwood bearing the Duchess of Morland, her brother, Viscount Elsworth, Governor Galton, Tristam, Lady Galton's niece, and Doctor Llewellyn. A wagon overfilled with servants came behind, and they seemed to be laughing and enjoying themselves every bit as much as the august company they followed.

The carriageway described a complete circle around the cone of the ancient volcano, rising gradually with each mile, and generally provided an excellent view of the island, though here and there stands of trees interfered. The day was sunny and the wind—ten knots, west-north-west Tristam estimated—was brisk, though not too cool. A shadow, from cloud that seemed to be perpetually forming over the island, would overtake them from time to time, but then the wind would tear a ribbon free and sweep it off toward the horizon, and they would again enjoy the sun.

As the party gained elevation, the smoke from the crater became more apparent, its tinge of yellow more obvious against the pure white clouds. Tristam gazed up at the crater rim and felt an odd chill. To think that molten lava had once spewed forth and run down these slopes, like a tide into a steaming sea. It was difficult to imagine on such a fine day.

"So this road, Sir Stedman, was built by the same race?" the duchess asked, and the sound of her voice called Tristam's attention.

Doctor Llewellyn answered before the governor could take a preparatory breath. "It does not appear as it once did, but certainly it was here at the time of the discovery, or perhaps we should say *rediscovery*." Knowing they would stop at Farrow, the doctor had spent some time reading about the history of the island. "There is a section, Your Grace, not far off, I shouldn't wonder, where some of the original stone that once paved the road can still be seen."

"I was about to say," Galton managed, showing only the slightest crack in his shell of overwhelming good humor, "that one can see the old paving stones just beyond these trees."

Tristam sat quietly pretending to listen to the conversation, though it was of little interest. He had made an effort to inform himself about Farrow's history and geology years previous and nothing new was being offered this day. His thoughts were entirely of the duchess.

It was the second day since the ball and Tristam had barely shared two words with the duchess since she had disappeared out through the curtains of his room. The subsequent night had not brought a visit, as Tristam had hoped. The idea of going to her chambers had began to obsess him, but he was quite sure that the duchess would not relinquish control over the timing of their assignations. It was entirely possible, he believed, that she might never allow such intimacy again.

The duchess continued to treat him as one might treat a cousin or friend of the family—as she had led the ship's company to believe she was—with some affection and familiarity, but not a single indication of attraction or intimacy.

Tristam tried to take his mind off the matter and back to the conversation. He also tried to take his eyes off the duchess—not an easy thing, for she seemed very beautiful to him that day. And no less so for seeming out of reach.

Sir Stedman was managing to hold the field. "We do not know how long ago the early inhabitants lived on Farrow. The other ruins found have been well buried and only discovered by the sheerest chance. There is even a ruin on Tristam's estate. The remains of a good sized building, it would seem. And when I say ruin, we must differentiate. The 'Ruin of Farrow,' as it is called, is not really a ruin at all. It is quite intact, as you shall see."

"They did not leave because of the volcano, I collect?" Galton's niece asked.

"It seems unlikely, for there is no sign that the ruins we have found were devastated by lava. No, they dwelled here long after the volcano became dormant. Here's the spot where the old road can best be seen."

Everyone climbed down from the carriage to look at the ancient paving stones. They were impressively large blocks, two yards square, worn and smooth, though seldom broken. Trees offered good shade here, and Tristam thought there must have been a spring nearby, for moss outlined each pale block as though it had been laid into a setting of green velvet. In some places hardy saplings had squeezed up through the cracks.

"You can see the ruts, worn no doubt by the wheels of carriages or wagons," the physician pointed out the smooth furrows, where water ran when it rained.

"No one has ever found evidence that horses inhabited Farrow," Tristam interjected, "though there were many other species introduced before our own history began here." He found the physician so annoying that Tristam could not help but dispute with the man on occasion, though he always felt childish afterward.

"But that does not mean horses were never here, my dear Tristam," the doctor said, as though addressing a child. "Not at all. But even so, it is possible that there were wagons. Drawn, perhaps by other beasts, or by slaves for that matter." He stood in the center of one of the paving stones, beaming, surrounded by his listeners; the world obviously as it should be, according to Llewellyn.

Tristam shrugged and bent to look more closely at a stone. He was annoyed that the physician had begun to use his familiar name—not an issue that Tristam usually had particularly strong feelings about. The fellow was maddening in the truest sense of the word.

"It is not far now," Galton said. "Fifteen minutes will see us at the Ruin."

Tristam let everyone board ahead of him and then said, "I must stretch my legs. Go ahead, I shall not be far behind."

"Are you sure, Mr. Flattery?" Galton asked, "the way is steep, or at least I find it so." He smiled and waved Tristam on. "But no doubt your young legs will not notice. We'll wait at the end of the carriageway."

Suddenly, the duchess stretched out her hand and said, "I will accompany you, Tristam, if you don't mind. I have been sitting long enough as well. No, no, Doctor Llewellyn, keep the governor company, please."

Tristam handed the duchess down, and the carriage and wagon rolled on to the creak of leather and the squeaking of springs. The second they were out of hearing the duchess released a theatrical sigh.

"My word, a carriage is far worse than a ship," she said. "There is no escape at all. I do hope I don't become ill. Can you imagine being trapped in a sick bed by that man? Or trapped in any bed at all. It is no wonder he has never married." The duchess looked up at Tristam from beneath her bonnet and laughed. "I am wicked, aren't I?"

Tristam said nothing, for he wanted dearly to resist the duchess' charm. It seemed to lead him only to confusion and something near to despair.

"Do not complain, Tristam. If I were not so wicked, you would not adore me as you do." She laughed and took Tristam's arm. "You have not yet paid a visit to your estate?"

"Tomorrow," he said, trying to ignore the soft caress of her hand on his arm. "Such as it is."

"Such as it is?" She looked up at him and smiled, her green eyes catching the sun in a most disturbing manner. "Why Tristam, did not Galton say it has its own ruin? The ancients dwelled in your very garden, perhaps. As our good governor would say, *'It is the most wondrous thing you can imagine.'* "

Tristam laughed in spite of himself.

"That is better," she said, taking her skirt in her free hand and swishing it in the breeze, one of those entirely unconscious, childlike acts that Tristam found so endearing. "I am your friend, you know, despite all that you think. On this journey a friend may be more important than wealth or even an uncle at court. So do not spurn me."

"You can't possibly think I spurn you."

"Well, you do keep fixing me with the oddest looks. One would think I had done you some irreparable harm. Did you not have the fullest pleasure of me this two nights' past?" She looked up at him as she said this, meeting his eye with no sign of embarrassment.

Tristam had never had a woman speak to him so candidly and found himself unable to respond. He felt his resistance melting as well. Perhaps she cared for him more than he realized, and he was simply acting like a petulant child because she had not chased after him like a lovesick girl. She was the Duchess of Morland, after all.

"Tristam?"

"I—I can't think what to say. Certainly I have hardly thought of anything else since. Why, it was . . . perfect in every way."

She rested her head against his shoulder for a second. "And though I will confess that I took pleasure from you as well—great pleasure, I might say—I thought it freely given . . . ?"

"Yes, certainly."

"Good. We do not have a misunderstanding, then." She waved off toward the sea. "Look. We have come full circle. I believe I can see the good bark *Swallow* lying in the harbor."

Tristam found it difficult to keep pace with the change in conversation, though he was relieved to have it stray into more familiar terrain. "So it is," he managed. "I am, sometimes, more than a little amazed to find myself on such a journey." It seemed an appropriate response to Tristam, a slight confession, but not too intimate.

"Those who cease to be amazed, Tristam, have placed one foot firmly in the grave, I believe. One should be wary of it." She pressed his arm close to her for a second. "I am so glad you are on this voyage. I should be mad without your company." She smiled at him, her lovely eyes holding his for a few seconds. She turned her attention back to the path again. "But, of course, naturalists have often gone on voyages of discovery, while I am certainly the first duchess to undertake such an enterprise. Imagine how strange I find my predicament."

Tristam found this small attention from the duchess had improved his mood remarkably. "What you say is true, but perhaps it will become customary, just as taking a naturalist is today. In the future we will hear great speculation: 'Who do you think will be the duchess on the next voyage to remote parts?' they will say. 'Perhaps the Duchess of Armond?' 'No, I don't think she's duchess enough to get the thing done.' "

The duchess dissolved into delighted laughter and kissed his cheek. "You make sport of me, Tristam Flattery." And then, " 'Ship's Duchess' has connotations that I do not care to consider."

They strolled on, talking of very little, and Tristam realized again that his normal resentment toward the duchess very quickly drained away in her presence. It simply could not stand up to her considerable charm. *So fell Dandish,* Tristam reminded himself, but to no avail.

The carriage and wagon came into view, wheels blocked, their teams led away to graze or drink. Lady Galton's niece waved a parasol, and the duchess swept off her bonnet and signaled in return.

"We might truly be on a picnic," Tristam said quietly, "rather than on the King's business."

The duchess pulled back and gave him a look of apparent amusement. "But we *are* on a picnic, Tristam.

Do try to enjoy yourself. Why, one of the serving girls has an eye for you. You might have her to bed, if you wish." With that the duchess released his arm, waved her bonnet again, and strode ahead.

As Galton had promised, it was not far to the Ruin, and it was just as well, for it was all the man could manage. He was terribly out of breath the entire distance, short as it was. Tristam and the viscount got a little ahead of the others on a stair and waited at the top.

"This is rather crude stonework," the viscount observed. "I thought these ancient engineers were said to be unsurpassed?"

Tristam ran his hand along the low wall. "This was done by our own Farrowers. The stone in the Ruin is unlike this—not even from the island. It was brought from some yet undiscovered quarries."

"Is that true?" the aristocrat obviously knew nothing of the Ruin for it was hardly a secret. "No wonder this is thought such a mystery. A race that has disappeared. Stone transported across how many leagues of ocean. Writing that no one can read. Worth the few days of bad weather and worse victuals to view such a site." The viscount stared down at the harbor. "What is our present height, do you think?"

Tristam dug into his fine memory. "The Ruin is at three thousand, five hundred feet. The peak of the crater is four thousand two, I believe."

"How do you know that?" the man asked, more impressed than Tristam would have expected.

"I believe I read it somewhere, Lord Elsworth. Barometric measurements were performed here several years ago."

"Ah, barometric measurements." He nodded. "That would answer." He looked back at the group following for a second and then turned to Tristam suddenly. "Would you call me Julian, Tristam?"

"I would be very pleased to," Tristam heard himself say, wondering if his tone sounded as false to the viscount as it did to him. *And while we're at it,* he thought, *precisely why did you murder Ipsword?* This viscount, Tristam had come to realize, was a complete cipher. A bit like a beast in the wild, apparently at peace but unpredictable and potentially deadly.

The viscount smiled at him. "You do have a prodigious knowledge, Tristam. I am in constant amazement. The duchess has the highest opinion of you, as well, and the duchess is a difficult woman to impress."

"Very kind of you to say." Tristam gave a small bow of the head. "In many of life's important fields, however, I'm just finding my feet, I'm afraid."

The viscount chuckled, a warm laugh much like his sister's. "Are you all right there?" he called down to the others.

"Perfectly fine. Don't wait for us," the duchess called back.

Tristam could see that they had stopped to allow Galton to catch his breath. The old man was redder than usual despite the fact that he was supported by two servants. Beside him, the duchess looked very concerned and the niece seemed not to know what to do. A few stairs farther down, Doctor Llewellyn was leaning heavily against the stonework, two of the servant girls hovering by, obviously anxious. Despite the condition of the two gentlemen, Tristam found himself wondering which of the servant girls was so interested in him, and then chided himself. *Don't be a fool; the duchess said that to keep you off balance, as she loves to do.*

Realizing that the two older gentlemen were in such straits, Tristam hesitated to go on.

"Well, let's be off," Lord Elsworth said, obviously not concerned. "I am eager to see this thing now." He set out immediately but had not gone four paces when he realized Tristam wasn't following, and turned, his look expectant. "They will be all right, I'm sure. The duchess is there with a gaggle of strong servants. They can carry the gentlemen up if need be. There is nothing for us to do."

Tristam's own curiosity overcame his feeling that he should wait for the others.

They set off at a good pace up the last slope to the Ruin. They were above the level of trees here and the grass was a bit thin, rock more prominent. Three hundred feet above them was the boundary of true vegetation; beyond that, flora existed only in small pockets.

Suddenly, quite close, the top of the Ruin came into view—a gray stone lintel bridging the gap between a column of light color and one of rose. Tristam felt a strange vertigo, as though he had passed through a portal into antiquity, for here lay the distant past, still living. The lintel, a simple piece of stone, appeared to be imbued with some mysterious quality that the naturalist could not name. Tristam had seen other objects that affected him thus. Lord Skye's pen and inkstand, though the most ordinary of objects, had more impact on Tristam then any religious relic ever could. Skye had written his great laws of motion with these very instruments!

The angle of their ascent revealed nothing further for a few moments and then they topped the rise and there stood the Ruin of Farrow.

Across a grassy common the columns rose up above a stone platform that was reached by a broad flight of stairs. Both men stopped to stare, for it was indeed the strangest sight, this artifact of stone rising out of the most pastoral landscape. But for Tristam it seemed more than that. Suddenly, he wanted to go no farther. He felt a wave of anxiety wash through him and realized he had broken into a sweat. The Ruin did not appear so innocent, but seemed to be a device imbued with terrible intent, like a guillotine or an implement of torture.

This is foolishness, Tristam told himself, and started forward again, though reluctantly. He was not sure if he was more unsettled by his response to the Ruin or by the knowledge that he could have such a reaction, for it clearly had no basis.

Upon the terrace columns had been placed to describe a half-circle and the slope behind had been cut back to create a wall which formed the other half. The ruin was truly incongruous in this setting, and the fact that it didn't resemble any known form of architecture made it appear even more alien.

As they walked, they could not take their eyes from the sight, and neither felt inclined to speak.

The stair had once been a graceful affair of white marble, wider at the bottom, curving toward the top like a perspective drawing, giving the impression that the stairway was almost infinitely long. The carved rail was shattered and several of the stairs were cracked and had been pushed askew.

Tristam forced himself to place a hand on the rail and once he had done this his anxiety seemed to evaporate as quickly and completely as a bead of water in the sun. He was not sure what he had expected—it was only stone, after all. Stone warmed by a mild Farrow day.

The two men mounted the stair slowly, almost reverently, as though they were believers entering a temple. Tristam almost felt they should remove their shoes.

At the stair's head they walked out upon a flat terrace, perhaps forty feet in breadth, bordered on the ocean side by seven tall columns joined by a gray stone lintel carved with the runes referred to by Galton. A section of the lintel lay broken on the terrace, and here the strange writing could be examined closely.

Tristam walked over to the first column and ran his hand over the off-white marble. It was not fluted as he expected, but its smooth surface was decorated by runes and carvings in relief. There were seven such columns, the two farthest out of white marble; the next two, on either side, of rose colored granite; the next pair were green marble; and the single center column shone black in the sunlight.

The terrace itself was patterned like a fan with lines running from the base of each column to the small fount that was built in a half-circle against the wall.

This was fed by a flow of water that issued from the carved beak of a raptor, though the head of the great hawk sat upon the shoulders of a man as though it were a mask. Above this, perhaps twelve feet up the stone wall, the unclothed forms of a man and woman appeared to bear a small platform upon their shoulders—a platform one could climb to by a narrow stairway that followed the curve of the wall. The countenance of both figures was hidden, for each had an arm raised to their face as though in great sorrow.

Tristam walked back toward the wall and gazed for a moment into the gently bubbling fountain, and then up at the two forlorn figures above. Although he could not even guess at the purpose of this place, the figures shielding their eyes would indicate its intent was not entirely innocent.

To either side, flat tablets had been chiseled into the wall and upon these, within an elaborate floral border, more of the strange writing could be seen.

There was a low stone bench opposite the stairway and Tristam went and sat there where he could take in all the wonder in silence until the others arrived.

It was not long until the voices of his party could be heard, and then their footsteps sounded on the marble stair. But the laughter and the buzz of conversation stopped as they reached the terrace and Tristam watched their faces transform. The group that had set out on a day's idyll was suddenly transformed into an assemblage of earnest converts.

Only Galton and the doctor did not seem so affected and as they collapsed on the bench, gasping, Tristam rose quickly to allow the women a seat as well. No one spoke for a time, and then the duchess turned to Tristam.

"Do you know the significance of these columns, Tristam? They are all carved with the most wonderful things."

Tristam hated to usurp Galton's place, for the man so loved to talk of his adopted home, but it seemed likely that Llewellyn would regain his breath first, and

Tristam could not bear to have the man take charge here.

"I'm certain that Sir Stedman can tell you much more than I, Duchess, but I have read something of the subject and shall be glad to relate what I can remember." He turned and cast his eye around the Ruin, looking for a place to begin. "The outermost columns, the white ones, indicate astronomical relations." Tristam walked over and began to point at the various figures. "The sun and the moon are obvious, of course, but some of the constellations are less so, for whoever created this place—and we by no means understand its purpose—saw the heavens differently than we do." Tristam borrowed a walking stick from the governor and used it as pointer. "These spheres would seem to be planets, indicating the builders knew something of our own corner of the heavens. This, I believe is the Great Mare, though joined by these lines it appears different than our own characterization. It is even possible that this constellation was seen as a letter of their written language. If you look at this." Tristam indicated the figure of a man set within a circle, his arms straight out at his side, legs spread. Tristam searched the characters that covered the lintel from end to end. "Here it is. Layel's brilliant contribution to solving the mystery was his realization that this human figure and this character were the same. Or perhaps it would be more accurate to say that the written characters are based on the human forms you can see carved here, though greatly abstracted. Look, here is another." This one was a woman in profile, arms up together, knees bent. "And over here you have the written character. You see; here the arms, the bent knee, et cetera. Though stylized and more elegant, you soon begin to see the way of it. And this first character is similar to the lines joining the stars in our Great Mare. So the builders may have found their writing in the heavens, so to speak."

"Yes, I see two alike," the duchess said, "the man

and woman together above your head and that character—third along. Most extraordinary."

Tristam looked and found, as he expected, that the duchess was right. Her quickness of mind never ceased to impress him. "Of course, despite Layel's great insight, we are hardly closer today to being able to read this script. We do not even know if these characters represent sounds or if they might signify entire words. We cannot tell. It is thought that these two columns represent the sky on a certain day of a certain year, but all attempts to prove this have, as yet, giving us nothing. It is difficult, even with what we know today, to accurately picture the sky at a given time in the distant past."

Tristam moved to the next column which was of beautiful polished granite of the palest rose. "There are, as you can see, a pair of these—one to either side. These granite columns seem to represent things geographical. It would almost be safe to say this is a stylized map or chart, though of a very different type than our own.

"You see here an island with two peaks—that is thought to be Farrow. Is that not so, Lord Governor?" Galton nodded. His breathing was still terribly labored and his eyes bulged from his efforts. Glancing at the physician, Tristam realized he had only a minute or two more before the man would be trying to wrest control of the situation.

"There are two other islands, here and here, which you can see should be nearby, though neither island exists. This was the cause of much debate at one time, and had many doubting the veracity of the ancients' geography, but recent soundings have shown that there are two sea mounts where you would expect these islands to lie. Many now think they were volcanic islands, like Farrow, that erupted and broke apart, disappearing back under the sea—though they are still comparatively close to the surface.

"This curving line is, without question, the coast of the Entide Sea, proving that the race that lived here knew of our own land. The harbor of Avonel would be somewhere here."

"But, Tristam . . ." the physician broke in, though he was still fighting for each breath.

"Now, Doctor Llewellyn," the duchess said, patting the man's hand. "You must save your breath. In a moment you shall have your chance. Do go on, Tristam. I am fascinated." She leaned forward as though not wanting to miss a syllable of what was said, which Tristam could see caused the doctor much frustration.

"If one stands atop that platform," Tristam pointed to the place supported by the two carved figures. "One can sight across the top of columns five and seven precisely toward the positions where the islands are thought to have existed. This may tell us something of the ruin's purpose. But it is also known that, on the summer equinox, the sun rises and sets in line with columns one and seven. And, at noon, is behind the black central column. At that point the sun's height can be measured as the angle between this intersection in the pattern and the top of the column. So the ruin appears to have served an astronomical purpose as well.

"The green columns are the most cryptic, for they are inscribed only with the written characters and the odd figures that seem to be the basis of this writing. Perhaps they are of a religious nature, or are directions to wondrous lands the ancients knew of. All guesses are equally valid, I should think. Poetry. A table of laws." Tristam threw up his hands.

"But what of the final column? The black one," asked Lady Galton's niece.

"Yes, Tristam, what is that material? I don't think I have seen its like before." The duchess continued to give Tristam her undivided attention, hanging on his every word, and Tristam was sure she did this to torture Llewellyn.

"It is obsidian. Glass, really. This is a natural column created, somehow, by volcanic means. Obsidian is the volcanic outpouring cooled so quickly that it does not form a crystalline structure. In a sense it is hardened liquid: glass. How this was formed so perfectly is a mystery. A natural wonder never seen before."

"It was not carved, then? Not polished?" the viscount asked.

Tristam shrugged. "Unlikely that it was carved, Lord Elsworth. Imagine carving glass. Polished? Possibly, though naturally formed obsidian often appears so. The plinth," Tristam tapped the column's base, "is polished basalt—or was polished long ago. One can see the difference. A crystalline rock formed from the volcanic outpouring but cooled more slowly."

Tristam turned toward the rock wall. "Now the fount is something else altogether. It is fed from a pool not far up the slope and drains through a waterway under the terrace. The stone is marble; white and variegated, as you can see. Its purpose remains unknown, if it had a purpose beyond the aesthetic. The man-bird form is not shown anywhere else in the carvings, and its significance is a mystery as well. The water is said to be quite palatable." Tristam dipped a hand in and tasted the water. It was warm but unremarkable.

Tristam felt he had lectured long enough. A fear of becoming like Llewellyn—in love with the sound of his own voice—haunted him.

"I'm sure Sir Stedman will have more to say, for I think our modest governor has been studying this site for many years and has theories of his own."

As Tristam finished, the others began a closer examination of the ruin, each drawn to some different facet. Galton's niece went to the fount and then cast a quick glance at the figures above. When she realized Tristam had seen her actions, she blushed furiously and went immediately to examine one of the columns.

A picnic was spread by the servants, who laid rugs and cushions on the marble terrace. Galton and the physician both regained their voices, and though the doctor tried his best to dominate the conversation, he had to give way to Galton's very real expertise on the subject.

The governor spoke as he ate, wiping his mouth

constantly, for the acts of eating, speaking, and breathing together resulted in a certain amount of spittle escaping onto his chin. "From the platform, as Mr. Flattery called it, one can indeed sight toward the sunken islands. Imagine that somewhere under the ocean lie ruins such as this. But there are other lines scribed into the top of the lintel as well and if one extends them back to the platform, or sighting balcony as it is also called, they converge on a central position. It is conjectured that these indicate geographic locations significant to the race that dwelt here. We do not yet know enough of the geography of this great globe to prove this yea or nay." The governor wiped his mouth and chin seemingly unembarrassed, perhaps even unaware, that everyone looked away. "One can climb to the sighting balcony easily. I've done it many times myself. The stair is narrow and the balcony does suffer from the lack of a balustrade, but if one is not too adversely affected by the fear of heights it is a most wondrous experience."

After the meal Tristam and Lord Elsworth decided to climb up to the balcony but, as the stair was so narrow and the platform so small, Tristam insisted the viscount have the honor of ascending first, for it would not take them both.

"Do be careful," the duchess called out as her brother set foot to the stairs.

Though he was a large man, the viscount was quite nimble and went up quickly, his back pressed hard to the wall. The platform was set at a height to allow a man to crouch, or kneel, and sight across at the top of the lintel.

"I see the marks you mention, Sir Stedman," the viscount called down. "Quite clear." He peered out to sea, shading his eyes. "I can't quite make out what it is they point to. I believe the one on the left might intersect the ale house by the bay."

The mood of the party seemed to be lighter now and this jest brought more laughter than it perhaps deserved.

Tristam ascended in his turn. The stair was only a foot and a half wide at the most and the wall, though surely vertical, seemed to overhang the stair slightly. Tristam immediately understood why the viscount had pressed his back to the wall, and did the same.

From a position crouched on the balcony Tristam could see the lines scribed across the lintel blocks. He stared out to sea and tried to imagine what distant, mysterious lands these lines indicated. Cloud on the horizon could have been snow covered mountains at the limit of vision, or a distant land thrown up above the horizon by some optical phenomenon. His own destination seemed suddenly unbearably far away. Months off yet. Thousands of leagues across open ocean.

Soon enough, he thought.

To Tristam's surprise, as he alighted, the Duchess of Morland insisted on ascending the stair herself— against the protests of both the physician and Galton. Her brother, wisely, Tristam thought, said nothing.

"I'm certain I can manage, Doctor, Sir Stedman. I will simply shed these shoes, imperfect for the climbing of cliffs, and proceed in my stocking feet. I must hitch up my skirt in a most unladylike manner, I fear. I trust that no gentleman will take unfair advantage, for my ankles will be most terribly exposed."

The duchess went up the stair easily and with no sign of fear, though her brother did walk below to break her fall should she suffer a slip. On the balcony Tristam thought she looked like a figure that had been made by the ancient carvers, for, if anything, she was more perfect in form than the figures chiseled out of the stone.

The duchess laughed with delight as she stood looking out over the Ruin and the island below. "Why, it is the oddest feeling. Imagine that someone from an ancient race stood in this very spot to view the sunrise of the winter equinox. It makes one feel all out of place. If you were not, all of you, here I would feel I had been magicked back into ancient times."

She came down, to everyone's relief, much elated.

Tristam wanted very much to look into the volcano, as he had never before had the opportunity to examine one that was at all close to being active. The climb was not steep or difficult and was quite short. "Easily managed," Galton had said, in two or three hours—both up and back. The rest of the party seemed content to spend this amount of time poking about the ruin, so it was decided that Tristam would make a foray up to the crater rim. Viscount Elsworth expressed a desire to see it as well.

At some length, Dr. Llewellyn expressed his regrets that he could not accompany the young gentlemen, and then explained in detail what it was they were likely to see. The young gentlemen made their escape as quickly as possible.

The day had grown warmer, so jackets and neck cloths were left behind, and Tristam carried his canvas satchel with his Fromme glass, notebook, and other tools of his trade. Above the ruin they stopped to look at the lie of the land and fix upon their best course, though the slope was nowhere steep. A plume of yellowish smoke wafted over the edge and swirled in an eddy just below the rim, so it was decided to stay south of this. They set off diagonally upward and soon settled into a comfortable pace.

"I must say, Tristam, that I'm most glad the doctor is not so able physically as verbally. It means I could accompany you on your botanizing forays and escape the man, at least for a time. That is, if you don't mind."

"Nothing would suit me better," Tristam lied, then ventured, "he does seem to be an odd choice for this voyage. Where in the round world did the Duchess find him, Julian?"

"I think he found the Duchess, is the truth of it. When Sir Benjamin Rawdon's wife was so very ill, Llewellyn replaced him for a few months as the King's Physician. Say what you will about the man, he is reputed to be an excellent physician—and that is not just his opinion. It was the King who insisted that the duch-

ess engage a proper medical man for the voyage and
Llewellyn was informed of this by Sir Benjamin. So he
put himself forward, as you can imagine. On paper, as
they say, he seemed the perfect choice. No family," the
viscount grinned, "perhaps no friends as well. A physician of note—tended the King. An amateur naturalist
of some skill, I gather. And a linguist into the bargain.
Llewellyn was very keen to go—wants to write a book,
apparently."

Benjamin Rawdon? The man who had intercepted
Tristam at the home of Baron Trevelyan. The man of
the dark, noble features, and terrible manners. "He ...
he does not lack talents, to be sure, but I am a bit surprised that His Majesty did not mention the good doctor's ... unusual manner in social situations."

The viscount nodded and walked a few paces before
he answered. "Not to criticize the King of course, but
I think even Doctor Llewellyn does not speak out of
turn in His Majesty's presence."

"No doubt that is it," Tristam nodded. "Rawdon. I
think I met him once. Dark-featured fellow. . . ."

"Yes, that would be him. Kindest gentleman in all of
Farrland. Would have to be to be a friend of
Llewellyn's." The viscount laughed.

The King's Physician had been treating Baron
Trevelyan. . . . Of course, the baron was a man of note
in Farr society, Tristam knew. Certainly the most famous empiricist in the land—well known to the King,
without doubt. Still. . . .

A tangy smell assailed his nostrils.

"Can you make out that odd odor? Sulfur, from the
vents in the crater."

They continued on, clambering over bare rock now,
vegetation confined to ledges. Tristam wondered again
if the viscount had taken his journal and Dandish's letter from his room in the Ivy. It seemed the most likely
hypothesis—the viscount or someone acting for him.
And yet here they were climbing a volcano together in
the midst of the Gray Ocean and speaking in the most

congenial manner. Jaimy had said the viscount would
not act without the knowledge of the duchess.

Blood and flames, Tristam thought, *what a despicable situation! Is there no one aboard this entire ship
whom I might trust?*

"Tristam?"

The naturalist had stopped unintentionally. "An odd
bird ... far over the shoulder of the hill. It's gone
now." Tristam pushed on. They passed above a small
pool, shaded by a scrub of bush.

They stopped two hundred feet below the rim so that
Tristam could hammer free a piece of the rock for his
collection. He also wanted to give the viscount a
chance to catch his breath, for although the man was
young and strong, he obviously had not spent his years
tramping overland as Tristam had.

The naturalist held up the piece of rock he had broken lose.

"Lava?" panted the viscount. He wiped his face and
neck with a handkerchief.

"Basalt. Lava cooled slowly, thereby taking on a
crystalline structure. Like the base of the black column." Tristam hefted it in his hand. "All to be worn
away one day."

"Did you feel that?" the viscount asked suddenly.
He placed both hands flat on the rock as though to
brace himself. The ground seemed to have trembled
beneath them.

"I'm not sure." Tristam dared not move.

They both remained very still for a moment, straining to sense any sound or vibration. But there was
nothing.

"Are they firing the guns at the fortress?" the viscount asked.

Tristam could see no smoke there. "I think we
would hear them from this distance. Wouldn't you?"

"I don't suppose this volcano could be about to
erupt?"

Tristam shook his head. "Volcanoes inactive as long
as this one seldom erupt without warning."

They remained still a moment longer and then they both laughed.

As the two men set off, a cloud enveloped them in a mist so thin that it appeared to be illuminated by sunshine. Only the sound of the wind and the scrape of their boots on the stone broke the silence.

"The top can't be far," the viscount offered, as though he thought Tristam needed encouragement.

The sulfur was suddenly quite strong, making Tristam's eyes burn and water. To his right, the viscount covered his nose and mouth with a handkerchief.

Through a spasm of coughing Tristam managed, "We should . . . make our way more to the left."

They began to traverse but did not emerge from the smoke as they expected; it seemed to cling to them and followed as they went. Suddenly, they both stopped as the earth vibrated beneath them.

"No mistaking *that!*" the viscount said. The man's eyes were watering so profusely that he appeared to be in tears.

Both men held their positions for a moment and when nothing else occurred, began moving laterally across the slope.

Not a dozen paces farther on, the earth shook again, violently and without accompanying sound. Both men lost their footing and slid, then tumbled a dozen feet, the mountain beneath them vibrating as though determined to throw them off.

In seconds it was over; they rolled to their feet and began an immediate retreat down the slope. In a hundred feet they came out into bright sunlight and fifty feet farther down they collapsed on the ground, coughing uncontrollably.

Tristam recovered first, pushing himself up into a sitting position. He wiped his eyes on his sleeve, having lost his own handkerchief. Around him the day remained perfectly calm; the prevailing wind blew, a sparrow sang nearby. The island appeared unaffected.

The viscount lay on his back on the slope, his arm cast over his eyes to protect them from the sunlight.

Tristam was so reminded of the figure carved into the wall of the ruin that he could do nothing but stare for a moment.

"Flaming martyrs . . ." Tristam managed, though, beyond that, he didn't know what he had begun to say. "Bloody flaming martyrs," he heard his voice mutter again.

Shaking himself out of his trance, he produced his water flask and offered it to his companion. In his turn Tristam tilted the flask, the warm water spreading through his dry mouth and throat like a priceless elixir.

He passed the flask back to the viscount who had struggled up to his elbows. "Finish it, Julian. There is a spring on our way. We should go back down to the others immediately, though I'm sure no one would have been hurt."

Julian nodded, then tilted the flask back and drained it, still breathing too hard to speak.

Anxious about their companions, they set off, though at a much reduced pace.

"Do you think we're in danger?" the viscount managed finally, looking over his shoulder at the crater rim.

"No. I think that was an earth tremor, unrelated to the volcano. There is no cause for concern here, though tremors can be followed by massive waves."

The Ruin came into view and Tristam took out his glass. "It seems there is no need for concern," he said, focusing on the columned terrace. "Nothing has toppled, everyone seems intact. There are no signs of people rushing about in panic. They seem rather unaffected, in fact."

"Well, I'm glad to hear it. If there were such a wave, Tristam, when would it appear?"

Tristam considered what he had read about such waves. "I don't know if it's possible to say. Our understanding of the relationship between the two phenomena is imperfect."

Water from the spring refreshed them and they covered the last section to the Ruin in good time. As they appeared on the stairs, no one seemed at all concerned about their safety and were greatly surprised to see their torn and dirty clothing.

Distress immediately appeared on the duchess' face and Tristam felt a sense of warmth toward her. "Whatever has happened?" she asked.

"Did you not feel the tremors?" Tristam asked. "There were at least two and perhaps a third."

Galton came up showing much concern for his guests. "We were not sure. Some thought they felt something and others not . . . but the horses were terribly spooked suddenly and the drivers barely managed to control them. You aren't injured, I hope?"

"Not at all," the viscount answered. "Barely a scrape or two."

"We had the oddest thing happen." The governor stopped in mid-sentence as though to catch his breath but, to Tristam, he looked out of sorts, as though he were trying to hide great alarm. "Just seconds before some of us thought we felt the . . . tremor, the strangest sounds were emitted, apparently out of the opening from which the water comes." He gestured toward the fount. "At the risk of seeming a bit mad, it sounded like the voice of some giant being speaking from the very depths of the earth. I've never heard anything like it in my life. Nor have I heard tell of such a thing happening here before."

Tristam found himself staring at the source of the fount's water, the man-bird carved out of marble. "I wish I had heard it myself."

"We had quite an adventure of our own," the viscount said. "Or it seemed so to me." He released his hearty laugh, partly from relief, Tristam thought, and partly from the sheer pleasure of adventure. "First we were lost in clouds, then the most foul smoke you can imagine drove us back just as we reached the rim. And then the whole mountain began to rattle as though trying to shake us off. Sent us skidding down the rocks." He laughed again. "Once that stopped, Tristam and I lit out like hares until we came into clear air. We were nearly suffocated, I should imagine."

Dr. Llewellyn saw this as his opportunity to take control and insisted the two gentlemen sit down while he listened to them breathe, took their heart rates, and percussed their chests. Pronouncing both of them sound was taken as a signal by the entire party and everyone began making their way back to the carriage and wagon. Tristam found himself supporting Sir Stedman as they descended the longer stair, though going down did not seem to tax the old man as ascending had. They were the last at the base where Tristam stopped to allow the governor to find his breath. Finally Galton nodded to him, but just as they set off, he drew the naturalist back, staring at him oddly. "Tristam, did you drink from the fount before you ascended the crater?"

"Why, yes. I believe I did."

Galton nodded once and walked on.

TWENTY-FOUR

Tristam was surprised to find himself sore and bruised the day after his climb to the crater's rim, for at the time the tumble down the slope had not seemed to cause much harm. He lay in the bath contemplating the excursion to the Ruin, the odd conversation with the duchess *("Did you not have the fullest pleasure of me this two nights past?")*, his strange reaction to the sight of the Ruin itself, and finally the earth tremor and the macabre "voice" that the others had heard.

"Where to begin?" he whispered to the empty room. The duchess. . . . There was no understanding the duchess. *"I am so glad you are on this voyage, Tristam. I should be mad without you."* Perhaps, but she had not visited him that night as he thought she might. One could predict the moods of the sea more readily than the actions and moods of the duchess. *"To open some small part of your heart will not bring you to ruin."*

Then why did he feel so wretched this morning? There might be more to life than the purely intellectual world of Tristam's past, but the world of the heart seemed to be composed of constantly shifting ground. It was almost impossible to keep one's feet.

With an effort Tristam tore his thoughts away from the duchess (knowing they would return soon enough). He still wondered about his reaction to the ruin; it had been such a physical response, as though his body had felt a fear his mind could not recognize. Like the feeling one had when awakened from sleep by a clap of thunder—terrified but unsure of the cause.

Perhaps traveling would always bring up unexpected

thoughts and sentiments as new things were encountered and assimilated. Nothing to worry about, he told himself, you are not suddenly losing your grip.

Now the "voice," well. . . . As he thought of the group's experiences, the strange feeling that the Ruin was an object of horrible intent crept over him, as though the bath water had suddenly turned cold. This propelled him out of the tub and he began to rub himself down vigorously, as though he could erase any unwanted feelings.

It is possible to think too much, he told himself, and realized no irony in this.

Another fine Farrow day was just beginning as he left his rooms, for he had risen earlier than usual that morning. It was his intention to ride the twelve miles to his uncle's estate that day.

A servant informed him that the morning meal had been set out in the garden and Tristam arrived there to find Lady Galton sipping coffee. The duchess was not in sight.

"The pleasures of the morning to you, Tristam," she said, a look of distraction disappearing immediately. "I hope you don't mind me calling you Tristam?"

"Not at all, Lady Galton." Tristam made a leg. "And the pleasures of the day to you, as well." He took the chair offered and Lady Galton served him coffee. Tristam noticed that her hands trembled as she poured.

Lady Galton was proof of the old saw that married couples grew to resemble each other over the years, for Tristam thought she could have easily been mistaken for Sir Stedman's sister. There was some quality about her—perhaps the look that at most times a remark of some wit was being considered, though almost never spoken—that reminded Tristam of the governor, and certainly her coloring was much the same, though her eyes were more hazel than blue and her hair tended more toward silver.

If Lady Galton had once been a great beauty, as the duchess had said, then age had slowly overcome that beauty until it was, in its entirety, concentrated in her eyes, still large and alive and bordered by dark lashes. Tristam could see hints that the woman's great natural poise was slowly being eroded by the ravages of age, but it was too strong, too much the habit of a lifetime, to surrender without a struggle.

"Our earth tremor does not seem to have precipitated a terrible wave, as we feared," Lady Galton said, though she did not sound relieved. "And that is something to be thankful for."

"It certainly is," Tristam answered, as prepared as anyone of his class to make small talk, especially with his hostess. "As the tremor was not felt even in the town, I should think it too small to cause such a wave. Still, we don't truly understand how one affects the other yet. So I will record this as another small bit of evidence."

Lady Galton sipped her coffee and gazed at Tristam thoughtfully. She opened her mouth to speak, and Tristam saw that she changed her mind and chose a different tack. "Sir Stedman has studied that ruin the entire time we have lived on Farrow, and the other ruins as well. It is his greatest interest, after the good of the island's people—almost an obsession, really. Yet the noises heard yesterday have never been reported before. He is beside himself with excitement. I think he shall have a camp erected there again as he did in the old days." A smile of great affection flitted across her face. "Though I don't suppose such a thing happens twice in a hundred years.

"Stedman is convinced that the 'voice,' as he calls it, is the reason the Ruin was built in the first place, or at least part of the reason. He has not given up on his theory that Farrow lies at the intersection of geological lines of stress—or perhaps 'force' would be a better word—but this voice has certainly caused him to consider the thing anew."

Tristam buttered a pastry as he thought. When he looked up Lady Galton's gaze flitted away as though she had been caught out in some way.

There is something she wants to say to me, Tristam realized.

"It is difficult to know, Lady Galton, why such an artifact was created—what it meant to the ancient builders. I suppose if they believed the noises being emitted from the vent were coming from a subterranean being—perhaps a god—well, that would be reason enough. If we could only plumb the mystery of the written language, we would probably have many, if not all, of our answers."

Lady Galton nodded and Tristam saw the tremor again, this time in the motion of her head. She touched her cup to her cheek as if in thought, and any sign of trembling was thus masked. "Your uncle was fascinated by the written language, as well. He and the governor spoke of it for hours on end."

"Really? I did not realize you knew my uncle."

"Oh, yes." She smiled again, as much with her beautiful eyes as with her mouth. "He visited us often and, of course, Stedman had his camp at the Ruin in those days, so they could not help but meet. They were both very keen on the same things. It was Stedman that set your uncle off in search of the new varietal and into his study of oenology. Not that we take any credit, mind you. The Erasmus Grape was the product of your uncle's very substantial genius, but the governor did plant the seed, so to speak."

Lady Galton looked around the small arbor. "I had hoped to see the duchess this morning. We have had so little time together." She looked closely at Tristam. "The duchess is a remarkable woman, is she not?"

"I believe she is." Tristam concentrated on dissecting an orange.

"This voyage has piqued my curiosity, Tristam, as you might imagine. Why do you think the Duchess of Morland would suddenly take this notion to join a survey expedition? It must be the talk of Farrland."

Tristam tried to keep his tone offhand. "I'm sure that it is. I believe the duchess has developed an interest in natural history, Lady Galton, as well as a great curiosity about the world itself. A sense of adventure cannot be limited to men alone. As you have said, the duchess is a remarkable woman."

"Yess. . . ." She stretched the syllable out tentatively. Tristam felt her lovely eyes on him. "I have known Elorin many years now—since she was a girl. And yet this took me by surprise. At first I could not believe His Majesty would allow her to go. In a way she is what keeps the King alive, I think. And she chooses to go off now, for as much as two years. I cannot understand what would possess her."

Tristam decided it would be best to evade the question, if possible. "Have you spoken to the duchess about this, Lady Galton?"

"We have barely spoken two words," she said, and Tristam could not tell if she was hurt or merely frustrated by this. "I have not been myself, of course, and I am sure the Duchess does not want to impose." She sipped her coffee, but Tristam thought he saw a hint of something—perhaps regret—on her aging face. "Or perhaps some matter has taken up her attentions entirely." She gazed at Tristam as she said this, her face purposely set to reveal nothing.

"Perhaps." Afraid he might give away more than he meant to if they kept speaking of the duchess, Tristam took this as an opportunity to change the subject. "I must say, Lady Galton that you and Sir Stedman have been most kind and hospitable. I am forever in your debt." As he was speaking pleasantries, Tristam was pondering what Lady Galton had said. It seemed impossible to him that someone of the duchess' sensitivity would not spend the requisite time with her hostess on such a visit. It was a terrible snub to both Lady Galton and the governor.

She smiled briefly. "It has been a great pleasure indeed. We get so few visitors and even fewer such as yourself—why, you seem to have become the object of interest of some of Farrland's most noted citizens. Sir Roderick wrote of you to the governor in the most flattering terms. And I have had the most charming note from Averil Kent who spoke of you as well." She smiled again, her eyes probing his. "I should have realized that you would know Kent."

"I only just met the gentleman in the summer, at an evening of the Society. I don't think there is a kinder man in all of Farrland."

Lady Galton nodded, her face suddenly troubled. "And Sir Roderick Palle?" she said very quietly, "what do you think of him?"

It was such an odd question, so disconnected to the conversation and so . . . bluntly asked as to be impolite, that Tristam was taken aback for a second.

"I am not sure what you mean, Lady Galton."

She looked up, something coming alive in her eyes—defiance, Tristam thought—as though she had made a sudden decision to cast aside caution, in a society where caution was as ingrained as the language.

"Don't you? Then I will try to be even more candid. I have come to distrust Roderick Palle, myself. What of you, Tristam? What of your own dealings with the King's Man?"

"He has been most kind to me, Lady Galton," Tristam answered evenly.

"Yes, that is the polite answer. But I am not being polite, as you can see. I think Palle has become involved in matters that . . . that are a danger to everyone." Her head trembled now, and she made no effort to disguise it. "I believe you are a man of principles, Tristam Flattery. Look carefully at what you are being asked to do. You are a man of reason, I have heard you say it. Why would you align yourself with those who seek to undo the efforts of reason?"

Tristam was so utterly surprised by this outburst that he pulled away from the lady before him, actually shifted his chair back.

"Lady Galton. I am a ship's naturalist engaged upon a voyage of discovery in the service of the King. I have no intentions other than to fulfill my duties to the best of my abilities. I was appointed to this position by Roderick Palle, yes, but I know nothing of any. . . ." He stumbled to a stop. "I don't know what it is you suggest. I am innocent of the politics of the court. Sir Roderick hardly seems the man to be involved in something . . . nefarious."

She reached out and put her hand on his arm, though gently. "You see, that is the myth, Tristam; 'evil deeds are done by evil men.' But it is not the truth. Evil deeds are done by those who mean only well or at least do not mean to do evil. Look at our history and you will see." She paused. "Good intentions, Tristam, as are your own, I am sure. That is why I have chosen to speak with you, because I believe, in your heart, you wish to accomplish only good."

She sat back slightly in her chair, removing her hand from his arm, and searched his face—looking for what, Tristam was not sure. He felt as though she were forming some judgment and he did not know how to react.

"If you are in league with Palle," she said suddenly, "then he will know that I stand against him. But if you are not, you need to understand that others have plans that you know nothing of or that you may only suspect." She leaned forward, speaking quietly, her voice wavering slightly. *"Do not bring this terrible bloom back to our world. Do not pass it into the hands of those who cannot understand its purpose."* She settled back in her chair as if this warning had sapped her vital energies. Her face had turned chalk-white.

She knew! Lady Galton knew of Kingfoil.

"Why?" Tristam heard himself say. "Why should I not? What is it that this . . . bloom will do?"

He thought her eyes widened a little as though she had been surprised. "Do you support Roderick Palle?" she countered.

"I do not know what you mean, Lady Galton. Certainly it was Sir Roderick who engaged me in this position, as I have told you."

She sat and regarded him for some time and when she spoke again she had recovered somewhat. "Your loyalties, Tristam, are unclear. Therefore, I shall not say more. I will not be so easily convinced to reveal what it is that I know. But consider what it is you do, Tristam. If you know as little as you claim, trust that this is no innocent errand you have been sent upon."

Tristam heard the sound of someone clearing his throat and looked up to see a servant standing down the path through the trees. Lady Galton nodded in return and then smiled at Tristam before lifting her cup to drink, her entire manner changed, all signs of distress carefully masked.

For a second Tristam thought it would be the duchess arriving, but it was Lady Galton's niece.

She kissed her aunt and curtsied to Tristam, taking a chair that would keep her pale skin from the sun.

"We have just been speaking of the Ruin, my dear," Lady Galton said and the conversation trailed off into the pleasantries that seemed to make up much of the social discourse.

Tristam found his mind wandering immediately. What in this round world had just occurred? In truth, Lady Galton seemed quite sane, yet she had just gone on about . . . what? It was not entirely clear, but one thing was certain; Lady Galton believed deeply in the warning she had spoken.

He realized that he had been addressed and had no idea how to respond. Something about the Ruin. "It is the oddest thing, isn't it?" he tried. Then, groping. "I . . . I was surprised to hear my uncle was interested in it as well." This, at least, was true. Erasmus, as far as Tristam knew, had always been completely reclusive, and the amiable Sir Stedman hardly seemed to be the type of companion his uncle would choose, or so Tristam would have thought.

Lady Galton nodded, smiling vaguely, alerting Tristam that he had been caught not listening. "You should really talk to Stedman, Tristam. He and Erasmus spent so much time together up there. I never go up myself—just the once soon after we came here. I do not care for the feel of the place. I'm like the native Farrowers in that." She hunched her shoulders slightly as if fighting a shudder. "It does give some an odd feeling. Have you ever been in a house said to be haunted?"

Lady Galton's niece had not, apparently. Tristam smiled. "No. Though I was told I met a ghost once in Merton."

The women looked puzzled for a second and then Lady Galton's eyes smiled. "Oh, yes. The ghost boy, was it?" She laughed, but it seemed forced. "Well, there you are. No doubt, it was similar. But if you want to know about the Ruin, you must talk to Stedman. The governor has been working on his own book on the subject." She gave a soft laugh, genuine this time. "Though I think it shall never be done. It has been written over and over these past ten years and is no nearer completion than it was after year three. And now this 'voice' . . . why that will set him back, who knows how long." She laughed again, a laugh full of affection. "It is rather like that old jest: do you know it? About the man who wrote the syllabus to be used in the education of his son—but the writing lagged always behind the growth of the child and so the boy never benefited from a single lesson. I fear Stedman's book is going the same way. Though we learn nothing new about the ruin for years on end, our increase in knowledge still outstrips his speed of writing."

Tristam laughed as well, but his curiosity was fired by this news. "I should like very much to see this book, Lady Galton, if the governor could be so persuaded."

"Perhaps he can. I shall ask. I know he did not speak of it to Doctor Llewellyn. Stedman will not show it to just anybody . . . but he likes you, Tristam. And you are the heir of Erasmus, after all. I shall ask."

Tristam poured more coffee for all of them. He was anxious to be off so that he could think—and for other reasons as well. Now that the decision had been made and the time set to visit his uncle's estate, he wanted to get on with it, but Lady Galton was his hostess . . . and he found also that his curiosity would not let him go. If only the niece would take her leave, he might find some answers—though Lady Galton may well have said all she meant to say.

"Do you know, there is an odd cult associated with the Ruin, or so it is said on Farrow. A secret society, I collect. No one knows truly what they do, but there are several of our islanders reputedly involved—as well as outsiders from all four nations, not just Farrland." Lady Galton lowered her voice as though she spoke dark secrets, but her eyes laughed. "It is said that the members of this society have had the secrets of the Ruin revealed to them . . . in dreams." She laughed. "They make it up, I expect. But they are rumored to go up there, on specific nights of the year, and perform rituals. Do you think it would be human sacrifice? I do hope they will leave our poor Farrow virgins in peace—they are in such short supply as it is."

The niece turned slightly pink at this, but Tristam laughed. "There appears to be no sacrificial altar, Lady Galton. I should not lose sleep over your virgins."

"Well, I hope you are right. You are off to see Erasmus' estate, I collect?"

"Yes, such as it is."

"Oh, Seabright is very comfortable. You will not be disappointed. Of course, it is not large, but then, this is Farrow, and there are no holdings of scale here. No, Erasmus' property is very good, and some of the noblest grapes are grown there, as should be. Seabright is quite fine, you shall see. And very well kept. The Borrows family have managed there since your uncle came by the place, and they treat it like their own. They are the best sort, I would not hesitate to say. No, Tristam, it is altogether a solid estate. I should send along some gooseberry jam to the Borrows. Cook makes the finest on Farrow. Have you tried it?"

❦   ❦   ❦

And so Tristam was sent off bearing gooseberry jam, his mind set to spinning like the wheels of a racing carriage by the events of the morning. Lady Galton . . .

of all people. It was difficult to believe that this gentle, aging woman was somehow involved in court politics, but the duchess had intimated as much. Was Lady Galton not a cousin of Princess Joelle, a woman who lived in the very center of Farr politics?

But what did Lady Galton know of Kingfoil? *This terrible bloom,* she had called it. What else could she be referring to? And Palle.... She spoke of him as though he were about to accidentally start a cataclysm. *"Evil deeds are done by those who mean only well...."* she had said.

"Blood and flames," Tristam muttered. "I am set off around the world on an errand, the significance of which it seems only I do not understand." *I can leave this ship,* he thought, *abandon the voyage. It is still possible.*

"That will save you from having to make any real decision in this matter," he said to himself. And then what would happen? He would return to his life in Locfal, a thought that he found did not cheer him. And something would occur in the larger world. Some event over which he would exercise no control. And he would be leaving the duchess, an idea he did not relish.

"I will go on," Tristam said to the wind. "But if I find *regis,* I will not consent to return it to Farrland until the duchess answers all of my questions."

He realized there was some advantage to being thought naive—if one were not. Roderick had his facade and the duchess hers. Tristam could hide behind the belief, firmly established he was sure, that he was innocent of people's motives.

Tristam brought Galton's gentle little mare to the cliff top and tethered her to a tree where she might graze. He stood looking out to sea for a moment and then pulled his notebook from his bag and sat down in the grass.

Taking out a mechanical pencil he began.

One: Valary's letter seemed to indicate that there might have been an herb that had something to do

*with the mages and their great age. Dandish de-
stroyed his plants immediately as well as every note
he had made except the one he had left to me in the
field glass. (Had the professor not written: "Do these
people understand what they have found? I must assume they do."?) Dandish had been growing Kingfoil
for the duchess.*

*Two: Roderick did not allow me to attempt to solve
the regis problem (which Dandish apparently did
solve). Why? Why would he not want regis seeds,
and yet send me out on this voyage to collect this
very plant?*

*Three: The duchess is Roderick's opponent at
court. Lady Galton just warned me against Roderick.
Yet the duchess does not seem to be aligned with
Lady Galton.*

*Four: Who else seemed to be involved in this mat-
ter? Trevelyan? (Or was he merely mad?) Rawdon,
who kept me from seeing the baron (and who is apparently a friend of Llewellyn as well as the King's
physician!)? Lady Galton (and by extension, Princess Joelle?). Prince Kori? The King. Kent (mentioned by Lady Galton)!?*

For an hour Tristam sat and mulled this over; at the
end of this he wrote:

*Mages. Erasmus. Regis. Rejuvenation. Struggle
within the court.*
Roderick . . . Prince Kori. Farrlander faction.
Duchess . . . King Wilam. Entonne sympathies?

It was a workable hypothesis. And if Tristam had
not had breakfast with Lady Galton, he might have believed it. The horror he had heard in her voice did not
support anything so common. Not that the possibility
of war was not horrifying—especially to those who
had seen war—but somehow Lady Galton's concerns
were not so simple. War she would not have hesitated
to speak of, Tristam was sure.

Tearing the page from his notebook, he set it afire

and then mounted his borrowed horse and set off, the words of Lady Galton still echoing in his mind: *"Evil deeds are done by those who mean only well. . . ."*

❦ ❦ ❦

The day was unfolding in what Tristam had come to think of as the Farrow pattern: eight knots of wind out of the northwest, a smattering of small clouds over the sea, a warm sun. The ever-present cloud that hung over the peaks of Farrow appeared to be wafting ribbons of rain over the highlands, feeding the numerous tiny streams and pools that kept the island green.

Occasionally wagons would pass, bearing precarious mountains of hay, for the islanders were at work taking off their last crop of the season. Winter, if it could be called such, slowed the growth enough that it was not worth harvesting again until spring—though, if properly managed, there was pasture all year. Everyone spoke to Tristam as he passed; many knew his name, in fact. No one was in such a hurry—even while making hay!—that they could not say hello or stop and gossip for a moment. If his morning had not been so disconcerting, he would have found this aspect of island life quite charming.

It had been Tristam's intention to see some of the island as he went and to make some notes in his journal, and he forced himself to continue this plan as a tonic against the tide of questions and fears that attempted to overwhelm him.

He left the road after a short while and crossed the open fields to ride along the cliff top. Several species of pelagic birds made their nests here in the spring, and many were still to be seen—northern gannets in particular were new to him.

The cliff ran down to the beach after a mile and here Tristam stopped and let his mare graze. He shed his boots and waded into some of the tide pools, losing himself until hunger, and the advancing tide, drove him up onto the rocks to eat. Here he spread his specimens to be examined more closely, deciding which would be preserved and which returned to the sea.

As was too often the case, Tristam found his thoughts turning to the duchess. His discussion with Lady Galton that morning had set him to wondering again why the duchess was aboard the *Swallow*. The duchess' own explanation did not seem as logical now as it had when she perched, unclothed, on the edge of his bed. Certainly the King might need his physic, as the duchess claimed, but Wilam VII was over one hundred years old! Did she really believe the *regis* physic would keep the King from aging? When considered objectively, her explanation made little sense. It was no wonder the duchess was avoiding Lady Galton—her charms would not so easily muddle that good woman's brain.

But now Lady Galton had made Tristam question what little he had been told about Kingfoil. What could it be that she believed the seed did that she would speak of it in such dire terms? Obviously, not something so innocent as the control of a disease.

Tristam shook his head. What a business! Valary's letter to Dandish. Mages.

Mages. . . . I seem to have been connected to them through my uncle, Tristam thought, and this disturbed him more than a little. His uncle. Whose home lay not far off. Thinking this, he collected up his specimens and returned them to the sea, then set out resolutely toward the home of his mysterious relative.

🜊   🜊   🜊

The lane which led to Seabright lay at the bottom of a tunnel formed of high-branched poplar trees. Leaves rustled and sighed with the sounds of deep summer, despite the lateness of the season, and smears of afternoon sunlight painted the lane bright and dark. The red dirt of the path blew off in small clouds where Tristam's mare landed her dainty hooves, for there had been no rain on the lower slopes for several days.

A low stone wall paralleled the lane—a highroad for squirrels, Tristam noticed—and, on the opposite side, a defeated old laurel hedge bordered the lane with faded greens and yellows. Past a bend in the lane a stone bridge crossed a running stream and into the pillar to either side a letter was chiseled—"E" to the left, "F" to the right. It was the only sign Tristam had ever seen to mark his uncle's passing through this world. Even the man's grave had, by his own request, been left without a headstone. Tristam stopped his horse for a moment and looked down at the two simple letters carved into stone.

If a man's deeds do not outlive him, of what value is a mark in stone? Halden, but it was a phrase that could have been spoken by his uncle. Tristam spurred his horse forward, trying to ignore the nagging anxiety he felt growing.

Come along, lad, Tristam chided himself, *this will certainly be the most tame adventure on such a voyage. Get on with it.*

A rhythmic squeaking became audible as he made his way along the drive, and then the sounds of a woman humming a tune he did not recognize. As he passed through an opening in a hedge, both sounds stopped abruptly and he found a large woman lifting a full bucket from a well. She did this one-handed, locking the crank-handle that raised the bucket in the other.

Tristam's mare whickered and the woman turned, a smile already forming as though she never had visitors who were not welcome. The whiteness of the woman's smile contrasted greatly with the dark tan on her round face, and brown eyes took Tristam in without a hint of suspicion. He found himself liking her immediately.

"Mr. Flattery?"

He doffed the hat he wore against the sun. "Tristam Flattery."

The woman curtsied, smiling as though she found his formality odd, but a bit charming all the same. "Welcome to Seabright. I am Elizabeth Borrows-Linn. Willis Borrows is my father. We have been looking forward to your coming, Mr. Flattery, for everyone who has had the pleasure to make your acquaintance has spoken very highly of you."

Tristam smiled. As he had been told, Farrow was very small. If there were a secret society centered on the Ruin, then Tristam would guess it was no secret . . . except perhaps to outsiders.

"And I have had only the kindest things said of the Borrows family. It is a pleasure to meet you at last." Tristam dismounted.

"I'm so sorry my father isn't here to meet you, but everyone is off to the Rowes'. The hay making, you know." She poured the water from the well-bucket into another, and then lifted a bucket in each hand, as though they weighed nothing at all, and set out, refusing Tristam's offers of help. She was not as tall as he, by five inches, Tristam guessed, but she would not be much lighter. Tristam was slight of build compared to this woman.

She passed through a garden gate and returned almost immediately, at a trot, to take Tristam's mare in hand. The horse went into a covered stall and was fed and watered in a manner that indicated Elizabeth handled stock often.

"No doubt you'll want to see your property, Mr. Flattery, but would you care to refresh yourself before or later?"

"I have a terrible thirst, but beyond that I am ready to tour the grounds, if you have time. Curiosity has the better of me."

"Father said to take you around if that was your desire. The others likely won't return until long after dark. There will be a bit of merry making if they get all the hay in. Father will be sorry not to have shown you about himself." She grinned as though she were playing a trick on the old man. "The house we just passed is the manager's house, the 'Grange' it's called, where the Borrows and our various in-laws dwell. It's a big old place and not uncomfortable."

Tristam could see little of the house above the garden hedge and surrounding trees, but it did seem to be a big old place and ramshackle as well, with wings and rooms added to no apparent design. The main roof had a distinct bow, indicating that the house was very old, probably built not long after the discovery some four hundred years ago. Stone houses with tile roofs lasted a long time in such mild climates.

"Your uncle's house is in the copse off there," she pointed down a long row of poplars and at the end he could just make out a terra cotta tile roof among a stand of amber beech and tall cedars. The house would enjoy a view down to the sea, Tristam noted.

"I left some ale there this morning, as we knew you were coming. Would you like to start there or in the vineyard?"

"The house and the ale seem to be calling to me, Mrs. Borrows-Linn. Do you mind?"

"Not one bit." Her brown face wrinkled up in a smile. "Though you must call me Beth, or no one will have the slightest idea who you are speaking to—least of all me."

They set off down the lane, Elizabeth setting a no-nonsense pace. Tristam was wondering how old this woman might be. Early thirties was his guess, so she would have been a child when Erasmus Flattery was a resident here.

"You knew my uncle, I collect?"

"Well, I was only a girl at the time, so I could hardly say I knew him, but I saw him often and spoke with him occasionally. I had strict instructions not to bother Mr. Flattery for he was always deep in thought. Your uncle was very kind to me, though—to all the Borrows children, in fact." She laughed as though at a memory. "My older cousins teased us—my sisters and brothers—with tales that Erasmus Flattery was a mage. We were all struck dumb in his presence, terrified that he would practice some enchantment upon us. In truth, we always hoped to see some magic, but of course we never did." She laughed again. "Children do love to believe such things."

Yes, Tristam thought, *children and sailors.*

They passed through a gate into a surprisingly well kept garden, still awash with bright colors. The house was at least as large as Tristam's home in Locfal, the stone showing through in places where the plaster had cracked.

"It is an old home, by Farrow standards," Elizabeth said when she saw Tristam's eye drawn to the broken plaster; but it was merely a statement of fact, not an apology.

She pushed open the main door, which was not only unlocked but appeared to have no mechanism to secure it beyond a latch. As Lady Galton had said, it was a comfortable home: Tristam liked it immediately. Though it appeared a bit uncared for on the outside, Tristam realized that this was not true of the interior. The walls were plastered and painted in pale shades, and the rooms trimmed in a dark wood Tristam did not recognize. Floors were polished wood or tile and, like other homes on Farrow, there were covered terraces and double doors with many-paned windows. The view was over fields to the sea and a small island not a quarter mile off shore. Tristam could see the tile roofs of several other buildings in their settings of green trees, and out on the blue ocean the sails of fishing boats were like a scattering of petals on a pond.

Elizabeth fetched ale for the two of them, and they sat in comfortable chairs on the main terrace. Off to the right, stretching up the gradual slope, were the vineyards, their vines cut back now as they must be each autumn. They looked like dark, twisted letters and brought to Tristam's mind the written characters he had seen at the ruin.

"We hope you will stop with us for a while, Mr. Flattery. I know Father is anxious to discuss the estate with you." She hesitated a moment, the wrinkles around her eyes pulling tight. "To be honest, we are all curious to know if you have plans for Seabright that we should consider." She was watching Tristam carefully as she said this.

"No, Beth, it is my hope that your family will continue to manage the vineyard, which you have done so ably. I hope to learn more of the business, one day, though that will have to wait for another visit, I'm afraid. I must return to the governor's tomorrow, for the ship will be ready to leave sooner than expected and I have much to do."

She smiled and Tristam could see a sense of relief there. "Well, I'm sorry to hear we will lose you so soon." She looked out over the vineyard and Tristam thought there was a sense of ownership in that look. Pride and ownership.

Just then Tristam heard a door thump open and the sounds of running feet. A girl, not more than twelve years, appeared. "Oh, Beth," she wailed, "come, come! Justy has swallowed a whole spoon!"

The woman leaped up. "Farrelle save us! Is he choking? Did you see him do it?"

"No, but it's gone. I turned my back and it's gone." The girl burst into tears.

Beth took her hand. "Well, I can't think he could swallow a spoon and not choke. But let's along and see." She turned to Tristam. "Do excuse me, Mr. Flattery."

Tristam sat on the terrace a while longer, admiring the view and considering the difference in this landscape and that of Locfal. *A painter,* Tristam thought, *would say the palette is cooler and the light warmer. I cannot quite describe it, but it is striking and very beautiful.*

Curiosity, as usual, called to him and he rose and went to explore the house even though he had the feeling he was sneaking around someone else's home.

Although it was much smaller than the Galton's mansion, Erasmus Flattery's abode was similar in style, as Tristam was beginning to suspect all homes on Farrow were. It was well appointed and showed signs of having been built by accomplished craftsmen. The first floor consisted of a small parlor, a morning room, library, drawing room of good size, a formal dining room and a breakfast nook as well. The kitchen, scullery, and pantry were a half-floor down, with high windows and stone floors.

Tristam was disappointed to find the shelves of the library almost entirely bare, though the few books there all related to the island of Farrow: its history; flora; fauna; agriculture, and even architecture. Three books dealt specifically with the Ruin of Farrow and its builders, but Tristam had read them all at one time or another.

A large desk was set before a window that looked out over the sea and, after a moment of hesitation, Tristam began to go through the drawers. Nothing out of the ordinary: bottles of dried up ink; pens of older design, though good workmanship; folders of yellowed paper; blotters. A small leather-bound notebook excited him for a moment, but he found its pages blank. It was, however, exactly the kind of book that empiricists favored for their journals and gave Tristam a bit of hope. Perhaps his uncle had kept a journal after all. But what had happened to all the volumes, if that was true?

He pushed the last drawer to and stared out the window. "Well," Tristam said aloud, resisting his disappointment. "I should have expected as much."

He wandered into the hallway, lost in thought, and then made himself mount the stair to the next floor.

There were six sleeping chambers—one obviously a nursery—with sitting rooms attached to the two largest. A covered balcony off one room offered a view and, from it, stairs led down to a terrace on the roof of the kitchen wing. Tristam realized that if he had not hoped to find some key to his uncle's character he would have been well pleased with the house, for it was comfortable and inviting. Looking out into the garden, he resolved to come and live here at some time in the future. "At least one could escape the winter," he said flatly, but the prospect did not seem to excite him.

As he descended the stairs to the terrace above the kitchen, Tristam heard someone call out.

"Hello," Tristam responded, not sure of the sound's source.

"Mr. Flattery?" It was a man's voice.

"On the terrace."

The sound of slow steps and a cane on stone was heard, and then an older man appeared on the stairway to the garden.

"Ah, Mr. Flattery. There you are." The man smiled, and Tristam knew immediately that this was Beth's father. Thick hair, white as snow, fell to the man's shoulders, a contrast to his thinning crown. Here a darkly tanned scalp showed through. Across the freckled forehead the man's skin appeared to have been stretched thin and taut. Heavy white eyebrows and an impressive white mustache, waxed to fine points, created a contrast to dark eyes. And in those eyes Tristam saw enough laughter to suggest that the exotic mustache was partly in jest. "You haven't been left on your own, I hope?" the man said, his concern apparently quite genuine.

"Only for a moment. A domestic emergency called Beth away."

The man laughed. "Well, we have only two hundred of those a day ... each one a crisis. Willis Borrows, your servant, sir."

"I am most pleased to make your acquaintance, Mr. Borrows. I have heard nothing but good spoken of you since I came ashore."

The man looked pleased at this. "Well, I'm sure you have met only the most generous souls. Wait a bit yet."

Tristam laughed.

"You have had a look about the house?"

"I have, and a fine house it is. I could not be more pleased with it."

Borrows gazed up at an ivy covered wall. "Your uncle was always very fond of this place, the garden in particular, and we have done our best to keep it much as it was. I believe there is a decent ale in the pantry, if you would care for a sip."

Tristam followed the old man, who was hindered by a serious limp, as he descended the stairs into the garden and from there into the kitchens.

"I came as soon as I heard you'd arrived. They don't really need me to make hay anymore." He tapped his leg with his cane. "I drive one of the teams, so someone quicker can work in the field or on the mow. But there are always more than enough able hands these days."

Ale was poured, and the two men walked back out into the garden where Borrows led the way to a wooden bench set in the shade of an ancient oak tree. They sipped their ale and talked of Farrow in general and Seabright in particular. Tristam was again surprised at how little interest the islanders took in Farrland, almost never asking, and, when they did, giving the impression that they were really just being polite. Farrow was an insulated little world.

Willis Borrows was obviously relieved to know that the new owner had not come to put the estate up for sale or replace the Borrows as stewards. Tristam felt a little odd holding the future of this family hostage to his whim, for the Borrows had managed Seabright since before Tristam's birth and, in a way, he felt it was far more theirs than his.

A tour of the vineyards followed and, finding in Tristam a willing and able student, Borrows explained viticulture and the managing of the business in perfect detail. Always a glutton for knowledge, Tristam was completely taken by this dissertation, and his excellent memory and training in horticulture impressed the old man.

The afternoon was well past when Borrows completed his lectures; by then he had led Tristam across the fields to the neighbor's where, in the wake of the haying, a massive supper had been laid out under the trees. Tristam was welcomed like an old friend and brought into the discussion as though he'd merely been abroad for a short time.

A dance followed the meal, two fiddlers, a whistle player, and a frame-drummer providing the accompaniment. Tristam found himself in great demand as a partner, for rumors of his skill had arrived before him. In this way the day and a good part of the evening passed without Tristam thinking of the true troubles that beset him.

It was late when he finally found his way back to his uncle's house, and he was gratified to find lamps lit in the hall. Though mortally tired, he went out to the terrace where he collapsed in a chair and stared out over the sea. The moon was a few days past full, and its distorted globe glittered on the waves. A warm zephyr curled about the house, its source undetectable.

After all the activity of the day, Tristam felt terribly let down. It seemed that Erasmus Flattery had managed his escape into the past as completely as yesterday's sunset. Only the imperfect memories of the few who had known the man remained. And even they would fade soon.

Part of Tristam's disappointment, he realized, was due to his growing hope that there would be some clue here that would reflect on his own troubles. It had been the letter from Valary. An unjustifiable feeling was growing in him that his uncle's time in the house of Lord Eldrich was somehow the catalyst that had begun his involvement in all of this. "Ridiculous," Tristam said without conviction. He could not shake the feeling though, and now, if he was to articulate what he felt coming here, it was. *"You got me into this, Uncle. Now give me a clue as to the way out, please."*

"Ridiculous," he said again.

Perhaps the truth is, Tristam thought, *that I love knowledge more than property and, though I am grateful for my material comfort, I would rather have whatever knowledge my uncle gathered over his long life. I am his heir in the physical sense but not in . . .* Tristam groped for a word . . . *not in spirit. I continue none of*

*his work. Pursue none of his passions except by
chance. If we had never met, I would know almost as
much about him.* He thought of the letter from Valary.
But what in this round world was the man involved in?

Thinking this, he fell asleep where he sat.

The dream began as so many did. Tristam became
conscious in half-darkness, a muted, unearthly light illuminating the stairs he climbed. The silence was so
complete he might have been deaf. Each step was an
effort, managed so slowly, as though he struggled
against an invisible current. On the landing, Tristam
came to a door which required all his strength to open.
Beyond the door was a bower, and beneath the trees, in
full summer leaf, falling snow filled the air so completely that Tristam could barely make out the scene.

Erasmus Flattery sat bent over a desk, snow covering his shoulders and hair. He was writing with a quill,
a long white feather, and Tristam could see that the
ink, too, was white. And instead of words appearing on
the page as the pen flowed, they disappeared—
disappeared into the eerie silence. As Erasmus came to
the bottom of a page, it seemed to explode into white
fragments, like fine down or ash, which floated slowly
to the ground. Tristam realized the "snow" was to his
waist and rising and he could not move. Another explosion of white. Snow rose to his shoulders. He fell
somehow and was held by the impossible weight bearing down on him—drowning.

I must wake up, he thought. *I must wake.*

❦   ❦   ❦

Tristam awoke gasping for air, his heart pounding.
He was in the chair on the terrace, but up and pacing
immediately. Agitated. Terrified.

"Blood and flames," he exclaimed. "Bloody blood
and flames!"

It was morning, and his neck was so stiff he could
not turn his head. He tried to calm his pounding heart

and clear his head, which throbbed with each beat of his heart.

"Martyr's blood," he breathed.

He began to walk toward the sea, trying to shake off the dream. *Do dreams haunt others this way?* he wondered. He broke into a trot, as though he could leave the dream behind.

The beach of pebbles and broken shell crunched gratifyingly underfoot, unlike the deep silence of his dream. Tristam stood for a moment, hesitating, then stripped off his clothing and plunged into the ocean. He came easily to the surface, breathing the welcome sea air. Twenty minutes later, he rose dripping from the sea, nearly restored to the waking world.

Willis Borrows was waiting in the garden when Tristam returned. Beth arrived moments later, supervising two younger women who bore coffee and food. Tristam was glad of company just then—the presence of others always helped him shake free of his dreams.

"You swim mornings, Mr. Flattery," Borrows said. "Just like your uncle."

Tristam stopped dead in his tracks. And then nodded, casting about for something to say. "You lost neither spoon nor child, I hope?" Tristam said to Beth.

"Sir? Oh, no. The spoon was found under a chair. It's the usual thing." She laughed, her brown eyes crinkling up in a manner Tristam found quite delightful.

Breakfast was substantial fare, food for those who did much labor, no doubt, but Tristam found his appetite was whole. Borrows was cheerful. And the day, now that he took a moment to look, was very fine.

Details of the business were harder to digest, but Tristam did his best to listen and remember what the old man was saying, for this estate accounted for a not insignificant part of his livelihood. He approved of everything Borrows planned for the coming three years and negotiated a slightly larger portion of the profit for the manager—well-deserved, Tristam was sure. That concluded, Tristam found himself wondering what best to do with the rest of the morning; he would not need to start back to the governor's until after dinner.

"You must have spoken often with my uncle?" Tristam ventured.

"Yes indeed." Borrows showed obvious signs of relief at having the business done. "Viticulture was dear Mr. Flattery's obsession, there was no doubt. We talked of it by the hour, and awfully knowledgeable your uncle was, too."

"Was he not often up at the Ruin, then?"

"Perhaps he went there, most visitors do. Farrowers don't go up often." He laughed. "Superstition I guess. Botanizing; your uncle was often off botanizing."

"Really. Sir Stedman told me he regularly saw my uncle up at the Ruin."

"Truly?" the man shrugged. "Well, I'm sure the governor knows what he's saying. Never spoke of it to me, though. Grapes and wine, that was all I ever heard." He lifted his stick suddenly and waved it like a lecturer. "And now, this talk has reminded me, I have something for you. Your good uncle wrote the year he passed on and asked that I give this to you when you came to Farrow. . . . And here you are."

The feeling from the dream washed over Tristam for the briefest second. "You have something for me? From my uncle?"

"Indeed I do. Come along up to the Grange and I shall give it to you at last, and a few other things as well."

"But what is it?"

The old man got slowly to his feet, hobbled by his bad leg. "Now, as we say on Farrow, Mr. Flattery, one should never ask after a gift—and right enough, too. It won't take us five minutes to walk up to the Grange."

It took ten minutes—Tristam was certain. They entered one of the attached sheds and here Tristam saw his first locked door. The old man located a key above the frame and drew the bolt, and then remembered they must have a lantern. Tristam insisted he could find one and rushed off, locating Beth hanging clothes in the garden. She was not in the same hurry as he was and Tristam realized impatience had him bristling even at her sunny disposition.

At last he returned to the shed where Borrows was sitting on the top step of a stairway that had been locked behind the heavy door. The old man looked rather frail seated there, hunched over his walking stick, looking down into the darkness.

"Mr. Borrows?"

"Ah, there you are, sir. Perhaps you should lead with the lamp, if you don't mind. Careful as you go. It's a steep old stair and twists off to the left."

Tristam began down the flight of stone steps, catching spider webs in his hair. He was careful to keep his pace slow and hold the lantern so as to light the steps for Borrows as well as himself. It was a difficult descent for the old man with his bad leg. Tristam could hear it in his breathing, sharply inhaled and then held, let out in a sigh, but Borrows did not utter a word of complaint.

The air was refreshingly cool and not as damp as Tristam expected, at least not by the standards of cellars in Locfal. There was an odd odor, not unpleasant, like good loam just turned by the plough. A rough stone wall on either hand allowed no view of what lay below.

They stepped down onto a floor of packed earth and Borrows sighed again, stopping with his hand against the wall for a moment. Tristam held the lamp high, chasing shadows into the corners. Before him stretched a cellar with walls lined by long racks filled with wine bottles.

The old man looked up as if to gauge Tristam's reaction.

"It is a fair sight, is it not?"

"I should say it is!" Tristam answered. His first thought was: *Jaimy would believe he had passed into a sort of paradise if he saw this.*

Borrows nodded, with great satisfaction. "Yes, there are some very fine wines here. We always take some of our payment in wine and it is a good practice. This is as fine a cellar as you will find on Farrow, though perhaps the governor's might boast to be the best. All the same, we have done quite well. See for yourself."

Tristam hung the lantern on a hook in the center of the cellar and began to explore. He was only moderately knowledgeable in the area of wines, but even his summary knowledge told him that this cellar would be the envy of . . . well, the Duchess of Morland.

After he had examined the labels of perhaps thirty bottles, he began to realize that his estate manager had understated the quality of this collection quite substantially. "My word, Mr. Borrows, you have a cellar fit for a duke."

"But, Mr. Flattery, it is yourself that has a cellar fit for a duke. Each and every bottle here is your own." The old man could contain himself no longer. He hobbled over to the nearest rack. "Look at this. A *Delisle Estate* red, from the grape of thirty-five. There can't be a hundred bottles like it in the known world. And here: a *Five Oaks,* twenty-nine. Even the King of Farrland can't boast such a wine! It is more rare than white crows, I'm sure." The old man could not stop himself. He went on enumerating treasure after treasure for a good hour. Tristam realized long before they were done that Willis Borrows was an oenophile of the first order.

"So this is my uncle's surprise," Tristam said when he had a chance.

"Ah, I'd almost forgotten." The old man curled his mustache unconsciously. "Now . . . it will be over here." He limped to a corner the lamp did not light. Stooping awkwardly, he slid a plain, wooden box from a low shelf. "Hah. There we are." Borrows cradled the box in one arm so that he might still use his cane and made his way to a small table set near the lamp. "Now here is something I'll warrant you have not seen before."

The box was hinged with leather straps and closed by a green brass clasp. Tristam realized he had gone rigid with anticipation.

"Yeess . . ." the old man said as he opened the lid. Inside was a wine bottle of such dark green glass it was almost black. "The only surviving bottle. Our own wine from the days when Seabright was a winery, made from the original crop of the true Erasmus grape." He removed the bottle carefully from the straw that protected it, bringing it into the light.

Tristam read the label: Seabright, *Regis, 1239.*

Regis!

Borrows held out the bottle to Tristam reverently. "It is the only bottle left, and there were few enough to begin with. A collector, like Roderick Palle, would pay a king's ransom for such a treasure." The old man watched him expectantly. "Mr. Flattery?"

Tristam tore his eyes away from the bottle and tried to smile. He searched for something to say, but his brain would not help him. *Regis?* The word meant king in Old Farr and was common enough, but the coincidence was still unsettling.

His eyes went back to the bottle, to the label in particular. An ornate border surrounded the lettering, vines and other flora intertwined—he knew it, he was certain. It was the same motif that bordered the text on the wall of the ruin. But it was the upper corners of the motif that caught his eye. At first glance he had thought them grapes and vine leaves, but now he realized that this was not so. They were not clearly drawn, but they bore a striking resemblance to the leaves of the *regis* plant he had seen in the King's palace.

TWENTY-FIVE

Kent felt that this task he had undertaken had been meant for a younger man. Too much travel, far too many nights passing without anything like his necessary sleep. He was sore from being battered about aboard the ship that had brought him down the coast, and now he was forced to stand in the cold and rain and wait for his carriage.

And yet, despite all of it, he was certain that he had not felt so alive in a very long time—more years than he could remember. Oh, yes—he was exhausted, but he felt vital! It was almost as if his youth were struggling to return, if only his body would awaken and welcome it as the rest of his being had.

He shook his head, spraying rain from the brim of his hat. It is the great temptation, he told himself.

But he had had his youth and very satisfactory it had been, too. He was not like some who had nothing but regrets for all that they might have done or might have seen. Averil Kent had so few regrets that he could enumerate them on one hand. More than enough, he felt.

Even as a boy Kent had felt driven to live every hour to the fullest, as if he thought he would die young and must make the best use of his time. But he had not died young, nor even in middle age. And now he was getting quite old indeed.

But here he was involved in an adventure. Oh, it was no lark, that was certain. No, he did not make that mistake. This was the most serious matter he had touched upon in his long life. Deadly serious. There were too many nights when he awoke in the grip of cold fear. But, blood and flames, he felt vital!

It is having a purpose, he told himself. Not that he had ever truly lacked purpose, but this was different. Much depended upon him. More than almost anyone realized. But it would be easier if he were younger. This journey was a perfect example. He needed to visit Valary more often—the debacle with Varese could have been avoided. Fortunately, no real harm was done. In fact, it had been a little comical. Massenet and Palle caught like amateurs!

A carriage came around the corner of a darkened building and bobbed along the rough stone quay. The old painter raised his cane and waved, hoping he would be seen in the darkness.

Blessedly, it was dry inside the carriage. Not far, he reminded himself. At least Valary did not have quite the fondness for solitude that the Countess Chilton displayed. Or perhaps it just was easier to achieve in this area of Farrland. Of course Valary had never been celebrated in four lands and, therefore, had no real need to protect his privacy. He was a historian of some reputation, that was true, but the countess. . . . Men had traveled across the Entide Sea for a glimpse of her—just one glimpse. And this was no exaggeration; Kent had met such men.

For a moment he fell into a memory of the countess on a certain evening many years ago. With his painter's recall of detail he could create a picture of her that was so complete, so near to real—why, he could see the individual lashes around her magnificent eyes. It had been the evening she had made a choice that had all but shattered Averil Kent.

So, in fact, he did have regrets—at least one that time could not dull. He would never become philosophical about that.

He thought of the woman hidden in the shadow of the screen. Occasionally, he felt some resentment toward her. How in the round world could she have hidden herself away for so long? *Farrelle's flames,* he almost said aloud, *the rest of us are bearing up. We parade our selves, faded and failing, before the world. What of it?*

But it was no use. Anger served no purpose—one of the lessons of age. The countess had made her choice, and some part of him understood. It was not merely an excess of vanity, as some believed. The countess had not been merely a beautiful woman, she had been an entire age's ideal brought to life. Gentlemen she had never even seen fought duels with complete strangers over her. It had been a madness, really.

Kent could remember the effect of her entering a room—the sound of every person, young, old, gentleman, or lady, catching their breath. Conversation stumbling to a halt. The arrival of a member of the royal family did not compare. He laughed aloud. Well, it was all past now. Done and past. And not since those days had Kent felt so vibrant.

"Just let me live until this task is done," he whispered to no god in particular.

❦   ❦   ❦

It was late and Valary had made them a second pot of strong coffee, for the night would be long yet. Kent stood with his back to the fire, sipping from a very dainty cup the historian had given him, some family heirloom, Kent suspected, for the cup was terribly old.

"Imagine that several hundred years ago a house was torn down," Valary said. He looked at some papers he had spread on a massive table that was all but hidden under piles of books and manuscripts and still more papers. Some part of his hair had escaped the ribbon which supposedly held it tame, and it had sprung up like long, gray wool from one side of his face. This rather comic touch contrasted with the seriousness of the man's manner. "Imagine that it had been demolished and all of its materials, every stone and brick and tile, every stick of wood, spread across the four countries, and even further, for some has reached as far as

Farrow. Some parts are used again in other houses, while other elements have been hewn into headstones or now make up parts of roads. Much of it simply was thrown into the bush to rot away, which it has done most effectively. Other parts went into foundations, which were then carefully buried; the tiles are on six dozen stables spread over a thousand miles; and still other parts were lost at sea while being transported." He looked up, peering over small spectacles. "Do you see? That is how difficult my task is. And I am trying to rebuild this house without even a sketch to begin with. Oh, I know where there is a depression in the ground where it is said the house once stood, but others say there was never a house there at all. That is the life of a mage-scholar. I put together scraps of conversations, perhaps inaccurately recorded; bits of letters; the scribblings of illiterate servants; glean some few half-truths from five hundred badly written books, all purporting to be true. That is why there are so few of us. So few who apply exacting standards, that is. There are any number of people who claim to know the secrets of the mages."

He turned back to his papers again, looking for something. The man had such a distracted manner that Kent wondered if he even remembered what he searched for.

"Ah, here it is." He held up a large sheet of paper, and smiled. "In the summer of 1407, three mages met at the castle of Locmeade." He looked up. "Three that we can be sure of—but there is anecdotal evidence that there were more. At least three more. Now Tenbaum always had a weakness for the ladies, and he almost certainly visited the Duke and Duchess of Ariss at their country home in Downe. A certain singer was a guest there at the time. Downe is a mere six miles from Locmeade Castle." He tossed the paper back onto the table; it had obviously jogged his memory enough. "Make of it what you will, but after this I have three separate references, two by Tenbaum in letters, and one by Lucklow in conversation with the Marquis of

Reme, that all make reference to their 'great endeavor.' " He held up both his hands. "Now in another area of study, I realize this would be considered slim evidence indeed, but in the study of mages—well, it is a contribution that would make a man's reputation. So, Kent, that was the beginning, you see. For over one hundred years—and Medawar said in a letter to Lady Henslow that he had been involved in a single pursuit for one hundred twenty years—they pursued some common goal. Do you see? Over a century, mind you. And with one exception these six were the last mages. Eldrich was not of their time, really, for he was merely in the service of Lucklow. And he was the last."

He crossed to the chair he had been in and out of over the last hour and picked up his cup of coffee; setting it down almost immediately without taking a sip. "The 'great endeavor.' And then . . . for no reason that we know, they stopped passing on their knowledge. Gave up the practice of . . . well, we don't know how long—but centuries, certainly. Every word, gone. Destroyed, it is said, and I think it is true. But Eldrich. . . . Why was he allowed to complete his training?"

Kent shrugged. Certainly it was a question he had asked many times.

"He was left to complete something, but not their 'great endeavor.' No. Eldrich was left to be sure that all the knowledge of the mages died with them. That was his task, I am sure. He intimated this to Flattery. Almost said it aloud."

"But did he manage it?"

Valary stood toying with one of the remaining buttons of his ancient waistcoat. Then he reached up and removed his spectacles, pressing his fingers to his eyes for a second. "I would have said yes. Unquestionably, yes. Eldrich was a thorough man." He replaced his spectacles. "But now. . . ."

The man lowered himself into his chair where he sat looking up at Kent, his face set into hard lines, the exhaustion he no doubt felt finally showing.

"You mentioned a language," Kent said softly.

"Yes." He raised his hand and waved a finger like a lecturer, as indeed he had once been. He was on his feet again, pacing, as though his passion for the subject animated him. "Now, as everyone knows, the four languages of the Entide Sea are all related. That is, they all descended from one common language. So long ago that the single root produced branches as different as separate species of trees. But still, to the philologist, there can be no question. I'm sure we can both cite a hundred examples to prove this. But there are other languages even more ancient, and if they are distant relatives of the tongues of our time . . . well, we know so little of them that in truth we cannot say. But the vowel shift! You see, the vowel shift is often consistent. This young man named Littel. Egar Littel. In a flash of great brilliance he realized that if the vowel shift was consistent, or nearly so, he could postulate words. Postulate whole languages, in theory. Now, of course, he is thought a charlatan, but I am quite sure he is anything but. I have applied some of his principles myself, and the results are impressive. Look. Look. I will show you."

There followed a half hour of Valary tracing words back into ancient tongues and Kent was impressed, for the historian then showed how he had translated an ancient fragment of a poem, and the result made perfect sense.

"So you see, we are closer. What I have done is comparatively simple, of course, and the language not so different from Old Farr. But there is no doubt that the mages spoke a language, or perhaps several related languages, that are unknown today, and certainly were unknown to all but them in ages past. Dunsenay was heard to call out in an unknown tongue at the Battle of the Midden Vale. But if they were related, even very distantly, to our root languages . . . You see?

"So, yes, if we had a text in this mage-language, and if—and I say *if*—it is related to the root language, we could, perhaps, begin to make sense of it. Of course the mage-language was recorded with its own script, I am sure, but even so. . . ."

Kent paced across the wide hearth. A sudden blast of wind caused a downdraft and Kent stepped away as a small cloud of smoke escaped the fireplace. "My fear is this." He looked up at the historian. "If we believe the mages practiced an art. . . . Well, Valary, if I were told that my own paintings would somehow cause inconceivable harm in the world, flaming martyrs, there are few pieces that I would be loath to destroy. We are talking about my life's work—their life's work. Could I not convince myself that just one piece, one small painting that bore my signature, could do no harm? Damn it all, Valary, they were men, just like you and me. Could you stand to have every word you put on paper destroyed?"

Valary seemed to consider this for a moment and then he shook his head, looking down at the fingers of one hand.

"A single text," Kent said. "Just one. That is all it might take. Erasmus Flattery. I will tell you true, I admired that man as few others but if he did this deed. . . ."

They both fell to musing. Another winter storm blew outside, and the house sat close enough to the sea that there was little protection. It almost shuddered with each blast of wind. Valary began the ritual of filling and lighting a pipe.

"I do not like this news of his nephew," Valary said, his excitement gone.

Kent shook his head, scowling. "No. It is not good. Though I am sure he is a man of principles, or at least he is not bad. It is difficult to believe, having met the young man, that he has talent."

"But you spoke highly of him." Valary puffed his pipe to light and blew out a long stream of smoke with obvious satisfaction.

"Oh, yes. He could become an empiricist of some stature. There is almost no question. But he seems . . . very much of this world. There is no mystery to him."

"That does not matter, I think. It is unlikely that we could recognize this talent. But it is in some people just as the ability to sing is there. You cannot look at a man and tell that he has a voice." He drew on his pipe for a moment. "Imagine that this power lies in the earth the way oil sits in the bowl of a lamp. Certain things are needed to make that oil give light. A wick must draw the oil up to the air, and, once there, a spark is needed to start the flame. Do you see? Those with talent are wicks, Averil. Like young Flattery; the power comes up through him, but what is lacking is the spark. The spark, I think, comes from ritual, and the ritual is dependent on language . . . and elements we are only beginning to understand. But even now he draws the power up. At least that is their hope. And if it is true, well, strange things will begin to happen around him. Virtually every mage had some affinity with the animal world. This falcon. It was the first sign."

"I was a fool," Kent said bitterly.

"No, no. Do not whip yourself, Averil. You could not have known."

Kent shook his head, taking no comfort from Valary's words. "Do you know I am worried about the boy, as well. I know he is the focus of this blind madness, but he is not part of it—at least not yet. What will become of him? Precisely what do the others aboard the ship intend?"

"It is a worry," Valary said quietly. "You can see it throughout our history. Those who showed any signs of talent too often were victims of ignorance and superstition. Stoned to death or cleansed with fire before a mage could discover them or before the talent had truly taken form. But once the power is manifest, it will begin to protect its possessor—though to preserve itself, not Tristam Flattery."

TWENTY-SIX

Tristam Flattery leaned heavily against a post on the balcony of his room and gazed out over the darkened garden. A warm wind, fickle in its attentions, swept across the lawns, rustling the leaves, first of this tree, then of that. It leaped down to play among the flowers, swaying the gladioli and foxglove in quick, circular patterns.

The moon, in its last quarter, floated clear of the trees, marking the hour—later than Tristam had realized. A farewell dinner had gone on longer than Tristam expected; the governor and Lady Galton were clearly unwilling to let their guests depart. The *Swallow*'s officers and passengers had been joined by the senior officers of the other Farr ships in harbor, and it had made for a lively evening. Among so many nearly identical dress uniforms the duchess had stood forth like a single blossom in a field, vivacious and witty and, Tristam felt, not a little flirtatious, surrounded by so many gentlemen. There had been something in her manner that had brought back memories of the night of the governor's ball, and Tristam found himself hoping that events would repeat themselves.

He swung himself easily into the hammock so that he could look out over the garden but found he could not remain still. The drop to the garden was not two feet and Tristam stepped out onto the lawn. He was not at all sure which window belonged to the chamber of the Duchess of Morland, but he walked out across the grass and, once he had reached the shadow of a tree, turned, hoping to find the familiar silhouette.

Nothing.

A few more paces took him to a bench which afforded a view of his own balcony—he did not want the duchess to arrive at his chambers and find him gone. The yearning he felt was stronger than he would ever want to admit. *I am lost,* he thought. *Though the Jacks think I am supernatural, it is I who am the victim of enchantment.* Tristam dropped his head into his hands and rubbed his eyes as though he could wipe away the vision of the duchess over dinner. She had the glow and demeanor of a woman recently in love— irresistible, Tristam thought.

A sound came to him above the whispering of the wind—a woman's laughter. Tristam turned around, listening. It came again, less clear but unmistakable. Immediately he feared the worst, and he felt his heart sink.

You are far gone, Tristam Flattery, he chided himself. This will be one of the Galton's maids and some young officer—the very men the duchess had disparaged the night of the ball.

The laughter came again and this time it propelled Tristam to his feet. Mixed into the wind it reminded him of the laughter he had heard in the arboretum when he had come upon the duchess and the King. Very quietly he moved forward, against his will it seemed, certainly against his better judgment. *You would be better not to know,* he told himself. But his feet kept moving, one before the other.

Not far into the copse he was stopped by the sound, very near now and he began to search the shadows. There, upon a square of darkness . . . movement. Tristam stood letting his eyes adjust and slowly the scene was revealed to him. Certainly he was at least half-right—the gleam of gold buttons could be seen on a jacket, tossed aside. The dark square was a blanket.

He could hear the harsh sounds of the lovers' breathing, the occasional half-smothered moan. *What am I doing?* Tristam asked himself: *if I am caught, embarrassment will be the least of my worries.* As quietly as he could he stepped back, one pace, then two. The couple before him rolled over out of the darkest of shadows and Tristam saw it was the very officer who had been courting Galton's niece when the duchess had given Tristam her little lecture about the unsuitability of navy men. And the woman lost in pleasure beneath him was surely the Duchess of Morland. Tristam stopped, against his will.

This is what your obsession with the duchess will lead to, always. He stood, staring, as though he must imprint this image in his mind, record the pain, like a child forced to look at the ruin he has made of some object. If he looked long enough, perhaps the memory would help him escape.

The man appeared to be in rut. Tristam could see white buttocks thrusting in a near frenzy. Strangely, it struck him that here was a man with no thought for anyone but himself. And the duchess, a woman who had revealed herself as a tender lover, seemed as lost in her pleasure as the young bull who mounted her.

Tristam tore his eyes away, took three silent steps back, and then fled. At the edge of the trees he lost his balance somehow and sprawled headlong on the dew-wet grass. He lay for a moment, suddenly out of breath. He tried to rise, but the ground seemed to shift beneath him. Struggling, Tristam heaved himself to his feet and discovered that he staggered like a drunk. He could almost hear the duchess' words: *"Hearts have never been safe with me."*

TWENTY-SEVEN

My Dear Jaimas:

We sail from Farrow this very day, so I must dash this note off to you. The position of ship's naturalist does not seem too far beyond my meager talents, and it is intriguing work and promises to become more so. One could do worse.

I have been to see our late uncle's estate; a small affair typical of the island, it seems. Not unsuitable for an eccentric bachelor, which is rather what I expect to become.

Life aboard our tiny ship is a bit claustrophobic, as you might imagine, but then one always has the machinations of the duchess to keep one amused. I have shipped you a second small wedding present which I hope will arrive intact. Remember me to all, especially your blushing bride-to-be.

Yours in haste,
Tristam

The motion of the open ocean had once again established its ascendancy over life aboard the *Swallow* when the peaks of the island of Farrow blended into a bank of cloud and were gone.

A light drizzle and cooling breeze had driven Tristam below into the confines of his tiny cabin, a rude shock after his room in the governor's mansion, but it at least offered some privacy—some safety. Having claimed that he felt a bit under the weather,

Tristam hoped that he would be left alone. He was avoiding the duchess. The memory of her, lost in pleasure beneath her sailor, seemed to dance before his eyes like the image of a candle flame after it has been snuffed. The pain this image brought to Tristam verged on the physical.

Did she not warn you? he asked himself. *She made you no promises, Tristam Flattery.* But logic had no impact on what he felt—complete and utter betrayal. If the duchess had been his innocent young bride, he could not have felt this more strongly. Nor could he have felt more a fool. How could he have thought for a moment that this woman cared for him? Obviously, she cared only for herself.

It was also painful to realize that she must have found him entirely inadequate as a lover. And even worse, she had gone to a young bull of a naval officer: a man so dense and insensitive that even Galton's niece had lost interest in him.

Why am I responding like this, Tristam asked himself? *Do I think I feel love for the duchess?* No. No, he was fairly certain that this was not so. *I am obsessed,* he told himself. *I am in the grip of a self-inflicted madness, as though an enchantment had been cast over me—but it is of my own making.*

Oh, certainly the duchess had done much to promote this madness; it had not come entirely from Tristam's desires and imagination. She had, after all, come to him in the night.

"Did you not have the fullest pleasure of me this two nights' past?" she had asked. *"Good, then we don't have a misunderstanding."*

Apparently only Tristam had a misunderstanding. The sheltered existence of an academic had not prepared him for the Duchess of Morland, that was certain.

He could understand why so many of the dons of Merton spent their lives behind the protective walls of the university, living their priestly, asexual existences, aloof from desire. The life of the mind—the life that Tristam had decided was inadequate.

Well, here is where that gets you, he thought. His tiny cabin seemed positively claustrophobic at that moment—a reflection of his life. There was no escape but to have stayed on Farrow.

And why didn't I stay?

He was not sure, but he feared that, even after what had occurred, he still followed in the wake of the duchess, like a magnet drawn to iron.

I cannot stay in my cabin forever. But perhaps a day or two of feigned illness will allow me time to regroup, at least enough that I can put a face on it. Unfortunate I did not inherit the craft of my mother.

A knock brought Tristam back to the world. His first thought was that it was the duchess, come to check on his condition.

"Yes?"

"Flattery? It is Osler."

The lieutenant had spent one year at Merton and had immediately taken up the common practice among the young scholars of addressing others by their family names. Tristam suspected that Osler felt some loss of his university career—though he was certainly an exemplary naval officer—and saw having Tristam aboard as a way of recapturing some of that life.

At a call from Tristam, Osler opened the door, a half-smile that spoke both amusement and concern appearing on his pock-marked face.

"Landsman's fever, is it?" he asked.

"I fear so, though it is not so bad. I'm sure I will be better in short order."

"No doubt. Odd that you were not troubled by it when we set out from Avonel—but then it is a mysterious ailment. I suffered it once for a terrible hour after I had been at sea for three years. I'd thought I was well over that." He smiled.

Tristam realized that he no longer really registered Osler's scarring—the result of the harbor pox—though he was quite sure the young officer never lost his awareness of it.

"Well, there is some news to cheer you, Flattery. You will have a great opportunity to see some sea birds in a fortnight. The captain is going to try to fix the position of Bird Island once and for all. It is presently charted in three different locations—surprisingly far apart. But apparently, as the name suggests, it is the home of some thousands of birds."

This kindled Tristam's curiosity, at least a little, but then a second thought occurred to him.

"This can't be on the common route to the Archipelago, surely?"

Osler shook his head. "No—farther north—but ships pass through the area often enough that the rock is quite a hazard."

"Ah. And we'll take how long to find it, do you think?"

Osler shrugged, leaning against the door frame, at ease on the rolling sea. "A week, perhaps. A fortnight at the outside."

Tristam nodded. He wondered immediately if the duchess knew of this. For a second he thought he should rush to her with the news, as though a threat to their common cause might rekindle the intimacy that Tristam had thought—or perhaps imagined—had been growing between them. But then he decided he had made a fool of himself over this woman often enough.

"Does the duchess know of this?"

"I don't think so," Osler answered, and then he brightened a little. "Do you think I should tell her?"

Tristam knew that both Hobbes and Osler looked for excuses to speak with the duchess.

"I'm sure that would be appreciated."

"I hope you're back on your feet again soon," Osler said, anxious now to leave. "The pleasures of the day to you, Flattery."

The door closed. Tristam laid back in his hammock, a bit jealous. Why had he done that? To see someone else look like a fool over the duchess; that was why. Tristam was not alone in being affected by this woman—though perhaps the others were not obsessed in quite the same way.

Tristam closed his eyes for a moment, but the image of the duchess beneath her lover came immediately to mind and Tristam could not bear that.

He must soon master this madness or he would be lost. The duchess would do this to him again and again if he let her.

A few moments later a second knock sounded on Tristam's door, this one gentle and tentative.

"Excuse me, Mr. Flattery. It is Jacel."

Tristam rolled out of his hammock and opened his door to find the duchess' maid clinging to the door frame, looking truly ill.

"Jacel, you should be lying down." Tristam felt his own fakery seemed absurd, suddenly.

"No, I feel no better. I must try to keep my mind on something else." She paused to breathe, barely controlling her illness. "Would you have a moment to speak with Her Grace?"

Tristam nodded. It was a very small victory—illusory really—but at least the duchess had called for him and he had not given in and found some excuse to go to her. Not that it would be any easier.

"I shall be along directly."

Tristam passed back through the empty wardroom and knocked at the door to the cabin of the Duchess of Morland.

This is what comes of having no escape, he told himself even as he waited for the door to be answered.

Jacel answered his knock, her pretty face still an unbecoming shade. It was difficult for Tristam to believe that the woman had chosen to continue the voyage, and though he had heard some citing the maid's devotion to her mistress as the reason, Tristam was quite sure it was the young Entonne's attachment to her mistress'

brother that had led her back to sea. And he thought
his obsession was fraught with trouble.

"Is that Tristam?" a voice called from within.
"Bring him in, please, Jacel."

In the bright cabin beyond, Tristam found the duchess propped up on her berth, a book in hand, her legs
covered by a heavy wool blanket. She smiled as
Tristam entered, but he could see that she searched his
face, reading him, he guessed, with little more difficulty than the book she held.

She pulled her legs up, making room at the foot of
her berth. "You look all out of sorts, my dear Tristam.
Do sit, and tell me what troubles you."

And here we are, Tristam said to himself, suddenly
she is kindness itself. One would think that the smallest inconvenience to me caused her great distress.

Seeing that Tristam hesitated to speak, she turned to
her maid. "Jacel? Would you mind."

The maid bent a knee and bobbed her head—a shipboard curtsy—and went out, closing the door silently.

The duchess set her book aside, and leaned forward,
hugging her knees as she had that night in Tristam's
room. He could not bear it, he realized, and looked
away. He did not see her nod, and then bite her lip.

"Tristam? It was a great risk for us to spend the
night together in Galton's house. I should have told
you." She reached out and tugged at his arm, forcing
him to look around at her. She smiled at him as though
there were nothing out of place in the world. "I dearly
wanted to visit you again, but. . . ." She paused, gazing
into his eyes for a few seconds, reading how much,
Tristam could not guess.

She pushed the blanket aside and rose gracefully in
the swaying cabin, crossing to the small desk where
she removed an envelope from a locked drawer. "The
King's Man," she said in the language of Doorn, "has
unlikely allies."

She slipped a letter from the envelope and handed it
to Tristam without a word.

He unfolded it and read:

My Dear Roderick:

Tomorrow (the sixth day of November) the duchess and her entourage will set out again, but what an interesting visit we have had! I have experienced something so overwhelming, so utterly unexpected that I fear I have not recovered yet.

I carried a party up to the Ruin, the duchess, Lord Elsworth, Tristam Flattery, and others, and gave the usual speech for visitors. Afterward the Viscount Elsworth and Flattery made shift to climb to the rim of the volcano. As they were about to reach their goal, a small tremor gripped the mountain and, in the gentlemen's own words, "attempted to shake them off!"

To us at the Ruin this was barely felt, but, along with a distinct emission of sulfurous gases, an eerie sound spewed forth from the mouth of the bird-man. A deep, rumbling, string of vowellike sonants that seemed for all the world an attempt at vocalization. We were all so shocked that every person there stood, staring at the sculpture, struck completely dumb.

I think that no one, not even the duchess, suspected what this might mean, for you see, I had noted that young Flattery drank from the fount earlier. And here he was, living under my own roof! Surely he is the candidate we have sought for so long. I tell you, Roderick, I am impressed with the young man, and not simply because of this unprecedented incident. We must make no mistakes. And I will say candidly, I question the wisdom of sending Flattery off on this voyage. Yes, I know the argument . . . but still, we should take no risks. Who knows how long it will be until we find his like again?

The duchess works her charm on him, I fear, though in the end this may not matter. Time will tell, and I am sure you have taken all precautions.

𝌆𝌆𝌆𝌆𝌆𝌆𝌆

Your servant,
Stedman Galton

Tristam stared at the page, unable to tear his gaze away, not sure what it was that disturbed him most: Galton's words or the single neat row of characters. *Runes!* Galton had written in runes! Was it a jest!

"Is this truly a letter to Sir Roderick?" Tristam was embarrassed by the incredulity in his voice.

"It is an exact copy. Including the runes at the bottom. Similar to the writing on the Farrow Ruin, it seems."

Tristam nodded. "How in the world did you come to possess it?"

The duchess made the tiniest motion, almost a shrug, a slight twist of her head. "I made the acquaintance of an officer aboard the ship which carried the government dispatches," she said simply.

The naturalist looked away to hide his reaction.

"Do you see? I realized my privacy might not be treated with proper discretion." Having returned to her former place, the duchess leaned forward suddenly and kissed the lobe of Tristam's ear. "I have not worked my charms on you as much as I would like, that is certain." She released her melodious laugh, taking Tristam back to the time he had first set eyes on her. *She cannot know that I saw her with another. It was her, wasn't it? The night was dark, after all.*

"Did you not warn me, Duchess, not to trust my heart to you?"

He heard her release a long breath, though he did not turn to face her.

She slipped closer to him, resting her forehead against his shoulder, taking his arm in both her hands. "You could have said no. I would have been hurt, but I would have survived. I have certainly suffered worse." She raised her head, and forced him to meet her eye. "And so will you, Tristam, unless you manage to run the gauntlet of human affairs differently than everyone else. It cannot be done without risk. Without some damage. And many suffer far more. My warning? I offered it in good faith. You chose to disregard it. *You* chose." She paused. "You may change your mind, however. But only once. Is that what you wish?"

Tristam could not think with those green eyes looking into his. *Vertigo,* he thought. He felt his head shake.

The duchess brightened a little, her seriousness disappearing like years. "I am glad." She leaned forward and kissed him softly. Then put her forehead to his, running her fingers into the hair at the base of his neck. Tristam heard her breath catch, and just that increased his pulse.

"We must not start rumors," she said, pulling free of their embrace, her face a bit flushed, he thought. She smiled as though teasing. "I have my good name to think of, after all."

She put her hand over his, tilting the letter so that she might read.

"Whatever does it mean?" Tristam asked, hoping words might disguise his state.

The duchess looked at him with a gaze devoid of emotion. "I had hoped, Tristam Flattery, that you might have some ideas. It is you that Galton calls *'the candidate we have sought for so long.'*"

"I haven't a clue." Lady Galton came suddenly to mind. She had spoken of Palle with some disdain—but this letter was supposedly from her husband to Sir Roderick!

"I think it is time we talked of your uncle, Tristam," the duchess said, her voice soft but so firm Tristam could not mistake the determination. She paused, waiting.

"I can't imagine what you would want to hear." Tristam felt a surge of unexplainable fear which almost immediately gave way to growing anger. "The truth is, I hardly knew the man, though it seems no one is inclined to believe me. I spent almost all my years in boarding schools," he said, some bitterness slipping into his tone. "Parts of three summers I lived at my uncle's home, and during those visits I was almost completely ignored. In my third year at Merton my uncle passed on and left me his worldly possessions, though this inheritance did not include a single written word. That is what I know of Erasmus Flattery. Less, I would guess, than many another." Tristam paused to catch his breath. "What did my uncle have to do with this?" He waved the letter.

The duchess, in her maddening way, shrugged, never taking her eyes from his.

Neither spoke for a long moment, and Tristam looked down at the letter again. His mind was in such turmoil that the entire letter might well have been runes—the words seemed to convey no meaning.

The duchess smiled suddenly. Then laughed aloud. "You have every right to such resentment, my dear Tristam. Why, you have been buffeted about, lied to by the King's Man. Sent on an errand that Roderick hopes will not succeed or at least not succeed in time. It is a wonder you have not exploded like a primed cannon." She reached out and caressed his shoulder. "You do not, I take it, understand what Galton thinks you are a candidate for?"

"I have not the slightest idea!"

She nodded, then leaned her forehead against his shoulder again. They stayed like that for some minutes, Tristam so entirely confused by the situation that he could not move.

"They have plans for you, Tristam Flattery," she said softly, causing him to tense up even more.

He felt resistance rise up in him like a rage. "Madness," Tristam spat out. "What kind of insanity has possessed these men I cannot imagine."

Nothing. She said nothing. Desperately Tristam wanted to hear her agree.

"But do you see, Tristam, what great significance Galton attaches to this *voice?*"

"Blood and flames," Tristam growled. "Foolishness, I tell you. Obviously a vent from the crater lies behind the figure of the bird-man. All that was heard were escaping gases."

"A belch, you say?"

Tristam thought he heard a smile in this question. He nodded and the duchess said nothing for a moment, then: "An empiricist's answer."

"Meaning?"

"Nothing more than said, I assure you."

Tristam's mind raced. "These runes? Have they deciphered them? Was this merely a jest?"

"Roderick seldom jests. Galton? Perhaps. But there is far more to our good governor than his ... jovial manner would suggest. Do not be deceived."

No, Tristam was tired of being deceived and he was beginning to think that it was everyone's intention—to deceive him for their own ends. *A candidate for what?* Tristam wondered.

"I doubt that I will persuade Stern to give up this search for his missing island," the duchess said, matter-of-factly. "You know how he responds when resisted." She still leaned against Tristam's shoulder. "A few days should not matter, but if this becomes the pattern of our voyage ... something will have to be done. We cannot well afford to waste months or even weeks. I can count on you in this, can't I, Tristam?"

Tristam could not answer for a second, then he heard his voice whisper, "Yes."

The duchess pulled away from him, sitting up as though she required some distance to think. "You see how cunning Roderick actually is? I realize now that Stern is not one of Roderick's minions. Our good captain is that rarest of species—a man of principle. An officer who will not be swayed from his duty. And if he believes that his duty is to carry on with the surveying of Oceana or the Archipelago, or to search for lost islands in the Gray Ocean, well, he will do it if he is at all able." She swung her legs off the berth and put the rug aside. "You see? Far better to send an ... honorable man. Someone who truly believes in the concept of 'gentlemanly conduct,' rather than merely dressing himself in the proper clothing and manners." She shook her head. "A man less formidable than Roderick would have sent someone he believed to be his creature—a man to whom he had promised wealth and titles. But I would guess Stern has been promised almost nothing: oh, perhaps a small promotion has been dangled before him, though maybe not even that." She looked at Tristam, her large eyes wide, as though to say, "do you see?"

"And this too-earnest dedication to 'gentlemanly conduct' and bull-headed devotion to duty—these are far more difficult to deal with than simple corruption." She shook her head, though Tristam thought this gesture indicated some admiration. "Stern is in a terrible position. If he returns from Varua with the seed . . . no one will know but Roderick and a few others. And Palle is notoriously ungrateful to those outside his own circle—something Stern may or may not be aware of. And within the navy this voyage might well hurt Stern's career. Returning without even having charted some new territory will give the appearance of having mismanaged his voyage. With no patron in the Admiralty or within the court, Stern has likely reached the height of his career—and I do not think he is unambitious." Tristam thought she was speaking her thoughts now.

"I could offer him whatever his ambition might desire—but you heard what he said about rising according to his own merit. I think he might actually believe that—and look where it has got him! If he believes the King's health cannot hold until we return, then any promises made by the Duchess of Morland will be a worthless coin." Her mouth tightened in mild anger.

She turned to Tristam. "But we must find a way to bring our good captain to his senses. It shall not be an easy task."

"If anyone can accomplish this, I believe the duchess shall manage it."

She tilted her head, looking at him as though wondering if he teased. Apparently she decided he was sincere. "You may call me Elorin, when we are alone. But do not do so in public, please, Tristam. It would not look right."

He bowed his head as though he had just been knighted.

He felt a kiss of the utmost tenderness on his cheek. "You are dear to me," the duchess whispered into his ear and then her arms encircled him and she held him close. "You must go before there is talk. Ships are such small places. Perhaps we can arrange a night ashore when we reach the Queen Anne Station: that is, if you are not tired of an aging woman?"

Tristam closed his eyes tightly—trying not to see a vision of the duchess beneath her lover in the dark. "I think you are the most desirable woman I have ever known."

Soft lips brushed his cheek again. "You are sweet. But you must be gone or I must call in Jacel. Take the letter, if you wish to puzzle over it, but whatever you do, keep it safe. Who knows who might be Roderick's agents aboard this ship."

❦　❦　❦

Tristam had returned to the comfort of his swaying hammock and lay there, lost in thought. Within him a battle seemed to be in progress—the memory of the duchess and her lover at odds with the words she had just spoken to him, with the affection she had shown and with the promises made.

Yes, she had warned him and, yes, he had chosen to ignore that warning—though it had hardly felt like a choice at the time. More a compulsion.

The duchess had slept with someone else, but then she had made no promises of fidelity—nor was she likely to. But had she lain beneath that bloody officer so that she might get hold of Galton's letter? Tristam did not know if this idea brought relief or whether he felt some distaste. His image of her did not allow such a common act. How desperate was the duchess to get her hands on this seed?

Given the other implications of Galton's letter, Tristam was surprised that things with the duchess seemed so much more important. What in Farrelle's name had Galton meant? A candidate? For what? Considering the warning of Lady Galton and her husband's letter together there was mounting evidence that some believed there was more to *regis* than its healthful properties or even the promise that it might extend one's years. This led Tristam into the area he did not wish to acknowledge. The dream of his uncle came back to him. *I am being drowned by the things he did not speak of.*

Deciding that he must make some effort to turn his thoughts elsewhere, Tristam pulled out the two packages he had been given by the Galtons upon leaving Farrow.

As he cut the twine from the first bundle, Tristam realized that his discussion with the duchess, despite the fact that neither had mentioned her encounter with the officer, had taken away some of his despair. She had raised his hopes again. *Or perhaps,* Tristam thought, *I have raised them myself.*

He pulled the paper off the first package. And it was a manuscript—Sir Stedman's perennially unfinished book about the Ruin.

"Well, well," Tristam said to his cabin. A letter from Galton lay atop the bundle and Tristam took it up.

My Dear Mr. Flattery:

I have a more recent fair-copy of my book, but Lady Galton insists it is identical to this one but for the placement of the commas; I fear she is not far wrong. I hope you find it of some interest for I am only a dabbler in the discipline of archaeology, as you know. Let me say again that it was a great pleasure meeting you and I do hope we will have the pleasure of your company again. Farrow has a way of getting

into a person's blood: I dare say you will find it so.
Good fortune to you on your adventures.

Your servant,
Sir Stedman Galton

Tristam began to leaf through the book; Sir Stedman's shaky hand covered page after page. Some rather plain but serviceable drawings of the Ruin accompanied the text as well as a complete compilation of all the runes carved into the ancient stone.

Tristam dug into a locker and removed the bottle of wine Borrows had given him. Galton's drawings were not so exact that Tristam could say for certain, but surely the pattern in the label was modeled from the border of the text on the Ruin. But did it represent *regis?* Without actually taking the bottle up to the Ruin, he could not say with certainty.

Tristam read bits here and there as he leafed through the loose pages. Though Galton's writing may have been stiff and formal, the work itself appeared to be exhaustive, something any trained empiricist would have been proud to have done.

Turning back to the first page Tristam began to read, but he realized that the words did not register meaning, almost as if they came from a language unknown to him. Images of the duchess kept appearing in his mind and with each of these his emotions would take a sudden turn—delight, arousal, despair, frustration.

"I *am* in a state," he whispered. At least the man she had been with was not an officer aboard the *Swallow.* That would be intolerable.

He forced his mind away from the duchess again though it took some effort of will. Thinking the second package might contain something that would draw his attentions more, he cut the string surrounding it. Inside he found a thick cloth-bound book, its title in Entonne: *A History of the Mages by F.T. Valary.* Valary's book! He opened it quickly and discovered an inscription.

For Tristam:

> *"Colder than starlight on midwinter's night,*
> *Dark, dark. My thoughts eclipse the sun.*
> *The silence comes, stealing, o'er the heart.*
> *But hear in the distance, the sea's tumble and run."*

Lady Galton

The lines were vaguely familiar though Tristam could not name the poet—a translation, he thought. Gently he put the book aside, almost afraid to go further. He felt that Lady Galton had somehow looked into his soul that morning as they had broken their fast in the garden. Did she know about his involvement with the duchess? Yes, he realized, it was likely that she did. Those beautiful eyes suffered no loss of sight—nor insight, it seemed. He hoped she was right about the healing power of the sea. Valary's book!?

But it is not coincidence. There is a pattern here. I feel that I am part of it, too much a part of it in fact—I can't step back far enough to see the design. He puzzled over the problem for some time, getting nowhere, as usual.

Tristam returned his attentions to Galton's manuscript, with only marginally better luck at first, but then his curiosity was awakened and he lost himself to it. Two hours found the last page and Tristam was pleasantly surprised by the text, for it was a work of some merit indeed. There was not, to Tristam's knowledge, a more complete work on the subject. Galton had done much to clarify the history of the Ruin's discovery, making some sense of the many stories that had long muddied the truth. The description and drawings were the most complete, if not the most artistic, he had seen.

Galton's careful observations on the other ruins on Farrow and how deeply they were buried were extremely well documented and raised the question again of how old the Ruin of Farrow was, compared to other remains found on the island.

Unquestionably the greatest original contribution of the monograph was the section that dealt with the shards of pottery found about the island. After Galton's years of collection and careful work, there seemed little doubt that much of the pottery was decorated with a written script that differed in fundamental ways from that found on the Ruin. Interesting indeed.

There was only one thing missing from Galton's work; a glaring oversight it would have seemed a day earlier, but now Tristam did not view it that way. Galton spent no time on the runes—they were barely mentioned in fact—only a paragraph saying they remained undeciphered.

TWENTY-EIGHT

In certain respects Averil Kent did not have the proper disposition to be a painter. The pursuit required long periods of solitude in which one focused on nothing but one's art, and Averil Kent had been born a most social man. The companionship of others was, to him, as necessary as air, and the more convivial the company the better. He savored the art of conversation as much as he loved the art for which he had become famous—perhaps even more.

The company of intelligent women, banter with men of good spirit, weighty discussion of matters most grave, wicked mockery of the pretentious—all of these delighted him in ways that solitude—his own company—did not. Oh, he loved to paint, there was no doubt of that. For most of his life it had been his other grand passion. But the time alone.... That was another matter. The irony in all of this was that Kent absolutely had to sequester himself away when he painted. There was no other way for him to make contact with his muse, whom he thought of as a jealous lover, unwilling to share him with anyone else.

So Kent was forced to alternate between periods alone at his country home, where he fought despondency and melancholia the entire time, and spells of travel or at his home in Avonel. Of course, when he was living the social life, he always felt a nagging sense that he was frittering away his time—something he no longer possessed in abundance—so after a few weeks this feeling would drive him back to work in the country ... and growing melancholia.

Sometimes Kent felt that he was a man whose needs would always be at war. Even that brief period when a canvas sat on its easel, complete, no longer produced a feeling of peace, for he believed, for some years now, that his work grew progressively less vital as well as less original.

The few months that he had been caught up in this ... *matter* had been an odd hiatus for the painter. For the first time that he could remember, Kent felt completely justified in abandoning his painting. Oh, he did experience the occasional twinge—the odd feeling that he should be standing before an easel, but these feelings were not overwhelming nor even that frequent. More a mere emotional habit, he thought.

Not that this was a holiday he had embarked upon. Not by any means. But all the same, he did feel a sense of freedom that was unique in his life. *"The muse,"* he told himself, *"is as difficult a mistress as any in this round world."*

This day he had come to his club, largely to see what he could learn of events that passed in both Avonel society and in the court. At such times he felt a bit like an insect, his antennae testing the air around him, delicately sensing the currents, ready to dart beneath a leaf.

He was well known here, as he was in most of Avonel and beyond for that matter, and the staff treated him with great respect and affection—"like a favorite uncle," a friend had once said, and he thought it was not far from the truth.

"The most innocent seeming of men," the countess had called him. Perhaps not a sobriquet that most men would choose, but it suited Kent's purpose admirably—his more recent purpose anyway.

The Brixham Club was not overly full at that time of day, but Kent wanted a chance to establish himself in a place where others would realize he was present, but he would still have enough privacy to carry on conversations—should this be required.

The squeaking of leather from his great boots accompanied Kent up the marble stair. The staff nodded politely as they passed, moving at a pace that never seemed so hurried as to be bothersome to anyone yet propelled them along at a surprising rate. A skill Kent would like to master in his life—never appear to rush yet be moving much faster than anyone realized.

The dark polished paneling, the finest eastern black walnut, gave the club a peaceful hushed atmosphere, yet the upper walls and high ceilings the color of new-cut ivory would allow no feeling of oppression to settle in. The place reminded Kent, in a small way, of his own home in Avonel.

Entering a large common room, Kent went to the periodical stand. Here he selected something to read and went up to the next level and took a table in a large bow window. It was the most private place in the great open room, and the most visible as well.

"Coffee, Mr. Kent?" came the soft tones of a servant whom Kent had known twenty-some years—perhaps it was even thirty.

"I know I should break my habits and dare something different. . . . But what would I enjoy so well? And at my age I have tried everything. Coffee; yes, thank you."

Opening the first pages of the city news, Kent realized he felt a bit of excitement, like a barely perceptible vibration somewhere in his center. It was not just this task he was so caught up in, it was the social life—or its potential—that caused this inner hum.

Kent had innumerable sources of information in the great city of Avonel. Something about his fame, his profession, and his personality led people to trust him with the most sensitive information. Everyone needed a confidant and who better than a man completely outside their sphere of activity? An artist, a man who had no involvement in the court or in business. A true innocent. And, even better, an intelligent and sympathetic listener. A person who invariably could see one's point of view, and—astonishing considering his pursuits—give remarkably sensible advise. And this proved especially valuable when it pertained to other personalities. Kent, after all, knew everyone. Was liked by everyone.

And here he sat in the window of his club, occasionally glancing out at the street and the harbor below, though out of the corner of his eye he kept track of who came and went in the room, and who arrived at the front entrance.

It was the height of the season in Avonel, soon to culminate with the anniversary celebration of the King's coronation, and everyone who was anyone had repaired to their city residences. The theaters offered their most elaborate productions, the major orchestras played almost every evening, and the small chamber ensembles were continually engaged. It was a time of year that Kent never missed, though this season he had other things on his mind.

A tiny, handsome man entered the room and nodded to Kent, his face showing the kindest look, and Kent bent his neck in turn. Lord Harrington, Chancellor of the Exchequer. A close associate of Roderick Palle and a man with quite a considerable mind. Kent was sure that no one would ever know the true amount of the monies Lord Harrington had put aside over the years. The man must be rich beyond imagining, Kent was sure. The chancellor took a seat at a small table near to one of the hearths—his customary place—and, like Kent, he began to pore over the periodicals.

A large carriage pulled to a rather hurried stop outside and from it appeared the Entonne Ambassador, Count Massenet: late for an appointment with the chancellor, Kent assumed by the way the man rushed. If only Kent could put an ear to the wall and hear what these two would say. It might have no bearing on the matter that interested him, but all the same, there were hardly two more central players in the great theater of politics. And formidable men! Kent would hardly want to run afoul of either. Wills as hard and sharp-edged as tempered steel.

The count appeared, stopping for the merest second in the doorway. A tall man, handsome, his appearance, Kent thought, as precise as his mind. Dark colored with a look not unlike the King's Physician, Rawdon, but leaner, stronger. He dressed in Entonne fashion, his clothing black and embroidered in silver thread. A silver sash ran from shoulder to hip and on his right breast he wore a jeweled medallion worth more, perhaps, than Kent would see in all his life. If there was one man in all of Avonel whose charms the ladies seemed unable to resist, it was this Entonne aristocrat.

As expected, the count crossed immediately to Lord Harrington, and though Kent was intently interested in what would be said between these two, it was certainly unacceptable to gape at men of such stature.

Reluctantly he went back to his reading, glancing out the window occasionally. A break in the cloud illuminated sails against a black squall and the drama of this caught Kent's eye.

"Mr. Kent?"

It was a very slightly accented voice. Kent looked up to find the Entonne Ambassador standing one step down, but still seeming tall. The man had the bearing of a military officer, Kent realized, but not stiff or overly formal.

The painter rose quickly, making a leg. "Count Massenet," he said, using the Entonne address. In Farrland an earl, the equivalent rank, would be addressed as *"Lord."* "The pleasures of the day to you."

"And to you, Mr. Kent. It has been such a long time since we have spoken. I trust you are well?"

"I am most certainly well, and I hope the count can say the same?"

"Life treats me more kindly than I deserve, I assure you. If you do not await someone . . .?" He made the slightest motion toward the empty chair.

"Do join me, please. Excuse my terrible manners. I thought you had come to meet the chancellor." Kent looked up and realized that the Farr minister had gone.

"Lord Harrington? No. A chance meeting, that is all." The count took the offered chair and a servant arrived almost silently. "I would join Mr. Kent in coffee, though make mine Entonne fashion, please." He turned back to Kent, smiling warmly.

"You are taking a well-deserved rest from your labors, Mr. Kent?"

"It is the season . . . I can't resist," Kent admitted, surprised that he felt a bit of embarrassment.

The count nodded. "I understand completely. Have you been to the opera? No? It is truly superb! And I do not say this because it is Entonne. No, it is a performance of the kind we might witness once in a decade. Not to be missed."

The servant arrived with coffee, obviously readied the moment the count appeared. Like Kent, perhaps, a man of habit.

"And your own affairs, Count? They go well?"

The man made an odd face. "Well enough. We continue to negotiate the treaty, endlessly apparently, to everyone's continuing loss." He smiled wryly. "You know how such things go. We no longer debate to gain real advantage but to come away from the table having created the perception that we have somehow won. 'Politics,' this is called. In truth, the losses in trade while this goes on more than erase any advantage. I confess, I am getting a bit bored with it all. Our interests do not exist in such opposition as some imagine." He raised his eyebrows, his look clearly saying that true gentlemen, such as he and Kent, were above such foolishness.

Kent found he smiled in return, honored to find himself momentarily a peer of Count Massenet.

It occurred to Kent that the count had probably never truly been bored in his life. His station would take care of that, even if his character had been capable of boredom—something Kent seriously doubted. Men of imagination were seldom bored and the treaty was only one of the man's responsibilities.

"Perhaps it is a function of age, Mr. Kent, but other matters seem more important to me lately. . . ." He glanced up from his coffee and met the painter's eye.

Kent said nothing. A man of Massenet's brilliance and position did not normally choose a Farrlander for a confidant. If he had anything to say to Kent that was not of the purest social intent, then the man had another purpose. Kent found himself leaning forward a little.

"Do you know a young man by the name of Flattery? A nephew to the great duke, I think?"

Kent nodded, feeling for a moment as though gravity had released its hold of him. Instinctively his hand clutched the table. "He is an empiricist of some potential."

"So I am told. And an intimate of the Duchess of Morland, as well." The count took a second to examine his fingernails on one hand. "Mr. Flattery is an acquaintance of one of my dearest friends, a musician and composer. I understand he is off on a voyage to the Great Ocean?"

It was hardly a secret of the crown but Kent found himself hesitating to confirm this. "I believe that is true."

"In the company of the Duchess of Morland and her savage brother."

One of the few men Kent could imagine who would have no fear of insulting the Viscount Elsworth. The count's skill with a blade had kept many a husband and father from calling him out.

"Yes. As all of Farr society have noted."

The count sipped his coffee. "I think there are strange things going on in your fair city, Mr. Kent. The favorite of the King—a woman—takes passage on a ship of the King's Navy and sets out on a voyage to the very ends of the earth. A nephew of the great Erasmus makes a journey to visit the Ruin of Farrow and then beyond with this same duchess. Certain members of the court have taken more than a passing interest in the doings of the mages."

Kent almost shut his eyes to hide the fear. What did this suave count want of him? What did the Entonne government want?

"Of course that is hardly new. Others have had this same fascination, even in Entonne. But this is not the same, I think." He glanced around the room and then back to Kent. He leaned forward so that the medal on his chest swung free. "You need say nothing, Mr. Kent. I do not ask that you confirm or deny—only that you hear me out, please." The man took Kent's lack of response as permission and went on. "These men have hopes of rediscovering knowledge long lost—and better lost, too, as we both realize. The people who are involved in this—they are not eccentric scholars or bored aristocrats desperate to amuse themselves. They are formidable men." He leaned back, touching his fingertips together—almost a feminine gesture it was so gently done. "Do you know what concerns me most about these gentlemen? Oh, not what you might think. I do not believe them bad. They are not even particularly greedy or selfish, for men in their station. No, what concerns me is the narrowness of their vision. It is a problem with men driven by the need to accomplish. They focus on the task at hand to the exclusion of all else—and it is an absolute necessity for them to do so. They walk a narrow road, and because the road itself is treacherous, they do not raise their heads to look to either side or into the distance—even to the next bend. *Never* do they turn their gaze back." For a second he paused. " 'Gentlemen who appreciate things Farr.' " A shrug and then he looked closely at Kent again, assessing the impact of his words, sensitive, no doubt, to the smallest facial tic. "Have you been to the famous linen factory of Hogarth? He is a great friend of your King's Man."

Kent nodded.

"Is it not a wonder? So many ingenious machines

laboring incessantly and producing ... well, I have forgotten the exact figure but an impressive yardage of fabric of the highest quality. Great profits for all involved, without question. That is what these gentlemen see. They do not look to either side—not for a moment. Self-doubt is not a quality that will assist a man in rising to the heights that these gentlemen have reached. Do you see? No one appears to have noted that the Wye River, once a beautiful waterway and aswim with fish, now flows like a rainbow stained with the colors of a hundred different dyes and bleaches. The fish are gone and the fishermen with them. A great wheel powered by the river current drives the factory and only a tenth the number of workers are needed to make the linen." He looked out the window for a second, as though to shake off the vision of the Wye Valley. "Many things are ignored when they paint their picture of this bright future, and it is their vision that all of Farrland—all the countries around the Entide Sea—will echo with the clatter of these precious machines. *To do a thing.* The mere act of accomplishing it.... That is everything there is to these gentlemen.

"Given a few new mechanical principles and look what these men do. Imagine if they were to possess a power greater than any of them can yet imagine? And not for a moment do I suggest they would set out to do evil. Oh, no, but all the same, those who serve them are not always so mindful, so eager are they to rise in the esteem of their masters. And those same masters may gain great advantage by turning their eyes away at critical moments. Of the world's great canvas they perceive only a corner—and even that is chosen with great care. A dangerous thing, I think."

The count leaned back into his chair, shaking his head gently. "The anniversary of the King's coronation is not far off. My own sovereign has sent a most generous gift, though this gift of long life can hardly be matched. Almost unnatural, wouldn't you say, in a family not known for longevity?"

Kent held his peace, afraid to hear what the man might say next, but the count did not speak. Unable to bear the silence, Kent heard himself fill the void. "These things happen, Count Massenet."

The count nodded, still staring at the old painter's face. "Yes. But if that knowledge can be recovered, what will be next?"

The painter shook his head. "I'm sorry, I do not take your meaning." Kent reached into his pocket and found his time piece.

"Mr. Kent," the man said, reaching out to stay Kent's hand, his voice both warm and vulnerable, like someone asking a great favor. "You are a man of enormous gifts. No one in all of Farrland is respected as well or trusted by so many. Even more, I know something of your activities, of your concerns. You will excuse me," he said, bobbing his head in a bow, "it is my function." He fell silent for a second, gauging Kent's reaction to his admission. "As fate would have it, my own concerns are not so different. I believe that we might be of some assistance to one another, Mr. Kent, and thus perform a greater service for all."

Kent felt his head nodding but not in agreement. *Yes, now I see.* "Our nations are at peace, Count Massenet," Kent said, "but that situation might change. I have seen it do so, and quickly, too."

The man nodded. "Yes. I can't deny it. But I do not ask that you enter into an alliance with my country against your own. This concern that we share. . . . If those involved were not well placed in the court, you would be less hesitant, I think. It is a question of perception. To oppose gentlemen so highly placed could appear . . . well, almost treasonous." He leaned forward again. "But do you not oppose them even now? They are not, after all, pursuing the policies of your government in this. Is not *their* treason the greater?"

Kent tore his gaze free of the count's, looking out the window for a moment. Danger. The wrong words could bring an end to everything he worked toward. Count Massenet would likely not hesitate to use whatever means were necessary to achieve his ends. Coercion would be nothing to him.

"I know what you are thinking, Mr. Kent, or I believe I do," the man said gently. "To ally yourself with a servant of the Entonne government. . . . Well, you are a man of honor and loyal to the land of your birth— qualities that I appreciate deeply—but it is possible that, if these gentlemen go too far, my own government will have no choice but to become involved. You remember what happened when Farrland had the cannon and Entonne did not. Mr. Kent, you could help avert this disaster." He raised his eyebrows as though asking, *Do you see?*

"Allow me to say only one thing more. I am not sure how much knowledge you have—a considerable quantity, I suspect, or I would not have taken this risk myself. Let me give you one piece of information—freely offered with no expectation of return. This will prove my sincerity, I hope, and convince you that an *'exchange'* between us would. . . ." The count pushed back in his chair suddenly and laughed. "I believe, Mr. Kent, that the ladies of Avonel must think you terribly wicked." He looked to his left. "Ah, Lord Harrington. You know Mr. Kent, of course."

Mr. Kent tried to keep his wits about him, rising to make a leg. Later he realized he hardly remembered a word of what was said. Social pleasantries, no more, and the chancellor had not appeared at all surprised that Kent spoke with the ambassador.

And then Kent was alone, left to his own devices by both men. For a moment he sat in something of a daze, unable to find his bearings. *You are in your club,* a small voice whispered. *You are perfectly well.*

A servant appeared.

"Ah. Yes. I believe I shall have dinner, and perhaps a bottle of wine. Do you have any of the Southern Estate 1251 left in your cellar? Excellent! And the sea bass, the way I always have it. Thank you."

Kent stared out at the open sea. Great towering clouds grew on the horizon, billowing upward and blossoming at the top. If one focused, he was sure, one could actually see the clouds change and spread. Change. Change happening so subtly and continually that one must not allow one's gaze to wander for a second. One could not even blink.

Well, it was not an entire surprise. Kent had suspected for some time that the agents of the count had interests other than the treaty and the other maneuvering of the Farr government. There had been signs. But that they were aware of him! After he had taken such pains to remain in the shadows. It was more than unnerving. Kent felt a rush of fear like a blast of winter wind. Oh, it was not his own life he feared for—at least not entirely—but it was his task, and the others he had involved.

Wine came and Kent dashed off a glass, which seemed to have no effect at all. Who else might know of his efforts? Suddenly Kent felt completely exposed sitting in the window, as though someone involved in the matters he pursued should never be out in broad daylight. Taking a grip on his nerves, he forced himself through his meal—not hurrying too much—and then made as jovial an exit as he could manage though he felt as if he were merely doing a poor imitation of Averil Kent.

At the Club's entrance his carriage waited by the curb. He nodded to his driver and climbed aboard.

As the door closed behind him, Kent realized there was a package, wrapped in silver fabric, sitting on the seat. A calling card was tucked into the fold, and Kent took out his spectacles to find the letters "AK" written on the card's back in a large, strong hand. The painter removed this and, turning it over, found, as he expected, that it was the calling card of the Entonne Ambassador.

Curiosity—the damned passion that had drawn him into all of this in the beginning—took hold of Kent and he lifted the small package, hardly longer than his hand and twice as thick. In a second he had the wrapping off. Inside was a finely made rosewood box, hinged and closed with a bronze clasp. This he opened and inside found a folded letter.

My Dear Sir:

May you accept this as a token of my esteem for you. In my country, after all, artists have fine avenues named for them and the most accomplished women vie for their attentions; which is as it should be. The letter that I have enclosed is very old, and it is the original. Please take your time in verifying its authenticity. Perhaps you know an historian who could assist you with this?

I remain, sir, your servant.

There was no signature. Kent removed an envelope from the box. For a second he paused with the paper in his hands as though it were some binding document and opening it would commit him to a course that he did not clearly understand or perhaps approve. The painter stayed like that a moment, even letting his gaze wander to the passing scene. A street in Avonel, the sounds of carriages and people talking. Familiar. Not a strange road at all but something he had known all his life.

He opened the envelope and from within removed a scrap of yellowed paper, as thin as an onion skin, almost transparent. Careful to cause no damage, he laid it on his open hand. He was surprised to find the language was not Entonne but Farr, and of a slightly antiquated nature as well. He began to read and realized that this was only a fragment, beginning in the middle.

I have been a witness to this horror and can tell you that our colleague exaggerated nothing. Children armed with fearsome weapons roam the streets as brigands, killing man or woman for little gain—often enough for none at all. Sky choked with a yellowish pall, noxious and unwholesome to the lung, it blots out the blue by day and the stars by night. The poor starve on the paving stones, and citizens shut themselves up in homes that have casements barred and doors of iron. In our darkest times we have not known such calamity, and this is the common day in this benighted land! At all costs we must end this fool's endeavor! We are tainted enough as it is.

In place of a signature Kent found only an elaborate letter "L."

"Lucklow," he whispered. Valary would have to verify it, but certainly that was the mage's manner of signing. He remembered the Entonne doctor at the society meeting. Varese had been his name. A man known to Valary. Had they found more correspondence after all? *Lucklow.*

Kent put his fingers to his forehead as though testing for fever. What a day this had turned out to be! His eye was drawn back to the box again as though hoping there would be some explanation there, but all he found was a small brocade purse, closed with a silver cord. Uncertain of what other revelation the count might have prepared for him, Kent picked it up gingerly as though it might burn his fingers. Working open the string, he tipped the contents out into his hand. A fine silver chain bearing a clear, cut stone the size of his thumbnail. Kent turned it over in his hand feeling the weight, watching the light refract through the facets and break into a rainbow on his palm. It was a diamond, he was quite sure. A gem of such size and perfection that its worth could hardly be imagined. All the monies Kent would make if he lived to be the age of the King would not buy it.

"Flames," he whispered. Was he now in the pay of the Entonne? Did they believe they had bought Averil Kent? He bent over the stone, half shielding it from view as though someone might see and know immediately his guilt. A delicate silver setting held the gem to its chain—filigree of leaves and branches.

He thought again of the fragment, part of a letter it would seem. If it had truly been written by Lucklow, Valary would not even notice the diamond were they laid side by side.

TWENTY-NINE

It was a perfect day to be at sea. From his position at the upper trestletrees Tristam surveyed this new world. The wind was consistent, and had been now for several days, blowing from the same quarter and creating seas that resembled each other so completely that they appeared to be merely an endless reoccurrence of the same wave.

And the world around him was blue. Dark blue of the deep ocean, and the sky a soft aquamarine around the horizon changing hue as one's eyes lifted. The graduation of aquamarine to the hard diamond blue of the sky overhead was so subtle that one could not mark a point where the changes occurred.

Blue. Aquamarine, azure, turquoise, cyan, ultramarine, lapis, indigo. Blue. At some time during the day every shade or hue appeared, if only for a moment, in the ever-changing sky.

Clouds, like the fluff from cottonwoods, tumbled slowly in the air, wool-white, and, high overhead, the mares' tales curled against the very dome of the heavens.

Tristam drank in the air—pungent, salty. *It is a beautiful world,* the ocean, he thought, *its essence so permeated with blue that one begins to think of even the air as blue. One almost expects to taste the color with each breath.*

He looked down at the deck far below. Things with the Jacks were not good, apparently, though they did nothing more than ignore him. At worst, he occasionally found someone staring with something like disdain. But his renewed intimacy with the duchess more than compensated. Tristam was sure he was the envy of every man aboard—something that might not be helping his position with the Jacks. The duchess continued to treat Tristam as she always had. There was no hint of impropriety, and of course there had not been any to speak of. Stolen kisses. Promises of what was to come when they reached the Naval Station—a fairly civilized place, by all accounts. An actual town.

Tristam wished they would find this damned rock and get on with the voyage. He realized his keyed up desires were beginning to make him a bit mad.

An indistinct, dark line blotted the horizon to the north. Tristam focused his Fromme glass for a moment and then cupped his hands to his mouth. "Squall to starboard, Mr. Hobbes," Tristam called down to the deck. The Jack supposedly acting as lookout on the other mast would not be pleased. *Farrelle take him,* Tristam thought. They did nothing to make Tristam's life easier; he was damned if he would do anything to help them.

So the days passed. Tristam was not easily bored and had enough to keep him busy, so the time did not weigh on him. Lord Elsworth, on the other hand, had gone through a phase of pacing the deck like a caged animal, his look a bit wild with frustration. Now he seemed to have fallen into somnolence—hibernating, apparently.

Tristam descended before the Jacks came aloft in case sail would need to be reduced. He went down to his cabin to keep his journal.

❦   ❦   ❦

It would have been considered an insignificant mass of rock had it not been the only piece of dry land within fifty leagues. There was no point of the island that could claim an elevation of forty feet above spring tides, and, on the entire four acres, there was not to be found a single tree or shrub.

Without a spring, or even a brackish pool, to slack a man's thirst, *Bird Island* was of almost no worth to mariners. Eggs of the innumerable birds that made their nests there could provide some sustenance, no doubt, but few ships strayed into this corner of the ocean without proper stores.

The island's only true consequence to the navy was as a hazard to navigation, and for that reason the *Swallow* had swept the ocean for two interminable weeks.

"Martyr's blood, Lieutenant," Tristam said to the ship's first officer. "No worth at all? Why, just look! It is the cradle of nigh on a dozen pelagic species. Thousands of birds, sir. Thousands! Why, it is a paradise."

The thickness of the navy men, even the officers, sometimes astonished Tristam. He leaned back to watch a species of fulmar pass close above the masts. He could feel his pulse racing with excitement—the King and his physic were not matters of concern at that moment. Even the duchess was not foremost in his thoughts.

"She holds, sir," the ship's master called along the deck.

"Clear away the starboard cutter," Osler called out. He leaned over the rail as he spoke and looked down at the heaving waters. Tristam could hear him muttering before he turned to oversee the hoisting out of the cutter.

Viscount Elsworth stood at the rail, almost itching to have some involvement. Action! Excitement. The man only came to life when there was something going on.

Jack Beacham appeared at the naturalist's side, looking uncharacteristically grave. "This is as poor an anchorage as I have ever known, Mr. Flattery. There is nothing but a stone bottom beneath our keel and not a whit of protection. What the anchor has bitten into is a mystery to every man aboard."

"It is a wonder." Tristam hardly registered the midshipman's comments. The clamor of the bird colonies could be heard each time a sea hissed by, a shrill crying and shrieking—eerie here in the middle of the lonely ocean. These were sounds that Tristam was certain could not have been heard by men more than a half-dozen times in all of geological time—millions upon millions of years. To Tristam it was a siren's call, compelling, irresistible.

"Walk back the falls! Lower away!" came the call and the cutter dropped onto a wave as it crested alongside.

"Mind yourself, Mr. Flattery," Beacham said. "There is a mean swell running." The midshipman relieved Tristam of his shoulder bag and dropped it into the hands of one of the Jacks in the cutter. "Now, sir, brightly."

Tristam slipped over the side to meet the rising cutter but, but just as he let go, a breaking crest grabbed the cutter's bow and opened a gap between boat and ship. Tristam flailed at the ship's side but only succeeded in twisting himself around. A resounding *crack* against the back of his head and he felt himself plunge into the cold ocean. Dark ... darkness rocking him, taking him in its soft arms and carrying him down, to safety he was certain, to the island girl of his dream. To warmth. Light.

🥚 🥚 🥚

"We almost lost young Beacham, as well, who took a dive after him. I don't know what possessed the boy," Stern said gravely. "He can't swim a stroke."

The Duchess of Morland stood in her cabin, both hands pressed to her face. Stern was certain she would cry and he did not know what he would do; call her brother or perhaps her physician.

"Tristam, gone!" the duchess managed. "It is *impossible*. I don't believe it! I. . . . He can swim. He told me so himself."

"He hit his head on the cutter's gunwale, Duchess." Stern spoke as softly as he was able, as though this would ease the blow. "It was a terrible misfortune."

He had seen this before; people unable to accept another's death. She was an old friend of the Flattery family—had known the young man for years. Poor woman.

But grief did not seem to be what the duchess was feeling at that moment. She fixed him with such a hard gaze—an irrational fury, without doubt. "It is impossible, I tell you! *Impossible!* It is not. . . ." She stopped, confusion coming over her now. "We will search for him," she said as though speaking to a servant.

Stern took a long breath. "Search? However will we do that? I am more sorry than you know, for I was very fond of our young friend. But the ocean has carried him off, Duchess, and will not give him up now."

There was a thumping alongside as the cutter returned from the rock. Osler had completed his sights.

"Bring the physician!" came a cry from the deck. *"Call Doctor Llewellyn. They've found him."*

Stern was physically thrust aside and was hard-pressed to keep pace as the duchess dashed up the ladder. Rain was lashing the sea, making the heaving deck slick, but the duchess rattled down the steps into the waist without breaking stride. Stern came to the rail to find the cutter scraping alongside, the drenched oarsmen all standing, looking down at the form of Tristam Flattery, laying in a heap in the boat's bilge water, his face white as a fish belly.

Taine, the ship's surgeon, was bending over him, feeling for a pulse. The surgeon stared up suddenly, his look deadly serious. *"He lives,"* he said, the certainty that this could not be true clear in his tone. "I don't know how, but he breathes."

"We found him on a scrap of beach," Osler said to the captain, his tone as full of awe as that of the surgeon.

One of the Jacks in the boat turned to his fellows. "I saw a flash of something white in the sea, I tell you—as he fell." His tone was filled with awe and fear. "Like the wings of a great ray. It carried him ashore." The man stepped away from the prostrate Tristam as though afraid.

"Enough of that!" Stern bellowed. "Rig a tackle and boatswain's chair and we will swing him aboard.

"There you are, doctor," he said as Llewellyn appeared at his side. "We will have your patient aboard in a trice."

"Captain Stern, sir," came the voice of Beacham, filled with urgency. "To larboard, sir."

"What?" Stern turned to look out to sea. "*Squall to larboard! Make sail!* Mr. Hobbes, buoy the cable and let it run. We will return for it. Mr. Osler! Get that man aboard and take the cutter in tow."

Apparently from nowhere, Viscount Elsworth dropped like a cat into the bobbing cutter, swept Tristam over his shoulder, and came up the ladder one-handed. The others swarmed up behind him.

"Take him to my cabin," the duchess ordered, and she and Llewellyn followed the viscount down the companionway, chaos breaking out on the deck as all hands were called.

Tristam regained consciousness to the smell of drying wool and the sounds of the ship plunging into a whole gale. Opening his eyes did not seem a good idea just then, so he lay, still as death, listening, trying to remember. It was not morning, he was sure of that. A voice registered, though it seemed distant.

"By every regulation of the navy I should have you flogged, Mr. Beacham. You abandoned ship, sir! Now how do you account for that?"

Beacham, Tristam thought, he was in some trouble, it seemed. Snitching pies, no doubt.

"But I could not let him go down, Captain. He is not a sailor, sir, but a landsman in our charge, as it were. And no one else made shift to catch him, sir."

"But you can't swim a stroke!" Stern roared.

"I did not rightly think what it was I did, sir," Beacham said so quietly Tristam could barely make out the words. The wardroom—they were in the wardroom outside the great cabin, where Stern conducted all such interviews.

A long silence followed and Tristam began to think it was only a dream he had just wakened from.

"Mr. Osler. Let the record show that Mr. Beacham slipped over the side while grabbing for a man who had the misfortune to fall overboard, and was then rescued by the men in the cutter who were standing by at the time. It is my considered opinion that he abandoned neither ship nor duty.

"Be sure in the future that you keep your foolish head aboard this ship, Mr. Beacham. Now return to your duty."

Tristam lay in the warmth and softness, floating slowly to the surface of consciousness. A hand rested on his forehead and then he felt blankets being tucked in around his neck. He sank down into warmth again, where a small child watched over him—a sullen boy, frightened and furtive.

🌢   🌢   🌢

Murmuring. Voices whispering above the sounds of a raging sea.

"I cannot give it credence with such little proof, Duchess. Certainly the sea pulled the bow of the cutter out and away: whether the men aboard did all they could to hold it is difficult to know. I was not there to see. Nor was the Duchess."

"But, Captain Stern. They managed to save Beacham, and yet no man made even an attempt to reach Tristam. There are several witnesses who say the same thing. And it was this man Kreel who held the line. You know he is the one instigating this persecution of Tristam."

"I do not deny it, Duchess. I do not deny it. But there are too many explanations of their actions. They were thrown off balance when the boat lurched. They were surprised initially and then recovered. You must put yourself in my position. Men will accept discipline from an officer they know to be fair. But this . . . ? Well, the Admiralty would certainly not uphold any ruling I make on such paltry evidence. And it is such a serious charge!"

"That is your answer, then? You will let an attempted murder take place under your command and do nothing? I might remind you that Tristam Flattery is the nephew of the Duke of Blackwater and the Earl of Tyne. I have heard the King speak of him on more than one occasion, Captain—and I would hazard that the King does not know the name Stern. And I do not even mention this matter we are to keep so secret. But I will say that without Tristam we will not accomplish it. Be sure of that."

"Duchess, I have the highest opinion of our naturalist, and am well aware that he is of a good family. I had a note from the duke before we sailed asking me especially to watch over his nephew. I shall bring him home unharmed. You may be sure of that. I give you my word as a gentleman. Nothing will befall Mr. Flattery while I command this ship."

"I dearly hope you are right, Captain Stern. For if you are not, there will not be a ship in all the known world upon which you will sail."

Silence. Stern had just been threatened aboard his own command.

"If the Duchess will excuse me." Very polite, entirely cold.

"There is still the matter we discussed earlier, Captain."

"And I have no more to say of it!" He flared up, anger showing. But then, calmer. "I have had my orders from the Admiralty."

"And a private conversation with Roderick Palle, no doubt."

"I am called by duties, Duchess. The pleasures of the evening to you."

A door closed softly. Tristam felt the cold sea envelop him again, but he could not move his limbs to seek the surface.

❦   ❦   ❦

Footsteps crossed the cabin in no regular rhythm, for Tristam could feel the gale pounding the ship, tossing it like a toy. He opened his eyes to find the duchess standing over him in a swaying cabin.

"I thought I heard your breathing change. Are you whole? Shall I call the doctor?"

"I believe I am here entire, though I have only the vaguest memory of what occurred."

She smiled down at him, not quite hiding a look of concern. Lamplight glinted in her hair and Tristam realized it was night. "You fell over the side as you boarded the ship's boat. You don't remember?"

"Ah. Did I hit my head, then? I have a powerful sharp pain in the back of my skull."

"Yes, you did. I shall wake Llewellyn."

"No, no. I am able to see perfectly well, I feel no nausea and I think the hurt in my head is in my skull only. No more than one would expect. Someone pulled me out, I collect. Who was it?"

The duchess put a hand gently on his shoulder. "I believe you owe thanks to some propitious tide or current—or so the captain thinks—for you were found a few moments after your mishap, washed up on a narrow little ledge. Something of a miracle. . . ." The look on the duchess' face did not convince Tristam that she believed her own words.

"I see." Tristam said nothing for a moment. "And what have the Jacks to say of that, I wonder?"

The duchess shrugged. "I think the poor crew are at sixes and sevens now, for Lieutenant Osler tells me that a man granted his life by the sea is thought to be charmed. You have given them something to ponder and fit into their way of thinking about the workings of the world." She forced a laugh. "I shouldn't worry."

"I missed the birds, then?"

The duchess laughed again, relief showing. "I see you are returning to your natural self. But, Tristam, are you shivering?"

"It does seem suddenly very chill. Is there another blanket, perhaps?"

"A blanket will be of no avail against a fever," she said feeling his forehead for the second time. Stepping back she shed her shawl and gown, and thus clad in her undershift the duchess lifted the blankets and slipped into the narrow berth beside her patient. Her soft arms encircled him and Tristam felt the warmth of her body as she pressed close to him.

"You are a block of ice, Tristam. Perhaps I should call Llewellyn, though he is none too well himself with this sea running."

"Wait a bit, I'm certain this shall pass." And he fell back into a troubled sleep.

🍎 🍎 🍎

Some unknown time later the wailing of the gale in the rigging brought Tristam awake. He felt neither cold nor hot and surmised that his fever had broken. Beside him the duchess breathed evenly, close against him. He brushed her hair gently back from his face and felt her stir.

"Mmmm." She pushed tighter to him. "You are recovered, I think," she said feeling his desire rising. The duchess began to kiss his neck. "Now here is a feat that will test our cunning," she whispered as the ship lurched, pressing them against the lee board, and then tossing them the other way. "Though I can cry out with utter abandon, I'm sure, for who could ever hear?"

🍎 🍎 🍎

Tristam spent part of the next day in the care of the duchess and then returned to his normal shipboard life. The gale had blown itself out by morning; when Tristam ventured onto the deck in the early afternoon, the sea was looking decidedly less threatening, though overhead dark clouds still hung heavily above a gray ocean.

The first lieutenant, Osler, nodded to him and smiled. Overhead, the Jacks were setting more sail, the master trying to make the most of a fair breeze, for they had encountered more than their share of head winds since leaving the island of Farrow.

The duchess and her maid were taking the air at the stern rail, but as Doctor Llewellyn accompanied them, Tristam descended into the waist of the ship, planning to perch on the spare spars. As usual, the duchess' manner toward him was completely opaque, and Tristam had to admire her skills as an actress—though these same skills made him wonder sometimes how genuine her affection might be.

He levered himself up onto the spar and leaned his back against the bow of the cutter. A panorama of a rolling, empty ocean stretched out before him. He closed his eyes and leaned his head back against the planking, wincing as his injury touched hard wood.

If I keep hitting my head like this it shall surely be weakened, I have not so much wit that I can afford to have it diminished. He felt more than a little exposed sitting there, out in the open. The Jacks working on the deck no longer seemed just ignorant and superstitious. But why in the world would the Jacks try to drown him? So they believed his uncle had been a mage. . . . So what? Why would this lead them to murder?

Somehow Tristam couldn't believe it would, but there was a part of him that kept whispering, "You can't afford to disbelieve it."

It seemed most likely that the act had not been planned in advance, but when he fell, no one had moved to save him. Not an act of murder so much as murder by inaction.

"Mr. Flattery, sir?"

Tristam opened his eyes and found Pim, the youngest Jack aboard, standing with a steaming mug in his hand and looking decidedly nervous. He proffered it and Tristam caught the odor of coffee.

"Cook's compliments, sir."

Tristam noticed that several Jacks stood about the

deck, watching. There did not seem to be animosity in their eyes but expectation.

Was it a peace offering? Tristam wondered. He reached out immediately and took the cup.

"My thanks to you, Pim, and to cook as well."

The lad bobbed in an awkward bow, already out of words, apparently. The others had gone back to their duties.

"With your leave, sir," he said, looking as though he would bolt.

Tristam smiled and the boy was off at a trot. The coffee was strong, unsweetened, bitter. The naturalist closed his eyes and sipped quietly. Pim had never been unfriendly to him. Just a shy boy, eager to please and very intimidated by the high-born passengers.

"Ah, Mr. Flattery, it is good to see you up, sir." Tristam opened his eyes again and found a happy-seeming Jack Beacham. "The pleasures of the day to you."

"And to you as well, Mr. Beacham. I am equally happy to see you whole, for I have heard that you plunged into the sea after me. And though I applaud your bravery, this was a foolish endeavor for a man who swims as well as the best of stones."

Beacham broke into a smile. "I did not think what it was I did, Mr. Flattery, until the cold ocean cleared my head. I could not reach you, but good fortune had a Jack hit me with a lead line. I have a prodigious bruise on my buttocks but grabbed the line and am here, as you see. They say I am the strangest sample they have ever brought up on the lead, sir, and I'm afraid I will be called 'Bottom Beacham" from now until I am truly dead."

Tristam laughed. "Well, I thank you for taking such a chance. Perhaps, when circumstances allow, I shall teach you the fine art of staying afloat and even making headway. It may stand you in good stead if such acts of heroism become common to you."

"I should like nothing better, sir, for I do not believe for a moment that it reduces one's constitution. I have been out in the coldest rain many times and soaked through until my skin wrinkled up, and I was never once sick afterward. It is a misguided belief, I think, and after all, I for one would rather reduce my health somewhat, if that were the case, than drown altogether."

"Well there is some sense in what you say. I am sure of that." An awkward moment when neither spoke. "Tell me true, Jack Beacham . . . are the Jacks set on doing me harm?"

Beacham looked around, suddenly more uncomfortable than Tristam had ever seen him. He took a step closer. "The hands are split, sir. There are those that think this has gone too far. They think the men in the cutter could have made shift to catch you, Mr. Flattery. And there is the undeniable truth that the sea has granted you your life. . . . There is a split in the forecastle that I have seldom seen, though fewer and fewer side with. . . ." He gave the slightest motion with his head toward the bow.

Tristam nodded, closing his eyes again. His wound had begun to throb. Kreel was a forecastleman.

Tristam felt a sudden chill as though his fever returned. *Blood and flames,* he thought, *they tried to murder me!*

"But, Mr. Flattery, with such luck as you have just shown I should not worry about anyone doing you harm. I have never heard of such a thing happening and there are a thousand stories of men saved from their end in the sea."

Tristam did not open his eyes. The tone in the boy's words was perfectly clear.

"It was a stroke of luck, Jack Beacham," Tristam said weakly, "nothing more."

Silence. Tristam knew Beacham would not answer because he would not gainsay him, but clearly he did not believe. As superstitious as the Jacks, Tristam thought.

"Now set me straight in a matter of ornithology, Mr. Flattery," Beacham said quietly, changing the subject.

Tristam opened his eyes to discover a Jack had begun working nearby. "I have made an observation that perhaps should go into your journal." The boy was making an effort to cast aside the seriousness of the moment. "Or perhaps it is nothing at all." He smiled, a bit embarrassed.

Beacham had taken an intense interest in natural history, questioning Tristam constantly. The midshipman had discovered that one did not have to be a fellow to get one's name into the *Society Annals* for a contribution, and he was hoping that Tristam would credit him for some yet undiscovered species or phenomenon.

"Yesterday, not long before we both plunged into the Gray Ocean, I saw, off in the distance, a bird dive out of the sky and strike another in the air, sir. Even at the distance I saw feathers fly and the bird, the diving one, took the other off. I don't know where, for there were such a prodigious number of birds in the sky that I lost sight of it. I have looked in the books, but I can't make sense of it at all."

"Have I pointed out a jaeger to you?"

"As we left Farrow? The one that chased the others for their catch? Too lazy to fish for itself?"

"Exactly. It is likely what you saw. A jaeger would not *take* a bird, that is *kill it,* but it might seem to have done so at a distance."

"Well, I did not have a field glass at hand, but it did seem so at the time. A white bird . . . just folded up its wings and dropped like a stone." Beacham demonstrated with his arms, "Though, as you say it was not near enough to be certain. I'm sure a jaeger is what it was, though, I confess, I had hoped it might be a species never before recorded."

"White you say? And diving?"

"That's right, sir. Just like this." He again demonstrated the bird folding up its wings and plummeting out of the sky. It was a good imitation of a hawk or falcon, there was no question.

"Well, that doesn't seem like any jaeger I know.

There could not be raptors so far out to sea. Unless there is some larger island nearby that is undiscovered. I shall mention it to Captain Stern."

Impossible, Tristam thought.

THIRTY

Another gale was blowing when Tristam woke, though he was sure it was not the storm sounds that had called him from sleep. He lay still in the darkness, mentally measuring the arc of his hammock as it swung in the confined cabin, and he listened. Hadn't there been a call? Perhaps a knock? He strained to hear above the din. The pounding of seas upon the bow and the creak of stretching cordage . . . but no sound of his name being repeated.

A dream, Tristam thought, and adjusted his position hoping to return to sleep. After this long at sea, gales did not really wake him fully. They merely registered in his mind, no more threatening than the storms outside his home in Locfal. He decided that his sleeping position was not the right one and tried turning on his other side, careful not to end up being pitched out of his swaying bed.

The wind moaning in the rigging brought back a memory of the gale during which he had made love to the duchess—the fever of the storm at sea like an echo. It was not a memory that would help him sleep, so he tried to push it from his mind. Part of the problem was lack of air, for the ship had been closed up against the weather.

Tristam decided he needed a breath of air. He rolled carefully out of his hammock and balanced in the dark. The cabin was so small and so well organized, that almost everything was within reach. In a moment he was pulling on oilskins over breaches and shirt.

Bootless, he crept out of his cabin into the glow of

a shuttered lantern. Up the companionway stair, and then out beneath canvas weather-cloths.

Immediately the cool wind lashed him and driven spray was dashed in his face leaving the taste of salt. Tristam almost laughed. On occasion the great absurdity of his life aboard ship struck him strongly. It was not quite the way he had lived in county Locfal.

So far the gale was not proving a bad one. He knew this more from the sound of wind in the rigging and the motion of the ship, for he could not see twenty feet—could barely make out the helmsmen in the light of the binnacle.

Tristam realized how accustomed to life aboard he had become. Only a few weeks earlier such a gale would have reduced him to sickness and to huddling in his cabin in real fear. But now the great seas, heard and sensed more than seen, did not seem the black monsters they once had.

The ship was lying to under reefed topsails, making no headway but holding her own handily. With such a small crew Stern often employed this tactic in bad weather as it allowed him to rest his crew and keep them fresh. The watches were small and frequently all but the helmsmen and one man on deck-watch would stay below ready to be called if needed.

Tristam stood, face into the wind, though it blew spray under his storm hat and cold tendrils of water felt their way down his neck and onto his chest and back. A distant flash of lightning illuminated an area of cloud and the crests of seas. For the briefest second Tristam could see the ship, bow high as it rode over a sea, and then it was utterly dark again.

He realized that if this were a larger storm, truly threatening to the small ship and crew, it would provide one benefit: it would drive all other thoughts, all other concerns and anxieties out of his rather overactive mind. Crises were cleansing in that way.

A sudden dull thumping up forward drew Tristam's attention—two hollow reports of impact on timber. Some piece of gear had probably come loose, and he set out quickly along the heaving deck. His growing competence in things nautical saw him taking such actions more and more often and he was surprised at the satisfaction there was to be gained from such simple tasks: belaying a loose line, tightening a gasket around a flapping sail.

In the darkness Tristam went hand over hand along a lifeline that had been rigged against the weather. Crests tumbling over the bow would occasionally wash past his bare feet, ankle deep, the sea here still cool, and feeling colder on such a night.

A larger sea rolled the ship until she all but buried her rail; Tristam was forced to halt his progress just to keep to his feet. He slid several feet toward the leeward bulwark, feeling the rope stretch. There was a precarious moment where the ship hesitated before beginning to right herself, and Tristam made ready to grab for the rigging if his lifeline parted which it seemed ready to do.

He heard the hiss of a crest breaking, washing over the forecastle and then sweeping along the deck. Water, thigh-deep, struck him with force, trying to tear his hands free of the sodden line he clung to with all his will. A series of thumps not a yard away warned Tristam that whatever had come loose was being swept his way, and he tried to pull himself up the slope of the deck.

A man, or perhaps men, blundered into him as they were washed, struggling, past. Tristam released one hand and made a grab in the dark but only tore away part of a shirt. He heard spluttering and coughing not two yards off as the water ran off the deck around him.

"Blood and flames!" Tristam spat out. "Are you there?" He made his way along the line, waving one hand before him as he went. There was a terrible thump of flesh on wood almost underfoot.

"Helmsman!" Tristam bellowed, hardly hoping to be heard over the moan of the wind.

Another flash of lightning, far off, and there was someone kneeling over the figure of Kreel, hands to his throat and the giant seaman struggling to pull those hands free. Before he could move or speak, Tristam saw Kreel's head lifted and driven down hard on the deck. And then darkness returned.

"Who called?" came a shout from the quarterdeck. Tristam stood riveted in place for a second.

"Speak up, forward."

Tristam jumped forward, guessing in the darkness, and threw his weight against Kreel's attacker. A massive arm swung around and sent Tristam skidding across the deck. He crashed hard against the bulwark.

Above the noise of the sea Tristam heard the ring of the bell which called the watch. A wave washed around him and he felt himself rising in a panic, coughing up salt water.

Dark. Too dark. He could make out nothing. A groan and the sounds of something dragging over wood. Tristam staggered along the deck, clinging to the rail for balance. He collided with someone, catching the person off balance as the ship heaved upright. In the darkness Tristam grabbed the limp form of Kreel and fell back from the rail. He hit the deck with the huge weight of the Jack half on top of him.

Sounds of men coming out the hatch.

"Here!" Tristam called out. He rolled the Jack onto the deck, clutching tight to his arms lest he be washed away in the dark. "To starboard."

A flash of lightning revealed the men coming, hand-over-hand, along the lifeline.

"He's not conscious."

"Call Mr. Taine," he heard someone shout. Strong hands suddenly lifted Tristam to his feet and others grabbed the inert form of Kreel.

"Flames, what's done for him?" a Jack hissed, looking suspiciously at the naturalist.

"I don't know. . . ." Tristam heard himself stammer. "I–I came out on deck for some air and I heard a thumping forward. Thought it was something come loose. I found him instead. Another few seconds and he'd have been washed clear over the side."

There was no time for talk. The men gathered their fellow seaman up and made their way, staggering, toward the hatch.

Alone on the deck, the naturalist stood clinging to the lifeline, his breath coming in deep gasps.

Flaming martyrs, Tristam thought, *I stopped a murder!* He hadn't seen the attacker's face, but he could think of no one powerful enough to take on Kreel except for the Viscount Elsworth.

"Flaming martyrs," he said again. "Murder."

🐦   🐦   🐦

Stern was seated at the small table with the ship's log open before him. To his right sat Osler, pen in hand and paper ready. Hobbes stood to his captain's left, and Tristam thought both seamen looked very grave indeed. Even Osler did not offer Tristam the slightest indication of a comforting smile.

"Mr. Flattery," Stern began, his voice at once tired and yet full of tightly controlled outrage. "This is a very serious matter, I must tell you. We are here," he glanced at Osler, "to take your statement and though this is not a hearing in the proper sense, nor is it a court of law ... still, everything you say will be recorded and duly reported to the Admiralty and the Navy Board. There is a possibility that, upon our return to Farrland, you will be asked to corroborate or to speak further on this matter. Do you understand what I'm saying, sir?"

Tristam nodded. "I do, Captain."

"Well, then begin by telling us what it was that you saw last night and why you were on the deck at such a late hour in weather so foul."

Tristam swallowed, not too obviously he hoped. "I could not sleep, Captain Stern. It is not uncommon for me, as almost anyone aboard can tell you. When I found that sleep would not come, I thought it might be due to the closed state of the ship—everything being so close and airless. I dressed and went up onto the quarter deck. Perhaps the helmsman saw me emerge?"

A nod from Hobbes.

Tristam looked down at Stern who stared up at him with a very cool and distant look. "As I stood taking in great breaths I heard a noise forward—a thumping—so I thought, as the crew were below, I would see if it was something come loose that I could easily tend to. I went down into the waist, and along the lifeline. Almost at the forward deck I was stopped when the *Swallow* took a great roll and shipped a large sea. As I stood, bracing myself, and clinging to the line, something, that I realized immediately was a man, washed past me and I made a grab for him." Tristam paused to look at the others, feeling, somehow, that his words did not sound truthful. There was sweat on his brow. What to say now? Did he tell them his suspicion?

"I came up empty-handed, but a flash of lightning revealed two men struggling, Captain, one whose face I could not see and the other was Mr. Kreel. I called out to the men at the wheel and they rang up the watch, who took Mr. Kreel below." Tristam paused, pretending to search his memory. "I can't think what else there is to tell, Captain Stern."

Stern looked down at his log for a moment, as though checking Tristam's story against another written there, and then he looked up. "You saw no one else? Or heard no one?"

"Not a soul, sir." Tristam felt a small surge of panic. "Though it was very dark."

"And you cannot identify this other man? Think, Mr. Flattery. Anything at all. Color of hair. A distinctive bit of clothing?"

Tristam shook his head.

Stern looked away, obviously unhappy with the answer.

Tristam tried to regularize his breathing.

"It is the damndest thing," Stern said, almost to himself. "Well, I will tell you Mr. Flattery—and I will have this go no further—there were others about last night. Oh, hidden by the darkness I'm sure. But there were others. One of the men at the helm thought he saw three men by a flash of lightning, though the other helmsman is not so sure. I will say this; Kreel did not receive such wounds from an accident—as he claims. The man was near throttled and the marks on his throat are plain to see. It is a wonder he lived." Stern slapped his hand down toward the log, but at the last second he pulled it back so that it landed softly.

"Mr. Kreel says it was an accident?" Tristam asked.

"Yes; the worst foolishness. The man will tell us nothing. Not a word. You are not a navy man, Mr. Flattery, so you have not seen this before. But I have seen whole crews split and turn on themselves. Turn murderous, too. And if the officers cannot get to the bottom of it. . . ." Stern thumped the log hard this time, but it was only punctuation—his temper was still in check.

"Despite the fact that it appears Kreel is the victim of this attack, I may have to flog the man and throw him in chains because he will not say who his attackers were. And that is a breach of the war articles, clear and simple. You see, Mr. Flattery, the Jacks have their own code, benighted as it may be. Kreel must deal with this himself or be thought a lolly-Jack by all the men before the mast. Bloody foolishness." It was the second time the man had sworn and knowing Stern's disapproval of such things made Tristam realize how deeply this attack affected the captain.

Tristam thought of Kreel and could still hardly believe that even the viscount could best such a man. Whoever it was had tossed Tristam across the deck with almost no effort.

"I can't think who the man could be who would dare face Kreel," Tristam said quietly.

"It was not one man," Stern asserted again. "You can count on that. The man took a savage beating. Kreel is a good and able seaman, but a great bully at times, and there are some who have had their fill of it, I would say. No, his own messmates, or some of them, took the man on in the dark, though there is not one among them who does not claim to have been elsewhere. If not for you, Mr. Flattery, Kreel would be sinking still. He has you to thank for that."

THIRTY-ONE

The Northeast Trades proved to be elusive winds that season and the Variables, the band of winds that lay between the Westerlies and the Trades, seemed to stretch on forever. As their name suggested, the Variables were unreliable in both strength and direction and at times disappeared altogether, leaving the *Swallow* wallowing on a windless sea.

Tristam lay in his hammock, the only position of comfort in his cabin, Valary's book open in his hands, but his mind elsewhere.

The past week had seen only fickle winds and little progress, and Tristam could feel the growing frustration of the crew and officers. Both Hobbes and Osler labored to keep the Jacks employed, for idle hands soon found their own endeavors and these were not always to the good of the ship. Tristam had made an effort to stay clear of the Jacks, not sure what the response to Kreel's attack might be, but the animosity the Jacks had harbored toward Tristam seemed to be diffusing. According to the code of the Jacks, Kreel was now in Tristam's debt, and this seemed to have brought an end to the enmity. Beacham had hinted that there was some relief among the Jacks over this.

Tristam had pumped the midshipman for information, trying to learn the scuttlebutt that passed before the mast. According to Beacham, Kreel, released from sick bay some days, would say nothing, leaving the Jacks at a loss; no one seemed to know who the guilty party was. An unheard of situation. If there was a feud aboard ship, Beacham assured Tristam, the Jacks, would know who was set against whom.

But Kreel would say nothing, and Tristam assumed that no one thought of Julian. The man was a lord. Peers did not engage in anything so common as a brawl.

Someone had suggested that Tristam was responsible and this joke had been popular for a few days. Tristam the giant killer.

The viscount had not so much as hinted at the matter in any conversation with Tristam, of which there had been several.

"The viscount is the trained falcon of the Duchess of Morland," Jaimy had said, *"and she carries him about on her wrist to be sure that all know it."*

And she had guaranteed that Julian would never act in such a manner again. And Tristam had believed her—though he wondered. Had the duchess only asked Julian to see that Kreel left Tristam in peace? And then things had gotten out of hand?

Was the viscount merely murderous? Some men were, it was said. Tristam found this a chilling thought—but then Ipsword's death had been utterly cold-blooded, monstrous really, or so Jaimy had claimed.

Beacham was shocked by the attempt at murder. *"Kreel would not be the first Jack murdered by one of his mates,"* the midshipman had said, *"but it is more commonly done in the midst of a fight, Mr. Flattery. An accident, really: done while the blood is hot. But this attack on Kreel . . . everyone believes it was coolly planned."*

But planned by whom? The truth was, Tristam could not positively identify the attacker. He had not seen the man's face.

He turned his attention back to his reading.

Contemporary accounts are in general agreement on the essential facts of the battle, unfortunately they tend to such a high-dramatic style (the style of the time) that they are often not credited. Here is an ex-

ample written by an observer, one Brenton Lace,
scribe to the Earl of Highgate.

The army of Farrelle came upon the field to the
trumpeting of horns and the waving of banners,
for their pride was such that each house should
be marked and none go unnoticed on this great
day. The Prelate Anjou made a fire to his god and
burned upon it the leaves of holyoak so that all his
soldiers might breathe the blessed smoke.

Upon the Midden Hill the gathered mages
looked down from their tower and knew despair,
for they could boast but one warrior for every ten
of Farrelle. But Lord Dunsenay went out of the
tower upon his gray steed and rode most brazenly
across the crest of the hill. Waving his spear at
the sky as he crossed one way and then the
other, stopping only to beat on his shield, great
crashing blows that unnerved the enemy in the
vale below. And as he rode he called out in ancient tongues, words that no one had ever heard.
In the valley the Farrellites stopped up their ears
for fear of bewilderment.

In midday the green sea-light formed around
Dunsenay, wrapping him in an unearthly green
fire as he stood upon the Midden crest and at this
the forces of the Prince of Delgarthy withdrew
from the field.

A great cloud came out of the west, then, as
gray as Dunsenay's steed, and the thunder shook
the Midden Vale.

The Prelate Anjou stood before his host and
called upon Farrelle to bring down the lightning
upon the tower of the mages. And as he called
out the thunder rolled and the lightning lanced into
the midst of the Army of Farrelle and they turned
and ran from that unholy place, crushing their own
in their terror.

Although the man does not seem to clear on the pri-
ority of lightning over thunder his account agrees in

*all salient points with that of another observer—or
participant in this case.*

Tristam closed the book and lay his head back. Children's tales.

His hammock hung almost motionless across the small cabin, for the ship only moved slowly up and down as though it rested on the breast of some sleeping giant. It was warm, though not unbearably so, but the lack of a breeze soon had the small ship stuffy and noisome.

The sound of someone pounding down the ladder outside Tristam's cabin came through the thin plank door and then the door itself reverberated to an ungentle knocking.

"Mr. Flattery, sir. The captain bids you come on deck, sir. Double time or they will be gone."

The man ran off. Tristam rolled out of his hammock and took up his Fromme glass—he had learned not to answer such a summons without it. Over the last few days there had been several species of whales about in numbers and the officers called Tristam whenever one was observed.

In unshod feet he mounted the companionway stair and came out onto the deck at a trot.

"Ah, Mr. Flattery!" The captain stood at the stern rail with several others. He motioned to the north where Tristam could see a dark squall, like a moving shadow, passing over the lead-gray sea.

Stern lifted his glass as Tristam came up. "They will certainly come this way, Mr. Osler. Do you see, Mr. Flattery? Waterspouts. A natural phenomenon I thought might be new to you." The seaman swept his glass across the horizon, missing very little, Tristam suspected. "There is a good breeze of wind beneath that cloud. Mr. Hobbes; call all hands. We should be ready to reduce sail."

Tristam searched the shadow bearing down on them and immediately found the spouts. Three: no, four of them, like elongated funnels spinning up into the dark mass of cloud.

A rustle of skirts told him the duchess had arrived and, like all the other gentlemen present, Tristam lowered his glass to make a leg.

In her hands the duchess carried one of Tristam's spare field glasses and she raised it, now obviously quite familiar with its use.

"Why, there they are!" she sang out. "Do you see three, Tristam? I can't quite make them out."

"Four, I think, though it is difficult to tell."

"They will be close very soon," Stern offered. "Perhaps closer than we might hope."

"Are they dangerous, Captain?" the duchess asked, not lowering her glass. Only aboard a ship would such an action not be considered impolite.

"No need for concern, Duchess, the *Swallow* is a stout vessel. But if such a spout comes aboard . . . well, look to our sails. It will tear them to rags in a trice. I have heard tell of spars coming down, but I believe they must not have been sound or their standing rigging was in a weakened state.

"Here is some wind now," Stern said, raising his hand. "We will have steerage way in a moment and move clear."

Tristam heard Hobbes giving orders to the helmsman and felt the ship slowly begin to make way, the *thuddle* of the steering tackles vibrating up the sternpost and into the deck.

"The tip of a wind vortex, Your Grace." The physician had arrived on deck. "They funnel water up from the surface of the sea. It is said that a cannon ball through the spout will cause it to collapse."

The duchess lowered her heavy glass. "Is this true, Captain?"

Stern seemed almost to grimace, Tristam thought, for he found the physician as annoying as Tristam did himself. "So it is said, Duchess, though I have not witnessed this myself nor have I known anyone who has seen it done—no one whose word was a steady wind, that is."

The duchess raised her glass in the ensuing silence, and Tristam tried not to grin.

"There is a whale spout, I think!" the duchess said, giving a little jump of excitement. "Do you see, Tristam? Halfway to the squall and to the right?"

"You have a knack for observation, Duchess. Whales they are."

This compliment pleased her more than Tristam would ever have thought, and he could hear it in her voice. "I have missed my calling, I think. Do you see them, Doctor? The great leviathan. What variety would they be, Tristam?"

Tristam made an effort to hold his glass still. "It is difficult to say at such a distance, Duchess. Baleen whales, I think, though I cannot say which species."

"Sperm whales," Llewellyn said firmly, contradicting Tristam, as was his usual practice. "*Physeter catodon.* Easily told by the shape of their spout, Your Grace."

"The squall is blowing the spouts off too quickly for my poor eye to tell," Tristam said, and then added, "though of course, the doctor might be right." Tristam was making an effort not to argue with Llewellyn; it was a great waste of one's mental energies, he had decided.

The squall overtook the whales and they disappeared into the darkness without any sign of concern. Perhaps, Tristam thought, they took pleasure from the rain upon their great backs, as other beasts seemed to take pleasure from the sun.

Although the *Swallow* had been nearly stripped of canvas, she began to make good speed, the burble of her hull moving through the water lifting the spirits of everyone aboard. Despite the ship's speed, the squall bore down on them quickly. As the gap became smaller, Tristam could see that there were more waterspouts than he had originally thought, half a dozen, at least, and these rose like strange columns upholding a maelstrom-dome.

A blast of wind struck the ship, almost rolling the lee gunwale under. Tristam grabbed the rail and at the same time steadied the duchess—almost losing his Fromme glass in the process.

He followed the duchess and the physician below, but once Tristam had secured the portlight in his cabin and returned his glass to its locker, he rushed back on deck wrapped only in a cotton square, and clutching soap in hand. Though they were in the midst of some chaos he stood by the stern rail and washed himself in the falling fresh water—a precious commodity aboard ship.

The *Swallow* ran steadily before the wind now and the waterspouts Tristam had seen were gone. A sail came free with a *crack* and the foretopmen were sent aloft to tame it—a dangerous endeavor, for a wet sail flogging in the wind might as well have been made of iron.

"Making the best of it, are you, Mr. Flattery?" Stern grinned at Tristam from beneath his storm hat. The captain was wrapped in his oilskins and may not have been much dryer than Tristam.

A great blast of wind threw the ship on her beam ends and Tristam slid half the width of the quarterdeck before his slippery hands managed to find purchase on the rail. Out of the corner of his eye he saw a shadow plummet from the upper yards.

"Man overboard!" Stern bellowed, his cry all but lost in the wind.

Tristam saw a flash of dark blue in the frothing sea. "I have him!"

"Mr. Flattery! No!" But it was too late. Tristam plunged headlong over the rail.

He hit the cool ocean two yards from the sinking Jack, and, not a fathom under, grabbed the flailing seaman by his hair. The air was so full of spray and rain that Tristam could hardly be sure if they reached the surface.

"Don't let me go, sir. I don't swim."

Tristam realized that it was Pim he braced under the arms—one of the greenest hands aboard.

"I shan't let you go. But don't struggle so! Lay back and kick your feet."

"Oh, Farrelle save us, Mr. Flattery. The *Swallow* is gone! They'll never find us. Oh, Farrelle." The boy was quivering with fear.

Tristam shook him, shouting over the wind. "Think what you're saying! They'll run free of the squall in ten minutes and about-ship right away. In less time than you can think, you'll be back aboard. Why, we won't even be properly clean. But we must save our strength. . . ."

Whatever Tristam intended to say was lost in the most horrifying roaring he had ever heard. It was caused by the wind, no doubt, but Pim's hair stood completely on end.

"Flaming martyrs!" Tristam whispered, for a waterspout spun toward them not thirty feet away. Both men were frozen by fear and it was only a mouthful of salt-water that had Tristam kicking to keep them afloat.

The waterspout roared toward them, its black, whirling mass tearing the surface off the water and sucking it into the vortex as though by dark attraction. Tristam heard Pim rapidly mumbling a prayer as though he raced to get through it before he was swallowed whole, but the waterspout passed them by.

"Well," Tristam heard himself say, surprised by the calmness in his voice. "I shall be able to boast the closest observation of a waterspout—by any man who lived to tell about it, at least—I'm sure of that." The terrified Jack looked at him as though he had gone mad, but Tristam could not help it. The encounter with the waterspout seemed to have exhausted his fear. In fact, he felt remarkably calm, almost lighthearted. "Don't look so downcast, Pim, the squall is passing and I think there shall be sun, which will make us easier to find."

The squall moved off to the south, hiding any sight

of the *Swallow*. Tristam hoped she wouldn't be carried too far off. Pim would drain him quickly.

The sun fell upon them suddenly and Tristam realized the squall had left the same conditions in its wake as had existed before—a windless calm—though the squall had whipped the sea into a short, confused chop, forcing Tristam to use a great deal of his strength to keep them afloat.

"Well, I think we should have a look while we are here," Tristam said, forcing confidence into his voice. Taking note of the sun's position Tristam began to side-stroke after the *Swallow,* towing Pim with one hand. "Kick your feet and do not struggle to keep your whole head out of water. You will wear me out. That's better."

I am fortunate, Tristam thought, *that he is too terrified to panic. For the moment he will do anything I ask.*

They made slow progress against the steep little seas, but Tristam could not bear to stay in one place and wait. Sharks would become a real danger in a short time, for it had often been observed that they would appear not long after a man was in the water—even here in the open ocean. *What senses they must have,* he thought!

Pim was growing calmer, and making more of an effort to kick his feet. He even moved his arms a bit. He was a strong boy, there was no doubt of that. It was unfortunate, Tristam thought, that it was not Pim's strength they were relying on to keep them alive.

With some effort he bobbed up to search the sea, and there he thought he saw the *Swallow,* almost hull-down on the horizon. The squall had carried them farther than he had estimated. *Well, this may not be as easy as I hoped. They will launch boats, but even so it could be some time. And I criticized Beacham for diving in after me. This was just as ill-considered. Though how could I have done otherwise?*

Towing Pim was already beginning to seem an effort, which caused Tristam's first real feeling of fear.

He knew they would have to stay afloat a good length of time, for they could not expect to be found immediately ... if they could hope to be found at all.

I shall not look until I have counted to three—no—five thousand, Tristam decided. And with each stroke he counted one.

"Mr. Flattery?"

"One thousand, six. Yes?"

"I am sorry you ... that is, I. . . ."

"Now you've made me lose count." Tristam swam a few stokes more. He could feel his companion was kicking less. "Don't worry, Pim. The ocean gave me back my life once. I can't think it means for me to drown: nor you. But paddle, lad! I can't keep you afloat if you won't help."

A renewed effort resulted. Tristam began to count again but lost patience at two thousand and bobbed up to look. He could not find the ship. Although it took great effort, he tried again. Yes! There she was! And perhaps he had seen a dot on the ocean as well. A boat, he hoped.

"The cutter has been launched," he reported, hoping to raise the boy's spirits.

"Farrelle be praised. I have been praying, sir. Praying as never before."

"That's good, Pim, so long as it doesn't take away from your kicking."

Row, you bastards! Tristam thought.

On the count of two thousand Tristam would look again. Keeping the leaden Pim afloat for any time was beginning to look impossible. The human body is almost neutrally buoyant, Tristam told himself. It takes only a few pounds of floatation to keep the average-sized man on the surface. It should not require so much effort!

One thousand, nine hundred, ninety nine. He pushed himself up.

"Damn!"

"What is it, sir?"

"There are two boats and they are making for the

wrong part of the ocean. We must swim." Tristam set a course he hoped would intersect the searchers. Pim waved his legs ineffectually. "Come on, damn you! Pim, we'll drown if you don't do better than that."

The terrified seaman improved his efforts again, but Tristam could not count on that happening forever. The cold water was sapping their strength.

Tristam lost count yet again. It was all he could do to keep his limbs moving as they should. After a suitable time he popped up. There was a boat, but it was going to pass them by! *Damn this sea,* Tristam thought.

The squall had been uncommonly strong and the short little sea it left behind would make them hard to spot, especially from the low vantage of the cutter. The sun had slipped behind a cloud and that wouldn't help either.

"Could you see them, Mr. Flattery?"

"Yes, we are on a collision course. Don't let off kicking."

If I can keep this up for ten minutes, it will be a miracle.

Pim went suddenly rigid. "What was that?"

Turbulence! Something moving in the water nearby. A great explosion of breath, followed by an inhalation that echoed in a massive chest. The smell of rotten fish oil.

"A whale," Tristam said, almost laughing with relief.

Suddenly they felt a tugging from the water as though a current pulled at them from beneath the waves. The whale had sounded directly under them.

Pim turned in a blind panic and tried to climb out of the water onto Tristam's shoulders. The naturalist went under and received a heavy blow on the forehead from the sailor's knee. He let himself sink a few feet more and then pushed himself away. The whale, he was sure would not harm them intentionally, but Pim could drown them both.

Tristam stroked to the surface five feet from the

frantic Jack. Pim was flailing about and barely keeping his mouth above water.

"Oh, Farrelle save me. Mr. Flattery. He'll et us both."

"It means us no harm, you bloody fool! I can't keep you afloat if you're going to drown me."

Pim was reaching out for him but Tristam kept just out of range. "I'm drowning. Oh! I'm drowning."

"Yes, you will, too, unless you take hold of yourself."

The whale surfaced once more, its glistening back rolling to the surface not fifteen feet away. Again the unmistakable explosion of massive breath. It was a baleen whale, Tristam was glad to see, and not a toothed variety. At least they could not appear edible to this giant.

"Mr. Flattery!"

Against his better judgment he reached out and took Pim's hand, and to his relief the boy did not try to climb onto his shoulders again.

The whale stayed on the surface and circled them slowly, blowing at irregular intervals. Tristam found himself making mental notes—a habit he would take to his grave, apparently. Small dorsal fin set in an area of mottled gray-white. Otherwise it was a black back. Length was hard to guess, strangely enough, for it was too close, but it was large.

A shout. Then another. Tristam bobbed up, almost at the end of his reserves. His tussle with Pim had drained the last of his strength.

The cutter was making directly for them, someone standing in the bow. The whale blew once more and then sounded, disappearing into the mysterious depths of the vast ocean.

❦   ❦   ❦

Tristam and Pim lay in a heap at the coxswain's feet, so relieved to find themselves rescued that both had tears in their eyes.

"Praise be, praise be," Pim kept saying over and over, though whether it was a prayer or simply an indication of how addled the boy was, Tristam could not be sure.

Lieutenant Osler sat on the gunwale above them, almost as joyous as the two castaways. He had given Tristam his jacket so that he might cover his nakedness.

"It was Mr. Hobbes saw you, Mr. Flattery." Osler nodded to the ship's master in the bow. "The whale spout drew his attention and then he caught sight of you with his glass. Blood and flames, but it was a near thing. If not for Hobbes' leviathan, you would be swimming yet."

Tristam shook his head. "I don't think we could have lasted another minute. We were at our end." It was all he could manage. The naturalist had never felt so entirely drained in his life.

🦗   🦗   🦗

Both seamen and officers alike clapped Tristam on the back as he came over the rail, wearing Osler's jacket tied around his waist like an odd skirt.

"I will tell you, Mr. Flattery," the captain said, pumping Tristam's hand, "I despaired of ever seeing you again. It was a nobly foolish act of bravery, sir. There is no doubt." He waved at the gathered crew. "Let him through, now. Let the man find his clothes."

The duchess stood by as well, clutching the rail for balance, it seemed. There was no mistaking the relief on her face. She put a hand on Tristam's naked shoulder for part of a second but took it away quickly.

Tristam tried to smile at her but had so little energy he could not manage it. Shaking as he went, he slipped below and into his cabin where he collapsed on the tiny square of cabin sole. A few minutes later, a knock roused him.

"Tristam? Are you whole?" It was the duchess.

"A moment." He managed to pull on breeches and a shirt before opening the door.

Distress was obvious on the duchess' face. She looked quickly behind her, where Osler stood at the bottom of the companionway ladder. The lieutenant discreetly exited.

Reaching out as though she would embrace him, the duchess took hold of his shirt front, then pushed his soaking hair back from his face. "How could you have been so foolish?" she demanded. "You risked everything for the life of a cabin boy."

THIRTY-TWO

Although he understood the principles of optics perfectly well, Tristam still found that he was attempting to see his entire six foot frame in a looking glass not five inches square. It made him laugh. With a great show of impatience he smoothed his coat as best he could and brushed haphazardly at his sleeves. It would have to do. The ship's officers, he was well aware, would arrive dressed impeccably, as usual—but they had stewards and other servants to look after their uniforms. Tristam had Tristam.

"And a miserable gentleman's gentleman you make, too," he whispered to his reflection in the looking glass.

It had been some three weeks since Tristam's act of heroic-foolhardiness—jumping into the ocean after a drowning Jack—and despite the considerable passage of time, the *Swallow* had not yet reached the pass that would take them through the Archipelago.

Those wholly honest, unfailingly steady winds that Beacham had sung praises to, the peerless Northeast Trades, had materialized only intermittently—a few precious days of fair breezes between complete calms, and gales which brought unyielding head winds. Even now Tristam could hear the sails slatting about in their gear, for the *Swallow* was becalmed again and had been since just after noon—the day's run a paltry twenty-five nautical miles.

The lack of progress was not only frustrating to all aboard, but it seemed to turn everyone's thoughts to the worst purpose. It had become obvious to the Jacks, and perhaps the officers, as well, that Kreel studiously avoided the viscount, almost as though he were afraid—or at least so the man acted. Tristam believed the Jack was making a silent accusation, though clear enough to anyone who was not blind.

Tristam hoped that Julian—if it actually had been Julian—was not still planning to finish the job. He didn't want any responsibility for Kreel's death, for Tristam was sure the viscount had been acting either to protect him or out of vengeance. But there was nothing he could do. He had not seen the attacker's face.

I have done enough for Kreel already, Tristam told himself. *I saved his life. One attempt at murder paid back by another. The accounts are balanced.*

But what would the Jacks do if they believed the viscount had tried to kill their messmate? It was hard to say. Kreel, the naturalist had come to realize, was not generally popular beyond his own small group of followers—feared, yes, but not liked. Most of the crew were probably happy to see him get his own back. For any of the Jacks to harm the viscount was almost unthinkable. Stern would have to hang someone for that—he would have no choice. But then, the hands had impressed Tristam several times with their inability to foresee the results of their actions. Some of them were little more than children in that regard. Julian should bear that in mind.

Over the past weeks Tristam felt he had been accepted by the majority of the crew. Beacham said the Jacks had begun referring to Tristam as "the professor," and that it was not meant unkindly. A good sign, apparently.

He pulled his frock coat down in the back in an attempt to straighten the shoulders. It would have to do. A sudden crack of canvas overhead stopped Tristam with his hand on the door to his cabin, but it was just the sails slatting as the ship rolled, not wind as he hoped.

In his search for fair winds Stern had been forced farther south than he thought ideal. As a result, the *Swallow* was far off her course. The bands of wind might be boldly marked on the Admirality charts, but, in truth, they shifted—not only from season to season but year to year as well.

Even so, this foray into the south had not improved their situation in regard to winds. As things stood, they would have to make up some distance to the north to reach the Queen Anne Passage.

Stern kept joking that at least there was no fear of meeting corsairs, and that was likely true for the marauders tended to patrol the sea lanes as close to the pass as they dared, hoping to catch one of the rich prizes coming from Farrland's silver mines.

Tristam heard little about the situation there and often wondered what had occurred for the Admiralty to send the *Raven* out to the station at such a pace.

He checked his pocket watch. Mustn't keep the duchess waiting. Meals had become less and less appetizing as the voyage stretched on, and had acquired an air of ritual. The most banal food would be served in the duchess' cabin upon silver and fine porcelain, the guests commenting upon this terrible fare as though it had come from the most noted kitchen in Avonel. Tristam knew that the duchess found this amusing, but he suspected that the navy men did not see any humor in it at all. They were too inured to life aboard. So much so that they believed this new tinned food to be "dietetically salutary"—an opinion the duchess made great sport of in private.

Tristam passed through the tiny wardroom that lay between his "closet" and the duchess' cabin and met Stern and Lieutenant Osler arriving at the same time, brass buttons gleaming, not a speck of lint in evidence. They entered to find the viscount and the physician, drinking port and perched on the ledge of the gallery windows, which had been opened to catch any breath of wind that might happen along. When they greeted the viscount, neither Stern nor Osler showed the slightest sign that they had sensed the mood of the Jacks or knew who it was they had come to suspect in Kreel's attack.

For his part, the viscount appeared his usual jovial self, perhaps a bit tipsy, but happy to see everyone.

With the skylight and stern windows open, the great cabin was a welcome change from Tristam's stifling accommodation. Even so the duchess suggested that they not stand upon ceremony and insisted all the gentlemen remove their jackets, which Tristam found a great relief, for they were far to the south now and winter was but a vague memory.

The duchess, Tristam noted, did not appear to be affected by the heat. In a white gown she seemed as fresh as anyone sitting in the shade in a breezy garden. A look of heightened excitement, as though she were newly in love, was something the duchess seemed to be able to achieve at will. Tristam found it very alluring and so did other men, he realized. Her glow of not-so-secret love had no apparent focus—she had no lover to anyone's knowledge—and perhaps subconsciously this fed everyone's fantasies, doubling the effect.

Tristam looked around the room at the present company: who was there who stood a chance against this woman? Not Tristam, certainly. He might be able to muster some resentment toward the duchess when she was not present (after all, she did manipulate him terribly), but he was beginning to concede that she could sweep the feeling aside with little more than a smile and a toss of her lovely curls.

With the exception of Stern, the others showed no more resistance.

Sunset began to prepare its spectacle just as dinner was served, casting a warm glow into the cabin—perfect light for a woman with the duchess' coloring, Tristam noted.

The salt pork and tinned peas arrived on silver chafing dishes. "Lovely," the duchess cooed, and cast a conspiratorial glance at Tristam. Fortunately wine kept well, and this at least was worthy of its serving vessel and cut-glass stemware.

"There is a rumor, Lieutenant Osler," the duchess began, "that just over the horizon lies the Archipelago, and that if the mainmast were only a bit higher we would be able to see islands from the maintop." The duchess said this with complete ease, the nautical language as much a part of her common speech now as the social discourse of the drawing room.

Tristam had noticed that the duchess had launched a new campaign; she had begun to focus her charm on the ship's officers, devoting noticeably less of her attention to Captain Stern. It was difficult to guess what she hoped to gain from her actions, but it was clear that the officers had become as devoted to the duchess as they could be to any sovereign. Stern tried to maintain his pose of gentlemanly dignity, but Tristam thought the captain might not bear up much longer. Here was a man used to being both in command and the person who set the tone of whatever social life existed aboard. The navy was the only life Stern knew and suddenly he must feel he was losing his place in it. The man was adrift. More and more it looked like he was merely in the employ of the duchess, around whom life aboard now centered.

"We certainly are close, Duchess," Osler said, obviously pleased to have her attention, "though perhaps not as close as rumors have it. But with any wind at all we could raise the Archipelago in a good day's sail."

The duchess smiled at Osler as though he had just said something that pleased her immeasurably. "Well, I will be glad to see it. There is some possibility of fresh food, I have been told."

"Well ..." Osler glanced at his commander, a bit sheepishly, Tristam thought. "If the captain chooses to land a party. . . . We have much northing to make up and may well find a shore breeze to take us on our way."

"What say you, Captain?" Llewellyn asked, unaware, as usual, of the undercurrents flowing around him.

Stern feigned slight surprise at actually being asked for his opinion. "I would not gainsay the lieutenant, Doctor," he said, more peevishly than he meant,

Tristam guessed. "We have much time to make up. But we will see. If the ship is becalmed near a likely landing place, we might put a party ashore. There is only one protected bay charted between here and the Queen Anne Station—it is a treacherous stretch of coast—so we cannot count on getting fresh victuals. But our crew is hale and we are not in real need."

An actress of the duchess' ability could speak to her audience with little more than a gesture, and she smiled, raising her eyebrows as though saying to the others, "Could we not have guessed?" Without a word she managed to make it seem that Stern had said something foolish . . . yet again. Tristam felt a bit sorry for the man.

What precisely she hoped to achieve by isolating Stern, Tristam could not imagine. There was certainly tension around the table. Was she merely angry with the man? Unlikely, Tristam realized. The duchess was far too calculating.

"How much longer until we reach the island— Varua, that is?" Llewellyn addressed this question to the table, apparently, for he did not look up as he spoke. Tristam thought the man looked a little under the weather, and he seemed to have reacquired the cough he had suffered from on Farrow.

A second's silence and then the captain answered. "If the winds in the Ocean Beyond are as fickle as those we have experienced so far, I would not wish to speculate, Doctor. Certainly the crossing is commonly thirty-some days at this time of year. There is, however, valuable work we might do along the way, for the Palle Island group, discovered by Pankhurst and our own Hobbes, has never been properly surveyed. A month and a half there, or perhaps a bit longer, would see a significant addition to our hydrographical knowledge. Not to mention what could be learned in the way of botany and the other disciplines." He nodded at Tristam.

"A month and a half?" Llewellyn looked up at this, his face registering the most remarkable change—like a patient who had received the worst possible news. Life aboard ship did not agree with the good doctor. "It . . . it seems an awfully long time, Captain."

Stern shrugged. "It is our business, Doctor Llewellyn. But once you are ashore in the Palle group, you will find much to interest you, for they are said to be beautiful islands with a wholesome climate. Uninhabited, too, though perhaps we shall find evidence that this has not always been so."

"Beautiful, but not on our course to Varua, I am told," the duchess said, looking at Stern over the rim of her wine glass.

Stern's color began to rise. He was not made to live with this situation, that was certain. Tristam expected an outburst, but Stern forced good humor into his voice, looking around the table as though he would cajole the company. "Come, come. We have an opportunity not granted to one citizen in a hundred thousand—or even fewer. We are seeing the new world! A world we have only begun to explore. If we can carry the lines of the globe's charts a bit farther into the areas presently marked *unknown*, we shall be taking part in history." He turned to the downcast-looking Llewellyn. "Consider, Doctor, if we continue the practice of previous surveyors, and I have every intention of doing so, then there will be a notable feature of the world's geography named for each and every one of us. Your name will not be inscribed on some bit of stone to be lost amongst the numberless others—it will be writ upon the world itself! There for all men to see, down through the ages. You can't ask for more than that, sir."

Llewellyn managed a weak nod and then returned his gaze to the table—unwell, Tristam was sure, for certainly such a suggestion should appeal to a man as vain as the physician.

"Yes," the duchess said dryly, "won't that be lovely."

Into the ensuing silence a call from the masthead

dropped like a rat onto the table. "Sail, Mr. Hobbes! To larboard, forward quarter."

The two officers erupted out of their seats and bolted out the door, the sound of their boots stomping up the companionway stair echoing back to the diners.

"Well, so much for our dinner party," the duchess said, tossing her napkin onto the table. She regarded her food with obvious distaste. "Shall we have a look, as well?"

At a more dignified pace, the others proceeded to the deck. The captain was perched on the stem, clutching a forestay, gazing off to larboard with his glass. In the failing light Tristam could make out the sails of another ship.

"Mr. Flattery," Stern said as Tristam mounted the forecastle, "would you be so kind as to lend me your Fromme glass? Tell Mr. Hobbes to have a midshipman carry it up to the masthead." Stern turned and walked back to the shrouds of the mainmast.

Tristam bolted down to his cabin, returning with his field glass. Shedding his shoes and stockings, he grasped the ratlines and climbed up after the captain, determined to deliver the instrument himself so that he might have some idea of the other ship's identity. All the sailors aboard had become very grim-faced and Tristam did not like that in the least.

Pulling himself up onto the crosstrees, Tristam found Stern and Osler sitting astride the main topsail yard.

"Ah, kind of you, Mr. Flattery." Stern turned Tristam's glass on the distant ship. The naturalist waited for a pronouncement, watching Stern's face for a hint, but the captain suddenly handed the glass to his lieutenant, without saying a word.

"It is a Farr flag, to be sure," Osler said, no hint of tension in his voice.

"That does not surprise me," the captain answered. "Give the glass to Mr. Flattery. He has keen sight."

Tristam quickly focused on the ship. Very distant, a dark hull under a pale cloud of sail.

"Is it bow toward us, Mr. Flattery?" Stern asked.

"Yesss, I believe it is, Captain. Or nearly so."

"Wind in its sails?"

"They are flapping, sir."

"It is hard to tell from this angle, I know, but does the stern seem unnaturally high and broad? Look carefully now."

"Well, the light is not good, sir," Tristam said, understating the case, "but it does seem to have a greater sheer than the *Swallow*. In fact, I am quite convinced of it."

"Lieutenant?"

"I'm afraid I agree, sir."

"It is the damnedest luck," Stern said quietly.

"But why would they be down here, sir?"

"Perhaps Nash or some other has chased them down. Or they might be seeking wind as we do." Stern took the glass again and had a last look before the darkness closed in completely. He swore an oath under his breath and then handed the glass back to Tristam.

"No lanterns tonight, Mr. Osler. We will keep the ship dark. Hoist out a boat and tow our head around to the north, and keep it there. If there is a wind, we must make the best of it. Perhaps by morning we will be far from here . . . and from them." He cocked his head toward the distant ship. "We can only hope."

"Shall we clear for action, sir?" Osler asked this terrible question in a calm voice.

"No, they will not close with us this night. If they are still within view, we will exercise the guns at first light." He made a move to go, but stopped. "Not a word of this to anyone, Mr. Flattery."

Tristam's cabin seemed particularly close and airless that evening and he rolled in his motionless hammock so frequently that he was sure he would wear a hole through. He wondered if others were suffering in the same way. For some reason he dearly longed for the company of the duchess—not as he normally wished but merely her presence. They could be a comfort to each other.

Corsairs.

It was difficult to believe. They were only an under-gunned survey ship with nothing of true value aboard—except, of course, the Duchess of Morland. No doubt, the King would pay any price to have her returned safely, though it was impossible for Tristam to believe she would be returned completely unharmed—and it could be much worse than that.

Tristam rolled over again, striking his ankle against some hard corner, reminding him of the box in which his uncle's rare wine lay hidden. Worth a small fortune he had been told. . . . Exactly how small? He rolled the other way, without further bruising.

Stern was a clever officer and had met corsairs before. There was every chance he would keep them at bay, at least until the Naval Station could be reached. The idea of running the *Swallow* in under the safety of the guns at Queen Anne Station gave the naturalist a moment's comfort. But it did not last. What if the enemy ship had found wind? Tristam knew it was possible. He had often seen the ripple of a breeze on the water not a mile off while the *Swallow* bobbed in a dead calm.

"This will never do," Tristam said aloud. Rising as silently as possible, he dressed and went barefooted up to the quarterdeck. It had become his practice, upon reaching the deck, to go immediately to the stern rail and look for any sign of a wake, and that night his hopes were higher than usual.

Without lanterns only starlight illuminated the deck, for they were just a day past the new moon. The *thirteenth moon*, the Jacks had noted. A year of thirteen moons was believed to be a time of ill omen, and the coming full would bring the most dreaded days of the cycle. Tristam, however, had not been infected with the superstition of the sailors.

He nodded to the helmsman, neither man speaking for they were directly above the cabin of the duchess.

Tristam was surprised to find a man bent almost double over the stern rail as though ill—ailing in a flat calm. Taken unawares by Tristam's nearly silent approach the man turned with a start. And it was Hobbes! A sailor who could not have known a day of seasickness these past thirty-five years—and his face twisted in fury.

Tristam was stopped in his tracks by the master's reaction, but the look on Hobbes face changed immediately, deep embarrassment or chagrin replacing the rage. With a perfunctory nod he left Tristam at the rail and made his way quickly forward.

Hobbes was so even-tempered that Tristam stood in some shock, wondering what could possibly have caused such a reaction. And then he heard the voice of the duchess not three feet below him. She whispered in Entonne, but Tristam could make out her words perfectly.

"It is most madding, Julian. If Stern realized what miracle lay waiting in Varua, he would drive this ship as he has never driven a ship before. There would be no more talk of 'contributing to the hydrographical knowledge of the sphere,' that is certain. I would take the man into our confidence if I thought for a moment he would believe me."

"He would not believe." Lord Elsworth said. "It is maddening, though; I agree." Silence.

What miracle, Tristam wondered?

"At least we have managed to keep Flattery out of their hands," the viscount said, causing Tristam to spread his hands on the rail as though needing support. "Though I must tell you, I am none too comfortable in the man's company. Farrelle's oath, I am glad I was not there when the whale came. Is it not remarkable?"

"Yes," the duchess shook her head distractedly, Tristam was sure. "One cannot alter one's view of the world overnight. Time. It will take time." The duchess paused. Tristam could almost see her nibbling her lip delicately as she did when deep in thought.

He felt a sense of dread, growing inside him like a tumor.

"We have no choice, Julian. We follow Tristam's course, now—blindly. You must stay close to him, as close as you can."

"Yes, I understand. But, in truth, we have greater concerns at the moment."

Tristam had come to know the duchess so well that he almost heard the sigh the silence masked. "Yes." A second's hesitation. "I almost hope they are corsairs. We are not such a great prize to them, so they should not be so difficult to discourage. The alternative is far worse."

A small ripple of water—a sea creature surfacing.

"Perhaps, but even marauders should not be taken lightly. This is not a ship of war. Stern has few men, fewer guns and a slow ship. You should not have such faith in old tales." Silence for a moment, making Tristam wonder if they had become aware of his presence. "I must sleep," the viscount said. "We will need our wits about us these next days."

The noise of people moving below. Tristam turned and silently made his way forward, not looking at the helmsman as he passed.

What had he just heard? "We follow Tristam's course, now."

He went down into the ship's waist and slumped against the bulwark.

Keep him out of whose hands?

The duchess had spoken of him as though he were charmed—or cursed. He covered his eyes. To hear her speak of him so coolly, so objectively. . . . "Farrelle's flames," he muttered.

What did these people want of him? They were as foolish as the superstitious Jacks! But Tristam knew the duchess was no fool.

THIRTY-THREE

The journal of Tristam Flattery:
this fourteenth day of December, 1559.

There is no sleep for me this night, and not simply because we have been discovered by marauders. What in this round world have I heard? Each time I believe I gain some understanding of the machinations that occur around me something new happens and I am thrown off the scent completely, find that I have been in the wrong track. What is it these people expect of me? How is it possible that they have come to regard me as having some role in their designs? This idea is so misguided as to verge on lunacy. Whatever the function of this seed that I seek I have come to regard it with some dread. I am of half a mind to say nothing even if I do find it—as Lady Galton suggested. I cannot imagine what has come over these people . . . whoever they are.

The eastern sky showed no signs of the approaching dawn, yet most of the *Swallow*'s people were on deck, peering silently into the darkness. A small breeze had reached out from the Archipelago during the night and Stern had taken the advantage to move north, hoping to sail beyond the corsairs, who lay between the *Swallow* and the Queen Anne Station. But the breeze had raised their hopes for only two brief hours. What the marauder had chosen to do under cover of darkness was the question that had brought so many on deck so early.

Tristam had been sent aloft as a lookout and perched, with Lieutenant Osler, on the topmast trestletrees. Below them the sails hung limp, wafting only to the roll of the ship, while overhead the fainter stars were beginning to disappear, hinting at daylight. Both Osler and Tristam scanned the dark ocean, looking for a light or the white of sails.

"There seems to be a dark line to the west," Tristam said, his voice hushed, for there was something very solemn about their situation.

The young officer kept his glass trained to the east. "I wouldn't be surprised. There is a strange current here that has set ships to the northwest in the past, and we sailed north and somewhat west during the night. That will be your Archipelago, Mr. Flattery. Wait a bit until there is no doubt and then you may call 'land-ho.' It may lift the spirits of a few."

As there were no signs of a ship in that direction, Tristam overcame his curiosity about the islands and turned his glass out to sea. There was a grayness in the eastern sky now, without question.

"Mr. Osler?"

"Sir?"

"Almost directly abeam to starboard . . . perhaps forward of that." Pale, ghostly, far out on the rolling ocean.

Osler turned his glass to starboard, searching carefully. "You have found our corsairs, Flattery, damn their eyes." He cupped a hand to his mouth and called down to the deck. "Sail, Captain. Two points and a half off the starboard bow."

There was a shuffling on the deck as everyone moved to a better vantage.

"We cannot make them out, Lieutenant," Stern called up after a moment. "There is no doubt?"

"None, sir. And there is land on the western horizon, as well."

The growing daylight illuminated the distant sails for all to see, and the peaks of the far islands, for only the peaks could be seen catching the light of the rising sun. In that few moments of the morning's twilight the island tops had little definition, an irregular line of deep purple spanning the western horizon, appearing to Tristam like an illustration of mountains in a child's book—unreal, naive, the details sketched in by imagination alone. Irrational though it was, Tristam felt these storybook islands seemed a haven from the distressing reality of the corsairs' ship to the east. The truth was, however, the *Swallow* was trapped against an impenetrable maze of shoals and channels.

Osler stared at the distant ship as though he would sink it with the intensity of his gaze.

"Is it the same ship, then?" Tristam asked quietly.

Osler apparently did not hear but, as if in answer to Tristam's question, the Jacks began to uncover and unhouse the *Swallow*'s guns. Of the distant ship Tristam could make out little, though it appeared an ominous sight in the empty ocean, reminding him of the *Raven* bearing down on them as they sailed toward Farrow. Where was the *Raven* now, he wondered?

"Is this a fast ship, our friend out there?" Tristam asked, raising his voice a little.

"Fast? No, but she has a longer waterline and with the wind free she will have the advantage over our little *Swallow*. And the corsair's captain can set more sail as well—right up to royals and sky sails. She is a bird of prey, if I might borrow from your discipline, Mr. Flattery, and she has her eye trained on us.

"That ship was once an Entonne merchantman: perhaps one hundred thirty feet in length of deck and deep in the hold. If properly strengthened, she could carry two decks of guns—ten- or twelve-pounders—in opposition to our few four- and six-pounders." He paused as if to consider more. Tristam was impressed with the man's calm detachment.

"But it is not all dark, Flattery, for the *Swallow* will certainly be faster going to weather, more maneuverable, and shallow water may be our greatest ally. You can be sure that Mr. Hobbes is searching the charts as we speak. An area of reefs or shallows will protect us better than a deck of twelve-pounders—especially with our crew. Hardly a man among them has been in an action, but for the Master and Captain Stern."

"You have not been in a battle?" Tristam was surprised. "You seem awfully calm. I wish I could say the same for myself."

"Not a fleet action, no, but several single ship actions. I have met corsairs before, perhaps even this very captain who chases us. Do not be concerned, Flattery, we carry no silver, as they well know. If we make the taking of us difficult enough, they will be discouraged—especially if chasing us draws them farther from the common sea lanes. It is bullion they seek, not a naturalist's collection." He smiled as he spoke but kept his glass trained on the far ship.

"Look carefully, Flattery, and tell me . . . does our sea hawk appear to have wind under her wings?"

Tristam turned his glass on the dark hull of the other ship. The sails did not seem to flutter and the ship heeled steadily. "I think so. There are waves cresting around it as well." Tristam felt his heart sink. "They seem to have found the trade."

"Not the trade, I think," Osler said. "Look how they go. That is wind from the southeast, I'm sure. Perhaps we will see the trades yet today, but until then this southeaster will have to do. It will reach us by and by."

"But this black ship will be borne on its wings."

"They can't sail swifter than the wind, or even nearly as fast. They will close the gap some, but we will be on our way soon enough." There was a shout from the deck. "We are called down, Mr. Flattery."

Tristam slowly descended by way of the ratlines as the Jacks scrambled past him on their way up to loose sail. Osler slid down a backstay, arriving at the deck in seconds and making Tristam vow to do the same at his next opportunity—if he was not to be captive of corsairs.

Mounting the quarterdeck, Tristam found Captain Stern standing alone at the after rail and the duchess leaning on the bulwark near the break in the deck.

Tristam was surprised to find that the duchess did not show the slightest signs of fright or of having spent a sleepless night.

"The pleasures of the day to you, Tristam," she said, as though they were not being pursued by men whose reputations must be deeply unsettling to a woman.

Tristam found himself unable to take his gaze from her face—the overheard conversation still echoing. Only the threat of corsairs kept his questions at bay.

A breeze rustled the duchess' hair and then a small gust filled the sails, causing the ship to heel and the rigging to creak loudly. The southeast wind Osler had predicted. There was an audible sigh from the crew.

"Wear ship as soon as we have steerage-way, Mr. Hobbes," Stern said quietly. Tristam knew it was a captain's responsibility to exhibit confidence no matter what the circumstances, but even so, he was struck by Stern's manner. The naturalist felt an easing of his anxiety.

Along the deck the Jacks jumped to their duties without any goading from the officers, and the ship answered her helm like a well-mannered saddle horse. The yards were braced around and *Swallow* spread her wings and began to fly from her pursuer.

Tristam watched as Stern stood looking aloft, then staring back over the rail toward the black ship, then to windward. He appeared, for all the world, like a gambler weighing his hand, deciding whether he would stay or ask for cards.

"May I look, Tristam?" The duchess nodded to his glass and he passed it to her.

"They seem almost to be on a different course from our own. Do you see? Almost parallel to our own way of going."

Lieutenant Osler stood nearby, watching the final stages of the evolution. "Though they are to windward of us, Duchess," the young man said, "they cannot sail directly to us for we shall move on, if you take my meaning. You will see that we are hard on the wind as we go, yet they have the wind on their beam—their course not so parallel as it appears. The captain of that marauder is steering to intersect our course, Duchess, and to keep his advantage of the 'weather gauge,' as we say. As we sail now, they cannot close with us much before midafternoon, I shouldn't think."

"Mr. Osler!" Stern said sharply, surprising Tristam for the captain's idea of gentlemanly deportment did not allow hollering at his officers—gentlemen themselves.

"Sir?" The young officer jumped to a rigid attention.

"See to your duty, sir." Stern said more quietly, perhaps surprised by his outburst. "We will exercise the guns."

Osler was off at a run, without looking back at Tristam and the duchess.

Garvey, the master's mate appeared from below just then, a rolled chart under his arm, and joined Hobbes and the captain at the rail. Tristam and the duchess moved a pace closer, almost without thinking, but still could not hear what the navy men were saying. Tristam thought Hobbes' manner to him was a bit cool that morning, though under the circumstances it was difficult to judge. No one was acting normally.

Stern pressed his finger to the chart, nodding and occasionally asking questions. Glancing down the deck at the men preparing the guns, the captain noticed the duchess and Tristam watching, and appeared to take pity on them. He bowed his head to the duchess in invitation, and she and Tristam almost rushed to the rail.

"You can see, Duchess, that our position is not impossible. We are not so far from the naval station that the coast has not been well surveyed. We may thank good fortune for that. The *Swallow* is here and our corsairs' ship would be hereabouts. You can see this cross. . . ." He gestured to a mark on the chart. "As things stand now, that is where the two ships shall converge—later in the day. Of course, much could change between now and then, and almost any change would be to our advantage. The arrival of our trade would put the naval station to windward, and we can certainly work our way to weather more handily than our marauder." He glanced off at the distant ship.

The duchess pointed to a pass into the islands. "Can we not go through there, Captain Stern, and hope to lose our pursuer in the profusion of straits and narrows?"

The area the duchess indicated, Tristam could not help but notice, was surveyed less than a mile in from the ocean shore. Beyond that the Archipelago was represented on the chart by a vast blank area marked *"Unknown."*

"Many of the passes are difficult to enter, Duchess, for the tides, though not great at this latitude, still create substantial flows in the narrows. Beyond such passes lies an area of extreme danger to ships. Or we might sail into a blind pass—a bay, for all purposes—where we would be trapped. I would enter the Archipelago only if no other course were possible."

"Captain Stern." It was Osler reporting in a most uncommonly clipped manner—still stinging, Tristam realized, from Stern's earlier rebuke. Tristam had never heard the captain speak harshly to his officers before and he wondered if the black ship affected Stern more than Tristam had suspected, or whether the duchess' attention to the younger officers was beginning to tell.

"We are ready, sir."

In the waist of the ship Tristam could see the gun crews of the larboard watch standing by their bronze machines of war. The men did not appear confident.

Stern spoke more kindly to his lieutenant. "The bow and stern chasers are still housed, Mr. Osler."

"I can man them only at cost to sailing the ship, sir. Shall I do so?"

"No . . . no. Our chief hope is in flight. We dare not reduce the efficiency of the ship. Press every available man." Stern turned to Tristam. "Mr. Flattery, I hope you will not object to joining in our defense?"

"I am yours to command, Captain."

"Good. And Lord Elsworth, and even the boatswain and carpenter, as long as we can spare them. Leave only the surgeon and Doctor Llewellyn to their specific duties."

"I am a competent archer, sir," Tristam offered, wondering what part he could play in such a situation.

"I hope we will not come so close, Mr. Flattery. Place Beacham in command of the larboard quarterdeck gun. He fancies himself quite a gunner. Mr. Flattery, you may assist Beacham though I will not have you swabbing or ramming powder."

A few moments later Tristam found himself under the command of Jack Beacham, who was himself under the watchful eye of the captain. The bow and stern chasers, as they were called, were small guns, throwing only a four-pound ball. Their range was not great, but for short distances they could be fired quite accurately by an experienced crew. They would not shatter a strongly built hull, yet they could do substantial damage if they struck the rigging—not to mention men.

"Lord Skye's terrible invention" the duchess had called the cannon and it was so, Tristam knew, for the naval gun had turned the tide of a war, winning great sea battles over the formidable Entonne navy, until the enemy had managed to forge their own cannon—though how they had managed it was still a great mystery.

The next two hours were spent in going through the drill of running guns in and out, swabbing, and priming. After these operations had become reasonably smooth, the guns were primed and fired, an operation that Tristam found surprisingly satisfying. Beacham had served aboard a ship of war and seemed to Tristam to know his business—incongruous in one so young and pleasant of manner.

The carpenter, a great bear of man named Tobias Shuk, had been sent to work the aft gun as well, and though he did not stint in his efforts, it was clear to Tristam that the man was greatly shaken by the entire enterprise. A landsman, like Tristam, the man had been a ship builder, lured into this voyage by the stories of

Varua. When the gun was finally discharged, and Tristam watched the ball throw up a column of spray, he turned to find the carpenter near to tears. Tristam thought it was because of the clouds of sulfurous smoke, but then he heard the man speak.

"What a great evil Skye brought into this world," he muttered, his voice taut with emotion, and then bent down to his labor and hid his face from the others.

Tristam looked back at the marauder just then and saw it enveloped in a shroud of smoke. Then a prodigious explosion rolled across the ocean, freezing every man to his place.

"It is an old trick, gentlemen," Stern's voice fell into the silence that followed. "They try to unnerve us, but they cannot enlist us to their cause so easily. Carry on."

And they did. The *Swallow* had only limited supplies of powder and shot, but they used what Stern felt they could spare and by midday they began to resemble a fighting ship, at least to Tristam's uncritical eye.

The black ship of the corsairs had come much closer and Tristam could easily see now that it was a substantially larger vessel. If it did not have the appearance of deadly efficiency the *Raven* had displayed, it certainly bore all the threat of a large man—unswift, perhaps even clumsy, but still immensely strong.

Tristam stood at the rail, drinking from a flask Beacham had given him, when the duchess came and stood at his side. Tristam nodded, too tired to make a leg, and then realized she was dressed in the uniform of an officer.

"Do not stare, Tristam. Stern ordered Jacel and me below, not wanting these marauders to see a woman aboard, but I could not stand it. Lieutenant Osler was good enough to lend me these clothes and Stern relented his earlier decision." She raised a glass and focused on the black ship. "They have come up quickly, haven't they?" The duchess turned to look to leeward. "Well, there is our Archipelago, Tristam. I had hoped to be more pleased to see it. I understand it will soon be what is called a 'lee shore'?"

A long line of low hills could be easily seen. Behind them, rugged peaks thrust up into the sky running both north and south like a range of distant mountains, for that is what the Archipelago was—an immensely long mountain range half-risen from the sea.

"A lee shore, yes, but not for a while, yet." Tristam tried to measure their angle to the distant land and decided they still sailed almost parallel to it. Even so, they had drawn much closer over the course of the morning—ships had a tendency to slide a little sideways as they made their way forward, "leeway" the sailors called it. If the coast bent outward to the east, even a little, they would no longer be able to stay clear on their present course, which would be a disaster. They would be forced to tack out toward the enemy.

Borrowing the duchess' glass, Tristam followed the coastline south and to his great relief there did not seem to be much deviation. If anything, the shore bent a little to the southwest.

The watch was piped to its dinner, and Tristam and the duchess stood on the deck watching the massive black ship slowly close the gap.

"Duchess, Mr. Flattery. . . ." It was Stern emerging from below, his manner kindly, Tristam thought. "You would do well to set yourself some task. Watching this ship will not bolster your courage, I can assure you."

The master and the midshipmen came on deck to shoot the noon sight and Tristam was enlisted to work the mathematics with the midshipmen.

This did not take long, for the midshipmen had benefited much from Tristam's earlier instruction and there was little deviation in the sights shot—which is to say they were all close to that of Mr. Hobbes. A cross was placed on the chart and Tristam could not help but notice it was uncomfortably close to the cross which marked the spot where the two ships were estimated to meet.

Returning to the deck Tristam found the carpenter

hard at work with his mate and several Jacks cutting gaping holes in the larboard bulwark and setting strong iron rings into the frame heads.

"What is this?" Tristam asked Beacham.

"I don't know, sir, but if I was forced to guess, I would conjecture that the starboard guns will be moved over beside their mates, doubling the weight of our broadside, so to speak. We might pray the ship will take the strain."

Tristam walked back to the aft rail where the captain stood talking quietly to Hobbes as though a ship full of corsairs was not bearing down on them.

"There will be scant room to fight the guns, sir," Hobbes was saying.

"No matter, we shall not stay to fire a second time, Mr. Hobbes: it would be the end of us. We will pump most of our water over the side as soon as the carpenter is done. The guns themselves may follow. If we can get to weather of them, we have a chance, but we may have to lighten ship considerably." He swept his gaze across the horizon. "These winds cannot be relied upon." The captain fixed on the enemy ship for a few seconds, and then he shook his head. "I see what you say. They are hardly the ragged band I had expected." He paused. "But I cannot think that war has been declared in our absence."

The two men stood watching the corsairs. Tristam could make out individuals on the deck now, especially on the quarter deck where there were fewer men, and certainly these men did not look the part of corsairs. What was Stern suggesting? Had war come to the nations of the Entide Sea?

The two rows of open gun ports, each framing a gaping mouth, made his stomach turn over.

"It will be a near thing. If this does not answer, are we prepared to wear and run in close?" Stern kept his eyes fixed on the marauder.

"We are, sir. Let's hope this barge is as unhandy as the rest of her kind."

The afternoon crept by. Tristam helped move the

three six-pounders from the starboard side to their new positions to larboard, more difficult than one would think for the ship rolled and pitched unmercifully. As Mr. Hobbes had suggested, there was scant room left to work the guns, but it could not be helped. To the surprise of the naturalist, half the guns were loaded with lengths of chain rather than with balls. Beacham explained that with such small guns they could do little damage to a ship's hull, but chain would wreak havoc in the rigging.

The bow and stern chasers were housed and their crews moved to the larger guns in the waist. Beacham assured Tristam that these guns were identical to the gun they had drilled with that morning, except for their larger size, but Tristam still felt some apprehension at firing a weapon he had no experience with.

By the time the *Swallow* had been cleared for action, the sun had cast the eastern shore of the Archipelago into shadow, stripping away all sense of depth and again giving the impression of a children's drawing. Tristam stood by his gun, watching. He dearly wanted his glass but had left it below out of harm's way. A soft rain misted his back, and he looked up to find Jacks out on the footropes, wetting down the sails and rigging—a precaution against fire.

At a quiet order from the captain, the master's mate put the helm over and the *Swallow* turned two points toward land, putting the wind just aft of the beam. A bubbling and rushing along the hull spoke of the increase in speed. The Jacks braced the yards and sheeted sails without a word, no shanties accompanying the heaving of lines.

The corsairs turned as well, falling into line almost astern.

"I would venture to stay that the captain knows his business better than the marauder who commands that forsaken vessel to windward." Beacham had appeared at his side. "Do you see? They have fallen in behind us as we hoped. Impatience and so many more guns have caught them out."

"Stand by your guns," came the order.

The cannon that Beacham and Tristam manned was farthest aft, at the foot of the stairs to the quarter deck, and Tristam could still hear some of what was being said by the officers. The duchess was sent below and Tristam saw her nod to the viscount who was stationed at a gun forward. He thought for a moment that he had been forgotten, but she paused and tried to smile at him—which meant more to him than he realized.

Tristam could see Julian, standing a head above the Jacks around him, intent on his duty, and then his view was blocked by another, equally large. Kreel was stationed at the gun next to the viscount's.

Better that they were farther apart, Tristam thought, but at least Kreel was far from him.

Stepping up onto the second stair, Tristam could just make out the masts of their pursuer. With each second he was certain he could see them drawing closer and this set his nerves to jangling.

"Take your place, if you please, Mr. Flattery." Lieutenant Osler smiled as though in apology for giving Tristam an order.

Stern came to the break in the deck then and addressed the men. "Do not fire before the command. We shall only have one opportunity and cannot afford to waste it. If we are fortunate, gentlemen, we shall be out of this within the hour. Let each man do his duty."

The men gave three cheers, in which Tristam joined self-consciously. He, for one, was decidedly frightened and wondered if it showed, for he could not even force a smile and felt his face drawn and tight. Worse, his bowels were in a tangle, complaining loudly on occasion.

An explosion sounded in the distance. To Tristam's great surprise he saw a cannon ball skip across the top of the waves not a hundred feet off.

"Just getting the range," Beacham whispered. "That will be their bow chaser—a little six-pounder."

The others laughed and Osler hushed them into silence with a stare. Tristam could feel the tension on the ship as they waited. Unlike the others around him, the naturalist had no real understanding of what Stern was about to attempt. Certainly if the captain let this great ship within range one broadside would destroy the poor *Swallow.* Yet he could see the corsair ranging up behind them. There was no need to stand on a step for a view now.

"There she goes," one of the Jacks whispered, nodding to the other ship. "Making leeway like a log."

Tristam looked back and could see that the man was right, the corsair was having to trim her sails and steer a higher course lest she lose the advantage of the weather gauge.

A second explosion and Tristam found himself half crouching. Nothing happened, but then there was a loud slatting overhead and Tristam looked up to see the mizzen topsail crashing about in its gear and a ragged hole torn in the canvas.

Beacham turned to Tristam. "Acceptable. They should find wood next time."

The helmsman began to work the ship up closer to the wind, and the Jacks trimmed sail accordingly. The sounds of the hull moving through the water had changed now and Tristam looked up to see their ensign was not fluttering as it had. The wind was falling light just as the sun began its final plunge toward the far mountains.

Beacham held out his hand and measured the distance between the sun and the horizon. "Half of an hour, no more," he said, and Tristam felt hopes rise at the statement. Darkness would hide them.

"Run out your guns," came the command suddenly, and Tristam strained on the tackles with the others, running the gun out against the heel of the ship. The carriage thumped up against the bulwark and Beacham put the firing cord into Tristam's hand.

"Not before I say, Mr. Flattery. Make no mistake." The midshipman took his fid and stood by to elevate the gun.

The men were utterly silent, every ear straining for the commands of their officers.

"Luff and touch her, Mr. Garvey," Tristam heard, and the *Swallow* swung suddenly to windward so that they were broadside to the corsair, broadside and on the marauder's forward quarter. Tristam had a clear view now and could see the corsair's yawing gun ports, and her men standing by their guns, as intent as Tristam himself.

The captain of the black ship ordered his own helmsman to put his ship up, to bring her massive broadside to bear, but she did not respond as the agile *Swallow* did.

Beacham pried the gun up quickly.

"On the roll!" came the order.

The *Swallow* crested a wave and as she did, Beacham gave the gun a last pry. "Stand clear, Mr. Flattery. . . ." He held up his hand, staring off at the enemy ship. *"Fire!"*

There was a great explosion as the *Swallow*'s guns roared and Tristam was blinded by a thick, choking pall. He felt the ship fall off and begin to sail again. A hand found him in the smoke and pulled him down. "Lie flat on the deck," the carpenter said, and Tristam did not wait to be told a second time.

With his face pressed hard against the rough planks, Tristam waited for the answering roar of the corsair's guns. And then he heard a cheer. Around him, men began to jump to their feet and he did the same. In the clearing smoke he saw the corsair was turning downwind, away from the *Swallow*.

"She has lost her fore topmast!" Beacham shouted over the cheering. "She is turning downwind lest she lose the mast entire."

The *Swallow* was gathering way, making a course to windward—her one superior point of sail. Men were clapping each other on the back and shaking each other by the hand. Osler led the men in a cheer for Captain Stern, in which, Tristam was sure, the Jacks shouted themselves hoarse. And then, abruptly, the deck was si-

lent. Something had changed. Tristam looked around
wondering what it was, wondering why the men's
faces had suddenly fallen so completely grim. And
then it struck him so powerfully, he almost felt the air
jarred from his lungs. *The wind had died.*

Like everyone else aboard Tristam turned immediately to the quarter deck, staring at the captain who
was appearing out of the cloud, standing as rigid as
Gregory's statue, Tristam thought, staring off at the enemy vessel. Both ships were rapidly losing way, but
Tristam knew their great momentum would slowly pull
them farther and farther apart—a condition which he
applauded. The ships now viewed each other stern to
stern.

The captain turned to Osler and in the hush his voice
carried forward.

"Reload. And hoist out the boats. We will tow ourselves out of range if we must."

Before the lieutenant could come to the rail and give
his orders, the Jacks were in a fury of motion. The
guns were spaced so closely that their crews were on
top of each other. Jumping to haul on a tackle, Tristam
knocked one of the Jacks from the next gun crew flat
on the deck.

As they finished loading, the first boat lifted off the
skids, Tristam could hear Hobbes calling orders over
the tumult, his voice loud but devoid of panic.
Beacham leaped up onto the bulwark, grasping the
boarding net.

"They are all a-scramble to stay the foremast, lads.
We shot the forestays clean away and some of the
shrouds as well, I think. Blood and flames, but we
could rake them stern to stem if we could fire now! I'll
wager we could smash their rudder to flinders."

"The lieutenant," one of the Jacks said quietly.

Beacham jumped down to his place again. As he did
so, the port beneath the steps to the quarterdeck opened
and the voice of the Duchess of Morland issued out
into the growing darkness.

"Is that you, Tristam? Please tell us what has happened. We are mad with ignorance below, and no one will let me into my cabin where I might have a view."

Tristam crouched down to where he could just make out the anxious face of the duchess in the gloom. "We have almost toppled the corsair's foremast, Duchess, and were about to make good our escape when the wind fell flat. Boats are being readied to haul us out of cannon range."

"Has anyone been hurt? Lord Elsworth is still standing?"

"I don't know if there were injuries, Duchess." Tristam popped up to look along the deck and could make out the viscount by his gun, a huge grin on his face. "Julian is unharmed—in fact, I believe he's enjoying himself."

The duchess shook her head. "He would. A sea battle is, no doubt, a dream come true. Will we escape them in the dark?"

The very question that was causing Tristam to despair. "It is very likely," he said as confidently as he could.

"Mr. Flattery," Beacham whispered and Tristam returned to his place, standing by, ready to fire. To his great surprise, he realized he dearly wanted another shot at the corsairs. His earlier dread and terror had been replaced by a great excitement.

The ship was beginning to roll, broadside to the waves, and Tristam could see the helmsman spinning the wheel to no effect. "We have lost steerage-way," he heard someone say.

The first boat crashed into the rail as it dropped over the side, eliciting a string of oaths from the ship's master. But the cutter had barely scraped down the topsides when the second boat swung into the air, as poorly controlled as the first. The small crew was being stretched too thin, Tristam realized—not enough hands to perform any task properly.

The carpenter and boatswain were called away to rig tow-lines at the bow.

"The corsairs have launched boats," a man at the

next gun whispered and it was obvious the news had come down the line from one gun crew to the next.

"Dakin caught it," someone else whispered, "got in the way when the gun reared back. Cracked his skull. It is a lucky thing there is a proper physician aboard, I say. You can't saw off a man's head!"

This brought a despairing laugh and the remark was repeated down the line. Tristam heard the distinctive sound of a knotted rope lashing into a man's flesh, and there was quiet again among the gunners.

Twilight was quickly settling, as though the light had been borne off on the disappearing breeze. There was a sudden murmuring along the deck and Tristam could see the officers huddled at the after rail.

"A white flag," someone whispered. "Their boat bears a white flag."

Too used to having the run of the ship, Tristam was going mad having to stand by his gun. Suddenly he was reduced to the level of the poor Jacks, not privy to any of the discussion that decided their fate. One of the *Swallow*'s boats was hailed and ranged alongside and Stern went quickly over the rail. No one could miss the fact that he bore a short standard and white flag.

"What kind of parlay can be held with corsairs?" Tristam whispered to Beacham, unable to stay silent, but the midshipman only shrugged.

The absence of wind was like the lull in a couple's conversation of impending divorce—a silence so full of desperation one could almost touch it. Only the regular noises of the ship lifting and falling on the swell. Along the deck Tristam could see the tense faces, all signs of elation gone; everyone wondering.

How does one parlay with a corsair? Tristam asked himself again. What could they possibly offer? He could think of only one answer. They knew about the duchess. Word had reached them through some agent in Avonel or Farrow—or worse yet; from the Queen Anne Station. Tristam was almost certain this was the answer. The marauder would let the *Swallow* and her people go if Stern would release the duchess into their hands. Ransom. A queen's ransom. That was their goal, and only a small survey vessel to fight to gain such a treasure. What foolishness had led the duchess aboard!

Darkness fell while the boats from the two ships met. Tristam had just a glance as the *Swallow* turned somewhat on a wave. The two white hulled boats out on a dark, windless sea, their oars dipping and backing as they held position a cable apart.

The thirty minutes Stern was gone from the ship passed so slowly Tristam was sure the hands of the ship's clock must appear nailed in place. And then a call and the boat thumped alongside. Tristam could just make out Stern as he came over the side. The man did not hesitate but went directly to the quarter deck, spoke briefly with his officers and then disappeared below, his manner so stiff and determined that Tristam could sense the anger.

"That does not bode well," one of the men whispered.

Osler crossed to the head of the quarterdeck stair.

"The Captain would see you, Mr. Flattery," he said quietly, and turned immediately back to his duties.

Tristam cast a look at Beacham who offered nothing but a lift of his eyebrows. Quickly the naturalist mounted the stairs to the quarterdeck and descended into half-obscured lamplight below.

Tristam was utterly mystified as to why he had been called, but hoped he might at least learn some part of what was going on.

Stern was not seated at the table in the wardroom, as Tristam expected but instead paced back and forth before the door to the duchess' cabin. He rubbed his short-cropped beard with one hand as though he searched for some lump or disfigurement hidden beneath, and his other hand was fisted upon his hip where his long navy coat had been thrown back. When he saw Tristam, he stopped his pacing and knocked on the duchess' door without so much as a nod to the naturalist.

Jacel answered and stepped outside, curtsying to the gentlemen, obviously not intending to follow them in, but Stern beckoned her.

The duchess no doubt understood from Stern's manner that his meeting with the corsairs had disturbed and angered him deeply but she stood with her arms crossed. If not looking completely defiant she at least did not look as intimidated as everyone else aboard when the captain was in one of his moods.

As soon as the door was closed, Stern turned on Tristam, his face unreadable in the unlit cabin. "I have just been promised safe passage for my ship and crew if I will but hand over one of my passengers to these Entonne marauders." Though the words were spoken quietly, there was no mistaking the passion in the seaman's voice. He looked around the group standing mute before him, then back to Tristam. "Tell me, Mr. Flattery. . . . What is it they want with you?"

"Me!" Tristam looked desperately at the duchess but in the failing light he could not tell if she showed any signs of surprise.

"Yes, *you,* sir," Stern answered, Tristam's response adding fuel to the slow blaze of his anger. The man slammed his fist on the table. "I will have some answers here. What is it that I have not been told? Are you so valuable to someone in Farrland that these marauders would take you to ransom before they would take the Duchess of Morland?—for they know the Duchess is aboard as well."

"It is not ransom they seek," the duchess said quietly. "They will do Tristam harm."

This stopped the officer for barely a second. "And why would they wish to do such a thing, Duchess?"

The woman looked down at the cabin sole, and perhaps shook her head, Tristam could not be sure. "Because they are as foolish and superstitious as your Jacks, I fear."

"That is not an answer that I can comprehend, Duchess," Stern said quietly.

She looked up. "Nor is there likely to be a better

one, Captain Stern, for I know no more than that. Roderick has kept you in great ignorance, I fear."

Stern stood, hands on hips, glaring at the duchess for a moment, but she did not give way at all. Tristam would have thought she was completely unaware of the captain's rage, or if she was aware, thought it unimportant. Stern was so accustomed to having everyone at the mercy of his moods that he clearly was thrown off balance. This was the Duchess of Morland he faced—the favorite of the King.

The captain turned on Jacel suddenly. "There were two Entonne ships in the harbor on Farrow. Did you take the opportunity to speak with those of your own nation?"

Tristam could see the poor maid stiffen. Her mouth worked, but no words came. Here was someone properly cowed. She looked over to the duchess and then back to Stern. She managed to nod—Tristam could just make it out in the dark.

"And did you speak of the other passengers—Mr. Flattery and the duchess?"

Again she nodded. Tristam could sense her fear growing—fear and understanding. "But, Captain Stern," she said, her voice quavering. "It was no secret. All of Avonel knew, I am quite certain."

"Yes," Stern said, deadly quiet, "one thing that was not a secret." He continued to glare at the young woman for a moment and then turned back to Tristam. "My ship and every soul aboard are in danger, because of you, Mr. Flattery. Why is that? I will have an answer, or, by Farrelle, I shall give serious consideration to granting this marauder's request."

Tristam thought of Lady Galton: *'Do not bring this terrible bloom back into our world.'* "I do not know, Captain Stern, though I dearly wish that I did." He wanted to look over at the duchess, certain that she had the answer that Stern wanted—that Tristam wanted.

Stern raised his fist as though he would shake it in Tristam's face.

"He speaks the truth," the duchess said, her voice

still calm. "Threats will gain you nothing." She turned to her maid. "Jacel, that will be all."

The maid gave the quickest curtsy and fled from the cabin.

Turning away, the duchess walked to the gallery windows and looked out into the dark night. Stars were clear above the horizon, but no other ship could be seen.

"Think, Captain; other nations have objectives and intentions we know nothing of." She turned back to the two men. "The life of our King depends upon the success of this voyage." Tristam could tell that she searched the shadows, trying to see the captain's face, to meet his eye. "I do not know what Roderick has told you, but I fear you don't understand the importance of this quest. This Entonne ship—for though it plays the part of a marauder, surely you have realized the truth—this emissary of the Entonne government can lose nothing by negotiating. After all, if you give them Tristam, we would almost certainly fail to find the seed. But once they have Tristam, they will still do everything within their power to destroy the *Swallow*. War is being risked here. They will have no witnesses."

Stern looked down at his hand gripping the table and he released his hold, splaying fingers almost gently on the polished surface. "This is madness," he said, so quietly Tristam barely heard. Distracted, Stern turned away, lost in his thoughts. Then he looked up at the duchess, his anger gone—displaced by the realization that the intrigues of ministers and governments had found them in the trackless ocean. And he was only a sea captain, not privy to the policies of his government. "The oarsmen all claimed to not understand Entonne," he said, his tone subdued, "so perhaps the Entonne captain's demands will not be known. I have sworn the boatmen to silence on pain of being charged with treason, but we can only hope the Jacks don't guess the truth." He looked over at Tristam, his anger gone but the questions still present. "Perhaps we will get free of them in darkness, though they are likely not alone. There will be other ships abroad with the same purpose. It is a vast ocean." And then, shaking his head, he left.

The duchess stood looking at the closed door as though her gaze had followed Stern to the last second, trying desperately to see something.

"Why do the Entonne want me, Duchess?" Tristam asked quietly.

In the gray light Tristam thought she looked over at him, as though she had not quite heard the question, for her thoughts had been elsewhere.

"Want you? Because you will keep the King alive."

No, Tristam thought, that was a lie.

We follow Tristam's course, now.

There was nothing Tristam could say. The duchess would admit to nothing.

"I have a gun to tend."

Beacham smiled at the naturalist as he returned and Tristam felt an immediate, all pervasive guilt.

Everyone here is endangered by my presence.

It was no wonder Stern had threatened the boatman with a charge of treason. Was it possible that none of them spoke Entonne? Sailors traveled widely and saw many ports. But most harbors that took the coin of seamen were prepared to accommodate—the people spoke the languages of the Jacks. Perhaps the Entonne request would go unknown. Even if they had spoken Tristam's name, it might not have mattered: *Flattery* spoken with the accent of Entonne was almost unrecognizable.

Darkness was now so complete that Tristam could not see his own gunmates. The shifting of men, a half-muffled cough—that was all there was to indicate the presence of the crew.

Tristam wondered what would happen to the *Swallow* if no wind came to rescue them. The waves would set them slowly toward shore, some five miles off, he surmised. There might also be a current here, though the charts did not show it.

He waited. Hunger began to replace excitement. But to Tristam's horror, the anxiety returned. Every creak of the rigging, every splash of an oar from the towing boats had Tristam straining to hear, fearing their position had been revealed to the marauder. Smells became more pronounced, as they often did when he was hungry; the caustic sulfur, and the sweat of the gun crews, mixed with the ever present smell of tar and the salt and decomposing matter that characterized the ocean.

Fear that the corsairs would suddenly appear alongside kept everyone on their feet, starting at every sound, imagining shapes in the darkness. A bucket of precious water came down the line, the captain's own steward rationing it carefully, for much of the water had been pumped over the side to lighten ship.

Along with all the agonies he shared with everyone aboard, Tristam kept coming back to the fact that the marauders wanted him. But why?

Sometime after midnight a breeze from the west began to rustle the ship's pennant and the yards were braced around as silently as possible. The *Swallow* was heading south and Stern elected to continue in that same direction, perhaps afraid to go too far from shore now that their water was low, or perhaps he felt there was always a chance here that his ship's ability to beat to weather would stand him in good stead close to a lee shore. A dangerous gamble, Tristam knew, but they had little choice.

It was most likely that the corsairs would assume the *Swallow* had turned north, hoping to reach the safety of the naval station. In which case the corsairs would use this same breeze to carry them north, hoping to find their prey still within sight come daylight.

There was great relief among the Jacks to feel the ship moving. Osler came along and divided the gun crews in half, letting one group lie down on the deck and sleep. Tristam drew the second watch and so leaned against the bulwark, spellbound by the swirls of phosphorescence streaming outward as the ship passed. *Phytoplankton,* he knew, caused to luminesce by the disturbance of the passing hull.

"Mr. Flattery?"

A whisper, but still a voice Tristam should know. *Kreel!*

The massive Jack appeared in the starlight, stepping near to Tristam. Reflexively, the naturalist drew back.

"Tell him I mean you no harm," the man said, so quietly Tristam could barely hear. "We are quits, thee and me." What was this he heard in the man's voice? Fear? "He did for Dakin in the smoke, thinking it was me. You have to tell him." Tristam felt a hand grip his shoulder strongly, but it was a pleading, not threatening, gesture. "He's mad, you know, but he'll listen to you. Tell him.... Tell him you saved me. We're quits for all time." The pressure of the hand was gone and the man faded into the darkness.

Martyr's blood, Tristam thought. *Dakin? Julian tried to kill Kreel and got Dakin?*

The naturalist stood by the rail in great turmoil, wondering what he could say to the viscount—if he could even find the man. A sudden fear that terrible things might be happening in the darkness made Tristam feel ill. Did Kreel speak the truth? Surely the duchess must realize who had tried to murder Kreel that night. Mustn't she?

If Kreel died now, murdered in the dark or in the heat of battle, Tristam would bear some responsibility. He left his place as silently as he could, up to the quarterdeck and down into the darkness below. There was a shuttered light at the base of the companionway, but Tristam found only darkness as he passed into the wardroom.

Feeling his way as silently as he could, Tristam came to the duchess' door and opened it without knocking. There were too many people lying awake this night, listening, Tristam was sure.

"Elorin?" he whispered crossing toward her berth. He heard coverlets move. "Who is it?"

"Tristam." He took three more paces and then dropped to his knees beside the berth. "It is Kreel. He swears that Julian tried to kill him in the smoke. The man says we are quits—Kreel that is—he will do me no harm. He was frightened when he came to me. I don't know if what he says is true, but if it is even remotely possible. . . ." Tristam hesitated.

He felt a hand reach out and find him in the dark and he clasped it tightly. The pressure was fear.

The duchess threw her covers aside. "Where is he?"

"Julian? He is at the forward gun, or should be."

The sounds of someone groping, clothing hurriedly arranged.

"Take me there."

Her fingers found him again, squeezing his hand once, and then Tristam led her across the dark cabin.

They came up onto the deck into starlight, faint shadows of rigging like a net thrown across the deck. At the forward gun the viscount was not among those sleeping or standing watch. Tristam paused, bewildered for a second, his heart pounding, thinking they were too late.

Kreel did not seem to be sprawled near to his gun, either.

I should not have hesitated, Tristam thought.

Someone materialized out of the shadow. "Mr. Flattery?" whispered Beacham. "They're on the foredeck." And then, just as stealthily, he was gone.

The duchess had heard Beacham and they both rushed to the steps, the slap of bare feet loud in Tristam's ear.

There. Two silhouettes on the bowsprit. Tristam could make out someone, clutching a forestay, brandishing a belaying pin, and then another dark form, crouched two yards away.

"Martyr's blood!" Tristam hissed. *"Julian!"*

He jumped onto the spar and started out along it, balancing precariously in his rush.

"Tristam! Stay back from him!" It was the duchess,

whispering urgently from behind. "Julian. That is enough! Let him be."

Tristam realized it was the viscount before him, and holding something in his hand, though Tristam could not tell what. The viscount turned quickly to look at Tristam, shifting his position as though Tristam were a threat. The naturalist stopped so quickly he almost slipped into the sea. Kreel had retreated to the very end of the jibboom where he clung to a stay, swaying with the movement of the ship.

The breeze was so light Tristam could hear the viscount breathing raggedly, as though with pent up rage.

"Tristam." It was the duchess. "Come back." She scrambled, on hands and knees, up onto the base of the bowsprit. "Julian, it is Tristam. Be careful what you do. Calm yourself."

The viscount made a slight movement back toward the ship and Tristam sprang back a step, his hands out as though to ward the man off. Flames! Someone was going to see this, despite almost total darkness. There were too many about.

Tristam could not make out the viscount's face, but he could see the man moving, his head weaving back and forth as though he struggled with the fire in his blood. He kept casting glances at Kreel, like the Jack was some prey snatched from his grasp. And Tristam felt this strongly—the creature before him was not quite human.

The viscount took a step in toward the ship.

"Back up, Tristam!" the duchess said sharply.

The naturalist did as he was told. He came up against the duchess and the two clung to each other, moving backward off the spar. Julian hesitated. Tristam thought that the man would make a rush out toward Kreel, but then he shook his head, and moved toward the ship. He sprang past Tristam and the duchess, landing easily on the deck, the shadow-net falling over him—and then he disappeared into the darkness.

Tristam heard himself let out a long sigh. He handed

the duchess down off the sprit, where she pressed herself against him for a moment, her shoulders shaking briefly.

"I must find Julian," she whispered close to his ear. "You deal with Kreel. He must speak of this to no one. I will guarantee his safety, now—and more if necessary. Offer him silver. Anything." She embraced Tristam and then went after her brother.

For a moment Tristam stood calming his heart. She assumed he would do as asked: protect her murderous brother. Had he really hit Dakin?

Kreel had slipped in along the sprit, still hefting his belaying pin.

"I heard Her Grace," the man whispered, hunkering down into shadow. "No word from me. Just keep that monster away from me and my mates. That's all we ask."

Tristam returned to his gun, and found Beacham standing in his place.

"How in the world did you get involved in that?" Tristam asked.

The midshipman's face was invisible in the darkness. "I couldn't sleep. I was lying awake nearby when Kreel spoke to you. I just sensed trouble, sir."

"Well, bless your sense, Jack Beacham," Tristam whispered.

"Things have been put to right, then?"

The question gave Tristam the feeling that Beacham knew quite a bit more than he'd realized. "I hope so, yes."

He saw Beacham's head nod. "It's my watch, sir. You should lie down and try to sleep."

Tristam did as suggested, though sleep was impossible. He wondered how many men had heard what went on. Flames, the ship seemed small to him suddenly. Dakin. Tristam barely knew the man to see him, but Farrelle save him. . . . The man had done nothing. *Should I go to Stern with this? I have no proof myself.* And Kreel would not be a witness, he was sure of that.

Tristam lay with his ear on the planks of the deck, listening to the small voices of a ship wallowing on a windless sea.

THIRTY-FOUR

Fewer people stood watching at first light that second day; most were exhausted by a night of fitful sleep. The atmosphere aboard was hard to discern, for only speech necessary to handling the ship was allowed. Even so Tristam could see the crew was decidedly surly and somewhat frightened.

Forward, the viscount stood at his gun, Kreel not a dozen feet away, both men apparently intent on their duties. If any of the other Jacks had heard what had transpired in the night, they were not letting on.

To his great relief Tristam was sent aloft with Osler to stand lookout, a welcome change from gun duty, and it also seemed a small escape—the best that could be managed aboard ship.

"I will wager, Flattery, that they have gone north on the same wind that carried us south." Osler was not looking so unruffled today. Lack of sleep and the tension of his position were leaving marks. His eyes were red, and his smile wooden.

"I don't think I'll take your wager. I'm sure you're right." Tristam answered, staring out to sea. "Were I Captain Stern, certainly I would have set my course to the north and off shore."

"Yes, and you might have sailed directly into the marauder in the dark of night. Still, it is the likeliest course. What captain wouldn't run for the protection of the naval station?" They were trying to convince themselves that all was well, Tristam knew. Both men continued to scan their section of the ocean, hoping not to find the white of sails in the slowly increasing light.

"Do you feel that?" Osler asked suddenly. "That will be our trade arriving, pushed along before the sun."

A pennant at the masthead began a slow dance and then streamed northwest—the anomalous southeast wind had arrived again. But the direction did not seem to matter to the crew, it was wind and the master had the Jacks on the run to take full advantage.

"But which direction are we to sail?" Osler asked, scanning the ocean. Without knowing the enemy ship's position they could set sail toward them.

To leeward the denser shadow against the gray sky was the shore. *How close are we?* Tristam wondered. Above the sounds of the breeze and luffing sail, Tristam thought he heard a slow rhythmical hiss.

"Do you hear surf, Mr. Osler? Far off, I think."

The officer leaped up, grasping the futtock shrouds, as though the increased height would enhance his ability to hear. Turning his head delicately from side to side, he looked like a seer attempting to gaze beyond his own time.

"Farrelle be damned! Keep the sharpest watch you can." Osler swung his glass over his back, grasped the backstay, and shot down to the deck at such speed that Tristam was certain he had flayed his hands to ruin.

The naturalist searched to leeward, struggling both to see through the darkness and to contain his imagination, which created reefs out of every patch of gray. But soon he was certain there was white, and then suddenly there was no question. A line of surf materialized out of the gloom, undulating like a dying snake. It was not an unbroken line, Tristam was sure, but nearly so.

The face of midshipman Chilsey appeared just at the height of the trestletrees, and below him, spaced a few feet apart, a line of men progressed down the ratlines to the deck.

"We've formed a whisper line, Mr. Flattery, direct to the captain. Tell us what you see."

"There is a reef to leeward, about two miles off and

barely breaking the surface. I cannot make out its extent, but it stretches away to both south and north."

The midshipman ducked his head and muttered to the man below. Quickly Tristam scanned the ocean to the east where the light was growing, but still there were no sails. The ship heeled abruptly to an accompanying chorus of creaking and stretching in the rig. Tristam reached out and steadied himself on a shroud.

"She's just sighing, Mr. Flattery," Chilsey whispered. "Stretching like a man fresh out of his hammock."

Osler pulled himself onto the topmast head at that moment. "We'll continue as we are, Mr. Flattery. Watch the larboard and aft."

Under the influence of a freshening breeze the *Swallow* began to spread a wake astern. Five knots, Tristam estimated, and not done yet. The sky was changing its hue and Tristam could no longer say if it was black or the deepest of blues as the night transformed itself into day.

There was no question in Tristam's mind now that if one stared into the semidarkness long enough one would find whatever one sought. What the eye could not locate the mind would manufacture. But there was a spot of lighter gray, he was certain . . . almost. Tristam hesitated a moment longer.

"Lieutenant? Would you look to windward." Tristam pointed "About four miles, I should think, and a little aft of abeam."

Osler searched for a moment and then lowered his glass. "There will be no need for silence now," he said, his face conveying the distress his voice tried to hide. "They're not on top of us." He leaned out and called down. "Sail, Captain! Half a point aft the larboard beam."

There was a groan from the men on deck as they moved about to catch a glimpse of the ship—all hoping it might be a ship from the naval station.

Osler checked the reef again and then turned back to the distant ship. "He outguessed us, Mr. Flattery. A damned skilled seaman even if he is a marauder and deserves to be thrown over the side with a fathom of rusted chain for a neck cloth." Osler looked back to his reef and then forward.

John Chilsey arrived at the masthead for the second time, a glass slung across his back. "Captain bids you gentlemen to come down, Mr. Osler."

"Well, stay awake, Chilsey," Osler said, swinging off the trestletrees to the shrouds. And then as an afterthought, "And don't go falling off. You are wet enough behind the ears as it is and Mr. Flattery cannot be expected to go aswimming after every Jack-fool aboard."

He disappeared before the midshipman could find a reply. Tristam followed the officer, impressed that anyone could make a jest under their present circumstances.

On the quarterdeck Tristam found the duchess dressed in her uniform again, listening to Stern and the ship's master, hands clasped behind her back as though she were imitating an officer. Tristam was almost certain he had seen such a thing at the theater.

Stern was waiting for Tristam and Osler.

"There was no end to this reef that you could see?"

"None, sir, though it does not seem to go on without interruption. There are many gaps in the line of surf, Captain, some quite wide."

Stern glanced at Hobbes and then at Tristam. "Our chart shows three rocks in a line—no more. And such efforts are called a survey! Damn the . . ." He stiffened suddenly.

As if to hide his embarrassment over this outburst before the duchess, Stern trained his glass on the corsairs' ship. After a moment he turned back to his officers.

"They will not let us make fools of them twice. If they can trap us against this infernal reef, they will pound us until we surrender, which will take no time at all. We will be lucky not to end up on the rocks." He cast a glance over his shoulder at the black ship and then turned back, his moment of indecision over.

"We'll find the likeliest looking break in this reef—I shall go to the masthead myself—then heave to and lower a boat to sound the pass. Lieutenant Osler, you are in charge of the cutter. Have it ready. There can be no mistakes. May I have your glass again, Mr. Flattery?"

Tristam accompanied Stern to the trestletrees, sending young Chilsey down. The sun had floated free of the horizon and the blue of the southern sky was spotted with the small clouds identified with the trades, though they had abandoned their parent wind and sailed on the southeaster that continued to blow. The depth of the ocean must not have been great, for the seas were higher and closer together, causing the ship to roll sharply. Every so often she would all but put her gunwale under. Tristam wedged his back against the mast and pushed his legs through the trestletrees, hooking his feet into the futtock shrouds, but, even so, he was forced to clap onto a line with his hands regularly. The motion up the mast was much greater than on deck.

Despite the extreme movement, coffee was delivered to both Stern and Tristam and the two men examined the reef the *Swallow* paralleled, paying special attention to changes in the color of the water in the irregular breaks in the line of surf.

Stern did not take his eyes from the reef for a second, even to speak. "We have little time before we are brought to by this marauder, Mr. Flattery. A hole in this reef must be found. If by some stroke of ill fortune we do not find such a pass, I will put the duchess, Lord Elsworth, and yourself into a boat, together with such men as I think appropriate—Mr. Hobbes, most likely, and Beacham as well. It is likely you can escape into the Archipelago and make your way north to the Queen Anne Station." Stern paused, leaning out as though to see over the side.

"Though we are not done yet. Not by any means." Stern kept sweeping his glass along the length of the reef. "It is time, Mr. Flattery, that we had a candid conversation." He kept searching among the breaking seas.

The naturalist wondered what was coming. *Dakin,* he thought. *Farrelle rest him.*

"I will tell you in all honesty, Mr. Flattery, that this has been the damnedest voyage I have ever conducted." He shook his head slightly, and then fixed on a single point for a few seconds. The ship heeled more than usual and Tristam grabbed the shroud. "You see, the Admiralty gave me to understand that this was a bit of a futile endeavor—undertaken to keep peace with the palace, but hardly expected to succeed in time. Do you understand what I'm saying? And then the duchess insists on becoming part of the voyage, apparently to be sure all haste is made to complete the task. I find you are the nephew of Erasmus Flattery, something bound to cause difficulties with the Jacks. Then a falcon comes to you fifty leagues from land. I hear tales of your trip to the Ruin—a 'voice' never heard before your visit. No one knows how you came to be lying on the rocks of Bird Island. The sea itself seems to have saved you. And then a whale rises out of the great ocean and circles you until your rescuers' attention is drawn. Most fortunate. And the list goes on. The duchess is utterly convinced that the Jacks attempted your murder, though she was not there to see. Someone tries to kill Kreel, the man who the duchess believes caused your plunge into the sea. Hardly a coincidence, I would say. Though you stopped that murder, didn't you?" A pause. "And now an Entonne marauder is out to sink us because you are aboard my ship—risking possible war. Or perhaps they will not sink us— perhaps you are too important for that. . . . All of this has one focus." Stern turned his gaze on Tristam. "You, Mr. Flattery. Perhaps you would like to tell me why that is?"

Tristam found he could not meet Stern's eye, and looked out over the foaming reef.

"I am waiting, Mr. Flattery."

"I wish I had an answer for you, Captain Stern, but

I will tell you truthfully that I am as much in the dark as you." Tristam shook his head, looking down to the deck. His earlier explanation—that some people believed Kingfoil would extend their years—seemed foolishly inadequate now. The catalog that Stern had just recited did not even include the other things that Tristam had experienced: Dandish, and all the events around the professor's home; Ipsword; the letter from Galton to Sir Roderick; the warning of Lady Galton; perhaps even the events at the Society evening. Tristam closed his eyes tightly.

"My ship, Mr. Flattery, is in danger—and I do not even understand why. I think I am entitled to an explanation."

"As do I, Captain Stern, but I have not yet found one. I will tell you, though, that I did not know my presence, or more likely our purpose, would bring your crew into danger. Sir Roderick gave no indication of it to me. I am not sure what he might have said to you."

Stern looked back to the reef. "I have never met the man."

The statement rang completely true, Tristam was certain. The duchess had been wrong.

Stern leaned forward suddenly, cupping a hand to his mouth. "Heave to, Mr. Hobbes. Hoist out the boat."

Stern handed Tristam his glass, a look of complete distraction on his face. The naturalist could see the man fighting to marshal his thoughts. "I shall bring you through this, Mr. Flattery." He swung himself around the futtock shrouds, the wind catching his coat and shaking it like a luffing sail. "But I would dearly like to know why I am endangering every soul aboard. Two years we shall be on this voyage. I do not intend to continue sailing onward, like a fool, unable to take proper precautions because I am kept in ignorance. You have a considerable intellect, Mr. Flattery. Even if you do not know all the reasons, I am sure you've spent many hours in thought. I will hear your thoughts before we go another league or I shall heave the ship to and wait." Stern looked down at the deck for a second, then back to Tristam, his determination unmistakable. A perfunctory nod of the head and then Stern disappeared.

Tristam sat for a moment, watching the officer descend to the deck, and then took the tin cup he had wedged between his knees and sipped at his cold coffee. A sudden lurch of the ship caused him to grab for purchase and he watched his cup hurl out over the waves, spinning as it fell, until it disappeared, its splash unseen in the chaos of the sea.

🍃　　🍃　　🍃

True to Stern's prediction the captain of the black ship was not so easily confounded. As soon as the *Swallow* hove to, the marauder altered course, driving straight toward its prey, setting every sail it could. Tristam stayed at the masthead, his gaze riveted to the charging ship. As she ran down on them, the corsair threw great arcs of white spray from her bows and these would occasionally refract the sunlight, breaking it into a rainbow. A most incongruous sight.

Whatever damage the *Swallow*'s guns had inflicted the previous day had been repaired during the night, for Tristam was sure she would not have been able to drive on so otherwise.

To leeward the cutter was hoisting its sails and striking out for the break in the reef. Occasionally a trough in the seas would be deeper than the others and Tristam would be allowed a glimpse of the glistening rock hidden beneath the confused surf. Stern was taking a chance heaving to so close to the reef, Tristam realized. He had learned enough of the handling of ships to know that one did not sail so close to windward of an obvious peril—and heaving to was even more dangerous. The captain was counting on the handiness of his ship and the skill of his crew—and he was desperate as well. If a squall should catch them in this position. . . . He did not like to think of it, for there had been squalls enough this past week.

Tristam turned his gaze back to the corsairs. Through his glass the men aboard were still only tiny automatons, their movements barely connected to any result that Tristam could perceive, as though the basic laws of cause and effect were breaking down before his very eyes.

The cutter appeared only through the gaps in the sails, now. One moment it was riding over the heaving seas, heeled to the rising wind, and the next it was surging into the foaming gap, picked up on a wave and racing ahead until it slipped behind a sail. How they would sound moving like that he did not know.

Turning back to the corsair, he realized that such haste was their only hope. The crew of the marauder could be made out now, even the men on the quarterdeck could be distinguished—officers standing out in uniform reminding Tristam that this was not truly a marauder but a well managed ship of a great nation. They had opened their gun ports and Tristam could see the gleaming bronze of the cannon, their mouths agape, ready to speak fire.

Suddenly the *Swallow* was sailing again, moving south, passing the break in the rocks. Tristam got a glimpse of the cutter, beyond the reef and sailing hard in the same direction as the *Swallow*.

"Mr. Flattery!"

Tristam looked down and saw Hobbes waving him to the deck. The men were mustering at the larboard guns. Tristam collapsed his glass and slung it over his back. Leaning out, he grasped the backstay, hesitated a moment to gather his resolve, and then sprang out, taking the cable into his embrace as he had seen the Jacks do. A bit jerkily he slid down the cable to the rail, Beacham giving him a nod of approval as he jumped down onto the deck.

"You have a moment, Mr. Flattery," Beacham said, his tone even but his face giving the lie to his voice, "if you would care to put your fine glass below. The captain would be at a loss without it."

Tristam vaulted up to the quarterdeck and almost fell

down the hatch. He threw open the door to his cabin and it struck something soft and heavy. *Something has come loose,* was his first thought. In a terrible rush, Tristam jammed the door back with all his strength, not caring what he damaged.

Poking his head in through the narrow opening, Tristam hit the back of his skull as he drew back in surprise, for he had Doctor Llewellyn pinned against the locker. Tristam's first reaction was to apologize, thinking there must be a perfectly justifiable reason for the doctor's presence in his cabin—after all, their situation was extraordinary—but then he noticed the man held a sheet of letter paper in his hand and other papers lay on the tiny bureau.

Tristam pushed the door open, crushing the cringing physician even further, then, reaching down, he hauled the man to his feet.

"Tristam," the man spluttered. "This is not what you think. . . ." Immediately he began to gasp for breath.

Tristam pressed himself through the narrow gap and into the cabin, banging the door closed behind him. "You mean my eyes deceive me, sir? That is not my personal correspondence you hold in your hand?"

Tristam reached out and jerked the letter out of Llewellyn's grasp. "Get out, sir! I shall take this up with the captain and the duchess. Gentlemen don't read one another's correspondence! Or had you forgotten?" Tristam opened the door and helped the doctor out with a hand under his arm. For a moment he stood, lost in confusion, and then he remembered his purpose and yanked open a locker and installed his glass. Quickly he gathered up the papers spread about and shoveled them into a drawer, but before he pushed the drawer closed, he was stopped by the realization of what Llewellyn had been reading—it was the copy of the letter Galton had sent to Roderick. *Gentlemen don't read one another's correspondence.*

A noise on the deck reminded him of his duty and he set out running for the companionway.

"They are almost within range," Beacham said as

Tristam took his place. The black ship had drawn much closer. "For their twelve-pounders, that is," he added.

Tristam turned to leeward, searching for the cutter, for the opening that would be their salvation. Still there was the undulating line of surf breaking on the reef, much closer now—too close Tristam thought. The cutter rose and fell on the seas, heeled so far that on the crests Tristam was sure he could see her keel. They were pressing their boat toward the next break in the reef.

"They need to take a reef in that sail," one of the Jacks observed, quietly, sounding utterly absurd to Tristam in their present situation.

"Stand to," Beacham said, his voice sounding much older and more grim than Tristam would have believed possible. "They are bearing up."

Off to the east the great black ship was indeed altering course to parallel the *Swallow,* bringing her two decks of guns to bear.

"Hold your fire." It was Stern standing at the rail. "If you see smoke from their guns, lie flat on the deck."

A hoist of signals shot up to the *Swallow*'s mast head.

"We are surrendering," one of the Jacks whispered. "Farrelle save us. We are done for."

"It is only to buy us time. To confound the bastards," Beacham hissed.

A blossom of smoke appeared at the corsair's side, and like many others Tristam dropped to the deck. When he looked up and realized most of the experienced men remained on their feet, Tristam scrambled up immediately.

"They have laid in a shot across our bow," Beacham said. "If the captain does not bring us to, the next shot will be in earnest."

"But will we not go on the reef?" Tristam asked.

"If we are damaged as we should be," Beacham looked at Tristam. "Unfortunate that you did not have the opportunity to instruct me in the art of staying afloat. . . ."

He said no more for all around them men fell to the deck and Beacham and Tristam did the same. The blast of the corsair's guns unnerved Tristam completely. He heard a voice whimpering and wondered if it was his own.

"Oh-please, oh-please," someone near him said over and over as though it were a chant. *"Ohplease."*

The sound of wood splitting and shattering drowned every sound. Something struck Tristam's back, but he dared not move to survey the damage. Silence, and then a rending sound overhead.

"Topmast coming down!" A crash somewhere behind him. The "thwung" of taut rigging parting.

"Up, lads! Fire as she bears."

Tristam scrambled to his feet. The sound of men crying out and moaning pierced his ears. A Jack from his own gun crew lay crumpled on the planks, unmoving.

Beacham was prying the barrel of their gun up, his hand covered in red. "Stand clear, Mr. Flattery," he said, his voice conveying no hope at all.

"Fire!"

The *Swallow*'s ragged broadside boomed across the waves and Tristam held his breath, waiting for smoke to clear. A moment later the corsair appeared out of the haze—some of her sails were shaking in the wind but otherwise she was apparently unharmed.

"Reload!"

Tristam took the shot given to him by the captain's steward and passed it to a Jack, then stood by a tackle, ready to run the gun out. Two Jacks carried a man past, his head split wide open, eyes rolled back to pure whites.

The men were going about their business, but Tristam could tell the fight had been knocked out of them. The next broadside would do for the *Swallow*, and all aboard knew it. Tristam felt a hollowness inside—fear seemed to have been replaced by numbness.

As he waited for the order to run the gun out, Tristam searched for the cutter and found it attempting to beat into a narrow gap in the reef, a man standing in the bow ready to heave the lead. In the pass Tristam could see a tight ball of gulls, hovering and diving. He could even hear their cries. And then, into their midst, fell a hawk, scattering them like feathers before the wind—*a winter falcon*. It did not give chase to its prey but spun about, hovering in the sunlight.

"We have to go through the pass," Tristam heard himself mutter. Without a further thought he vaulted up the steps to the quarterdeck and crossed to Stern who stood beside the helmsman, a glass focused on the opening in the surf.

"Captain! We must go through," Tristam said.

Stern looked up, his face twisted in anger. "Mr. Flattery! Take your place, sir!"

"The corsairs have run out their guns," someone called.

Tristam grabbed the man's arm and stepped close, staring into his eyes. He was not sure what he would say—whatever was necessary. "You asked why they pursue me. . . . My uncle was a mage. The falcon. The falcon that came to me at sea." He pointed, but the bird was gone. He turned back to Stern, desperate. "It hovered in the pass—a sign. We must go through."

The gap was almost abeam. Stern hesitated.

Tristam was certain he must sound like a madman, unhinged by the sight of battle—raving. The captain shrugged off Tristam's arm and turned to windward to stare at the great ship as it prepared to fire. Calm, the man seemed desperately calm.

"Take us through, Mr. Garvey," the captain said quietly. "Mr. Hobbes, trim to run before it." Having made his decision, the captain turned his back on Tristam, on the black ship, and focused on the opening in the rocks.

Tristam stood by the wheel, bracing himself against

the roll of the ship. They came around slowly. To windward he could see that the corsairs were passing on now, their captain caught off guard. He did not expect Stern would put his ship through the pass before the cutter had sounded for bottom.

The ship came around until the fresh wind was on the larboard quarter, and then she lifted on the swell and was carried forward by the sea, only to settle in the trough as though resting before her next effort.

As they rose again, the corsair fired. Despite their great exposure to the enemy guns, not a single man on the quarterdeck did more than flinch. No one crouched and Tristam stood among them, waiting to be blown to pieces, but the corsair had fired hurriedly as they turned to follow their prey and the shot had fallen harmlessly into the waves.

The seas piled up before the reef, their crests building until, too high, they tumbled into foam. The cutter had beat into the gap now and the Jack with the lead was sounding furiously. Suddenly, a black flag went to the masthead of the cutter and the men in the boat all turned and stared at the ship bearing down on them.

"What is it?" Tristam said. "What does it mean?"

Stern stared at him for a second, his look unreadable, and then he turned back to the pass. "There is not enough depth for the *Swallow* to pass, Mr. Flattery. Hold your course, Mr. Garvey, we have no choice now but to go on."

Another sea lifted them, carrying them in its powerful grasp. The ship began to rush down the face of the sea, and then this wave, too, passed beneath them, rushing forward to hurl itself upon the rocks. The motion was extreme now and Tristam reached for the binnacle to steady himself.

"Mr. Flattery!" the helmsman grunted. "Take hold!"

Tristam did not wait but grasped the spokes of the wheel.

"To me," the man said, his voice strained. "We'll broach to."

Tristam wrestled with the wheel, putting every bit of

his strength into it, feeling the resistance, the spokes cutting into his hands as the ship began to yaw to larboard. Slowly they forced the helm over and the ship answered.

"Back the other way, now—brightly," the man said and Tristam helped him spin the wheel back as the strain came off.

Again a breaking sea overtook them and again they fought the wheel, struggling to keep the ship on course. Even as he worked to steer the ship, Tristam watched them sweep into the narrow pass, the seas so great that foam ran in through the scuppers as the ship rose. To either side waves broke in confusion.

"Clap on!" Hobbes yelled. *"Brace yourselves!"* Both the master and captain took hold of the shrouds, and Tristam waited for the ship to smash down upon the rocks lying below.

The sea rolled out from beneath and the ship settled her great weight down into the trough, searching for the bottom. *But they were through,* carried on a crest!

Each and every man aboard stood, so surprised at their good fortune that none had voice to speak.

"Mr. Hobbes, is it possible for us to heave to?" Stern asked, apparently unaffected by their near ruin.

Tristam saw the gray old master look up at the rigging. "Not without losing our foretopmast and perhaps the whole of it, Captain."

Stern looked back over the rail. "Then we shall have to hope they cannot follow."

The master looked back at the corsair following now in the wake of the *Swallow.* "We could rake them from stem to sternpost if we could heave to, but I fear it would leave us unable to control our vessel."

Stern nodded. "Carry on as you are, Mr. Garvey. Where is our cutter? Who can see?"

"They are on our beam, sir," Garvey reported, "and giving her everything they have."

"Signal Mr. Osler to follow us. We certainly cannot stop to pick them up until we see what course our black friend chooses."

Tristam went to the stern rail and stood with the captain and Hobbes. The duchess appeared beside him and if Stern noticed he said nothing.

The corsair's ship, with the wind free, was charging down on the foaming gap in the rocks. Tristam could see men standing on the forecastle, apparently benumbed by the crashing of the waves, and the swirling, foaming eddies in the pass.

"They must draught more than we," Tristam said.

"Substantially," Stern answered. "We are about to see a marauder go up on the rocks, with very great loss of life, too." There was no hint of pity in his voice. "How long until our foremast is stayed, Mr. Hobbes?"

"We are running cables now, sir. Half of this hour will see us able to heave to. An hour will put us mostly to rights." Hobbes waved a hand at their pursuer. "I think they have lost their nerve. See the Jacks all a-scurry to shift their yards."

"Tristam!" the duchess said suddenly. "You are hurt." Tristam felt her pull his shirt away where it stuck to his back. Fingers probed the muscles, and he winced involuntarily. "You will live, I think. Take off your shirt and I will bind this." Tristam did as he was told and the duchess bound the garment about his middle.

The two ships were not more than half a mile apart, Tristam guessed, and he could easily see crew standing by to shift the yards, but still they held their course.

Stern spread his hands on the rail like a man stretching days of strain out of his limbs. "They will not come through," Stern said with obvious satisfaction. "We shall be away. Shape our course north, Mr. Hobbes. Heave to and take in the cutter as soon as we are able."

Hobbes began to turn toward the man at the wheel but stopped. The corsairs had not altered course, though the men stood at their stations prepared to do so. For a moment no one spoke. With no change in her great speed the corsairs' ship plunged on toward the passage.

"The captain is a fool," Stern spat out. "They have no choice now."

The marauder yawed suddenly and Tristam thought they would broach to but their helmsmen won the struggle and the ship lifted on a wave and swept into the gap between the rocks. Tristam held his breath and the duchess reached out and grasped his arm.

The massive ship seemed to hang in the chaos between the rocks and then it slipped into the trough. For the briefest second it appeared to stumble and plunge its bow, but then rose again, gathered way and sailed into clear waters in the *Swallow*'s wake.

The captain smashed his fists down upon the rail. "Will we never be shut of them?" Stern cried out, but his outburst was lost among the anguished cries of the crew. "A chart, Mr. Hobbes."

The master was off at a run. Stern turned to Tristam. "You might work some magic for us, now, Mr. Flattery. It is our only hope, I fear."

Tristam said nothing, for he could not tell if the officer spoke out of despair and grim humor or if he was truly hopeful.

What madness possessed me? Tristam wondered. But the falcon.... How could it have been a coincidence?

A chart appeared and Hobbes and the captain bent over it. "I had hoped we should not be forced to this," Stern said quietly.

Hobbes put a long finger to the chart, his manner equally grave. "We might trap ourselves into a false channel or a bay. There is no way of knowing."

Stern looked up, regarding the pursuing ship, and then went back to the chart. "Set course for the narrows, Mr. Hobbes. It looks like we might fight a small tide in, but with any luck the wind will follow us. Signal Mr. Osler. They must come aboard as we go. We will tow the cutter or lose it, if we must. The bow and stern chasers are to go over the side. Lighten ship, Mr. Hobbes, lighten ship. Once into the narrows, I will turn our broadside out to sea, then we shall know how badly this marauder wants to take us. They shall have only their bow chasers and we will rake them three times over as they come." He clapped Hobbes on the arm. "But we cannot be caught out here or all is lost. Nothing is more certain than that."

Tristam was enlisted to help heave the small stern guns over the side. Despite their size, they were not light and the few men set to the task were almost not equal to it. Inside the reef the seas were smaller, but still there was a surge, rising and falling, and they struggled to accomplish their task upon a rolling deck.

Despite all, the guns went over the side with only minor injuries sustained, and Tristam found that he was now truly mad with thirst. Immediately he went to haul lines with the Jacks and was surprised to find himself sending the studdingsails aloft with the Duchess of Morland. When the studdingsails were drawing and the lines coiled, the duchess looked up to find Tristam staring at her.

"If you dare call me 'Jack,' I shall belay you sharply with that pin," she said, nodding to the pin rail.

"I believe the term is, 'lay one out with a belaying pin,' Duchess." He bowed.

She tried to smile, but her gaze slipped off over Tristam's shoulder and he turned to see the corsair bearing down on them. Each time the *Swallow*'s bow rose on a wave, the marauder appeared to those standing in the ship's waist—and at each revelation the black ship grew larger.

"If we had a topmast . . ." Tristam heard a Jack say, but they did not and that meant the main topgallant could not be set as well as at least one staysail, and the ship's speed suffered for it.

Tristam realized that one of the officers standing on the quarterdeck, staring astern, was Osler, and then, in the ship's wake, the cutter appeared, crewless, lifting on the waves and slewing off the crests, its helm swinging free. Somehow the cutter's crew had come aboard while Tristam's attention was elsewhere.

Forward, the Archipelago lay closer than Tristam expected. The dense green of the shore was resolving into identifiable trees, bluejack oak and cedar, but even so the distance was too great. Tristam could see that. The corsair might not beat them to the shore, but certainly the marauder would pull within easy gun range any moment. The duchess mounted the stairs to the quarterdeck and Tristam was about to follow when the gunners were piped to their stations.

Beacham mustered his gun crew, still one man short. "What of Telman?" the carpenter asked.

"He folded up his cards, lads," Beacham said, "it sorrows me to tell."

One of the Jacks made a sign to Farrelle, a hand splayed flat on his breast, head bowed.

"That's two," Beacham said. "Dakin and Telman." He bent over and examined the flintlock, blowing into the mechanism. When he rose, he looked out to sea and then up at the yards—his interest feigned, Tristam was quite sure.

Dakin had died—murdered, perhaps, by mistake. Tristam could not bear to look at the men around him. Beacham had overheard Kreel. Had anyone else? *I am protecting a murderer,* Tristam thought.

"No one else, I hope?" Tristam asked, and got a shake of the head to ease his conscience.

"They're luffing!" someone hissed.

The corsair was indeed, though not quite head to wind they were turning out to sea and their sails began to luff and slat about.

Osler hurried the duchess down the companionway. The *Swallow*'s stern lifted and Hobbes yelled out. *"Down on the deck!"*

Tristam did as he was bid, glad of the break in the deck which afforded him great protection from the coming broadside. The deafening crash of the corsairs' guns reached them and then the crash of steel smashing wood. The mizzen topsail yard swung wildly, creaking and squealing, battering the lee shrouds, its windward end broken off into a jagged butt, the sail trailing off to leeward and shaking so violently the rigging vibrated.

Around him men were rising and Tristam did the same. Smoke swept down on them from the corsair, though it was only a thin film. Something black shot across the deck as the ship rolled and Tristam saw men leap clear as it thundered into the bulwark. Two men pounced on the object and raised it aloft triumphantly.

"There's a good view of the twelve pound ball," Beacham actually laughed. "I've heard tell of the favor being returned, so to speak."

"Firing it back?" Tristam said.

"Right back, yes." Beacham slapped the breach of the gun. "Ours're too small, though."

"I would like to do that!" one of the Jacks said. "Return the favor." He laughed.

"Silence there!" Hobbes shouted. "This is no bloody frolic."

The men fell quiet. Astern the corsair had fallen into their wake again, unable to reload before the *Swallow* was out of range. Not far off Tristam could see a line of breaking surf and beyond that a long, sandy beach. No opening could be seen, but there was a place where hills seemed to run down and meet. In the chains a Jack swung the lead, letting it fly with all his strength, and calling out the depths. Overhead the hands had already bowsed the swinging yard to the shrouds and were running a cable to the shattered end to act as a brace.

Suddenly Hobbes was off the quarterdeck. *"All hands to shorten sail! House those guns and bowse them tight!"*

"Martyr's blood!" Beacham spun around. "What . . .?"

"Let go the lee sheets and slack the topgallant and topsail halyards!"

One of the Jacks pointed aft and there Tristam saw a mass of cloud or perhaps a whirling fog—opaque, lit brightly by the sun yet dense to its center with scud breaking away around its edges. It was passing over the line of surf that marked the reef, tearing the crests off waves and churning the sea to spume and foam.

"A white squall," Beacham said and jumped to his station to shorten sail.

Tristam and the carpenter were left to bowse the gun up to the rail, and if the man had not been so powerful, Tristam was sure they would not have managed it.

"They do not see it . . . the corsairs," the carpenter breathed. "Look."

Tristam ran up the steps to the quarterdeck and realized that Tobias' assertion might have been true, but it was true no longer. The corsairs had been so intent on catching their prey that they had not kept watch astern, but the sight of the *Swallow* shortening sail alerted them, for they were in a mad scramble to pull down canvas.

Tristam was called to help brail in the mizzen, taking hold of a sheet that tore at his hands. Before the squall hit, Tristam had a view of the corsair, thrown onto her beam ends, enveloped by roaring white. . . .

A gust caught the mizzen sail and it broke free, lifting Tristam and Tobias off the deck and throwing them hard against the shrouds. The sheet ran through Tristam's hands as he fell and, immediately, the sail began to flog itself to pieces.

Blinding rain hit just then, driven before a powerful wind, the drops pelting them like grape-shot. The *Swallow* ran toward the pass as the squall struck, wind shrieking in the rigging, waves breaking on either side, and then the pass, too, disappeared in white.

"Steer your course, man!" Tristam heard Stern yell and then saw the captain jump to the wheel, tearing it from the tired hands of Garvey who had tended it all that long day.

Tristam grasped the shrouds and stood, back to the wind, battered by hard rain, almost blinded by the fury of the squall. Suddenly he was thrown forward, his hands almost torn from the shrouds. The *Swallow* seemed to hesitate, as though she stuck, and then she slid slowly free and continued.

No corsair will follow us here, Tristam realized, *that was the earth we just touched.*

The sea was suddenly calm, and above them the sun began to break through the white. The downpour slacked to a pleasant rainfall and Tristam tilted back his head and opened his mouth, feeling it soft on his face, wet on his tongue. The squall rushed on, and out of the cloud the new world appeared, green and fresh. It was as though they had passed through a portal and left the black ship, in all of its cruel reality, behind.

THIRTY-FIVE

Tristam became aware that something was not right. He opened his eyes, glancing quickly around. He was in his cabin and it was daylight. But there was a quiet, a stillness, that whispered of lack of motion. No surge of the ship pushing her bow into the seas. No gurgle of water passing along the hull. No wind sounds or creak of cordage. His hammock hung still, like the pendant of a clock that had run down.

We are in the Archipelago, Tristam remembered; *safe.*

Unless the ship had been moved while he slept, the *Swallow* lay in a protected bay not far from the mouth of a stream of sweet water. Stern had found his way in here the previous evening, his ship battered, his crew suffering from lack of hydration, want of fresh food, and from the strains and pressures of battle. The corsairs had not followed. When a boat was sent to the mouth of the pass, they saw no sign of the marauder: both a comfort and a source of anxiety. Where were they now?

They were after me, he remembered suddenly!

Tristam continued to rock in his hammock. He had no emotional response to this realization, as though his mind were unable to consider the implications. But that was not true—his mind seemed particularly clear that morning—filled with an odd silence.

My emotions have been swept away by battle, Tristam thought. And he lay exploring this, attempting to find words to describe his state. *Hollow. Calm. Silent. Still.*

In some corner of his mind Tristam expected to find a few embers of emotion that he could prod back to life. He tried turning his thoughts to matters that he knew affected him deeply. The image of the duchess beneath her brute of an officer—no response. The duchess leaning forward to kiss Tristam softly—the touch of her lips. Nothing.

Empty. Motionless. Drained. Becalmed.

If he had only felt half-alive in the past, now he felt less than that.

Perhaps I should have stayed at Merton and become a professor like Dandish and Emin, he thought.

But this thought, too, created no emotional resonance.

It occurred to Tristam that this state was the opposite of his father's. Where Morton Flattery had responded to all events, all matters, with extreme emotion, Tristam now had no response at all. Neutral to everything—even to his loss of feelings. For the first time he thought he had some small understanding of what had controlled his father's life.

Perhaps there is merely a sluice gate within each of us, Tristam reasoned, *controlling the flow of emotion, and some are born with it opened wide. And others are born like me—with it closed off but for a trickle.*

It was only a reaction to battle, Tristam told himself again, to surviving a surfeit of emotion. It would pass.

He closed his eyes and imagined he was floating beneath the surface of a cold clear pool—or had it been a dream?—animated only by the smallest eddies and currents. No sound. Just thoughts as clear as crystal, appearing in his mind without weight, utterly free of any emotional gravity.

No irony, no sadness, no humor, no warmth.

I am an automaton, Tristam thought. *Perhaps this is what occurs inside the viscount at all times.* But then he remembered the beast in the darkness; the man did not seem to lack passion, as perverted as it might be. An emotional compass that deviated, attracted to something darker.

*And right now my own compass spins as though
there were no magnetic field at all.*

In his present state, the events that carried him along
did not seem disturbing. He could even contemplate,
quite dispassionately, the string of strange happenings
that had brought him here. The Entonne ship had been
after him. Galton's letter to Roderick came to mind.
These people had some very strange ideas about
Tristam. But instead of immediate denial, he began to
explore. He remembered Stern on the crosstrees reciting his list—a list Tristam could easily add to. Not so
disconcerting, really, if looked at coolly.

Assuming the duchess was correct, then the Entonne
marauder was no marauder at all but under orders from
the Entonne government. If it was their intention to
stop Farrland from acquiring more Kingfoil, then they
would need to do more than take the ship's naturalist.
It was Tristam whom the Entonne had wanted to keep
from Oceana. They did not want *Tristam* to find the
seed.

We follow Tristam's course, now.

These words would not stop echoing in his mind.
The duchess, at least, did not think Tristam was without an internal compass.

Again he thought of Stern on the masthead—the determination in the man's voice. The captain was tired
of being kept in the dark, as though he were a fool. Oh,
Stern would carry out a voyage for the Admiralty understanding absolutely nothing of its purpose, Tristam
was sure, but to have his ship and crew endangered
without even having been warned—and to be sure that
the civilians he carried knew the reason. . . . Poor Stern
could not bear that. Even a career naval officer must
get tired of being used eventually. Especially when this
unquestioning loyalty had clearly brought him almost
no recognition.

I do not want to end up like Stern, Tristam thought:
the dutiful servant, silently chewing his resentment,
hoping, pitifully, that his sacrifice would one day be
rewarded.

This thought seemed to ignite a flicker of warmth, a small glow of feeling. It appeared somewhere near his core. Resentment, perhaps. He reached down inside himself and fanned the coals, realizing that this emotion could burn away inside him until one day there would be nothing but emptiness—as was happening to Stern.

I will not allow that, he vowed. *Let me use these coals to forge something else: iron determination.* That would be his compass. He was not going blindly to Varua to fulfil someone else's purpose. He was damned if he would do that.

A rhythmic scraping began in the stillness, vibrating through the very bones of the ship, resonating in the great drum of her hull. It sounded to Tristam like the heartbeat of a massive beast and it seemed such an affront to his present state that he could hardly bear it. An attempt to stop his ears with his pillow did nothing more than lower the sound's register.

It was no use. He realized he would have to rise, and swung stiffly from his hammock. He fumbled through the pockets of a waistcoat until the smooth metal of his watch came to hand. *Half-two!* He had been in his hammock some sixteen hours. Lack of sleep, thirst, exertion, and, yes, fear, had consumed all of his reserves.

The scraping grew suddenly louder, carried on the breeze into his open port like irritating insects come in to buzz about his ears. A curl of wood shaving tumbled in the port and lit in Tristam's hair.

A clean shirt did not exist, so he settled for one "less dirty," which did not seem to matter to him—Tristam the fastidious.

Searching through the lockers for clothing reminded him of the encounter with Doctor Llewellyn, and he dreaded the idea of going to the man to have his injury examined, though a quick probe with his fingers indicated that he was probably not badly hurt.

Another puzzle. Llewellyn? What had he been looking for? Tristam realized he had no idea. He would have to bring it up with the duchess.

I must stop keeping other people's correspondence, he thought; *it leads to nothing but trouble.*

Tristam went in search of food, locking his cabin as he left—a practice he intended to keep up in the future.

Coming into the bright light of day, Tristam saw Tobias, the carpenter, and his mate shaping a new topgallant yard from one of the spare spars. The two men worked in the ship's waist, using adze and draw-knife, tapering the spar toward either end.

"The pleasures of the day to you, Flattery."

Tristam turned to find Osler, shading his hand and looking at the naturalist, a bemused smile on his face.

"And to you, Mr. Osler. You are undamaged, I assume?"

"Yes, thank Farrelle. Though I think fatigue has crept right into my soul. I feel ... odd. As though removed a step from the real world." The lieutenant shrugged.

"I thought it might just be me," Tristam said, relieved to hear he was not alone. He noticed the cutter, heavily laden with men, setting out across the bay, a white bundle amidships.

"Dakin, and Telman, Farrelle rest them. They'll lay them to rest above the high tide line on that small island. Can't have a pyre when we don't know what has happened to our marauders."

Tristam watched the oars dip and lift as the boat passed over still water, the reflection of its white hull following, cloudlike, on the surface.

> *"And they laid him in a small boat*
> *Beside his helmet and sword*
> *And set it aflame as it took to the waves,*
> *Fire and sea carrying off their lord."*

Tristam and Osler turned to find the carpenter standing below them, a draw-knife in his hands, his eyes fixed on the distant boat, and then he went back to his work.

The younger men shared a look.

Osler bent his head toward the stern rail and Tristam followed him there, his eye drawn back to the funeral boat.

"Do you know any reason why the captain and duchess would have a row, Tristam?" the lieutenant asked quietly, using the naturalist's first name.

A row? "Not that I can think of. What has happened?"

Osler shrugged, his eye turning to the boat now.

"I don't know for sure. It happened ashore, well away from everyone. I just happened to be out in one of the boats and saw, at a distance. There is no mistaking the captain in a rage, even if one can't hear his voice. I just wondered what might have caused it. We will be two years aboard, as you know. . . ."

Tristam shook his head. "I was dead to the world myself. I hope it was resolved." Had Stern gotten wind of the viscount's attempt on Kreel. When had that been? The previous night? Or had suspicions developed about the death of Dakin? He would ask the duchess.

Tristam turned to look at the nearby shore. If he were not in this strange, emotionless state, he would be beside himself with excitement. The new world.

"Would you like to go ashore, Flattery? We will likely be here a few days. The captain wants to rest the crew, and then we will water the ship, hunt food, cut some firewood. You will have an opportunity to practice your trade."

"Yes. Yes, I'd like nothing better. But first I must find something for my stomach. I feel like I have not eaten in a week."

❦   ❦   ❦

The boat ground up onto a beach of fine gravel and sand and Tristam set foot on the new land. The beach was a scene of great activity—Stern obviously had a peculiar idea of resting his crew. Jacks were drying fish on lashed-together racks while others butchered a small deer. Beyond this the captain's observatory tent was being erected, indicating they would stay a few days, for Stern was going to establish the accuracy of his chronometers by the method of lunar sights— *lunars*—an exacting process that required some time. Trees were being felled along the beach and sawn into firewood, and water was being ferried by the barrel out to the ship.

Not too far in the distance, on a grassy rise over the bay, the duchess and her maid sat on chairs under a sail cloth awning. But Tristam's emotionless state persisted, and he found he had no interest in the company of his own species—even the Duchess of Morland. Tristam was also afraid that he might find the viscount there, and not be able to escape the man afterward—a terrible thought.

No, he would go alone, to wander in this place where perhaps no man had ever walked before. The sound of a gentle breeze through the trees would be a welcome change from the howl of wind in the rigging.

Tristam set off along the strand, his unstrung bow in hand, and a battered canvas bag over his shoulder. Thayer's swallow-tailed kite passed overhead, low to the seagrape trees, and Tristam took out his glass to watch. It was, without a doubt, the most graceful raptor the naturalist had ever seen. Rather than riding on the breeze, and subject to its vagaries, the kite seemed to be borne upon its own currents, sailing where it chose with only the occasional beat of its long wings. Tristam watched, noting how the deeply veed tail flared and cocked, steering constantly.

What a clumsy thing a ship is, he thought, *when compared to such a miracle of design. Sailing upon the winds more easily than a cloud.*

The kite disappeared and Tristam walked on, stopping at the stream to drink.

"There is a pool at the next stream, Mr. Flattery," said one of the Jacks, waving down the strand, "not far back from the beach."

Tristam took the man at his word and followed the

small stream, not more than a long stride in breadth, up into the green forest. There was no path, but the underwood was not dense, and Tristam easily made his way. All around him stood trees unlike any he had seen and yet he knew them from his studies; *seagrape* and the *bluejack oak, tallowwood, strangler fig,* and something Tristam thought was called a *doveplum,* though not really a plum at all but a member of *Polygonaceae.* And there, beneath an awning of swaying branches, held aloft by the trunks of gracefully curving trees, he found a shallow pool. The water was clear, as though untouched by man and his works.

Shedding his clothes onto a carpet of moss, Tristam slipped into the water, cool enough to wash away his lethargy but not so cold as to drive him quickly out. The image of floating beneath the surface came to him, causing a second of uneasiness—perhaps his emotions were beginning to come back to life, to surface again.

He lay on his back and looked up at the trees, full of small birds and squirrels, and listened to the music of the place—the delicate melody of the birdsong mixed with the gurgle of the stream over stones and the whispering and sighing of the breeze in the trees.

Here I will stay, Tristam thought suddenly, *give up this foolish voyage, and build a home. I will become a true part of the world I study, making my living from the forest and the sea.* He closed his eyes and saw the kite drift across the sky again.

The falcon, he thought. *I saw it, among the gulls . . . thousands of miles from its native range. But how?* Perhaps, he reasoned, it was only a light-colored hawk of the new world. Without doubt there were many species not yet noted by man.

But in his heart Tristam did not believe this explanation. He turned his thoughts away from this subject—something for which he could contrive no rational explanation.

Soap and articles for his toilet had not been included in Tristam's necessities for a trek ashore, so he washed as best he could and combed out his tangles with his fingers. He stretched out upon a rock to dry in the sun and breeze and had the good fortune to capture a strangely marked beetle which was so cooperative as to walk onto the palm of his hand.

As he dressed, Tristam heard the sounds of movement in the bush and paused to listen, thinking it was some large beast. The rhythm of the movement convinced him this animal was bipedal—a member of the crew or a member of a hitherto unreported native race. A flash of sudden fear—emotion—what if this were men from the Entonne marauder?

A branch swept aside and Doctor Llewellyn appeared, puffing terribly, his face scarlet. It was the only time Tristam could remember being happy to see the man.

"Tristam. Ah ha. We need ..." he wavered as he stood. "I must ... sit," he managed. He lowered himself partway to the ground and then collapsed the rest of the way, to sprawl, gasping for breath so desperately that Tristam was tempted to run for the ship's surgeon.

"Are you all right, Doctor? Shall I get help?"

The man raised a hand. "A moment. . . ."

It was several moments, but the physician slowly gained control of his breathing. Tristam found himself edging away from the wheezing man even though he knew the doctor could not be consumptive—the entire crew would have been infected long before now.

Llewellyn fumbled at his neck cloth, pulling it open, and then wiped a square of linen over his face, for he was sweating profusely.

"I am better, I think."

Tristam sat on a stone where he looked down upon the doctor.

"Mr. Flattery, I realize that I have done a contemptible thing, but when I have explained myself I hope you will at least understand what has driven me, even if you cannot bring yourself to excuse my actions." He searched Tristam's face for a second as though assessing the impact of his words. As usual the doctor's tone rang false, overly obsequious, and insincere.

"I have, no doubt, mentioned that I served as the Royal Physician briefly during the absence of Sir Benjamin Rawdon. Benjamin and I studied together and he has always been a friend to me even when Llewellyn was perhaps the least popular student at Merton." The man paused to take several long breaths.

Rawdon, Tristam thought, the man who intercepted me on my visit to Baron Trevelyan.

"Benjamin's wife fell very ill," the physician went on, "and he asked me to examine her to corroborate his diagnoses. Lady Rawdon had a form of the cancer, Tristam. I shall not go into the details but suffice it to say that I thought she would not live out the year. I was most disconsolate, both for the gracious lady and for my friend and colleague, for his devotion to Lady Rawdon has always been unwavering. When Benjamin asked me to take his place in Tellaman Palace, I agreed immediately and made arrangements for my own practice.

"During the next few months I had only two brief letters from Benjamin. In the first he said Lady Rawdon was 'getting on very well' and in the second he wrote that she was almost completely recovered. I remember hoping, for both their sakes, that he was not deluding himself, as people in such situations are apt to do: physicians are not immune to such folly.

"During this brief time I had occasion to serve the King only twice—minor complaints from which His Majesty recovered extremely quickly. The King, as you no doubt know, is astonishingly well preserved . . . for a man who has passed his centenary by more than a decade. In fact I would venture to say he is physiologically no different from a very healthy man in his late sixties, which is truly remarkable.

"My consultations with the King were very brief and His Majesty never spoke to me directly but rather whispered to an old servant who then related the King's words to me. I marked this as very odd, but then the sovereigns of Farrland have had stranger eccentricities.

"During my second attendance upon the King, I had opportunity to make a small jest, such as physicians do to put their patients at ease, and this amused the King enough that His Majesty laughed. I cannot describe this laughter to you but it was of such an odd character that I asked leave to look into His Majesty's throat. The King would not allow this, which worried me somewhat. Later, Benjamin assured me that there was no cause for concern. That is the sum service required in my time as acting Royal Physician.

"A month later Sir Benjamin and Lady Rawdon returned to Avonel from their country seat and, to all appearances, the lady's remission was complete. I did not examine her, mind you, but a physician can tell much from signs others do not mark. Such recoveries are not unknown, though I have never seen one so swift or complete from so serious an illness. When I asked Rawdon to tell me of his course of treatment, he said that nature had effected his wife's cure, and would add nothing else." Llewellyn looked off as though he were seeing some part of the story he told. "Now I have known Benjamin Rawdon for thirty-some years. In fact, I think there are few who know him so well. There was something out of place in his response, I had not the slightest doubt. He was not lying to me—Benjamin is almost incapable of such a thing—but he was avoiding telling me much.

"I flatter myself that I did not perform my duties at court too poorly, for some months later Llewellyn was again requested to act as physician to the King—Rawdon and his wife travelled to Uppcounty for the marriage of their middle son." Llewellyn stopped his tale at this point and looked down at the ground for a moment.

In his new state of disinterest, Tristam could almost see where the story was leading.

"It shames me to admit what next occurred." The doctor began to work the sleeve of his jacket between thumb and finger. "I had seen two rather remarkable recoveries while in the service of the King, and though the King's own ailment was not of a serious nature, even trifling diseases can be most devastating to the very old, and yet the King recovered more quickly than a man a third his age. Llewelly's natural curiosity—a trait that you share, I think—was aroused. I had access to Sir Benjamin's office and I confess I began to poke through it, looking for what I did not know. I found nothing obvious, but rather than leaving the affair to rest I began to feel a strong fascination, almost an obsession. One day I forced access to Benjamin's locked drawers and cabinets." The man pushed out his lip, a small gesture of defiance, Tristam thought.

"I came upon a monograph concerning Lady Rawdon's recovery. Sir Benjamin had treated her with an herb, Tristam, and noted in careful detail how his good wife responded. Although one could hardly consider this to be empirical evidence—her recovery could have been coincidental—Rawdon, a careful professional man, did not even consider this a possibility. It had not been nature that had managed her recovery: Lady Rawdon had been cured of a disease hitherto invariably fatal. *Rawdon had a cure for the cancer and he was not shouting it to the world!* In all of his notes there was but one sentence that threw light on this: 'it is the saddest thing to think that the Kingfoil is so rare, even in its native Oceana, that there will never be sufficient quantities of the physic to do general good'.

"So wrote Rawdon. Sir Benjamin returned and a year passed. I thought much of this matter, Tristam, I can tell you. My imagination was afire. Everyone in the palace knows of the locked arboretum, though none, I think, suspect what I do. I had begun to wonder if it was this physic kept the King in such good health for so unnatural a span of years. So often the old are broken by one illness coming upon another—minor afflictions to the young, but to the aged each one is like a heavy blow driving them ever down until they are beaten into the grave itself. But the King . . . the King recovers from each affliction as though he were a man of youth and vigor—or so I conjecture.

"I pondered this long and most often late at night, for I was driven to insomnia by my thoughts. And then one night I had a fever and the sweats. And then the next as well. 'Nothing,' I thought but it did not abate and then I began to feel this. . . ." He placed a hand on his breast and then rubbed it as though trying to assuage pain. "It is not the consumption, as you might think. It is the *black lung*—a form of the cancer, some think—here in my left lung to start and now spreading in the right as well. But for a miracle, I knew I would be dead in a few months . . . a terrible wasting death, too: I have seen it. But, Tristam, I knew of a miracle." He looked around suddenly as though it occurred to him that someone could be listening. Reassured by the quiet, he continued.

"I went to Rawdon and confessed what I had done— that I had read his notes. I told him what I suspected of the King. He denied it and said his wife's recovery was a miracle of nature." Llewellyn put a hand over his eyes for a second. "I called him a liar and a false friend. . . . I named him my murderer. I begged. I wept. And he wept as well, saying finally, 'Llewellyn, I should do anything for you. But this one thing I cannot do.' He admitted that he had possessed some small quantity of the herb for his wife—granted to him by the King—but that he had no more, and that the King would soon have none as well, for the plant had ceased to bear the seed that was the healthful part. I believed him now, for I could see he had opened his heart to me and was greatly distressed by my condition. I allowed myself to be sworn to secrecy." He looked up at Tristam. "But I began to read everything ever written about Oceana. I learned the language. I traveled far just to look at obscure documents and journals. I learned nothing of this plant I so desperately sought.

"My condition deteriorated, not so quickly as I feared, but still it was not so slow that one could begin to have hope. And I had no hope. I considered writing a pamphlet telling what I had learned—letting all of Farrland know what the King kept in his palace. But this was only spite and anger and would accomplish nothing. I confess as well, though I know you scoff, I found comfort in the Church of Farrelle." He shrugged.

"And then I heard of this voyage. Again I went to my friend Rawdon and begged him to help me find a position on this ship, for it could only have one purpose—to find more of the plant that bears the miraculous seed. Benjamin took pity on me, and through his influence the King was convinced that the duchess should not make such a voyage without a proper physician—a position which I obtained. And so I have come here, through great trials—I dare to say through greater suffering than any soul aboard.

"But I would suffer ten times as much to find this seed, Tristam. Not just for myself but for all of mankind. A cure for the cancer and what else we do not know!" He looked oddly at Tristam. "Or perhaps we do know. . . .

"You are the ship's naturalist. A trained botanist, expert in the flora of Oceana. I knew you were the one sent to find this herb. And so I took an opportunity to search your cabin, Tristam. A shameful act, but I am a desperate man, as you see. I would venture to say that nearness to death will rob most of their dignity and honor . . . and Llewellyn is dying—a little more each day. Foolishly, I hoped I might find some of this seed." He shook his head sadly. "And in my search I found the letter from Galton to Roderick Palle. How is it, Tristam, that you came to possess such a document?"

"I feel no need to explain my possessions to another, Doctor."

"And quite rightly," Llewellyn said quickly. "I only asked because of the runes, you see. I could not help myself. Can Palle and Galton read them, then? Have they broken the cipher and told no one?"

Tristam stared at the man, wondering if his emotionless state was reflected on his face. "This seed, Doctor Llewellyn, you say it is a cure for several diseases, and protects its user from the ordinary death by common ailments?"

"Yes, exactly. It somehow strengthens the body's natural defenses against disease—at least that is what Rawdon thinks."

"So why has the duchess come?"

"I do not know for certain." Llewellyn shook his head, and looked down as though considering the question again. "Loyalty to the King. Fear that other factions at court have influenced the voyage. The King is very well preserved—it might lead one to believe the seed had other effects. The duchess would give much to preserve her youth."

We follow Tristam's course, now.

Llewellyn appeared to have arrived at the same conclusions that Tristam had once reached—before he overheard the duchess' conversation with her brother.

"You may be greatly disappointed when we reach Varua, Doctor. Sir Roderick Palle told me that any Kingfoil found was the property of the King."

"But, Tristam!" the man cried. "I need only the most paltry amount. So little, surely, that no one could miss it. Rawdon cured his wife with less seed than would fill the bowl of a wine glass. From all the plants in all of Oceana I require so little. Could you truly possess this and watch me die?"

Tristam looked down at the man, so pathetically sprawled on the ground, and knew that, normally, he pitied the man somewhat. *I could not stand by and watch Pim drown,* Tristam remembered. He had already decided that he would not surrender Kingfoil to anyone before he understood their purpose. He had already decided to risk treason.

"Doctor Llewellyn ... this seed is more rare than you realize and what little is found by the islanders is the property of their own king. It is very possible that we will return with nothing. . . ."

Llewellyn did not wait for Tristam to finish. "But, Tristam, I can help you," he cried out, his anguish apparent. "I speak the islanders' tongue and I am a trained empiricist, as are you." He looked up, and Tristam could see tears glistening in his eyes. "We are brothers in our quest to press back the borders of ignorance and bring forth the age of understanding. A world where disease and poverty and ignorance will be banished. A world where you and I will be recognized for what we are and what we have contributed . . . and what a contribution we can make, Tristam! To overcome the cancer and who knows what other scourges. Our names will live on with Skye and Marsfield and Boran. And to overcome such disease will mean the lengthening of our short lives. As empirical medicine has added a decade to those lives, so we shall do again—perhaps more. . . ."

Tristam was afraid the man would begin to sob.

"A handful of seeds, Tristam." He was begging now. "The smallest handful. That is all I ask."

Tristam hefted his canvas bag onto his shoulder and went and offered his hand to the physician. "Allow me, Doctor," he said quietly. "I was trying to say that I will give you what help I can. But it may be less than you hope for—the plant is difficult to find."

The man looked up in surprise, almost afraid to believe what he had heard, but then he took Tristam's offered hand and struggled awkwardly to his feet.

"I—I thank you with all my heart Tristam. . . ." and it was the first time Tristam had heard sincerity in the man's words.

THIRTY-SIX

The naturalist stepped out from under the green canopy of the forest and stopped to survey the cove. A smaller island nestled up to a larger one formed the bay— roughly rectangular, a quarter mile in width by three quarters long with a narrow entrance at either end. Stern had chosen it mainly for that reason—if the corsairs found their way into the Archipelago and discovered the *Swallow,* they could not bottle the Farrlanders up, for prevailing eastern winds would allow escape through either entrance. It was as safe a location as could be found.

Tristam lowered his shoulder bag gently to the beach, mindful of the specimens waiting to be preserved. He had spent the afternoon botanizing, suspended in the strange state of inner calm. His emotions were still absent. Tristam had also spent the afternoon in thought, an odd experience when one's thoughts engendered no feelings.

And to think I used to worry that I was without emotion. This *is what it's like to be without emotion.*

Swallow lay at anchor on the calm water, sails furled, her ensign wafting in the breeze, the crew at work on her rig. There were still gaping holes in the larboard gunwale where they had set the guns and signs of the enemy's marksmanship on the hull, but she floated, proudly, Tristam thought. *"A game little ship,"* Stern had called her with great affection, and that seemed an apt description to the naturalist.

There was talk of careening the ship, for her copper was beginning to foul, long tendrils of weed growing on her hull, but the tidal range was so small that it would have been a difficult task, if not impossible. There was also a fear that the corsairs would appear and catch the *Swallow* heaved down on the beach.

On the rise of the point Tristam could see the duchess under her awning, shading her eyes and waving.

It is time, he thought.

He raised an arm in return. Hefting his bag to his shoulder Tristam set off along the strand, passing among the Jacks who worked on the beach. They nodded as he passed; no sign of animosity now.

The abandoned cutter had been found that morning, cast up on the sand not too far outside the narrows and miraculously only in need of small repairs. For all her lack of a helmsman she had come through the surf intact. Tobias Shuk had taken the boat in hand and had her blocked up on the sand where he was in the process of replacing a section of her gunwale and a broken frame.

"The pleasures of the day to you, Mr. Shuk," Tristam greeted the man.

"And to you, friend Flattery." The man was a member of the society of friends: a transcendentalist. He had joined the voyage to Oceana so that he might see man living in his "unspoiled natural state."

The carpenter leaned over and put his bearded face close to the cutter's rail and sighted along its top. "Built by men who knew their business," he pronounced with satisfaction. "She'd never have survived being tossed up on the beach otherwise." He took up a carefully shaped piece of hardwood and flexed it into place, showing his great strength. "That will do," he muttered.

"I believe it will more than do," Tristam said. "I could not make out a seam where the ends butted. How do you do that?"

The man smiled, almost shyly, Tristam thought. "Well, friend, I have been at joinery since I was little more than a boy." He paused and looked at the strake in his hands. "And I understand the wood. Now, that will be my secret—if I have one. Wood is a gift from the world of nature to we undeserving men." He nodded down the beach to the Jacks sawing firewood beside a great pile of branches, their leaves wilting in the sun. "One should be thankful for such gifts, take no more than we need, and waste none of that."

Tristam nodded. He wondered what Tobias would say about the bag of specimens he carried.

"Do you know if we will begin to survey here? Is that the captain's plan?"

Tristam shrugged. "I don't know the captain's mind, and I have heard nothing."

Tobias nodded. Picking up a small plane, he addressed his beloved wood with a few tender strokes. "I wondered, for I will have to build the longboat if we are to begin the survey in earnest."

"Build a boat? Here?" Tristam looked around at the shore and the edge of the wild forest.

Tobias grinned pleasantly at this reaction. "Well, not out of the forest. We carry a longboat in parts stored in the hold. It is a large boat and awkward to have on deck for long passages. That is why we wait and do not build it until we are at our destination. I had thought it would wait until we were in Oceana. Then we would leave the boat there—a gift to the King. Though the Varuans have their own shipwrights." Tobias looked up at Tristam. "Did you know the shipwrights in Oceana are priests—or very near. Building a boat is thought to be a spiritual act, a creative act, like writing a poem, only more so. There is as much ritual as craft goes into each boat, for the boat itself has a spirit passed down from the tree, which is thought a great living being in itself."

Tristam nodded. "Perhaps the Varuans will set you up for a god, Mr. Shuk, when they see what a skilled shipwright you are."

The carpenter turned back to his work. "I am only repeating what Doctor Llewellyn told me, friend Flattery," he said quietly.

"I jest, sir," Tristam said, a bit ashamed at baiting

the man, who was good-hearted in the extreme, despite his odd ideas. "I'm sure the Varuan practice is as it should be. Craftsmen do not get their proper due in our world—and I say that quite honestly."

Tobias gave him a half-smile. "Kind of you to say, Mr. Flattery." Tobias took a worn oilstone and began to sharpen a plane iron. "What do you make of the doctor, Mr. Flattery?" he asked overly casually.

The carpenter's manner was always so genuine, so lacking in guile, that Tristam was immediately aware of the change. "What do you mean, exactly?"

The carpenter hesitated for a moment. "He is a learned man, or so he appears to one as ignorant as myself. But do you think he is ... 'well found,' if you take my meaning?"

Tristam felt his mouth go dry. "What has he been saying to you, Mr. Shuk, that you would ask?"

The man shrugged his heavy shoulders, looking a bit alarmed by Tristam's sudden seriousness. "We have talked much of Varua and the islanders, for friend Llewellyn has read more about the islands than any man living, I think. I should venture that he knows more about the islands than Hobbes, and the master has *been* there.

"The doctor has been kind enough to instruct me in the language, and has shown great patience, I might add. I was never the best of students, though I venture to say that I read as well, and as frequently, as most educated men. In return, I have promised to help the doctor find some herbs and shrubs that the Varuans use for healing—I believe he wants to write a monograph on the subject."

Bloody fool! Tristam thought, but it made sense. The doctor was enlisting the assistance of the most serious and able man who was not an officer. "Something seems amiss to you ...?"

"Well, I cannot be sure." He reassembled the plane without looking, his skills residing as much in his hands as his head. "But you know the good doctor has the cough and the shortness of breath. . . . I may be out in my thinking, but it is my belief that he has fixed his hopes on finding a cure in the islands." He looked up and said quickly, "Now I believe that much is known by people who live closer to the mysteries of the earth—for they healed their people long before empirical medicine came to be—but I think the doctor has his hopes set very high, though he tries not to show it. Just as he tries to hide the seriousness of his illness, friend Flattery. This sickness. . . ." Tobias looked up at Tristam, compassion clear in his eyes. "I have seen the doctor spit blood. It is a terrible thing, I know. I saw a man—a strong, good man—taken with the black lung. A ship builder such as myself. He did not last the half-year." The carpenter paused for a second, his normally serious nature suddenly even more grave. "It seems cruel to us, but it is the way of nature." He met Tristam's gaze. "I fear that friend Llewellyn may not have strength enough to sustain him until we reach our destination—or he will be so reduced when we arrive that nothing can be done. And I will be left seeking some herb that I know nothing of, for the doctor does not think the good islanders will share their healing skills readily with strangers, and he knows much of their ways." The man took a long breath, picking up his piece of wood again as though its feel reassured him.

"I am much concerned, Mr. Flattery." He looked up at Tristam. "Have you knowledge of these herbs? Will I be able to help our good doctor? I should hate to have his death on my hands?"

Tristam almost said, *but it is the way of nature*. He stopped himself for he could see great concern on the man's face. "There are many herbs on the islands, Mr. Shuk. I have books that can tell us much. But I am concerned, too, now that I have heard you out. The doctor may have been driven by desperation to wild hopes." Tristam toyed with the buckle on his bag. "Perhaps we should not speak of this to others; the doctor's dignity . . ." He did not finish, but the carpenter nodded.

"I think that would be wise. The doctor has suffered much at the hands of others, for he is one of those who can never be easy in the company of his fellow men. Though I warrant he is no worse than the rest of us when you come to know him."

"I am sure you are right." Tristam walked around the boat slowly, his eye caught by the skill of Tobias' work. "I shall look forward to watching you build a boat entire, Mr. Shuk, for I am almost as in awe of such skills as the Varuans are said to be."

Tristam set off down the beach, barely watching where he walked, the conversation with the carpenter almost ringing in his ears. Llewellyn was a desperate man. Desperate men bore watching.

The duchess came a few paces down the knoll to meet him, her smile broad. "We have survived," she said. "Most of us anyway. How are you, Tristam?" She reached out and took his hands as a woman might her brother's. "Your injury is not too serious."

"It is nothing." Tristam thought she looked a little tired—a relief to know that there was something that might distress the duchess enough that some ill effects could be seen. "And the Duchess?"

"Oh, I'm undamaged." She looked down at Tristam's bag. "But you have been botanizing. . . . I am most curious to know what you have found in this new world. Have you made any great discoveries? Is your name already made?" Her teasing had an air of artificiality, as though the duchess tried to imitate her usual manner.

Tristam set his bag down and began pulling at the buckles. With great care he unwrapped a small package and from it took three identical blossoms of such beauty—exotic in both shape and color—and as unlike the domestic flowers of Farrland as to be almost fey.

"*Orchidaceae Cattleya Elorinae,* if you will allow me to name it for you. An epiphyte I believe previously unknown."

"Why, how very presumptuous of you," she said, obviously pleased, and took the blossoms from him with great gentleness. "I will allow it this once." She leaned forward as though she would kiss his cheek, then caught herself. "But I shall have to thank you properly another time. And what other treasures have you collected?"

Tristam crouched down and began removing his booty from the bag. Several bird skins came to light, a dozen and a half insects, rock samples, fossils, nine different mosses, thirty or so leaves of various trees, seed pods, bark; and finally, carefully rolled into Tristam's handkerchief, the intricately patterned skin of a snake.

The duchess almost took a step back, revealing the normal response to reptiles. "My, what is that?"

"A type of adder, I believe. I had such a time killing it. I thought it was going to bite me before I did for it. But I finally managed to catch it on the skull with my staff." Tristam broke into a grin. "It convulsed and turned belly up and then fell still. Fortunately, I had read of this subterfuge before and turned it over with my stick. And what did it do? It turned back belly upward, for it was only practicing upon me! Had I picked it up, it would have bitten me. But such snakes believe that, to appear dead, they must lie on their backs, and so they will always roll back to that position when turned." Tristam laughed. "What a time I had, for I didn't want to damage his fine skin."

The duchess put her hand to her mouth. "You could have been bitten."

"Oh, unlikely." Tristam held up the head, opening the mouth to reveal the fangs. He went to test the sharpness with his finger, but the duchess jerked his hand away and then laughed at her own reaction. Tristam realized that the snake was unsettling to her.

"Shall we call it *Viperidae Pallei,* Duchess?" he asked, trying to lighten the mood.

She laughed, a bit too loudly. "That may not be wise—though not inappropriate, of course."

She fixed Tristam with her searching gaze, making Tristam wonder if she sensed his state. Perhaps she felt something similar herself. Osler had admitted to not being himself earlier.

"Shall we walk along the beach?" the duchess asked. "It feels so good to stretch one's legs."

Duchess and naturalist set out along the edge of the bay. They held their silence as they went, only stopping to view a pod of porpoises through Tristam's glass.

When they were far enough down the beach that no one would be able to guess even the tone of their conversation, they sat on the trunk of a fallen tree. They watched a flock of terns feeding over the calm water, crying out and diving, then leaping nimbly back to wing.

The silence did not bother Tristam, who still felt nothing—not even the things he would expect to feel when alone with the duchess.

"I know you are upset about what happened with Julian. I am myself." The duchess broke the silence, trying to guess what was on Tristam's mind. As she spoke, she watched his eyes carefully, as though she was ready to change what she would say, adjust the emotional tone, depending on his reaction. "Tristam, I want you to know I did not give Julian instructions to harm Kreel. I just wanted to be sure you were safe. The man tried to murder you at Bird Island; do not doubt it. And Julian claims it was Kreel tried to kill *him* in the heat of battle. He showed me the most gruesome bruise on his shoulder—another man would have had shattered bones." She reached out and squeezed his arm. "But we stopped the worst from happening."

"No," Tristam said, surprised by how flat his voice came out. "The worst happened anyway. Dakin. Kreel swears that, in the smoke, Julian killed Dakin, mistaking him for Kreel."

The duchess put her hands over her mouth. "Do we know he's telling the truth?"

Tristam shrugged. "No. Kreel's word, only. But Dakin's skull was crushed by a severe blow. The Jacks think he got in the way of the gun when it reared back." Tristam paused for a second. "If I question them more closely, they will certainly wonder why. They may be uneducated, but they're not all fools."

"Say nothing, please," she almost whispered. The duchess turned her gaze away from Tristam, staring out over the bay. Her anguish was genuine, Tristam was sure. And for the first time that day he felt a trace of human emotion—compassion.

For several moments they sat silently together, Tristam feeling that vast gulf that sometimes opened between two people, like a fault in the earth.

The duchess reached out and took his hand again. "What you saw in the dark—he struggles against his nature, Tristam." She whispered now, her voice pleading. "Kreel *must* have provoked him. The damage to Julian's shoulder is very real. He . . ." Her eyes closed tight. Tristam watched; the odd sense of being removed from the world began to dissolve slowly.

"Surely you can see, Elorin, that he is unnatural?"

"Yes," she said emphatically. "And you have no idea the anguish this brings him. Separated from us, always. He knows he is not like us, that if people knew his true nature. . . . That is why he has learned to control it. He would give anything to be like us. Like you, Tristam. You see how he has created this persona: the good-natured fool. It intimidates no one. He can move freely through society. He is terribly handsome and women are drawn to him. They sense he is hiding something— some secret. It is part of his allure. If ever they find out what it is . . . they are gone, terrified. But he is not without feeling, Tristam. These women hurt him. His situation is agonizing. He hunts often, knowing that much of his need is dissipated in that.

"He did not set out to injure Ipsword, Tristam. Yes, I know what everyone said. It *was* less than an accident—but less than intentional, as well. His nature . . . it is complex."

Tristam never thought he could feel sorry for this woman, so strong and so vibrantly alive, but he felt sorry for her now. Clearly she allowed Julian an occasional lapse—an expression of his "true nature"—as long as it was someone like Ipsword or Kreel . . . or Dakin. Someone of little consequence, in her scheme of things. Had she not called him a fool for risking his life to save Pim? Tristam felt a little ill.

She squeezed his hand.

I don't want to be drawn into this, he realized; *watching out for her unnatural brother.*

Already he had become too involved, not telling Stern about Kreel's claim—about Dakin. *An accident of battle,* the duchess clearly thought, Kreel more responsible than her precious brother.

She looked so very fragile, suddenly, clinging to his hand as though afraid he might abandon her—now that he knew. He had only the word of Kreel. . . .

"Men are killed in battles," Tristam heard himself saying, his pity for the duchess winning out. "Kreel is no saint. He would have no reason to tell me the truth."

The duchess nodded quickly. For a second she moved closer to him, resting her forehead against his shoulder, caressing his back. But then she pulled away, afraid they might be seen.

Tristam looked for some change of subject. "Did Stern give you a difficult time this morning?"

"Does everyone know?"

"By now? Probably. Osler told me."

She raised her eyebrows and forced a smile. "It was much the same conversation that took place after his parley with the marauders. But he was more adamant this time. He is determined not to move the ship an inch farther until he knows why the Entonne were after you." She looked at Tristam now, her anguish passing, the vivacity quickly returning. "My previous explanation does not seem to have satisfied him. I believe Stern thinks *you* unnatural, Tristam."

Receiving the same description as the viscount would normally have unsettled Tristam, but not that day. "But I am unnatural; don't you know? My uncle was a mage. Governor Galton believes I caused the voice at the Ruin. A whale rose out of the sea and offered to take me on its back. A falcon marked the break in the reef—the same bird that came to me at sea. And it is a longer list than that. You believe it as well, don't you, Elorin?"

Stern has made his attempt, Tristam thought, *so I will add to the pressure.* He still felt that the world around him was devoid of its normal emotional resonance. He could think and say things that he would usually not even contemplate.

"This is no time to jest, Tristam," the duchess said, but Tristam could see the change in her face. She looked at him oddly—apprehensive, perhaps.

" 'We follow Tristam's course, now' " he said quietly, watching for her reaction. This did not give her pause, as he expected.

"You have taken to listening at my door?"

"No. I came upon Hobbes bent over the stern rail one night. Embarrassed him terribly, for he was listening to your conversation. I heard my name. You know how it is when you hear others speaking of you." He shrugged.

The duchess stood and walked to the edge of the bay, her gaze cast down. She crouched, pulling back her sleeve, and retrieved a shell from the water's edge, shaking it and her hand dry as she returned. She held it up to Tristam.

"Terebra maculata," Tristam said. "The spotted borer."

The duchess turned the shell over in her hands. "Nature usually achieves such perfection," she almost whispered, and then she looked out over the bay.

"You said, a moment ago, that my brother was unnatural—and you were right. But if even my dearest friend had suggested that to me years ago, I would have slapped their face. I would have shouted them into silence. Of course they would have been as right as you, but I was not ready to hear the truth then.

"Despite the empiricists' vaunted objectivity I don't think you would have listened to me before now." She turned to see how Tristam had taken her words. "I

showed you the letter from Galton. I am not certain
what Palle and Galton and their group are doing. Obviously, they have another use for *regis,* or believe they
have. It has something to do with your great-uncle and
Eldrich, and the Ruin on Farrow—as surprising as *that*
may seem. Galton called you 'the candidate we have
sought for so long' but I understand they have another
name for you as well. They call you their 'lodestone,'
Tristam, and have sent you on this voyage to seek out
something they want. *Regis* is part of this, but I think
there is more. They believe you are 'charmed' in some
way, and I am beginning to agree. Even Stern suspects
this." She fell silent, watching Tristam, her beautiful
green eyes revealing nothing now.

"Why were the Entonne after me?"

"Because you set a rose afire in my dining room,"
she said without hesitation. "I am to blame, Tristam. I
never would have suspected Bertillon. Massenet, you
see, has agents everywhere. If I had realized what Bertillon was up to. . . ." She shook her head. "It was a
test, I believe. Did you recognize that language? The
nonsense rhyme?"

Tristam shook his head.

"Neither did I. I fear the Entonne know more than
perhaps even Palle and his group."

"Flames," Tristam heard himself mutter.

"Exactly. But you see, Tristam, that is why I was
forced to come. His Majesty's needs are of little importance to Palle. He has other concerns. And, I say this
honestly, I was worried about you. I don't know what
they expect of you, but I fear it." She looked around
the quiet bay as though it were not the place of refuge
it had been named. "I have become suspicious of any
coincidence—especially where you are concerned. I
have begun to suspect even the winds. I wonder how
the Entonne found us on so large an ocean. I wonder
why we have come to this place. I fear where we might
go. We must proceed with such care. I don't know
what Roderick wants of you, but I am afraid that you
might accomplish it and we would not even know."

She looked over at Tristam, concern clear on her face. "Keep the viscount close, Tristam. Please."

She must have sensed his revulsion.

"You are safe from him. Julian would lay down his life for you, Tristam."

"Why would he do that?" Tristam found the thought appalling.

"Because I have asked him to protect you. And because he does not value his life, overly. And because he admires you, Tristam. He knows you are good and honorable, and intelligent, and that you have an open heart. All of the things he would choose for himself—had he been able to choose.

"Your good nature has even won over the superstitious Jacks, who think, now, that you are their good luck charm and that no harm can befall the ship while you are aboard."

"They don't know that the marauder was after no one but me," Tristam said, a little bitterly.

The duchess shrugged. "Even if they did, they would likely justify it somehow. Resent the Entonne for trying to steal their good luck, or some such thing. Once people have truly taken an individual to their heart, that individual can do no wrong. Look at the terrible rulers who have been adored by their subjects."

Yes, Tristam thought, *and look at your own relations with your brother, Duchess.*

"But what about Stern?" Tristam asked suddenly.

"I am not sure." She fell into contemplation for a moment. "He is not ready for the truth—so far as we know it. I tried to tell him about Bertillon and the rose but he thought that I mocked him. He would have none of it." She shook her head—an admission of error. "Stern is not old enough to have fought in the last war, but, even so, the navy men consider the Entonne their natural enemy. This incident with the marauder has unsettled him deeply. I tried to use that to convince him that our voyage is of more importance than he was led to believe. I am not sure what he will do." She looked up at Tristam. "Although an officer, and a man of

527

some education, Stern is, in his way, as superstitious as the Jacks. He has half a mind to leave you at the Queen Anne Station, just to have you off his ship. But at the same time I think he is afraid that this action might bring him bad luck.

"I tried to convince him that without a trained naturalist we could never hope to find Kingfoil. He is sure there are things I am not telling him—despite the fact that when I tried to tell him what I knew he would not listen. He is not ready. I think he will spend a few days here, stalling, hoping that one of us will tell him a 'truth' he can accept. He knows that this is the one area where he has leverage: I want the voyage to proceed as quickly as possible, and he has it in his power to thwart me. He might do it simply out of frustration, or resentment."

What explanation would Stern have believed, Tristam wondered? The man had almost accused Tristam of being . . . unnatural. And yet he refused to believe the duchess' story. Did Stern know something that Tristam did not?

Tristam realized that *he* did not believe that what the duchess had just told him was the truth—or perhaps she had told him the best lie: half the truth. There were things she was keeping back, yet. But she would not tell more now, he was certain of that.

The duchess seemed to rouse from her thoughts for a second. "I am not sure what to do about Hobbes." She shook her head as though rejecting some idea. Silence again. The distant sound of the Jacks calling out—the long rending crack of a tree falling, its final crash to the beach, branches breaking.

So marks the arrival of men to paradise, Tristam observed.

"I had an odd conversation with Llewellyn," he said quietly. "Something else you should know." He told the story of finding the doctor in his cabin and then of their conversation earlier in the day. The duchess turned her shell over and over in her hand as she listened, and when he was done she flung the shell into the bay.

"That explains some things," she said, and no more. Picking up the orchids Tristam had given her, the duchess went to the water's edge. She crouched down suddenly on the narrow strip of wet beach that followed the ebbing tide. Very deliberately, she set the blossoms on the surface, like a child would do—to see if they would float—and when they did not sink, she let them go and, gently, the current drew them away. She stood to watch them go, standing very still for many minutes, all of her attention taken up by the flower's voyage.

"Such perfection," she said quietly, but without resignation.

The journal of Tristam Flattery:
This seventeenth day of December, 1559.

It has been a day of strange conversations and experiences. My emotionless state seems to be slowly giving way and the return of "feeling" brings me great relief.

I do not know which I found more strange, the duchess comparing me to her brother, or her admission that she believes we have not come to this place—to any place, in fact—by accident.

If I am indeed a "lodestone," what is it that I seek? I would turn aside, but I'm now afraid that any course I take will be the one predestined. I am almost afraid to take a step. This area of the Archipelago no longer seems the pristine and innocent new world, but has begun to seem ominous, forbidding, full of secrets. I wish we had not come here. I wish I had not taken ship at all.

THIRTY-SEVEN

Stern showed no signs of moving the *Swallow* from Refuge Bay, and on the third day he sent out the boats to begin a survey of the area. As ship's naturalist, Tristam went along and was left on one island or another so that he might determine something of the geology and add to his rapidly growing collection.

Names were given to prominent features of geography as they were added to the chart and Tristam soon had an island named for him *(Flattery Island),* as well as a headland *(Professor's Point);* the latter he thought would give visitors pause for as long as the name persisted.

When he could not manage to avoid it, Tristam was burdened with the company of the viscount on these outings and it was all he could do not to show his discomfort. Not that Julian acted any differently—he remained utterly good-natured—and he was eager to assist, carrying large loads without complaint. Tristam soon found that he could not accomplish nearly as much without the man. But Tristam could not forget what he had seen that night on the bowsprit, nor could he stop wondering about the fate of Dakin.

On the third day the *Swallow* lay to her anchor in Refuge Bay the lookouts spotted a sail out on the Gray Ocean. It was well beyond the reef and to the north, so distant that they could not say with assurance that it was the marauder; though no one seemed to think it could be another. And this meant Stern would definitely not move to go north.

The evening of the third day—a day when the natu-

531

ralist had managed to get away without the viscount—
Tristam returned to the ship late. While the others went
to find their hammocks, Tristam spread the result of
his day's effort on the afterdeck in the dull light of the
ship's lanterns. He, too, was in a frenzy of assigning
names, and so far had named a particularly beautiful
flowering bush for Jaimy's fiancee, a bird for his uncle
(the Blackwater finch), a new species of willow for
Dandish, and this was barely a beginning. This day's
haul had been particularly rich. In the poor light he
entered his findings in a notebook beside the date, location, and a brief description of the habitat.

Since the day after the battle the state of Tristam's
emotions had continued to be odd. The feeling of
numbness persisted, but then he would have waves of
intense feeling—anger, joy, despair—and these were
completely beyond his control. They would last minutes sometimes, hours occasionally. And then the
strange emotional silence would return. He felt his
emotions ebbed and flowed like tides, but were not
subject to the regulation of sun or moon.

Tristam tried to keep his mind on his work, hiding
his state as best he could, hoping he would wake one
day with his equilibrium restored. Tales of men returning from the wars and acting strangely for years, going
mad sometimes, began to haunt him.

A faint shadow fell over Tristam's notebook as he
wrote and he looked up to find the Viscount Elsworth
standing above him.

"From the duchess," the man said, proffering a small
envelope.

The viscount did not leave after he had made his de-
livery, as Tristam expected, and a second of awkward-
ness ensued. The lamplight flickered orange on the
viscount's face, giving it a garish cast, and causing it to
change and vary. It was an eerie effect.

"I missed you this morning," Tristam offered, trying
to sound at ease. "I'm not sure where you got to."

The viscount nodded. A longer silence. "Do you

know the true difference between you and me, Tristam?" he asked quietly, his voice completely natural.

The naturalist found that he shook his head, not quite sure he had heard correctly. *What?*

"I am more in control of where I go and what I do. It is not *you* that should fear my company." Saying this he nodded, stepping back out of the lamplight, and then disappeared below.

Tristam stood, looking after the viscount. "Blood and flames," he whispered. "The man is a ghoul." He felt a quick flaring of intense resentment. *Unnatural.*

Farrelle save me, Tristam thought, *look who I have become brother to!*

Remembering the letter, he tore open the envelope as though it offered an escape from the viscount.

My Dearest Tristam:

I have moved ashore into a commodious new abode—a tent—for the duration of our stay in this place. Although the stern captain has set sentries to watch over me, I don't think they are as devoted to their duty as one might expect. I'm certain that any man who could swim and made his way to my tent by the western approach would never be seen—a situation of great concern to me. Might I have a visit from you soon? Your explorations are of great interest to me.

Yours,
Elorin

Tristam hesitated for only a second, and then he began throwing his specimens into a bag. Morning would be soon enough to deal with these. In a moment he had stored the bag in his cabin, locked the door, and was back on deck.

Slipping past the anchor watch was not difficult, and Tristam went quietly over the side and into the cutter. He paused there to look down at the opaque surface of the bay. Stars hung, suspended in the calm waters, a mirror to the depths of the heavens. Thoughts of what might swim in those waters caused not the slightest ripple of fear and Tristam slipped, seallike, in among the stars.

The bay was surprisingly warm, the water seeming dense to him, as though it were some other liquid with a different viscosity. As silently as possible, he began to paddle toward the shore. He felt the depths below him as something tangible, like a presence. The increased coolness of the water at the low point of his kick seemed, in its way, like the heat one felt from another body in the darkness—there was much life below. A thought of the great whale swimming near him in the ocean caused Tristam to suddenly pull his limbs in as though the fetal position would protect him.

He almost turned back to the ship in a panic. *Why is this happening to me?*

With an act of will he forced himself to swim on. *I will be afraid of the dark next,* he thought. *But how can I control this ebb and flow of emotion?*

The shore couldn't be far. The coals of a fire glowed on the beach and a jagged line of blackness cut off the stars at the edge of the forest. Tristam focused on the dark area of the knoll and thought of being in the duchess' arms, which did not excite him as he thought it should.

If anything can reawaken my emotions, Tristam told himself, *it is the duchess.*

He kept this focus for perhaps a hundred feet, then he felt turbulence beneath him.

"Blood and flames!" Tristam cried aloud. He spun about searching the surface for some movement, but there was nothing. Steeling his will he forced himself on, his belly and genitals feeling suddenly very exposed.

A few more strokes and he heard the sound of voices—the Jacks camped on the beach—a comforting moment of laughter.

Turbulence again. Something broke the surface a yard behind, causing him to spin around.

"Blood and . . .!" Tristam spat out. A dolphin released its breath into the air, accompanied by a squeal. Another surfaced a few feet away, and then another. The air was full of the rank smell of rancid fish oil and the squeals and squawks of the dolphin tongue. They began to gambol around him, splashing water into his face and brushing by him so closely he felt the occasional rub of soft skin. Tristam could sense their excitement, like children greeting a loved one.

A man! A man among us in the dark waters!

Glowing green trails of phosphorescence marked the dolphins' passing, and these would swirl into confusion and then fade away, only for another to appear, and then another.

He controlled his breath and swam on, his heart banging inside his ribs, beating against the water's pressure on his chest. The beasts swam about him at such speed in the dark waters that he was afraid they would strike him—but remarkably they did not.

A few more strokes and he was close enough to shore to stand. The dolphins continued to play around him, swarming about his legs, their motions more frenetic now, their voices more insistent.

Do not go yet! You have just arrived.

But I cannot live among the race of dolphins, Tristam thought, stood a moment and walked into the shallows, leaving the gamboling mammals behind. For a second he stopped and turned back, looking for them in the dark, but it only seemed to take a second for them to forget him, and they were away.

He stepped up onto the beach and collapsed for a moment, catching his breath, calming his beating heart. Then, dripping, he hurried along the sand. The rocks and moss of the knoll passed underfoot, first coarse and brittle, then soft and yielding. The white of a tent appeared in the dark, its shape blurred, apparitional.

Tristam paused, looking for the sentry, listening for sounds, but heard nothing. The man would be on the knoll's opposite side where there was some chance of a drunken sailor coming from the camp on the beach. Such men would not venture into the forest at night for fear of the unknown, and they did not swim, so guarding the beach was all that was required.

Sure that no one stirred, Tristam went toward the white haze of the tent which seemed to float on the rise of land. The door was only a flap and after a few seconds of exploration Tristam was able to pull it aside. Inside was utter darkness. He listened but could hear no sound of breathing.

"Friend or foe?" came a whisper.

"It is Tristam." In the darkness he could not see her, but the rustle of coverlets led him.

The duchess had risen to greet him and she giggled when she touched his skin. "You are sopping! Have you swum the fierce Bosapool for me, my love?" she teased.

Tristam was feeling decidedly chilled now for he wore only his soaking breaches. He was about to ask for a square of cotton when the duchess pressed herself close to him, stroking him almost fervently. She kissed his chest and then peeled off his breaches—and drew him further into the darkness.

At first Tristam was afraid he had made a terrible mistake, for he did not seem to react to the duchess' attentions, and then suddenly something awakened in him, but not the feelings Tristam associated with his heart. His breath came hard, and he felt that mysterious force take hold of him—desire. It washed through him and he felt as though he were in the surf, in the soft clutches of something overwhelming. It lifted him and he tumbled and turned, disoriented, losing his sense of time.

🌰　🌰　🌰

It might have been the middle of the night, Tristam did not know. The duchess lay beside him and they spoke in whispers. It was the first time Tristam felt that they were lovers, lying close, sharing their thoughts, making absurd jests, stifling their laughter. He hoped morning was not near.

The duchess nestled her head into his neck, hair tickling Tristam's face. "Is it difficult? To swim, I mean?"

"Not difficult. The human body is buoyant. Boran estimated that less than fifteen pounds of floatation would keep the average man aswim. So it takes a little effort to stay on the surface and some small amount more to move forward. Easily learned once the fear is conquered. Did I say that I swam among the dolphins on my way from the ship?"

"You did not!" She pulled back a little as though to look at him, but darkness was too complete. "You're not teasing me?"

"Not at all. They came and played about me as I swam, so close that I felt them brush against me on occasion. They had no fear at all and wear the softest skin you can imagine."

"You have the softest skin I can imagine. It must have been a feeling like no other."

"It was too dark to see much. I couldn't even tell the species, let alone make any useful observations, though it was remarkable how quickly they swam and how close they came and yet not once did we collide. What eyesight do they have that would allow this?" He would have fallen to musing, but the duchess interrupted his thoughts.

"You are a hopeless empiricist," she chided him. "You have such an experience and it sets you wondering about their senses! Are you always like this, Tristam? Do you make mental notes as we have love? Will you publish your findings? *An Inquiry into Copulation in the Human Species* by Tristam Flattery, Esquire." She bussed his cheek. "You are no poet, Tristam Flattery, I will tell you that much.

"You do me an injustice," he whispered close to her ear. "I am transported when we have love. My mind has room for nothing else."

"Ah, Tristam, occasionally you do say what a woman wants to hear." She kissed him tenderly.

An owl hooted and in the silence Tristam was sure he could hear the *"pooshh"* of a small whale blowing in the bay. It came to Tristam that he could not have moments like this with the duchess without the burden of her brother: one did not come without the other.

"Julian gave you my note, I suppose?" she asked, suddenly, as though she had sensed his thoughts. "Did he tell you about today's discoveries?"

"No."

"There is some debate, I understand—I think only you will be able to say one way or the other—but they found what might be stone work on a point of land."

"Stone work?"

"Yes. Though Osler thinks it is a natural formation of some kind—and that would seem most likely."

Tristam thought for a moment. "The Archipelago is largely unexplored, but in the known sections we have found no signs of men. It is likely nothing." Tristam felt a tug of anxiety. What had brought him to this place? A marauder. A falcon. A white squall.

"I'm sure you're right. The other discovery will interest you more, for I'm sure it's real. There is apparently a smoking volcano a few miles off. That might reveal something significant of the islands' geology."

"Now that is news." Tristam felt his interest kindle. "All I have seen is stratified rock raised up out of the sea. Today I found fossils in stone at three thousand feet—fossils of sea creatures. A volcano I will have to see."

The duchess began to kiss his neck, and then his ear. She pressed herself to him, running a finger along the curve of his neck. "I thought that young men on voyages were said to be insatiable when they finally reached land. . . ."

"Absolutely true. I was only acting out of consideration for the Duchess' dignity and years."

She grabbed hold of his hair close to the scalp and shook his head gently. "I'll show you how advanced I am in years, you insolent wretch."

This twentieth day of December, 1559.

The islands are yielding up their secrets: a new and noble species of Quercus (which I have been all but forced to name the Elsworth oak: Quercus Elsworthi). (If I find a new beech I shall name it for Beacham! The Beacham beech!) A vole, I believe (I shall have to get some more expert opinions in classification in some areas. Oh how I miss Professor Dandish.) A variant of the peregrin falcon: not a new species I am sure, though lighter in color and smaller in size. Some striking butterflies and another beetle. Only just missed a snake of the most lurid green: too quick for me, especially as I did not know if it would prove a poisonous variety. All in all a grand day.

I want to have a look at this stone formation the survey party found, though I'm sure it will amount to nothing. Still, it would be the find of the decade if it was the work of men. I am subject to the emotional tides even yet. Three days now. I hope it will not last much longer. Had an evening like no other, this night. Daylight is not far off now, but I don't want to sleep— don't want to let this feeling escape.

THIRTY-EIGHT

Alissa Somers had never felt so entirely divided in her life. Her mind told her that she was managing perfectly and that only someone who knew her well could guess the truth—but inside she was quaking. She felt so completely out of place. Reminding herself that these were merely people, far less accomplished than many of her father's guests, did no good. In the company of famous empiricists and scholars she was at home—in the midst of aristocrats she felt her confidence evaporate like spilled preserving spirits. And this left her with a tiny echo of a question: had her confidence always been so illusory?

I should not care so that they approve of me, she chided herself. But these were Jaimy's people and she found she did care, though her father would be appalled to hear her say such a thing.

Alissa had been left in the company of three of Jaimy's female cousins her own age—nieces of the duchess, Jaimy's mother—and though Alissa was certain this had been done to make her feel more at ease, the plan was not working. It was difficult for her to believe these . . . *girls* could, in fact, be her own age. She was certain that she had never been so . . . well, *girlish,* so concerned with trivial things. It was almost impossible to keep her attention on the conversation and she found herself scanning the crowd, praying for Jaimy's return. Suddenly she brightened.

"Oh, please do excuse me. There is an old friend of my father's. I must say hello." And with a perfect curtsy she swept off, leaving the "girls" to discuss her in her absence she was sure.

"Mr. Kent?"

The man in the old style wig turned around and his kindly face took on a look of the greatest joy. "Miss Alissa, I have been so looking forward to giving you my congratulations in person! I will say that this young lord is more fortunate than he deserves by a great deal. Does he have any idea how lucky he is?"

Alissa was surprised at how soft his lips were when he kissed her hand, holding it with obvious affection. Kent actually was a close friend of her father's, and in years past had been often at their home.

"I believe I am the fortunate one, Mr. Kent," she said, believing every word. "And even more fortunate now, for I have found you and we can have a real conversation." She cast a look over at the gossiping nieces, glad to have made good her escape.

The Duke and Duchess of Blackwater, Jaimy's parents, were having their annual celebration of the duchess' birthday—no small affair—and everyone with claims to being anyone in Farr society was in attendance, including the Prince Kori and the Princess Joelle, though they had made their appearance and already departed—their visit being brief not out of disrespect for the duke and duchess but because the members of the Royal Family were aware that their presence had an inhibiting effect on such gatherings and took the focus away from the person in whose honor the celebration was planned.

"You can have a real conversation here, if you are determined and know precisely whom to approach." Kent waved a wrinkled hand toward a man by the windows. "The Marquis of Sennet is one of the four most skilled ornithologists in Farrland, and a fine and interesting man as well. Ask him about his study of the nesting habits of *Falconiformes* and you shall have all the 'real' talk you can possibly manage.

"Or if you would rather talk politics and the affairs of nations, there are any number of people present, foremost among them Sir Roderick Palle, of course, and the Chancellor of the Exchequer." He nodded toward the King's Man who stood by the fireplace, gesturing with a wineglass to a very small man. "But then I think it is *bivalvia* that is your particular interest, if I am not mistaken?"

Alissa wondered what he could possibly mean and then she realized—the Society meeting.

Kent went on quickly. "Oh, do not look so concerned. Your secret is safe with me." He lowered his voice. "But surely you did not think you could hide such charms from everyone? I pray you take care with such adventures, Miss Alissa. I am in complete sympathy with your father's, and no doubt your own, position. I should like nothing better than to open attendance at Society gatherings. But do be careful, there are others almost as aware of small details as painters. A small curl escaping from beneath a wig will eventually alert someone." And then, as though her surprise were enormously gratifying, he laughed quite heartily. He had caught her out and was quite pleased with himself. Alissa's relief was great, and his mirth so genuine and fully felt, that she found herself laughing as well—sharing the jest.

"There," the painter said wiping a tear from the corner of his eye, "now you look less like a frightened fawn and more yourself." Motioning with his head toward the room in general he went on. "An impressive company, is it not? The Earl of Mandbridge and his countess. . . ." He stood taller, casting his gaze around the room. "And his mistress—the plump woman over there. The one with too much rouge and the ghastly jewelry. Of course they are near paupers you know—they've spent everything. Only the largesse of relations stands between the earl and the gutter. And they are not the only ones here in that situation. Do you see that very lovely young woman over there? The one looking around, rather sadly? She searches for her husband who has disappeared with the wife of the drunken gentleman by the window."

He bent his head slightly toward her so that Alissa could smell the powder in his wig. "Never," he said firmly, "be intimidated by a person because of the size of house in which they were born." He nodded at her, as though confirming this advice.

Alissa felt a wash of warmth toward the old man. He had sensed her state and was making a valiant effort to make her feel more comfortable. Alissa had known Kent so long that she had learned his tricks over the years; his appearance of being a little inept in this effort to put her at ease was part of the design, part of the charm of the man. People were often deeply touched by his apparently simple and open manner. Even Alissa, who had long been aware of his subterfuge, had enormous affection for him. He always meant the best.

"Mr. Kent, I am sure you are the kindest gentleman in all of Farrland," she said.

"You have no idea how much gentlemen dread hearing those words from the mouths of young women. It is like a sentence. 'Old, old.' And I have been hearing them now for some considerable sum of years." He shook his head, but she could see that he still smiled.

Alissa drew herself up primly. "But, Mr. Kent, I am engaged to be married. I have my reputation to think of. Put yourself in my place, sir."

This made him chuckle, and she was glad.

"Why, Miss Somers, you are the kindest betrothed woman in all of Farrland, and beyond I think." He cast his eye around the room for a second with that look of great affection he almost always wore. A man at peace with his world, she thought.

"But of course if it is real conversation that you want, I should not send you elsewhere and lose the opportunity myself." He looked down at her, the wrinkles appearing around his eyes as he smiled. Wrinkles from a life of joy, Alissa thought, not from care.

"I will tell you something of great interest," Kent began, and the change in his manner suggested that he was no longer merely playing—this *was* a matter of real interest. "Have you read Chatterton's journals?"

Alissa had not, though she was dying to do so. Chatterton had been the great novelist and pamphleteer of the older generation—Kent's generation—and now, more than ten years after his death, his sister was overseeing the publication of his journals and letters. It was the type of event that delighted the educated of Farrland. Editions would be snapped up faster than the printer could create new ones.

"Well, I have read the first volume," Kent stopped, his look distant, "and I can tell you that Chatterton's writings have been expurgated . . . sanitized."

"You knew him," Alissa said flatly, not meaning it as a jest. Kent knew everyone.

"Oh, yes. I knew him well, I think. Well enough that he occasionally read me excerpts from his works in progress and from his journals. Brilliant, irreverent, scathing toward pretension. The man really was a genius." Kent stopped, looking down at the shine on his boots. "But his sister, Mrs. Hidde, has taken her own pen to his works. It is a crime. The efforts of his lifetime—a life of thought and insight . . . gone."

Alissa could see genuine anger taking hold of the man. She had not thought Kent could be anything but pleasant, but then she understood his resentment—it was a terrible thing.

"And the great man's thoughts have been replaced by the woman's own . . . insipid maunderings! Do you believe it? She has taken her brother's journals and used them as a stage for her own empty ideas. Now there's a heresy for you. She should be thrown on the pyre herself."

Alissa felt her own anger begin to flow. Injustice was something a Somers could not bear. "What has been done with his actual writings, do you think? Has Mrs. Hidde destroyed them?"

"I pray not, but nothing she did would surprise me now." Kent took hold of himself, pushing his sudden anger down. "Can you imagine a worse travesty?"

At that very moment Alissa could not. "I believe the works of great minds belong to every thinking person, Mr. Kent. They should never be shut up, altered, denied. It is like cutting out a man's tongue, and worse, for Mr. Chatterton is dead and cannot defend himself."

Kent nodded, casting his glance around the room as though checking on his children. "And it is not the only case, not at all. I know of others. Too many, in fact."

The painter fixed his gaze on her, though not unkindly, searching her face. "I may even know of a similar incident very close to home. Could you, Miss Alissa, be enlisted in the undoing of such an injustice? *'The works of great minds belong to every thinking person,'* you said. Do you have the courage of your convictions?"

Alissa found herself looking around, feeling more uncomfortable than she had all night. People stood so close by that she wondered if they could be overheard. Exactly how close to home did Kent mean? And whose home, exactly?

"I must hear more," she said, almost too quietly.

Kent cast his gaze around the room again, his look of great warmth cooling a little. "Of course I would never ask that you compromise your principles in any way." He must have sensed the source of her discomfort. But then he hesitated, too long, as though afraid to speak his request—making Alissa fear what it might be.

"I must ask that you treat what I say in confidence, whether you choose to answer yea or nay."

She smoothed a seam on her gown. "That, at least, I can agree to."

Kent nodded, approval not acknowledgment, she thought. "It begins with Erasmus Flattery. . . . I knew him somewhat." The painter wet his lips, speaking now very softly. "He told me, not long before his death, that he was engaged in a project of great significance, yet, according to his nephew, the duke, Erasmus left no notes or writings beyond a few monographs. It is my belief that the duke might not understand the importance or significance of his uncle's work. Oh, certainly the duke is a fine man, but not an empiricist, not a scholar. Families have hidden many things that they did not understand—novels written by wayward sons, important works of philosophy thought to be blasphemous texts. Many works suppressed by families for many reasons—most misguided." He looked around again, forcing a smile back onto his lips. "I think it is possible that the works of Erasmus did not simply disappear." He paused, catching her eye. Alissa could feel his yearning, but still he asked nothing specific of her.

She had hoped it would be a far more innocent request—some research at Merton College, perhaps. Something only her father might have access to. But this was Jaimy's family he was talking about.

Were there really extant works of the great Erasmus? This thought was almost spoken in her mind—as though her curiosity had its own voice.

She realized that Kent had considered carefully before choosing her. If it had not been Jaimy's family. . . .

"What you ask, Mr. Kent. . . ." She paused, knowing she must refuse. "It is more than a little presumptuous. I. . . ." She felt a wavering, confusion. She was a Somers at heart, and would remain so no matter what family she married into. "I will give it some consideration," her voice said quickly. "I can promise no more than that."

Kent nodded, showing no disappointment. "But we will keep each other's secret?"

"Torture could not drag it from my lips," she said, mock sincere.

The old man looked a bit alarmed. "I hope it will not come to that," he said softly.

Kent stood watching Alissa—as she made her escape. Was this a foolish risk? He had known Alissa Somers for most of her life and thought highly of her. And this request he had made. . . . It was merely a hunch and would likely come to nothing. He also tried to comfort himself that, though she did not know it, Alissa was already caught up in this matter.

Kent stared at the walls, hung with overly-flattering family portraits. Ministers, admirals, King's Men, ladies of letters, but no Erasmus Flattery. It was telling.

She will help me, he thought.

A young couple greeted him as they passed.

She will help me and come to no harm, I'm sure. Not that he could afford to let his feelings about acquaintances get in the way of what must be done. Not now.

Sir Roderick caught his eye from across the room. The King's Man nodded, his smile tight-lipped but amiable.

I am quite sure I know your purpose here, Kent thought, *but are you equally aware of mine?* He could not say how dearly he hoped the King's Man still thought him, to quote a friend, "the kindest gentleman in all of Farrland."

Now where was this young lord? Not too far from his betrothed, Kent was certain. He should like a word with the young man before Roderick found him.

The painter discovered Lord Jaimas Flattery in conversation with the Marquis of Sennet. The two men were wedged into a corner of the library, where most of the well known empiricists and writers had gathered among their admirers. It was a sign of the times that these gentlemen and ladies had been invited to such an occasion.

"Mr. Kent," the marquis said, "we were just speaking of falcons, if you can believe it." The man beamed at the painter. Kent had always liked the way the ornithologist made mild mockery of himself and his own obsessions.

"You must know Lord Jaimas."

"I do indeed, Lord Sennet, and I have come to offer my sincere congratulations, for Lord Jaimas is about to marry a young woman I esteem very highly. Almost a niece, in fact."

Jaimas gave a slight bow, a smile spreading across his face. He looked more like his cousin than Kent had remembered.

"And I shall be proud to call you uncle, Mr. Kent, for anyone who thinks so highly of Alissa is as dear to me as a member of my own family."

Kent wondered exactly how great the similarity was between this young man and Tristam Flattery. Did Sennet say they were discussing falcons? He would have to corner the marquis later and find out just what had been said.

"And I have congratulations to offer, as well," the marquis said, lowering his voice, "though I must tell you, it is not yet official. But Sir Roderick assures me that you are to be raised up, Kent, granted a baronetcy by His Majesty. And more than well deserved, I might say. *Sir Averil Kent.* Does it not sound completely natural, Lord Jaimas?"

Kent was sure that the blood drained from his face. It seemed that Roderick Palle was more aware of him than he had hoped.

THIRTY-NINE

"Well?" Osler asked, impatient for a verdict.

Tristam bent over the rock formation, scraping away lichen. He shrugged, hoping that would be answer enough for a few moments.

Flames, Tristam thought. *Look at this!* The tide of his emotions had turned again and the hollowness was, at least for now, replaced by an irrational and rising sense of dread. The naturalist could not shake the feeling that the incoming tide of emotion flowed out of this jumble of stone and into his heart.

Ridiculous.

But so strong was this feeling that he feared it would soon overwhelm his reason altogether. It was all he could do to keep his mind focused on his efforts.

But look at it!

"Mr. Flattery?" It was Osler, his voice sounding odd.

Tristam realized that he had rocked back on his heels and crouched there, doing nothing but staring.

"Just thinking." Tristam did not move. "I will tell you one thing, Mr. Osler, the surrounding rock is altered volcanic, and this is very old marble."

Marble once hewn by men.

Tristam was of half a mind to lie. Tell them it was a natural formation after all. Get them out of here. Get *him* out of here.

All along he had thought the battle and close brush with death had affected his emotions but now he realized that this was not so: *it was this place.*

He looked around, hardly aware of the others staring at him. The islands of the archipelago spread around the horizon like the work of a great artist, their sweeping silhouettes and wavering reflections creating a composition of great beauty, Tristam was sure—but the scene did not seem beautiful to him. It was this place. . . . If Tristam was Palle's lodestone then the iron that drew him was buried here—or very nearby—he could feel it, somehow.

They had come here that morning, leaving the ship at first light, winding their way westward through the hidden channels of the Archipelago, and had slipped silently between islands until the cone of the volcano had appeared. That thin shroud of smoke had seemed terribly ominous to Tristam. And then they had landed here on this point and scrambled up to this jumble of rock . . . this unnatural formation.

A streak of sweat ran coolly down Tristam's neck. He looked up to find Osler standing over him silently, touching his lip with a finger as though exploring a sore—not looking at Tristam.

I am behaving oddly, Tristam realized—unsettling the others. The naturalist forced himself to stand, brushing hair back from his face.

"Who has the spade?" he asked, forcing his voice to sound normal—almost succeeding. But this place unnerved him completely.

Tristam pushed the blade into the soft earth, gingerly, stopping as soon as he felt resistance. In half an hour he handed this work over to a Jack who proceeded as Tristam had and the naturalist stepped back, crouching again; watching, feeling the dread still growing inside him. Each time the spade revealed more of the stone Tristam felt a bit more of his own facade was stripped away, exposing something unknown beneath. Revealing the creature who had been drawn to this place.

I am their lodestone. But what have I been led to?

More marble was revealed and Tristam shifted uncomfortably. He forced himself up again. Struggling against this incoming tide of feeling. Struggling to stay on its surface. He heard himself breathing raggedly.

Using his hands Tristam began to work at exposing rock. Everyone joined in as they could, even the most uneducated Jack a little in awe of the possibilities. They worked silently for the better part of two hours and it became more and more obvious to everyone that there was a regular shape to this formation.

"Well, Mr. Osler," Tristam said, finally. "Do you still think this natural?"

Osler stood for a second, looking down at the rock, his serious face suddenly a little sad. He shook his head. "No. Though what it is the remains of I cannot begin to guess."

Tristam nodded agreement. "It is very ancient, I think. Far older than our oldest cities." As he spoke he used a square of cotton to wipe the grime from a small white shard he had unearthed. He held this out in his hand, turning it in the sunlight. "Do you see this?" Tristam pushed the object on Osler. "It is a fragment of pottery. Do you see how fine it is? The ridges indicate that it was turned on a wheel. Those are the marks of the potter's hands." He found he shuddered as he said this, as though he had been touched by someone long dead.

A ghost.

Tristam looked around at the faces of the men present. They were as silent as mourners, unable to find words for something so momentous. Men had been here before them.

But why have I been led here? Tristam asked. *What is it Roderick wants me to find? Could there be Kingfoil in this place? Or is it something else altogether? Something perhaps even Roderick and his followers do not suspect?*

"If this were Farrland," Jack Beacham said quietly, "we would put a navigation beacon on such a point."

A few men gave half a laugh, but no more. Did they feel some of what Tristam felt?

Tristam tried to smile but could not. "It is as good a guess as any, Beacham."

He remembered the strange feeling that had almost

overwhelmed him as the Ruin of Farrow had come into view. Turning, he tried to look off through the trees. The cone of a volcano lurked somewhere not far off—as on Farrow.

Osler set the fragment of pottery down on the stone work, suddenly. "We have our survey to continue. You will want to be left here, I should imagine, to continue searching. Meet you here two hours before sunset?"

Here. Yes, here. The feeling of dread surged in him like a sudden dark wave, but Tristam felt himself nod to the lieutenant. "Two hours before sunset."

I should go with Osler, he thought. *Run from this place.*

But some part of Tristam knew this would not work. His presence here had a sense of inevitability about it. If he went to some other island that would be the place he was meant to have gone.

Tristam realized suddenly that he was not afraid. Fear was not what was growing in him. He felt *dread,* which he had not realized was so different. Fear could make a man turn and run or not allow him to continue, but this feeling Tristam experienced was made up in large part of acceptance. Deep apprehension of what was to come, yes, but coupled with a knowledge that it could not be avoided. Roderick had set him off, searching, and he had been drawn to this point. To this island. Perhaps even on this very day. There was nothing that he could do.

The Jacks began to collect up their tools, quietly as though they had unearthed a sacred place. Or perhaps they were observing silence for Tristam and his companions who were to be left behind.

As they began to pick their way down the rock to the boat Tristam thought they resembled nothing so much as a burial party, armed with implements of their trade, respectfully silent.

"Mr. Flattery?"

Tristam turned to find Beacham staring at him.

"Are you well, sir?"

Tristam nodded, bending to lift the worn bag to his

shoulder, and then set off to forestall further questions. Beacham had managed to have himself detailed to assist the ship's naturalist that day, so Tristam had a boy and a murderer for bearers—and he wondered if that was inevitable as well.

My faithful servant, Beacham . . . , and this dark brother—both of us unnatural.

Tristam felt as though his movements were no longer managed by his own will but proscribed, the scene unfolding like history. The mountain, smoking vaguely at the island's center, did not help. It was like a presence, casting a shadow that followed them as they went.

What has happened to me, he wondered suddenly. Very recently I was an empiricist, struggling against ignorance and superstition. And now . . . ?

Am I sinking into madness? Is that what befell my father?

"It would be easier going along the beach, Mr. Flattery," Beacham offered. "Or do you plan to set a course inland?"

"The beach," Tristam said, knowing it did not matter.

They scrambled down the rocks of the headland onto a curving margin of sand that formed a wide bight in the island's flank. Here they trudged on, three abreast, Beacham stopping to retrieve shells and other bits of flotsam from the tide line. They made their way slowly, the midshipman bringing Tristam his finds like a faithful retriever.

At Beacham's insistence they stopped to wade in the shallows and cast a net. Tristam sat in the shade of a tree and stared at nothing, uninterested in the practice of his profession. Occasionally he glanced over to the midshipman and the viscount. Their activities seemed so normal that Tristam could not quite understand why he no longer felt like a ship's naturalist. It was as though these strange changes in his emotions had swept away the core that was Tristam. But who was emerging?

Finishing with their net Beacham and the viscount came and sat for awhile, eating in the shade of this previously-unknown species of tree, and then they set out again along the sand.

Thoughts of his night with the duchess began coming back to Tristam like fragments of a dream or long forgotten memories. He clung to these like a sailor grasping at the shrouds in a gale. Had he had love with the duchess only the night before? It seemed an age ago.

"Who is it has the cough?" the viscount asked, suddenly. "I thought he should hack his lungs up. I believe he kept me awake half the night. Have we taken aboard some new world consumption?"

Beacham kept his eye fixed on their surroundings, taking his duties seriously. "It is the physician, Lord Elsworth. Now that we are quietly in port his coughing can be easily heard. He has an illness of the lung, as I'm sure you've noticed. It strikes him down and then lets him be for a time. Last night was the worst I've heard." He was quiet for a few seconds. "Though it is the good doctor's nightmares that most often wake me. I have never known a man for nightmares like Doctor Llewellyn." He pointed off toward the crown of a nearby island. "Is that a kite, Mr. Flattery?"

Tristam studied the bird for a moment, little more than a black dot against the pale blue—a bit of animated punctuation that had taken wing from a page and was making its escape heavenward. A raptor, perhaps. A falcon?

"Only a gull, Mr. Beacham."

They walked on, Tristam separating himself from his companions so that he could have silence.

A headland rose up in front of them and they scrambled over the rock and into bush, climbing a short section of cliff. Here Tristam left his companions behind briefly, so convinced was he of the inevitability of the day that he could not believe he was meant to fall to injury. He had scaled the rock like a man who believed he could fly.

Beyond the headland they found another beach circling a shallow bay. It was some hours past noon, Tristam judged by the sun, for he had come away from the ship without his timepiece. The sun was passing into the west and the nearby islands were falling into shadow with only the highest points catching the direct light, creating subtle patterns in green and gray. The afternoon was perhaps more advanced than he had thought. The hour of their meeting with Osler was not so far off.

I will escape this place, Tristam thought suddenly. *Osler will come and take us away and nothing out of the ordinary will have happened.* But this thought did not alleviate the feelings he had borne all that day.

The songs of unknown birds filled the air and the wind spoke among the trees, a mysterious tongue. Small waves lapping the shore added to the discussion.

Along the beach, trees pressed close together, branches spreading in ways both familiar and slightly alien. New world trees filling niches similar to those at home.

Black willow, bayberry, and a species he did not know, stood near at hand. Bluejack oak spread its hardy branches in several places along the shore, and *Planera aquatica* grew near to a stream mouth. Tristam forced himself to name these as he went, like a litany. The litany of a man of reason. But they seemed only words—perhaps not even words but just sounds—arbitrary and a little absurd. Their meaning draining away at each repetition, as though it were dissipating like old magic.

They came to a stream, and Beacham dipped a finger in and tasted—apparently approved—and cupped his hands for a longer drink. The others did the same, for it was a warm day.

Crouching by the stream's edge Tristam's gaze followed the flowing water back into the trees where it descended a slope in small, regular steps. And there, perched on a branch, was a small owl looking down at him with large, dark eyes set within multiple rings; one black, one white, the next the color of dried blood. The body was whitish, and flecked in brown, almost rufous. Brown eyes stared back at Tristam sadly. Blinking occasionally as though struggling against tears.

Beacham followed Tristam's gaze, and seeing the owl he stood suddenly, setting the bird to wing. It disappeared silently into the dark shadows of the wood.

The midshipman shuddered. "We had no need of *that*."

"That was a new species," Tristam said, expecting to see the midshipman's face light up.

"New or old makes no matter, sir," Beacham said, his tone uncommonly serious. "It is terrible bad luck. Owls are often augurs of death, Mr. Flattery. There is no surer sign."

"Not even the cessation of breathing?" the viscount asked, but neither Tristam nor Beacham laughed.

Tristam began walking up the stream's edge, looking at the rock formation over which the water ran.

"Look at what regular steps this waterfall takes," Beacham said suddenly.

Unnatural.

Tristam stood staring up into the dark forest, listening to the ancient song of water running over stone. His companions joined him, all three gazing up the watercourse, which fell in even steps, each just less than a foot. The stream itself lay between stone banks, the low, steep bank on either side so covered in moss and fern that they seemed solid walls of vegetation.

Beacham stepped into the flow and mounted the first steps but Tristam found himself watching with a growing horror, and it wasn't fear that the boy would slip. The viscount moved away, examining the corner of the cliff, which was covered in mosses and fern. He pulled away a clump of green from a ledge and stood back.

"It is a slick stair," Beacham called out, "but it can be climbed."

Tristam turned away, suddenly feeling as though the incoming tide was winning. In a moment there would be no air to breathe.

Can I not refuse to go, he thought. Can I not stop what is unfolding?

The viscount swept away more vegetation, pulling free the clinging vines. Several ancient roots defied him but bare stone was appearing.

"What have I found, Tristam?" the viscount asked, his words jarring the naturalist. A root broke away suddenly and the viscount staggered back.

Beacham had stopped on the stair and was looking back down to his companions. "Surely this is not the work of nature," he said.

Tristam wanted to cover his ears, wanted to dive into the sea and swim away from this place, from these men who did not understand what they were doing. But he stood, fixed to that place, no more able to turn away than to take to the air.

Beacham came down from the falls and stood looking on. "Well, Lord Elsworth, you shall have your name in the history books yet. Do you see? There is an eye. And here would be its brow."

Tristam stepped back while the two cleared away more of the covering vegetation. He felt ill, suddenly, and sat heavily on the sand. He glanced up the water-stair, for he knew that's what it was—a stairway carved by the hands of men.

Why have I been led here?

As he sat there he felt the numbness begin to creep back in, as though the water flowing down the stair trickled into his soul.

Beacham and the viscount stopped to look at what their efforts had revealed. "Is it an animal?" the viscount asked.

"Avifaunal," Tristam answered. He did not even need to look. "A hawk. *Raptor. Ravisher. Plunderer.* And that is what befell this." He waved a hand at the rock. "It has been smashed by men." He turned away and gazed at the watercourse. It led up into the shadows of the primeval forest, into the heart of this mystery.

'We follow Tristam's course, now.'

"What does it lead to?" Beacham asked, his voice subdued.

The inevitable, Tristam thought.

"I don't know," Tristam said softly. "Let us follow your owl and see."

❦   ❦   ❦

Water running over stone like an ancient song, the rock so worn now that the song had almost returned to its natural form. Still, there were vestiges of the regularity that the even steps had imposed but this was in the background now, a quiet harmony.

Tristam was reminded of the dream from his uncle's house on Farrow—pushing up a stair against an invisible current.

The three men went slowly up, concentrating on their footing, not speaking, their breath soon coming hard. The constant sound of water running and the wind in the trees were like whispers and sighs.

Tristam slipped and the viscount grabbed his arm, pulling him upright with that massive strength. Perhaps the man was here for that sole purpose.

In places the stairs had been eroded to mere irregularities and here the climbers were forced to drag themselves along the walls using rock or root or vine.

The stair continued up, its angle of ascent unvarying as far as Tristam could tell, for perhaps two hundred and fifty feet, making a slip potentially disastrous. Occasionally they halted their progress and examined sections of wall that were exposed through the covering of green. Once these surfaces had been richly carved, though time had effaced them.

A gust of wind moved the branches overhead causing patterns of sunlight to dart in a mad array across the stream and the underwood, and at the same time a haunting tone, like a deep note from a massive woodwind, sounded somewhere in the forest above. All three of them cringed as though this sound presaged some calamity, but the note ended in a dying fall, leaving only the sounds of water and breeze.

"Martyr's blood!" the viscount said. "I did not like the sound of that!"

They stood, rooted, for some minutes but when the sound was not repeated they worked up their nerve and went on. Beacham fell and slid several feet before he managed to catch himself, coming up wet and bruised and a little unnerved. He progressed more slowly after that, testing his footing with care.

Finally they came to a place where they could no longer see the stair ascending above them and Tristam felt as though a cold stone had grown in his stomach.

But when they reached what they took to be the stairhead it proved to be only a landing—thirty feet of level stone covered in water, and then the stair went up again, disappearing into the green of the forest.

Not far above this they found a natural arch of rock spanning the stair, and in this they could see a number of holes, natural or manmade they could not tell, but here could be heard an eerie breathy drone. They stood waiting and catching their breath for some time but there was no long note such as they had heard earlier and they pressed on.

Not thirty steps further the wind came up suddenly and, after a moment of vibration on the edge of audibility, the strange wail sounded again, causing them all to stop, jarred by the power of the sound so close to its source. Tristam had felt the note in his chest.

"I should not like to hear that on a dark night," Beacham muttered. "Why it would stop the heart of a man thirty years at sea. Freeze the saltwater in his veins."

They pushed on and found that the rock wall had fallen away in one place, choking the stair with debris, and constricting the flow of water so that it rushed through a narrow gap, growing deep and swift. They wedged their way through this, dragging themselves over stone, afraid all the time that the rock would shift and the whole dam give way.

Around them a strange world was slowly being revealed. Massive ferns, twenty feet in circumference and taller than a man, sent out a hundred elegantly curving fronds. Unknown vines and flowers crept up trees, twisting about the trunks and branches like mad lovers intent on suffocation. Thick beards of moss hung from branches and spread in carpets over much of the ground. The sun fell in shafts through the dense canopy overhead, illuminating tiny portions of the forest as though nature were drawing attention to itself. *'Look. Do you see the perfection? Can you recognize the miracle?'*

The burble of water flowing down the giant stair drowned most other sounds so that the wind or the calls of birds seemed eerie and distant, marking their ascent with another note of strangeness.

As they went they surprised a water snake which slipped silently into a crack in the wall, its long tail whipping once as it disappeared into the earth. After that they kept to the stair's center, proceeding in single file.

Under the arch of trees that overhung the great stair there appeared a crescent of sky, raising the hopes of the explorers.

"I hope it is not just another resting place," Beacham said, laboring in the rear. "Not that I couldn't use a resting place. . . ."

The naturalist should have felt the same—his legs were burning with the strain—but something forced him on now. It was as though he longed to get whatever was going to happen over with. He found he had taken the lead.

The final arch of trees was only yards away. Tristam glanced back and saw that his companions had stopped, bent double, gasping for breath. Tristam looked up at the blue sky framed in the portal.

He had been in the chill water so long that the cold seemed to have crept into his bloodstream. Tristam felt a certain detachment, as though he watched himself calmly from a safe distance.

I might not go on otherwise, he thought.

Best to have it done. He forced himself up the last steps, as though it were the finish of a race.

A blast of wind funneled up the stair, stirring the ferns and the branches overhead, sounding the long moaning note. A bird fluttered out of the trees above and Tristam thought he caught another glimpse of the owl—Beacham's owl.

With a final burst of energy Tristam stood upon the stairhead looking out over a topography of jumbled white stone and tangled forest. *A ruin,* he realized. *A lost city.*

Someone heaved himself up onto the stair at his side and cursed under his breath. Tristam realized that the viscount stepped away from him, his gaze fixed on Tristam, not the wonder before them. Unable to bear the accusation in the man's eyes, Tristam turned away.

What appeared to be a plaza opened up before them: paved in marble, utterly overgrown to either side with dense forest. A shallow stream ran from the plaza's opposite side where water fell between two stairways half-smothered in vines and mosses and tanglewood.

Beacham arrived at the stair head. "Well, sir," he said, his voice subdued by awe, "we shall be known all our lives for this discovery. I never dreamed . . ." But he could not finish.

I dreamed, Tristam thought, *up a stair against an invisible current and then into an arbor. . . . I have come, Sir Roderick, but to what purpose?*

Before him spread the ruins of an alien city, overwhelmed by the forest which sent columns of vines and roots twisting out onto the small remaining area of barren stone. Here they trapped soil carried by the wind and the rains and anchored this with scrub grasses and ground cover, patiently collecting enough soil for the trees—like courtiers preparing the way for their king's return. But beyond this small area the forest had pushed far into the city's borders in its relentless campaign to reclaim a lost kingdom.

There were no sounds of men, here; only the whisperings of the world of nature, which men often called silence. Tristam imagined he heard the language of the forest itself. *Have men returned? Are all our efforts to be undone?*

Around the small plaza the ruins of shattered buildings lay covered in a carpet of green, reminding Tristam of objects buried in snow, their true shapes disguised, in time to be lost entirely. But in places sections of stone wall could be distinguished—a window casement from which trailed a wild vine covered in exotic crimson blooms. The remnants of a high portico could be seen, tapering columns supporting a lintel and a roof of curling branches. Even the pale marble had begun to take on the colors of the forest, stained to pale shades of green and dusky brown.

Further on Tristam could see the city rising up to a second level and here the tumbledown ruins of truly massive structures stood, though they were now so covered in undergrowth they seemed almost natural outcroppings, part of the strange landscape.

Above the double stair, the top of an enormous building could be seen in the distance—higher than any other, almost a pyramid, flat-topped and stepped, crowned with a swaying tree, branches waving like a conqueror's banner. The triumph of the ancient wood over this abode of men.

Wind came up the water-stair again, voicing strange words—chanting an eerie tonal scale, and all three men moved away from the stairhead.

Areas of exposed stone lay to either side of the flowing stream—the result of regular flooding, Tristam surmised, swept clean by water—and they were glad to feel hot stone under foot. The gentlemen stooped to pull footwear from their bags but Jack Beacham was content to go barefoot.

Crouched down, pulling on his boots, the viscount could not take his eyes from the decaying city. "How long do you think it has been lying so?" he asked. "Abandoned."

Tristam ran his hand across the weathered paving

stones, and looked around at the height of the trees, the overlying layer of soil. He shrugged. "Centuries? I don't know."

Here? To an ancient, abandoned city. Why?

The feeling of dread seemed to crest like a wave, and Tristam found himself walking on, nearly unaware of the movements of his body.

They skirted along the stream heading toward the double stair and the next level—what appeared to be the city proper—Tristam choosing this course without discussion, the others following. The sound of their boots on the stone did not echo but was muffled by the surrounding forest. Even so, Tristam could not help but feel the sound was terribly out of place, intrusive. The city did not seem merely empty and abandoned, but ominously so.

Beacham stopped before the half-hidden sculpture of a woman which leaned out from the corner of a building, held from falling by dense vines. The three gazed up at the headless figure, her one remaining arm reaching out from among the sinuous vines and leaves like the last sight of one drowning. A spray of white flowers could have been wave crests.

The hand was perfectly rendered, and expressing such forlorn need that Tristam wanted to reach out and rescue the woman from the overwhelming forest. But they were too late—she had drowned long ago.

They went on.

Avenues branching off to either side were now choked with forest, the pale boles of curving trunks appearing here and there in the dense tangle of branches and leaves. These ancient streets curved back into the darkness of the wood like canals of vegetation flowing into an ocean of unbroken green. Streams that led into a mystery so old, and so well buried that men could no longer pass inside. Glints of stone appeared in places where the sun penetrated the canopy of green, and in some of these surfaces were shattered openings that Tristam found so disconcerting he could hardly bear to look at them, as though something would be revealed to him that he did not want to see.

He forced his attention back to the remains of the vast city that had once thrived here, to the scraps the forest had not claimed as its own. What race had dwelt here? What had been their commerce, their arts, their science?

He had been led to what might prove to be the greatest mystery known to man. He, Tristam Flattery. But why?

At length they came to a pool, perhaps thirty feet across, that lay at the base of the double stair, fed by a falls between the steps. Here, at least, the mystery of the water-stair was solved, for the pool was broken and choked with rock and gravel and debris from the forest.

"The water once fell into the pool and was likely carried off beneath the plaza by a conduit," Tristam said. "Our stairway was dry in the past." He waved at the ruin of the pool, water flowing through the broken rim out into the plaza. "Unless it was flooded intentionally for defense."

They stood for a moment looking back down the broad avenue with its shallow stream, the fallen buildings beneath their carpet of green to either side. Tristam did not know how his companions reacted, but his own feelings were torn between complete awe at such a discovery and this terrible sense of dread that had sent its tendrils into his heart the way the forest overwhelmed the ancient city.

At the stairhead lay a massive tapered pillar of black stone, broken in three. The width of the column was fully eight feet, two feet taller than Tristam as it lay, and in length perhaps fifty feet. Tristam ran his hand along the worn stone.

"Do you see," he said, feeling he should break the silence. He sighted down the length. "A single piece of stone. Black marble. And once richly carved." What Tristam said was no doubt true, but whatever design had been etched into this stone was now all but lost to time.

The points where the column had been broken were now polished smooth by wind and rain. Tristam began to think that the city might have been lying abandoned far longer than he had imagined. Beacham wedged himself into the gap and climbed quickly up to the column's top where he scraped off some of the grasses and thin covering of detritus.

"It is not so different from the columns we saw at the Ruin on Farrow," the viscount said as he too pulled himself up onto the stone. "Though far greater in size."

"Yes," Tristam said, "but round columns can be found in our own antiquities. The shape is too obvious to confirm a link between the ruins."

Farrow. Races of men had preceded Tristam's own by centuries, perhaps millennia. He thought of the bottle of wine Borrows had given him. Were the vines carved on the Farrow Ruin depictions of Kingfoil?

Tristam went over to examine the base where the column had once stood. It was six sided, perhaps four feet in height and a dozen feet across. Each side had a sculpture in relief but they were all but gone now, and not just from the wearing of the years. Tristam was sure that men had made an effort to obliterate what had been carved here.

On one side he thought he found a constellation represented, and on another what might have been oddly shaped sails, doubly pointed at their peak.

He turned and stared out over the plaza. To either side, fifty yards apart, lay the ruins of two massive structures. A row of weathered columns stood before one, the lintel long since fallen and consumed by the forest. Neither structure was now more than three stories, Tristam thought, but their bases were enormous. Here and there green hummocks jutted above the trees suggesting that once the buildings had boasted towers. Other than that it was almost impossible to guess at the original shapes and styles of these structures. The forest had smothered them completely. Tristam thought it would take years of excavation to lay bare the stone work but it was possible that some of it that lay buried might in fact have been given better protection from the elements. Under the layer of green some parts of the city might reveal much more than what still stood above ground.

Behind these mounds of stone and greenery the forest had swallowed any other signs of the structures, but Tristam had the impression that the city was not small. The builders had chosen a site in the draw between the cone of the volcano—which seemed to hang over the city like a dark being—and a lower hill. The city could easily step up either side of the valley some distance, there was no way to tell but to explore.

Directly before them, across the terrace, lay another double stair and Tristam could see water falling between these as well. Behind that, on the next level, the central pyramid rose grandly above the surrounding forest.

"I don't know where to start," the viscount said, looking around, bewildered.

Tristam turned in a circle, like the needle of a compass. There. He pointed at the far pyramid. "From there we will have a view." *Up,* he thought; *up into the air.*

In the center of the plaza Beacham was crouched, examining the paving stones, brushing his hair out of his face as the wind whipped it like a flag.

"What is it, Mr. Beacham?" the viscount called out. "Have you found your likeness there?"

"Not quite, sir. But I have found something." Still staring intently down, Beacham stood and moved slowly to one side.

Tristam realized that there was a pattern in the plaza floor here, made up of marble and basalt, the darker rock running like striations across the plaza.

"This will bring joy to the captain's heart!" Tristam said as he came and stood beside Beacham. "If it is what I think."

"I believe it is a chart, sir. Though I'm sure Mr.

Hobbes would name it more properly a map. The scale is not true, I would say, and . . . I don't know how to say it, sir. . . . All the islands have been rounded off, so to speak. The roughness of the shores is gone. But nonetheless it is a chart and of the Archipelago, or at least this part of it."

The three men all bent over the plaza floor, searching the pattern. Five yards further on Beacham stamped his feet on the stone.

"And here we are, gentlemen, or my name isn't Jack Beacham." His face lit in a grin, and turned a deeper red so that his freckles seemed to grow larger. He was pointing at piece of basalt set into the marble. It was badly scarred and cracked.

"Are you sure?" the viscount asked.

"As sure as sure, Lord Elsworth. Here is the narrows we passed through earlier. He began tracing their route as though he were a ship. "Here is where the *Swallow* lies to her anchor, and here is the pass we followed into the Archipelago from the Gray Ocean." He paused, studying the chart intently. "It is not properly scaled, but look. . . ." He crossed to the west. "Here are the hidden channels between the islands. And the Great Ocean beyond! The captain will be the happiest man in the King's Navy when he sees this."

Immediately the midshipman began to plot a path through the archipelago.

"This chart would save us from many a wrong turning, Mr. Flattery. Do you see?" He tapped his toe on a blind passage to illustrate.

Already the viscount was bored, wandering away. He walked twenty feet and stopped to survey their find. "What area does your chart include, Beacham?"

The sailor jogged off toward the distant stair but stopped long before the stair was reached. "It might be two hundred miles, sir. Certainly no more and I should not be surprised to find it less."

"Their kingdom," Tristam said, "if kings they had." Tristam bent down and looked at the small crater where the city would be situated. "This. . . . It was caused by man, not nature. I would say this city was not abandoned—but sacked and defaced."

Beacham had stopped fifteen feet away. "Do you see, sir? There was another stone here."

Tristam went to look and found a small cavity in the basalt—a shard of blue still to be seen in its bottom. He bent and blew some sand from the hole. *"Lapis lazuli,"* he said. "It marked something of significance. Perhaps another city." He shook his head. "Perhaps we have found an ancient nation. What became of it, I wonder?"

"There are no fortifications to be seen," the viscount said, turning in a circle. "Perhaps war found a people who did not practice its arts." He shrugged his shoulders as though to say that speculation was not in his nature.

The viscount kept looking at Tristam oddly and though the man did not stray far from Tristam's side the naturalist got the impression that Julian tried to keep a few feet between them.

"Let's climb up," the viscount said, "and see what is to be seen."

The pool at the base of the next stair was not so damaged, but it was filled to its upper rim and they could see that debris from the forest lay thick in the bottom.

"The rain this morning would have caused an overflow," Tristam said, looking out over the plaza. "That is what keeps your chart so clean, Mr. Beacham."

A stream of water fell into this pool from the next terrace, a height of perhaps twenty feet. The decorations on this pool were not so damaged, though they had not escaped the wearing of the elements. Tristam was sure there had been a motif of vines and leaves encircling this fount. Columns had been toppled to either side of each stair and these, too, once bore a similar design. The left hand stair was much broken by the incursion of roots that lay among the jumble of blocks like thick curving fingers. From somewhere in the forest came the lonely notes of a hermit thrush, a muffled echo sounding along the abandoned avenues.

As they ascended the intact stair, Tristam looked up at the sun and realized they would have to push on if they were to return to the beach that day.

The third plaza was over three hundred feet across, ending at the foot of the pyramid that dominated the city. Tristam stood looking a moment, trying to understand what this view might have meant to one of the original inhabitants. Was this a seat of government he looked at? A temple?

From the pyramid's base a narrow canal flowed straight across the plaza and Tristam realized now that the face of the structure was dominated by two long stairways reaching to the top. Between the stairs water ran down a steep flume, feeding the canal. The plaza stepped up to both right and left, Tristam thought, but the forest hid anything else that may once have completed this plaza. A series of evenly spaced columns lay on the edge of the trees to either side, some lying on the ground, others still keeping their vigil.

A sense of purpose seemed to have taken hold of the explorers now and more than just wandering at whim, they pushed on toward the structure before them. Tristam looked into the canal as they went and found it less than a yard in depth and only twice that across. The sides were worn and smooth, and fluted by the countless years of erosion. Over the centuries the water had slowly eaten away the rock until the paving stones were undercut by almost two feet, another sign of the age of this place.

"How is it, do you think, that the water flows down from the pyramid?" the viscount asked suddenly.

Tristam was surprised that he had not noted this immediately. He scanned his surroundings. "I cannot say from where the water comes, Julian, but certainly the source must be a lake or pool higher up the slope."

The viscount nodded. "The engineers who built this city knew their business."

They were hurrying now, Beacham almost breaking

into a trot. To find a vantage to view it all was what spurred them on. Tristam turned his attention to the plaza floor, for in places the stones were cracked and broken and subsiding or were being lifted by some unknown force beneath, making treacherous footing. A faint tang of sulfur pulled Tristam's gaze up to the peak. He remembered his retreat from the volcano on Farrow, how the mountain had seemed intent on shaking them off and this reinforced his feeling of disquiet.

Perhaps this is the source of the fear that nags me, he thought. *This is too much like our day at the ruin: mysterious structures, a smoking cone above. . . . Enough to unsettle the mind.* That would explain some of this anxiety. The brain, Tristam knew, had its own, more primitive, memory of past experiences.

The edge of a block caught Tristam's sole and he stumbled forward but recovered and went on. As they came to the foot of the long stair, they slowed for no apparent reason, then each looked to the others, wondering who would lead.

Tristam's course, the naturalist thought.

To both left and right of the stairs there were broken fragments of stone from sculpture but the stairs themselves appeared to have been attacked only by the slow assault of the ages.

Tristam put his foot to the first tread as though testing to see if it would bear his weight. He looked up at the steep pattern of lines formed by the rounded edges of steps, resettled the bag on his shoulder, and began to climb.

The treads of this stair were not wide, and Tristam did not look forward to descending. As it was, traversing back and forth as they went would almost have been easier, for the original inhabitants must have been created with feet smaller than Tristam's. They rose up to the level of the tree tops and here the trade wind blew freely, catching at Tristam's hair and luffing his shirt like a poorly trimmed sail.

"There is wind up here, sir," Beacham said, catching

his breath. "That is why the clouds can outsail our poor *Swallow*."

The pyramid itself stepped up in seven tiers, the little stone that could be seen closely set and perfectly shaped. Here on the walls, some of the carvings were undamaged by whatever tragedy had befallen the city. Tristam could make out a horizontal motif of the natural world—vines and leaves and the great bowls of trees. And on the next level, stylized fish and whales and perhaps the heads and wings of birds. A great cat crept across one section of wall and above this lay a mountain with a cloud at its peak, no doubt a portrait of the smoking cone above. But there was no representation of people, leaving of the inhabitants a mystery.

The narrow steps were too treacherous to allow one's attention to wander, so the climbers did not spend much time examining the structure. Later there would be time to admire carvings and speculate about the meaning of symbols . . . , perhaps.

The viscount collapsed to a stair for a moment to catch his breath and Tristam stopped to wait, taking the opportunity to look out over the city. He suffered a moment of vertigo and lowered one knee to the stone. The strange instrument on the water-stair howled and the trade wind whipped at Tristam's clothes and shoulder bag.

They were just high enough now that the shape of the ancient city was beginning to appear, towers and turrets of green standing up above the forest: the suggestion of a pattern being revealed. A cloud floated across the sun, chasing a shadow which flowed over the ruins with surprising speed.

In a distant strait between islands Tristam could see one of the ship's boats, heeled to a breeze of wind. The sight reduced his anxiety until he realized how very far away the boat must be. What did this city look like from a distance? Had he looked up here himself and not realized?

Lord Elsworth nodded to Tristam and rose to go on. Beacham had become terribly silent and Tristam caught a glimpse of the boy's face as they set out. *Yes,* Tristam thought, *how large and strange the world turns out to be.*

Again the head of a stairway drew near and Tristam was half-prepared for it to prove another false end to the climb.

What was it the inhabitants of this city placed so high?

His legs were still responding to his urgings, but not willingly and he feared that he might fall if he could not rest soon. Suddenly he could see over the rim of the pyramid's top and he realized that the black slope must rise higher, making the front appear cut away. Here, raised only a step, was a half-circle of smooth stone, like a terrace, set between polished columns— the two farthest out made of white stone, the next two of rose, the next of green and the single column before Tristam shone black in the sunlight.

All three men stood there, fighting to fill their lungs with air, staring at this strange apparition.

"So," Tristam heard himself mutter. *"So."*

Why am I not shocked? Why am I not horrified? Because I am on a track cut into the globe that leads me to its own ends. Here, clearly. Perhaps beyond. But here.

"You wanted to see the ruin of Farrow, Beacham?" Tristam asked softly. "Well here it lies."

The viscount had shut his eyes tightly—tendons stood out on his wrists and his hands appeared to have spasmed into claws. Tristam heard his own breath coming in gasps, felt himself swaying where he stood. *Dread.*

Twice now he had been brought to this same artifact though he had not the slightest understanding of its significance. What did Galton know? What had his uncle learned?

Tristam wondered if Roderick had known that this was where his journey would lead. 'Their lodestone' they called him. But to what had he led them?

The viscount looked around as though there might

be some threat, something of which to be wary. Tristam stepped away from the man, turning his attention back to the artifact—the seven columns joined by a gray lintel.

Had the builders of the Farrow Ruin lived in this city?

Beyond the smooth pattern of marble, water bubbled into a small fount and above that perched a tiny platform that appeared to be braced upon the limbs of a tree carved out of the stone.

Tristam felt himself walking forward, dazed, then stepping up onto the marble terrace. Something on the floor moved with the wind, and Tristam's eyes darted down to find white feathers, stuck in dried gore. Some animal had made a meal here, it seemed. Some raptor, Tristam feared.

As though it might burn him, Beacham reached out and touched a column. *"Stone,"* he said, as though he had expected it to disappear at his touch.

The fount caught Tristam's eye, for it was formed from the stone coils of a massive snake that raised its head up behind the fount—but instead of the viper's jaws Tristam expected, the snake's body ended in the head of a raptor. And from its curving bill flowed clear water.

"It is not precisely the same," he said, certain he sounded a fool. Somehow this did not seem the place for fools.

Along the lintel, characters were marked, and these, too, bore a resemblance to those on Farrow, but were not identical. Nor were the columns decorated the same. It was as though the Ruin of Farrow had been recreated by a slightly different sensibility, or the plans had not been entirely precise.

Which is the copy, Tristam wondered?

He followed Beacham's example, touching a column gingerly. Sun and moon were recognizable on one, and the constellation of the Great Mare as well, but on the same column—one dedicated exclusively to the heavens in the Farrow ruin—there was a fine filigree of vine work that twisted about its base and then wound lightly upward, joining the stars and planets.

But is it Kingfoil? Tristam asked himself. It was impossible to say. Perhaps.

"This place appears completely undamaged," Lord Elsworth observed, his voice sounding calm—much to Tristam's relief.

"Only the elements and time have been at work here," Tristam said, "and even they seem to have had little effect. As though it has been preserved somehow." He looked up at the characters spanning the lintel. "I should never have thought to find such a thing had I. . . ." He shook his head. "It is beyond imagining."

The naturalist felt a sudden need to sit, and walked over and perched on the rim of the fount. The viscount continued to examine the columns, running his fingers over the black pillar.

"What is this, Tristam? It is certainly not the same material we saw on Farrow."

"Marble. Black marble, like the great column we found lying broken below. But you are right, the central column on Farrow was obsidian, and featureless." He would need the drawings in Galton's book to compare, but this artifact differed, and the black column in the center—on it was carved a horseshoe shape, like a gate, or so it appeared. An arch, carved with stars, the supporting pillars shaped like twisted horns, and between these a gate carved with the same runes that could be seen above.

A gate.

I have come, Tristam thought, as though announcing his presence. *But I do not know my purpose.*

Beacham had mounted the stair to the balcony and went up gingerly, for this stair was even narrower than the one on Farrow.

Tristam dipped a finger into the water and put it to his lips. Cool, unremarkable. He cupped his hands and drank, thinking of Galton.

The columns were casting long shadows across the

terrace as the sun descended toward the western horizon. The day was quickly disappearing. Tristam did not think they could make it down the water-stair in darkness and the thought of spending the night in the dark city was terrifying.

We arrived here late, he thought, *we are meant to stay.*

"Can you see if there are sighting lines, Beacham?" the viscount asked.

"Not yet, sir."

Although Beacham would ascend to the main tops without the slightest hesitation, this narrow stair and drop of twelve feet had slowed him considerably—the strangeness of the place had shaken his confidence.

"Mr. Flattery?" Beacham had reached the balcony and the tone of his voice indicated some surprise.

"Sir?"

"I believe there was a man at the head of the water-stair just now." He spoke quietly and calmly just as Tristam had heard men do immediately after they had sustained grievous injury, as though maintaining an appearance of normality would somehow help—*'Everything is all right, do you see? I'm really undamaged.'*

"It is Mr. Osler come after us," Tristam said.

"I don't think so, sir."

Tristam and the Lord Elsworth went to the head of the stair and looked down over the city.

"Are you certain, Beacham?" the viscount said. "I see no one."

Beacham was scrambling down from the balcony, slipped and half-jumped, half-fell the last five feet. "It was not a trick of the light, Lord Elsworth. A man, just at the stairhead." Beacham peeked over the rim as though he did not want to be seen.

"Well, let us wait a moment and see," Tristam said.

"Could it be the corsairs?" Beacham asked.

Do they seek me yet? Tristam wondered.

The viscount stepped back from the edge suddenly

and turned back to the Ruin as though searching for something. "The wind often drops at night," he said. "If we crouch back against the wall, we shall have some protection. I, for one, will feel better about going down at first light. Here, at least, it would be difficult to approach us without one of us knowing. We have food. Shall we make a supper as we can?"

Tristam could not eat. He sat in the fading light, wrapped in his jacket as the day quickly cooled, and listened to his heart racing.

Martyr's blood, he thought. *Why did I come here?*

Across the western horizon, above the peaks of the Archipelago, the sunset lit the sky in gold and red, setting a long snake of cloud aflame.

"It is an eerie place, is it not, Mr. Flattery?" Beacham huddled over his meal, his collar up to the wind, looking for all the world like an old man. "What did they use such a place for, I ask myself. And this snakehawk? It makes my blood cold, that's for sure."

Tristam shrugged. He was expending effort to control his breathing. *What will happen to me,* he thought. *What will happen to us all?*

"Is it not strange that we have been to the Ruin on Farrow and now we find ourselves here? Like a pattern don't you think?" Beacham ventured.

"Coincidence," Tristam said reflexively, not believing for a second.

"Well," Beacham said, almost to himself, "Mr. Shuk claims there is no such thing as a coincidence in this world."

"Yes," Tristam said, his voice heavy with sarcasm, "carpenters know all about such things." That stifled the conversation, to Tristam's relief.

Light faded quickly once the sun was down, and as the light went, the city below fell into shadow as though the forest spread silently at night.

In time the conversation resumed, though it fell to near whispers. The wind almost died away and a moon, waxing toward full, floated in the eastern sky, casting the palest light on the distant water. *The thirteenth moon,* Tristam remembered. *Flames!*

They took turns going to the edge to gaze down the dark stairway, but each time one of them returned, there would be a shake of the head and the conversation would be picked up again.

Tristam remained silent, lost in the labyrinth of questions. He worried that he had brought his companions into danger. But had there been any choice?

Against the stars, smoke curled out of the volcano, tinged with a dull orange glow which Tristam was certain came from within the volcano itself.

Lord Elsworth surprised Tristam by talking easily and earnestly with Beacham, and despite what the midshipman knew of the viscount he responded in the same manner.

As the night wore on conversation was punctuated with silences of increasing length. Even with the wind reduced it was a cool evening and the explorers huddled into their jackets, trying to find comfortable positions—impossible in their present situation.

"Perhaps here we shall have an opportunity to look into a volcano," was the last thing Tristam heard the viscount say before the man began to snore softly.

❧   ❧   ❧

"Are you sleeping, sir?" Tristam heard Beacham whisper. Perhaps he had been. Either that or he had been in a different world—where a hawk battled a fiery snake in the air.

"What is it?"

"A light, Mr. Flattery. Well, not properly a light, but a glow, I think. You should come see, sir."

Tristam rose stiffly, pulling cold hands from his sleeves. He shivered. The moon was gone.

"Have you been awake all this time, Beacham?"

The midshipman nodded. Tristam stopped by Beacham's side and stared where he indicated. It took a moment for him to decide, but he agreed—there was a glow.

"That is the water-stair," Tristam said. He could pick out the arch of trees at the stair's head. And the glow seemed to flicker almost imperceptibly. "Fire."

Beacham nodded.

"I hope it is our own people," Tristam said. "Wake Lord Elsworth."

Beacham disappeared leaving Tristam staring into the dark. The glow was growing brighter, he was sure. Branches were beginning to take shape and the line of the stairhead appeared straight and clearly defined.

"Mr. Flattery!" Beacham said, his voice full of fear. *"He will not wake.... Sir?!"*

A single flame flickered into being below the arch of trees, and then another. Torches.

Tristam swore and tore himself away. He had not gone two steps when he heard the midshipman cry out.

"Flames! My hand!"

Tristam ran. In the starlight he could just make out Beacham, kneeling over the viscount, holding his hand up before his face.

"What...." Tristam couldn't finish for there was a sharp pain in his cheek and jaw. He stopped, stunned. With his tongue he could feel a shaft in his mouth—through the cheek and hard into his gum. And then his tongue went numb.

He wrenched a dart from his mouth as he sank to his knees. A noise above him.

"Sir?" Beacham whimpered, and then was silent.

Tristam tried to rise and felt himself float free of the earth. Movement to his right.... The soft hiss of a snake in the darkness.

FORTY

Lieutenant Osler and midshipman Chilsey stood atop the water-stair gazing at the ruins of the city. Osler was a bit ashamed to admit not insignificant jealousy: he dearly wished he had come upon it first—even if he had argued against men in the Archipelago. He cupped his hands to his mouth, hesitated and then shouted.

"Hel-lo, Mr. Flattery! Hel-lo!"

There was nothing, then a small cry in answer: the last syllable of the naturalist's name—an echo. Both men stood in silence a moment, straining to hear, and then moved out of the water onto the dry stone of the lower plaza.

Osler looked up at the sky. Local noon, he would guess. They had found the stair while looking for their companions that morning. Obviously Tristam and his companions had come up—probably the previous day—so Osler had sent the cutter off to carry news of the find to the captain and he and Chilsey had climbed up to find the others—and to see for themselves what lay above.

"I wonder where they are, sir?" Chilsey asked. "I hope they've found a treasury full of gold and silver and are rolling around in the stuff as we speak."

Osler smiled. The lad was pretending to joke, but Osler could tell he was more than half-serious. Myths of lost cities usually involved riches. A university man might hope for artifacts and lost knowledge when he considered such a find, but the uneducated thought immediately of gold and silver.

He was also becoming a little worried, probably unwarranted, but concern was growing all the same. The strange arch that moaned and cried when the trade wind blew had set his nerves on edge and ever since then he felt a disquiet that he could not explain. But no doubt he would find them, tramping about like excited children, not only unharmed but without a care in the world.

He finished pulling on his boots and looked up at the city. There had been a civilization of great sophistication here. A city not much smaller than Avonel, it seemed. And that long stair carved through solid rock. . . . It must have taken a hundred years! "Where shall we start, do you think?' Chilsey asked.

"The open areas first."

Chilsey nodded his head in quick agreement with this plan. "I hope they're not in the forest," he said. "Did you see that viper Mr. Flattery killed?"

"Yes. Bloody mean looking." It seemed they were of one mind in that matter. Stay out of snake terrain if at all possible.

They set off toward a distant stair beside a shallow stream that flowed across the plaza.

    🐚   🐚   🐚

The Duchess of Morland braced herself against the cutter's heel just ahead of the helmsman and across from Captain Stern. Though wrapped in a sailor's oilskin she was still getting wet from spray and certainly her hair must be a sight. The instant word had arrived that a stairway had been found, Stern had readied a boat to go see this wonder for himself. The thought that an important artifact might have been discovered by his voyage had cheered him quite considerably, though the duchess could see that he tried to protect himself from disappointment yet. "It is likely nothing," he had said when he spoke to the duchess, "but I must look into it. Would the Duchess care to accompany me?"

So here they were, beating into the now consistent

trade wind, headed toward a smoking mountain. She worried about the missing men—out through the night. *It is likely nothing,* she told herself. But if that was true, why did she feel like an over-wound watch spring?

A wave caught them smartly on the forward quarter and a sheet of water came over the rail. She pulled her head inside the oilskin and felt the water hit her like a hard slap. She emerged cautiously.

The coxswain, an impertinent young man, grinned broadly, water dripping from the end of his nose. "It isn't getting hit by water that we mind, Your Grace, it's the fish."

Stern gave the young man a withering stare, and the boy went back to steering intently, his color suddenly a bit gray.

Poor lad, the duchess thought, smiling despite Stern. *The fish: ha!*

They were drawing near to an island and she dearly hoped it would be their destination. Of course, one could never tell, for sailing boats often went off at the oddest tangents from their true destinations. She checked the wind. They had been tacking since rounding the tip of a long low island. But certainly this must be the volcanic island, for there was the smoking cone above.

In the bow the duchess could see Llewellyn doubled over, soaked through no doubt, and miserable from the sea sickness—but the man would not be left behind. As an empiricist he simply must be present at such a discovery—thinking of his reputation, no doubt. She shook her head; if this stair had more than a dozen steps, the physician would never be able to ascend and would have suffered in vain.

When told of Llewellyn's search of Tristam's cabin, she had initially been tempted to confront the doctor, but something had stopped her. Better to have him wonder what she knew. To observe him. Even better to have the physician think Tristam had kept his secret. She stared intently at the man, hunched over in the bow. Ever since Llewellyn had been maneuvered aboard she wondered whose interests he served— though she was fairly certain she knew.

Palle, she thought, *you would follow me to the ends of the world.*

She looked back over the blue sea. Certainly the cutter was making for the beach.

She regretted every second they spent among these islands—every second that was not used to carry them forward—but to find signs of a civilization here. . . . It was the stuff of dreams. No sign of inhabitants on the beach, apparently. Gone—she wondered where.

A memory of history: Avonel being razed and rebuilt. If the King had ordered Avonel to be located elsewhere, the ruins of the city would have been left to the elements, to be buried eventually. Such thoughts made her own civilization suddenly seem a tentative arrangement. A shiver ran through her and it was not just from being wet in the wind.

The foresail was lowered suddenly, and the boat glided in toward the shore. A gust of wind caught the sail as it came down, shaking it quickly, and a deep, sonorous moan sounded in the forest—like a great horn.

"What on the round earth is that?" she heard a voice ask.

Stern caught her eye, the same question clear on his face.

The cutter ground to a gentle halt on the sand beach and the Jacks jumped over the side to pull it up another few feet. She could see the look of relief on Llewellyn's face. He had bent over the rail twice during their sail and wore that terrible look of desperation which those who suffered the sickness of the sea quickly acquired. She almost felt sorry for him.

The captain and coxswain helped her ashore and she shed the oilskin, for it was suddenly quite warm now that they had some shelter from the wind. It appeared to be a beach like many others, the thick green of the forest leaning out over the sand as though the wood were so crowded the trees along the marge were being pushed out.

One of the Jacks shouted from the edge of the trees and everyone converged on the spot where the stream disappeared into the rising forest.

Even the physician managed to cross the few feet of sand, but he stood looking up at the flooded stairway and the duchess heard him mutter, "What a tragedy. I shall never have the wind to climb such a slope."

The duchess was seized by panic as she stood, staring up into the wood. She thought immediately of the Ruin on Farrow. Tristam's course led here. Here. And she did not know if that boded good or evil.

🖤 🖤 🖤

Osler stood looking up the steep stairway of the pyramid, wondering if it was the best course of action. Certainly there had been no response to their repeated calls. Flattery and his companions might be inside one of the ruins, he reasoned, and unable to hear.

"It will give us the best vantage," Chilsey offered.

The lieutenant hesitated a second more. "I think you are right. Let us go up and set a watch. They will have to appear in time."

The two men mounted the stair, glad of the cooling breeze, for all this climbing was proving hot work. They stopped to catch their breath after a few moments, and Osler looked out over the ruined buildings, thinking what a great city it had once been. Plazas as large as any he had seen in the countries surrounding the Entide Sea. And here it lay for who knew how long, mysteriously emptied of its people. It would fire the imagination of the dullest mind.

Jon Chilsey looked over at him and forced a smile. Life aboard ship did not build up the lungs and both men were short of wind. Strands of the lad's dark hair were plastered to his forehead with sweat, and his face, though deeply tanned, was red from his efforts.

"Ready?" he asked gamely.

"A moment more," Osler said, wanting to give the midshipman a chance to find his breath.

He looked up the rise of stairs. They had completed perhaps half.

ꙮ ꙮ ꙮ

Stern left the impertinent coxswain on the beach to watch both the boat and Dr. Llewellyn, but everyone else, six sailors and the duchess, accompanied the captain up the water-stair.

The Jacks led the way out of consideration of the duchess' modesty, for she was forced to hike her skirts up to her knees or they would have been sodden. Stern accompanied her, giving her his arm and carefully averting his eyes. It made the duchess smile, for Stern took his dedication to gentlemanly conduct more seriously than many lords and princes. She suspected he was a prude—a sad state for a man on a voyage to Varua where the maidens were said to be both comely and unhindered by the mores of sophisticated societies. The place, perhaps, where she should have been born.

They had discovered that the loud moaning noises came from what appeared to be natural wind-pipes in a stone arch that spanned the stair. The trade wind would gust and the deep sound would begin, echoing up the stairway in the strangest manner. It reminded her of wind blowing across the mouth of an empty bottle.

The stair was long and treacherous and in one place partially blocked, but she was not about to turn around because of a little water and dirt. Who knew what lay ahead, after all, and if she was not the first one there, she was at least directly on the discoverers' heels, and that was something. If she had not felt a growing sense of anxiety, she would have been truly elated by her situation.

ꙮ ꙮ ꙮ

They would have collapsed on the top step if Jon Chilsey had not cried out, for there was Jack Beacham, half-hidden by a pillar, stretched out on the shining stone of a strange terrace.

Both sailors stumbled forward and found Tristam Flattery and Lord Elsworth there as well. All three lay in a scattering of white petals, though over Flattery, who lay along the central meridian, a down of white and dark red plumules mixed among the petals.

Their faces were painted a reddish brown that Osler suddenly realized was blood. He found himself stepping back and looking around, his heart acting oddly.

"Are they dead?" Chilsey whispered, horrified.

Osler forced himself to go to Flattery's side and kneel. For a moment he was almost afraid to touch the man, so cold and still did he appear. The naturalist had been stripped to the waist, his face smeared with blood, now dry, and delicate shells laid over his eyes. The fingers of his left hand curled around his field glass, which had been placed on his chest, and the right hand pressed to his heart, a coil of red tattoo winding around the wrist.

Chilsey came and stood beside him, looking down, his breathing ragged. Osler thought the lad mumbled a prayer.

Putting his hand near Flattery's mouth and nose, Osler could feel no breath, nor did the chest seem to rise and fall. Gently he moved Flattery's hand from his breast and discovered the wrist had been gashed and was red and swollen, the entire hand appearing bruised.

"He is not cold," he said. A sudden moan from the distant stair caused him to start back, but then he put his ear to the naturalist's chest. "It beats, I think—quick but faint."

He examined the other two in the same way and found them not so badly off. There were no cuts upon them and their hearts beat more strongly and regularly.

Chilsey half-crouched, looking around them constantly, hovering near to his friend, Beacham. "Who did this?" he asked. "Flames and blood: I feel as though I am being watched. My heart is a-pounding worse than it did in any action." He touched Beacham's arm tentatively. "Jack," he pleaded, "wake from this."

When Beacham did not stir, Osler thought the lad would sob.

"What has been done to them?" Chilsey cried out. "They are so near to death. . . ." He fell into a frightened silence.

Osler felt sorry for the terrified midshipman but could not think what to say. Nothing he had learned in the King's Navy had prepared him for this. He looked around at the terrace. There was no question of what it resembled—the Ruin on Farrow. He found this almost as disconcerting as the three men who lay stretched out so carefully on the meridians etched into the floor.

❦   ❦   ❦

"Did you hear that?" Stern asked. He cupped his hand to his ear and turned his head. The sound echoed again. A shout, certainly, but the words were unclear, distorted. He could not discern their origin.

"Captain!" One of the Jacks pointed. "Atop that . . . great pile of stone, sir."

Someone was waving an article of clothing from the top of the pyramid.

"It is Julian, I think," the duchess said, relief in her tone.

Stern took off his hat and waved it in reply. He had been sure there was no cause for worry. Flattery and his party had simply come upon this place late in the day and made a camp for the night. He was a bit annoyed that they had not made shift to inform him of their find earlier, but it was almost understandable.

Stopping only to put on shoes, Stern and the duchess set out in the wake of the barefooted Jacks who walked close together, silent, their eyes wide, tripping over each other as their gazes flitted from this to that, never having imagined in their lives that they would find themselves in such a place.

They had mounted the second set of stairs before realizing the man calling from the top of the pyramid was Lieutenant Osler and that he was shouting for help.

Stern started off at a brisk walk but soon realized he was leaving the duchess behind in this strange place and slowed his pace. The duchess hurried as best she could but was hardly dressed for an expedition. Damned nuisance, Stern thought, why hadn't she waited down on the beach, or at the ship? Or in Avonel!

Glancing down, the captain almost tripped. He stopped so suddenly one of the Jacks ran into him.

"What is ...?" The duchess stopped in midsentence. "Is it a chart?"

"Yes, of sorts."

Osler cried out again, having seen them stop, perhaps, and Stern pulled his gaze away. Farrelle's flames! It was a map of the Archipelago, or at least some part of it. He forced himself to hurry on, conscious of the shapes of islands and narrows and sounds passing beneath his feet.

By the time they had reached the base of the pyramid, she and Stern were both forced to sit for a moment, and the water running in the channel was most welcome. He moistened his handkerchief and gave it to the duchess to wipe her face and neck.

They could hear Osler now, shouting to them. "We'll need help to get them down."

"What has happened?" Stern called back. "Is someone hurt?"

"They have all been rendered ... unconscious, sir. They cannot be stirred from it. We must bear them down. Do you have a rope?"

They did. Stern had brought one from the cutter thinking to use it as a kind of lifeline if the stair proved too slick underfoot.

After a moment the duchess rose, ready to go on.

She looked sick at heart but, if nothing else, Stern had to admire her courage; nothing seemed to stop her.

"Unconscious?" she muttered. "Whatever could he mean?

It was a difficult climb, with no handholds the entire way. The poor duchess had to hold up her skirts lest they trip her. Stern saw her look back once, and then she reached out and grasped his arm to maintain her balance.

"Don't look down," he said, repeating the instructions given to green sailors going aloft.

The captain felt a certain dread creeping over him as they pushed their way up the stair. Unconscious? All three of them? Flattery might claim to be no spawn of a mage, but Stern was not so certain. The captain had been at sea many years and had never known a man around whom strange things occurred so regularly.

The duchess swayed again as they reached the stairhead and, once he was sure she had her feet beneath her, Stern looked up and almost reeled himself. Before him lay the Ruin of Farrow in barely altered form!

The sight of her brother lying upon the cold stone jolted the duchess into motion.

"They are alive, but we cannot rouse them," Osler said, almost apologetic. Stern was surprised by the lieutenant's manner. Osler was not a man easily rattled.

"We have seen no one else, Captain," the lieutenant managed. "We found them lying thus, but there is no sign of who might have done such a thing."

The duchess knelt beside her brother. Stern could not see her face for blowing hair, but her motions were slow, tentative. Tenderly she wiped at what appeared to be blood caked on Lord Elsworth's face.

"Where is that fool of a physician when he is needed?" she muttered coldly.

Stern took a few moments to ascertain that Osler was correct in what he said. All three men were sunk in a deep torpor, Tristam worse than the others. He was no medical man to know the best course, and the doctor could certainly never make it to this place under his own power, but it might prove foolish to move these men in their present conditions. He just did not know.

Stern looked up at the sky, gauging the hour and the likely weather. Hesitation, he knew from long experience, could often prove as calamitous as any other course. There was no help for these three to be found here.

"We will make litters and bear them down," he said. There were nine men and the duchess; it could be done. The viscount was a large man, but both Tristam and Beacham were of only average weight. It could be done, though it would take the rest of the day.

"Lieutenant. We will want some stout poles. Our jackets and shirts will be needed as well. Be quick. By the time we have sent for help, we can have them on the beach—if we set our wills to it. Mr. Flattery leaped into the ocean to bear a man up, and we can make no less effort here. Let no man say we have shirked our duty to our shipmates."

❧   ❧   ❧

It was near dusk when the exhausted Jacks finally brought the unconscious men down to the beach. They set their litters on the sand and collapsed where they stood—strong men drained of all reserves. The great fear that had beset the Jacks as they made their way through the city and down the stair had also taken its toll, for the sailors were almost sure that they would be attacked and treated like the men they carried. And for men as superstitious as the Jacks that was a terrifying prospect.

Whatever ritual had been performed in the ruined city—for ritual it obviously had been—had unnerved the common sailors.

Only Stern's strong will had carried them through. The duchess thought each one of them a hero, for they had performed their labor without faltering or complaint. The captain had taken his turn bearing the litters and proved more powerful than she would have ever expected—resolute and strong. She had helped as she could, but these were men who did hard labor every day of their lives and were toughened by it in a way that she had never fully understood.

When they arrived at the beach, Llewellyn, as she had seen before, went through a transformation; from ineffectual little man to confident physician.

Each man in turn was carefully examined, but it was over Tristam that he lingered. Finally he turned to Stern and the duchess and spoke quietly and calmly.

"Lord Elsworth and the young Jack are in no danger, I am sure. Each has a mark, the smallest puncture, in their skin. They have been struck by a bolt or a dart tipped with a substance, perhaps derived from some relative of the genus *Strychnos*. They will recover fully, I believe." He glanced over his shoulder at the three prostrate men. "But I am in fear for Mr. Flattery. The radial artery has been slit and he has lost much blood. His pulse is weak and rapid, and his color pale. The laceration has already grown septic. Putrefaction will spread its miasma into the blood. Already he is burning with a fever. We must take him to the ship immediately."

The duchess saw Stern look around as he did when sensing wind upon his face and neck. He shook his head. "The trade is falling. We might be forced to man the oars." He cast a look of concern toward his crew. "And they are all in as it is." He shook his head again, then caught the duchess gazing at him. "I swore I would bring this young man back unharmed and I will." He went to the cutter and took out the tin box of victuals and set it on the beach where his crew sprawled. Opening the box he began to distribute food.

"We are not finished yet, lads," he said, his voice more touched with kindness than the duchess had ever thought to hear. "We must use what wind there is, so we cannot tarry or take time to rest. These men are terribly ill and must be carried to the ship without delay."

❧   ❧   ❧

It was near to morning, though still dark, the stars bright outside the windows of the great cabin. The sounds of a ship at anchor—the working of timbers and the creaking of the rig, the muffled sounds of the rudder moving to the current deep below—all had become as familiar to the duchess as the sounds of a sleeping lover.

Llewellyn had left to rest and the duchess took the watch over Tristam, exhausted herself, but worry would not let her sleep. Gently she wiped the naturalist's brow with a damp cloth. His condition was deteriorating, she was certain. Julian and Beacham were mending quickly and though they were yet unable to speak they had regained consciousness and some small control of their limbs. But Tristam was burning up and had barely moved since Osler had found him on that alien pyramid. And she was frantic with fear.

As quietly as possible she paced across the cabin sole. The ship was so small and the walls between the cabins so thin that almost any noise was transmitted some distance—a lesson she should have learned earlier.

She perched on the ledge of an open gallery window and looked out at the dark night. An owl hooted somewhere on the shore and the sounds of some large mammal breathing on the surface came to her.

"He has more place in my heart than I knew," she said to the night.

If Tristam died, she was quite certain the voyage would end in failure. She could not hope to succeed without him—no one else realized that as she did. For no reason other than that she knew he must be saved, no matter what the cost.

She pulled the cord that summoned her maid. Poor Jacel. Julian's illness had driven her to anguish. Fool of a girl.

The maid appeared almost immediately. Obviously she had been awake and fully dressed.

"Your Grace?" she said quietly.

"Llewellyn," the duchess said, and the young woman curtsied and ran off.

"At any cost," the duchess whispered.

In a few moments the physician arrived, rubbing his eyes, the neck of his shirt open.

"Your Grace," he said, crossing toward Tristam.

"His condition is unchanged, Doctor Llewellyn."

"Oh?" The man pulled up short, trying to show no annoyance at being wakened to no purpose.

"There is a matter we should speak of, Doctor." She thought she saw signs of apprehension in his face. He continued to stand dumbly in the middle of the cabin, the light from the shaded lamp casting odd shadows around him.

"I have often wondered," she said quietly, "why Roderick Palle was so determined to maneuver you aboard the *Swallow*." She fixed him with her gaze as he started to speak. "I would prefer you did not insult my intelligence with denials, Doctor. I know your friends, perhaps better than you do yourself. Wells, Rawdon, Noyes. They are not so hidden as they think, nor are their intentions so artfully disguised." She stepped near to Llewellyn so that her height might be felt and so that her voice could be used to greater effect. "I'm certain no one else has glimpsed the actor behind the character, Doctor, but I for one do not believe this pose. You are neither bungler nor fool." She held his eye for a second. "What did you find in Tristam's cabin besides Galton's letter?"

The man did not answer for a few seconds, but stared at the duchess as though he were making a careful assessment.

"I have asked you a question, Doctor," she said, making her voice so cold it hurt her throat. "Be assured I will have an answer. I am more resourceful than you know."

He shook his head. "Nothing but the treasures of a naturalist."

"No *regis* seeds?"

He hesitated for a second and then cast his gaze down.

"So you have only what Rawdon gave you?"

He looked up in surprise but then shook his head. "I don't know to what Your Grace refers."

"Doctor, let me assure you . . . I have no use for you. You are more than an annoyance, you threaten my purpose. I have twice decided to rid myself of your presence; once in Farrow and once since. You do know of my brother's reputation?"

He said nothing, but his posture answered her question.

"But twice I have decided to wait and see what time would reveal. And look what such prudence has brought? I suddenly find I have a use for you, after all. You will save the life of Mr. Flattery. You have *regis* seeds. Do not deny it. I have seen you begin to sink beneath the burden of your illness and then rise like a martyr from the flames, renewed in health and vigor. I have more intimate experience of the effects of the seed than anyone in Farrland—save one. You will use it to save Tristam, Doctor Llewellyn, or I will have no use for you at all."

Llewellyn rubbed a hand across his cheek, as though he had been struck there. For a long moment he said nothing. He looked up as though in silent appeal and finally he managed to speak. "But Your Grace does not understand. Without the seed, I will certainly die. What choice have you given me? The death of the black lung or a death by . . . drowning, will it be? It seems that Llewellyn sinks either way . . . and the sailors say drowning is not accompanied by pain." He shrugged.

The duchess walked across the cabin slowly, considering. She had known he was not a fool, but she had also been certain he was a coward. When the corsairs had chased them, she had seen it—he was more than terrified. Gently she pressed her hand to Tristam's brow. He was on fire.

"What is it that you want, Doctor?"

"I have been reduced to that most basic of animal desires, Your Grace. I want to live."

She continued to look down at Tristam, his beautiful young face glistening in the lamplight, his color high, as though he glowed from the fire blazing in his veins.

"You are telling me you don't have enough seed to save Tristam and to keep yourself alive until we reach Oceana."

Another long pause, then a rasping whisper. "We do not know how long it will take to find the seed, Your Grace, nor do we know when we shall arrive. I fear I will die before we find this island." A pause. "There is also a possibility, Your Grace, that the seed will not be the physic that Tristam requires."

"Yes," she heard her voice come out in a flat whisper, "I know." She wiped Tristam's face. Held her hand briefly over his heart and then went and rang the bell for her maid.

"If I do not have coffee, I shall expire. Will you join me, Doctor?"

Llewellyn looked up in surprise, and then shook his head.

"Captain Stern," she whispered in Jacel's ear, and sent her out with a hand upon her arm.

"He will not live, will he?" she said when the maid closed the door.

Llewellyn looked over at the naturalist and she thought she saw some compassion there, but only a little: Llewellyn did not care for the human species. He shook his head a little distractedly, far more concerned with his own situation.

She reached out and placed her hand on Tristam's shoulder, thinking that her heart might break—for the first time in many years. "What did they do to him?" she whispered.

"They took his blood," Llewellyn answered flatly.

And the duchess shut her eyes, so tight that no tear could escape.

Stern entered, his gaze flitting from the duchess to the doctor. And then he stopped in mid-stride—

faltered, really. "We have lost him," he said, his voice filled with real regret. "I am so sorry, Duchess."

"He lives yet, Captain, though he cannot continue much longer. Tristam's cure, however, is within the power of Doctor Llewellyn, for he has stolen from Benjamin Rawdon some of the Kingfoil seed that sustains our King."

Stern's look of compassion turned immediately to suspicion: his natural response to the duchess. "Doctor Llewellyn?"

Llewellyn, she could see, was frightened now. His face was ashen. She thought he would have to sit, for he wavered where he stood.

At any cost, she reminded herself.

"I assure you that a search of his cabin will prove me right, Captain."

"What say you, Doctor Llewellyn?"

The physician lowered himself awkwardly into a chair. For a moment he did not speak and the duchess could see that his mind raced to find a way out of this trap. In the end, he looked up, appeal on his face. "But what of my life?" he whispered. "It sustains me." He nodded to the duchess. "She would have me die, Captain. I would do anything to save this young man, but you cannot ask me to give my own life."

"Llewellyn has the black lung, Captain. He has enough seed to keep him alive—until we reach Varua, at least. It is his hope to find more when we arrive, enough to cure his disease entire. Ask him yourself. You might ask him as well if the King will live until we return from this voyage, for the good doctor knows far more than you might guess."

Stern said nothing but turned his gaze on the doctor who supported himself on the table, even though he sat.

He waved his head from side to side, eyes pressed closed. "There is not enough for us both. Not enough, I tell you."

"How is it you have come by this seed, Doctor?" Stern asked.

Llewellyn glanced angrily at the duchess. "I am no thief, Captain. It was given me freely. I tell this as the truth."

"By Sir Benjamin?"

The little man shook his head. "I cannot say, Captain."

"Doctor Llewellyn," Stern said, his anger coming to the fore, "aboard ship I am King's Barrister, judge, and jury all. I shall have answers to my questions, sir."

The look on the physician's face seemed to say: *here it is again: persecuted, humiliated, robbed.* "Sir Benjamin Rawdon took pity upon me, Captain Stern," he whispered.

"The King knows of this, then?" Stern reached up and grasped a beam as though to steady himself.

Llewellyn hesitated a moment and then shook his head.

Stern cast a glimpse at the duchess.

"Then this seed you have is the property of the King of Farrland?"

"Captain," the duchess said in real alarm. "Let me remind you that without Mr. Flattery we are unlikely to accomplish our purpose. Dr. Llewellyn is certainly incapable of searching for the plant himself, which would leave us dependent upon the generosity of the Varuan king. You have found your lost city, and a passage through the Archipelago as well, that is accomplishment enough for one voyage. But return without the seed, and the King will die. Llewellyn will tell you this is true. Whatever your orders, the truth is that speed is our greatest need. If we return too late, even if we bring the seed, you will pay the price for the King's death. Count on it. No one in the Admiralty will shoulder the blame, as you well know."

Stern wavered. He did not trust her, the duchess knew this, but he was not a fool—and Stern was well acquainted with the workings of the Admiralty. "But, Duchess, would you have me condemn Doctor Llewellyn to death?" Stern fixed her with a gaze like an accusation.

She felt her anger rise and she spoke very carefully. "And when we reach Varua, will you give him the seed that is, as you have just said yourself, the property of the King? Will you ignore your orders to save his life? Or will you bring every seed back with you, and watch the doctor die?"

Stern glared at the duchess, but she met his gaze without blinking. She would not be intimidated like some midshipman.

Finally, quietly, he said. "What would you have me do?"

"It is possible you might save them both. Treat Tristam with the *regis* physic and sail on with all haste. Drive your ship across the Ocean Beyond. Time is what will kill Doctor Llewellyn. He must have the seed, but so must Tristam. And Tristam must have it now." She turned to Llewellyn. "You are a physician, sworn to sustain life. Will you not take this risk, Doctor? I will tell you true, without Tristam you won't find your cure in Varua."

Both Llewellyn and Stern fell into silence and indecision. It was a moment balanced like a goblet on an edge. If she reached for it now, it might upset, but if she hesitated, all could be lost.

"What say you, Llewellyn?" the captain asked.

The doctor closed his eyes and she could almost hear his thoughts: *persecuted, put upon, robbed—it was always the same.* She was certain he valued his life more than anything: more than honor, good character, love. . . . More than the regard of his fellow men. It was the only thing he truly cared for. *Does he not see that without Tristam his hopes are dashed?*

He nodded suddenly. "I will use my few seeds to treat Mr. Flattery's condition if the good captain will agree to carry me with all haste to Varua." He paused as though summoning courage. "And allow me the seed to effect my cure."

Stern turned away to look out the great windows of the cabin: the captain's cabin. Over the bay the sky was no longer black, casting shades of gray into the cabin. "You ask a great deal." He glanced at them both. "I have never gone against the orders of the Admiralty. Never forsaken my duty."

The duchess could not hold her peace. "Let me make a shrewd guess, Captain Stern. Your orders instruct you to sail to Varua and return with the seed. That is what has been committed to paper. But what has been said to you is somewhat different. Survey as you go. Haste is not required. But if you return too late ... only what is written on paper will be brought forward—as evidence of your incompetence. And if you let die the only naturalist aboard, you may not even find the seed." She turned to Llewellyn, then back to Stern. "Have either of you even seen this plant we seek?"

Both men looked down. She crossed to Tristam again and felt his brow. For a second she thought he did not breathe, but she could just feel a hint of it upon her fingers.

"Consider much longer and the decision will be made for you!" she said angrily.

"Doctor," Stern said, his confidence shaken, she could tell, "you attended the King. Will His Majesty live until we return? Is this possible?"

Llewellyn looked up, confusion on his face. The duchess suddenly realized that he might not know the truth. Did he have the wit to understand there could be only one answer here?

"It is as Her Grace has said," the physician managed.

Stern shook his head. "Then use your arts to save our naturalist. I shall carry you to Varua without further delay, and if we are able to find this herb we seek, I will spare what, in good conscience, I can. I promise no more than that."

Llewellyn looked at the duchess, a look of the greatest relief on his face.

"Your patient, Doctor," she said.

He took Tristam's pulse, and then went quickly out. The duchess and Stern regarded each other for a moment. They had many thousand leagues to sail together yet, she reminded herself.

"I thank you, Captain. I am sure you have made the wisest decision in a difficult situation."

He nodded as though any compliment from the duchess was of dubious value. "There is one other matter, Duchess, now that you have achieved your ends."

"Sir?"

The next words came with some difficulty. "I would have my officers back."

She almost smiled and was forced to hide it by dipping her head in a mock bow. "Captain Stern," she said with all the grace she could summon, "they are yours."

FORTY-ONE

After endless struggle Tristam awoke to the sounds of a ship at sea. *Had he found his way back, then?*

A gentle breeze funneled down from above and cooled his face, but he was warm, tucked into a bunk under a weight of blankets.

Do I dream, Tristam wondered, *or have I wakened into another world?*

The ghost boy ... he had been following the ghost boy, had been almost a ghost himself, thought and feeling so ephemeral they seemed to drift off, like smoke on the wind, leaving only the smallest scent behind. An endless dark maze of alleys and tunnels, and shattered, ancient stairs. Where had he been?

Nowhere. Lost.

And through that endless night he had clung to his awareness of self lest it drift away with his thoughts. *I am Tristam,* he chanted to himself. *Tristam.* And at the worst of times; *I am me. I am me. I am me.*

Following the boy who slipped silently along in a silent world, squeezing through holes so small that Tristam thought he would never follow. And then overhead the viper battled the white bird.

Tristam would echo this battle inside, as though his heart were a hollow drum, reverberating to an outside will. A thought drifted into Tristam's mind; *my blood is on fire and that is the battle to quench it.*

Follow the ghost child, slinking furtively along a darkened, dead street. Afraid, always afraid. Looking for springs to quench their thirst—just a few drops of blackened water, like blood dripping from a wound.

And then light, and soaring strength. Tristam would lift on great wings, stretching into the sky, looking. Searching for the viper, and the battle would be engaged among the clouds.

And then he would plummet, twisting within the coils of the biting snake, crash back to earth where a small boy waited, leading Tristam away from the fire.

A sound of a man laughing foolishly, like a returning memory. *I am a naturalist on a voyage of discovery.* Or was that a dream also?

The creaking of the deck overhead as footsteps passed. Water gurgling close to his ear. A ship at sea.

I have wakened into that other world, he thought. *I am alive in that world of light and air and men and women. And I am Tristam. I walked up an endless stair and passed through the gate. . . . And now, I have returned, somehow. Led by a small child.*

Water, I must have water.

Opening his eyes he found the glare of light on the white beams overhead too dazzling and pressed his lids closed again. *Water.* He felt as though the dryness began in his mouth and spread to every corner of his being, as though the snake biting him had drawn out all of his life fluids—as spiders did of their prey.

An attempt to move brought on a wave of dizziness, near blackness.

"Tristam?"

Yes . . . I am Tristam.

It was a warm voice—one that he knew, or had known long ago. A hand touched his forehead.

"Do you wake?"

His mouth was too dry to speak, but he nodded, which caused more vertigo.

The hand was removed to his chest and he felt a soft kiss upon his brow. "Perhaps I shall begin to believe in gods," the voice said, and he could hear a change in its timbre, spoken through a constricted throat.

"Duchess?" he managed. A memory from that world of light.

"Elorin."

"I must have drink."

"Yes, of course."

A moment later a hand slipped behind his head and raised him up and the wet rim of a cup touched his lips. *Glorious water.* He felt it run cool down his throat. He thought it should hiss when it reached his stomach.

"That is enough for a moment. I believe too much at once will not be good. Oh, Tristam, I am relieved beyond imagining. I have been frightened nigh on to death myself. But you are well, aren't you? Your fever is broken?" She shook him gently. "You frightened me, you frightened me! You have been raving and muttering and lost in delirium."

"Lost . . . yes. How did I come here? I have been battling the bird-viper for night upon night. I can't think how I have survived." He opened his eyes to slits and suffered the pain of adjusting to daylight.

The duchess bent over him, running her hand gently through his matted hair. "Llewellyn," she said, almost a whisper. "He had some of the seed. It saved your life, I'm sure. Terrible nightmares are one of its less salutary qualities. But you are out of danger now."

Tristam closed his eyes. *Out of danger? Regis. They had given him regis.* Drinking the water, dark as blood, and then soaring up into light. *I should never have taken the regis seed,* he realized. *Never.*

He felt his body had been invaded—had become a host, like a body into which parasites burrowed. He felt ill and hollow and corrupted. And something else. A yearning more powerful than he had ever imagined. The *regis.* . . . Dandish had become addicted.

"You should have let me die," he whispered.

"Tristam?" Distress at his words. Confusion.

"I should never have taken the seed. Not me." Horror. Despair. But why? Why did he know this?

Silence. Thinking. A sharp mind hovering over him. A hand took his own, gently. The softness of it, the warmth, reduced Tristam to tears. He did not know why.

"Tristam . . ." his name, spoken with such tenderness. "What happened up there?"

Up there? He tried to order his thoughts. The city. He had gone up into the abandoned city with. . . .

"The others?"

"They are well, Tristam, do not be concerned. They did not suffer the same injuries as yourself."

Injuries? A memory so horrible he turned his mind away. *"They slit me open . . ."* he said, mouth dry. "Farrelle save me, Elorin. They let my spirit bleed out and tried to make it take another form. . . . But I escaped into the air. And the child led me. Through the streets of the ruined city and through the city that lays beneath."

A hand on his brow. Fingers wiped a tear off his cheek.

"You have had terrible dreams, Tristam," she said, voice wavering. "The fever from the wound on your wrist. And the physic."

She took his right hand out from under the cover and touched his wrist as gently as she could, her fingers cool. "I will tell you true that we thought you would not keep this hand for the putrefaction was terrible."

Tristam opened his eyes and saw that a tattoo encircled his wrist, winding out of an ugly wound—red and tender but closed, already healing.

"It is where the snake . . . the bird struck me," he said.

"In your dream."

Dream?

The duchess shook her head, her curls catching the light. "The King suffers horrific nightmares as well," she whispered. "So powerful they seem more real than . . . reality. But they are dreams. Nothing more."

Tristam flexed his fingers and the snake tattoo appeared to squirm. He felt a wave of nausea and shut his eyes.

"You have no memory of what they did to you, Tristam? What was the purpose of this?" She touched his wound.

"I can't separate the dreams from memory, I think. But do you see, it is the bird-viper from the pool atop the pyramid. There is an artifact, like the Ruin on Farrow. . . ." He opened his eyes and stopped, seeing that she knew. "You have seen it?"

She nodded. "Yes, we brought you down. I think better of Stern for it. He took his place among the Jacks to bear you down the flooded stair. They are a coarse lot, the hands, but their hearts are true. You would be there still without their efforts."

She caressed his chest and shoulder. "I have orders not to tire you when you wake, Tristam. Drink some more and I shall try to find a broth that will not endanger your life."

He drank again. Sleep was calling to him, but he feared slipping back into that netherworld. This one was so light, so warm. "Tell me where we are."

The duchess' face lit in a smile. "Can you turn your head a bit?"

With her help Tristam managed to look out the stern windows and there, on the horizon, mountaintops glistened white in the sunlight. "Do we sail back to Farrland?"

"No, Tristam, we are in the Great Ocean Beyond. We have passed through the Archipelago by a new route and we point our bow to the west. You cannot see, but we sail in the company of small clouds, a fleet of them spread across the blue sky, traveling, as are we, toward Oceana. And the western horizon seems vastly far away, as though we can see a hundred leagues and all is blue and empty, the sea running up into the sky."

Tristam lay his head down and his eyes closed of their own volition. He felt a kiss on his brow—so soft and full of tenderness that it was almost a word. And then another on his cheek, and then, even more softly, on his lips. Three words.

Tristam felt himself drifting away again—not into darkness and fear—but into a warm dream of rocking on the ocean, embraced by a soft breeze that was the love of this woman named Elorin.

Outside the stern windows a bird cried and Tristam let go completely, slipping into a fair dream: a white bird sailing in the ship's wind, looking down upon him from an empty sky.

Tad Williams

Memory, Sorrow and Thorn

THE DRAGONBONE CHAIR: Book 1
☐ **Hardcover Edition**   0-8099-003-3—$19.50
☐ **Paperback Edition**   UE2384—$5.99

A war fueled by the dark powers of sorcery is about to engulf the long-peaceful land of Osten Ard—as the Storm King, undead ruler of the elvishlike Sithi, seeks to regain his lost realm through a pact with one of human royal blood. And to Simon, a former castle scullion, will go the task of spearheading the quest that offers the only hope of salvation . . . a quest that will see him fleeing and facing enemies straight out of a legend-maker's worst nightmares!

STONE OF FAREWELL: Book 2
☐ **Hardcover Edition**   UE2435—$21.95
☐ **Paperback Edition**   UE2480—$5.99

As the dark magic and dread minions of the undead Sithi ruler spread their seemingly undefeatable evil across the land, the tattered remnants of a once-proud human army flee in search of a last sanctuary and rallying point, and the last survivors of the League of the Scroll seek to fulfill missions which will take them from the fallen citadels of humans to the secret heartland of the Sithi.

TO GREEN ANGEL TOWER: Book 3
☐ **Hardcover Edition**   UE2521—$25.00
☐ **Paperback Edition, Part I**   UE2598—$5.99
☐ **Paperback Edition, Part II**   UE2606—$5.99

In this concluding volume of the best-selling trilogy, the forces of Prince Josua march toward their final confrontation with the dread minions of the undead Storm King, while Simon, Miriamele, and Binabek embark on a desperate mission into evil's stronghold.